LIONEL said with caution, "You act as if you've got a wonderful secret. What is it, darling?" He forced himself to smile.

Patricia clapped her gloved hands together in joy, and her smile was wide. "I have, I have!"

"Tell me," he said, and wanted to slap the silly fool. An awful premonition came to him. There had been that one time, just that one accident. Though one time was enough to knock a woman up.

"We're going to be married!" she exclaimed, and now tears rushed into her eyes, tears of happiness. "Right away!"

He said, and even his knees felt cold with fear, "Right away?"

She wanted to say, "We're going to have a baby."

But she could not. Her throat worked, but a hot shame came to her, an enormous embarrassment. Her face turned red, and seeing that, Lionel was aghast. He thought of her father, Patrick Mulligan. He was ruined, ruined, because of this idiot, this...creature. He wanted to kill her!

"But your father wants you to marry Jason Garrity."

"I'll never do that," she said. "Never."

TAYLOR CALDWELL

Answer As A Man

A Fawcett Crest Book Taylor Caldwell No sale

Published by Fawcett Crest Books, a unit of CBS Publications, the Consumer and Educational Publishing Division of CBS Inc., by arrangement with G. P. Putnam's Sons.

All rights reserved that printed in the United States of America. Simultaneously in a Heritage of Random House, Inc., New York and of Canada by Random House of Canada Limited, Toronto, Canada.

ISBN: 0-449-20050-5

ISBN 0-449-20050-7

Printed in the United States of America

First Fawcett Crest Edition: December 1981
20   19   18   17   16   15   14   13   12   11   10

For my beloved husband, William Robert Prestie,
who always "answers as a man."

PART I

Then the Lord asked Satan:
Have you considered My servant Job?
—*Job 1:8*

1

Jason Aloysius Garrity was awakened rudely, as usual, by the clamor of the 5:30-A.M. bells of the little church almost next door: St. John the Baptist Church. The bells were ringing for Mass, and they awakened all the workingmen and their families in the neighborhood, whose remarks, when aroused, were less than reverent. But the bells were their only alarm to rise and pursue another depressing and somber twelve hours of toil, so the cursing was relevant. The day would be exhausting and stupefying, and they hated the prospect with dull resentment, and justification.

As did young Jason. But he had youth and hope and stamina and determination, which made him considerably different from his neighbors. However, he was depressed and gloomy, which also was usual in the dawn of a weekday. He recalled that today was his birthday. He was fourteen years old on this morning of November 11, 1900. He was now of an age to work a full day in the factories—for four dollars a week—and was permitted to leave school. The prospect was less than pleasing, but Jason was not one to bemoan anything, especially something which was desperately necessary. He faced life with composure and resolution, accepting all that it was without whining or protest; at least, not out loud. He kept his resentments and complaints to himself, out of consideration for his mother, Kate Garrity, who had miseries enough of her own. She would often say with love, "Jason is the only one in this family who is cheerful, I'm thinking, no matter what happens, God bless him."

To which his grandfather, Bernard Garrity, would reply with a grunt, "Well, then, he's young and he's got his dreams, but life will settle that, for sure." He remembered his own dreams when he had been Jason's age, and if his small cold gray eyes watered, only he knew of it, and his natural irritability would increase. His neighbors called him a "miserable old bucko," for he rarely if ever smiled and would shake his stick at the Saturday-night drunks and curse them, or bring down that stick on the shoulders of a spalpeen who was unusually noisy or impudent on the street. He was not universally loved. Nor did he love anyone, except of course the

8

Blessed Mother, his widowed daughter-in-law, Kate, and Jason. He was famous in the neighborhood for his intolerance, violence, irascibility, skepticism, and "a tongue like knives." The priest was certain, with sadness, that he was a lost soul, for he never went to Mass, except for Christmas Eve, and made a very sketchy Easter Duty, and was not known otherwise to go to confession. But then, as Bernard would remark sourly to his daughter-in-law, "the boyeens were born in America and know nothing of that damned Famine in Ireland, and so they still have dreams." When the new young pastor called—very timidly—the occasion would conclude in loud arguments, which Bernard always won, and headshakings on the part of the pastor, who would go immediately into the church and deplore his own recent sin of explosive bad temper. He would also pray for Bernard's soul, and not without a little human vindictiveness. Had Bernard known, he would have growled deeply and loudly, his closest approach to laughter.

Bernard was seventy-two. He swept and cleaned the floors of neighborhood shops for a living, and washed their windows, and kept the little church tidy, and shoveled snow in the winter, and emptied ashes. It was a lucky week if he brought home four dollars. As he had had a stringent, starving, laborious, and very lean boyhood in Ireland, he was as healthy as new leather, and as tough and resilient. To him weakness and sloth were mortal sins, never to be forgiven by man or God, in whom he did not entirely believe.

He had no compassion for beggars, or liars, or hungry thieves, or any softness. His only compassion, well hidden, was for women, whether naughty or virtuous. He had seen their desperate courage and valor in Ireland, and he had not thought it evil when a colleen sold herself for a loaf of bread for her family, or a turnip or a bit of lamb for the pot, or to feed her child. In fact, he thought such women more noble than others, for Irish women considered sexual congress out of marriage the most mortal of all sins. They felt they had bartered their immortal souls to the Devil to keep a loved one alive during the Famine, and though they wept, they did not turn aside. If anyone deserved an improbable heaven, he would think, it was such women, and he hoped, for their sake, that there would be a recompense somewhere, even if he doubted it.

The dim gray-blue of a false dawn was invading the tiny bedroom where Jason slept on a narrow hard bed, next to the

9

cot of his brother, John Xavier, who was thirteen years old. It was very cold in the room, for there was no heat in this small cramped house except in the kitchen, with its coal-and-wood stove, and there were no curtains at the window and no rugs on the floor, and only one small lithograph, unframed, of the Sacred Heart of Jesus, hanging on the wall. The icy air still vibrated with the sound of the bells. St. John the Baptist Church might have been the most minute of churches in this nondescript meager city of Belleville, Pennsylvania, but it surely had the loudest main bell of any church, strident, admonishing, arousing, and belligerent. Even when it frequently tolled for the dead it was stern and angry. It had come from a train, and had cost three dollars, which it appeared to resent with considerable and clamorous fury. It apparently believed it had lost status, though it had been duly blessed. Jason felt it was really the voice of the young pastor, Father William Ralph Sweeney, and he sometimes amused himself by conjecturing that that voice was directed entirely against his grandfather, whom he dearly loved.

The blankets on Jason's cot were thin and patched and old, and he shivered in the early-morning cold and stretched his long young body in the area of warmth his flesh had created. It was time to get up and deliver the load of washing his mother had done the day before for distant and more affluent women. Her laundry was celebrated for its excellence, and she often made up to six dollars a week for doing it, so meticulous it was. Delicate articles were washed and ironed with genuine love, for Kate was appreciative of fine fabrics and lace. It was Jason's daily job, before and after school, to return the laundry to its owners and collect the money. He knew almost all the luxurious houses in Belleville. The ladies had their own laundresses, but they had discovered that Kate Garrity could be trusted with the most fragile of silks and voiles, and that she returned them in blooming condition. After the afternoon deliveries were made, Jason earned a dollar a week by helping out old Mr. Joseph Maggiotti—who had the corner grocery and dry-goods store—slicing sausages and selling threads and needles and pots and pans and lengths of cotton and secondhand shoes.

This job went on from four to eight every day and the whole day Saturday. Mr. Maggiotti, who was even poorer than his neighbors, was old and widowed and lived in two rooms over his shop. He could pay Jason only that one dollar a week, but often he would give him a quarter of a pound of butter, the end of a bologna sausage, a yard of cloth for an apron for Kate, a pair of black cotton stockings, a loaf of day-old bread, and sometimes a steaming pot of spaghetti with a pungent sauce, or a slice of Romano cheese, all of which were received with thanksgiving by Kate. Heathen food, old Bernard would say abrasively as he devoured it with relish.

Mr. Maggiotti was the only person on the street Bernard could tolerate, and he could sometimes be found chatting inside with Joe or sitting on a chair outside the shop more or less peacefully smoking and glaring at passersby, who found him formidable. He washed Mr. Maggiotti's windows and swept his shop for free, despite the owner's protests. He would accept a chunk of buttered Italian bread, however, and a little tobacco, with the graciousness of a bishop. Mr. Maggiotti would, with furtiveness and an eye for a reproving passing glance, give him a glass of very acid Chianti wine. They quarreled constantly, and loudly, and had an abiding affection for each other, these two old men. They also had respect. They both had nothing good to say about their young pastor, whom they considered an ignorant bucko teeming with ridiculous goodwill and earnest illusions about the innate goodness of humanity. They knew better.

"You gotta good grandson, that Jase," Mr. Maggiotti would often say.

"He'll do," Bernard would grunt.

"He no hate work," Mr. Maggiotti would protest.

"Sure, and you're right, Joe. Not like his damned brother, Jack, who says he wants to be a priest. Lazy way out. That boyeen is supposed to have two paper routes, but half the time he's at Mass or vespers, and Jason's got to deliver his papers in the morning, besides carting his mum's laundry. Then Jack's delicate and has a weak stomach, Kate says, and so Jason delivers his evening papers, too. Must be a magician, Jason, getting everything in, and on time, too. Moves like a jackrabbit. Well, then, it'll do him good. Perhaps. Work never killed a man. It's only the travail of his soul that kills him. Kills us all eventually."

Mr. Maggiotti would reply with sadness, "*Si.* Grief—it killed my wife. All the bambinos . . . died—one year, two year. No food. Bad times. God rest her soul."

Bernard would say with unusual cheerfulness, "Thank God, we all die. That's one blessing."

Mr. Maggiotti, a buoyant soul, did not entirely agree with this, though being a polite man with manners, he would dolefully shake his head, as if in assent. He loved the infrequent sunshine in Belleville; he loved the trees and grass and flowers and the voices of children, and the rising dawns and the scent of good food and cloth, and the texture of the coarse lace he sold, and the winds of heaven and the silence of a moonlit midnight and the cheap gaudy statues in the church and the glimpse of a pretty face and the sound of the rain on his tin roof and the slow falling of the miracle of snow. And Mass. But he never betrayed these weaknesses to Bernard, for whom he had respect. A man did not argue with a valued friend, except when it came to politics, a matter on which Mr. Maggiotti was vehement. Mr. Maggiotti thought that most politicians should be quietly assassinated. Bernard thought they should be publicly hanged. It was a subtle difference, which they never resolved. But then, Mr. Maggiotti was a Sicilian, Bernard an Irishman, and they had clashing codes of honor.

On Christmas Day they both got drunk in the back room of the shop. Bernard would supply a pint of very bad cheap whiskey and Mr. Maggiotti would contribute a bottle of cherished wine and roasted chestnuts and ham and his own ravioli. The shopkeeper would sing Italian songs in a beautiful resonant voice and Bernard would sing Irish ballads and they would weep on each other's shoulders, deliciously. It was their happiest day. Kate would gently say it was a scandal, but she did not mean it. She loved Bernard as a father and was happy that he could enjoy himself. Her husband, Peter, had, as he said, left his father in her hands. She always felt that Bernard, instead, was her protector, the iron gates in her harried life. Peter had been too much of a dreamer to protect anyone. He had written poetry, none of which he could sell. He had also played the violin in taverns in Ireland, which never netted him more than a shilling or two at the best. Bernard, in comparison, was an oaken shillelagh.

A number of their neighbors were Germans who had fled Germany under Bismarck. Mr. Maggiotti thought them grim and joyless. Bernard respected them for their relentless industry, their cleanliness, their hard acceptance of life. Germans had few illusions. Germans hated sloth, and of that Bernard approved. They also had a local band, all rugged brass, which made Mr. Maggiotti wince. But Bernard considered it a furious defiance of fate, and he had always defied fate. Defiance was man's answer to chaos. And, perhaps, to God. Germans never begged Mr. Maggiotti for credit. They paid cash, or went without. Mr. Maggiotti thought credit was a pact between gentlemen. Bernard thought credit was a sign of fecklessness. "Never a lender or a borrower be," Bernard would quote from Shakespeare. "One must trust," said Mr. Maggiotti, who gave credit to some of his customers and suffered for it. "Trust," said Bernard, "is all very good, but make them put it down on paper and make them honor it."

"You hard man," said Mr. Maggiotti.

"Learned it the hard way," Bernard would reply. "Men are bastards."

"God loves all men, Bernie."

"More fool he," said Bernard.

Mr. Maggiotti would then bless himself and lower his ardent brown eyes piously. Bernard thought him a bit of a hypocrite. After all, a man did not live this long and remain an innocent fool. But Bernard forgave him. A man was entitled to his hypocrisies if it made life a little easier for him. It was like pretending wax flowers were real—if one looked and did not touch. It brightened corners, though Bernard preferred to scowl at dark, hollow, empty ones. Irishmen might become sentimental after a few drafts of whiskey, but they did not bring that sentimentality into the affairs of the world. They knew, as the Holy Bible said, that money is the answer to all things. It also said that "be surety for a stranger—you will smart for it." Bernard had given "surety for a stranger" once in his life, and sure, he had smarted for it. Credit was the invention of the Devil. And banks, which were the edifices of the Devil. What few coins Bernard could save were put into a tin tea box, under his bed. Interest? The Holy Bible was against it. Interest mocked a man and devoured his spirit. There were other ways to increase your "fortune."

Jason, on his cot, became aware of a very familiar sound: his mother was scrubbing on her washboard. Rub-ba-da-dub. She arose at five. His door was partly open. The kerosene lamp from the kitchen wavered its feeble yellow light into his room. He could smell the naphtha soap, and steam, strong and suffocating. On this morning of his fourteenth birthday he rebelled against it, though he did not know why. He looked across at the cot of his brother. John was not there. So, he had gone to Mass again to avoid delivering his morning newspapers, and that, now, was left to him, Jason. After Mass, Jack was usually in a state of static ecstasy, absorbed in the adoration of God and his hoped-for vows. Kate reverenced and honored that, with awe. Jack would often say, refusing his breakfast of prunes and oatmeal, "No, Mum. I have received our Lord, and that is enough for me." Jason suspected that he ate as heartily as possible before going to school, and Jason was right. He more than suspected his mother "stuffed" Jack with food to "keep up his strength," after others were absent. A man of God needed nourishment.

Jason heard a soprano whine of complaint. That would be Joan, his crippled sister, complaining pathetically from the bedroom she shared with her mother. There was a growl from Bernard, who was not susceptible to whiners, and then Joan whimpered. She both hated and feared her grandfather, who was not beguiled by her frail beauty. Jason loved his eleven-year-old sister and did not know why. She despised him and was open in her derision and contempt, whereas she adored her brother John, who prayed over her with a solemn face. "Moochers," Bernard would say. "They'll have their way, from the flesh and the bodies of others. Did not St. Paul say, 'He who does not work, neither shall he eat?' Kate has too soft a heart."

To Bernard, those who did not earn their bread were anathema, whether young or old, whether sick or well, whether whole or disabled. There was always work in some form or other for them to do, to the limit of their capacity. "Parasites," he said once, "lose their ability to move, to live on their own. They should be destroyed, like lice." Kate had shuddered at this and had spoken of immortal souls. "Hah," said Bernard, "the good Lord himself condemned them."

Jason hated to get out of bed before dawn, for he was always tired and never had enough food for a lad of his height, which was already five feet eight inches, and he only fourteen, with years of growth ahead. "He'll top my six feet," Bernard would say with pleasure. "All the Garritys were grand men, and no dwarfs among us, except for the women, poor souls." To be short, and to be a woman, in Bernard's opinion, was to deserve the compassion of God. Jason had Bernard's somewhat small, deep-set, cool gray eyes, his mother's short straight nose, his father's long Irish lip and wide smiling mouth with excellent teeth, and a round firm chin with a dimple. He had Kate's bright complexion and her black curling hair and her cheerful expression—which did not always reflect their thoughts. He already had the broad brow and shoulder, the long strong arms and sturdy legs of a man, and he was all muscle, quick and sure on his feet, and instant with his fists when absolutely necessary. Few boys now dared to challenge "that damn mick," though in the first grade many had tried. For all his calm and genial air, Jason could be terrible in just anger. But never was he petty or petulant, and never did he complain of his life and responsibilities. The hardship he endured was only temporary, he would say to himself. There was a way out, in America, and had not he been born in Belleville two months after his parents and grandfather had arrived? He was American and entitled to his heritage, and though Bernard's remarks about the country were cynical, Jason did not believe them.

He glanced again at his brother's cot, annoyed at its emptiness. He was constantly repressing his impatience with John Xavier and his often urgent desire to "bash him a good one." He also suspected that John's claims to a vocation were for the purpose of avoiding work, though Father Sweeney emphatically declared that "it is a true vocation the boyeen has." Kate's poor thin face, harassed though it was, would glow with pride and tremulous devotion. A priest in the family! What greater honor could a mother receive than that her son entered the priesthood? It announced to the world that the mother was a heroic and noble woman, a sister in joy with the Blessed Mother herself.

Unlike Jason, Jack was "delicate" and "unwell," to quote innocent Kate, though Bernard would scoff and remark that so was a willow sapling, all sinew and flexibility, bowing meekly before the wind, then springing upright faster than any other tree. In height, John was almost as tall as his older brother, but he appeared emaciated in spite of his truly enormous appetite, an appetite which seemed to have escaped his mother, who was always forcing food upon him even at the expense of others in the family. John would protest—but he always ate, claiming it was only to please Kate. He also had a cultivated cough, which he hinted was due to his grandfather's pipe, a hint he dared not mention in Bernard's presence. John used that cough to great personal advantage and even had the stern nuns at the parish school pampering him, they who would not have pampered Jason had he come in with a broken leg. "Jack has a way with him," Bernard would admit, without admiration.

John had gray eyes, like his brother and grandfather, but his were open and deliberately candid, and he would stretch them because they were somewhat sunken on each side of a nose which, while well-formed, was rather large. His complexion was pale, though he was very healthy, and his face was hollowed out under broad colorless cheekbones. A long thin chin and a pallid strictured mouth added to his appearance of austere illness and asceticism. His hair was light brown and thin and shining on a skull which seemed fragile, for it was small and narrow, standing on a neck as slender as a girl's. His shoulders were narrow also, his arms and legs spindly. All in all he had a spare look, though he was nearly as quick as his brother. He stood straight and with some stiffness, and his glance was unbending and severe. He was a good and dedicated student, which Jason was not, and the nuns assured Kate that he was every inch a budding priest. He had not a single vestige of humor, and his smile was astringent.

"Not a Father. A monk, with a tin cup," Bernard would jeer. "Much easier than earning an honest living." Tears would come to Kate's soft brown eyes, and then Bernard would awkwardly pat her shoulder and say, "Now, now, it's a mean old bucko I am, Katie, and a priest he will be, though God knows where we'll get the money to send him to a seminary." "The Good Lord will provide," Kate would say, and Bernard would suppress a snort.

Then there was Joan, crippled from infantile paralysis since she had been an infant. Everyone loved Joan, except that unregenerate curmudgeon Bernard, her grandfather. Even the self-absorbed John loved her, after himself, and he loved no one else, not even his devoted mother, whom he exploited. Joan was beautiful in spite of her useless legs. The disease had not marred her otherwise, and she had a face like that of a marble nymph, smooth and white and miraculously carved. There was an other-world exquisiteness about her face, a certain dainty polish resembling pearl. At times her flesh appeared translucent, especially in a sharp light. All her features were perfect: her large and shimmering blue eyes with their long black lashes, her elegant little nose, her full red lips, her brows like bird's wings half-lifted in flight, her docile expression, and her billowing mass of satin black hair, brilliant with waves. She had small round arms and hands and a body which promised a charming miniature pulchritude in later years.

"Resembles all the Garrity women," Bernard would say with reluctance. But who would want to marry a crippled colleen? Joan could move about with the aid of canes, though with difficulty, and slowly, and no one saw the legs under the long frocks Kate made for her. She was never in pain, though strangers believed she was and therefore pitied her. Joan, who was very clever under all that lovely quiet, took advantage of this solicitude. Only Bernard suspected an innate shrewdness, a watchful cunning, a greed, and an enormous selfishness coiled in wait like a viper in Joan's shriveled little heart. It amazed him, disillusioned though he was, that one so young and untouched and cosseted and petted could be so ruthless of temperament, so avid.

I have only one true grandchild, he would say to himself with some sadness, and that is Jason, God help him. A true Garrity, Jason, but the others are not, and their father was not, either. Nor are they Shanahans, like poor Katie, all gentleness and kindness and faith. Where do they come from, these changelings? It grieved him that he could not love John Xavier and Joan Eleanor.

He looked up, this gray, gritty morning in November, when Jason entered the kitchen on his way to the outside privy, his face flushed with vexation. "I see Jack's run away again, the third time this week, and it is only Friday," he said.

"Mass, dear," said Kate. Jason went out through the kitchen door, slamming it after him. Kate gave Bernard a helpless look, and he said, "Well, then, he has reason, Katie, and this his birthday. It's too much to hope that Jack will say a prayer for him, I'm thinking." His voice was deep and strong, as sure and loud as that of a much younger man, and his brogue was rich as peat. He was long and upright and solid of body and appeared much younger than his seventy-two years. Constant exposure to wind and weather had permanently browned his complexion, which was vital in spite of the dry folds on his lean cheeks. He had a tight and furious mouth and flared nostrils and black brows like bad-tempered crows, and his thin and curly hair was an absolute white, arching over his powerful face like a snowy cliff.

Kate loved him more than she had loved her own father, and so did Jason. But John only feared and hated him, and Joan despised him, though she feared him also. She thought he was crude, and had he known this, he would have been pleased, for he was a man of no pretense, though he could be courtly at times.

He said to Kate this morning, "We'll be giving him his presents tonight, and not before?"

"He'll be too busy to enjoy them before tonight," said Kate, and felt a thrill of pain in her gentle heart. Perhaps, today, it might have been well if Jackie had not gone to Mass, and so given his brother a little time, on this his birthday. But God came first, did he not, before any human consideration? Still, Kate was hurt for her elder son. Bernard studied her with his own sadness. Katie Shanahan had been such a sweet and lively lass, happily singing in spite of famine, illness, and despair, and the damp little shanty in which they had lived in Ireland. But she had stopped singing when her husband, Peter, whom she had considered the noblest and most gifted man in the world, and the loveliest, had died of "the consumption" in America. Small of stature, and very thin, she had lost most of the brilliance of her complexion, and her large and luminous brown eyes had a haunted expression, though she was usually smiling. Her thick black hair, and those eyes, were all that was left of her endearing young appeal. The tender and touching mouth, once so rosy, was now pale and often tremulous. Her teeth needed attention, which she could not afford, but no one heard her pain, except Bernard, who could only guess it when he would see a swollen cheek.

Bernard was positive she was a saint, and the only saint in whom he believed. The small body, almost breastless and meager of hip, was neat and tidy under a gray calico dress with a sprightly apron starched to the stiffness and texture of cardboard. She moved about her sorry little rooms like a darting mouse, always busy, and to Bernard she seemed to move in light. There were times when he had to grunt and bend his head with a savage motion to hide his tears. He would think, for a moment, that he had caught a glimmer of radiance in the coiled masses of her black hair, which was always combed and neat.

We could not be worse off if we'd remained in Ireland, Bernard thought. But Pete *would* come, yammering this was a free country. Is it? Free for what? To starve in, to be reviled in, to be treated with contempt? Even the blackamoors were accorded better in this land than the Irish. Still, men and women and children were not killed on the streets here for their religion, or for stealing a loaf of bread, and their churches were not wrecked by evil creatures. Were they? There had been rumors of such in the Boston papers, and a few months ago old Joe Maggiotti's polished shop window had been shattered by a stone. A free country.

Bernard pondered. There was no freedom, at all, in this world, and never would there be, for man was vile. The most terrible enemy of his brother, less merciful than a tiger, more to be dreaded than the plague. An alien in a world otherwise beautiful. Freedom was a delusion. Man was the slave of his own appalling self, and a slave enslaves others. Why had the Lord died for such? It was a mystery which no priest had explained to Bernard's satisfaction.

There was a shrill splatter of rain against the one kitchen window, and Kate anxiously glanced through the glass for her son. The blue-gray shadow of the morning had not lightened perceptibly. The wind was palpitating in the polished black stovepipe; then it brutally hit the side of the little house, and the thin wall shivered.

"Where's Jason?" Kate said.

"Sure, and he's not dreaming," said Bernard.

2

But Jason was, though he could not be seen as yet in that shifting dull light before the sun rose. He had left the white-washed outhouse which Kate kept so absolutely sanitary and scrubbed and limed, and stood for a moment just near the door. He looked up at the sky, striated now, in the east, by alternating bands of black and gray and faint white; weight of darkness, bloated, here and there, by shapeless and tenebrous clouds. A gray rain had begun, the drops as sharp and cold as splinters of ice, and a wind like a huge knife-edge cut through them. Jason stood and looked at the back of the little house which his family inhabited. The yellow lamplight did not lighten the gloom, brave though it shone from the kitchen window. The house was built of aged clapboard, with a shingled roof which Bernard and Jason had to repair frequently, and it was the color of the sky itself. The house contained but three rooms, the large brick-floored and brick-walled kitchen with its wooden ceiling—which Bernard frequently shellacked to keep it bright—and two bedrooms, one for Kate and Joan, the other for Jason and John. Bernard slept on a narrow cot in the kitchen, and under that cot lay his thin tin trunk which he had brought from Ireland and which was filled with his few articles of clothing and other necessities. During the day the cot was covered by a many-colored wool afghan Kate had knitted. It served Bernard as a blanket in winter and added gaiety to the room all year long, and so the cot was also a comfortable couch or a place for a furtive nap during the day when Kate was overcome by exhaustion. Joan frequently usurped it, however, and Kate never rebuked her. There was a long wooden table which Bernard had made for himself with exactitude and love, though it was only soft wood. He had painted it a brilliant green with a yellow edging. He had also made the five chairs that surrounded it, which he had painted in the same colors.

He had also built the large cupboard, again in green and yellow, and Kate, out of scraps gathered over several years, had made a round braided rug for under the table. It protected feet against the chill of brick in the winter. Someone had given Kate some old lace curtains, which she had sedulously mended, and they covered the one kitchen window. Kate was saving pennies for curtains for the other two rooms. They would cost four dollars; she had saved two. In the meantime there were cracked canvas "blinds" at those windows, with ragged edges.

Jason gazed at the house where he had lived since his birth. It stood at the rear of a larger house, where the landlord lived. The landlord was little more prosperous than the Garrity family and had a wife who "ailed." He was a tinsmith, and could barely walk with his "rheumatism." He charged the Garritys four dollars rent a month for their house, and supplied the coal for their stove. Mr. Carson was a sour old man with a justified hatred for the world, and he resented Bernard's painless mobility and his "popish drunkenness." The two old men were not friends, though they were polite to each other. "You don't know what trouble is," Mr. Carson had once grunted to Bernard. Bernard thought of his three brothers and one sister who had been publicly hanged in Dublin by the English, and his mother who had died of starvation during the Famine, and his father who had fought in the streets for the right to practice his religion and had been bayoneted. He thought of himself who had accepted the "queen's shilling" and joined her army, in order to survive and procure bread for another sister and her brood. He had spent his youth in an English barracks, had married an Irish girl who was a servant in a London mansion, had produced one feckless son, Peter of the Poetry, and had then taken his young family back to Ireland at the end of his service. He had also brought with him four cherished pounds sterling, and three gold sovereigns.

He had learned carpentry in the army and made a stringent living in Dublin, until his wife had taken "the consumption" and had died swiftly and uncomplaining in his arms. There was none to care for ten-year-old Peter except an "ould widow woman" in the shanty next door. Bernard's tough heart had almost literally broken when his Agnes had died. He had not been able to buy enough blankets to keep her warm during her agonized illness, nor had he been able to buy the "nourishing food" the doctor had sternly recommended.

On the occasion when Mr. Carson had complained that Bernard did not know what trouble was, Bernard had grimly nodded, had filled his noxious pipe. "Sure, and right you are," Bernard had said, and had walked off, followed by the reproachful eyes of his landlord. Irishmen, according to Bernard, had their pride.

The street on which the Garritys lived was narrow, cobblestoned, and never was free of the odor of coal gas, dust, horse manure, outhouses, and stagnant water caught in backyard pools at every rain. Belleville had little in the way of sewers, and gaslight had come here only recently, mainly for the streets. It was the rare house which had the luxury of gas lamps and running water and indoor bathrooms. There were a few concrete walks, but mostly the sidewalks were composed of planked wood, uneven and rotting.

Bernard, accompanied by his son and Kate, had hoped to reach Pittsburgh, where he could practice his trade and where Peter might be able to find employment as a clerk in some office or shop. But the money did not last long enough to take them to that city. Peter had worked intermittently and listlessly at random employment, and then, shortly after Joan's birth, had given up living, literally and figuratively. At night he had written many very bad poems, hoping someday they would be published. With what could be spared he had bought books, the only virtue his father could find in him. No one but Bernard himself, and now Jason, read those books. A number of them had been secondhand copies of great poets, and "useless novels," as John called them. To John, all books without a religious theme were not to be considered worthy. Shakespeare's sonnets and plays were "indecent." "Wonder why he doesn't find a lot of indecency in the Holy Bible, then," Bernard had once remarked to Kate, and had laughed his grudging laugh. "Plenty of naughty tales of fornication and adultery and murder and such in the Book, none of which seemed to bother God very much. But then, I'm thinking Jack has a suspicion he's purer than the Lord himself."

There was no need for a craftsman like Bernard in Belleville. Most furniture was now made in factories, and came from a place called Grand Rapids, in the state of Michigan, and was much cheaper than handmade furniture, as Bernard had discovered. He could not compete at even the smallest profit. Belleville was not a prosperous little town. It was not near any mining section; it was not on a big river; there was little lumber in the vicinity to support a sawmill. It had no assets but its proximity to the Poconos. It lived on the rural community, which was not prosperous either. It did have three small factories, which manufactured machine tools and horseshoes and sundry other articles, but they would hire no "foreigners," and especially not "papist" ones. They had a warning sign on their walls to this effect.

Belleville's water system was provided by incredibly lavish wells, which fortunately never became dry, as its water tables were an underground stream.

The town had no "opera houses." But it did have several Baptist and Methodist churches, the one Catholic church, and one surprisingly active brothel. It did have church suppers and lawn fetes and strawberry "festivals," and six saloons which did a very good business, especially on Sundays, via the back doors. It was, Bernard thought, a very mean little town, for he was a Dublin man. It was also very shabby and had a special dreariness of its own. There were times when Bernard felt a silent, furious claustrophobia.

There were two newspapers, a morning one, an evening one, owned by the same man, whom Bernard loathed for his politics. The papers were sprightly and optimistic—and childish to him. Bernard was well-read and too worldly to be euphoric about anything, and the papers' bounding enthusiasm over almost everything revolted him. Occasionally he wrote acid letters to the papers, for which he was roundly abused by other readers. "Da," Kate would say with smiling love, "you are a caution." "So's all truth," Bernard would reply happily. "Besides, I'm literate, and nothing vexes the illiterate as much as literacy." Bernard, like many Irishmen, had intensely considered the priesthood, and had, before his sojourn in England, spent two years in a seminary in Navan. The priests, not Bernard, had decided Bernard had no true vocation. He was too intransigent. He assented to almost nothing, and repelled any attempt at rigorous discipline. He thought most of the saints a boring, maudlin, and two-dimensioned lot, and said so. They had, as he openly remarked, no guts. He was not unhappy at being expelled.

Until recently there had been only two large public schools in Belleville; then compulsory education had been inflicted on the people. Why people incapable of rational thought should be "educated" was a mystery to Bernard. Before compulsory education, only the intelligent, and those who longed for literacy, were educated beyond the first two or three grades. The others went out into the fields or the factories, to their greater peace of mind and their superior incomes. But now they were forced to attend school until they were fourteen, and so the number of schools and teachers had increased. The general thought behind it was contained in the

Constitution, which declared that all men were equal before the law—that is, a man's financial or social position had no impact on justice. A new and pernicious interpretation of the Constitution—that all men were equally endowed with intelligence and ability and excellent heredity at birth—resulted, in the schools, in a lowered curriculum. To rescue their children from this debacle, a number of financially able parents opened two private schools, where education was truly education. There was one Catholic school near the church, St. John the Baptist, where the nuns demanded the highest performance from their pupils, or expulsion. A boy or girl kept up with all the class, did all the strenuous homework, was subjected to intense and implacable discipline, or, to the humiliation of parents, was ousted.

In this formidable little school, John Xavier Garrity was the star pupil of the eighth grade and therefore cosseted and admired and encouraged by the nuns. His brother, Jason, was the scorn of Sister Mary Margaret, teacher of the ninth grade—which had sixty pupils. He was threatened with expulsion at least twice a month, for falling asleep at his splintered desk out of absolute exhaustion, which he neither complained of nor explained. He did not feel unjustly treated; it was a part of the life he lived. It was something to be endured—for the time being.

On this lamentable morning of his fourteenth birthday, Jason, hardly aware of the smarting particles of half-frozen rain which stung his face and bare hands, stared at his home and for the first time in his life knew an acute and adult depression, heavy as death. There was something about the forlorn scene, the wet wooden walls of all the houses, the livid light on their roofs, their meager feathers of smoke rising from huddled chimneys, the sound of the first vehicles on the street, the echoing rumble of wheels and the plodding clop of horses' hooves which added an almost supranormal melancholy to the whole atmosphere. Glancing at the garbage pails at the rear of the houses, Jason felt rather than saw the running furtive rats. Frail yellow lights were now appearing at other backyard windows, intensifying Jason's somber despair. He was unfamiliar with such an emotion, for he had a brave heart, and its impact, therefore, was intolerable. Behind those thin wet walls, he felt for the first time, were lives as stagnant as old water caught in a leaning barrel, lives immobilized in poverty and misery, never to escape. Were the lives of his family, and himself, as mean and insignificant

24

as these? Their only common denominator was pain and hunger. He felt all the devastating horror which confronted his neighbors, the irremediable suffering, the comfortless dejection.

For the first time in his young life he felt caught up in a common humanity; he experienced empathy, and it ripped up his emotions and assaulted his heart. He wanted to weep not only for himself but also for strangers. He had no words to express his feelings. When the big bell of the church growled its surly note to the cold wet air, indicating the lifting of the Host, it only added to the lonely dusk, the crushing sadness of the surroundings.

Jason, whose black curls and shoulders were already wet—he was shivering—could not move. He raised his eyes again to the doleful sky and the clouds behind which the morning sun was still hidden. He did not know he was crying, not with the tears of a child, but of a man stricken with the pain of his spirit, infused with a universal grief, a loss of something never known but only suspected in some deep oceanic depth of the soul.

A few clouds parted and a pale white sun looked down, silvery pallid, giving very little light, and no brightness, no warmth, no suggestion of a new day. It merely floated, an enormous flat sphere, in the darkness surrounding it.

Suddenly, from that cheerless orb two long colorless but sharply defined paths of misty radiance darted earthward. All at once, Jason's heart exploded with a huge mystical joy, inexplicable, without form, without boundaries. It was an ecstasy of discernment, of total understanding, of infinite awareness and comprehension, as if he had immediate knowledge of all life, of God himself. All the unknowable was explained, all shown. He was enraptured, stilled with bliss and exultation, caught up within himself, transfigured, powerful, exalted, as though he had glimpsed, for one eternal moment, the Beatific Vision. He had no impulse to kneel, to venerate, to worship, for what he experienced had no name, no frame of reference in piety, no connection with the world of men at all. It transcended time and place and flesh. It was only Itself, revealed utterly, possessing no human awareness. It was Revelation, and its awareness of its revelation was sufficient for it, demanding no acknowledgment.

Then it was gone, and with it the Revelation. Jason stood, trembling, conscious of something too tremendous to understand, though for an instant he had understood it entirely.

But he could not remember what he had understood when he had been caught up in that ecstasy. He could only remember some vast and limitless jubilation. He felt as if something had moved irrevocably in him, as a mountain is moved, or a sea diverted, and all the desolation about him was only an illusion. Life had lost, for a time at least, its power to hurt him.

He had heard of the "rapture" of saints. It never occurred to him that he himself, for one endless instant, had experienced rapture. He was not famous for devotion to his religion, or for his earnest practice of it. Yet, as he went toward the house, he was suddenly aware of God in the simplest and purest sense.

He ran in to the warmth of the big kitchen, shaking rain off vigorously, like a dog. He saw his mother's face, her tired eyes; he saw his grandfather eating prunes and stewed figs in absorption; he saw that Joan had come to the table, her glowing black hair neatly combed, her beautiful face as still as snow.

"Why did you stand out there in the rain, Jason?" asked Kate as she put a bowl of porridge in front of him.

"I was thinking," said Jason, wiping his face with the big family towel at the sink.

"Ugh," said Bernard. "Bad for a man's bowels, thinking."

But Kate was studying Jason with her usual anxious smile. "You were thinking of your birthday, dear? Tonight we'll have a little celebration."

Jason sat down at his grandfather's left and poured the thin blue milk over the oatmeal and was careful not to use more than one spoonful of precious sugar. Bernard did not look at his grandson, but he was sharply conscious that something had happened to Jason. There was nothing in his appearance or his manner to show what it was, though Bernard, with his Irish intuition, knew that in some manner Jason had changed. Was there a more compact outline to the boyo, a more vivid emanation? Well, at fourteen he was no longer a lad; he was a man. Perhaps he had just realized that. "More tea, Katie, please," Bernard said. The kitchen was quite warm and comfortable, bright with color. Bernard happened to glance at Joan. Was there a deeper malice in those beautiful blue eyes than usual when she stared at Jason, a more focused slyness? Sure, and it's just my imagination, thought Bernard. The rain was turning to snow; great white flakes were mingling with the drops. The wind increased in rage, and the window shook.

Jason said, "Why isn't Jack back from Mass? It's over now."

"Hah," said Bernard, "he's gone into heavenly discourse with the saints, perhaps."

"Da," pleaded Kate, pouring more tea into his cup.

"The trouble with you, Katie, is that you're a grand innocent woman," said Bernard. "It's a cold wet morning and his lordship doesn't feel inclined to do his paper route. Leaving it to Jase. And niver a copper does he leave for his brother, in thanks."

Joan spoke for the first time, in her high and childishly lovely voice. Kate thought it sounded like the tenderest note of a harp. "Jack has chosen the better part," she said in a very trenchant tone.

Bernard looked at her without love. "And now it's you quoting the Holy Bible, is it, then? Get it from Jack and his hypocrisies?" His dark face swelled with a rare anger, for he was almost always gentle with the female sex. Kate was distressed. "Da, Jack is no hypocrite. You've never said that before."

"Better if he was. There'd be some hope for him then," said Bernard. He rattled his spoon in his cup. "A man can outlive his hypocrisies, but niver those convictions which give him pleasure. Jack's pious convictions give him the privilege of shirking his duties. What do you say to that, Jason?"

Jason was hurriedly gulping his breakfast. He not only must deliver his mother's laundry before school, but also John's papers. It was now a quarter past six by the alarm clock that stood on a shelf near the sink. He said, "One of these days I'm going to kick his..." He looked at his mother and sister and said, "...his teeth down his throat."

Bernard laughed his loud, abrupt laugh. Joan said, "That sounds just like you, Jase. You don't understand about Jack, and never will."

"I hope you're right," said Jason, but his voice was softer. Joan's beauty always entranced him. She rarely, as Bernard would remark, had a civil word for her older brother, yet it was obvious that he adored her, and Bernard felt uneasy. Jason was no fool; how was it possible that he could not see that his sister despised him? Bernard had long suspected that Joan felt herself "above" her family, as if she were a damned princess. But then, even the rough brown wool robe she wore

27

at the table gained a certain air and aristocracy on her perfect
little body, a certain patrician dignity to which Bernard himself was not immune. Jason, he would reflect, no doubt felt
that also. It was a strange thing that beauty effortlessly received love, even if it were possessed by the unworthy, while
a noble soul was frequently disdained if it lived in an un-
prepossessing body. Bernard might have his doubts about the
existence of God, but he never doubted the existence of Satan.
His presence was only too evident in the world.

Jason swallowed tea so hot it burned his mouth. He jumped
to his feet, went to the wall where coats hung, and put on his
grandfather's warm dark tweed coat which Bernard had
brought from Ireland. It was hideous and too long, but it shed
rain like glass. Jason wore it, by permission, only on stormy
days. He hastily kissed his mother, patted Joan's averted
head, struck a heavy affectionate blow on his grandfather's
shoulder, and ran out. Bernard watched him go. Yes, there
definitely was a change in Jason today. It could not be defined,
but it surely was there, almost palpable.

Jason ran briskly down the desolate wet street; the cob-
blestones glistened with dirty moisture even in this dun early
light. He had pulled a woolen cap over his head; his boots
splashed through puddles of black water. The tiny lawns before the old beaten houses were but trampled mud, for there
were too many children in the harsh neighborhood. Some
housewives were not too careful about their outdoor privies
and the smell of human offal was pervasive. Jason reached
the small corner shop of Joseph Maggiotti and pushed open
the door. A bell tinkled wanly. Old Mr. Maggiotti appeared,
holding a buttered crust of his own bread, peering gnomelike
in the unlighted gloom of his shop. He was very old, very
emaciated, and absolutely bald. His small face was but a dark
wedge of pain and patience, but his black eyes were as vivacious as a youth's and brilliant with intelligence. He
grinned at Jason, and his bright white teeth shone even in
that murky light.

"Again? For the papers?" he said. "Jack's with the angels,
si?"

"Si," said Jason. "I'm going to kick his ass off one of these
days."

"Good," said Joe, nodding vigorously. "And one for me, eh,
too?"

"Si." The newspaper wagon was waiting. It was already
heaped with papers. Mr. Maggiotti covered the papers with

a length of cracked brown oilcloth. "You're a good boy, Jase," he said. "And a successful man you'll be." He tapped his forehead. "I know it, here."

"I hope so," said Jason, tucking the oilcloth around the papers.

Mr. Maggiotti looked at him shyly with affection. He reached into the pocket of his long striped apron and brought out a small object wrapped in brown paper. "For you. For the birthday," he said. Jason took the object, unwrapped the paper. There was a new silver dollar in it.

"I can't take all that money, Mr. Maggi," he protested.

"You take it. Saved for a long time. Went to the bank for it." Mr. Maggiotti shone with delight.

"A whole dollar!"

"Pretty, no? A silver dollar." Mr. Maggiotti preened. "Saved for a long time. For you, Jase."

Jason almost cried. He wanted to drop the coin on the aged wood counter and refuse it, but he saw the shining eyes of the old man, the pride, the pleasure. He said in a rough voice, "Thanks, Mr. Maggi. I've never had one before. I'll keep it all my life. I'll never spend it."

The old Sicilian nodded. "A dollar saved, it is good." He lit the gas jet near the till. The yellow light spewed out and lit up every spotless corner of the minute shop, showing the jars of cheap penny candles, the packages of Bull Durham, the rolls of poor gay cloth, the burnished pots and pans, the barrels of pickles neatly covered by white napkins, the glass case filled with black cotton mittens, pins, needles, thread of various colors, shoelaces, buttons, scissors, secondhand shoes of all sizes brightly polished and mended by the old man himself, and a meat counter containing thick Italian sausages, pungent cheese, homemade bread, small buckets of butter, a few cans of sardines, and various other sundries. There were drawers behind the counter where pressed glass dishes waited for purchasers, and rosaries and cutlery and knives. On the distempered wall hung a sign, "In God we trust. All others, cash." It was a wise motto which Mr. Maggiotti often forgot when confronted by a child or woman who was hungry or a man who had just lost his poor job. He was usually repaid, sooner or later. Very seldom was he cheated. After all, a man must eat, and so must a child. He knew that if he was not repaid, payment was impossible, so he forgot.

"I've got something for the Mama, too," he said, and he gave Jason a very oily brown package which smelled exceptionally appetizing. "Not every day we have a son with a birthday, no?"

Jason carefully put the package in the big pocket of his grandfather's coat. The shop was deathly cold. The little iron pot stove was never lit until almost Christmas. Mr. Maggiotti, in consequence, had a frightening cough all winter. He coughed now. But he smiled glowingly at Jason. Without speaking again, Jason tugged the paper-filled wagon outside. He could feel the old Sicilian's eyes watching him, and he was afraid to look back. Near the entrance was nailed a small wooden cross. Jason looked at it with a dark, closed face and said, "Nobody should be as poor as this, nobody. It isn't right." He felt the silver dollar in his pocket and he wanted to cry. But this would mean two dollars this week instead of the one Mr. Maggiotti paid him every Saturday.

He tried to whistle as he bent his head against the rain and the wind. But it was a dolorous sound. He had forgotten what he had experienced that morning. Somewhere in the back of his mind it lingered, waiting. He went down the street, turned into Tunbridge Avenue, a grandiose name for a street meaner than the Garrity street. Deftly he rolled the newspapers tightly and tossed them on broken porches or against paintless doors. It was quite light now, but there was no sun, only the shriek of the wind. At the end of Tunbridge Avenue he was hailed loudly, and saw his best—and only—friend, Lionel Nolan.

Lionel was a merry soul, blithe, mischievous, shrewd, intelligent, and cynical even at his age, which was thirteen. He was the "bad fate" of the nuns, who loved him just the same for his jolly nature, his wit, his willingness to run errands for the harried women, his exuberant healthfulness, a rare thing in this section, and even for his "naughty tricks." When he entered the classroom, invariably late, he brought an excitement with him, an ebullience, which made the sourest old nun smile unwillingly and cuff him in affection. Ancient Sister Agatha, the principal, who was called some very unpleasant names by the pupils in private, would smirk on Lionel after administering the proper severe punishment. She would say, "You're a rare bad spalpeen, and that you are, my lad," and send him off with a heavy bang on his back. "And mind you don't come back for more too soon."

He was an altar boy, very severe of face and perfect in manner when serving, but his parodies of Father Sweeney had a touch of lewdness about them, which delighted the more unregenerate of his companions. Father Sweeney was certain Lionel had a vocation, which made Lionel risible among his many friends, and many friends he had. He could outbox, outrun, outwrestle any other boy his age, some even older, and it was done with no overt malice or arrogance. He was also generous when he had a penny or two to spend, and no one, not even Jason, suspected that this was to buy approval, friendship, and a following. He was famous for his "tall tales," which no one ever thought to call outright lies, for the tales were so amusing, so obviously extravagant, that to most people it appeared that Lionel did not intend them to be believed, but only to be enjoyed. He could also sing like an angel, and there was no game with which he was not familiar. He was as active as a monkey.

Lionel was "red Irish," in contrast with Jason's "black Irishness." He was shorter and more muscular than Jason, and of a sturdy build in spite of poor food and the adversity in which he lived. He had a plump, wide face with a very impertinent nose and a big laughing mouth and jumping yellowish eyes always mirthful and very observing. His hair was violently red, and he had two deep dimples in his face, one on each side of his mouth, plus a dimpled chin. He was considered very handsome and fascinating, except to his father, whom he called "Gloomy Gus." Mr. Colin Nolan possessed a certain Irish puritanism and inflexibility which did not endear him to his one son. He had been known as the "heaviest hand in County Mayo." Certainly Lionel felt it frequently, which did not seriously disrupt his enjoyment of life. The Nolan household was the grimmest in the neighborhood. Mrs. Nolan, a tall flat woman, had never been known to smile. Not even beer was permitted under that dark roof, and Mr. Nolan never went to the local saloon.

Jason loved Lionel, for Lionel literally lit up the atmosphere whenever he appeared, making the most somber day an expectation of pleasure and amusement. He was much attached to Jason, though he rallied him frequently and made good-natured fun of him before others. He thought Jason too serious, in spite of Jason's cheerful smile, which he guessed too often concealed anxiety and worry. But Jason forgot his worries when he was with his friend. Lionel made him laugh. Jason was not of a naturally confiding disposition, but he confided in Lionel, and it never occurred to him that Lionel, though he would listen sympathetically, never confided in him at all. He believed that Lionel was "light," and refused to accept trouble, which was a relief to Jason, who often felt his own troubles were unbearable.

Lionel had a sister whom Jason avoided. Her name was Molly, and the name suited her. She was twelve years old, and like her brother, she was "red Irish," with a pert and pointed face, large eyes the color of clear honey, a mass of red curls, and a spirited rosy mouth usually uttering sardonic remarks. She was still small for her age and showed no signs as yet of nubile curves; her slight figure was boyish and restless. Her lean little arms were spotted with enormous freckles, the same kind that covered her face and her neck, and she was disapproved of as a "tomboy," for there was no pole or tree she could not climb with remarkable speed, and no fence she could not leap over with an unseemly display of lank thighs, and hardly a boy she could not soundly thrash when needful. Vivacious, keen, smart, and direct, she was not loved as her brother was loved. Though she was an excellent scholar, the nuns felt no fondness for her. She was too derisive of fools in the classroom, and could be impudent even to the most formidable nun. She had a way of defiantly tossing that rioting blaze of curls, and her eyes could be challenging.

Her father adored her. Her mother was afraid of her. Lionel treated her with smiling indulgence, and joked about rather than with her. She would look at him sharply, her golden eyes intent, and there would be something grave in her expression, if only briefly.

Jason thought her a nuisance when he thought of her at all, and disliked her. She would tease him and push him and laugh at him loudly. He did not know that even if she was only twelve she was deeply and maturely in love with him. In comparison with Joan, his sister, she was an active squirrel full of chattering. He thought her extremely ugly, whereas Joan was a haughty nymph in spite of her crippled state. In order to see Jason, Molly would visit Joan and help her with her homework, but between the two girls there was much hidden animosity.

Between old Bernard and Molly there was a profound empathy, an understanding, and an intense fondness. They seemed to speak to each other without words. Kate considered the child "very noisy, but clean and well-mannered," and that was all. Kate was incapable of disliking anyone, and she was grateful to Molly for her kindness to Joan, and was hurt when Joan uttered a cleverly malicious remark about the child in her absence. Molly's animation made Joan realize her own affliction and limitations. She believed Molly to be vulgar and coarse, and never saw the bright softness in Molly's eyes, and the compassion. Molly was not deceived by Joan; she knew her thoroughly, as Bernard knew her, and pitied the crippled girl not only for her affliction but also for her nature. She saw that Joan despised Jason, and this outraged the girl. For John she had a smiling contempt; he amused her.

On this drab and storm-swept morning, Jason was glad to see his friend, and hailed him in return. "What're you doing out so early," he asked Lionel, "and in this damned weather?"

"Thought you might be delivering the papers Jack should be doing," said Lionel. "Here. Give me a load for across the street."

They often met like this, and the somberness of the day lightened for Jason. He felt rich in the friendship of the most popular boy in the school. He could not understand why he, the least popular, attracted Lionel. Gratefully he filled Lionel's arms, thinking that time would be saved and he would not be late again for school. "You're dippy for doing this for ole Jack," said Lionel. "I'd kick him in the crotch, myself. Why do you do it?"

He often asked this question, and Jason invariably replied, "Well, there's my mother." Lionel would nod sympathetically, as if he understood mothers. He did not like his own mother at all. But his apparent sympathy was consoling to Jason. "I know," he would say, and run across the street and deftly distribute the papers, all with extravagant gestures and whistlings. His bare red head was like a spot of fire in the murkiness, blithely bobbing along the wooden walks and up the porch steps.

Jason never thought of Lionel as enigmatic, if he had even known the meaning of the word. Molly often thought of her brother as this, though she, too, as yet did not know the word itself. Bernard Garrity mistrusted him. "There's more to the bucko than appears," he would say. "These laughing men need to be watched." But Kate was fond of Lionel; Jason would brighten openly at the sight of him, and she loved Lionel's constant stream of jokes. She found something heartening in one who found life amusing and bearable. To her it meant a sort of reassuring nonchalance and strength. The Nolans were every bit as poor as the Garritys, if not more so, yet Lionel never complained, was never downhearted or resentful. Nor was he stupid and blandly accepting. He had insouciance.

As for Joan, her face would become enchanting when Lionel appeared, her voice more musical, her smiles ready and waiting. She even acquired a dainty animation. Lionel taught her to play Old Maid and checkers, and showed her a genuine patience and a desire to please. He was not insensible to beauty, and Joan was all sweetness to him.

Once Lionel had asked Jason, "What do you want most out of life?"

Jason considered this for a long moment and then said, "Money."

"So do I." Lionel rubbed his fingers together lovingly.

"But how're we going to get it?" asked Jason with some desperation.

Then Lionel said a strange thing. "You'll find a way, kid, you'll find a way." For once he did not laugh; he did not even smile. He had only stared long and hard at Jason, his yellowish eyes, not as clear as his sister's, but disingenuous, very intent. Years later Jason was to say to himself, "He knew. He knew all the time."

There were two papers left in the wagon. One was for Bernard, as Jason knew. It was old Joe's gift to him each day. The other one was for Jason's favorite customer, Patrick Michael Mulligan, the owner of Mulligan's Inn-Tavern, which even the most rigorous called "a nice decent place." Though, as an Irishman, he was not accepted in what passed for Belleville society, he was respected and personally liked. He could be counted on for any charity, for he had a great kind heart and was genuinely affable and kind. His employees loved him, though he could be stern with incompetents and those who considered a job a place for social encounter. He demanded loyalty and gave it in full measure. The Inn-Tavern had thirty clean bedrooms, comfortable and warm, and visitors from out of town usually filled it to the last room. Patrick was a concerned host; he regarded his guests as valued friends. He was as round and comforting as a warm muffin fresh from one of his own ovens; he had a charming open countenance, like a summer rose, flashing blue eyes and thin blond hair and several chins, for he was a marvelous chef and ate immense servings of his own dishes. He was famous for his corned beef and cabbage—always fresh and well-spiced—his sauerbraten and potato pancakes, his homemade breads, his roast beef and stuffed geese, his cutlets and pork chops, his delectable fried chicken as crisp as a nut on the outside and soft and luscious within, his herby stews and pastries, his fine rich coffee. His dining room always immaculate, his waiters always obliging and polite.

His tavern, attached to the building, was conducted with decorum, and no one criticized even the ladies who patronized it with their husbands or fathers. It was "respectable." He had been born in Ireland; he knew how to make a pub the neighboring meeting place for friends. On Saturday night there was a fiddler and a piano for dancing. All was demure, invisibly regulated, and friendly. He was considered a rich man, and owed not a penny, having the Irishman's aversion for banks and mortgages and debts.

As he was a widower, with one child, no one thought to rebuke him for having a discreet mistress, a middle-aged widow of property, who was the very soul of prudence and good conduct, and of an excellent family with robust bank accounts. No one ever caught them in public impropriety. They addressed each other formally—no use of Christian names before others. Sometimes they soberly mentioned marriage, which never took place. Mrs. Garden did not intend to jeopardize her financial standing by marriage, for in the commonwealth of Pennsylvania a wife's money still automatically belonged to her husband on wedlock. Besides, secretly, both had had disastrous marriages and did not desire another such, though they loved each other dearly.

Mr. Mulligan's daughter, Patricia Mary, had been born when Mr. Mulligan had been forty-four. She was now thirteen years old, and the heart of his life. She was never called Pat or Patsy, for she was a most aloof and dignified young lady, "a bit of a snob," as her father would say with love. Tall, if too slender, she had a cultured presence for a girl so young, and was extremely—and consciously—graceful. She had a private tutor. Her father would boast that she could quote Shakespeare "by the armload" on the slightest provocation. She thought Patrick crude and was somewhat ashamed of the Inn-Tavern, believing it unworthy of her pretension. Her mother, she would say, had been the daughter of an Irish knight, a fiction which the doting father did not dispute. "All the Irish are the sons of kings," he would say, winking and patting his very rotund belly.

Patricia, contrary to her father's convictions, was not very pretty, though she had great style even at her age. Her father bought her clothing in Philadelphia. She had a cloak lined with white ermine, and her undergarments were of silk or the softest linen, handmade, and cascading with lace. She had a buggy of her own and a sleek mare. She rode about town with an uplifted profile and an expression of chronic disdain. She had fine straight light brown hair, always elaborately curled, a thin sharp face with a large nose, thin colorless lips, and her dead mother's agate eyes. In her case, however, the eyes were cold and perpetually scornful.

She took riding and dancing lessons, went to Philadelphia frequently to visit an aunt—also with pretensions, whose husband was a "damned Sassenagh," according to Patrick—and elegant cousins who pretended to be English. She had no intentions of spending her life in Belleville. She loved nobody but herself, not even her fatuous father, whom she endured as a lady must endure her elders. She thought of herself, not as an Irish Catholic girl, but as an Episcopalian, her aunt having converted to that religion on her marriage. Patrick insisted on her attendance at Mass on Sundays and holy days of obligation; on this he was very firm. Patricia "suffered." She thought Father Sweeney proletarian and unlettered.

She had few if any friends in Belleville. She had fawners, whom she tolerated. Had it not been for Patrick, no servants would have remained in the ugly if luxurious house he owned near the Inn-Tavern, for Patricia was pettish, overbearing, and extremely demanding. The maids hated her, but they loved Patrick.

Jason had seen her a few times, in her polished buggy and sometimes at the door of her father's house. It was inexplicable that this proud Irish boy, with his own dignity and sense of worth, should have fallen in love with this dim girl. Lionel had guessed this. He had laughed at Patricia, ridiculed her openly to Jason, rallied him about her—this had led to their first fistfight, which Jason had won, to his later contrition. Lionel no longer teased him about Patricia. Jason, he believed, had too much sense to be long infatuated with that "silly, homely, daffy girl."

Jason, to Patricia, did not exist. He was someone who brought papers occasionally, and delivered the exquisite laundry—her own—done by Jason's mother. She read constantly. She dreamed of a Continental nobleman, or an English lord at least. When she saw Jason he was faceless, a lumbering cheap Irish nobody. Her father spoke of him fondly, but then Patrick spoke of almost everyone fondly and ap-

36

provingly. That her father was a "grand darling of a man," as Bernard called him, she did not know or care. Patrick's brogue offended her; she had tried to correct him a few times, but had, to her dismay, encountered blue eyes suddenly hard and fierce, and had been frightened. Calculating, if not very intelligent, she knew when to retreat.

Patrick had a houseman, whom Patricia called "our butler," but Patrick was always first up and liked to receive the morning newspaper himself. So he appeared at the heavy double oaken doors of his house when he heard Jason pound up the porch stairs. "Top of the morning to you, boyo," was his invariable greeting. He gave Jason his personal sunny smile, but his glance was keen and knowing.

"Mr. Mulligan," said Jason, and paused. Mr. Mulligan waited. Then Jason said, "I'm fourteen today, sir. You promised me a job."

"So I did, Jason." Mr. Mulligan regarded him fondly. "When can you start?"

"I want to finish school, in June. Ninth grade."

Mr. Mulligan nodded. "Good, then. In June, we'll talk. Start you in the kitchen. Three dollars a week and all you can eat." He saw Lionel racing across the street, still delivering the last papers. "Promised him one in June, too, when he's fourteen. Make a good waiter, I think. Too flighty, perhaps. Time will tell."

"He's not flighty, Mr. Mulligan. He's got a lot of sense."

Patrick thrust out his lips. "Yes, I know. A bold lad. Bright. Best be careful, Jason."

"Why, sir?"

Mr. Mulligan shrugged. "Not for me to judge, boyo. I've been wrong before."

"He's my best friend, sir."

"And many's the man who was betrayed by his best friend. Remember Judas, who betrayed our Lord."

Jason smiled. He thought Mr. Mulligan fanciful. He touched his cap and ran down the steps. It was snowing heavily now. Mr. Mulligan lingered in the doorway. Like many Irishmen, he was prescient, intuitive. He wished, for a moment, that Jason was his son. He closed the door and felt a vague melancholy. Then he was annoyed at himself. He reopened the door and called to Jason, fumbling in his pocket. Jason returned. Mr. Mulligan thrust a five-dollar gold piece in his hand, the first Jason had ever seen. Jason stared at it speechlessly.

"Happy birthday, Jason," said Mr. Mulligan, and closed the door in Jason's face. He did not answer the long, angry pealing of the bell. He chuckled to himself. When the gold piece dropped into the mailbox Mr. Mulligan nodded.

"He'll do," he said aloud.

Jason told Lionel of this episode. His face was dark with outrage. Lionel stared at him, then burst out laughing, and gave no explanation for his merriment. He loved Jason, in his way, but thought him a bit of a fool. He filed this information away in his formidable memory. Lionel never forgot anything of significance. He wondered, for an instant, if Jason had displayed a prodigious cunning. Pride, to Lionel, was self-indulgence, or an astute self-serving.

3

The day was all white when Jason arrived home: sky, earth, even the bare trees. A vast cold chill now lay windless in the streets, and a deep silence, for Belleville had no streetcars. The stillness was disturbed only by an occasional rumbling wagon and horses or a hoarse cough from a hurrying workman. No children were abroad; it was too early yet for school, and housewives were busy in the kitchens. Lionel had returned to his home for breakfast and Jason heard his own footsteps crunching on the new snow. Mr. Carson hailed him as he went down the alley to the little Garrity house. "Got a spare newspaper?" he asked, leaning from his narrow rear doorway.

"Only the one for my grandda," he said. Mr. Carson grumbled and slammed his door in umbrage. Jason went into his house. Well, at last John was back from Mass. He was sitting in the warm cheerful kitchen at the table and was devouring a very big dish of hot porridge. He looked at Jason remotely with his small gray eyes. As usual, he appeared to be freshly scrubbed with harsh soap; he was excessively neat and his slight body was always rigid.

He offered no thanks to his brother for having done his morning work. He gave off an air of preoccupation with unworldly things, which always irritated Bernard. "As if he is being served by invisible altar boys," Bernard would say. Joan did not look at Jason either. She was busy buttering toast for John and smearing that toast with marmalade that Kate had made in the summer. Kate looked worriedly at the alarm clock on the shelf near the sink. "Jason, love, you'll have to hurry with the laundry," she said.

"He'll have a hot cup of tea first," said Bernard, and deftly took the teapot from his granddaughter, who had been in the act of refilling John's cup. She tossed her beautiful head and regarded Jason with the air of one resenting an intruder. "And one of those pieces of toast, then, Joan," added Bernard.

Jason, standing, drank the cup of tea and glanced at the clock. He then remembered the parcel Mr. Maggiotti had given him and fished it from the huge pocket of his grandfather's coat. He gave it to Kate, who reddened a little and

39

then opened it. It contained nearly half a pound of fat bacon, a slab of salt pork, a thick length of salami sausage, a slice of yellow cheese, and a chunk of butter. "Oh, how kind," Kate murmured.

John stared avidly at the bacon. "I think I'll have a little of that," he said. "If you please, Mum."

"It's for Jason's birthday," said Bernard. "I know that."

"Let him have some," said Jason, seeing his mother's face. "A priest has to keep up his strength, you know."

Bernard laid down his spoon and regarded Jason sternly. "He'll have none of that, Jason, unless you have some too."

"No time," said Jason. Joan gave John a pleased smile.

"Then," said Bernard, "Jack has no time, either. He'll take Joan to school himself this morning, in her chair, and not you, Jason."

"Da," said Kate.

Bernard was rarely abrupt with Kate, but he now said, "Quiet, Katie." Jason, usually indifferent to injustice, smiled. "I think I'll have a piece of my birthday cheese, Mum. I do find I'm hungry after all. Da, will you have some with me?"

Bernard winked at him. "Thanks, lad, but I'll wait for tea. Put it all away, Kate, for our feast tonight. Except for giving Jason a slice now—on some of that toast, Joanie, which you are kindly buttering."

Joan felt a thrill of hatred for both Jason and her grandfather, but she silently thrust the fresh toast at Jason, who took it with the slice of cheese his grandfather had cut for him. John had assumed an appearance of proud martyrdom. He sipped daintily at his tea. Joan touched his arm in sympathy. "Mr. Maggot must think we are beggars."

Bernard said in a slow, hard voice, "Don't call him that again, Joan. Ever."

She flinched. Bernard did not use that tone often, and it was threatening. He had slapped her lovely face more than once when she had been unusually impudent. He did not consider her crippled state to be any excuse for cruelty.

Jason remembered something else. He withdrew the silver dollar from his jacket pocket. "Mr. Maggi gave me this, too, for my birthday." He held it in the palm of his hand and it glittered in the lamplight.

"A rare bucko, my friend," said Bernard. "You'll save it, Jason?"

"How very kind," said Kate as she closed the cupboard door where she kept her small store of foodstuffs. "A whole dollar. He must need it for himself, poor soul." John and Joan stared unblinkingly at the coin. "We could use it," said John.

"And Jason could save it," said Bernard. "It can inspire him."

Jason hesitated. He glanced at his mother, at her sweet exhausted face. He went to her and put the dollar in her hand. She tried to refuse it. "No, Mum," he said. "It gives me pleasure to know you can buy a new length of cloth for a Sunday dress, and you need it." Kate's eyes grew large and bright with tears. She looked at Bernard, who smiled at her. "A good enough use for a birthday dollar, Katie. Take it."

"Joanie needs some new petticoats," murmured Kate. Bernard promptly reached out and removed the coin from her hand. He tossed it in the air and it shone. "A frock for you, Katie, or back it goes to Jason. Take your choice."

"Oh, Da," she said, but accepted the coin and put it on a shelf.

Jason, eating hungrily, told his family of the gold piece Mr. Mulligan had attempted to give him. They stared at him dumbfounded and incredulous. Jason said, "I dropped it back in his post box."

"No!" cried John with new outrage. "Five dollars! A gold piece! It could pay this month's rent. You must have been out of your mind, Jase!"

Jason said in his grandfather's own hard, slow voice, "It was alms—charity. Mr. Mulligan isn't my friend, he's only a customer. He isn't a relation. He is a stranger. Alms."

"You did right," said Bernard. "It was the only thing to do. I'm proud of you, Jason."

But John was thinly excited and trembling. His whole body quivered. He regarded his brother as one regards an enemy. "At the very least, you could have dropped it in the poor box in the church!"

Bernard leaned back ponderously in his chair, and his eyes, as they looked at John, were icily bitter. "It minds me I heard that before—about giving a gift to the poor," he said. "It minds me someone was given a lesson concerning that. Or you, with your Bible, Jack, know nothing about that."

"We are obligated to give to the poor," said John, who winced at his grandfather's look. But he had some courage of his own.

Bernard uttered a sound which was neither a grunt nor a laugh. "Well, tell me, then, what our Lord said to Judas when Judas complained to our Lord that the gift of ointment

41

which Mary Magdalen was rubbing on the good Lord's feet was a waste. 'The money should have been given to the poor,' said Judas. And what did our Lord say to that, Jack?"

Stains of scarlet appeared on John's gaunt cheeks. He was silent at first. Then he said, "In this case it doesn't apply, Da."

"Who are you to judge?" replied Bernard with a contempt which forbade any further argument. He smiled briefly at Jason. "And proud am I of you, boyo, for not believing you are poor. A man's only poor when he thinks he is, poor devil."

John swung on Jason. "You didn't think it 'alms' to take that food from Mr. Maggiotti! What's the difference?"

"He's a friend," said Jason. "We give him things, too. But I had nothing to give Mr. Mulligan, who's not my friend."

Jason put his coat on again. His mother's neatly wrapped laundry was waiting, four thick bundles of it. If he hurried now, he might not be late for school. He ran out.

Something happened to him, mused Bernard. There's a grand difference in him today. He has become a man. It was not only the very hot tea which made Bernard's eyes suddenly moist. For some reason he looked at the plain wooden cross on the wall, and did not know why he looked. He usually avoided it. He and God had some very violent differences of opinion. He said, wholly out of context, "There's one thing the Sassenagh will never forgive the Irish for. We survived."

John shrugged. He was not proud of being Irish. He was proud of nothing but his own piety.

Jason was late for school after all, in spite of his running on the errands. Mrs. Sturgeon had been too slow in finding her purse to pay him the seventy-five cents she owed.

"Heedless, wretched, dilatory boy!" Sister Mary Margaret scolded when Jason erupted into the silent classroom of some forty-five boys and girls. "No sense of duty, of obligation, of common politeness and consideration for the other scholars! Hold out your hand, Jason Aloysius Garrity, and a shame on you!"

She smartly used the ruler on Jason's extended hand. His palm, fortunately, was numb with cold, so he felt little pain. The nun was a short, plump woman with an irascible face and glittering pince-nez and belligerent eyes. "This is the third time this month. I'll have a talk with Sister Agatha, or perhaps with Father Sweeney. This carelessness must stop."

Jason attempted to say something, but he was out of breath. "No excuses!" cried Sister Mary Margaret. "To your seat with you, and get out your arithmetic book! Page twenty-five. Not that it will do you any good, with your slothful ways."

Jason, frankly, was not a good scholar. He read with joy all the books that belonged to his grandfather, and some which he could buy for a penny or two in some frowsy old bookshop. He could write "a fine hand," which the nun admitted herself, and his compositions were imaginative and grammatically correct, and he was greatly interested in history and poetry and literature. He had a discriminating eye and was aware of nuances and hidden meanings, and was intensely alive to sensations and color. But mathematics, civics, and geography appeared dull and pedestrian. Unlike his brother, John, abstractions did not interest him. He could do sums well enough, after sweaty struggle, but life impinged on him too acutely for mathematics to hold his attention. Curiously enough, what little science he learned in school engrossed him. He did not connect it with mathematics. He knew exactly how far the moon was from the earth, but how that knowledge had been acquired never occurred to him. He believed it was by some occult intuition.

In short, as Bernard knew, Jason was involved with mankind. He was endlessly fascinated by the changes on men's faces, the intonations of their voices, their guessed motives, the way they tried to compromise with the grim circumstances of their existence. He did not always sympathize. A man accepted his life, or if it were unbearable, he tried to change it for the better. Like Bernard, Jason detested whiners. A man should never say, "Oh, pity me, for I am a poor soul and the victim of my fate! Or of society!" No. A real man said, "This is where I am, but I need not stay in the gutter. It is my duty to change what is evil or intolerable in my life. I was given the strength to choose my way, and I will choose it. To do less is to degrade myself by my own will."

He did not, as yet, put this exactly into words, but he knew it with all his soul.

He was approaching confirmation. His knowledge of the catechism was uncertain. He could never recite the seven sacraments in the correct order. He could not understand penance, for he rarely, knowingly, did anything to demand penance. There was simply no time for wrongdoing. He could not completely grasp the difference between venial and mortal sin. He could not quote the Ten Commandments in order, either. As for the rosary—he understood the Five Joyful Mysteries, but the others confused him, except for the Sorrows of the Blessed Mother. After all, his own mother had her sorrows. There were times when he felt a vague but deep resentment at her undeserved suffering. He also hated injustice and cruelty and malice, which he observed were all about him. He often asked himself, "Why are people like that?" He had seen that these things were not inspired by poverty, but came out of the dark souls of men themselves, mostly unprovoked. He had been taught of evil. He felt it more powerful in the world than any "innate goodness of man."

The nuns considered him a dullard and sighed over him.

Out of sheer weariness he fell asleep at eleven o'clock, and was awakened painfully by a box on his ears. "Lazy, stupid boy!" cried Sister Mary Margaret. "You think of nothing but eating and sleeping—a great big boy like you! Look at your smudged paper! Haven't you learned how to use a pen yet? What a trial you must be to your poor mother!"

She added, with a deep moan and with uplifted eyes, "But she is comforted by your brother, for which we must give thanks to God."

Jason was still more than half-asleep, for he said in a loud if sluggish voice, "My brother needs a kick in the ass."

The class exploded with delight. Sister Mary Margaret retreated a step as if at a sacrilege. Some of the boys clapped, some booed. Some of the girls pretended shock. Jason was sent down to the office with a note for Sister Agatha.

Sister Agatha, an ancient lady with a rigorous view of mankind—quite justified—was in a rare benevolent mood that morning. She had just given young Father Sweeney what she called "a piece of my mind," which had been extraordinarily eloquent due to her arthritis. Ordinarily she regarded Jason with a less-than-kindly eye. She was old and she was harassed and her constant pain made her impatient, and she was always hungry. She could not recall ever having had a good satisfying meal in all her life. She was convinced that humanity had no authentic reason for existence, for which opinion no acts of contrition on her part could ever make her sorry. Tiny, active as a cricket for all the arthritis—she did not believe in "Giving In"—she had a wizened face like a parched raisin, wise fierce old hazel eyes leaping with life, a pale cherry of a nose, and a baleful mouth full of obviously false teeth. Even in repose her expression was wrathful and suspicious, and her wimple crackled loudly like winter ice underfoot when she was disturbed, which was almost always.

Her office was small and extremely shabby if savagely clean and tidy with its files and bare floors and two bare uncurtained windows. One showed the nearby wall of the church with its sooty bricks now painted with streaks of snow, a bleak sad scene hardly four feet away, which blocked the light from her office. But the other window revealed a glimpse of mountain splendor, white and dark blue against the wan sky. Suddenly a crown of gold touched the brow of one peak, and Jason, in spite of his exhausted condition, felt a faint memory of what he had experienced earlier that morning. Sister Agatha, always acute, saw that subtle change on the youth's face, and she sat back in her creaking chair and gazed at him intently.

"Well, and what have you done now, Jason lad?" she asked. She pretended to study the note Sister Mary Margaret had sent her. Jason had never heard her speak so mildly. It was invariably the case, with Sister Agatha, to administer punishment first and then, very occasionally, to suffer explanations afterward. "'Never a lick amiss' is my motto," she would say.

"You cursed, it says here, Sister Mary Margaret. No." She peered at the small writing. "You used vulgar language in connection with your excellent brother, John." As she had employed vulgar language to young Father Sweeney only half an hour ago, she felt what was for her an expansive glow. "What did you say? What inspired it?" Her voice was loud and husky for so minute a woman.

"I was asleep," said Jason. "Sister."

"Again? Third time this month."

Jason hesitated. He was too proud to explain what had caused his sleepiness, but there was something now in Sister Agatha's voice which made him say, "I was tired."

"Lollygagging with worthless spalpeens like yourself most of the night, instead of sleeping?"

"No. Sister." Then, in spite of his reticence, a tinge of exasperation came into his own voice. "John, my brother, was off to Mass this morning, and I had to deliver his papers for him, second or third time this week, and then deliver my mother's laundry."

"There's nothing wrong with going to Mass so often," said

the old lady. "Perhaps 'twould be better for you if you followed John's example."

"Then there would be less to eat in the house," Jason said with a reckless anger she had never heard from him before. "Everyone works in our house except Jack and my little sister, who can't walk well. My grandda works all hours, and so does my mother, and so do I. We wouldn't eat or have a roof over our heads if we didn't." He had begun to breathe hard and his tired face flushed deeply with a renewed anger. "If Jack would make up for his going to Mass when he should be delivering his papers and helping Mum, it wouldn't be so bad. But he doesn't."

Sister Agatha put on her glasses to see him more clearly. "'Render unto Caesar,'" she began, and then was taken aback when Jason made a most unusual gesture, as of dismissal. "I know all that, Sister. 'And to God the things which are God's.' But I heard once that our Lord worked as a carpenter, and I bet he did that after praying, and didn't make prayer the only thing."

"Um," said Sister Agatha.

"My grandda says to work is to pray, anyway," said Jason. "Someone should tell Jack that."

Sister Agatha again studied the note. "'Vulgar language.' What did you say to Sister Mary Margaret, Jason?"

Jason slowly remembered and then could not help smiling. "Sister mentioned Jack, and I said he needs a kick in... uh...well, something like a donkey."

As Sister Agatha had thought something perilously like that about poor young Father Sweeney that morning, she began to cough and covered her mouth with her handkerchief. The hazel eyes twinkled. She was not an unworldly old lady. She had heard hearty language from her brothers and father in Ireland when she had been a young girl, and she guessed, very knowingly, exactly what Jason had meant to convey. She knew John Garrity very well, indeed, and though she virtuously admired his piety and devotion and his ambition to be a priest, she had thought him somewhat of a prig, not unlike Father Sweeney, for whom she had no affection at all, and a less-than-ardent respect.

Again she studied Jason, the intense gray eyes and thick black lashes and brows, the inherent strength of his features, and the set of his body. She saw his hands, big and raw and chapped, calloused with labor. She said, trying for severity, "I hear your arithmetic hasn't improved lately."

"I don't understand it very much," he confessed. The nun had made no move for the switch, though it lay near her hand. Sister Agatha recalled that Father Sweeney did not seem to comprehend the relationship between money and life either. He had complained that morning of "undue expenditures." She knew it was useless to explain to him that the meager sums at her disposal covered barely half of the expenses, and that she had, as she had said, to "rob Peter to pay Paul," an allusion that seemed to puzzle him.

"Well, then," she said to Jason now, "you know there has to be money for the rent, for clothing and food. That's mathematics."

"Then I don't have to learn it," said Jason. "I know all about it. I've known about it for years." He seemed relieved.

Sister Agatha found herself nodding, then severely came to herself. "And civics. That's government and such, Jason. A literate man needs to know all about it."

"Da says government should be hanged," the boy replied. "That is, politicians."

"An unworthy sentiment, Jason. And a stupid one, I am afraid. You must live in this world, unless it is your hope to be a monk?" Her mouth quirked with humor.

The thought was so appalling that Jason blurted out, "Christ, no!" Then he slapped his hand over his mouth. Sister Agatha did not feel she had been exposed to a blasphemy. She felt that Jason had been quite sincere, even reverent, in his denial. But she believed it proper to raise a stern hand.

"That will do, Jason." She looked at the switch. She had no desire to pick it up. "Go back and apologize to Sister Mary Margaret, and see you do better—in something. Anything." She waved her hand at him and took up some papers and frowned at them. She sensed, rather than saw, that Jason was hesitating near her, as if he wished to speak again. But she did not look up; she felt very moved, though she did not know why. In a moment or two he was gone.

Had she failed the lad as perhaps she had failed many others? She reflected that God had not promised man joy in this life, but only labor. Yet, it was a lovely world—if it were not for man. She had a profound faith, but still...I am a sinner, she thought, and tried to feel guilt and contrition.

She was not very successful.

Jason returned home in the bitter dark after his work at the shop of Mr. Maggiotti. His eyes burned hotly and he was

47

also full of rage. He had detected that Mr. Maggiotti had neatly covered two large breaks in his window with a court plaster and cardboard. The damage was in a corner, and the old man had put a jar of candies in front of it to conceal it. When questioned by Jason, Mr. Maggiotti had shrugged deprecatingly and had said, "I'm an old man, Jason. Careless."

Jason went outside and examined the break. He came back, his eyes sharp. "Did you throw this stone when you were playing this morning?"

Joe spread his hands eloquently. "It was the jar."

"You threw it at the window?"

Joe bent his small head in distress and mumbled something. Jason hitched up his knickers and tightened the buckle just below his knee. He still glowered at his friend. Joe said, "What can a man do when he is no liked?"

"He can 'no like' himself. Did you call the police?"

Joe held up his hands. "The po-lece? What they do with bad men and boys? They say, 'Did you see them?' I say no. I only heard. One poleceman, a boy, said, 'Kill.' He look very mad. Irish like you, Jase."

Jason thought of his brother's quotation from the Bible: "The wages of sin is death." There was only one answer to crime: dire punishment. He looked at the broken window. Joe had no money to replace it. He had had to go into debt for the last vandalized one.

Exposed now in his dereliction in not reporting the vicious act, Joe brought out a crushed and half-torn piece of paper from one of the drawers near the till. It had obviously been wrapped about the thrown stone. On it in dark ink was a crude sketch of a hand dripping with inky blood. Beneath it was printed, "Get out, Black Hand! Go back to Wopland!"

Jason felt the atavistic male lust to savage and to murder for the first time in his young life. He looked about the tiny shop, so immaculate, so clean and orderly. He saw the flickering yellow lamplight. Joe could not afford to use any of the gas mantles he sold, so the light was uncertain here and full of roaming shadows. To Jason every shadow concealed a grinning malicious enemy of the helpless, and the first true hatred he had ever known rushed into him with a taste of hot metal. He turned to see Joe's large eyes looking at him imploringly. The old man shook his head and said with simplicity, "No, Jase. No."

Jason thought of what he had been constantly reading in the newspapers, the general public hatred and suspicion of immigrants, no matter their race. It was strange that a nation of immigrants, which had deprived the Indian inhabitants of their homeland, should so despise those who followed them. "Except," Bernard would say, "we later ones weren't transported because we were criminals and were crowding the Sassenagh's jails. We came of our own will; *they* were yoked together like dangerous cattle. 'The basket girls' of Virginia were whores swept up from the streets of English cities, most of them; who speaks now of the white bondsmen—really slaves—shipped to these shores to be sold and bound to white masters until their sentences were completed?

"And the gentlemen who signed the Declaration of Independence: many of them Catholic gentlemen, and Irish, to boot. The Carrolls of the Carolinas, who had suffered so much in England, to name but a few. Ah, and this is an evil world, boyo. It is natural, I'm thinking, for man to hate his brother, and to kill him. It says so in the Holy Bible. Cain and Abel."

"It is more natural for man to love his brother," John had said with a cold affronted glance at his grandfather.

"Such as you loving your brother so much that you put your own burdens on his back," Bernard had replied. "A fine example, sure and it is, of brotherly love. Tell your brother you love him, and pray for him—and the poor sod can be persuaded to give you his heart's blood out of gratitude, at no cost to you."

"Da," Kate had said. "Jack's too young to understand."

"The hell he is, Katie. He's got it all figured out, haven't you, bucko?"

John had risen with great calm and majesty and had gone outside to vomit. That had been six months ago. Kate, wailing, had followed him. "I hope," said Bernard, "that he throws up all his bile, too."

Joan had begun to cry, but Jason had smiled wryly. "Da, think of what Mum feels when this goes on."

"Ach," said Bernard. "It's wimin who muddle things up. Should live apart from us. They ruin our manhood." But he had gone outside to bring Kate in, with his big arm about her waist and her wet face on his shoulder, though he had ignored his retching grandson. "Sure, Katie, it's the bad tongue I have," Bernard had assured his daughter-in-law, "and you'd best forgive me."

"Jackie is so delicate," Kate had wept.

"Delicate as a turnip," Bernard had hardheartedly replied.

"There, there, no more tears, Katie. After all, I am an old man."

This had so amused Kate that she had smiled involuntarily. "As old as a newborn baby, Da." Jason had heard this and somewhat agreed. His grandfather would never grow old. He had the lustiness of a strong child, and a wisdom beyond mere literacy. He had felt a huge melting love for Bernard then. Bernard's invincible spirit was the wall about the house, the warmth of the stove, the shelter of the roof, the weld that soldered the family together.

But Jason knew that Bernard was right: man was the enemy of his brother. All the pious homilies were only pleading cries in the darkness, protesting the truth in its red rawness, its primeval savagery, its irrefutable verity. Cain had far more sympathizers than did Abel.

Jason knew all this by instinct, but tonight he only wanted to know the identity of those who had injured his old friend. He wanted to kill. The thought did not horrify him. It exhilarated him, for he understood that the wicked were deliberately so and must be punished severely, even with death.

Joe Maggiotti watched Jason as the boy silently left the shop. There was fear in the old man's eyes. There was something about Jason which had upset him. Jason emerged into the dark cold; little snow devils were whirling up from the walks. The arc lamp on the corner of the street was spitting and hissing out a strong bluish light. Otherwise the street was dark, except for the yellow streetlamp on the next corner. Jason walked to that corner and encountered a young policeman on his beat, bent before the gale. "Mr. Clancy," he said. The policeman turned up the collar of his inadequate uniform coat and peered wet-eyed at Jason.

Jason said, "Somebody broke Mr. Maggiotti's window this morning. Again."

"Sure, and I know," said the policeman, who was all of twenty-one years old. "I heard the crash. I ran to the shop, and three big bastards were running off, laughing." He paused and stared at the distant arc lamp as if in thought.

"You didn't catch any?"

"Well, then, it was this way, Jase, boyo. I did, and then I did not." By the flickering light he saw Jason's eyes, and to him they were like the points of gray-steel knives. He shrugged, rubbed his hands together. "There's justice, and there's justice," said the young policeman. "I got one. The others made off. Now, then. If I had taken the one big brute, a man about sixteen, to the station, what then? Like as not he's brought before a magistrate of the same mind as himself, and he's on the street again, laughing his bloody head off." Mr. Clancy himself had arrived from Ireland only six years ago with his parents.

He fumbled for his club and regarded it reflectively and with appreciation. "Sad, that. The bastard will not be on the street for a long time, I'm thinking. Perhaps never. They must have dragged him off after I tucked his cap over his head. Of course I didn't see anything. He must have fallen. A bad gash, and in Christian mercy I pulled that cap over the cut. Bleeding very hard, you understand, and he wasn't...awake just then. Wound might have been touched by frost."

Mr. Clancy shook his head in commiseration. He tossed his stick in the air very skillfully. It whirled in the darkness, then descended to his hand. "Yes, boyo," he sighed. "There's justice and there's justice. A man has to choose. A good night to you, Jase, and you'd best be getting home. Streets not safe any longer. And my regards to your grandda."

Something tight and almost unbearable relaxed in Jason. He smiled as he watched Mr. Clancy walk off with a perceptible swagger, whistling to himself. Jason ran home, oblivious of the wind tearing at his face.

He entered the big warm kitchen, comforting with its color and lamplight. Bernard and John and Joan were sitting at the table, Bernard reading his newspaper, his two younger grandchildren playing dominoes amicably together. Kate stood at the hot stove and the air was thick and delicious with the odor of boiling corned beef and cabbage. She gave Jason her usual anxious sweet smile and said, "You're late, love." Jason went to her and kissed her on the cheek, and she patted his broad shoulder. Bernard looked up from his paper, but John and Joan pretended to be absorbed in their game.

"What's up?" asked Bernard on seeing Jason's face.

"Someone broke Mr. Maggiotti's window this morning."

Bernard took off his glasses and regarded Jason thoughtfully. "I know, then. I saw it."

"Mr. Clancy heard the crash and—"

Bernard suddenly had a gust of coughing. He looked at Jason intently and then led the boy's eyes to John, who was now listening. "Too bad Mr. Clancy didn't catch them," said Bernard.

"Perhaps it was some poor soul who was hungry," said

51

John in his censorious voice. "Such should be fed, not put into jail."

"Seems to me," said Bernard, "that there's the Salvation Army and the Church feeding the 'poor,' as you call them. And there's public charity here, too."

John said, "Punishment is only revenge, Da."

"And where did you pick up that damned idea, Jackie, bucko? Best read your Bible. Best remember penance, too. It's not educated you are."

John's pale face reddened. "It was Father Sweeney's own saying."

Bernard shook his crest of white hair, and it seemed to rise. "It's not his sister he saw hanged in a public square in Dublin by the Sassenagh," he said, and now his small gray eyes seemed to shoot sparks. "He'd change his damn tune if it had been. Or perhaps he'd get on his knees and kiss the Sassenagh's arse and thank him. Wouldn't surprise me what could happen in this damned stupid world."

"Da," said Katie, speaking in a voice of entreaty.

Bernard shrugged. "It's not your poor fault, Katie, that you gave birth to a fool. His father was one, too."

"I remember my dada," said John, his hard color deepening. "I hope I will be like him."

Bernard lifted a fork and pointed it at him. "No worry, Jackie. You already are, God help you." He paused. "Well, not entirely, perhaps. There's a stone in your heart, and that may be the saving of you after all."

"It's Jason's birthday," Kate pleaded as she watched Jason shake out his snowy coat and hang it up. "Fourteen years old."

"And not yet confirmed!" said John. "Not even approaching confirmation."

"So he's still innocent, which is more than you are," said Bernard. Then he relented. "Well, God made us all as he designed, so perhaps you aren't entirely to blame for what you are, Jackie. Well, then, let's not talk any more about it."

He looked at his newspaper. "McKinley! As strong as weak tea. Glad I didn't cast my first vote for him. Now, there's his vice-president, Roosevelt. A man after my own heart. Tells the Russian czar, outright, to stop the pogrom just started, and damned if the czar doesn't stop it! And the man's not even president! And here's the silly wimin screaming for the vote again, in Washington. Think their votes will change the world. Nothing will, except maybe a holocaust from heaven."

Listen to the wimin. If they get the vote, there'll be no more wars, no more poverty, no more child labor, no more injustice, no more drunkenness, no more riots, no more exploitation of labor—nothing but paradise on earth. Katie, your sex is no brighter than mine."

Jason sat down at his place near the table and saw a little heap of packages awaiting him. Everyone became silent as he took one up and unwrapped the brown paper. It was a red woolen scarf his mother had knitted for him, and a woolen cap to match. When had she done this, she who worked every moment of the day? At night, Jason thought, his eyes smarting, when we were asleep. He opened another little parcel. It contained a penwiper made by Joan, his sister, composed of layers of pinked wool scraps. In silence he opened another package. It was a new missal from his brother, John, a well-bound one to replace his ragged one, and Jason was moved. Then came his grandfather's gift, a fine jackknife, which he had long coveted. It had cost all of a dollar, a fortune.

He looked about the room, and even John and Joan were smiling at him. "Thank you," he mumbled. "Thank you a lot." He got up, kissed his mother again, kissed his grandfather, hesitated, bent and kissed John's rigid cheek, then kissed his beautiful adored sister, who shrank only slightly.

But John always ruined such occasions. He said, "Had you kept that gold piece from Mr. Mulligan, Jase, you could have bought a new window for Mr. Maggiotti. But you just thought of yourself, as usual, and of no one else. The sin of pride, too."

"Holy Mother of God!" Bernard roared, and threw down his fork. Kate cried out, and so did Joan, and John turned away with horror. "Even for a poor man like old Joe, a man doesn't sell his soul!"

Jason, seeing his mother's face, was distressed. He said, "Had I known, I would have kept it, Da, and given it to Mr. Maggiotti."

"Well, it's too late now," said Joan spitefully, and there was a pleased smile on her angelic face.

"I did mention the poor box," said John.

Bernard was too angry to speak. Jason said, "Never mind. I've thought of going around and collecting a few cents here and there to help Mr. Maggiotti get his new window."

Bernard silently plunged his hands into his trousers pocket and brought out a handful of coins, which he noisily spilled on the tablecloth. "Nearly two dollars," he said finally. "We need only four more. We'll get it, sure and we will!"

"Yes," said Jason, who was less than hopeful, but he wanted peace tonight for his mother's sake. Bernard had often remarked that Irish families find their greatest enjoyment whetting their tongues, like knives, on each other. But Jason did not enjoy it, and neither did his mother. He said, "Where did you get that money, Da?"

"Went around," grunted Bernard. "Not everybody's got a heart like a stone."

Jason involuntarily glanced at his brother. For the first time he noticed how John's gray eyes had a curious fixed glare in them, like the colorless shining of glass, oddly dilated and intent, and disturbing. The thin black brows lay almost on top of the eyelids. It was a truly immobile and merciless face the boy possessed, the face of a fanatic. Why didn't I see that before? Jason thought, and was uneasy. Had he ever seen his brother smile, heard him laugh? Jason could not quite remember. There was something like violence in John's very stillness, which was rarely shaken, a violence which had never burst into honest rage or uncontrolled gesture.

Then Jason looked at his sister. He saw that she was watching him with a strange intensity, and he recalled that often she would do this. But never had it shaken him as it did now, and he did not know why. It was as if she were trying to hear all his thoughts, not with affection and concern, but out of an imperative necessity, and with some secret design.

Kate said, with a pleading look at Jason, "Jase, love, would you mind if I returned that dollar Mr. Maggiotti gave you this morning for your birthday, so you can help with his window?"

Jason said nothing. Bernard loudly cleared his throat. "No, Katie. Joe gave it to Jason, and Jason gave it to you. We'll find the money, dear colleen. That we will."

"You always know, Da," said Kate with such absolute trust in her voice that Jason, for some reason, wanted to cry.

Bernard said, "Don't elevate me, Katie. I'm a bad old bucko and always was."

Jason wondered how long it had taken his mother to save up pennies to buy that considerable piece of corned beef for his birthday. He felt sick with love, rebellion, and pity. She sat there at the table, her hands wrapped in her apron, and Jason saw their rough redness, the cracks in them which appeared filled with her blood. She had caught cold two weeks ago and her cough was heavy and racking and drops of sweat would burst out over her anxious face. Mr. Maggiotti had sent her a mixture of thyme, honey, and lemon juice, which she gratefully declared had helped her, but Jason could often hear her cough in the night. She hardly touched the food on her plate, but John, Jason noticed, had eaten at least one-third of the meat and two of the large potatoes and a huge wedge of cabbage. But then, he thought with bitterness, he has a "weak stomach."

When the dinner was finished, Kate stood up with a proud smile and went to the cupboard and brought out a seed cake in which had been embedded one large candle. She held it up triumphantly. "Jason's birthday cake!"

Bernard clapped; after a moment or two Joan and John clapped. Kate set the cake before Jason and kissed him soundly. "Happy birthday, love," she said, and her voice broke. He took her hand, brought it to his lips, and kissed it. "Oh, Mum." She leaned her cheek on the top of his head and closed her eyes.

"Cut it, what are you waiting for?" demanded Bernard in a very husky voice. "Now, then, I'll light the candle, and you must blow it out and make a wish, and it's said it will come true."

He struck a wooden match against the sole of his patched shoe. The candle made a brave blaze in the lamplight. Jason leaned forward and said fiercely to himself, "Money, money, money!"

He drew a deep breath and blew it out, and the candle flame guttered and disappeared. "Good," said Bernard, "you'll get your wish, and I hope it was a good one."

Kate had not been able to put enough eggs in the cake to make it moist, but it was sweet and palatable. Bernard said, "That minds me. I'll take a wedge to old Joe, and I've got a little of the creature left. It'll warm his heart this bad cold night." He looked at Jason, and the many clefts on his face turned into an astonishingly gentle smile. "Fourteen years old, eh? It'll do ye no harm, boyo, to have a drop of the creature with Joe and me tonight. You're a man."

Kate thought of her husband, Peter, who had, on too many occasions, taken the last copper in the house to the local saloon. "A man's got to soothe his misery at times, Katie," he would say to her, and she would never tell Bernard. She suspected Bernard knew, and that he, in turn, was hiding the truth from her as she was hiding it from him. She looked at Bernard and he said, "Niver you mind, now, Katie, he'll

55

niver be one for the bottle." When he was very touched his brogue became unusually strong.

Jason, to please his mother, put on the red woolen cap she had knitted, and wound the scarf about his neck. He would have preferred to go to bed, but he put on his own worn coat, far too short for him now in length and sleeve, and his grandfather shrugged his way into the long tweed coat. A half-filled pint of cheap whiskey peered from one pocket. Katie wrapped a good piece of the cake in a white piece of cloth and Bernard put that in another pocket. "Katie," he said, "they'll never call you 'blessed.' But I do. It's a real saint you are."

Grandfather and grandson went out into the cold black night. The sharp blizzard sliced into their faces and the wind brought tears to their eyes. The narrow street was empty and desolate in the storm.

Bernard said, "It's hell to be poor if you have a family, but it's more of a hell to be poor and have nobody. That's the case with Joe, but he doesn't complain. Comes to me often—why were we born?"

"Well," said Jason, struggling to keep his coat closed, "it does say in the catechism that we're born to know God in this life and serve him, and then join him forever after death."

"Hum," said Bernard, with no reverence. "He goes the wrong way about it, sure and he does. On a night like this you think of selling your soul to the Divil for comfort."

"At least they say it's warm in hell," said Jason, laughing. The howling wind tore at the back of his throat, and he choked. The man and boy leaned into the gale, bent almost double. Each step was a struggle against an unseen icy battlement. In that short distance their eyelashes and brows were thick with snowflakes. The wan yellow light from Joe Maggiotti's small shop was only a wavering shadow in the night. "He's still up, then," said Bernard. They heard a steady banging of a swinging door even above the shrieking of the wind.

Then the pale dancing lamplight of the shop blew out. "Ah," said Bernard. "We're just in time."

They had almost reached the door of the shop when it came to Jason that it was the shop door itself which was wildly swinging in the wind and making that crashing sound. He stopped for an instant. Bernard went on. Then Bernard uttered a rough oath and fell heavily on his knees. Jason ran to him and by the arc light saw that a log of wood, covered with snow, was lying near the raging door, and Bernard had fallen over it. Jason took the old man by his shoulders; he was lying prone over the log. Bernard struggled to rise. "Some bastard put it there," he said. "Curse him."

Then Jason cried out. Bernard's body had disturbed the snow on the log, and now Jason saw it was no log, but Joe Maggiotti, himself, lying on the wooden walk near the pounding shop door, Joe as silent as death, and as still. Bernard saw, also, and was frozen on his knees, staring.

"Jesus, Mary, and Joseph," he stammered. "Joe! Joe?"

"Oh, my God!" Jason shouted, as the arc light flared up. "It's...it's Joe...and his head is all bleeding!"

Dazed and stunned, Bernard took off his woolen mitten and touched Joe's face. It was already deathly cold and stiff. He pulled his hand away; the congealed blood was like a dull red jelly on his fingers. Joe's open brown eyes gazed fixedly at nothing; his jaws had fallen apart. There was a bloody gash on his chin, and the whole top of his head was crushed.

Jason was fourteen years old and a large boy, but he suddenly was weeping. "It...it was the door. It must have hit him. We've got to get him out of this."

Bernard was silent, swaying on his knees, his hands clenched against his broad chest. He had closed his eyes. Then he said, "No use. He's dead. Joe." The slow painful tears of grief and pity began to roll down his cheeks.

Bernard opened his eyes and looked at Jason. Never had the boy seen such a terrible face before. Bernard said, "He's been murdered. Killed. Get Dave Clancy."

Jason pushed himself to his feet. He felt weak and shocked, and his breath seemed to have solidified in his throat. He tried to make himself run to the corner; he tried to shout in his despair and terror and sorrow. He had had nightmares like this, full of deadly fear when his legs felt held down by quicksand and he could not move them to flee, to flee from a thing to horrible to be faced but which menaced him.

He reached the corner, gasping, swung about it, and immediately fell over something that appeared, in the dimmer light, to be a big dog moving very slowly on the ground, shaking its head. Wildly he seized the head and felt a hot liquid running over his hands. Then he heard a groaning.

The nightmare of darkness, storm, and terror expanded about Jason. He lay, panting, where he had fallen. He knew now it was no dog which had caused him to fall. It was young Mr. Clancy, bareheaded, his helmet having rolled into the gutter, a bleeding slash on his forehead. The policeman was scrabbling on his hands and knees. His club had gone. He stared up vacantly at Jason and muttered something. One of his hands fumbled at a pocket. Blood was running into one of his eyes and he blinked. He muttered again, and Jason, feeling burning vomit in his throat, rolled over on the snowy walk and tried to hear. "Whistle," Clancy muttered again.

"Yes," said Jason. He clawed his numb fingers into the policeman's pocket and found the whistle. He pulled with all his strength, for he was steadily succumbing to shock. The first blast was feeble; Jason closed his eyes, prayed, and blew again. Now the sound was penetrating and bounded back from the brick wall of the small warehouse near where Mr. Clancy lay. Over and over Jason blew until he could blow no more. He dropped the whistle, tore off the red woolen scarf his mother had given him, and rolled it into a little pillow. Gently, crying, he put it under the policeman's bleeding head to protect it from the frozen sidewalk. He said, "Please, please, Mr. Clancy, hold on." He took one of the policeman's hands and held it as tightly as he could, as if dragging the young man from a pit. Mr. Clancy stared at him sightlessly.

He did not hear any running footsteps or shouts or exclamations, but all at once he was surrounded by men, shawled women, children, and two policemen who had come running from other streets. Someone was lifting him to his feet. He struggled. "Help, help. Mr. Clancy. My grandfather...Joe's shop...Joe's been killed. They must have tried to kill Mr. Clancy, too."

He burst into great tearing sobs, and a man put his arms about him and said, "It's all right. We'll take care. Jase Garrity is it, then? Yes. Your grandda is all right, too. We'll take care. Let's go home now, Jase. Home."

Jason saw Mr. Clancy being carried into an ambulance. He saw flickering faces milling in the darkness; he saw distended eyes, gesturing hands. A woman was holding his hand. Someone was wiping his face.

He said, out of his new manhood, "Get them. Kill them. Joe. Mr. Clancy. Why, why?"

He did not remember reaching home. He found himself in bed, his grandfather sitting beside him, holding his cold hand. Bernard said, "We'll find them, boyo, we'll find them." Bernard was trying to smile. Long silent tears ran down his cheeks. "We'll find them, niver you fear." Jason swallowed, gasped. He had been given a huge draft of whiskey.

Jason whispered out of a hurting throat, "Why, why, Da?"

A little light seeped in from the kitchen, and Jason saw Bernard avert his head. He was staring at the door. "Yes. Why, why? There's never any real honest answer to human wickedness. Dave Clancy won't die, Jason, though he's badly hurt. He woke up in the hospital and said he heard a screaming—Joe screaming when he ran from his shop to escape the murderers—and Dave started to run and he was knocked down with his own club. He sends his thanks, Jason."

There was a deep silence in the house, except for Kate's soft crying in the kitchen beyond the bedroom. It seemed to Jason that her mourning filled the whole world, and there was no comforting.

He looked at his grandfather, and was suddenly frightened. For Bernard had lifted a clenched fist toward the ceiling and his mouth moved in ferocious and silent execration. It was not Bernard's face raised to the ceiling. It was a face of vengeance, hatred, repudiation. It was a face full of memories; it was as if he were taking a solemn and dreadful oath of blasphemous defiance. Jason closed his eyes in an awful fear and fell abruptly asleep.

Bernard rose heavily and slowly and for the first time walked like an old man. He went into the kitchen, where Kate was sitting alone at the table, weeping. Her son John and her daughter were not there. And John was not in the bedroom with Jason. Bernard put his hand on Kate's shoulder, and she felt the iron weight of it. She looked up, and her weary face was scoured with tears and pain.

"Jason's asleep, Katie. I gave him . . . something."

"It minds me. Like Ireland, Da."

"Yes, Katie. Like the whole cursed world. Jack still with that young bumpkin of a priest in the rectory?"

"Yes, and Joan's in bed. Da, Jack is praying for—"

Bernard said, "I'll kick Jackie boyo out of bed meself in the morning. He'll not only deliver his damned papers but the laundry, too, and if he dares to shirk by going to Mass, I'll break his blasted head, that I will."

He added in a changed, ponderous voice, very slow and calm, "And where was his God tonight? Yes, where was his God? When is he ever there when he is needed?"

"Well, then," said Bernard to the young priest, Father William Sweeney. "You sent a lad for me. What is it you want?"

It was the next day, and even Belleville, that dull little

town, was radiant with the light on the new snow, its ugliness almost obliterated. The white mountains scintillated with white fire and leaned against a sky the color of delphiniums, innocent and pure.

Father Sweeney was both intimidated by Bernard, as usual, and resentful. He felt a powerful antagonism today against him personally, or, possibly, against the entire world. Bernard had a brutal look this late morning, a harshness of expression, and a most direct and formidable gaze. Father Sweeney moved uncomfortably in the straight kitchen chair in his dolorously bleak little study, which was nearly as cold as the day outside. He was a small man, twenty-nine years old, and almost fleshless, for he never had enough to eat. He had the long head of the Irish, and in his case it appeared fragile as an eggshell, and it was covered by a tentative mat of curling auburn hair which seemed quite childlike. His face was small and sensitive and not very worldly, though he usually wore a look of conscious determination or hopeful expectation. He had round brown eyes; Bernard thought them evasive, but they were only timid, for Father Sweeney was a shy man and he suffered all the misery of the shy. He had a short broad nose, and it was always wet because he had a chronic catarrh caused by inclement weather and his own frail constitution. His devoted mother, who lived in Pittsburgh, often sadly—if somewhat boastfully—said Billy had never been robust like other, rude boys. For the rest, Father Sweeney had the long Irish lip and so tremulous a mouth that he had trouble making it as stern as befitted a dedicated priest. He looked all of eighteen years old, and a young eighteen at that.

His habit was shiny with long use, and made of cheap material. It was discreetly patched and the seams were always being restitched. But his collar was as stiff as an icicle, and immaculate. He had little chapped hands, which he usually kept clasped tightly, for they had a tendency to tremble when he was agitated, and he was agitated by Bernard, whom he feared.

He had a weak, almost girlish voice, and many complained that they could hardly hear him at Mass. He had a "throat condition," and it was painful this morning because of the cold.

"A great tragedy, poor Joe Maggiotti," he said.

"Yes," said Bernard, and his look, to the priest, was most terrible. "And why did you send for me, Father?"

"Joe was your friend, wasn't he, Bernard?"

"That he was. Well?"

Father Sweeney could not bear Bernard's eyes, which were both gelid and unresponsive. He had seen that appearance in the eyes of an old embittered bishop from Ireland, and it had terrified him. To avoid those eyes, the priest stared down at his battered desk, which had been polished until it shone. He said, and his voice shook in spite of himself, "It was very strange. Joe brought an envelope to me only two weeks ago. He made a peculiar request, which he did not explain. He said that immediately on his death, and before his burial, I should give the envelope to you, his old friend." Father Sweeney cleared his throat. "I don't know if it is legal—"

"The hell with law," said Bernard. "Made by the unjust against the just. Well? Let me have the envelope...if you please, and I'll be on my way to Joe's house, where the neighbor wimin laid him out."

Again the priest cleared his throat. "He made another request. That you read it in my presence."

"He did then? Why, I wonder?" Bernard's eyes took on a gleam of cold contempt.

"I don't know, Bernard. It is what he said. Perhaps funeral arrangements."

"He had nothing but his shop," said Bernard. "It'll be sold, likely, to keep him from a pauper's grave."

He tore open the thick brown envelope with a rasping sound. A sheaf of papers fell out onto the desk. They were all covered by Joe's thick black handwriting, painfully composed, but if the English was crude, the intent was clear, and the directions. Joe had spent weeks on the composition, sometimes asking the help of nuns.

Bernard picked up one paper. "This is an old insurance policy. Three hundred dollars, for funeral expenses and for Masses for his soul." For a moment Bernard could not speak. "Twenty years ago. Six dollars a year. He must have starved to pay it." Bernard took up all the other papers. "Dear Friend, Bernard Garrity," the first began. "My own true friend."

Bernard's eyes clouded. He could not speak. He could only read. Father Sweeney gazed at the big powerful man who appeared like an impervious gray boulder, without sensitivity or emotion. Father Sweeney had heard from Kate that Bernard's father had been a teacher in Dublin and that Bernard himself had studied two or three years for the priesthood. It seemed incredible to him that this coarse and muscular man could even read and write. He resembled the raw uncouth Irish peasants of which Father Sweeney's mother had told him with some scorn.

Children were pouring out of the parish school on their way home for lunch, and their shrill voices made a ringing in the frigid air outside. It was the only sound which invaded the study. Bernard slowly and carefully read every sheet of paper. Finally he put them down and looked at the priest.

"Joe's left me his shop, its contents—everything," said Bernard. "He owned the property. He left me his only treasure, a large cross which hung over his bed, made of olive wood from Jerusalem, with an ivory Corpus. He brought it from Italy. It is very old...and very beautiful. He would have died of starvation rather than sell it. It is valuable."

"I saw it once," said Father Sweeney, thinking of the big cross, which would look beautiful over the high altar.

Bernard went on. "There is the deed to that property here. And a deed to fourteen acres of land, right near here, on the mountain. He wrote that he bought it forty years ago, for twelve dollars. He had hoped someday to have enough money to build a house for himself and his wife, and the children— who never lived. He's deeded it to my grandson Jason."

Father Sweeney said, "It is worth much more than a few dollars now, Bernard. Houses are being built on the closest mountains—"

Bernard said, "A man doesn't sell land. He buys it."

Father Sweeney was silent. Bernard said, "I will sell everything else Joe left to me, except for the cross, and use the money as a reward to anyone supplying the police with evidence that will lead to the arrest and conviction of Joe's murderers. I should like to put a bulletin on the board in the church to that effect."

Father Sweeney was aghast. "No!" he exclaimed.

Bernard folded his massive arms across his chest. "And why not, if you'll be so kind as to tell me, Father?"

Father Sweeney saw that Bernard had appeared to grow larger and almost to fill the tiny study, and that his formidable look had increased and had become more terrible. The priest wet his suddenly dry lips. "To find the murderers is the work of the police, not of a layman."

Bernard's gaze was appalling. Only a dark avenging angel, thought Father Sweeney, with renewed fear, could look so.

Bernard said, "Money has a way of stimulating interest

in catching criminals. It saves time. It helps the police, when an informer comes to them."

"It is...corruption, Bernard."

"And is it, now? Catching criminals has become a crime?"

"The police, the paid police—it is their work, not yours."

"It is the work of every man who wants justice."

"You want a man with guilty knowledge to inform the police, and that, again, is corruption. Corrupting the informer."

Bernard laughed. "A man who withholds knowledge of a crime is already corrupt. Informing, by money or by conscience, eases that corruption in his own mind. I know human nature, Father, and you do not."

The young priest clasped his damp hands tightly in his lap. "You are looking for revenge, Bernard."

"I am looking for retribution, or has retribution become a crime, too? And justice. And your famous law. If so, then let's disband the police, the courts, the prisons, and kiss the murderer on the arse and forgive and love him."

He pointed a thick strong finger at the priest. "I have no right to forgive a crime committed against a friend. I have only the right to see that justice is done."

"Our Lord forgave those who executed him."

Bernard lifted fists and struck the desk. "You speak irreverently, Father, and I will not ask your forgiveness. God punishes, does he not? And does he not use men to act as his agents of punishment? Punishment, sure and swift, deters the criminal. Our Lord was not only divine—it is said—but was veritable Man, also. Have you forgotten what he said about criminals, murderers, thieves, liars, betrayers? I suggest you read your own Bible, Father. He was a man in all ways, and often a very angry man." He gave that fearful laugh again and said, as if to himself, "Is it I who would explain him, to whom I am not reconciled?"

Before the priest could speak, Bernard continued, "Eileen, my sister. Sixteen years old. When English soldiers were looting her parish church, she tried to intervene. She threw herself at the feet of the Blessed Mother and defied the soldiers. She was hanged three days later—a beautiful colleen. Who avenged her, Father, a child protecting her faith? Your God?

"I saw her die on a scaffold in the public square, a rope around her little white neck. She was not even permitted a shriving. She had been 'interfering with the duties of the military police.' Have you a sister, Father?"

The priest nodded. "Margaret, fourteen years old." He seemed about to cry.

Bernard leaned back in his chair. "See her, Father, in your eye now. A lovely little colleen, fourteen years old, hanging from a shameful scaffold before the jeering faces of a hating crowd. Would you ask forgiveness for them, Father? No, don't speak. It would only be hypocrisy."

He stood up. "I will use the money for notices in the newspapers. A good day to you, Father."

During the next few days the nuns remarked that Father Sweeney seemed preoccupied and less carping and severe. When Sister Agatha heard that he had also become less irritable, she nodded with satisfaction. "He is growing up, then," she remarked. "And it is about time."

Joe Maggiotti had what his neighbors called "a grand funeral." It cost one hundred and fifty dollars, and he had a respectable stone too in St. Elizabeth's Cemetery. That cost fifty dollars. The rest of the policy money was given to Father Sweeney for Masses for the repose of Joe's soul and his swift release from purgatory. Bernard laughed at that, and even Jason felt uneasy at the laughter. Bernard hung the beautiful cross over Jason's bed, and John felt not only slighted but insulted.

The shop and contents and all Joe's property in the building were sold, for eight hundred dollars. Bernard at once posted notices of reward in the two Belleville newspapers. A week later an informer went quietly to the police. Two youths were arrested for the crime, subsequently convicted and executed. They were not "poor." They were twin brothers, seventeen years old; their father was a prosperous blacksmith and horse dealer and they lived in a comfortable house with many amenities. They had been inspired by hatred of "the foreigners and papists." Their father was a member of the Know Nothings. He had hired a well-known lawyer to defend his sons, who pleaded their youth. The prosecuting attorney was a sensible man. He informed the jury that youth was no excuse for adult crimes, and that the murder had been senseless, excited by irrational hatred and malice and criminal minds. He was not reappointed.

Two months after Joe's death, Jason approached his grandfather and suggested that Joe's cross be given to St. John the

Baptist Church for the high altar. Bernard was outraged. "Joe would like it," said Jason.

"You've turned into a fool like your brother," said Bernard, and did not speak to Jason for three whole days. Then, on the fourth day he thrust the heavy cross into Jason's arms and said, "Oh, give it to the spalpeen, if it pleases you!"

It was noted that Father Sweeney began to grow in dignity and was less censorious and open more to reason. This puzzled and disturbed John, who had regarded the priest as his mentor.

4

Bernard had no trust in any government, and he despised politicians and invariably referred to them as "rascals" or "imbeciles." When President McKinley was assassinated in 1901, Bernard remarked, "I wonder what powerful men he offended in Washington and New York." When questioned by an acquaintance to explain, he replied, "I read, boyo, I read. The newspapers. Didn't your Benjamin Franklin say that reading one's newspaper regularly was better than a college education—that is, if the newspaper was an impartial and honest one, and they are few, that I can tell you." He subscribed to magazines also, notably *The Saturday Evening Post*, though it frequently deprived the family of meat. He read everything with at least a modicum of cynicism, and would debate loudly, at the dinner table, with a writer with whom he disagreed—as if the writer himself were present. He wrote to some writers, who often replied, and the resulting correspondence was lively and acrimonious.

Bernard had thought the Spanish-American War "outrageous, disgusting," and had so written to newspapers. This had resulted in an interview with Bernard by a lesser government agent, and Bernard had routed him with facts. But the newspapers mysteriously ceased to publish his vehement diatribes. "Disagree with government at your peril," he said to Jason. "A free country it is, then? And it will get worse, rather than better." He had become one of the new president's greatest admirers, though he loudly debated with him on the merits of the Panama Canal. "There'll be trouble there someday," he told what few friends he had. Bernard approved of the canal itself, but he heartily resented the new president's remarks concerning the Central Americans, whom he had called "monkeys," one of his less vituperative epithets. "Sounds like the Sassenagh concerning the Irish," he said. "Politics is dirty enough and foul enough, God knows, without sneering at a man for his race, which is God's business only, is it not? That is, if there is a God at all," he would remark, more out of a desire to annoy than personal conviction. His feud with God had become more vehement, especially at the dinner table in John's hearing. John was beginning to vex him more and more, and the dislike between grandfather and grandson increased. "It's not his damned piety I hate so much," Bernard said to Kate. "Let a man believe he has the Almighty's personal ear, and I'll not contradict him, unless he attempts to force his convictions on me or anyone else. It's frightened I am when a man publicly asserts his own holiness and verity. I begin to wonder what deviltry he is up to in secret, and keep out of his path. I mind me of an old priest in Ireland, a saint if ever there was one, and he was always bewailing his own worthlessness and always calling himself a sinner. That I respect. That I trust."

When Father Sweeney expressed his horror that many young people were "being lured into Oriental mysticism and religions," Bernard asked him, "And what is the reason, then? Do you of the clergy ever ask yourselves why? What is it the boys and colleens find in Oriental mysticism that they don't find in their churches? What consolation, what hope, what spiritual values? What is the lack they feel in their parents' religion? You lads of the clergy had best discover the answers, before our Lord calls you false shepherds."

Bernard approved of the "new woman" in America, who was concerned with the exploitation of very young children who, between the ages of six and twelve, were working in the factories and cotton mills for as much as twelve hours a day, six days a week, for less than to keep them fed. The "new woman" was also passionate against the enforced prostitution of little girls, against the crowding of people in filthy tenements, against the general and widespread use of drugs among the young as well as their elders. He had not, as yet, come to agree that women should vote, unless they, as well as their men, were intelligent and understood for what they were voting. "Many's the man, too, who should not be permitted to vote. The majority have the intellect of cattle, if I may insult the poor beasts by comparing them with humanity."

When a magazine writer condemned "the new working woman," Bernard raged in a letter to the editor: "And what in hell have women been doing for all these thousands of years but 'working'? On the farms, in their houses, in the fields, and God knows where else. The only difference is that they didn't receive wages for their work, and their work was despised, though it kept the country running." He thought of Kate, who not only held her household together but did laundry for "strangers" to "make ends meet." He thought of the many thousands of other women who did the same. Their labor was lightly called "cottage industries." Bernard wrote furiously of the "sweatshops" where young girls labored for almost nothing, becoming consumptive in the process or starving to death. He wrote of the thousands of women in the factories, since the Industrial Revolution, and in the coal mines.

Like all full-blooded Irishmen, Bernard respected and loved women, and their wrongs infuriated him. When John said coldly, "I thought you believed that women should remain out of men's affairs," Bernard had grinned wickedly. "They've been in our affairs since Adam and Eve. We've been trying to get them out, too, but, by the grace of God, we haven't succeeded. Now, then. I do not like aggressive women who hate being women, and also hate men and want to displace them in the so-called scheme of things. Women, God bless them, are more powerful when they use their power in less noisy ways. Such as kicking their men gently in the arse to reform things. Niver was a man who didn't fear his woman, with good reason, but niver was the man better for not fearing her. A man may not listen to other men, but in bed he listens to his female—or God help him."

He added, "If women lose their power over men, in their own clever way, the world will be the poorer, and then we will have chaos, and a godless society."

"You keep contradicting your own convictions, Da," John, now fifteen years old, would remark. Bernard would grow expansive and look at his grandson with an inimical sparkling of his eyes. "A man who doesn't change his opinions occasionally has become petrified," he answered. "Like burying himself in cement, too. When I was a lad I thought that every successful politician should agree to be hanged on the conclusion of his term of office. Now I think he should just be exposed for the scoundrel he is and outlawed from decent society."

Once John, driven by his cold and silent rage, discussed with Father Sweeney his "fear" that his grandfather "might be excommunicated." Father Sweeney, with new chilliness, had replied, "I certainly won't start the process, Jack. It is not that I agree with your grandfather, but he has a right to his opinion, and so long as he does not oppose doctrine or dogma, he has nothing to fear."

"He fears nothing," said John with enormous rage.

Father Sweeney had involuntarily smiled. "He is an Irishman, Jack." He began to wonder if John had a true vocation, for all his piety and tenacity. He even, to his own dismay, searched for flaws in John. He began to think of the Spanish Inquisition, so sternly condemned by the Church fathers in other countries. Extreme piety, he thought to his own shock, can be a sin in itself. Did not the Church condemn scrupulosity? He saw, with new clarity, that John confessed to sins which were not really sins but an expression of human nature, and not entirely sinful. John thought human nature, even at its best, despicable. He had once confessed that he believed congress between men and women was evil, and had waited for the priest's approval.

Father Sweeney had replied, "God himself blessed the union between men and women." He had a sudden thought at which he winced. Was John masturbating? The priest was now two years older. Often his thoughts disturbed him. Was he growing too tolerant? Certainly old Sister Agatha sometimes smiled at him and answered him civilly. He prayed on the subject. He confessed to himself that he was feeling more comfortable and that his people were confiding more and more in him. He was becoming confused. But he was happier. He still, however, disapproved of Bernard, who often deliberately mocked him.

Mr. Mulligan was highly pleased by his employees Jason Garrity and Lionel Nolan, though he was careful not to praise them too highly. Praise had a way of disconcerting and disillusioning the praiser, for those praised often began to feel "above themselves," to quote Mr. Mulligan. They "took advantage." Mr. Mulligan had had long experience with human nature, and though he was the most affable and just of men, he carried some bitterness in him. One of his late employees, highly praised, had become arrogant, impertinent, and slothful. Men had a way of overestimating themselves if too lavishly "appreciated," Mr. Mulligan realized.

He had discovered that Jason's cheerful expression was more a formation of feature than of cheer itself. Jason, he found, had a sturdy character and a steadfast will, as well as possessing an admirable quality of not expecting too much of others. He could tolerate a gibe with good nature, if not accompanied by malice. But malice drew his implacable hatred and was never forgiven. There were times when his face took on an iron aspect, and it was this face, not often shown, which inspired both respect and fear. He was "Irish proud," as Mr. Mulligan expressed it. He never complained. He was anxious to learn. The cooks in the kitchen liked him and taught him. They were frequently irascible with less intelligent workers under them, but in some way Jason had the ability of soothing both sides of a hectic quarrel. This led to more harmony in the kitchen, to Mr. Mulligan's relief, and he had promoted Jason to general manager.

Lionel was now headwaiter, and the ladies loved him for his blazing smile and blazing hair and natural courtliness and willingness to serve and even assist fellow waiters. He could deal smilingly with the most fractious of diners. Slights, brutal remarks from bellicose males, the impatience of the unusually hungry, meager tips or none at all, could not upset him. He shrugged off meanness and even malice as being comic, and this was no pretense. He found humanity to be infinitely amusing, even at its worst. His yellowish eyes always had a glint of humorous enjoyment, even when he was deliberately provoked by a man who had had too much to drink and who wished for a fight. Amiable and light in manner as he was, few ever noticed a certain sharpness on his alert face, a certain watchfulness, a certain cold keenness. Jason was intuitive about people, and avoided the malevolent and brutish. Lionel smiled, and no one knew that he remembered.

Between the two youths, Jason eighteen and Lionel a year younger, their earlier friendship was deepening into the friendship of men. If Lionel found Jason's often unbending ways, when it came to honor, somewhat hilarious, he never remarked on it. Honor, or principle, had many faces to Lionel. He was more gregarious than Jason, not out of affection for others but for his own entertainment. Where Jason found life grim and harsh, Lionel found it interesting and diverting. Jason was repelled by grossness; it was risible to the buoyant Lionel. Lionel quickly learned of lewdness, and also was amused by it. But Jason had much of the puritanical nature of certain of the Irish and would turn away in disgust at an overly obscene joke or remark. This was soon noticed in the kitchen, where he spent twelve hours a day, and had he not had a pugilist's physique and a certain icy stare when offended, he would have been mercilessly taunted. Lionel only laughed, and with enjoyment, and he would tease Jason for being a "prude."

"That's life," Lionel once said.

"So is the privy," Jason had replied. "But you don't make jokes about it. At least, I don't."

They had just been told, during the lunch period, a most putrid joke about women in general. Jason had said nothing;

his handsome dark face had remained impassive. But Lionel laughed and slapped his knee. "There are girls in the world, you know, Jase."

Jason thought of his mother and sister and said, "I know. I'm not blind. But they're...defenseless, all of them, and a dirty joke is an attack on them. It's not...manly."

Lionel thought of his own sister, Molly, with whom he was never *en rapport*. Molly had his own sharpness of inner vision, which he sometimes found irritating, for it was a sharpness looking for duplicity, whereas his was exigent. He did not love Molly and often disliked her, and he felt the sentiment returned. Molly was rarely amused by him, and he thought her humorless and bad-tempered. He did not dare repeat any little sexual jest before his parents, to whom he was indifferent. But his father had a hard hand and his mother was "straitlaced." Being good-natured and flexibile, he attended Mass with his family every Sunday and holy days of obligation, for it was easier to accept boredom and inconvenience than to quarrel. Lionel hated quarrels, of which there were plenty in his home. He found them pointless and tedious.

If Lionel ever wondered why he was so attached to Jason, Jason had no such speculations. Lionel was his friend; he had proved that on many occasions, and the proof had been sincere. They both despised John Garrity. Lionel had an easy way of inquiring about Joan, but the youth loved the crippled girl. There was something intense in Joan which responded to something in himself and he knew that Joan was aware of it too.

Jason more than suspected that Molly, Lionel's sister, did not overly like her brother, and this Jason resented. She had what Jason called a "spiky" voice when speaking to Lionel; she was the only one who could make his smile disappear, and Jason resented this also. He felt his friendship for Lionel attacked by a "nasty snip of a girl" who was too quick with her tongue and who would often look at him with what he thought was mockery.

Jason was now deeply in love with Patricia Mulligan, who thought of him, if she ever thought at all, as "Papa's kitchen drudge." To Patricia, those who worked in humble or menial positions were hardly human and not to be considered by those who lived in her world.

Jason, though quick and sure of movement, gave the impression of being somewhat ponderous. But Lionel reminded people of a fox, and they admired his deftness. Jason often felt compassion even for the cruel, if they were ignorantly so, but Lionel possessed no compassion at all, except, oddly enough, a twinge of it now and then for Jason. Never one to explore his own motivations or emotions for some subtlety, he merely accepted the fact that he infrequently pitied his friend. He did not ask himself why. Jason accepted life in all its aspects, not always with happiness and often with grim forbearance. Lionel accepted it, in all its aspects, as highly diverting.

"I'll niver know why Jason likes that Lionel," Bernard would remark to Kate. "I wouldn't trust him around the till."

"They say opposites attract," Kate would answer.

But Bernard was not satisfied. "It would be interesting to know why that redheaded spalpeen is like Jason's shadow. I can't fathom it."

Nor could Joan, his granddaughter. She had come to the conclusion that Lionel was so often present because of her, but certainly not for "stupid old Jason." She would have preferred that Lionel like John, but she was early aware of the antipathy between the two. This puzzled her.

Mr. Mulligan had been reduced, by sad experience, to expressing his appreciation of employees by giving them cash. Jason was now receiving fourteen dollars a week, all the food he could eat in the kitchen, and the implied permission to take some of it home. Jason, who now felt that Mr. Mulligan was more than an employer, availed himself of this permission, but prudently. He often took home the end of a smoked ham and its bone, a loaf of slightly stale bread, a bucket of soup, a head of cabbage, the remains of corned beef or a lonely chop or two, and some pastries. But never did he take a roast or steaks.

Lionel was receiving twelve dollars a week. But there were his tips, and often his income for a week was fifteen or even eighteen dollars. He had no complaints. He gave his father his wages, but kept the tips for himself, unknown to his male parent, who knew nothing about tips. Lionel now had a secret savings account. Jason gave all his money to his family, and with Bernard's help had forced his mother to limit the laundry to some extent. Out of those wages Bernard paid the small real-estate taxes on the fourteen acres of land which Joseph Maggiotti had left Jason. "Someday that land will be valuable, mind my words," he told Jason. But Jason did not think of that. He only thought that old Joe had not been properly avenged. His hatred for the executed murderers never abated.

Because Jason did not receive tips, Mr. Mulligan had taken to slipping a twenty-dollar bill in the boy's pocket at Christmas. On the first occasion Jason had wanted to return it. But Mr. Mulligan had affectionately patted him on the arm, saying, "You deserve it, bucko." Mr. Mulligan knew he would not mention the gift to his friend.

Lionel's parents had no friends, no visitors. They were absorbed in work, in their religion, and in saving what they could. There was little conversation of a family sort in the house, no small jests, few if any smiles. To the adults their children were bewildering. Molly would quarrel vivaciously with her parents, and they thought her impudent, but preferred the girl to their son. Lionel's easy laughing ways affronted them. He was "heedless." He was light-minded. He was not serious. Lionel avoided his family as much as he could.

Jason found the art of cuisine fascinating. Not infrequently one of the cooks would show his appreciation of this interest by teaching Jason the intricacies of his particular specialty. The cooks considered themselves artists, and would preen at Jason's admiration. One of them, a very elderly man, would boast that he had worked as a chef in one of Philadelphia's better restaurants, but age had finally overcome him and he had returned to Belleville, where he had been born.

"You got to have a feeling and respect for people when you cook," he said to Jason. "No one who ever hated folks was a good chef; he kind of puts pizen in the food, even if it tastes all right. Their stomachs feel it."

Jason understood. He told this to Lionel, who laughed. "You don't believe that, do you?"

Jason thought, and he nodded. "Yes, I do. You can do...things to people the way you think. There's more ways of 'talking' to people than with your mouth."

Lionel had laughed again. "Well, I 'talk' to them in my mind about tips, and sometimes it works," he said.

Being very intelligent, Lionel knew that his friend had changed in some deep if inexplicable way since Joseph Maggiotti's murder. His laugh was not so frequent; his jokes were inclined to be heavy, his confidences were rarer. Lionel could not understand this. After all, old Joe had been dead "for years." It was not as if he had been a relative, a member of

73

the family. In Lionel's opinion Joe's death was no great loss. He had been old and tired and very poor. When Jason talked of "justice," Lionel was bored. Justice had been done. The murderers were dead, too. Why brood? Life was for the living. He saw that others respected and trusted Jason, whereas they did not respect or trust him. He only charmed them, and he found that much more to his interest, and far more profitable. There would never be any tips for Jason. He would have to earn every penny. Jason had "character."

"Character," Lionel had once heard, "is everything." Lionel did not believe that for an instant. Never self-deluded, he knew he did not possess that famed "character," and he was glad of it. It could get in the way of fortune and be boring into the bargain. He honored it in Jason, for Jason would never cheat him. Lionel was convinced that, given an opportunity, all men were cheaters, with the exception of a very few, and one had to be on guard. He did not have to be on guard with Jason. He wished there were more men like Jason in the world so that he, Lionel, would not have to be so vigilant, and could then direct his mind with greater concentration on his own future.

No one ever questioned his real devotion to Jason. It rose partly out of gratitude that Jason was as he was, partly out of trust, and partly out of sincere affection. It was also the accolade the amoral give to the moral in their hearts. Years later Lionel was to say with insouciant cynicism, "How could the conscienceless survive and flourish if there were no men of conscience in the world?"

One granite January night Lionel said to Jason, "Come on. Let's have some fun. I've found a place."

"I'm sure you have," said Jason, with no amusement. "You always do."

"Nice clean girls. Only two dollars."

"No. Besides, I don't have two dollars."

"I'll treat you."

"Thanks, no."

"Thinking of being a priest like your damned brother?"

Jason's wide smile was infrequent these days, but now he treated his friend to one. "Let's say I'm helping my grandda save a little money for Jack's seminary—when he can get in. Say. I thought you were coming home with me to see Joan and play cards with her after dinner."

Lionel hesitated. "It's eight o'clock. She's probably in bed."

"No. She's expecting you. She helped Mum bake a cake."

Lionel shifted on his dancing feet. "Give Joan my regrets. Tell her I have to stay here on a special party."

"No. I'll just tell her that you couldn't come."

"You and your goddamn truthfulness. You're dippy, you know. All right. See you tomorrow."

Jason said, thinking of his sister's disappointment, "Shall I tell her you'll see her tomorrow night?"

"Fine. Bully. Give her my love."

Lionel waved his red-freckled hand and cantered off, whistling. Jason left the Inn-Tavern, frowning thoughtfully. Joan was sixteen, a woman. She was also frail and crippled, housebound except for school. For a minute or two he worried about her future, dreaded her inevitable hurt. He knew now that she was in love with Lionel, and he felt a touch of uneasiness. Lionel was gallant with all females, no matter their age. Jason had often seen him bowing in a most courtly fashion to little girls in pigtails and hair ribbons and ruffled frocks, and to very old ladies. They had been enchanted. Jason had not yet decided whether the courtliness was derisive or genuine, or simply a manifestation of good nature and natural charm. There were times when he suspected that Lionel was a complete stranger to him, enigmatic, smiling, with thoughts he would never reveal, and emotions, if any, he would never betray, not even to his best friend. Never had Jason seen him really angry, or melancholy, or heavily thoughtful, or conjecturing.

But, there was Joan, of the angelic beauty, helpless, dependent, with eyes that seemed to glimpse a beatific vision. When she looked at Lionel her beauty became luminous, her mouth trembling with smiles, her flesh translucent. Lionel would kiss her lightly on the cheek like a brother—but he would hold her hand often on the table as they played card games or dominoes together, and the hold, Jason had seen, was not casual, but firm and lingering. At parting, he would put his hand on her gleaming black head and would gently stroke the tumbling bright mass of her hair, appearing not to be aware of what he was doing. Often he would just smile at her, and his lively face would change, but what that change was, Jason did not know.

Jason often wished to ask him bluntly, "Do you like my sister?" But something prevented him from doing so. He was afraid that the answer would be a gay shrug, a wave of a thin freckled hand, an offhand word. He was afraid that Lionel merely pitied Joan, was trying to be generous, or endured Joan out of friendship for himself. Once Jason had said to his sister, "Lionel likes all the ladies, all of them. I see it in the dining room. It doesn't mean a thing." He had been almost shocked at the way her eyes had suddenly filled with a fierce sparkling, but he did recognize the blue-steel glint in them as hatred. She had replied, "What do you know about Lionel, anyway? You're too stupid to know anything about anybody."

It was then that Jason had realized what he had always refused to admit—that Joan had nothing but contempt for him, and aversion. He had been confused and amazed at the pain he had felt. She had added, "You're just a countrified Irish bumpkin like Da." Her pretty fluting voice had changed to the ring of a thrown hard stone on concrete, and she had turned her head away from him. John, listening, had smiled thinly, but he had said nothing. For all John's affection for his sister and his dislike of Lionel, he would not add his warning to Jason's. He had even been faintly amused by Jason's stricken expression. Why hadn't the big fool known long ago? John's congenital selfishness had solidified and increased with his years.

Jason, in spite of his new knowledge, continued to love his sister and did not know why. His urge to protect her, to prevent harm from touching her, remained with him, and he worried often about her. Jason knew that his grandfather worried also, despite his quite open dislike of the crippled girl and her dislike of him. Jason knew his mother's anxiety about her daughter, her fear for her, though Joan was often discourteous to Kate and seemed to regard her as her personal attendant, valuable for her services but not to be taken with seriousness. In some obscure and senseless way she half-consciously believed her mother guilty of her condition, and was resentfully bitter in consequence. Jason had once hesitantly mentioned this to his grandfather, and Bernard had gloomily grimaced and had remarked, "Who knows all the hell in the human soul? Best to accept it, then ignore it, unless it attacks you."

5

One Monday night shortly after eight, Jason was preparing to ride home from the Inn-Tavern. He had every other Sunday off and on Mondays—a slow evening—he could leave at eight o'clock instead of the usual ten o'clock. As the Inn-Tavern was a long distance from his home, and there was still no public transportation in Belleville, Jason had bought a third-hand bicycle so that he would never be late. But he did not buy this until Lionel had appeared with a very fancy new model, all shining and lavishly equipped. "We're not clods any longer," he informed Jason. "Besides, it saves shoe leather, and a bicycle gets you home quicker." After some thought, this seemed reasonable to Jason. When Lionel appeared one morning, during a rainstorm, in a fine new mackintosh—"saves your clothes"—Jason went to a secondhand-clothing shop and bought a rather grimy one for himself. This also seemed reasonable. Lionel's coat had cost an extravagant twelve dollars—it was very stylish—but Jason's had cost but one dollar and fifty cents. Kate had done her best to make it presentable, but had not been too successful. However, it was an adequate protection.

Mr. Mulligan was not unaware of these transactions.

On this Monday night Jason wheeled his bicycle out of the back employees' entrance. He had tied a bag of food to the handles of his vehicle. Since Mondays were slow, the meals served were leftovers from Sunday. Mr. Mulligan's establishment did its best business on Sunday in spite of the righteous frowns which were bent on him in this very religious little city. On Mondays Jason's home-going bag was very heavy since he knew the food would be stale the next day. Mr. Mulligan himself sent large baskets of perishables to the little local convent on Mondays. But on Sundays, Father Sweeney had a basket of delicious edibles, given with generosity and invariably concealing, in its depths, a few dollars in an envelope, in addition to what Mr. Mulligan gave at Mass collections. Father Sweeney was now able to afford a new habit once a year; he also had a bicycle, a Christmas gift from Mr. Mulligan. Father Sweeney suspected that Jason

Garrity had had something to do with this, and he was not far wrong.

Father Sweeney also suspected that quite frequently Mr. Mulligan's transient rooms were occupied by prosperous married men and pretty, well-dressed young ladies of ambiguous reputation. So long as they did not "paint their faces" flagrantly, and were genteel of manner and low of voice, the townsfolk did not too vociferously object, for the "friends" of these females owned the factories and the few fine shops and businesses of Belleville, including the four banks which held mortgages. But Father Sweeney was a different matter. He had once spoken to Mr. Mulligan quite sternly, and Mr. Mulligan had listened with a respectful and indulgent smile.

"Hell, Faether," he had said, "and is it my affair? Or yours, if I may say, with all respect? My establishment is no whorehouse..." Father Sweeney flinched. "Decorous, it is. So long as there is no open bawdy display or behavior, and all is discreet, who am I to judge? I've seen some of the wives." Mr. Mulligan shuddered and raised his eyes to heaven. "It is the husbands you should pity. Seems to me our Lord had something nice to say about Mary Magdalen, then. Didn't he?" Father Sweeney was frustrated, but he had become much milder over these four past years, and not so rigorous as before. Besides, many ladies from out-of-town accompanied their husbands on their business in Belleville. Who could tell one lady from another, whether wife or doxy? Many was the doxy who was more of a lady than the wife she had displaced. Open sin was not to be tolerated, especially cheap and offensive sin, which violated the sensibilities of others, but this sin was not obvious at Mr. Mulligan's, nor would it have been permitted. But Father Sweeney wistfully wished that some of the prosperous gentlemen were Catholic. He could then severely admonish them in the confessional. But almost all Catholics in Belleville were very poor, and most were Irish.

The barrooms in the rear of the Inn-Tavern were supposed to be closed on Sundays. On those days the windows were heavily blinded with thick draperies, and no light shone through them. There was an inconspicuous door to the bars in the rear, which silently opened and shut with astonishing frequency, admitting many gentlemen accompanied by their ladies. The dining room, of course, did its best business on Sunday, and everyone had ruddy cheeks and twinkling eyes, though there was but water on the tables, or "tea." Children were notably absent. The majority of wives were at home, sleeping off enormous noontime dinners, while their husbands were ostensibly out for "brisk long walks" with their friends of the same sex. Sometimes the "friends" invited husbands home later for a "light supper," which was appreciated by the wives, still sluggish from the early dinners.

Jason, half-mounted on his bicycle, looked back affectionately at the Inn-Tavern. Mr. Mulligan often bragged that the shell of his establishment had been built over one hundred and twenty years ago. It had been an abandoned wreck on a street which had once been the most majestic and prosperous area in the town. After Mr. Mulligan had bought his property, many other old ruins had been bought and refurbished. Now the street had a certain style and liveliness, though it was suspected that the house on the corner did not really shelter a stout jeweled widow by the name of Mrs. Lindon, with her several pretty young daughters and handsome young nieces who were "just visiting from other parts of the state." Mrs. Lindon had an extraordinary number of nieces, it appeared, and "young cousins." The "daughters" were more permanent. If well-dressed gentlemen, late in the evenings, came to call—well, a mother had a right to look for excellent marriages for her daughters, did she not, and to do the same kindly thing for the "nieces" and "cousins"? They were all good patrons of Mr. Mulligan's, including Mrs. Lindon, who had well-bred manners, much jewelry, and was very proper and kept a careful eye on her protegées. She had a most stately air and a fine big bosom, and her deep voice was refined.

She was also one of the richest depositors in all four banks. Her "husband" had been an "importer" in Philadelphia. She had moved to Belleville to "live a nice quiet life with my girls." No one openly contested this. When any of her more beautiful charges married bachelors or widowers of distinction, only the best people were invited to very opulent wedding parties—held in one of Mr. Mulligan's private dining rooms. The marriages were always celebrated in Belleville's more affluent churches, and the brides all wore veils and virginal white and kept their eyes modestly down.

The remaining girls were soon joined by more "nieces" or "cousins" who had decided to spend long visits with Auntie Clementine, or who had been "suddenly orphaned." If the authenticity of all this was universally doubted, no one openly complained. If the widowed mayor of Belleville and other gentlemen like himself came to call on Mrs. Lindon—well, she was a wealthy widow and a great catch herself. Wasn't she? Mrs. Lindon was the largest benefactor of local charities and went to church every Sunday, always accompanied by several "daughters, nieces, and cousins." She had a new motorcar, too, a Stanley Steamer, and a victoria with two sleek black horses. She looked like a queen in them, and her silks and furs, it was rumored, were all bought in New York. She had a number of servants of the utmost discretion, for they were paid incredible wages and were very loyal. They loved Mrs. Lindon and all the girls.

Jason, as he stood looking at Mr. Mulligan's establishment, doubted, with a wry smile, that Lionel was visiting any of Mrs. Lindon's enticing young relatives that night. He could only afford two dollars. Jason never condemned Lionel's small excursions into sin. He had long since learned that there was very little joy in the world. So long as the joy hurt no one else, and brought no overt evil with it, then it should be tolerated. Jason had also discovered that there was more real evil among the ostentatiously virtuous than among the lovers of joy.

The Inn-Tavern, usually called "Mulligan's Place," comprised three and a half stories. In the attic, an incongruous squat box with a single window, lived some of the help. The lower stories had balconies, ornate with wooden lacework, painted an immaculate white, carved and stained-glass windows or windows with fretted iron over them also painted white, and little openings, hardly windows, tinted a brilliant gold. There was a lone tower to the left of the attic, perched on the third floor, with a candle-snuffer roof. The doors were of heavy wood, overlaid in carved bronze. Mr. Mulligan had had the roofs of all painted a soft green, but the wooden walls of the house had been painted such a dark green that it appeared almost black. There were porches here and there where permanent guests could sit on pleasant evenings and look at the passing people, the motorcars, and the carriages. Though the edifice was directly on the sidewalk, it had an air of rich, reserved elegance, and it had a strictly ordered long thin garden in the rear, also for guests. The garden held white wrought-iron benches and chairs. Mr. Mulligan had gone deeply into debt to restore the house, but had paid off the debt in five years and was now very prosperous.

All the floors in the huge house were of pegwood and as shining as mirrors, and were partly covered by Oriental rugs in quiet and luxurious shades. The bedrooms were ample, well equipped, the china of the best quality, hand-painted. Mr. Mulligan had enlarged the one bathroom and had added another, and had embellished them with marble fittings. There was also a "ladies' retiring room" with couches and chairs and a lavatory, which was the admiration of the town. Here ladies could comb their hair, gossip together between courses at dinner, touch up very inconspicuous "paint," and scrutinize each other's gowns.

People drove from miles around Belleville to dine at Mr. Mulligan's. It was famous not only for its cuisine but also for its imported wines and warmth and prudence. There was nothing else like it in Belleville or even in other nearby towns of much larger populations. It was not a hotel. Mr. Mulligan had introduced the first fine "family establishment" outside of the resort areas.

Tonight all the roofs glittered with hard snow under a bleak icy moon. All the windows glowed with golden light. Two, on the first floor, shimmered with rosy reflections from the huge fireplaces. Jason felt proud to belong to such an establishment. Yet he felt that something nameless was missing, and he did not know what it was. He contemplated the improved position of his family over these past four years. The man who had bought old Joe's shop and building had hired Bernard to work there waiting on customers and cleaning the displays and the windows, for six hours a day six days a week. He was paid eight dollars a week, and was permitted to take home partially stale bread and other sundries. Bernard himself had painted the shop in a bright yellow trimmed with green, his favorite colors, and his arrangement of the one window was tastefully graced with offerings of pink ham, long Italian sausages, neatly polished secondhand shoes, and shining copper pots.

Bernard had demanded that John work also, after his school. He delivered both morning and evening newspapers, and worked on Saturdays in the office of a small factory. On occasion he also went there after school hours, to his distress. There was his homework, he would plead, and he needed his sleep. Bernard had only shrugged. "At your age, boyo, you need but four or five hours' sleep a night. That is all I had when I was seventeen, in Ireland, when I was in the seminary studying for the priesthood. And my father, who was a teacher of astronomy in the University of Dublin, slept even less. Too much sleep makes a man fat and lazy and softens his brain.

The world is too interesting to waste time in too much sleep. On with you."

Kate had taught the protesting Joan to embroider artistically, and her linen doilies, dresser scarfs, and centerpieces were now on display at the shop, and sold well at good prices. Joan might murmur that she was "tired," to which her grandfather would say with bluntness, "Tired of what, miss? Staring at your face in the mirror and dressing your hair, and eating? It's time you helped your mother." To Bernard every soul should work to its capacity, even the handicapped. So, added to the embroidery was another task for Joan: Bernard had negotiated with the new local manufacturer of "fine shirts for gentlemen" to permit Joan to do the dainty hand stitching necessary on visible seams, cuffs, and buttonholes.

"You're helping your brother to go to his damned seminary, and that should comfort you," Bernard had remarked with a not very affectionate grin. "All for God, and for that you have probably cut off a few years in purgatory." This did not console Joan. She thought her crippled state should suffice to waft her into heaven immediately. Bernard had disillusioned her, he hoped. "You are no saint, Joanie, and you reek with the sins of selfishness, self-pity, vanity, and greed, and that you know in your heart—if you have a heart."

Poor Kate was ailing, though her sweet smile was not extinguished. Her eyes were too bright, and her complexion had grown too vivid, and her chronic cough never was alleviated, despite bottles of Beef, Iron, and Wine. Bernard would watch her, brooding. He had compelled her to give up her laundry. "Money pouring in now," he would say. "My money, Joan's, Jack's, and Jason's. No need for you to work that hard. Enough to do at home." She was very thin, much thinner than before, though Bernard would force her to eat the good food on the table. Joan and Jack loved plentiful quantities of milk, but Bernard limited them to half a glass a day and insisted that Kate drink a pint and a half herself. They did not like him the more for this, and considered themselves abused. After all, they worked, did they not? Mum did nothing but the housekeeping. Gas had been installed in the stove, and there were gas lamps, too. Why did Mum need all that food? She worked very little, they grumbled to each other. "One of these days she'll be going to matinees and the nickelodeons, like other idle women," John would mutter to his sister.

"Da bought her a beautiful store dress for Christmas,"

Joan answered with resentment, "and a pair of kid button shoes and gloves. If he has all that money, why should we work so hard?"

Bernard did not agree with conservative doctors that "the consumption" was not contagious. Though it was a conspicuous Irish disease, the results of the past Famine, Bernard knew that Kate had contracted it from Peter, his son. So, without explanation, he had bought a cot for Joan and had placed it far from Kate's bed, and he had gently taught Kate to cover her mouth when coughing and to burn the rags she used for sputum. "But they're good cloths, Da," she would say. Bernard would reply in a voice she did not protest, "Burn them, Katie. You never know."

As Jason pedaled home this dark, very cold January night, he thought of all these things. The streets were empty. No one was about, though it was not yet half-past eight. The moon sailed in black emptiness. A far lonely dog barked. The bicycle wheels crunched loudly on the crust of snow. Suddenly Jason, without warning, was assailed by a terrible melancholy, profound and paralyzing. It was so intense that he had to halt, one foot on the slippery street.

He tried to understand this invading spiritual agony, but he saw no cause for it. It was only there, like an encasement of black stone over his spirit, which held him imprisoned and motionless. His thoughts vaguely scampered about in his skull like terrified mice, vainly looking for escape from the tenebrous gloom in which they raced. Jason could not catch them in their panic. He would think he had hold of one and then it slipped from him.

Things were so much better than they had been four years ago. Then why this amorphous sorrow of soul, this pressing weight on his chest, this wet burning of his eyes? He looked about him. He had halted near a clump of black firs close to the street. There was a hollow place under them, without light or even shadow, though a streetlamp was burning nearby, pale and yellow and flickering. Beyond the trees was only the blank staring of shut houses. He was alone. A kind of terror seized him. He was not a young man ready with prayers and incantations for comfort in a comfortless world. He was too pragmatic. But he mumbled aloud, "For what am I living?" This new thought was a fresh assault on his soul, and his terror increased.

He still stared at the empty hollow under the trees. Then all at once he felt a "shifting," a movement, though there was no movement anywhere. Suddenly, like a giant wave of light, he was engulfed in brilliance, though he did not see it with his mortal eyes. He was only aware of it, a glory, an opening, a vastness of being, of understanding, of love, of promise, of secret but incredible hope. Above all, of a tremendous love, supernatural, filled with eternity, without boundaries; personal, consoling, joyous, ecstatic. Warmth enveloped him, like embracing arms. He was not only released, but he felt an expanding, as if aware of his membership in something beyond life and duty and grimness and pain. He was swept, in that blinding glow, into rapture, tenderness, strength, and grandeur. Everything was explained, everything known, all terror lost, all peace encompassing.

He began to cry with happiness, wordlessly prayerful. He tried to hold it, but as quickly as it had come, it was gone, and there was only the lonely dark and the cold.

However, the melancholy and fear had left him, as if a parent had lifted him from a sightless bed and had held him and had told him something he could not remember and only knew.

He went on his way, but now smiling and singing aloud the Irish ballads his grandfather had taught him. He felt that the future was no longer menacing, but fulfilling, and he was part of it. Then, without his volition, he said aloud, "Our Father..." For the first time it had meaning. It was personal. It was protection. He was not alone. A "thing" now walked with him, was his eternal companion.

Bernard saw it at once when Jason entered the house. He saw the exaltation. If he had not known his grandson, he would have thought the youth drunk. Bernard had the spiritual understanding of the Irish, the occult awareness. "Something" had touched Jason. Bernard had heard of such occurrences, though he had not experienced them himself. The priests had talked of it, as the prerogative of saints. Jason was no saint. Yet, "it" had come to him as it had come four years ago. Bernard felt awe, and also fear. He could not ask Jason. Jason himself would not know. It was a visitation, a spiritual revelation.

No one else in the warm little house saw this. Joan, sipping her hot tea, was sadly contemplating her wrongs. John, as usual, was furtively devouring everything in sight, even lifting the slice of bread off his mother's plate. His gaunt face, as always, was withdrawn, tight, and gray. His ascetic cheekbones gleamed in the gaslight; his fleshless fingers were deft and darting. He looked up quickly at Jason and said, "What did you bring us tonight?"

But Joan said with sharpness, "Where's Lionel?"

Jason gave the weighty bag to his mother. He looked at his sister, hesitating. Lionel had again begged off for a night on the town. At last he said, under the stare of her suspicious but glorious eyes, "He couldn't come."

Her face changed darkly. "You mean you don't think your friend is good enough for your crippled sister, so you didn't mention I was expecting him tonight."

The joy was faintly echoing in Jason, so he said with urgent kindness, "No. He just couldn't come, Joanie. There was something he had to do. Honest. He'll be here tomorrow, though."

He saw that his sister was wearing her best blue Sunday dress, beautifully embroidered by herself, and that her long hair was held back by a blue ribbon and that she wore the imitation-pearl beads Bernard had given her for Christmas. Her beauty was supernal. Jason felt pity for her, and anger at Lionel. "He'll be here tomorrow," he repeated. Joan looked about to cry. She gave Jason a malevolent glance. "You'd do anything to make somebody unhappy. I know you, Jase. You hate your family, me and Jack. You plot to yourself all the time to make us miserable. I know you."

Bernard pushed back his chair, and his great face was crimson. "You damned little snot!" he exclaimed. "You whining little besom! You should be thoroughly thrashed, for once in your life!"

"Da," Kate implored.

"Katie, that colleen is a monster! She has no appreciation of the sacrifices of others. She sees only her face in a mirror, and what is that worth, then?" He glared at John, who was avidly exploring the bag Jason had brought home. "Hands off, bucko! You're another one. Worthless. Katie, take the bag from him. We need it for our supper. If you don't take it, it will disappear down his throat in a twinkling, for all he has had three servings of sauerkraut and potatoes and sausages, and half a loaf of bread." Bernard snatched the bag from John's grasping fingers. "Wish it would choke you," he muttered, but everyone heard.

"A growing boy," Kate pleaded.

"So is Jason, who works harder than anyone in this family."

"I've had dinner," said Jason, though he had not. The joy was fading from him, but all at once he saw his family with unfamiliar clarity. The faces of his mother and grandfather became brilliantly clear to him, as if light had been thrown upon them, and his joy was mixed with pain. He saw the truth of his brother and sister, then refused to see it. It would be too terrible. A man had to believe in his family. What else was there?

Bernard laid the contents of the bag on the table. A fourth of a ham, a dozen Parker House rolls, half a pound of butter not yet rancid, five baked potatoes, half a head of raw cabbage, a package of roast beef in slices—Jason had not wanted to take this, but the chef had told him it would be spoiled by tomorrow—a tin of boiled turnips with nutmeg and butter, a few apples, two oranges, a package of greasy bologna, an opened can of condensed milk, half a roast chicken with dressing left on someone's plate, a paper of boiled brussels sprouts, a huge slice of cake, some slightly stale pastries. "A feast for us," said Bernard.

"It's Monday," said Jason, taking off his coat. "It would be bad tomorrow."

"So. Let us eat it, then," said Bernard, licking his lips ostentatiously. "And what's this? A half-bottle of wine!"

"I didn't notice that," said Jason. "The chef must have put it in."

"Leftovers, for beggars," said John, taking a large slice of ham.

"A disgrace," said Joan, taking two of the pastries.

"A grace," said Kate. "Thank you, Jason, dear."

"Your boots, Jason," said Bernard. "You need another pair. Get them tomorrow."

John smirked at his sister. She shrugged delicately in reply. She began to eat with exaggerated gentility, as if every bite offended her.

Bernard said, "Katie, if you don't share this magnificence, I will be very vexed with you."

"I'm sure," said Joan, "that Lionel doesn't have to take scraps from other people's plates to his house."

Bernard laughed his harsh and grating laugh. "No, indeed. He'll just take flesh from other people's souls, that's all. Or eat them alive."

"He'll be a success, not a drudge," Joan said, with rare courage against her grandfather.

Jason listened with discomfiture. Then he had a thought. He turned to his grandfather. "I had an idea tonight. It was . . . something. I can't remember . . ."

"You never had an idea in your life," said John, taking a slice of roast beef.

Bernard looked at him. With a kind of fury he reached across the table and struck his grandson violently across his face. "And what have you but cant!" he shouted.

"Da," said Kate, in tears.

Bernard lowered at her, but with love. "Katie, you have only one real child, one human being of a child. Jason. God love him." He filled a tumbler with wine. He looked at Jason and his hard little gray eyes were very bright. "To Jason," he said. "A toast from the heart. God bless you, boyo. You'll need all the blessings you can get."

Jason was embarrassed, but his heart lifted. He poured a glass of wine for his mother. "For Mum," he said. He hesitated. "For all the good women in the world."

"Amen," said Bernard. The others said nothing, but Kate's eyes were filled with light.

John touched his smarting face. He seethed with hatred. What a boorish family for a priest! No wonder he had to pray so hard.

6

Father Sweeney, with trepidation, asked Bernard to see him in his study. Spring spread outside, all golden and exuberant.

"I am wondering," said the young priest. "If John has a true vocation."

"For the Spanish Inquisition, yes," said Bernard heartily. "What is the trouble?"

"He is too scrupulous, Bernard."

"You mean he condemns practically everything."

Father Sweeney stroked his rapidly thinning auburn hair with a hesitant hand. He lifted a letter from his elderly desk. "I have a letter here from the seminary in Pittsburgh where John is studying for the priesthood. Father O'Connell. He mentions that John is a most exemplary seminarian, in terms of faith and hope..." The priest paused again.

Bernard said, "But he doesn't know the meaning of love." When Father Sweeney did not answer, Bernard went on, "But I knew that from the time he was in nappies. Strange that others didn't seem to know."

The priest was pained. "We thought as he grew older that he would learn, from example, in the seminary."

"Hah," said Bernard. "Minds me of some of the old—the old—priests in my seminary where I was studying for the priesthood, in Ireland."

As Father Sweeney was also "minded" of certain old priests he had encountered in his own seminary, he grew more and more uncomfortable. "Well, then, Bernard. It is not only that. John doesn't seem to comprehend the difference between venial and mortal sins. Intellectually, yes. Otherwise, no. He seems to believe, most of the time, that there are no venial, that is, ordinary human daily sins. All sins are deadly."

"And a worse sinner I never met," said Bernard.

Father Sweeney chose to ignore that. "We've spoken before of his extreme scrupulosity. He...he was found wearing a hair shirt."

"Good!" said Bernard. "I'll buy him drawers to match."

Father Sweeney compressed his lips to stop a short laugh. He was a very serious young man. "He also engages in self-flagellation when he is alone.

"Now, does he?" said Bernard with interest. "Making up for lost time. A clout or two a day, which I used to wish to give him when he was home, would have prevented that. But better, as the Americans say, late than never."

"We don't approve of it," said Father Sweeney. He coughed a little. "Father O'Connell is under the impression that John is striving for sainthood."

"Nothing but the best for Father Garrity, is it?"

"Bernard, you're taking this too facetiously."

"Not I! I told you so two years ago when he first went there. But who listens to an old bucko like me?"

"A year ago Father O'Connell suggested a Trappist monastery to John."

Bernard held up a hand. "I know. That wouldn't suit Jack Garrity. He'd have to keep his mouth shut most of the time instead of talking about 'sin.' And he'd have to work like the devil. He wants to be out in the world denouncing everything that is pleasant and lovable and laughing. He wants to inflict pain on others, or at least rule their lives, which would be the same thing, I'm thinking." He smiled at the priest. "There was a touch of that in you, too, once upon a time, Father. But you learned, that you did. Jack will never learn. What other crimes has he been committing? In another family he'd have made an excellent burglar or a confidence man. He has the talents for it."

Father Sweeney sighed. "He doesn't seem to understand the doctrine of limbo. He believes in infant damnation, or implies that at least."

"So did the old missionaries, both Catholic and Protestant. He is just reverting to type, as they say."

"This is a grave matter, Bernard. You don't seem to grasp the gravity."

"Do I not, indeed! I was one year, only, from ordination, and then was booted out. Well, boot Jack out, too."

Father Sweeney was suddenly interested. "Why were you booted out, Bernard?"

Bernard leaned back in his straight rickety chair. "There was an old priest. Like Jack." He grinned. "I clouted him."

"Dear me," said the priest, who had wanted to do that several times during his own studies in the seminary.

"It wasn't only that," said Bernard. "I didn't agree very often, either. I didn't think a man and his wife should live together if they hated each other, even if there were brats in the house."

89

Father Sweeney gasped. "You believed in divorce?"

"Better divorce than murder, and burying a body in the cellar, as so many desperate husbands—and wives—do. A hell of a shock to the nerves, that is. Too much after a lifetime of strain. Yes, I know. 'These whom God hath joined...' Now, there's the question! A man marries a hellion, or a poor soul of a woman marries a drunken brute. A vile sinner marries a saint. Did God join them in the beginning, or did the Devil? That's the question!"

Father Sweeney closed his eyes wearily. Bernard said, "Now, then, Father. Should a good man or woman be condemned to a long hell on earth in a bad marriage? Yes, yes. You would say such suffering 'elevates' the soul. I don't believe it; never did. As I said, it often leads to murder. There're few saints who revel in suffering, Father. Or enjoy it, except if they're deranged."

The priest was aghast. "You mean you think that the multitudes of faithful souls who died for their faith were 'deranged'?"

"Some," said Bernard hardily. "But as I have never met a saint, except one old priest in Ireland, and my son's widow, Katie, I am not one to judge. But many's the saint that goes unrecognized and unsung. It takes a little touch of the music hall to be recognized as a saint, humility or not. You will notice that the saints were always loudly praised for their 'humility.' I often wonder who started the rumor in the beginning." He paused and looked surprised. "Perhaps that spalpeen of a grandson of mine has the makings of a saint after all! He was always jabbering about 'humility,' and a prouder young ass than he I never saw!"

Father Sweeney, feeling somewhat agitated, stroked his hair again. He reached for his clay pipe, and took his time cleaning and filling it with cheap tobacco. Bernard did the same. He saw that the sky outside was effulgent with blue light; the window had been opened a little, and a sweet breeze entered the little study. Out of the corner of his eye Bernard regarded the priest with compassion. What the good Lord saved me from! he thought.

"Yes," said Father Sweeney with some sadness. "John is proud. He seems to think that he is without the usual sins, and so is far superior to the other young seminarians and even to some of his teachers."

"Well, let them boot him out, as I said."

"I thought you could offer some suggestions, Bernard."

"I just did."

"You can't be serious!"

Bernard considered. "Well, then. If you boot him out, he'll be back on our hands, and that's a thought to squeeze the soul. I blessed the day he left with his bags. I have a thought. Add some iron balls to the ends of the whips he's using on himself."

"Bernard."

"Or set him to cleaning all the middens every day."

Father Sweeney blew out a large puff of smoke. "John decided one day, as a penance, to scrub the kitchen from ceiling to floor, and all the cupboards, and the contents of the cupboards." The priest coughed delicately. "Unfortunately, the soapy, dirty scrub brush fell into the kettle of soup old Sister Mary Elizabeth had on the stove."

"And?" said Bernard, leaning forward.

The priest kept his face sober. "She lost her temper, I am afraid. She beat him about the head and shoulders with a heavy iron frying pan. It was thought, for a day or two, that he had a concussion."

"And he didn't?" said Bernard after a fit of hoarse laughter.

"No."

"Sad, that. Might have improved his intelligence. What if I write him a letter and tell him that if he's booted out he's not to come back to my house, but get a job, say, in the coal mines? That should give him thought."

Father Sweeney thought so too. But he said, "Do write to him, Bernard, as I will, too. He's determined to be a priest. I must remind him of certain virtues—"

"He doesn't believe in virtues. But he does believe in sins."

"I wish you would ask his sister to write him, too."

"Joanie." Bernard considered, and his hard old face became tough. "Now, there's two of a kind. They recognized that in each other. Yes. She is the only one who could influence him. I'll tell her tonight that Jack will be booted out and put on the street if he doesn't improve. She's so proud of the idea of her dear brother being ordained. A threat that he might not be should frighten the—"

"Bernard," said the priest with haste.

"Well. Yes, that should be enough. She might take time to think of the consequences, if she can pull herself out of her dreamings about that redheaded rascal Lionel Nolan."

The priest said with rebuke, "It was only last Monday that Mr. Pat Mulligan remarked how fortunate he was to have

Lionel in charge of the dining room. The lad is not yet nineteen, and is very ambitious and efficient and untiring—rare attributes these degenerate days—and is full of ideas—"

"Schemes, you mean, Father."

"Which have excited the approval of the patrons, Bernard."

"Oh, he does love his work!" Bernard's face heavily darkened. "He's after Joanie, and she's after him." He reflected. "Come to think of it, they'd make a good pair, though I hate to think of a Garrity woman married to such as Lionel."

"Lionel has had his salary increased to twenty dollars a week, and Mr. Mulligan is not rash with money. He says Lionel is worth every penny, including the tips."

"Jason's also getting twenty dollars a week, Father."

"Diligent," said the priest. "Yes, Mr. Mulligan told me." The priest spoke with some reluctance. "Well, diligence does make up for a lot of lesser things."

Bernard regarded him with gray fire in his small eyes. "I resent that, Father. Jason has more intelligence in his...his finger than Jack and Lionel have in their whole brains! A better boyo was never born! He has more than 'diligence.' He has a mind and a heart and most of the heroic virtues the Church is always talking about. Pity you never saw them. That beautiful old crucifix hanging there over the high altar, Father, that old Joe left to Jason—"

Father Sweeney broke in, astonished. "But Jason told me that you had insisted he give it to my church!"

Bernard's face changed to a softness rarely seen by anyone but Kate. He nodded. "Yes, he would say that. It's just like Jason. Never wanting any credit for himself. Kind, generous, quiet about himself. He'll go farther than that Lionel devil, mind my words. And always with honor. Slower, but with honor." He added, "Pat Mulligan told me that Jason is his—what was it?—yes, second in command. That's what he said. Oversees everything. When Pat had the lung fever last winter, Jason took full charge, and nothing went wrong." But Bernard asked himself: When did I last hear him laugh? Why doesn't he go dancing on a Saturday night with the other lads? Why is it only work, and books? That is all he talks about, and his poor mother. "And that minds me, Father. My poor Katie must have a room to herself in the Sisters' Hospital. We can afford it now, if not too much."

"You must speak to Sister Maria Francis," said Father Sweeney with pity.

"You can put in a word, Father. I talked to Sister last

week, and so did Jason. She said there was no room in that damned poor little place. They can make room! Katie's dying, and she wants to die in dignity, with no one but the good sisters there. She doesn't want Jason and me to see how she is now..." His strong and resonant voice almost broke. At Kate's pleading, he tried not to think of her condition. He tried, but he could not look on that haggard face with its feverish bright cheeks and eyes and see all that sweet patience without anguish.

The priest sighed. "We need only twelve thousand dollars more for the new small wing," he said. "We have five thousand. That is, we did have until we bought those two old houses next door. Twelve thousand dollars is a lot of money, I am afraid. The parishioners do try very hard, but they are all so poor. Mr. Mulligan gave a thousand dollars at Christmas. We used that to renovate the roof and put in a new furnace and put down concrete sidewalks. But the rooms will have to wait."

"And the papers are talking about a panic next year," said Bernard. "Things are pretty bad now as it is. But let us cheer up. We are going to have a war. That should make things prosperous." His voice had become bitter.

Father Sweeney was astounded. Was Bernard out of his mind? "War? What war? With whom?"

Bernard shrugged. "Father, I read all the papers. The bloody Sassenagh said in his Parliament, just recently, that Germany was 'invading all our traditional markets in the world.' That's what wars are always about: markets. Call it territory, as they used to do, but it is markets in these days. Sure, and it's the same thing. And there's the bankers. They always invest in wars. That's what Lincoln said, too. He hated and feared them like poison, and with good reason, Father. You should read more than your breviary and the religious rot... Sorry, Father. But there will be a war. D'you think the Spanish-American War was fought for some damned nonsense such as honor or 'being attacked'? They're just excuses. We got Cuba and the other islands, didn't we, out of that war? Well."

He stood up, and he stared at the silent priest grimly. "I'm thinking of Jason, Father. He's twenty now. Old enough for a war—to die in—for the bankers and the munitions makers, and national prosperity."

"I'm afraid—" the priest began.

"So am I, Father. But not about the same thing. You'll put

in a word for Katie? Jason and I are paying five dollars a week for her. We'll try to make it more, when she has a room of her own."

He walked out into the warm spring air. Even the ugly old street seemed to shine with happy light. But Bernard did not see it. He was thinking of too many terrible things. The world had never been a good place in which a civilized man could live in peace. But the future glared into a far greater hell. Bernard knew that in his soul. He went to the shop where he worked.

There were twenty-eight dollars a week "coming into the house," as Bernard said. But there was Kate, who cost five dollars a week, and her doctor, whose bill was never less than ten dollars a month, and her medicines which he prescribed, and the rent had been raised two dollars a month, and there was John in his seminary, and a "woman" who had to be paid three dollars a week to care for the house and Joan now that Kate was no longer there, and fuel—the landlord no longer supplied coal, for the house now had gas—and food and clothing and repairs, and many other devourers of money, including dentists and offerings on Sundays and holy days of obligation. Joan's embroideries brought in very little, for "times were hard," as people complained. The cost of food had increased, too, and as Joan was "delicate," the doctor said, and as Bernard was fearful that the girl might come down with the consumption, she must have good nourishment. She had developed a faint little cough like John's when her brother and grandfather were present. There were also the small taxes on Jason's fourteen acres of land, and the cost of living was steadily rising in 1906.

The food from the Inn-Tavern was a tremendous help, but Joan lately had come to despise it vehemently and to declare she would rather starve than eat it. Jason, afraid himself, had yielded, as had Bernard, and she had the food she preferred, and the creamy milk she drank copiously. Jason often thought of his grandfather, who was seventy-eight, and though Bernard hardly was infirm and seemed to discount his years in his appearance, Jason knew that age would inevitably strike him down. He often fell asleep over his newspaper, and his enormous vitality was less.

There were five people, which included the "woman," to be cared for on twenty-eight dollars a week, not a poor sum in itself, but it could be extended only so far. Bernard put a dollar a week into his tin box under his bed. Jason had no savings at all. He knew his wages were far larger than those received by the average workingman, but he could not wear a workingman's cheap patched clothing in the Inn-Tavern. He had had to buy a good wool suit for fifteen dollars a year ago, which the "woman" pressed and cleaned once a week, and he had to have immaculate shirts and stiff white collars and cuffs every day, and "decent ties," two of them. Then, there was the barber. Bernard cut his own hair, but Jason had not that alternative.

There were times when Jason silently gave in to despair. His only pleasures now were his own small store of books and those he borrowed from the public library, and his visits to his land halfway up the mountain. He could visit it only once or twice a month, on his Sundays off, but the land was his refuge, his renewal, his blessed silence after a long week of human voices and clamor and worry and work. Last Christmas Mr. Mulligan had given him, "for the family, too, Jase," an inexpensive phonograph, and somehow Jason had contrived to buy four cylinder records, two by Caruso and two by Galli-Curci. He could only play them when Joan was out for an airing, pushed by the "woman." She preferred ragtime. She called opera "dreary, like a funeral." She spoke with admiration of the gramophone Lionel had recently acquired for his own house, and the lively tunes. Joan had taken to visiting Molly frequently and called her "my one and only dear friend"; Molly, on hearing this remark once, had crinkled her mouth unbecomingly but had held back her sardonic remarks.

On this particular mild Sunday in April 1906, Jason took his bicycle to the foot of the nearest mountain and rode it up as high as possible on the wandering dirt road. When the road ended, he left his vehicle and climbed the rest of the way. How sweet and fecund the air was, how warm and tender the sun on his bare head and shoulders! What a blessing the silence was, stirred only by the sounds of birds, the movement of wind among the fir trees and the oaks and wild birches and elms, chartreuse in their early leafings against the bright blue sky. The quiet here was the quiet of a cathedral, and the choir was the music of the holy earth, simple but profound and implicit with promise. In dim spots among the trees, trailing arbutus made gentle carpets, and there were patches of wild crocus and buttercups and purple pitcher plants and new brilliant grass. Somewhere there was a little spring, and it sang to the radiant air and its waters trickled over small stones down the mountain. Jason drank of its sweetness often; it was as clean and fresh as flowers themselves, and it was like an elixir to the youth.

Tree toads sang, a celestial chorus celebrating life, and Jason paused to listen. He said, aloud, and somewhat sheepishly, "Hosanna!" The singing stopped for a moment, then resumed. A blue jay fluttered across his path and screamed; sparrows asked questions with irritation; a robin suddenly lifted his silvery voice. A rabbit scuttled nearby; a fox looked at Jason from behind a big stone. There was busy life here, but it was harmonious and had a meaning, unlike the world of men. The shining silence was everywhere, and the scent of the earth increased as Jason climbed. He stopped for a moment to put his hand on the warm bark of a great oak; it seemed to him that a slow heart pulsed under his palm, answering. To him, as to his Irish ancestors, trees were holy things, the home of druids, not to be violated. He wanted to worship, but he did not think of the God of the fervid cities. His impulse was toward Something more intense and immanent—indwelling yet immense and boundless and universal. He felt the immediacy of the godhead, listening, aware, burning with Being, young and joyous yet timeless, swelling with a love and mystery not to be comprehended by man. Here was all explained, even to the dark mind of humanity—if it would listen, which it rarely did. Here, indeed, was the peace that passed understanding, the eloquent peace of a majestic eternity, which knew nothing of death or pain or tumult.

The earth, Jason would sometimes think, was a temple, sacred and dedicated not by any priest but by...What? For an instant something flashed across his mind, as incandescent as the sun but more vivid—a wing of light, which also brushed his flesh. But it was gone at once; it left only a shadow of resplendence behind it. Then it also was gone.

Halfway up, the mountain sloped to a wide undulating plateau, and Jason reached his acres, surrounded by other virgin acres, about eighteen of them. Here were green grass and clumps of trees and wildflowers, animal trails and outcroppings of warm sentient rocks gilded by sun. Here everything seemed ignited by light. Jason sat on a boulder and contemplated his surroundings. Slowly he pulled out his package of Bull Durham tobacco and his folder of rice paper and made a cigarette. He struck a wooden match on the boulder and lit the cigarette and tranquilly watched, for a moment, the rise of blue smoke in the unstained air. The climb had been long and warm; he was sweating lightly, though pleasurably. His young muscles throbbed with life. Happiness came to him, seeping into his flesh like soothing water.

Below him the mountain drifted down to the valley. There was Belleville, far now, a cluster, a grouping, a crowding. But it was made golden and silvery by the sun and appeared to shift in an aureate haze, so its ugliness was transformed. There were three new factories in the little city, but today no smoke rose from their chimneys. Beyond them was the stream, too narrow to be called a river, a shining topaz, liquid and bending. And all about was the greening countryside. The mountains formed a crescent around the valley, tumbling with various shades of purple, mauve, heliotrope, lilac, and emerald, wavering under cloud shadows, then brightening into vivid glory.

Contentment filled Jason like fragrant nectar. He folded his arms on his shabby knees. He listened to birdsong and the small laughter of the spring. No noise approached him from the town. A larger spur of the main railroad had now reached Belleville, and Jason saw the toy freight train on its glittering tracks, but he could hear nothing of its passing. He did not glance farther up the mountain, where a few summer houses had been built, though not many. To him they were an intrusion, a violation, even if they were prettily designed and white and red-roofed in the sunlight. He did not know, or care, who owned them. Here was his empire, on his own land. Here he could forget, for a while, his harassed life. His black curls shone, his dark round face became colored with an olive rose. His gray eyes were those of a happy child. The strong hands were as relaxed as if he were asleep.

Suddenly, he became aware of voices, and all peace left him. He turned his head, and waited, frowning. He heard footsteps on the stones and grass. Then three heads rose up, followed by three masculine bodies, all strange to Jason.

Now the men stood on the plateau and looked with umbrage at Jason, and he stared back in waiting silence. They were apparently prosperous city men, for their clothing was fine and tailored and their boots expensive, their white stiff collars glistening in the sunlight. They had rings on their fingers. One man was short, stout, and middle-aged; the other two were younger and alert. The oldest man carried an ebony cane with a gilt top. The ties of the men, though narrow and black, were pierced with costly pins. The three mopped their sweating faces with linen handkerchiefs, but they did not stop their outraged staring at Jason.

"Who are you?" asked the oldest man in an ugly voice.

Jason said, "Who are you?"

The man was freshly angered. "Never mind. What are you doing here?"

Jason said, "What are you doing here?"

The man said, "Get the hell out."

Jason said, "Get the hell out."

One of the younger men said, "Throw him off, Elmer."

Jason smiled unpleasantly and flexed his arm muscles. "Try," he said.

The oldest man said, "Now, let's not fight." He lifted a fat hand. "You've got no right here, son. This is private property."

"Yes," said Jason. "It's mine. So, you've got no right here. Trespassing."

They gaped at him in a sudden uncomfortable silence. Then the oldest man took a few steps toward Jason. He smiled pleasantly, but his small brown eyes were not smiling. "You Jason Garrity?"

"Yes."

"I've been looking for you, son." He held out his hand, but Jason did not take it. "Why were you looking for me?"

"Well, it's this way, son. We'd like to buy your land. Fourteen acres, isn't it?"

"Yes." Jason thought of the harsh poverty of his life. "What are you offering?"

The oldest man, in his large-checked black-and-white trousers and black broadcloth coat and silk vest, considered Jason sharply: a laborer, in his overalls and blue cotton shirt with the open collar, and dirty boots. "Well, we found the land was bought by a Joseph Maggiotti, a long time ago. He paid three dollars an acre. But times have changed," and he laughed throatily. "Things have gone up. We know it isn't worth it, but I'm willing to give you twenty dollars an acre. That's a lot of money for this worthless piece of land on the mountain."

Two hundred and eighty dollars! That would ensure great comfort for his mother, thought Jason, and better medicine. Then he looked about him, down to the valley, up to the mountains. He had thought of something a year or two ago. He became quietly excited, but he showed no evidence of this.

"Why do you want to buy this?"

The man gave him his card, a thick ivory-tinted smooth

oblong. "Elmer Schultz." He said, "I own three hotels, two in Pittsburgh, one in Philadelphia. We had the idea of building a...little family-resort hotel here. Inexpensive. For the folks around here. Just an idea. May come to nothing. Who would come from the big cities here in the summer? Nobody. Just for the local people."

Jason smiled. "Now, that's very kind of you, Mr. Schultz, building for us yokels here. We're not a very rich town, you know."

Mr. Schultz changed his opinion of Jason. This was no "yokel." His accent and his words were not rural. Mr. Schultz became wary. He put his foot on the boulder on which Jason was sitting. He assumed a "folksy" attitude.

"Well, sir, I was raised in a little city like Belleville. No one gave a damn for building a resort for the people there. I've got different ideas."

"Magnanimous, eh?" said Jason. The other two men glanced at each other.

"Well, sir," said Mr. Schultz, falsely beaming, "you can say that. We've got to think of the common folks these days. Ain't that what the president says, himself?"

"Good old Teddy, rich Oyster Bay Teddy," said Jason. "I get awfully suspicious of rich people sobbing their hearts out over the 'suffering working class.' I wonder what they're up to. Nothing good, and you can bet on that. So, you're sobbing, too, over us poor yokels with our miserable lives?"

Mr. Schultz pulled out a heavy huge gold repeater watch from his vest pocket. "Got to make the four-o'clock train. All right, son. Twenty-five dollars an acre. Take it or leave it."

"I left it five minutes ago, Mr. Schultz."

"Why?" The rich voice had become bellicose. "You need the money, don't you?"

"No," said Jason. "I'm thinking of building a hotel here myself."

"You?"

"That's right. I...I've got good backing, too."

Mr. Schultz glared at him. Why, the dirty Irish mick! "Who the hell would back you?"

Jason shrugged elaborately. "Perhaps I don't need the backing." He yawned. "Good day, Mr. Schultz. You'd better run or you'll miss your train."

Mr. Schultz drew a deep, very audible breath. "Let's talk this over...Mr. Garrity."

Jason studied the card. "Tell you what, Mr. Schultz. I'll think about it. That's all I can tell you."

Mr. Schultz said in an ominous voice, "I give you one week. Here. I'll write my address on the card." He drew out a gold fountain pen and scribbled on it. "One week."

"Thank you," said Jason, and Mr. Schultz heard the mocking note in his voice. Mr. Schultz held out his sweating hand, and this time Jason took it and shook it with such strength that the other man winced.

They went away, muttering to each other. At the edge of the plateau they paused and looked slowly all about them. Then they were gone.

Jason stood up. His excitement almost choked him. He waited; then, when he knew the men had left, he ran down the mountain, fleet as one of the mountain deer.

7

Lionel was eating an early dinner in the big bright kitchen of the Inn-Tavern. He was not one to savor food or good wine. They were of no interest to him personally, though he realized the deep importance of them to the guests, and so had made himself an acute judge of liquors, wines, and viands. He could taste a dish and decide on its excellence or mediocrity, and a wine for its fragrance and body, but he craved none for his own enjoyment. He ate merely to satisfy hunger. His teeming mind was centered on other matters, and his eyes would move from side to side restlessly as he ate his own meals. His quick face turned everywhere, his fork moving very fast, and he was mostly unaware of taste. The two chefs eyed him, as usual, with no particular favor, offended as they were by his lack of appreciation. From time to time he would take his watch out of his vest pocket and study it sharply. It was Sunday, and the diners would soon be entering. He must be ready to greet them. The chefs did not like the Sunday crowds, for usually they had drunk too much in the back rooms so that their taste was numbed.

Lionel had never seen Jason in a disheveled or emotional state since old Joe Maggiotti's death. So when Jason, in soiled overalls and patched blue shirt, exploded into the kitchen by way of the employees' entrance, Lionel was astonished. Jason's face was actually afire with excitement, and sweat ran down his cheeks. His body emanated frenzy and disarray. He was panting, breathless. As the others in the kitchen also stared, he shouted, "Where's Mr. Mulligan?"

"Hey!" exclaimed Lionel, putting down his fork and half-rising in his chair. "What's the matter with you? It's your Sunday off. You can't come in here...in those clothes."

Jason waved his arms. "The hell with my day off, with my clothes! Mr. Mulligan—where is he?"

Lionel, studying him for an intense moment, felt a strange excitement. His yellow eyes became alert. Intuitive, he had an odd premonition. Jason would never get into this state over a minor matter. "Put down that damned fork!" Jason yelled. "I've got to talk with Mr. Mulligan, and you come with me!"

The chefs gaped from the stoves. Lionel put down his fork and stood up. "Mr. Mulligan's in one of the upstairs private dining rooms with Mrs. Lindon and a couple of her...young relatives and two banker friends. You can't go up looking like that...Can't it wait?"

"No! It can't." Jason took his friend by the arm and began pulling him toward the staircase in the kitchen, which led up to the three private dining rooms on the second floor. "Lionel. I can't tell you here. No time. You can hear me tell it." He then laughed, a loud, almost hysterical shout. "If things go right...we'll be rich, rich!"

Lionel stared even closer at Jason. Jason was never extravagant or enthusiastic in speech, but he was today. The air seemed to vibrate about him. Never hopeful or expectant, but always judicious and thoughtful, he was not one to catch at rainbows or to believe mica was made of precious metal. All his judgments were sound. So Lionel followed him. At the top of the stairs, Jason turned and said, "Which dining room?"

"Here," said Lionel, and knocked on the shut door, forgetting to be wary. Mr. Mulligan said from behind the door, "All right. Come in. Who's there?" Lionel pushed the door open on a pleasant scene. The room was large and nicely decorated, with white-painted walls, gilt moldings near the ceiling, a bright chandelier gaslit even this early on a spring evening. It was a circular room, for it was in the base of the building's tower and so was called the Tower Room. The round rug was blue and gold, the furniture excellent, the big table covered with linen with a lace overlay, the sofa and chairs upholstered in yellow velvet. There was a fine rich odor of roasted beef and onions and potatoes floating tantalizingly in the air, mingled with the scent of wines and brandies and broiled new mushrooms and hot cream and fresh warm bread. The weighty silver gleamed in the gaslight. The guests put down their wineglasses and stared with amazement at the sight of Jason in his workman's cheap clothing. Mr. Mulligan stood up, frowning. "What the hell," he said. "Jase, what's this? Lionel, what's he doing here today, dressed like a farmhand?"

Mr. Mulligan strove for umbrage, but he did not feel it. He simply wanted his distinguished guests to believe he was angry. His bald head shone with perspiration induced by the warmth of the day, good food, and copious drafts of wine. His black broadcloth suit, very sober and proper, his subdued cravat with its pearl pin, his embroidered vest, all very expensive, could not conceal the fact that here was a hearty, even gross man who loved life and knew how to make it enjoyable, and that, in spite of grim experience, he also loved people.

"What the hell?" he repeated, then bowed to the three ladies present. "Pardon me," he said. The ladies nodded graciously. The two middle-aged gentlemen with them inclined their august heads. The rings on their thick fingers glittered under the chandelier. Lionel recognized them, of course, as Mr. Gordon Rumpell of the First National Bank and Mr. Edward Sunderland of the Belleville Savings Association. They were both presidents of their organizations, and were very distinguished indeed. They could have been brothers in their mutual rotundity, their florid coloring, their disillusioned and watchful brown eyes, their black eyebrows and their carefully waved white hair, their discreet cologne, their fat avid hands, their polished boots. Sons of prosperous farmers, they had done well for themselves and had gone to college. They were despairingly hated by those who owed them money, for they were men completely ruthless even when they smiled and were most agreeable.

Mrs. Clementine Lindon was at her imperial best today, clad in a very costly dress of black silk with many ruffles and much lace. A long string of pearls lay on her big and handsome bosom, and there were diamonds in her ears near her vast pompadour of redly tinted hair. A white velvet hat, broad and very chic and swaying with many-colored ostrich plumes, perched on that fraudulent but tidy mass of polished strands and curls. Mrs. Lindon was extremely dainty and fastidious, and her voice was refined, her airs ladylike to parody, her scent advertising Paris, her shoes handmade, and her rings and bracelets testifying to wealth. But all of this could not overcome the coarse complexion, the hard if smiling eyes of an indeterminate hazel, and her thick and sensual mouth coated with shining red paint. Here was a woman, it was evident, even more ruthless than the bankers, and far less kind and sympathetic than Mr. Mulligan. She gave out an aura of corruption and exigency which her splendid apparel could not hide. However, she had moments of tolerance and even generosity. She had cultivated an aspect of gentility and graciousness which would have done credit to the late Queen Victoria—whom she had greatly admired—though she was at least a foot taller than the deceased monarch. She could even appear brutal in a nice way, and was very intelligent, and was known not to endure nonsense. No one had ever been known to successfully cheat Mrs. Lindon. Attempts were greeted with implacable vengeance. Foolishness was not to be tolerated. She was a lady of immense common sense. She had invented a genteel background and a well-bred family in Philadelphia, but her remarks on this subject were pleasantly vague and dismissing, as if she were too modest to boast. No one persisted in any questioning. Mrs. Lindon was too rich and her eyes too threatening when confronted by inquisitiveness which she proclaimed was vulgar anyway. Vulgarity was her favorite epithet, and condemnation. Mrs. Lindon could be very formidable when the occasion required it, and her corsets would creak in subdued agreement.

Her young "cousins," seventeen and eighteen, respectively, were like fresh daisies beside her; Mrs. Lindon was fifty-three, or so she claimed. The girls were her prettiest, and were the dear friends of the two bankers, who had exclusive rights to them by careful negotiations with Mrs. Lindon. Mr. Sunderland, a widower with two adult sons in their thirties, was much enamored of little Loraine, with her innocent blues eyes and thick flaxen hair, the latter overpowering in its high rolled pompadour above her delicately tinted little face with its fine bones, its soft babyish mouth, and its fragile skin. She exuded an air of tender virginity, though she had been a whore since she was fourteen. Mrs. Lindon was very fond of Loraine, and had hopes that Mr. Sunderland would marry the girl.

The other girl, Elsa, was a sprightly and lively brunette, as pretty in her way as Loraine, for she was all dark sparkle and vivacity, with a dark rose complexion, a lovely figure approaching womanly opulence, and a lot of perfumed black hair. She had a merry smile, very charming, and her teeth were sound and white, and she was known for her wit and quick laughter. She was eighteen, at the height of her beauty.

Both girls were demurely clad, if one did not look at them too closely, for their white silk blouses, with the boned high necks and the ruffled tops to the chin, were of an extraordinary seduction and lewdness, composed of exquisitely frail handmade lace, almost imperceptible over nude flesh. At fleet moments one could glimpse rosy nipples, coy and rapidly disappearing. Their waists, however, were tightly corseted and seemed like the stems of flowers. Their skirts were of black velvet, their belts of silver leather. Each wore only a jeweled watch pinned precariously on the lace blouses, and each had a feather boa, as white as the blouses, dexterously used to reveal and conceal.

Mr. Rumpell was enchanted by Elsa. He was very generous to her—and to Mrs. Lindon. He had a short, lumpish wife, extremely sullen and unamenable, and three dowdy daughters, all much older than his young paramour, who, like Loraine, had been an experienced whore from the age of fourteen.

Mrs. Lindon felt it incumbent now to lift her regal lorgnette—only plain glass—to survey the young men who had so precipitately burst into the dining room. She knew them well. She especially favored Lionel, whom she had designated, not without admiration, as a scoundrel, but she respected Jason and had often told Mr. Mulligan he could be "absolutely trusted," a trait that did not always appeal to her. Trustworthy men could often get in the way of clever negotiations, if these negotiations required a certain fleetness of foot and manipulation. However, she preferred, as lawyers, trustworthy men, and searched diligently for them, well understanding that law and trustworthiness were frequently mutually exclusive. But a lawyer one could trust personally was one the law could trust too, which led to difficulties. Semantics, too, often were inconvenient, and trustworthy lawyers were apt to keep doggedly to the plain wording of the law. Well, she would say, one cannot have everything in this world, though she did, herself, do rather well.

"Lionel...and Jason, I believe," she said pleasantly. Though a heavy drinker of good whiskey, she did not possess the deep and husky voice of cheaper women. Jason might appear at this moment as a lout, and Lionel might seem apprehensive, and stood in the background, but Clementine was not perturbed. She could see under appearances. That Jason was excited and agitated also excited her, for solid men were not easily made excitable. One had to beware of such as Lionel, who were very temperamental at times, and hasty. They were optimists, and Clementine did rarely trust optimists. They usually cost one money in the long run.

"Well, what's all this?" demanded Mr. Mulligan, trying to make his voice irascible.

Jason pulled a wide slim book from under his arm, a book Lionel had not noticed before. "I want to talk to you, Mr. Mulligan. Now. It can't wait." It was as if he and Mr. Mulligan were entirely alone, though Lionel was acutely conscious of Loraine and Elsa, and their shirtwaists.

Mr. Mulligan slowly seated himself, but he continued to stare at Jason. He, too, was now aware of something unusual. He said, "I'm among friends, Jase. Say what you will."

For the first time Jason became fully aware of others at the table. Two were...bankers. There was also Mrs. Lindon, whom he liked in spite of his knowledge of her. He ignored the girls, who eyed him favorably. They were too accustomed to effete men, whom they described in a less elegant term never used in polite society. Jason exuded masculinity, and a certain roughness. Both girls had had one encounter with Lionel, whom they designated to each other as "strange," with very naughty giggles and some disapproval.

"You might as well sit down," said Mr. Mulligan. "Pull up a chair, Jase." He hesitated. Then he filled one of the glasses with good wine and pushed it across the table. "You need calming down," he said. "Drink it up." He glanced at Lionel. "Reckon we don't need you, Lionel."

Jason drank impatiently. He hardly tasted the wine. "Yes!" he said. "I want Lionel here. It'll be his business, too."

Clementine fixed her light hazel eyes with some compassion on Jason. Here was another innocent, always looking after a friend's interest. Well, he'd learn, God help him. Lionel, all fox's ears now, stood deferentially in the doorway, his dancer's feet vibrating to the music from downstairs.

Jason produced Mr. Schultz' card and gave it to Mr. Mulligan, who stared at it in perplexity. But when he passed it on to the bankers, they became immediately tense and alert. They gave the card ceremoniously to Mrs. Lindon, then exchanged long glances. But they said nothing.

"What's it all about?" asked Mr. Mulligan. "What's Schultz got to do with you, Jase?"

Jason kept his voice quiet but strong. "You know the Shoulder, Mr. Mulligan? Yes. I own fourteen acres of it, smack in the middle of the other eighteen acres. The best part."

"Oh," said Mr. Mulligan, at sea.

"Mr. Schultz wants to buy them from me, to build, he said, a resort hotel for us yokels here in Belleville. I don't believe him for a minute."

Mr. Sunderland said, "I know of Mr. Schultz. He owns very fine hotels, which he built in Pittsburgh and Philadelphia. I also believe he owns family-resort hotels in others places in the Poconos. Farmhouse types, all clapboard and porches, which are full of children in the summer, and dogs and such.

And croquet for the ladies, and tennis for the gentlemen, and ponds nearby for rowing. Very...rural."

Mr. Rumpell coughed. "Mr. Schultz, I believe, was looking for you, Jason. He came into the bank. We, by the way, hold nine of the acres on one side of your...property—estate dealings, I believe, and—"

Mrs. Lindon said, "And I own the other nine acres on the other side of your property, Jason."

"Good God!" said Mr. Mulligan. "Why did you buy them, Clem?"

Mrs. Lindon lowered her eyelids. "I did think of an elegant establishment on the Shoulder, Pat. Fine food. Entertainment. But there were those fourteen acres right in the middle. I didn't know who owned them. Your deed offices in Belleville are very slack, Patrick. And there is no decent road up to the property."

Mr. Sunderland gave Jason an understanding smile. "So, your land stands in the way of Mr. Schultz. Did he offer anything for them?"

Jason told him, and Mr. Sunderland nodded. "Are you considering selling them?"

"No, Mr. Sunderland. I have other ideas."

Mrs. Lindon leaned her great bosom on the table. "What do you want for your land, Jason?"

His gray eyes studied her. "I'm not selling, Mrs. Lindon."

She smiled at him. She was so acute that she comprehended, and her regard for Jason increased. "I know," she said. Her bosom heaved with excitement, and her mind with visions.

"Why would anyone want to build a resort of any kind on the Shoulder?" asked Mr. Mulligan. "Nothing here in Belleville to attract wealthy people."

"The view," said Jason. "A marvelous view. I go there often, and I can see it. I even go in the winter. Beautiful. Secluded. Quiet." He hesitated. "I've been reading about skiing."

"Skiing?" asked Mr. Mulligan, now completely perplexed. "Isn't that a Swiss sport or something? Nobody would be interested in this country."

When Clementine spoke, everyone paid attention. "A magnificent exclusive year-round hotel! Summer sports. Dancing. Gowns. Jewels. Pretty, entertaining young...ladies. Shops, such as they have in Paris. Boutiques..."

"Shops, in a hotel?" asked Mr. Mulligan, floundering.

"Indeed, Pat. An exquisite restaurant. Wine cellars. Promenades, with a view. Tennis courts. Entertainers from New York. Hairdressers. Fashions. Oh, I see it all! Pennsylvania never had such a thing before! A whole center in itself! Who would need a city nearby? And, of course, the elite in Belleville and the surrounding towns and country would be lured there also. And people would come from New York, as well as Pittsburgh and Philadelphia. And even from Virginia. Just as they go down to Palm Beach. Flager did a wonderful job there, Pat. Built in the very middle of a jungle and marshes. People laughed at him. Now they are laughing on the other side of their faces. They could have bought the land. One must use one's intelligence..."

She saw the hotel she had in mind in a glorious fantasy. Four or five stories high, gorgeous suites, a ballroom, an arcade filled with expensive shops, soft green grass and gardens and grottoes and fountains, discreet dining rooms, luscious food, moonlight dancing, elegance, a small theater, a pool for swimming, tennis courts, rooms for gaming, a gracious European atmosphere. There were ten acres beyond the Shoulder. She would speak to Mr. Sunderland tonight. A golf course. Golf was becoming fashionable.

Mrs. Lindon was too pragmatic to be entranced by mere visions. She had it all laid out in her practical mind. It only needed financing. And experience. She looked fondly at Mr. Mulligan.

"No children," she said. "A resort hotel such as I have in mind would be no place for children. Children do dirty up beauty and elegance. And the people who would come would not like the presence of screechers."

"But resort hotels always mention they are good for children," said Mr. Mulligan, who felt he was quite out of his depth. What would a summer resort be without children?

"Does it ever occur to you, Dear Pat," said Clementine, "that not all people want the presence of children? No children are admitted to Delmonico's in New York, or other famous establishments. They belong in nurseries and schools, not the sort of resort hotel I have in mind." She coughed delicately. "And the gentlemen. They are often in flight from wives and children. They would be guests of the hotel."

Oh, no, thought Mr. Mulligan. Not a gilded brothel!

"The fine wives of New York, and their husbands, would find such a hotel a lovely escape from city life and families," said Clementine. Mr. Mulligan felt appeased, but still was uneasy.

"We could invite French designers," said Clementine. "To show their offerings."

They had forgotten Jason. He said, "I own those acres right in the middle, Mrs. Lindon."

Mrs. Lindon regarded him. "So you do, Jason. Would you consider fifty dollars an acre?"

Jason looked at her long and coldly. "No. I want to be part of this." He pushed his book toward her. "My grandfather, who lived in England for a time, bought this book."

Clementine slowly inspected it. "Um," she said. She had forgotten exteriors and furnishings. Slowly she turned pages, while the gentlemen, fascinated and mute, stared at her intently. Elsa surreptitiously fondled Jason's knee, and he was oblivious. Loraine widened her blue eyes at him, and he did not see them. They were very perspicacious young ladies. They thought of their savings.

The book concerned Hadley Hall, near Ipswich, and was luminously illustrated by drawings, hand-painted, of its appearance and interior. Built in the latter part of the eighteenth century, it was constructed of a very pale yellow brick and stucco, the center retracted between two large wings. It was two and a half stories high, with latticed windows and a great bronze door in the center, and a red-tiled roof and huge brick chimneys. It was definitely Georgian, but still had a light and airy atmosphere, strong yet not ponderous. Masses of enormous trees were gathered at the side of the wings and reared from the back, though the facade was clear and bright and open. A long straight driveway marched between clipped lawns and flowerbeds.

Clementine turned the pages to the gardens. "Ah," she said, musing wistfully over red brick paths, grottoes, statues, fountains, flowerbeds of celestial color and beauty and form, topiary trees clipped in whimsical designs, and flowering hedges, and pools in which was reflected the tranquil foliage.

"Yes," said Clementine very slowly, "I've seen this for myself. It's even more charming. I visited there for nearly two weeks." No one thought to question her about this, which was just as well, because it was not true. She looked at the others with a sweet smile and passed the book to the gentlemen, who looked on it together, murmuring under their breath in appreciation.

They came upon drawings of the many rooms, some very

massively furnished with invaluable antiques, enormous carved staircases, or moldings of silver and gold, painted ceilings, floors like brown mirrors, wideplanked and satiny, pillared doorways with cornices of blue or white or green marble, azure walls or walls of the purest white or the most sanguine red or minty green or pale sapphire, imposing fireplaces with brass andirons, Oriental rugs of subtle and delightful shadings and designs, draperies heavy with tassels and hung over filmy pale silk, portraits and landscapes and seascapes or serene mountains and valleys decorating every free space on the walls, candelabra of glittering silver and chandeliers dripping with prismatic light. There were a library, ballroom, and music room, faultlessly designed and equipped.

"Must have cost millions, millions," said Mr. Rumpell in a reverent voice. "Of pounds, that is."

Clementine leaned over to examine a page of text, and her swift eye read it all. "Well, no," she said. "Five hundred thousand pounds in 1788, which even now would be only four million dollars."

"Four million dollars," Mr. Sunderland breathed, even more reverential than Mr. Rumpell.

Mrs. Lindon slapped her jeweled hand loudly on the book. "We can build it for not much less than that on those thirty-two acres on the Shoulder."

Jason did not hear this. He was dreaming, and his gray eyes were fixed on his dream. For over two years now he had pored over this book, studying the pictures of every room, the garden, the house itself. He thought of great bedrooms, silks, velvets, laces, canopies, commodes, carpets, carved doors, ornate glass lamps, marble bathrooms, a vast dining room with crimson damask walls and a yellow marble fireplace and round tables with gleaming linen and cutlery. He had thought of this, vaguely, but it had not come alive as a possibility until today. Now he looked at the others with passionate eagerness, and Lionel leaned from the doorway, his yellow eyes sparkling.

"There is nothing like it in all of Pennsylvania, perhaps not in all the rest of the country," said Mrs. Lindon. "Why, presidents could be entertained there! Ambassadors! We could call it..."—she glanced at the text again—"Ipswich House."

Mr. Sunderland cleared his throat. "There is the matter of money," he suggested, and wet very red lips under a white mustache.

"And this mansion was built over one hundred and eighteen years ago," said Mr. Rumpell. "The cost today would be nearer seven million dollars."

"The Dow Jones averages are going down in the stock market these days," said the other banker. "Everyone is prophesying a monetary crisis in 1907."

"Pish," said Clementine with a large wave of her hand, superbly dismissing the crass talk of money and panics. "You must take the spacious view, gentlemen." She smiled kindly at Mr. Mulligan, whose mouth had fallen open. "How much can you borrow, Pat?"

"Me?" Mr. Mulligan stuttered. "Five hundred thousand at the most, and that'd include all my assets, I'm thinking. Everything."

"That's a good start," said Clementine briskly. "I can borrow a million or so." They all knew she was rich, but only the bankers knew of the several lavish and prosperous brothels she owned in Pittsburgh, Philadelphia, New York, and Washington. Only the bankers knew that judges had respectfully suggested she remove her colorful presence from those cities, in lieu of onerous incarceration. She had left her properties in the very competent—and honest—hands of a gentleman rogue who was wanted in various other cities for some peculations and embezzlements, and whose history only she possessed.

The stout bankers leaned back in their chairs and waited. Clementine turned to them. "Gordon? Edward? What do you say? How much can your banks lend Pat and me? With good interest, of course. Or, you could become partners, using your own money."

"Clementine..." said Mr. Sunderland, as if she had used a vulgar phrase.

She shrugged. "Well. We can do it, one way or another. We don't need the whole sum. Dear me. You'll have to figure those odious things out for yourself."

Mr. Rumpell wore a glazed expression, and he sweated rather noticeably. "Clementine, dearest, you must be mad."

"So are the Rockefellers, then, and the Morgans and the Belmonts. Faint hearts never made fortunes, and this could make us incredibly wealthy. Only the best people. The best prices. Discretion guaranteed."

Mr. Sunderland lifted a meaty palm. "Clementine. This wouldn't be a...a..." He glanced at the avid young ladies.

"Not what you have in mind, my dear. Discreet, yes. Secluded, yes. Refined and cultured, yes. Distinguished, yes."

"I'm happy to hear some yeses," said Mrs. Lindon merrily. "How much, Gordon, Edward?"

Mr. Mulligan came to himself. He looked at his two employees. "Jason, Lionel. I think it's time for you to leave. The Sunday guests will be arriving in about half an hour." He looked with disapproval first at his watch, then at the young men. "Jason. I'll forgive your blundering in here in that...cowshed attire, if you leave at once."

"I think," said Jason in his firm strong voice, "that you have all forgotten something."

"And what is that, my lad," said Mr. Rumpell with condescension.

"I own fourteen acres of land right in the middle of your site. Without my land, all this will come to nothing."

The bankers glanced quickly at each other. "Very well," said Mr. Sunderland after a very long and silent pause. "I'll make you an offer for them. Fifty dollars an acre. A fortune."

"No," said Jason. Lionel took a step closer to him.

"Good God, what impudence," said Mr. Rumpell. "Don't you realize, young man, that we've offered you a lot of money, more money than you've ever seen before?"

Jason's cheeks colored and his gray eyes became like polished stone. "I realize," he said. "I also realize that nothing can be done up there without my acres. Mr. Schultz knows that. He wants my land." Jason lifted his book. "I'll let him see this. And I thank you for your interest, and for what I've heard you say. You've filled in spots I wasn't certain of, so thank you again."

The bankers clenched their hands on their knees. "How much, then?"

"I want to be a partner. I want to manage it—under Mr. Mulligan, of course. And I want a chance for Lionel up there, too, as manager of the dining room and kitchens. All under Mr. Mulligan, of course." He smiled at the confounded Mr. Mulligan like a son.

"Dear me," said Clementine, whose mind had been going like fireworks and whose thoughts had been as colorful. "Jason does have a point. And I know how competent he is, and how trustworthy, and I know all about Lionel, too. They may be young, but they are sharp. And with Pat managing everything...why, it could be wonderful!"

Mr. Sunderland leaned toward Jason and deliberately let

his eyes wander over his oafish clothing, his scoured hands, his dusty workman's boots, his soiled blue shirt. "I think the less we have to say to this bumpkin, the better," he said.

"Now, see here," said Mr. Mulligan. "He's like a son to me, Jason. You can't insult the lad like that, in front of me, even though you're a friend. Jason's got a damned fine mind, and a lot of character." He paused, for he was scarlet with anger. "And Lionel, here. You couldn't get a better boy in any of your fancy cities, to do what he does." His brogue had thickened.

The bankers looked at him with incredulity. "Pat," said Mr. Rumpell, "do you understand the...the magnitude of what has been proposed to us, the money? And you let this...this young man prattle about partnerships and whatnot, he who probably hasn't two pennies to his name!"

In spite of his indignation, Mr. Mulligan was not without common sense. His dangerous color retreated. He gnawed a thumbnail and his eyes blinked furiously. He, too, for two years had been thinking of a certain matter. He suddenly beamed like a fat and rosy angel. He said, "Well, a partnership for fourteen acres—it does seem like too much, doesn't it? Jason, we are talking of millions of dollars—and you want a goddamned partnership for fourteen acres."

"There are ladies present!" Mr. Rumpell said sternly.

Mr. Mulligan waved grandly. "My apologies. Jason, don't you understand? For those fourteen acres you will get fifty dollars apiece. A fortune! And I guarantee both you and Lionel fine positions up there, with splendid salaries."

Jason looked at him with dogged pain. "Mr. Mulligan, why not put out shares? I've been reading the papers—"

"You mean, Jason, go public?" asked Mrs. Lindon, who knew all about stocks. "But a closed concern? Better?"

She had lost Jason now. But Mr. Mulligan had been listening. "Shares," he said. He sat up very straight in his chair to impress the bankers. "Small salaries, but some shares. Lionel, you can put in some money if you want to."

Jason looked aside, and the pain was deeper on his face. "I have nothing," he said.

"Yes, you have," said Mr. Mulligan, loving him like a father. "You have yourself, Jason, you have yourself. And that's worth more than money."

"You talk as if this...preposterous matter is already settled, Pat," said Mr. Sunderland. "Ridiculous, of course, the whole thing. I'm willing to talk about it, if Gordon also is willing. It will probably come to nothing. Millions of dollars are involved. Chairmen of the board to be consulted. Investors. Other banks. It's a wild dream! We haven't even broached the whole matter. We're not playing tiddledywinks. We're talking about money! And the land hasn't even been surveyed yet!" He pursed his lips in outrage at all this nonsense.

Clementine became very cheerful. "I think everyone has forgotten that I own nine acres on that Shoulder. Gordon, would your bank sell me the other nine?"

Shaken but smiling, Mr. Rumpell said with loverly indulgence, "And what would you do with them, Clem?"

She took up Mr. Schultz' forgotten card and studied it thoroughly through her lorgnette. "I think I will talk to this Mr. Schultz," she said.

8

As Jason and Lionel went down the stairs, Lionel said, "My God, my God! Jase! Am I dreaming, or dippy, or drunk?"

"I feel the same way," said Jason. "I don't know what will come of it, but I'm sure there'll be something."

"They were talking in millions," said Lionel, awed.

"And I was thinking of a modest hotel!" said Jason, stunned.

"Never tell them that," said Lionel. "Or they'll have you by the balls in two seconds. Think big, as the president says." He laughed almost hysterically. "When it comes to millions, what are a few more or less?"

"I thought of a smaller resort than Hadley Hall, Lionel."

"Think of a bigger version. Well, back to work. See you tomorrow."

Jason slowly rode toward home on his bicycle through the Sunday-still streets, where only the sounds of raucous gramophones could be heard and the muted whine of children and the annoyed complaint of some harried mother. Jason automatically winced at the new "ragtime" pouring through open windows. Church bells had begun to ring for early-evening services. A few men sat on the steps of small porches or on stoops, conversing quietly together and smoking, or indulging in some half-suppressed male laughter. Wheels ground at a far distance, and occasionally there was an explosive snort from an automobile. Otherwise the quiet was undisturbed.

Usually the squalid atmosphere of Sunday in a small town depressed Jason. Today he saw and heard nothing of it. At moments he felt incredulous; at other moments he felt a surging exhilaration which resembled drunkenness. Sometimes his breath caught short in his throat; sometimes he felt he was wheeling on air, far above the pavement. Money. What would it do for his family? Everything. His grandfather had once said, "If money can't buy happiness, nothing else will, and niver you mind the nonsense of 'poor' happiness. That is for the very young or foolish, or for one who lives only for the instant sensation. How can one be happy if hungry or with the rent not paid, and no job? Only a baby wetly bubbling in its cradle. Money will give freedom; freedom must be bought in this accursed world, and mind you, bucko, freedom is worth more than life itself."

Freedom.

Jason thought of his mother in the hospital. He had visited Kate that morning. For some mysterious reason, she had appeared fragilely radiant, as if expecting some wondrous boon or joy. Her poor haggard face had taken on a hectic bloom; her ravaged lips had been pink, her hand not so hot. "Yes, love," she had said. "I feel much better."

Jason had looked about the small wretched room which was so determinedly clean, at the two sagging beds, one of which his mother occupied, at the curtainless little window, at the two commodes and the single kitchen chair. Poverty. The other bed contained a very old woman, a gray shadow of a human being, senile, muttering, sobbing, unaware, abandoned flotsam of a grim world, forgotten, nameless. She had stared sightlessly at Jason and then had called him "Jim." Her almost inaudible cry had been full of longing and despair.

It was from this atmosphere that Jason and Bernard wished to remove Kate: a room of her own, undisturbed by the anguish of another human being. Kate worried about her roommate and the natural indignities of very old age and abandonment. "Mrs. Flood doesn't know," Jason had told his mother, and his mother had gazed at him with pain in her fever-bright eyes. "Who told you that, then, Jason?" she had asked, and he had no answer. Kate also worried about the money being spent for her in the hospital. She never said a word, but she hoped she would die soon so as not to be a burden on those she loved. A week ago she had received extreme unction, and had rallied, a miraculous event not unknown to priests. The next day she had actually been able to sit in a chair near the window. From that day on she had coughed less than usual, and the blood did not appear so often from her riddled lungs. She claimed to "enjoy" the miserable food, the food of a poverty-stricken little hospital. Never once had she complained during the weeks of her confinement here. The nuns said she was a "saint," at which Bernard had nodded his head.

Jason's strong pedaling legs slowed. There would be money—but it would not be in time to help Kate. He thought of his fourteen acres, so necessary for the phantom hotel gleaming in pale gold on a far horizon, a horizon in the future. He had time; Kate did not. He had been offered fifty dollars an acre. It was an enormous sum. It would remove Kate immediately from her disheartening environment. It would provide her with better food and a nurse for herself—at home. It would give her the comfort she never had had. It would restore her to her family and lessen her worry.

His heart sickened as his dream retreated. But his mother was more important than dreams. She had never asked for anything. It was time for her to receive, late as it was. The pedaling came to a stop at a corner. Dusk was increasing; the forlorn street melted into it. A chill wind chased away the day's earlier warmth. The mountains became mere ashen ghosts against an ashen sky, and most of them faded into obscurity. A gust arose, bringing grit against eye and teeth.

I must think of my mother, said Jason to himself, and it seemed to him that his heart sank like cold lead with this resolution. But above all there was his mother—he could wait.

Something stirred in him as if someone had spoken, but he could not distinguish what was said. He went on more quickly, without hope but with less pain. The euphoria was gone; he moved as one under a drug. He would tell his grandfather only what was needful. Some instinct warned him that the pragmatic Bernard would not agree with him, for above all, Bernard was a realist, and not even love could delude him. There would be hundreds of dollars for Kate. That would be enough to tell Bernard.

The kitchen gaslight had been turned on in the dreary small house. His grandfather, at least, should be there. It was not time for him to take up the last hours in Mr. Saul Weitzman's shop, the shop Bernard had sold years ago on inheriting it from Joe Maggiotti. Joan should be there, home from her outing with the "woman." But Jason had the alarming sensation that the house was empty. He did not, in his haste to go inside, notice a bicycle leaning against the wall.

He flung open the door of the kitchen. There at the table, sat Bernard, not moving, with a bottle of cheap whiskey at his elbow on the table. And there, also, was Father Sweeney, as silent, as impassive, with a glass in his hand. The two men looked up at Jason as he entered, and he felt that something calamitous awaited him.

"Where have you been, then, all these hours?" asked Bernard, but his voice was without emphasis. It sounded both indifferent and exhausted.

"On the mountain, as usual," replied Jason. He glanced at the priest, and a chill ran over his flesh. "Joan?" he said.

117

"Something's happened to Joan?" The gas mantle was suddenly surrounded by a wavering halo. He felt a nauseating drop in his stomach.

"No," said Bernard, and he shifted in his chair. He took up his glass of whiskey. A tear slowly ran down his cheek. "It's your mum. She is dead." He drank deeply. His head dropped, and he looked old and broken. The priest gazed at Jason compassionately. "No," said Jason.

Bernard began to speak, as if he were alone in the chill kitchen and was talking only to himself, remembering. His voice was slow and hoarse and without emotion. He looked at nothing but the glass in his hand. Jason stood near him, motionless. The brick walls, the varnished ceiling, all the furniture in the room became stark, strange, unfamiliar.

Bernard had worked that morning and until two o'clock at Mr. Weitzman's shop. Then he had gone to see Kate at the hospital. She had greeted him with her own sweet and gentle smile. He had sat beside her, holding her hand, while the very old woman in the next bed peevishly complained about her children "messin' up my kitchen." She had been unusually restless.

Bernard had seen too many consumptives to be deceived by Kate's brightness and soft chatter, her quick lucidity, her appearance of restored life. He had gone out to the elderly nun who patrolled the hospital. She had assured him that Mrs. Garrity was "much better today," though she had not got out of bed even once. Bernard had said shortly, "Send for Father Sweeney." But Father Sweeney had been called in an emergency and was not expected back soon.

"I sat there. I looked at her. She chattered. She even laughed. She talked of you, Jason, and Jack and Joanie. She said, 'You'll be looking after them, won't you, Da?' I said I would. She sat up, and kissed me, and smiled. She lay down, still smiling, still looking at me with those dear eyes.... Then I knew she was dead."

Bernard took another hard swallow of whiskey. "The old lady near Katie—she said, 'An angel just walked out of the room,' and she clapped her hands. I knew she was right. An angel...left."

Jason blindly reached for a chair and fell into it. He could as yet feel nothing.

"So," said Bernard. Now he turned ponderously to the priest, and there was fire far in the deep sockets of his eyes. "Tell me, bucko," he said. "What did Katie do to

118

deserve her life and her death? Tell me!" and he struck his clenched fist with sudden violence on the table, and the glasses and the bottle jumped. "Tell me," he shouted, "damn you!"

"Bernard..." said the young priest.

But Bernard shook his head like an old wounded bull. "Give me none of your homilies, Bill. Tell me no lies of the 'sufferings of the just.' Why should they suffer? Are they an amusement to your God, Bill? A sacrifice—to what? Why don't the wicked suffer? It's in your Bible, isn't it, that the wicked flourish like a green bay tree and their children dance with joy in the streets? Why is it that the gentle and the good and the innocent are tortured? Why are the faithful always deceived, the trusting betrayed? Don't talk to me about Satan, the prince of this world! Who made him the prince, who allowed him to be the prince? Your God. So...our Lord suffered on Calvary. Was it worth his sacrifice? Who made this evil world, this murderer of the sweet and pure and honest and just? Your God, damn you!

"Katie knew no comfort in her poor loving life. No peace, no laughter. Only work and pain. What did she do to offend your God? Did her virtue outrage him, and so he sent suffering to her in revenge? Don't tell me that she's now at peace, among the angels, playing a harp! Is that a reward for her blameless life, then? Christ!"

He put his veined hands over his eyes and wept the racking and terrible tears of the old. "There is no God," he said behind his hands. "There is only the Devil. Perhaps we should worship him instead of—"

"Bernard," said the priest, who would have been horrified only four years ago, but was now only dismayed by the old man's pain.

"I've lived a long time," said the hidden Bernard. "And niver have I seen the good protected and rewarded. But I've seen the wicked given the fruits—I've seen the innocent hanged and stabbed. I've seen the bad drink, laugh, and wench while the women and children starve. I've seen the noble despised and kicked, and looted and driven to starvation. I've seen thieves prosper and die a holy death." He dropped his hands and his whole face was ablaze. "Tell me! Tell me your lies, your excuses, your fairy tales!"

Father Sweeney drew a deep breath. He thought of his

119

teachings in the seminary. He said, "I don't know. God help me, I don't know."

He would not have said this earlier. Something in his voice alerted the desolate Bernard. Pity moved into his eyes. He reached for the priest's hand and held it. "For the first time you're honest, Bill."

The priest said in a low voice, "Job asked the same questions."

"And what was the answer, then?"

The priest's young face saddened. "God's own questions of Job are more...enlightening, more inspiring, than any answer." He looked into the distance. "'Where were you when I laid the foundations of the world—Arcturus with his sons—'"

"Shit," said Bernard. "We're only men, only human. Did he expect us to converse in eternities?" He threw the priest's hand from him.

"Yes," said the priest, "because we, too, are eternal."

The priest looked inspired, uplifted, as if he had heard a question that was an answer. "Do the wicked have the consolation of God? Do they hear his voice? No. But the good hear him in their dark night of the soul. That is the gift of life. The evil have only death. In the end they are betrayed by themselves."

"Silly lies," said Bernard, and he wept again.

The priest stood up, and his youthful face looked very old. He said to Jason, "Console him."

"I?" said Jason out of his stupefied agony.

The priest contemplated him for a long moment. "Yes," he said. "You."

He walked to the door, paused, and said, "It is vespers. I will return in the morning." He left the house. Jason drew his chair closer to his grandfather. He felt his own grief lifting like a torch in his chest. He looked about the kitchen; he heard the silence in the house; he felt the loneliness. Always he had believed that his mother would return here, restored to health. That she was dead was incredible to him, not to be believed. Mum, Mum? he said in himself. Where are you, Mum? At any moment he expected to hear her loving voice in answer. The chill breeze outside had become a wind. It hammered at the wall, against the windows. The gaslight flickered in a draft. The stove was cold; the brick walls had become remote, freezing. Bernard's loud weeping had diminished, the now silent tears testifying to a sorrow too deep for words. When Jason put his hand on his shoulder Bernard started.

"Da," said the youth.

Bernard said in a voice totally devoid of any feeling, "I've sent a telegram to Jack. Joanie will stay the night with Molly Nolan. The woman will be here in the morning."

"Da," said Jason again. Now his face became like carved old wood, hard and harsh. "You were right. God is the ... adversary. We can't contend with him. He's our ... enemy." He thought of the bankers he had just left, Mrs. Lindon and her pretty little harlots; he thought of the wine and the rich sauces and the silver. Jason added, "That is, if there is a God. I don't believe it. The world would be a different place if he existed. Let's forget him. Mum's safe from him—if he lives. He can't hurt her any longer."

Bernard stared. The tears dried on his cheeks. His mouth became tremulous. He rubbed one calloused hand slowly over it. His eyes never left Jason. "Jase," Bernard said, and then halted. He rubbed his mouth again. "If there is no God ... there isn't anything for Katie, either. She deserves a God."

"She deserves rest and peace more, Da."

Bernard's vivid gaze moved about the room. He listened to the silence, disturbed only by the hollow thud of the wind. He said, "I'd like to think there is a God—for Katie. The woman in the other bed—she said she saw an angel.... I'd like to believe it was Katie, going home."

Jason looked down at the table with its oilcloth covering. "Let's believe it, then," he said in a voice as emotionless as his grandfather's had been.

"I don't want to believe in lies," said Bernard. "A lie is the cruelest thing in the world, I'm thinking."

Jason said with loud bitterness, "What is it you are always saying is the motto of the Irish? 'We endure.' That is all we can do. It's the only truth any man has, the only hope he has—to endure."

Bernard poured more whiskey into his glass. He turned it about in his fingers, staring down into the contents. "I couldn't think, I don't want to think, that six feet of dirt is all Katie is going to have."

Jason shivered. "Better that than the life she's had."

Bernard sipped a little. "She had some moments, Jason. She loved us. Perhaps she still does. Who can tell? And we loved her, you and I. If you love someone, you never forget. You never move far away."

Jason went to the sink and pumped himself a glass of water. Oh, Mum, he thought. He felt the tears burning behind his eyes. He looked at the wall above the sink and saw his face in the little mirror that hung there. He saw the mountain and the valley as he had seen them this morning. He saw the sudden unearthly incandescence on them and felt the peace. There was something he had forgotten. What was it? Mysterious, exultant, promising. A lie, he thought, and dashed the water into the sink. He felt Bernard's big hand on his shoulder. He felt Bernard slowly turning him to face himself.

"Jason," said the old man. "All we have left . . . is to believe. In God, even when we hate him and demand of him and scream at him. What else is there? A wilderness full of stones. A desert. For our own sakes, we must believe."

"We must be cowards and believe in a lie?"

Bernard moved his hands down to Jason's arms, and he gripped them. His eyes filled with tears again. "Can we prove he is a lie? The invention of priests? What can't be imagined doesn't exist, never comes to the mind of a man. I was niver one with words. If a man thinks there is Something, there must be something. How else can he think of it at all?"

"Being afraid," said Jason.

Bernard gently shook him. "'The fear of God is the beginning of wisdom.' Why do we have fear? Is it in our souls, then, that we fear what is? Can you imagine being afraid of something that has no . . . verity, and never did? No." He looked down earnestly into Jason's tormented eyes. "No one has proved the existence of God. But no one has proved he doesn't exist, either. It is better for a man to hope that he is than to deny that he does."

Jason turned away his head. "Then, Da, you believe in him."

Bernard dropped his hands. There was a little silence. Then Bernard said, and his voice shook, "I believe . . . I believe . . . even when I hate him."

Jason made a sound in his throat, the beginning of derision. Then he remembered those moments of awesome enlightenment, of glory, of encompassing love, of complete understanding. From what source had they come? He had not invited them or even desired them; he had never known there were such things. He wanted to tell Bernard, but how do you describe the ineffable, that which cannot be comprehended but only known?

"Da..." he began. Bernard looked at him, waiting. "Oh, Da!" Jason groaned.

They fell into each other's arms and cried together, and were comforted.

9

"We must all come to dust," said John Garrity after his mother's funeral. He spoke with the cold and unctuous voice of reproving authority.

His brother looked at him with considerable of the grandfather's bitter rage and disgust. "So we do," he said. "But why should Mum have come to it with so much misery, eh, and so much pain? She never had, in my memory, a truly pleasant day."

"She—" began John. Bernard lifted his hand. They were sitting in the kitchen on this dull April day so unlike the day Kate Garrity had died. Rain slashed the windows, and storm clouds, black and heavy, rushed across the sky like galleons with open sails. It was only three in the afternoon of Kate's burial day, but the weather had turned chill and dank. Joan, wrapped in a shawl, was whimpering in the background. Bernard sat at the table, wearily slumped, with a bottle of whiskey at his elbow, and Jason drank tea laced with the whiskey. The "woman," overcome, as she said, by the funeral, had left for the day. John sat stiffly upright in his chair in his black seminarian's suit, white shirt with stiff collar, thin black tie, and stiff white cuffs. He looked fleshless and ascetic, as usual, and his prominent cheekbones gleamed in the gaslight like polished stone, and his small slate-colored eyes were remote and censorious. His hair was cropped. He was only a seminarian, and one on probation, yet he resembled an archaic priest of the Inquisition, a zealot, an icy fanatic, and Bernard, looking at him through an alcoholic haze, wondered if his grandson had bowels and blood and human flesh, or possessed any human emotions whatsoever. Bernard doubted it. This was an alien presence, and always had been, Bernard pondered in his sorrow, never a grandson or a son or a brother. He had been as apart from the family as a statue, except for a great fondness for his sister. On a few occasions Bernard had had unpleasant and unspeakable thoughts about this. He had encountered such in his own seminarian days.

Bernard said, "Katie's life has made me an atheist, to some extent."

"We must accept the will of God," said John, and glanced at his sister for approval. She nodded eagerly at him.

"If we do, always, we're damned fools," said Bernard. "Seems to me, I'm thinking, that we get out of the mud and stench by our own will, and God, it was, who put us in the mud and the stench—by his will. Should we stay there? Ah, shut up, Jack. Don't give us your homilies on this tragic day. You noticed, did you not, that Father Sweeney did not tell us of the 'blessedness' of poor Katie's life, nor did he suggest she was singing her head off in heaven now. He said, with truth, that she was at peace at last and was resting from her labors. Sure, and he's made progress from the early days, when he was almost as stupid as you are, Jack."

His red-rimmed eyes sparkled derisively at his grandson. "And a fine altar boy you were, too, glaring at the younger lads who were fumbling their best at Mass. What Christian charity! But you never heard of that, did you?"

Jack had clasped his slender bony hands on his black fleshless knee, and those hands involuntarily clenched with affront. He looked at his grandfather's hostile face, at the closed hard face of his brother. Hastily he directed another glance at his sister, at her pale luminous face, her black-lashed blue eyes. For a moment he wanted to weep, but it was not for his mother. Not even his mother had understood him, he thought. Only Joan. Kate had been a loving, foolish woman whose duty it had been to serve her family. John granted that in most instances she had done her duty, feeble as it was. I truly tried, he thought, to be forbearing and patient with her ineptitude. I have tried and prayed, in connection with Da and Jason. But they are intransigent and obstinate and dull of wit, and often impious. I can only pray for them now.

Bernard said, "Thank God I had saved a bit of money over all these years to pay for a funeral for Katie so she wouldn't lie in a pauper's grave. And there is enough left as an offering for a few Masses for the repose of her soul, though I doubt she needs them."

"We all do," said John. He was already restive. He wondered how soon he could decently leave for his seminary, where there were no sardonic men like his grandfather, no louts like his brother, who sat staring like a great black Irish bull. John was hungry. He had always been hungry, from the earliest childhood, though he had invariably eaten much more than his brother. In fact, he had eaten far more than his brother, grandfather, sister, and mother combined. Yet,

125

never had he been comforted and replete. There had always been a hunger in him, which he now believed was a hunger for God and godliness. Yet, still, even in the seminary, that hunger did not abate. He believed, however, that when he was ordained, this tearing hidden appetite, this consuming desire, would be satisfied, as it was never satisfied by food. He had heard much of the rapture and ecstacy of the saints, and he lusted for it. It would come, he was certain, when he was ordained.

Jason said, "I hope, my only hope, is that Mum doesn't remember anything of her life. I hope she is dead, completely dead. That's the only way she can have peace." His young man's voice was almost brutal as he looked at his brother.

"That's a sinful thought," said John. He would never have admitted that he hated Jason; that was a mortal sin. But the hate, a lifelong hate, was there, though John called it disapproval. He often prayed that Jason's soul might be saved.

He looked at the two huge baskets, covered with white linen, which had just been delivered from the Inn-Tavern, courtesy of Patrick Mulligan. The linen could not completely smother the rich fragrance of roasted beef and fresh bread and fruit and cake and ham and baked beans. John's mouth watered. It was going on for four, and his hunger gripped his middle like iron fingers. When could he suggest eating? There was no sign of hunger in the rest of the family, he thought with resentment. The wind rattled the stovepipe; the rain was a long drumming on the window. The day steadily darkened. Suddenly there was a roll of thunder, surly and threatening, and a flash of lightning.

Neighbors, who had called to console the family, and who had attended Kate's funeral, had long departed. Bernard had shown, unmistakably, that their absence would be appreciated. It had been a grand funeral. Mrs. Lindon had given all the flowers for the altar and for Katie's simple wooden coffin with the brass handles. Katie's grave had been heaped with flowers from the same source. Mrs. Lindon and all her young relatives had been at Mass, wearing solemn and decorous faces. John thought it a scandal, and he wondered why Father Sweeney had permitted this evil intrusion. When he had protested the flowers, Bernard had looked at him with a threatening face.

"Seems like our Lord was grateful to Mary Magdalen when she brought him ointment to soothe his feet," Bernard had said. "But then, and for sure, you don't understand that, do you, Jackie lad? Think on it. There's many a Magdalen who is purer than all the fine ladies who bedded down only with their husbands."

John had forgiven his grandfather, who, of course, was only a rude peasant, for all he had had a teacher for a father and had studied for the priesthood. John was always forgiving his family. It made him feel very holy.

None of the family knew, of course, that Mrs. Lindon, who had been a caller after the funeral, had looked at Joan with thoughtful shrewd eyes, saying to herself, "There is one of us, and that is certain. I'm never mistaken. If it weren't for her crippled state, she would be a very successful courtesan, not a mere whore. I wonder how twisted her legs are? There're some perverted men who like disabled women, even ugly and deformed women. This girl is the most beautiful thing I've ever seen, and no. doubt she is a virgin, too." Mrs. Lindon always detected corruption; she knew that Joan had a corrupt, if still inexperienced, soul. Corruption had nothing to do with experience. It was a matter of spirit.

Joan, who had heard some vague rumors that Mrs. Lindon was a scandalous woman, did not quite understand where the scandal lay or what it implied. The "woman" had mentioned "men," but Joan had had no explicit understanding. Kate, of course, had had no words with which to instruct her daughter, nor would she have thought it necessary. But Joan had looked at Mrs. Lindon, and the two had felt an instant kinship. Mrs. Lindon, thought Joan, was "nice" and "kind." And very stylish and handsome. Joan had looked covetously at Mrs. Lindon's jeweled hands, her beautiful suit of dark blue wool, and her fur and her smart hat and her rope of pearls and her well-coiffed hair. Joan had been much impressed that Mrs. Lindon had arrived in a new automobile, followed by another containing her young cousins and nieces, all richly and suitably clad, with kid gloves and feathered hats and boas and pearls. Joan thought them lovely and magnificent. Some were younger than herself, she thought enviously, but none was prettier. How wonderful to have wealthy parents! How wonderful to have such a cousin or aunt! Joan had heard of dances and parties in Mrs. Lindon's house. She nurtured a dim hope that someday Mrs. Lindon would invite her, too. So she had fawned sweetly on Mrs. Lindon and had given shy radiant smiles to the young relatives, who were much amused both by her recognized depravity and by her naiveté. Joan had seen people whispering behind their hands, and had been impatient. It was only envy, of course. What on earth were such as Mrs. Lindon and her relatives doing in Belleville?

Mr. Mulligan and his daughter, Patricia, "that stuck-up girl," had been at the funeral, though they had not gone to the cemetery. Mr. Mulligan had put his arm about Jason, but had given John only a brief nod. This had puzzled Joan. It was true that Jason worked for Mr. Mulligan, but John was studying for the priesthood, and that was a vast difference in status. Joan had resented Patricia's haughty air and condescending nod, but had consoled herself with the silent observation that Patricia was very plain, and no match in appearance for Mrs. Lindon's beautiful young relatives. Patricia had drawn her velvet skirts aside when Mrs. Lindon and her charges had passed her in the pew, and Joan thought that had been very rude and was no doubt inspired by jealousy. Patricia had given Joan a swift look of acrimony because of Joan's beauty, but was mollified when she saw Joan's wheeled chair, pushed by a small nondescript woman, obviously a servant. A slight contemptuous smile had lifted Patricia's pale lip.

Lionel and Molly had been there, of course, and Joan's shriveled heart had expanded at the sight of Lionel. He in turn was freshly struck by Joan's imperial loveliness. What did it matter that she was a cripple? Her body itself was perfection, and his experienced eye had penetrated beneath the coarse brown frock, the old wool coat. Joan's blue eyes were spectacular. She made the young whores look like drabs and strumpets. There was a regality about her, an untouchable delicate splendor. Lionel, too, had long ago sensed Joan's innate corruption of spirit, just like his own, and he loved her and was determined to have her, one way or another.

When Joan had passed him in her chair, Lionel had bent and kissed her chastely on the cheek, and had touched her shoulder in consolation. Joan wondered at the sudden wild fire in her vitals, and her trembling. Lionel had felt this even more violently in himself, but he had not wondered. Molly, with her acute perception, had sensed something of this exchange between Joan and her brother, and she had been disturbed. Innocent though she was herself, she felt something wicked had transpired, or that dangerous people had touched each other in a manner inexplicable to her, and had known each other with absolute surety. As Joan was wheeled down the aisle to the door, Molly had seen that Lionel's eyes followed her and were filled with a curious deep longing and

128

a forgetfulness of where he was. It was the first time he had kissed the girl. There was still a tingling on his lips, and a sharp thirst. When he finally turned and looked at his sister, he was surprised to see alarm in those clear yellow eyes. Molly's hair, like his own, was a blaze of red in the shadowed gloom of the little church. The organ moaned dolorously, but Molly continued to eye her brother with that confused apprehension.

Jason, one of the pallbearers for his mother, had gone before, but Molly had looked at him with yearning, and he had not seen her. She had wanted to touch him, desperately, but that was not possible for a girl so innocent, so truly innocent. The peal of the bell tolled, in her heart, like a dark premonition, leaving desolation behind. She felt bereft and alone, though Lionel took her arm and guided her out of the church. Their parents were not there. They were too busy.

Joan had watched, in the approaching rainstorm, the lowering of her mother's coffin into the wet brown grave. She had cried. That was not hard, thinking of Lionel and his kiss and the ecstasy it had brought her. They were the first tears she had shed, and people thought them very touching. Even Jason thought so. Bernard was not deceived, though he did wonder at the source of the tears. They were certainly not for poor Katie. Nor was Joan sentimental, nor could she produce tears at will.

There were but two real mourners at that funeral, Bernard and Jason. They were not resigned. They had not been consoled by the funeral Mass. They were consumed by bitterness and sorrow. They were almost alone at the cemetery. Rain struck their faces.

John was becoming ravenously hungry. The fragrance of the waiting food was unbearable. He had to wipe his mouth free of saliva. It was then that Father Sweeney came in to console the bereaved family. Jason and John rose, Joan stirred in her chair, but Bernard surveyed the priest irascibly, and merely leaned back in his chair.

"I congratulate you, Bill," he said mockingly, lifting a glass of whiskey in salute. "You didn't utter one hypocritical or pious word at Katie's funeral."

John said, dropping to his bony knees, "Your blessing, Father."

The young priest hesitated. He looked at Bernard's bitterly smiling face, at the silent Jason. Father Sweeney thought that he would have preferred to give the old man and Jason his blessing, rather than John, and he was alarmed at this, which was surely uncharitable and unfitting. Coloring a little, he murmured the requested words, but he felt a faint coldness in himself. John was improving somewhat at the seminary, but he was still on probation. The old fathers were still ambiguous about his vocation. He was constantly confessing to the "sins" of unworthiness and sloth. The fathers were inclined to believe in the "unworthiness," considering his scrupulosity, but they could not condemn him for sloth. "A busier bee was never known here before," one old priest had said, with some dissatisfaction.

After the requested blessing, Father Sweeney looked about him with some helplessness. "You'll be having a drink with us, Faether," said Bernard, lapsing into his richest brogue. "To Katie, for her blameless life, and in hope for her peace, at last." He poured a large dollop of Irish whiskey into an empty glass and extended it, as a challenge, to the priest. Father Sweeney, like all Irishmen, could not resist a challenge. He took the glass, still standing, and said thank you. He saw that John was regarding all this with coldly furious umbrage. So the priest lifted the glass, sipped at it with the other two men, and said, "Amen." He was covertly pleased to see that John was horrified.

"This family was blessed in Kate Garrity," Father Sweeney continued. "A noble lady in all her ways. Her memory will be cherished, her presence dearly missed. I have never known, Bernard, a more tender and gentle soul, devout and kind, almost sinless. If sins she had, they were the sins of putting her family before all else. But I do not think our Lord will hold that against her."

"If he did, he would have to hold it against his blessed Mother, too," said Bernard.

"There is a difference," said John. Bernard gave him one of his formidable looks. "There is, eh?" he replied. "And how would you know of any difference, you who never loved anyone?"

John involuntarily glanced at his sister, who gave him a slight sympathetic smile. Then his hunger assailed him. He went to the cupboard for plates. "Will you join us, Father?" he said, turning from the cupboard with a certain stiff grace.

"Ah, yes," said Bernard. "It seems you always did have a fork in your hand, bucko. Well, get at the victuals. Your damned mouth is watering."

Jason sat, his big arms folded over his chest, and he looked at his brother with open hostility. Joan said, "We haven't had anything since breakfast, after the funeral. I'm hungry, too." Her usually delicately tinted cheeks were flushed with remembrance of Lionel.

The priest sat down after furtively inspecting his watch and then replacing it. "I have about half an hour," he said. John was eagerly uncovering the hampers of food.

"I'm going back to the seminary tomorrow, Father," he said.

"Thank God," said Bernard, putting a slice of ham and another slice of roast beef on the priest's plate. "A small blessing, but an appreciated one."

"Da..." said Joan.

"Ah, shut up, Joanie," said Bernard.

Jason looked at the food and felt repelled. His sorrow was like an iron ball heated to fire in his chest. He would never, now, be able to do anything for his mother, to make her life more pleasant, less painful. He felt her presence in the kitchen, that gentle, tender presence, and his eyes darkened with tears. There was no mercy for the blameless, the kind, the trusting. Yes, God was the adversary. Man had to contend with him all the days of his life.

But even in his pain Jason thought: Better a terrible world with God in it than a painless world without him. He was stunned by his own thought.

John, forgetting everything completely, devoured the food piled on his plate. His expression was orgiastic, his eyes fixed and glazed and intent on what he was eating. He bent over the table as a priest bends to kiss the altar.

Observing this, Father Sweeney wondered with sudden and shocking suspicion: What is it he wants, what is he really devouring, what is the source of his hunger?

He was not revolted by John. For the first time he felt an awful compassion for him. Of all the Garrity family, he was the most needful of pity.

As if in counterpoint, the wind howled dolorously in the chimney.

10

Patricia Mulligan sat with her father in the huge ugly dining room of Patrick's house. It was a warm Monday afternoon in late May 1907. Patrick felt it was his paternal duty to dine with his daughter once a week, instead of eating at the Inn-Tavern. Besides, he liked his own dining room better than the one at the hotel, with its lighter furniture and its numerous windows and scintillating chandeliers. His taste, and the public's, collided; he conceded gracefully to the public. But he was happiest here, among the enormous furniture of dark red mahogany, brown velvet draperies and wavering gaslight.

Patricia thought her father's table manners repellent. He never lifted his little finger daintily. He gulped at his wineglass; he shoveled in his food, in a very ill-bred haste. He was also getting very fat, she thought with distaste. He ate in his shirtsleeves, despite her protests, wearing his vest open, his watch chain strained across his ample belly. He often took off his collar, too, and his tie, in what his daughter thought was a deliberate affront, and often she was right. But she was the center of his heart, for all, he would reflect, the poor colleen did have her airs and pretensions and lack of real intelligence. He gave her no credit for her secret shrewdness, for he did not know she had any. While she was not corrupt in spirit, as was Joan Garrity, she knew the world much better than did the other girl. She was also sly. And she had a Problem, which must be handled with dexterity.

Her agate-colored eyes studied him tonight. Though he had little taste for formality in himself, he demanded it of his daughter, so Patricia was always dressed elegantly at the table. Today she wore a white silk shirtwaist, buttoned to the throat, with a pearl-and-diamond pin and pearl-and-diamond earrings, and two pearl-edged combs upholding her brown pompadour—filled out with "rats"—and a black silk skirt and soft kid buttoned shoes. There was a pearl ring on her finger which had belonged to her dead mother. She looked almost pretty; there was a pink tint in her thin cheeks, and her eyes had an unusual sparkle and her tilted nose gave her an expression at once haughty yet flippant. She had a slightly dreaming expression, alien to her, for Patricia was a very practical girl. Though she had little of a figure, she had discreetly filled it out on the chest with pads of cotton under her camisole. There was also padding over her narrow hips. Patrick thought she had begun to "bloom." He did not know of the artifices, of which he would have disapproved. Glancing fondly at her today, as she daintily toyed with her food, he thought again of something he had been earnestly considering for over two years. After all, she was twenty years old now, and an heiress. Her own mother had been a wife and mother for two years at this age. Patricia was getting on. She had nothing but disdain for the eligible young men in Belleville, and never encouraged them. But she did speak too often of the fine young gentlemen who courted her when she was visiting her aunt in Philadelphia. Patrick distrusted them. He would not have his daughter leave him for another city, and for what were rakes in his estimation. Opportunists. Adventurers.

Patricia said, in her light voice which was always a little petulant, as if she were chronically displeased, as she was, "Dada, I do think that, as your daughter, I should visit the Inn-Tavern occasionally for dinner. In your company, of course."

"No," said Patrick. Then he looked at her with surprise. "You never wanted to go there before, Patricia."

She shrugged her shoulders. "I never thought it concerned me, Dada. Now I know it does. After all, I will inherit it, won't I? I should know about it. You agree with that, don't you?"

Patrick was about to disagree; then all at once, and for the first time, to his surprise, he saw that Patricia's eyes were quite sharp and knowing, and not soft and girlish at all. He was not entirely pleased, however, for girls should be vague and soft and womanly, not concerned with business or the world. But then, she had a point there. She was his heiress. He decided, with sudden pleasure, that Patricia resembled him in spirit.

But he wavered. He refilled his wineglass, before the housemaid could do so, and Patricia frowned. Really, Dada's manners were execrable. Her thought did not distract her. She leaned toward her father, waiting.

Patrick studied his daughter, and was more pleased with her every moment. "It's time you got married, my girl."

As he had hinted this—more than hinted—several times,

133

to Patricia's cool indifference, he was surprised to see the sudden hot flush appear on her cheekbones. She also averted her eyes. "Who?" she murmured. Her heart was making her silk shirtwaist tremble with its quick pounding.

Patrick reflected. Too soon, perhaps, to tell her whom he had in mind? "Well," he said, watching her, "there's Dave Muirhead, Frank Flaherty, and others." He paused. "And my young assistant, Jason Garrity."

Patricia was about to say, throwing up her hands, at the last-named, "Oh, my God, Dada!" But she was a very careful girl. She knew of Patrick's affection for Jason Garrity, whom she despised as ill-bred like her father. He was not in the least elegant; he was not, coming down to it, a gentleman. He had no graces, no delicacies, no subtlety, no fascination. He was a lout. His hands and feet were too big, his body too forceful in appearance, his step too hard and firm, his face too overtly male. So unlike...

So Patricia merely folded her hands on the table and looked at her father with meekness. "I don't really like any of them, Dada. But...give me time, won't you? I do so want to be your little girl for a while longer. Please?"

Patricia could be very artful and she knew how to manage her father. Patrick's rosy face blushed more deeply as she continued. "And I don't want to marry someone who does not live in Belleville or who would take me away from my home."

Astonished delight shone on Patrick's face. "And I thought you always wanted to get out of this town, love! I was always afraid you would marry someone from, say, Philadelphia."

Patricia gave him her sweetest smile, which was an effort for her. "I've come to my senses, Dada. I don't want to leave you, ever."

"Love, love," said Patrick, sentimentally close to tears. "And I'll have grandchildren to dandle on my knee every day!"

Patricia blushed violently, and her whole meager body tingled and her heart bounded. She dropped her eyes in a virginal fashion, and seeing this, Patrick was remorseful. A man should not speak to his daughter in any way which suggested Bed. He was touched by her deep blushes. He was a crude bastard, that he was, to offend her maidenly sensibilities in this fashion. It was bad enough for a poor colleen to face the realities of matrimony on her wedding night, without implying them beforehand. That "good" women ever had lusts of their own, Patrick did not believe. Passion was reserved for mistresses and whores. "Good" women merely endured conjugal assaults. Only "bad" women courted them.

"Forgive me, love," he said to Patricia now.

Patrick was well-softened, to Patricia's satisfaction; she said, "Well, may I dine with you once a week at the Inn-Tavern, Dada?"

Patrick thought. He would have to ask Mrs. Lindon not to come to the tavern too early with her young relatives, of a Sunday. That Patricia had any idea of Mrs. Lindon's profession, he would not have believed, even if she had told him herself. "There are characters, Patricia, who come to the place that I don't want you to know."

"But you will be there, Dada. I'll dine with you." She smiled at him.

"I'll think on it, my dear," said Patrick. His daughter sighed gently. She had won. Now she could relax and remember the day that had so changed her life.

It had happened on a sweet Sunday afternoon of flowery trees and warm grass.

It had been a perfect day, marred only by Dada's insistence on High Mass, which was too long and boring, as usual. Early dinner at home had been tasteless and heavy, and Dada had gone promptly upstairs at two o'clock for his Sunday nap before he left for the Inn-Tavern. Patricia, who was supposed to occupy Sunday afternoons with a Sunday nap, also, and to read an improving book, or to visit one of her few female acquaintances, was restless. There were strange urges in her twenty-year-old body, and her mind was filled with amorphous fantasies of knights in white armor. Patricia was not, by nature, romantic, but her body had its secret and imperious impulses. She knew, by intuition, far more than her innocent father would ever have suspected, though the intuitions were not explicit. She understood that men were different from women, and her female instinct was alerted. But exactly in what lay the "difference" was still not understood by her. She had viewed fig-leafed statues of men in the galleries and museums to which her aunt in Philadelphia had taken her, and had wondered what the fig leaves concealed. That they concealed something "naughty" but delightful, she was positive. She had heard the girlish giggles of her young cousins, and had listened to their whispered comments. All this had stirred and excited her without informing her.

She had seen a celebrated painting of Adam and Eve in one of the galleries. Adam, of course, had a decorous fig leaf. But Eve had had one, too. One of the cousins giggled and whispered, "Why does she have one, for heaven's sake!" Patricia had smiled knowingly, and had inspected Adam's fig leaf intensely, if covertly. What did it hide? It bulged. But what did it hide? There were no overt contours. However, she instinctively guessed that it had importance for women. At this thought she had felt a dismaying hotness in her virginal loins, and had been ashamed, if deeply excited.

Because her cousins knew almost as little as she did, there was no fully informed instruction from them. Her aunt, sorry for the motherless girl, had attempted some instruction, but it was mostly of warnings about men. A girl did not allow any intimacies, such as kisses in lonely places, or embraces. A girl kept herself "pure" before marriage. Men did not marry bad girls. There were dark hints of unwanted babies, and fates worse than death. In some fashion, babies were implicit with intimacies, but exactly what those intimacies were, Patricia did not know. Did one have babies if one sat in a chair a gentleman had just vacated? Did a kiss, however innocent, bring about a child? Finally Patricia guessed all this did not. It needed Something Else. But no one told her exactly what. Her aunt had, with an embarrassment which intrigued Patricia, gone through the routine of the birds and the bees, without details except those concerning stamens and pistils, and Patricia knew she possessed neither.

Patricia had finally resorted to the dictionary in her father's library. "Sexual intercourse." What did that mean? There was another word pertaining to something which only men possessed. Patricia looked it up in the same dictionary. There was no illustration, just babble about "glands." That was the extent of Patricia's knowledge, while her young body demanded insistently, again without exact information. So, though Patricia was baffled, she was still confronted by the imperatives of her young flesh, and grew increasingly restless.

Her aunt had told her that men were predatory and they put upon unwary girls. Patricia yearned to be put upon, though her aunt had warned of dire consequences such as "unwanted children." Too embarrassed at last, the aunt had burst out, "There are good girls and bad girls! Men don't

136

marry bad girls! Bad girls show their legs and entice gentle-men!" Patricia began to long to show her legs. Her aunt had warned of "the pit." Patricia wanted to peer into it. She began to massage her tiny bosom with butter and honey, hoping to increase it. She had noticed that men discreetly stared at the fronts of shirtwaists and dresses. She envied the women in portraits who had large white bosoms. Apparently men liked them, though in Patricia's opinion they were neither beau-tiful nor useful except to nurse infants. But how, exactly, did women get infants?

She found herself dreaming at night, but when she awoke, sweating and trembly, she could recall nothing of what she had experienced in her sleep except that it had been body-shaking.

She was ripe for seduction. She had guessed long ago that Mrs. Lindon's young relatives were not relatives at all. She had come upon servants who whispered and snickered behind their hands. Mrs. Lindon's girls were evidently "bad," and were to be avoided by "good" girls. What did they do in the bed-rooms of that house? wondered poor Patricia. That they did something very deplorable, but interesting, was evident, and there was money involved. But how, and why? Patricia held her skirts when encountering the young "relatives," but for what explicit reason, she did not know. They did things only married women did—but what the hell was *that?* Patricia was shocked at the sudden vehemence of her own question.

Once, half-asleep, she had involuntarily masturbated. The wild explosion had unnerved and profoundly shaken her, and she had gasped and sweated and had thought of evil. Some-how, in some mysterious way, men were involved in this savage experience. She took to reading the Bible. "Adam knew his wife, Eve." How?

On this lovely May Sunday, Patricia had not gone upstairs for the customary afternoon nap after noon dinner. Her rest-lessness overcame her. She had got out her bicycle from the stable and had furiously ridden off, pedaling with all her strength. That she was desperately seeking an encounter she did not know. The exertion exhilarated her and she pressed for the outskirts of the town. The gentle heat made her sweat; her breasts tingled wetly against the camisole and the shirt-waist, and the sensation excited her. Her loins, on the seat of the bicycle, began to burn. She took off her straw hat and tied it on the handlebars. The wind lifted her light brown hair and she laughed. She felt alive and vibrant as never before. She felt her femaleness and was proud. It was naughty, of course, but in what way?

She passed carriages and automobiles and did not see or hear them. She was intent on something, though it remained hidden from her. She searched with her eyes, and did not know for what she was looking. Her heart was beating very fast. An unimaginative girl, she had never noticed beauty before. Now she was entranced by the countryside which bordered the narrow road. Everything elated her, the new green of the trees, the scent of the warm grass, the sight of wildflowers shyly clustered in the shade of great trees—purple, yellow, red, and blue—the mauve glisten of the mountains in the distance, the fragrance of hot stone and hot dust, the comfort of the sun on her face and her hands. She smiled, and she wanted to cry in her delight. Patricia Mulligan had discovered life. She felt she was part of it and that she was beautiful, too. Her heart expanded. She began to sing.

There was a break in the thick trees lining the road. Patricia got off her bicycle and entered the break. There were shrubs here, but beyond them she could see a small oval glade surrounded by trees that threw cool shadows on the high grass. It was shiningly silent here and secluded and very still. Patricia pushed her bicycle to the end of the shrubbery and looked about her with pleasure. Buttercups and tall wild daisies mingled with the grass, sweetening the air with aromatic if rank fragrance. To Patricia it had a compelling fierce power which excited her. The leaves of the trees were polished by the spring so that they seemed to be coated with a green lacquer. She touched a trunk; it was alive and warm to her hand. She leaned her bicycle against it. Beyond the glade she could see the green-and-purple mountains and the small distant walls of the rising Ipswich House. It was not being built very fast; that, she had heard. It had something to do with the Panic, lack of credit, and money, and other tiresome things with which men engrossed themselves. Dada had a mortgage now, on his Inn-Tavern, for the Ipswich House, and was depressed by it, which seemed silly to Patricia, who had no idea what a mortgage was. When she had last gone to Philadelphia, the money her father had given her was less than the year before, and when she had wailed he had said, "There's a Panic, love, and money is short." She had pouted for two days, but Patrick, though sad over this, did not increase the gift. He had not tried to explain.

Ladies should not be concerned by Finance, even if they were hurt by it.

Patricia sat down in the yielding high grass. Then she pulled the pins and rats from her long fine hair. She laughed aloud with a nameless exultation. She unbuttoned the high lace neck of her blouse and turned it down. Her heated flesh accepted the cool breeze with gratitude. She took off her shoes and stretched her toes. She stared at the hot blue sky through the leaves, and laughed again. She picked a buttercup and rubbed her nose in the yellow pollen. She yawned and lifted her arms and observed their thinness. She wanted to hug something, she wanted to embrace with all her tall lanky young body. She pulled up her skirt, now dusty from grass pollen, and surveyed her long lean legs and thighs, which were not at all voluptuous. She sighed. She had a prodigious appetite but never gained weight, though she stuffed herself with pastries on the sly and drank cream. Her aunt in Philadelphia had comforted her by saying, "You're just slow in developing, dear," and then had added in a lower tone, "Marriage will cure that." That was another exciting thought. An hourglass figure was much to be desired.

She had not noticed another bicyclist less than a quarter of a mile behind her, which had paced her. That bicyclist was Lionel Nolan, for he had the Sunday off. He was an extremely gregarious young man, most of the time, but when he wished to think, and plot, he looked for solitude. He had seen Patricia Mulligan pedaling fast on the road and had been surprised, for she usually drove her buggy. Always curious about other human beings, he had followed her, amused by her agility, for she usually gave the impression of ladylike languor. On the few occasions when he had seen her, she had hardly glanced at him. The encounters had almost always been in church. Lionel had chuckled to himself. Who in hell would want such a skinny tall girl, with nondescript brown hair, a constricted face in which the nose was too big, a pale mouth and cat's eyes, and with no bust and no hips, and with a neck that was like a stem? Of course she was very stylish in her rich clothes and had a certain contrived grace of movement but to Lionel she was only amusing in her pretensions and airs, and "old-maidish" in her gestures. Her voice was without resonance or sweetness or beguilement, almost a monotone, which she apparently considered refined. A very dull and uninteresting girl, Lionel had concluded, and had often wondered at Jason's continued preoccupation with her. She had no feminine lures, no flirtatiousness, and did not know how to use her eyelashes or her smiles, which were reluctant and without warmth. But then, he would conclude, with his usual lack of self-delusion, people would probably wonder why he himself loved a cripple. True, Joan Garrity had a beauty which entranced all who saw her, but that was not enough, according to general opinion. It was more than enough for Lionel. But had Joan been a silly simpering girl of no intelligence, and as drab as Patricia Mulligan, Lionel would not have spared a moment's thought on her. So he was sorry for Jason Garrity and felt himself very superior to his friend, who apparently was obsessed by a girl with a mind as small as a hen's.

It was odd that Lionel, so astute about the majority of people, and who had known that Joan was extremely intelligent and aware, had not even guessed at Patricia Mulligan's exceedingly sharp shrewdness and ability to exploit. She was as clever a plotter as he himself, and he did not know it and would have laughed at anyone who had told him of it.

He saw that Patricia had left the road. He stopped his bicycle at the gap. Should he follow her, or not? It would give him some secret hilarity to intrude himself upon her and watch her discomfiture at his presence. He dismounted, and as quietly as possible pushed his vehicle through the shrubbery, and then he stood at the edge of the glade. His mouth opened wide in a silent grin of mingled incredulousness and suppressed laughter.

For Patricia had pulled her skirt and petticoats to the top of her thighs, revealing drawers of shimmering satin and lace. She was lying back on the grass, her lifted folded arms shutting out the light. Her hair was spread in astonishing disorder about her. Her blouse was unbuttoned down to the camisole, which was a mass of cascading lace and pink ribbons. Patricia had an air of innocent abandon, childlike yet female. To other than Lionel this would have appeared touching. He was not touched. He was just entertained and curious. His foxy yellow eyes narrowed; his wide freckled face broke into lines of mirth. He thought: I am not a gentleman; a gentleman would cough and move himself back a few paces, to give her time to rearrange herself. But as I am not a gentleman, I won't do that. So he whistled a ribald cadence and strode into the glade, laughing.

Patricia flashed upright, pulling down her skirts, pulling up her blouse, and turning a most unbecoming red. Her agate eyes bulged with mortification and embarrassment. She flung back her hair and fished in the grass for pins. "How...how dare you!" she cried.

Lionel advanced slowly and casually into the glade. "Why, what are you doing here?" he asked pleasantly. "This is my favorite place. Did you find it too? Nice, isn't it?" He sat down in the grass, not too near her, and his smile was ingratiating. "Glad to find someone who likes this little spot. I often come here," which, of course, was a lie. He had never seen the glade before.

Patricia's scrambling had put her out of breath, but now she was decently covered. Her hands closed on a "rat." But ladies never let men know they wore "rats" under their huge pompadours. It was almost as bad as showing legs. So she began, in flurried hot silence, to braid her hair. Her one desire was to leave as soon as possible.

Lionel tilted his head with its high burning crest. "You have pretty hair," he said. "It glistens like polished wood." He was pleased by his own poetry. He must use it on Joan, with greater veracity, except that he would mention polished jet.

"And pretty hands," he added, and this was not an untruth.

Patricia paused in the braiding of her hair. Young men in Philadelphia, and in Belleville, had always told her how stylish and fashionable she was, and how superb was her taste. But they had never mentioned anything complimentary about her physical person. She had hungered for such compliments.

"I've always admired your fine teeth," Lionel added, seeing he had made an impression. The poor dippy stupid girl, he thought. She can be fooled by a few kind words.

Patricia was staring at him as if seeing him for the first time. She saw his slender trim body, taut and vibrant as the body of a fox, his slim restless hands with their clean buffed nails, his long vital legs neat even in their old trousers, and, above all, his knowing intelligent eyes and springing red hair, which was carefully combed into large waves. He wore no collar or tie; his shirt was open at the throat, and Patricia could see his strong freckled neck. She had never really seen him before. He had been only one of Dada's "help," and therefore not worthy of consideration. Now she saw him clearly, as a man. Her eyes dropped briefly and involuntarily to his

141

crotch, and Lionel grinned to himself with both surprise and fresh secret hilarity. This was becoming interesting. He was even more amused seeing sweat appear over the girl's upper lip.

"I've got to go," she muttered, but she did not look away from him.

Lionel lifted his red eyebrows. "Why? It's early yet. And it's cool here, and refreshing."

He took out his package of "tailored" cigarettes, extracted one, put it slowly in his mouth, and struck a match on the sole of his dusty shoe. He did not ask permission to smoke. For some reason this fascinated as well as vexed Patricia. He was not awed by her, nor subservient to her, as were Dada's other employees. His voice was not fawning and placating, anxious to please. He was treating her boldly—and rudely. Patricia, to her dismay, felt a passionate excitement, and her breath caught. She should reprimand him, she told herself. But she suddenly understood that a reprimand from her would not disturb him at all. He would only laugh at her. Her agitation grew. She felt a tremendous urge toward him, and she cowered in confusion and alarm.

Lionel shifted a little nearer her. He looked at her feet in their black silk stockings. "You've got pretty insteps, too," he remarked idly. "And very pretty feet. Aristocratic."

Patricia gasped. She had forgotten her shoes. She pulled them on with trembling hands and with primal seductiveness managed to reveal a well-shaped if not luxurious calf. It was all instinctive, and not deliberate. Lionel knew this. Women were easy to understand, if one took the time, and Lionel always took time. He had long ago found that women could be exceedingly useful to him.

She said in her thin voice, "I think you are very forward."

He pretended bewilderment. "Why? Are compliments, if sincere, forward? What've I got to gain by telling you the truth, Miss Mulligan?"

Patricia's heart throbbed. She fumbled in her pocket for her handkerchief to wipe her wet palms. Suddenly Lionel was extending his own, a very white handkerchief, carefully folded, and of good quality. Dazed, Patricia took it. She found herself wiping her face and her hands; the cloth smelled of tobacco and fine linen. A sweet warmth filled her. She mutely returned the handkerchief to Lionel, and the gesture was faintly pleading, as if she were asking a question. All her hauteur had become humility. Her keen mind reminded her that he was only "help." Her instincts told her differently.

Lionel decided the time had come to give her a little indifference. He turned his fiery head and looked at the mountains, and thoughtfully smoked, one hand hanging on his bent knee. He frowned slightly. "It's taking a long time to build the new hotel," he said, as if to himself. "And too much money, which we can't get just now."

"We?" murmured Patricia. He turned to her as if surprised. "Why, yes. Didn't you know, Miss Mulligan, that I have a share in Ipswich House? Jason Garrity got that for me. He wouldn't sell his fourteen acres to your father, but took shares for himself, and me, in the hotel. If we ever get it built, we'll have our fortunes made."

Patricia was alerted. Dada had told her nothing of this. Her eyes widened in honest and overwhelming interest.

"I'll have charge of the kitchens and the dining rooms," Lionel went on. "And the menus. Haven't you seen the plans?"

"No," said Patricia, and was angered at her father, who told her nothing. He thought she was too fragile! For the first time Patricia resented that.

Lionel was shaking his head as if both amused and disbelieving. "An intelligent girl like you, too!" he said. "Your father's old-fashioned, isn't he? I always thought of you, Miss Mulligan, as one of the 'new women.'"

As Patricia had thought of herself as that, too, she was overcome. But she stammered, "I...I don't...I don't believe in votes for women."

"Why not?" asked Lionel. "Many women are as bright as men." He studied her. "I'm sure you are."

Patricia flushed again. "Well, I'm a girl..." she began.

Lionel treated her to one of his invincible tricks. He let his eyes wander very slowly from her eyes to her lips, let them linger on her small breasts, dropped them to her narrow waist, then her thighs, her calves, her feet. A violent trembling invaded Patricia's flesh. She felt she should be outraged at this insolent long survey. Instead, she was intoxicated. All at once her body felt seductive, enticing, irresistible, steaming with virginal passion.

"Obviously," Lionel said. His yellow eyes brightened as if with desire, and Patricia saw this and trembled even more violently. She did not know that this was another of Lionel's

143

clever tricks. He really desired her as much as he would have desired a gargoyle. But she could be valuable to him, even more valuable than other women. Shyly, as if unable to resist his impulse, he touched the high instep of her buttoned shoe, then withdrew his hand with a quick gasp. "Sorry," he said.

He could seduce her, he thought. He could manufacture a reasonable facsimile of lust. He considered. But...there was Dada. A man had to be careful. Ensnare a girl, for one's own advantage, but not a complete ensnarement. That was dangerous. It committed a man, and often ruined him. A playfulness, perhaps, implying future intimacies; a few tragic sighs at the hopelessness of it all. A woman never tired of deception, for she never knew she was being deceived until the last devastating and hopeless hour. By that time she was powerless to do anything but grieve and despise herself. Lionel understood women too well. If all worked well, he could make a lifelong slave of Patricia; that is, if he himself worked well. It would take finesse, and Lionel possessed a lot of that. He had had experience, even with Mrs. Lindon, who was now devoted to him and who gave him access to her pretty "relatives" without cost.

Mrs. Lindon had once said, "You have all the ways of a gentleman, my dear Lionel, but you don't have much education. It doesn't take a lot of study to give the appearance of education; it just needs a little reading, a lot of listening, and a knowing air." So she had given him books to read, and though they bored him, he had gained considerable polish. She taught him phrases to use to imply erudition.

Thinking of this, with gratitude, Lionel almost forgot Patricia, who was fixedly regarding him with moist eyes. Her mouth had fallen open. She was like one bewitched. Lionel, with pretended humility and hesitancy, reached for her hand. He pressed it. Pleading with his uplifted eyes, he timidly kissed that hand. Patricia shivered. Her little breasts swelled and tingled. His fingers burned into her hand. She wet her mouth, and her lips became tremulous.

Well, thought Lionel, that's enough for now. He said, "Forgive me, Miss Mulligan. But I couldn't help it."

All the longings and nameless urges Patricia had been lately enduring gathered in her with a tremendous force. She wanted Lionel's arms about her. She wanted...She did not know just what she wanted, but her instincts urged her. She wanted to lie in his arms, close to him, held by him. In short, she was in love, entranced, helpless, overcome. She had a sudden vehement desire to take off her clothing, to reveal herself to him. In the black hot whirlpool of her female yearning she wanted his hands on her body, seeking. Lust dissolved her; she felt herself helplessly surrendering.

Lionel, sighing heavily, released her hand. Through a mist she stared at him. She saw his sad face, his ardent eyes. "Forgive me," he murmured again, and averted his head. Then he stood up.

"I must go," he muttered. "If...if I've offended you, Miss Mulligan, please forgive me. But I just couldn't help it! You are so...beautiful...so desirable! Forgive me for a momentary weakness..."

He passed his hand despairingly over his forehead and shook his head as if stricken. Then, uttering a slight sound of sorrow, he turned and ran away. Patricia heard the crashing of shrubbery. Then he was gone and she was all alone in a brilliant daze of light and ecstasy and shaking passion.

That is how it began. She had not seen Lionel for three weeks. She dreamt of him, desiring her, embracing her. Now her dreams became more explicit, except for the final act. She could not bear it. Her days were filled with visions of him...and beds. And, of course, marriage. Patricia began to live in a world almost too exciting. The aspect of things changed. They became portents, full of leaping promise and joy. The world filled with music. Even Dada's grossness became less exasperating.

But Patricia had a very shrewd mind. It was all very well to dream. But one had to plan to make those dreams come true. Patricia was nothing if not practical.

She had now succeeded with Dada. She would see Lionel often. Her heart melted with tenderness for him, for his pain. She would soon let him know that his suit was not unwelcome. She began to plan the fine house Dada would build for his daughter and her husband.

Happiness surged in Patricia. She acquired a sort of radiance. Jason Garrity saw this in church. When he shyly smiled at Patricia, she smiled back. He did not know that she did not really see him. She was always looking for Lionel. She went very often to the glade. That she did not find Lionel there only confirmed her blissful belief that he was avoiding her to avoid his own pain. Soon she would console him. Soon she would let him know she loved him. She did not see him in church. She guessed he went to an earlier Mass, because of her. She sighed with joy.

Of course, it was impossible for her to know that Lionel had counted on all this, and was biding his time, waiting for her to make the next move.

11

On a hot July day, Patrick Mulligan called both Jason and Lionel into his office. Lionel for one startled moment had the fear that Patricia had blabbed. He was almost overcome with fear and his red freckles stood out vividly on his suddenly pale face. He said to Jason, "What do you suppose he wants us for?"

"Probably to discuss the hotel and the finances. Things aren't getting any better in this Panic, you know."

"I don't have a damned cent in that business," said Lionel, "so why is he calling for me?"

"Come on, and we'll find out." Jason was impatient. He had been in the kitchen for half an hour—a place he loved— and had tasted and approved a new dish the youngest recruit had invented. Unlike Lionel, he enjoyed food and had subtle discrimination. The menu was definitely improving since the new arrival in the kitchen, with touches of wine here and there, and brandy on duck. The Inn-Tavern's reputation was at its highest, in spite of the Panic. That is, the dining room was comfortably full except for Monday, but there were no longer many late guests for supper. Sometimes, at ten o'clock, there would be hardly more than a dozen people at the tables. Jason had introduced a very elegant addition to the dining room, a pianist and a violinist of fair competence, and this was much admired and appreciated. But recently these musicians were engaged only for Saturday and Sunday nights, much to Jason's regret and his sympathy for the employees.

This was a Wednesday evening, and again the dining room was practically full except for a table near the kitchen door. Jason sighed at the silent piano. The musician had wept when he had been told that he would play but two nights "for a while," and had mentioned his five children. Jason had put a five-dollar gold piece into the man's hand and then had run off to escape gratitude.

Mr. Mulligan's office was very cramped and dark—for it had no window—and smelled of dust, old paper, and ancient plaster. It was equipped with Mr. Mulligan's rolltop desk, reminiscent of Sister Agatha's with its crowded pigeonholes and general clutter, a set of filing cabinets always half-open, and a table which caught the overflow from the desk, and another small table at one side where Mr. Mulligan's "typewriter" sat six days a week, writing Mr. Mulligan's business letters, desperately trying to reduce the daily devastations of the files, and answering his telephone. It was also her duty to keep the office clean, to wash the globes of the gaslit chandelier hanging from the mildewed ceiling, and to carry messages to various places in the hotel when the matter was urgent. She had done her best on the faded Brussels rug in a turkey-red shade, and this was the real cause of the dusty atmosphere.

The "typewriter" was Molly Nolan, and Pat called her "the smartest girl I ever knew. Does everything right." He had had a male clerk previously, a pimpled youth who had a habit of falling asleep several times a day, and another habit of slinking out to the kitchen to snatch food at odd moments, though he was obese, and, as Mr. Mulligan said, "damned stupid." Mr. Mulligan equated fatness with stupidity, but no one had courage or malice enough to indicate that he himself was hardly a skeleton, except, of course, his daughter, Patricia.

Lionel fully expected to see Patricia there when he entered the office, but to his profound relief there was only Molly, busily clacking away at her two-tiered typewriter, and a stranger, a man, about thirty years old. He was sitting near Patrick, who was swinging on his swivel chair, and he did not seem to resent the stiff old chair in which he sat, though he was obviously a young man of substance. He turned his head as the two young men entered, and regarded them with sharp interest.

"Boys," said Patrick, his rosy face happy and pleased, "meet my favorite nevvy, Daniel Dugan, from Philadelphia. Danny, this big black Irisher is Jason Garrity, and the one whose hair looks like a burning bush is that rascal Lionel Nolan. Couldn't get along without them." His voice was rich and heavy with brogue, and there was a bottle of whiskey on his heaped desk and it was evident that he had been sampling the liquor in unusual quantities.

Daniel Dugan rose and shook hands with the two young men. "Uncle Pat's been telling me a lot about you over the past two days. Glad to make your acquaintances." He stood, smiling at them, tall and broad-shouldered and as at ease as only an urban man of some competence and considerable education and poise could be. Though his movements were measured, he gave the impression of agility and great strength and innate self-control. His expensive boots shone like black glass. He wore a loose jacket of fine gray flannel, but apparently there was something unrestrained in his nature, for his trousers were of a violent and very large green-white-and-maroon plaid. His linen was immaculate and heavily starched, and his red tie bore a tie pin in which was set a flamboyantly big diamond, which winked in the gaslight. His watch chain had many trinkets, including a Phi Beta Kappa key. His cufflinks were also set with diamonds and there was a diamond ring on his big left hand.

He had a blunt rectangular face, and the flesh was firm and slightly browned, as if he had spent much time in the sun. This implied that he was an athlete, an impression enhanced by his disciplined movements. He had prominent eyes the color of shining brown marble, and they were penetrating and restless under thick arched brows. His nose was very Irish, strong, short, and a little wide, with flaring nostrils. His mouth was unusually pink for a man's and very sensual, and he had magnificent white teeth, which he was displaying now to Jason and Lionel. His wavy brown hair was thick and glossy.

Jason thought, as his hand still tingled from the other's emphatic clasp, that here was a man who was not as friendly and as amiable as he appeared, and that under certain circumstances he could be ruthless and daunting and without compromise. He was a man to be feared. I don't like him, Jason thought. I wouldn't want to get in his way.

But Lionel was more impressed. He, too, had come to the same conclusion as Jason; however, he felt only admiration and respect for Daniel Dugan. He was more than worth pleasing.

Both young men were still wondering why they had been called from their duties to meet this paragon of importance and wealth. The typewriter clacked away like a score of castanets. Molly gave all her attention to it, her riot of red curls tied back with a huge blue ribbon. Her tall slender body rested, with her brother's alertness, on her chair; her waist was firm yet delicate, and encircled by a broad gleaming belt of patent leather with a brass buckle. She wore a neat if coarse shirtwaist of unblemished white cotton, with pearl buttons and a loose black tie, and her brown skirt had no wrinkles in it. She had beautiful feet and hands, which Daniel Dugan had observed with appreciation when meeting her.

This appreciation had increased at the sight of her scrubbed face with its bright freckles, its impudent snub nose, its pretty, resolute mouth and small white teeth, and, above all, her unusual eyes, the color of fresh honey, large and honest and direct. Here, he had thought, was a young lady of breeding and wit and bravery, one whom the world would never conquer. Daniel liked brave men and women. He had no patience for the weak, the uncertain, the tentative. He saw that Molly looked at life clearly and openly and would never be deceived. She also had the strength of integrity and disillusioned innocence. Compared with Molly, his cousin Patricia was colorless and without the vitality this girl possessed in unusual quantity. There was a verve emanating from her, an intrepid verve which would meet evil head-on and probably rout it.

"Sit down, sit down, buckos!" exclaimed Patrick, his hearty voice somewhat blurred. "Bring up the chairs! This nevvy of mine," and he jerked his thick thumb at Daniel, "is named for me, his middle name, Patrick. His dad did that, and a grand man he was, Mike Dugan, may his soul rest in peace. My brother-in-law. Married to my sister, and I never knew why, a measly colleen with a whining voice, and airs. My God, her airs! Worse than her sister, that Episcopalian. Not that I've got anything against Episcopalians," Patrick continued, waving his hand largely in a gesture of tolerance. "But that sister made a joke of her new religion, that she did." He beamed at Daniel with moist affection. "If this lad weren't my nevvy, and Patricia's cousin, I'd arrange a marriage, then."

Daniel laughed. He had a deep loud laugh, but it was not offensive. It often inspired trust in others.

"Almost got disbarred in Philly," Patrick went on, as if this had been something to be proud of in some fashion. "Too sharp for those Philadelphia lawyers you hear about. Sharp as a needle, Danny. Knew more law and how to get around it than a barrel of lawyers, there in Philly. Got to know most of the judges, too. A politician, like all us Irishers. That's what got him in trouble."

"Uncle Pat..." said Daniel, and his wide smile was not too pleasant. But he winked at the silent young men seated near him. "My uncle can exaggerate at times."

"I do, eh?" Patrick bellowed, and reached out and slapped his nephew vehemently on the shoulder. "Who diddled the chief of police, eh, with a nice fat bribe!" He beamed at Jason and Lionel. "Couldn't prove it, though. Danny's got too many friends. Danny's a criminal lawyer, knows all the tricks. That's what vexed the lads in Philly. Well, then, and it's a happy man I am! Danny's going to handle all my affairs, legal and"—Patrick chuckled juicily—"and illegal. For a long time, perhaps, until things cool down in Philly and he can run for Congress. Need him in this business, what with the new hotel and all. I've got ideas. I'm not going to stop with this Inn-Tavern and the Ipswich House, though God knows when it'll be ready, with this Panic. Can't get credit for love nor money. Country's in bad shape, and that it is. Well, then. Danny will be here for a long time."

Molly had been listening intently. The clacking slowed on the typewriter. She pretended to be absorbed, at last, in a file on her table. She had seen her brother's pallor when he entered the room, had seen the fright in his eyes, and had wondered with a quick spasm of dread in her heart. She had never seen him apprehensive before. What had he expected in this room? An accuser? But of what? She knew her brother very well; he would never be guilty of small, or even big, pilfering. But she knew he was exigent and often reckless, in spite of his natural caution. A cold uneasiness came to her in this small, stifling room. Then she looked at the silent Jason, and her heart was full of pain. She had hoped, when taking this position for five dollars a week, that he would come to notice her and eventually like and admire her. This had not happened. When he came across her, he would look at her remotely if courteously, but he never stopped for a word, and rarely smiled at her. It was as if she did not exist for him, and Molly, with grief and despair, guessed that she, indeed, had no impact on him at all. Lionel, with brotherly malice, had hinted that Jason was "mad about" Patricia Mulligan, who, in Molly's opinion, was a dreary girl of no character and certainly not pretty, and who possessed a voice like tin struck by a pencil. She was also, Molly would tell herself bitterly, stupid if sly. But Molly, unlike others, had noticed that Patricia sometimes had a piercing gleam in her agate eyes, a calculation.

"Well," said Patrick with jovial impatience, "aren't you buckos going to say something about all this?"

Jason colored with embarrassment. He had been studying Daniel very closely, and his dislike for the older man had increased. "What is there to say, Mr. Mulligan? I'm just your assistant, and Lionel here manages the kitchen and the din-

151

ing room. Are you asking us for our opinion about this...this new arrangement?"

Patrick scratched his neck. "Well, then. I just wanted Danny to meet you. You're important boys here, and are going to be more important—if that damned hotel ever gets built." He looked at Lionel. "Anything to say?"

Lionel smiled. His admiration for Daniel had become intense. He bowed his head quickly. "We are glad you will be here, Mr. Dugan. Of course we know that, with the new hotel, and expansion, Mr. Mulligan will need all the assistance he can get, an experienced lawyer and"—he looked inquiringly at Daniel—"business administrator?"

"Yes," said Daniel. He had not underestimated this young man with the swift comprehension and ingratiating manner. This one would bear watching. But he was more interested in the quiet Jason, and curious. He had sensed the tight malaise in Jason; he had seen bitterness in that strong mouth; he had more than guessed at a maturity beyond Jason's actual age. Life would never hurt such as Lionel. Not so with Jason Garrity.

Patrick puffed at a very huge and rancid cigar. Daniel produced a silver case of cigarettes and lit one. Jason's embarrassment grew. He said, "I must get back, Mr. Mulligan. We were taking inventory of the linens and inspecting the rooms. We're expecting the summer people."

"All right, then, all right, you young buckos can go. Just wanted Danny here to meet you, seeing we'll all be working together." He smiled happily at his nephew. "Rumors got around about the new hotel, and now we've got a few summer people from the big cities coming in for a week or two at a time. Sharpies, they look like. But gentlemen. Walk around up the mountain. They bring their wives, or doxies, too."

Mr. Mulligan did not often watch his language when Molly was present. He knew that the girl was no innocent, that she had a mind like a man's. So he was very fond of her, very open with her, and felt paternal toward her. A nice girl, and no fool. A real lady, one with whom a man could be honest and not watch every word he said. She had brought much order to his slovenly office, and her bookkeeping was perfect. He would give her an extra dollar a week beginning Saturday, though the wages of a "typewriter" in Belleville averaged much less than that. She had been working for him for two months, and he appreciated and relied on her. Sometimes he would pat her shoulder, but it was a fatherly pat and she never resented it. Lionel bowed deeply to Daniel, and Jason nodded briefly, and the two young men left the room.

Patrick poured another drink for himself and his nephew. "What do you think of them, then, eh?"

Daniel glanced at the absorbed Molly, whom he had noticed had not turned a page in the folder for several minutes. He inclined his head toward her, and Pat said, "Molly, love, would you leave us alone for a few minutes?"

Molly rose at once, and without a glance, left the room. "Lionel's her brother," Patrick said. "How'd you know it?"

"The resemblance, of course, Uncle Pat. And the way they looked at each other. Now, that Lionel. He was frightened when he came in here. The interesting question is, why? I don't trust him. He's not one who'd ever get his hand in the till. Too careful of himself for petty business. You could even trust him around the safe. He'll serve you well—as long as it serves his own interest. He would never diddle you. Not that his conscience would bother him. It's just that he's after bigger things than petty larceny, or even big larceny. But he's a trickster, for all that. He's got a criminal's soul, but he would never be involved in anything questionable. It would all be nice and legal."

Patrick scratched his nose thoughtfully. "Well, I had an idea about that when he was just a spalpeen. I gather you don't like him?"

"Of course I don't. But that won't interfere with my appreciation of his cleverness and his real value to you. He's got imagination. He's a runner. The other chap is inclined to plod, under ordinary conditions. No, I don't like your Lionel. I'll be watching all the time. A very complicated character, and complicated characters interest me. Criminals are fascinating. They've got gusto, the big ones, and Lionel's a big one."

Patrick grinned. He said, without malice, "You recognized a kindred spirit, then?"

Daniel smiled. "A big criminal is quite a study. All our important and powerful entrepreneurs are like Lionel Nolan. And gentlemen, all, though even the president fears them. It's the little criminals I resent and hate, the little mice and rats, with no brains, no courage, no derring-do, no intellect. They're hardly human. Yes, your Lionel will go far and be very valuable to you. As long as you are valuable to him."

"Hum," said Patrick. He blew out a huge cloud of noxious smoke. "And what of Jason Garrity?"

Daniel reflected. "I like that young man. I admire him. There is a rock of rectitude and honor. He's not clever and volatile like Lionel. But his mind is far superior. He's not self-serving; you could trust him with your life. He's the kind great saints are made of, and generals, but never politicians. Ambitious, yes. But always with honor. It'll take him longer to get where he wants to go than it will take Lionel. But he'll be a fixture. The other's a dancer, a prancer. Jason never even danced in his soul." Daniel paused. "There's something there I encountered only once before, and I still remember it, though I was only about eighteen at the time. It was when my dad and I took the long tour of Europe, during my holidays from Groton. I met an old priest in a tiny village in Italy. The poor people thought he was a saint. He was, too." Daniel's expressive face changed, became almost somber. Then he shrugged. "Saintliness can be hard to endure for more than a minute or two. Your Jason's no saint. There's violence in him, hidden and held, but there. There's bitterness in him, too. And he's very perceptive. But...he can be deceived, especially if he loves someone."

"He'll be your right-hand man, Uncle Pat. You can stake your life on that. You can rest easy with Jason Garrity. Meanness is beyond him. It is impossible for him to betray anyone. A good man, and when I say that, it is an accolade.

"I like him. But he doesn't like me. The other does. We'll see."

"He's got a brother who's studying for the priesthood." Patrick laughed. "Now, there is one of your real rogues. Jack Garrity. Looks like a monk hoping everyone else is going to burn in hellfire. Gives me chills when I see him. His grandda told me about him. He detests the lad, and no wonder. Yet he was never in trouble, that Jack, and all the nuns loved him and predicted great things for him. Jase doesn't love him much, and I think Jack *hates* him."

Patrick sank into momentary thought. Then he said, "I'm going to have Jason marry Patricia. I love him like a son."

"Oh?" said Daniel, sitting up with interest. "Are they engaged?"

Patrick frowned. "Now, then. Patricia is a very strict little girl, and loves her dada. Told me she doesn't want to marry and leave me. I keep mentioning Jason, and she turns up her nose. But she'll marry him, and that I am going to make sure of. He is just what she needs. I have only to say the word."

Daniel doubted that. He knew his cousin very well. Like

154

all her kind, she could be very obstinate, and her father adored her. It would take a mighty effort to get her to marry Jason Garrity, a very mighty effort. He said, "I've noticed she is blooming, Uncle Pat. Really maturing. She's got a kind of glow she never had before. It makes her pretty, and Patricia is no beauty, you know, even if you think so. Aunt Moira introduced her to many young men of family and money in Philadelphia, and gave parties for her. But the young men weren't interested. Now, I'm not trying to insult you. I'm just giving you facts. Patricia's no siren. She hasn't any charm. Let's be honest. She's got style, which she was taught, and she'll make a very shrewd wife for someone, and knows her pennies. A pragmatic girl"—even if she has no spirit or real character, Daniel added to himself, and no real virtues. She's not like that Molly girl, sad to say. He had never met anyone like Molly Nolan before, at least not any woman. He smiled faintly to himself.

Patrick was annoyed. "You never did like my girl," he said. "Not even when she was a toddler and you were fourteen years old."

Daniel came suddenly back to his present situation. "Oh, after all, could you expect a young boy to notice a baby? No. I am trying to tell you that there is a lot to admire in Patricia. She'll make an excellent wife, watching out always for her husband's interests, which she'll make her own. I know you think of Patricia as a soft little girl, but she isn't, Uncle Pat. There's granite in her, somewhere, believe me." He had a sudden thought, and was surprised. "And I'll tell you something else about Patricia. If she ever falls in love, it'll be for life. No flightiness about her, except superficially."

Patrick was appeased. Yet, he felt some uneasiness. Patricia had become very absentminded of late. She often smiled to herself, and her smile was excited. And as Daniel had said, she had taken on a sudden and noticeable bloom. She had become softer in speech, and her eyes sparkled. Patrick had heard her sing early in the morning, when she usually was the most irritable.

Daniel said, "Yes, she'll make a very loving, if very practical, wife. I hardly knew her this time. She looks like a woman in love."

Patrick laughed. "I hope it's Jason. Even if it isn't, I'll make it so. It can't be some bucko in Philadelphia. She'd mention it fast enough if it was. And she never gets any letters, except from her aunts. And she doesn't go out with any young fella in Belleville, at least not often. She doesn't like the fellas she knows here. They send her flowers and candy and she never even looks at them. She knows I want her to get married; she's old enough. And she'd tell me if there was anyone. No. I think she is just thinking of a wedding. We'll put Jason there as the groom."

Well, thought Daniel. Perhaps. He was amused at himself when he thought: I hope for Jason's sake that Uncle Pat doesn't succeed.

There was a knock on the door, and Molly entered. "May I come in?" she said.

"Seems like you're already in, Molly, love," said Patrick, and his kind face beamed brightly. "Now, love, will you get me out the Schultz folder? I want to discuss some things here with Mr. Dugan."

Molly passed Daniel on the way to the files. She moved lithely, he noticed, like her brother. And she had a lovely rear, like a young Psyche, full of innocent seductiveness. The movement of her thighs under the poor brown skirt was supple and enticing. It was most evident she did not know this. She had no voluptuousness that was overt, but it was there just the same, for all her slenderness. Daniel was charmed. He was more than charmed. And he was interested by his own emotions. Not a beautiful girl by any standards, but there was something alluring about her, something strong yet pliant. When she came to the desk to lay the folder before Patrick, Daniel noticed her hands again. And he wanted to take them and hold them against his cheek.

That she was unaware of him, and did not look at his virile handsomeness as all other women did, and had never once smiled at him, stirred him. He thought of the girl in Philadelphia to whom he was tentatively engaged, and she was suddenly vapid and without form. He could hardly remember her features now. She was dissolving in his memory.

Patricia, fulfilling Lionel's expectation, had "made the first move." She appeared in the dining room with her father on Sunday, almost two months before her father arranged the meeting with Daniel in his study, meticulously arrayed in a blue lace dress draped enticingly about her narrow hips and over her bosom, which had acquired extra padding. This enhanced her waist. She wore blue silk shoes and silk stockings. Her pompadour was really enormous, and shining, and upheld by tortoiseshell combs studded with blue stones. One tubelike curl was permitted to lie on her shoulder, and her lavaliere, very dainty, was of gold inlaid with diamonds and aquamarines, as was her bracelet. She, indeed, had style and taste, and her nondescript face had a pretty glow in the light of the chandeliers. Lionel was impressed, and pleased, and for the first time felt a quick desire for the girl, which made him inwardly laugh at himself.

She pretended to be haughtily unaware of Lionel as he bowed and presented her with the menu. She looked about the dining room with pretended ennui. It was too early— Patrick had planned this—for the Sunday-evening guests, who were in the rear bars or upstairs in the private dining rooms drinking and discreetly roistering. The diners were still few, and rather elderly and very decorous.

"The duck with brandy and oranges is very special today," Lionel murmured to her. Patricia gave her father a quick glance; then, seeing he was bowing and smiling to some guests, she whispered to Lionel, "In the glade? Later?"

Lionel also glanced at Patrick. He whispered in a very fast tone, "This is my day. I will be here late. Next Sunday? I will be off then."

Patricia had not known of the Sunday arrangements. Her bright color faded a little with disappointment. Then she nodded. Patrick turned to his daughter. "We have a grand chef, young and with ideas. Try the duck, love. And the burgandy. My special vintage." He said to Lionel, "Jason left yet?"

"Yes, sir. An hour ago."

Patrick felt his own disappointment. He said with unusual irritation, "I don't know you young fellas. Always running off." But Patricia was relieved. She simply could not bear that lout, so big and stupidly silent and always staring at her. She knew her father wanted her to look on him kindly as a possible husband, and this outraged her. Her father just didn't have any sense, to think that his daughter would even consider such an oaf. Why, she had been courted in Philadelphia by young men of the very best society! She had not encouraged them, of course. Patricia, like almost all of humanity, had the human capacity to deceive and flatter herself.

Patrick, always perceptive, noticed that his daughter's glow had faded somewhat. He said, with solicitude, "Not feeling well, love? If so, we'll leave. There's a good dinner at home."

Patricia was jolted. Leave Lionel? Even if he were only in

the room as the headwaiter, his presence, however directed to others than herself, was a source of contentment and tenderness. At least she could watch him. She said, almost sweetly, "No, Dada. It is just the heat. I feel...rosy." Ladies did not sweat. Gentlemen perspired. Ladies became "rosy." She glanced up at the slowly rotating fans on the ceiling. Patrick had lately installed electricity even in the chandeliers, which now had too hard a light. The fans created a hot breeze. Patricia's neck became wet. She wiped it daintily with a perfumed handkerchief; then, as she consulted Lionel again, she discreetly permitted him to have a waft of the carnation perfume. Lionel thought of death; for some reason carnations were always at funerals, pungent and overpowering. He wrinkled his pointed nose, but smiled.

"I think, Dada," she said, "that I'll have the chicken broth and the broiled bass." A lady always pretended she had little interest in food; her physical necessities were never gross. Patricia had a great appetite, but never revealed it. "And only a little lettuce, with lemon juice and oil." Her mouth watered. She would have dearly loved the luscious duck and mashed potatoes and dressing. But Lionel would be offended by such plebeian taste. Later, at home, she would have cold beef sandwiches and would pilfer one of the servants' bottles of beer, and some pickles and vinegar-flavored onions and cucumbers, and a slab of huckleberry pie and a lot of coffee. Later would come tea itself, with attendant pastries. Patrick, of course, would be at the Inn-Tavern, and she could eat in peace and savor every morsel. Patricia was really a hearty girl. But she could never gain weight, as was the fashion, and her legs were long and slender and not fleshy as other girls' legs were. She craved fat. She lingered over newspaper drawings of Lillian Russell, so enticing with her white double chin and portly little arms. Patricia hated her own height and thinness. She had noticed that gentlemen were attracted to obese girls, especially if they were short. "No higher than my heart!" as the song went. She hated her eyes. "Five-foot-two, eyes of blue"—again the popular song. She envied her father for his bright blue eyes. Why could she not have inherited them? Why did she look like her dead mother, who had been so unfashionable. That her mother had been soignée, she did not know.

Patricia's face became discontented as she surveyed the chicken broth put before her. She drank it, her little finger stiffly thrust out. She did not know it was a vulgar affectation.

Patrick said, with concern, "You're not hungry, love? Do you feel unwell?"

"Oh, Dada," she said with impatience, "you know I have no appetite."

Patrick sighed. "You should fill up, Patricia. You look like a girl of thirteen." Patricia flushed with vexation. She knew that only too well.

Lionel, with great ceremony, came back with two small slivers of broiled bass with a slice of lemon. Patricia closed her eyes for a moment. She kept swallowing water. Then Lionel presented her with a dish of hot buttered mashed potatoes, and her stomach lurched. She took a small spoonful. There were fresh peas. Another austere spoonful. There was scrapple. She shook her head, and her stomach protested and grumbled. She loved rich cream on lettuce. She poured a little oil on it, and squeezed a drop of lemon on the green leaves. Her hunger grew. But when she looked at Lionel, she was overwhelmed with sweetness and innocent desire and her eyes became wet with love and longing. She almost forgot her hunger. Her father, of course, had an immense slab of hot red beef and gravy, and he heaped his plate with a mountainous serving of mashed potatoes and peas, and he was also devouring cornbread muffins with melting, dripping butter and taking vast drafts of wine to wash it all down. Patricia felt faint. When he had a side dish of scrapple, she became fainter. It was one of her favorite dishes, especially with maple syrup.

For dessert she had a few scarlet strawberries dusted with fine sugar. Patrick had a truly gigantic slab of hot apple pie surmounted with ice cream, a dish newly fashionable. Pie à la mode, it was called. Patricia adored it.

But she was certain Lionel admired her for her ladylike lack of appetite. She did not know he was thinking: That girl has no bowels. Maybe she hasn't anything else, either. The thought made him smile. Perhaps, soon, he would find out for himself. He wondered if her bones would bruise him. But...there was Patrick. Lionel knew how to be careful. He would use the girl for his own purposes, but Patrick must never know. That would result in his instant dismissal, the end of his dream.

Patricia was torn between two desires—to rush home and gorge, or linger to look at Lionel. It was a measure of her yearning love that she preferred to see Lionel and suppressed her urge to run to the kitchen at home, while the servants

159

dozed in their third-floor hot rooms sleeping off their own heavy dinner. Later, later. She was sick with hunger—and love. It was true that Lionel was only a glorified waiter, but she had begun to delude herself that he was really a prince in disguise. He did not even look Irish, she would think with happiness. He looked like an Englishman. He was so elegant; he had such graceful gestures. He spoke like a gentleman. She remembered her father's stories that most Irishmen—except Dada, of course—were convinced they were descended from Irish kings. She believed it. Dada was only a peasant. As for that clodhopper Jason Garrity, he, too, was a peasant, with such big hands and feet and gloomy, craggy face. But Lionel, to Patricia, looked like a thoroughbred horse.

Patrick looked at his watch. "Time to go, love," he said, as he patted his lips. He wanted to get back to his guests in the lounge.

Patricia rose. Now her hunger was impelling. Lionel materialized from the front of the room and slowly helped her put her white feather boa over her shoulders. She looked at him from under her lashes. Her heart trembled with bliss. As if he knew, he pressed her upper arm as he arranged the boa. Patricia closed her eyes for a moment, swimming in ecstasy and with what she did not know was healthy lust. Her face was luminous under the wide blue silk hat with the pink silk roses on it.

Driving home in the new Oldsmobile, which snorted and exploded and belched out smoke, she sat in a dream, smiling, and her thin lips became lustrous. Once there, and Patrick gone back to the Inn-Tavern, she rushed to the kitchen and devoured quantities of food, standing by the icebox in an ecstasy of voraciousness. She drank two bottles of beer; then, unusually sleepy, she went upstairs to her huge ornate bedroom and fell on the bed, to dream of Lionel.

Daniel Dugan sat in the narrow Mulligan garden and smoked, and thought about the new hotel. Nothing moved there. The whole damned country had come to a stricken standstill. He thought of the hunger riots in the streets. He thought of the foreclosed houses and frantic people selling their goods, or finding their claptrap furniture on the street. He was not a man of compassion, but he did think of the starving faces of women and children, encountered everywhere.

He knew the causes, and he felt a deep hatred and anger.

He knew what was in the air. The Panic had been contrived. It had been arranged several years ago, and Daniel knew why. War. Or slavery. Perhaps both. He himself would profit, but he was not old enough as yet for this to give him full satisfaction. That would come later.

From somewhere in the neighborhood came a doleful wailing of a gramophone that delivered a popular song, a negro spiritual:

> O Lord, remember the rich and remember the poor,
> Remember the bond an' the free.
> And when you done rememberin' all 'round,
> Then, O Lord, remember me!

Yes, indeed, thought Daniel Patrick Dugan sourly. Yes, indeed.

A soft wind suddenly swept the warm garden and the street outside, and Daniel heard the startled jingling of the Chinese wind crystals that hung on every porch. Then there was silence again except for the distant clatter of wheels, a drowsy clatter. Everything was so still, so warm, so shimmering with yellow sun, so peaceful.

What an innocent country we still are, in spite of the politicians, thought Daniel. Regrettably, it won't last much longer. Regrettable?

Not for people like me! thought Daniel Patrick Dugan.

12

To Patricia, the long days crawled to the next Sunday. She counted each hour. What if it rained? She prayed ardently for the first time in her life that it would not rain. She even visited the Blessed Sacrament on Friday to make that naive petition. She amused herself by considering what clothes she would wear. As she did so, she hummed:

Sad news; bad news;
Anything but glad news!
What do you suppose they're saying
At the fashion show?
They declare the shirtwaist girl
Must pack her trunk and go!

But even in Philadelphia and New York they were still wearing shirtwaists, according to the *Bazaar* and *Mode*. Really, she mused, she couldn't go on her bicycle in a plain frock, and certainly not in an afternoon dress. She pondered if she should take her buggy. Then there would have to be an explanation to the stableboy, who reported to Patrick whenever Patricia used her vehicle. Patrick was under the happy delusion that as females were so weak, they could not go far on a bicycle; they had not the strength for it. But a buggy was a different matter. For the first time Patricia was faced with a dilemma common to other girls: how to hoodwink a guarding father, how to go to a rendezvous furtively. She had heard of rendezvous; very romantic. The lovelorn damsel rushing into her lover's arms. Beyond the "rushing," she knew nothing. The lover's arms were all that mattered, and Patricia tingled, then shivered with a nameless anticipation.

She decided on her best silk shirtwaist, green, with puffed sleeves and a high ruched collar and much tucking over the bosom, and lace at the wrists. With it she would wear her white duck skirt, daringly cut to the ankles, and a silver belt, and white slippers. The shirtwaist had cost, said Patrick, a fortune—twenty-five dollars—and had been imported from New York. But it was all handmade, all hand-tucked. Even the lace at the wrists was "real" and was not the cheap machine-made kind. The garment was crepe de chine of a very superior kind. "A man could buy the finest overcoat for winter, for that," Patrick had said ruefully, remembering the Panic now devastating the country. Patricia had shrugged.

With the outfit finally determined, Patricia looked over her jewelry. Mama's large cameo for the throat, with a rim of tiny diamonds and emeralds. And her pearl earrings. She had a new watch, too, to be pinned on the shirtwaist. Patrick had given it to her on her recent birthday, and it was very small, though heavy, and the pin was an enameled butterfly with ruby eyes. Gloves? That was a serious question. Gloves it was, then. A lady did not go to a rendezvous gloveless.

All week long Patricia had expanded like a rosebud. Her cheeks glowed with new color; her lips became ardently pink, thin and tight though they were. Her brown hair took on a gloss, and her eyes widened, showing golden specks in their agate depths. Daniel, who lived with the Mulligans while he looked for a house for himself, regarded her with amusement. Miss Prim was beginning to look very naughty; she had an exalted appearance, as if preparing herself for bed. An unknown lover? That, of course, was impossible in this dreadful little town, impossible for a protected girl like Patricia, who probably had not the slightest idea about sexual congress. She wouldn't even know the words, thought Daniel. He would watch his cousin covertly. She had begun to move like a woman suddenly conscious of her thighs for the first time. His disillusioned eye had perceived that the newly swelling bosom was not entirely natural. Well, he would think, good for the poor homely little thing, so long as she doesn't bring a bundle home. By Friday he no longer believed that it was impossible that Patricia had a lover unknown to her father. I hope it's no one disreputable, for Uncle Pat's sake, he said to himself. But girls did not sneak off with respectable and approved young men. So it was most likely an unacceptable scoundrel, and for a moment or two Daniel felt uneasy. Should he hint something to Uncle Pat? No, he finally decided. Let the girl have her fun—provided she had the sense not to go too far. Daniel was somewhat afraid that Patricia did not have this sense. Well, it was no business of his. He was a selfish young man who prudently minded his own affairs.

He began to watch Patricia, however. Patrick said to his daughter on Saturday, "Looking forward to tomorrow to have dinner with me again, love, at the Inn-Tavern?"

To his surprise, Patricia looked undecided, a new deceit of hers. Then she shook her head. "I think not, Dada, not tomorrow. I've had a headache the last day or two. I think I'll stay home and rest." Daniel looked on with amusement. He saw that she fluttered her short eyelashes demurely. "Take a tablet of that new aspirin," said Patrick, worried. Patricia promised she would, and tried to appear fragile.

Because of the "headache," she was excused from attending Mass on Sunday, a rare thing. But Patrick, who stayed home for Sunday dinner, was cheered that his daughter had quite recovered at noon, when Mass was safely over. Daniel was always inwardly hilarious at Patricia's enormous appetite, though Patrick insisted that she "ate like a bird." After dinner, in the warm still afternoon, Patrick went up for a nap. Daniel said to his cousin, "Would you like to take a walk, Patty?" He was the only one who "vulgarized" her name.

She said, with haste, "Oh, no thanks, Daniel. I think I'll take a nap, like Dada." There was an apprehensive glint in her eyes as she stared at him. But he said with kindness, "Well, so I will take a walk alone. I'd like to look at the hotel again, on the mountain, though God knows when it will ever be finished." Patricia sighed deeply. She did not like or trust Daniel, but this time she gave him such a happy smile that he was touched. He wanted to say to her, "Take care, Patty old dear, take care." But he refrained. Why weren't girls, these modern days, informed about the result of indiscretions? This wasn't the age of Lincoln, for Christ's sake. It was the new twentieth century. The young ladies he frequented, some younger than Patricia, were well-informed indeed.

Patricia carefully covered her light costume with her duster, put on a sailor hat with a red ribbon, and a heavy veil to protect her complexion, pulled on her best white kidskin gloves, and crept down the stairs, avoiding every step that might creak. She heard the snoring of her father and relaxed. She looked for Daniel and saw the smoke of his pipe in the garden. So, she was safe. No servants were around in the hot Sunday quiet.

Her bicycle was in a shed behind the house. She wheeled it out. Once on the street, she mounted it and swiftly pedaled off. The streets were deserted. There was no sound but the dry rustling of trees and an occasional whining of a phonograph or the mechanical tinkling of a player piano. Sunday in Belleville was truly a torpid day of rest, religiously kept.

No children skated, laughed or shouted, or played ball. Instead they rocked silently on porches, smoothing dolls or reading an improving book, or moved with prim sedateness in back gardens, or sat miserably on the curbs shuffling the dust in the gutters with their feet. Everyone hated Sundays, if he was young, and especially if it were summer. Local stores were tightly closed, shades drawn, awnings up, and passersby saw only languid reflections of themselves on glass. Patricia loathed Sundays. One could "call" on "at homes," but she found these visits dull, sipping lukewarm tea and eating damp sandwiches and tasteless pastries, and talking about politics and scandals.

The one other permissible Sunday activity was a picnic. Anyone who had a carriage or a buggy or other vehicle was out on the road looking for picnic spots, which Patricia found equally as depressing, with hordes of children, baskets of cold fried chicken, potato salad, greasy ham sandwiches, crumbly cake, milk, flies, bees, hornets, ants, and mosquitoes. Patricia, as she pedaled, did not escape the dust of the well-traveled road, and soon there was a yellowish deposit on her duster and on the beautiful white kid gloves. She kept shaking it off. She was hot under her veil, but the sun was burning, and no lady ever had sunburn, or, heaven forbid! did she ever acquire a parched, tanned complexion. Her eyes began to smart even in the shade of the white straw sailor hat. She was becoming too "rosy." Carriages and buggies clomped past her and automobiles belched a stench of gasoline in her face. Patricia kept blinking her eyes free to search for the entrance to the glade. It seemed to elude her. What if there were picnickers there, too, with their screaming children, dogs, and baskets and tablecloths on the grass? She felt outrage that such a lovely place would be violated. Then, just as she was getting desperate, she saw the narrow opening between the trees and brush.

She dismounted, looked about her at the traffic, then wheeled her bicycle through the breech, walking on tiptoe as if frightened of causing any noise. She found the glade, and murmured a sound of thanksgiving that no one was there. The trees thick, the grass tall, and the fragrance of the hot grass and wildflowers floated intoxicatingly on the air. Beyond, the green-and-purple mountains were painted against a sky too brilliant for the eye to endure. Patricia took off her duster, veiling, hat, and gloves and shook them. The disturbed dust made her sneeze. She was dismayed. She had earlier coated her nose and chin with rice powder, but had forgotten to bring the bag. Carefully she wiped her nose and wet eyes.

Lionel was not here as yet. She consulted her watch. Half-past two. For a terrible instant she wondered if he had forgotten. Or had he another lady-friend? Her heart quailed, then lifted. He had no one like Patricia Eleanor Mulligan, so rich, so stylish, so desirable! She pushed the long pollen-filled harsh grass aside and tramped her feet on what remained, making a hollow.

She sat gingerly and spread her white duck skirt about her to avoid creases, opened her purse, and brought out a little mirror. What she saw therein was an old human illusion: she saw beauty, not real reflection. She puffed up her pompadour, smoothed the long brown curl on her shoulder, assumed a posture of careful grace, and waited, her heart thudding against her spare chest. She heard the muffled rumble of traffic and distant voices; she heard the lethargic drone of insects, the subdued comments of birds too sluggish in the heat to go searching for food.

Patricia, leaning back in her hollow, felt the pressure of her elbows on the flattened grass, the prickling of stiff twig-like stems. But she did not move. She kept her eyes on the break in the wild shrubbery. She looked at her watch again. Had the minute hand crept only ten minutes? It seemed an hour. Still, it was almost three o'clock, and she had learned from her father that the "Sunday lads" left the Inn-Tavern at one. What was keeping Lionel? He ought to have been here nearly forty-five minutes ago, waiting for her, not she for him.

Lionel was making her wait. Let the little fool wonder if he was coming or had forgotten her. He had learned that a lover's promptness received a woman's disdain and made her condescending. But delay made her more eager with concealed relief when he finally arrived. He knew how to time such matters. Women were such imbeciles, except for Joan Garrity and, he admitted, his keen-eyed sister, Molly. Joan might love him passionately, as he loved her, but she was never carried away by her love. She was always there, her magnificent blue eyes seeing everything calmly and coolly even when her hand was warmest, her lips the sweetest. As for Molly, Lionel had never loved his sister, or even liked her, but he respected the steadfast bedrock of her spirit, her inability to deceive, her scornful awareness. He had a suspicion, however, that Molly was far more vulnerable than the crippled Joan, and in this he was correct. Molly, in spite of her inner strength, could be devastated by love, which Joan could not. Merely thinking of Joan made Lionel's whole body throb, but almost with reverence. Joan was sheathed steel. But Molly could be bent under severe circumstances. Lionel, as yet, had never seen her bend, not even when her father—her favorite parent—had died a year ago. Lionel also suspected that under Molly's intrepid exterior, her refusal to compromise on a matter of principle, was the gentlest heart, a heart Joan did not possess. So Lionel had more honest respect for Joan than he had for his sister. He could not imagine Joan melting mawkishly at the sight of a man—not even himself—but he had seen the golden lovelight in Molly's eyes when she encountered Jason Garrity, the helpless drop of her capable hands, the sudden weak aspect of her compact body.

On the few occasions this past week when he had seen Daniel Dugan, he had also seen Molly, and with great alertness and conjecture he had observed that Daniel always greeted Molly in a special tone of voice, and then, as she passed him in the hall, looked long and intently after her. Lionel had carefully put away this most intriguing and possibly valuable piece of information.

People were Lionel's "business." They were participants in a great game on which he could gamble. Only Jason Garrity had ever come close to Lionel in real friendship, and Joan was the only creature he had ever loved. Jason he could trust, and Joan was part of himself. He had known, even as a child, that villains had more in common and were more loyal to each other than were the virtuous. His father, who was rarely profound, had once said, "There are no quarrels in hell; only in heaven." Lionel had wondered, briefly, what unspoken terror had inspired that remark. But he was not to know. His father was too silent a man, and he had never before or after made such a subtle remark. If anything had distinguished that dedicated workingman, it had been his stolid indifference to people, his belief that toil was all. He had left nearly all he had to his wife, some two thousand painfully saved dollars, one hundred dollars for his funeral, and fifty dollars for Masses for his soul. He had never known that his son had thousands of dollars in savings. He might have approved, but he would not have been interested, so long as the source was honest.

These things ran through Lionel's mind like a thin streak of mercury as he pedaled—not too fast—to his meeting with Patricia Mulligan. He never doubted that she was waiting for him. Then, as he neared the entrance to the glade, he went over his planned approach to her. Should he, or should he not, seduce her on this second lonely meeting? He would see. Lionel was seldom precipitous. He tempered all things by nuances. Forcing matters was often disastrous and defeating.

Pedaling along easily, he was suddenly startled by the loud rasping horn as an automobile roared past him. The passengers looked back at him and grinned. With high good nature he yelled, "Get a horse!" They waved at him, and two women jiggled their parasols. No one was offended. Lionel was careful not to offend people.

He found the entrance to the glade. He had picked out landmarks the Sunday he had met Patricia there, and so was not uncertain. Lionel had a very orderly mind. There were rare occasions when he could be reckless, but he always got away in time, and to his advantage, leaving others confused.

He was careful to move as soundlessly as the fox he so resembled, stirring hardly a twig of the scrambled shrubbery and hardly bending the tall grass he crept through. He left his bicycle against a tree and slipped like a tawny shadow to the edge of the glade. There was Patricia in what the poor girl thought a most beguiling posture. She had practiced this sedulously at home, studying reflections in her large mirror. The padding artfully thrust up her tiny breasts. Her legs were extended but bent at the knee to show curves under the duck skirt. Lionel was highly amused, as usual, on encountering human pretensions. He never had compassion, no matter how innocent they were. He studied the unaware girl, and wanted to laugh. It still seemed unbelievable that he had seen passion in those unattractive eyes, on that meager mouth. The rice-powdered nose stuck out glaringly from the pallid complexion. Well, he had seen worse in the cheaper brothels, where starving girls waited hopefully for a dollar or two. Last Sunday, elegantly clothed, Patricia had seemed passable. In less lavish and bejeweled dress today, she seemed more like an ordinary girl than a fine young lady. Still, she was Patricia Mulligan.

He stepped back a few paces, as silent as a drifting leaf, then began to whistle rollickingly. He reached the glade again. Patricia's pale face had turned pink, her eyelids drooped alluringly, her cheeks gained color. She opened her eyes as if greatly startled, but kept her pose.

"Hello," said Lionel in a warm voice. He had a good tenor voice, very lilting, which he often used to advantage. He wore a neat summer suit of light linen, his best, and his straw hat was tilted over one merry eye. Patricia saw him in his Sunday finery from under her eyelids, and her heart pounded very heavily now. She murmured something which she hoped was nonchalant. Lionel advanced on her, removing his hat and revealing the blaze of his hair, which had been carefully combed into glistening waves. His new white shoes were immaculate with chalk.

He sailed his hat on a bush, grinned to show his excellent white teeth, pulled up his trousers so as not to wrinkle them, and in one sinuous movement sat down, crossing his legs. "I didn't expect you today, Miss Mulligan," he said.

Patricia did not know what to say. What did a girl say to her "lover"? She frantically tried to remember romantic phrases from some novels she had read, but she could not recall them.

"Beautiful day, isn't it?" said Lionel. He looked about swiftly for a less open spot where "the dark deed," as the nickelodeons called it, could be consummated. He saw one, some feet to the left of Patricia. He was quite clever in discovering such hidden spots. Would the girl be amenable? Or would she, at a strong overt gesture, get indignantly to her feet, slap his face, and run home to Dada to complain? He studied her closely. He would not be too aggressive. He would let her show him the way, all by her ignorant self, and he would follow very judiciously, alert to genuine resistance. For a moment or two he was bored; then he remembered this would be quite a conquest if he could manage it. Of course, the girl was a virgin, and virgins could be difficult in the clinch, and they always cried—or worse, they screamed. He listened intently to the distant traffic. It would continue for some time, and he could always keep one hand hovering over her mouth to muffle any shriek. Besides, he was too deft and experienced to really hurt her.

He said, "I thought you were the most fascinating lady I had ever seen last Sunday, Miss Mulligan." Then softly he added, "Patty?"

Patricia's breath became choked. "Thank you." She had no coquetry, so it was with sincerity that she added, "And ... today?"

"Lovely, too. But different. You are always different, every time I see you."

Patricia's face glowed quickly, as if light had flashed upon it. She smiled. When she smiled like this, which was rare, there was a certain shy sweetness on her face, and Lionel was pleased. She murmured, "Don't call me Patty." She thought of her cousin who called her that. Then she stammered, "Patsy...perhaps?"

"Charming," said Lionel, and shifted neatly on his buttocks to within a foot of her feet. "It suits you. Devilish." He waited. Patricia's face glowed. How well he understood her! No one else did. For a moment her eyes moistened with self-pity. Lionel imperceptibly moved a little closer. Finally he reached out, as with a timid uncertainty, and put his hand lightly on her ankle. She started like a young deer, began to move her foot, then let it remain. She trembled.

"Forgive me," he said in a very humble tone, though keeping his hand on her foot. "But you have the most delicate...ankles I've ever seen."

"Thank you," she replied in a voice that was genuinely fragile and shaking. His fingers felt hot through her white silk stocking, and a long thrill ran disconcertingly up her leg. More tears came into her eyes, and her breast heaved. She could hardly bear these new sensations, yet longed for more.

Lionel, the expert in seduction, let his hand reach a little higher, and he felt the girl's increased trembling. But she did not recoil. He looked about him, as if absently. "It's hot out here," he said. "You must be uncomfortable...Patsy. Over there, there's more shade, deeper, under those bushes and under that big tree."

Patricia's instincts caused her to pause. A young lady never went into a secluded spot alone with a gentleman. Never. That was very compromising. Suddenly Patricia wanted to be compromised. The fingers were tightening on her calf, urgently, pleadingly. Then Lionel was on his feet, smiling down at her and holding out his hand. She hesitated for a long warning moment, then recklessly gave him her hand and let him pull her to her feet. She let him draw her, stumbling, through the high grass to the shadowy spot. Her whole body was suddenly shaking, and this was both frightening and importunate. Obsessed with sensation, she was vaguely surprised to find herself half-sprawling on thinner and gentler grass, the fronds of a willow drooping about her. Again, she was dimly afraid as she stared at Lionel. He was

170

casually taking off his coat; he carefully laid it at a small distance. Then, laughing happily, he was sitting beside her. He took her hand and said, "This is nicer, isn't it? And no one can see us."

There was a duskiness here, a smell of moss and toadstools, infinitely exciting, like musk, to the entranced Patricia. Lionel had opened her hand. He was slowly and enticingly stroking her palm with one finger, and watching her. More thrills ran up her arm, across her breast, down over her corseted belly, and then to what were referred to as private parts. Shameful, indecent! But how overpowering, how sweetly paralyzing, how tenderly voluptuous! Her eyes, stretched and distended, her mouth open and wet, her throbbing throat, confronted Lionel, and he was full of triumphant satisfaction. This was going to be easy. He had come prepared. But . . . how to prepare under her gaze? Well, that would be easy too; the girl knew nothing. That she was in love with him, most terribly in love, did not occur to him, or, if it did for an instant, he dismissed it as irrelevant. He wanted only to arouse her so he could take her with the least possible difficulty to himself.

Watching her very closely, he slipped his fingers under the lace-covered wrist; he felt the wild throbbing of her pulse. Good. She was ready for more liberties. "What a stylish shirtwaist," he said.

"Silk," she whispered. For the first time in her young life she felt heat in her underdeveloped breasts, a sharp rising against the satin of the camisole, and a frenzied desire for more intimate contact. Lionel was slowly unbuttoning the tiny crystal buttons of the shirtwaist. Patricia moved, distantly shocked; then her whole body became as defenseless as water, and profoundly flaccid. She could hear nothing but the roaring of her heart, compelling, demanding, surrendering.

The camisole was rolled down with gentle mothlike movements, and then Lionel's lips were on a bare little breast. Patricia cried out once, then was helplessly undone. "Beautiful, beautiful," Lionel groaned, and proceeded. Patricia's body arched. When Lionel's hands were on her drawers, untying the ribbons, she blindly and without real volition assisted him. Now his own ready passion was obliterating even his caution. He closed his eyes and thought of Joan. He had his own fantasies. He began to sweat in his urgency. The girl's flesh under his seeking hands was wet also. He unbuttoned his trousers. His cold mind still was in control, however, and he thought: No need to rumple them if I'm careful. He fumbled for something in a pocket and with one hand covered himself with experienced swiftness. Patricia did not see this. His body was above hers, not yet touching. She could see his face, very close, and to her chaotic senses it was the most beloved in all the world.

In the turbulence of her unfamiliar emotions, she was lifted into desiring joy. Her head was on the grass; tears ran down her cheeks. When she felt the weight of Lionel's body on hers, she closed her eyes with rapture; without her knowledge, her arms lifted and enclosed his chest. The heat of his flesh became hers.

Then, without warning, she felt an intense and piercing pain, and was struggling, her legs thrashing, her arms and hands pushing him away in terror. But he was stronger; the pain became more unendurable. She opened her mouth to scream, but a quick hand was on it, smothering her. She was certain she was being killed.

All at once the pain was gone. She could hear Lionel panting in her ear; his sweat mingled with her tears. She saw his face, his eyes shut and teeth clenched. It was a strange, absorbed face, alien yet again exciting. It was then that she felt an explosion of ecstasy, unbearable, blinding, violent beyond all violence, running in tides over her body.

She did not know that Lionel's passion was far more than her own, and that it was the untouched Joan he was deflowering and to whom he was making savage and adoring and total and tumultuous love. It was Joan Garrity's beautiful face he was kissing. It was Joan's full red mouth he was devouring. It was Joan's body he was possessing. His own tears now joined Patricia's, and he cried over and over, "My darling, my love, my darling, darling!" His chest pressed Patricia down; it was as if he were trying to absorb her half-naked body into his, merging it into himself. In the final climax he felt that his blood had joined the blood of Joan, and it was, running riotously together in an ardent stream, rising in a fountain of joy, swelling, engulfing. For a moment he was strangely reverent, awed.

Patricia came to consciousness first. Lionel's arms were gripping her with a pain that was also joyous. She did not feel unclean. She had loved Lionel before; now she loved him with her new womanhood, her new knowledge. He was hers—forever. That he had not made love to her but to another girl never occurred to her, and never would. That he had taken, not herself, but another woman, would have been beyond her comprehension. She was only sure, with elation and selfless delight, that she was loved and that this love would never end. The pragmatic Patricia Mulligan was no longer practical. She loved as a woman, as she would never love again. She would give herself, over and over, with no end to the giving.

She felt Lionel rolling off her body. Leaning on his elbows, he looked down at her with astonishment. He was fully shaken for the first time in his life, and in some peculiar way, felt betrayed. His face was absolutely white; the freckles seemed to start out upon it. He swallowed hard, catching his breath.

But he came back to reality very fast. He covered himself hastily, after removing the object he had put on, burying it in the grass. He reached for his coat, and took a handkerchief from it. He thrust it into Patricia's hand. He averted his eyes from her exalted face. "Here," he muttered. "Wipe yourself."

Patricia thought he was overcome. She waited for more kisses, for touches of tenderness. But Lionel was buttoning his trousers. His hands were shaking. Patricia saw this with gratification. Her heart became tumescent with adoration and fresh desire. She wiped herself. Then she was horrified to see blood on the handkerchief. She cried out, staring at it.

"It always happens. The first time. Nothing to be frightened about," he mumbled. Well, it hadn't been too bad. He sighed deeply. Of course, it had been Joan all along, not this miserable girl whose face had begun to pucker, preparing for tears of fright. "It isn't anything," he said roughly, then remembered that the girl was Patricia Mulligan. "Always the first time," he added, more gently.

"Will it...will it last long?" Her voice was faint and weak.

"No. It's just about over. Don't be afraid."

He knelt, dressing himself. He heard her say in a changed and timid voice, "Do you...do you love me, Lionel?"

Oh, goddamn, he thought. The silly bitches always ask that! There was only one reply. He patted her flank, smiled, and said, "Why, of course...Patsy."

"I'll love you always," she whispered as she buttoned the shirtwaist and pulled down her grass-stained skirt. "I'll love you always."

And they always said that, too. It was a ritual. It made

them feel less dirty, less used. Continuing with the ritual, he said, "I hope so."

Putting her hand on his shoulder, she said, "How soon can we be married?"

He looked at her and was aghast. Married!

"You did say we'd be married..." She faltered. "Over and over."

But he had been crying that out to Joan Garrity. It had risen spontaneously from his enraptured heart.

He knew that he was in danger. He shuddered in spite of the heat of the day. He said, "Patsy, we must talk of that later. Later, much later. We have so much to think about. Don't we?" His voice was actually entreating, he was so fearfully alarmed.

Her head still lying on the grass, Patricia nodded in submission. She stroked his arm, and he shuddered again, but did not draw himself away. His eyes were fixed fiercely on hers. "And we'll never talk of this to anyone, will we? It...it is too...precious. Isn't it?"

"Oh, yes, yes!" cried Patricia. "Too precious! It's ours alone." She was almost lovely in her meekness, her understanding.

He helped her to her feet and brushed the grass blades off her clothing. She held up her face, like a child, for his kiss. Closing his eyes, he obeyed. She did not feel the kiss was dry, reluctant.

"And...the Sunday after next?" she pleaded, her eyes glowing.

"And the next, and the next, and the next," he said.

Patricia never fully remembered pedaling home. She was not on a bicycle. She was being carried on wings, her body tingling and content.

Lionel, cautiously taking another road home, was very thoughtful. He was not at all on wings. His mind was running with cold purpose. The next time, he would mention to the girl that his salary was very low, too low as yet to acquire a wife. Step by step. That was the way. Of her secrecy he could be sure, for she had a father. Had she had a mother, that would have been dangerous. Girls did not confess indiscretions to a male parent.

He looked at his watch, a "turnip," as it was called—for it was nickel and cheap—and saw it was five o'clock. He smiled again. He would go to Joan, as he always did on Sunday evenings, and he would look at her, and remember.

174

His mind, always orderly, was teeming with plans. If that damned hotel ever got built, he could marry Joan. He had not asked her, as yet, but he knew that she was waiting for him and would always wait. He thought of her face again, the face he had really kissed with such terrible ardor in the glade, and his cold heart softened. It was always Joan with whom he lay, never the girl of the moment.

Joan, Joan, he thought. My darling, darling, darling.

My darling, thought Patricia, and even as she smiled on her bicycle, her eyes filled with happy tears.

13

Patrick Mulligan and his nephew Daniel Dugan sat in the garden of Patrick's house this golden late-September day. The mountains were the color of oranges against a benign and gentle sky tinged with gilt. The autumn flowers in the garden flared with violent color, as if in denial of their coming death. And, why not? thought Daniel. Even in mid-season they had not been so vehement; each petal glowed with light and hue; each flower face lifted itself to the warm air and the scented wind, a wind that had not been so pungent a month ago. White butterflies and the great black-and-yellow striped monarch butterflies blew from bush to bush, from blossom to blossom, their wings luminous. A tranquillity lay on the garden, a sweet thoughtfulness. The trees basked, heavy with their leaves, which were turning to scarlet and bronze. It was Sunday, but the sabbath peace had dwelt on the land since the end of August.

Daniel smoked his pipe, and Patrick smoked one of his thick black cigars. They had not talked for several moments, content in silent companionship. But Patrick's face had an overcast of anxiety. He said, "This damned Panic. When will it end?"

Daniel said, "When our invisible government wants it to. You know, this was contrived, to force the passage of that private organization of bankers, now calling themselves the Federal Reserve System, which has nothing to do with government at all. The bankers call it 'federal' to deceive the people. Under our Constitution, only Congress has the right to coin money, but the bankers don't like that. They want to coin money themselves. We've been over that before, Uncle Pat. Once that amendment to the Constitution passes—the Federal Reserve System—the bankers will be able to control our currency and bring about the rule of what they love to call the 'elite.'

"So, now we have a Panic which was planned a long time ago. The plotters are now telling the American people that if there is a Federal Reserve System there will be no more panics, no more depressions. They will 'control' that. Teddy Roosevelt knows what they are up to. William Jennings

Bryan, that passionate and incoherent bumbler, knows, too, and that's why he is screeching about crucifying mankind on a cross of gold. But he is too hysterical to be taken seriously."

"Ah, God," Patrick said.

Daniel nodded. "And along with that amendment there is proposed another: a federal income tax. The government has promised that 'only the rich' will be taxed—for the people's social benefits—but the people will discover that the real victim is the 'little man.' Like Ben Franklin once said, a national income tax will make us slaves."

"I know," said Patrick. "That happened in Ireland. The Irish were taxed to the death, Danny boy, by the English aristocrats. Queen Victoria said that after the Irish were eliminated in Ireland, by taxation and starvation and confiscation, of course, she would help the English aristocracy to 'resettle' our country with their own kind. I know, I saw it for myself."

"I know it, too, Uncle Pat. And it can happen here."

"You don't have any faith in the American people," said Patrick. "They won't allow a federal income tax."

Daniel laughed, and the laugh was not pleasant. "Oh, yes, they will! Their greed will be appealed to. Envy, one of the deadly sins, is very deeply rooted in human nature, Uncle Pat. And God always punishes it. This time the punishment will again be slavery through taxes—as it has always been." He looked at his uncle kindly. "And it is the pressure of the bankers behind the Federal Reserve System, and the financiers behind the federal income tax, who will cause the passage of those two amendments to the Constitution. Very soon, too. As I've told you before, a government needs money through taxation to conduct imperialistic wars. There's something brewing in the world, a war of governments against each other to control the world."

Patrick shook his head. "Danny boy. No American would go to war."

"Yes, he will. There will be wonderful slogans. The old Romans were expert in that. 'The Senate and the People of Rome.' 'One nation, one government, one people.' Yes, indeed. But all the time, it was only the government, and the men who controlled it, who wanted more and more power. This will happen to America, too."

"I hope I die before it does, Danny."

Daniel looked at him with affectionate commiseration. "I'm afraid you won't. But don't look so miserable. This is too nice a day. Let's enjoy it. As the Roman gladiators said in the bloody arena, 'Hail, Caesar, we who are about to die salute you.'"

"'We who are about to die...'" murmured Patrick. He paused, then looked at the distant mountains. "Lord, have mercy, Lord, have mercy, Christ, have mercy—"

Daniel said, and his face was grim, "Yes, I know the kyrie. I wish every American knew it. And there'll be the day, in America, when the despairing will chant it, without hope, I'm afraid. For the despairing will be responsible for their own doom."

Patrick rocked heavily in his chair, his bright blue eyes clouded with thought. He said, "That damned hotel. I've gambled all I had. Mortgaged the Inn-Tavern. Everybody's up to their ears in debt, for the hotel. And we can't get credit to complete it."

"Cheer up," said Daniel. "The big chaps are careful. If this Panic goes on much longer, there'll be a revolution. They'll stop short of that.

"Didn't Mrs. Lindon buy thirty acres each side of the property? Don't worry too much, Uncle Pat."

"Easy enough for you to say, Danny."

"I've put half a million of my own money into it, haven't I? I believe in it. Half a million, Uncle Pat, is a big investment, and I'm not an optimist. I don't invest in losing propositions."

Patrick gave him a smile of love. "Wish you were my son, bucko."

"I am, almost. I've been studying this business of yours. It will be a great thing, Uncle Pat. I know it will."

He stood up, yawning and stretching in the golden warmth. He looked at his watch. He thought of Molly Nolan. But he said, "Patty is blooming like the fabled rose. She's got a sheen on her. She's actually getting some flesh on her bones. Like a woman in love. Where is she today, by the way?"

"Gone off on her bicycle. She does that, sometimes, on Sundays."

"Where does she go?"

"Well, today she's with the Sinclair girls. One of their teas."

Daniel glanced at his uncle, and then away. "She's becoming more sociable, then?"

"Yes. Glad of it, too. Patricia always was... well, a little snobbish. She's improving." Patrick laughed fondly. "Know what she told me a week ago? She said to me that I wasn't paying the boyeens in the dining room enough. And the ones helping me manage. That spalpeen Lionel Nolan, and Jase Garrity. In this Panic, too, when a man's lucky to have a job! Made me promise to raise their wages next week. Never thought she even looked at Jase, but now she's telling me how poor he is. Who isn't? Well, I promised. Anything to please my little colleen."

Daniel studied his uncle. "And so you are going to increase the wages of Jason Garrity...and Lionel Nolan?"

"Well, then. I promised the girl."

Daniel put his hands in his pockets and looked at the mountains. "I thought she didn't like Jase Garrity."

Patrick smiled fatly. "Seems like she does, doesn't it? I'm that glad, Danny. It's a lad after my own heart."

"But Lionel isn't?"

"Can't raise one without the other, now, can I, Danny?"

"I suppose not." Clever Patty, thought the young man. Clever, indeed.

He thought again of Molly, and the conversation he had had with her a few days ago.

For several weeks he had been inviting Molly to take a ride with him on Sunday in his new automobile, a luxurious Packard, and she had politely declined with a remark that her widowed mother needed her. Daniel loved her voice; it was lilting and musical, a feminine copy of her brother's, but hers had a sometimes disconcerting sharp edge to it, like the point of a knife in honey. She was all business, swift, efficient, clear-minded at all times, and would tolerate no shiftlessness in others. When Daniel called her into his own office with some question on general procedure, she was almost instantly there with a file folder under her arm, and she would respond crisply and without hesitation, looking directly at him with her extraordinary eyes. He had never known a woman like Molly Nolan before, forthright, frank, honest, and without coquetry or pretense or pretended coyness, and with an intelligence, he thought, as acute and discerning as any man's. Yet, with all this, she was certainly not a "new woman." She had an allurement that to him was irresistible, and she was most unaware of it. It was not a deliberate charm like her brother's; she was never ingratiating; she rarely smiled, she did not try to please everyone; she was deft in every way and often implied impatience with fools. In short, Daniel had observed, Molly was a realist and could be domineering. Still, under it all, he had guessed there was a kindness, a fidelity, a tenderness, even an innocence, all hidden for fear of appearing weak.

Once a young assistant cook appeared in Patrick's office, only to find him out for the day. He then told Molly, on her insistence, that he needed more wages. Molly had stared at him. "Times are very bad," she said, "and Mr. Mulligan has not reduced the wages of anyone, though other employers have had to do it. He takes the loss himself. But why do you need more money?"

The cook had mentioned his five children. Molly had raised her gold-red eyebrows. "Mr. Mulligan is not responsible for your children," she had said, with that knife point in her voice. She had then swiftly motioned with her hand in dismissal. No one argued with Molly, not even Patrick.

Daniel had first been intrigued and amused by the girl; then he had come to respect and admire her. There were no blurred edges on Molly, no ambiguities. A little later he was captivated by her. If I don't take care, he would tell himself with humor, I shall fall in love with the damned girl, and then God have mercy on me. He did not find the prospect disagreeable, however.

He had soon found out that Molly disapproved of her brother, and he guessed why. He also knew, to his vexation, that she was in love with Jason Garrity, and he knew that it was hopeless. Daniel was by nature a keen investigator, and as a business administrator and lawyer for his uncle, it was his duty to observe, clarify, and understand others and come to certain conclusions, and with no dangerous delay.

He knew all about Lionel and Jason now. Patrick had told him of the incredible beauty of the crippled Joan Garrity. Once Molly, in a moment of unusual despair and fear, had confided to Patrick that her brother was besotted by Joan, "who is just like him, I'm afraid. He needs a better wife than Joan is; they will just aid and abet each other. I know exactly what Lionel is; I know exactly what Joan is." Patrick had told Daniel of this confidence, not out of a desire to gossip— one didn't gossip about employees—but because of his fondness for Molly, who should not be upset. "The colleen takes life too seriously for her age."

Patricia appeared with her father for dinner every other Sunday at the Inn-Tavern, and it had not taken long for Daniel to see that Jason Garrity was in love with her. This amazed him. He had come to an increased admiration for Jason, for all the boy's short answers. Daniel was impressed by Jason's total lack of falseness, his tremendous intelligence and integrity, his profound depth of character. That Jason disliked and mistrusted Daniel himself was only too evident. Daniel knew himself to be exigent, but in this world a man had to be, or he perished in his weakness. Jason had an almost feminine intuition. What he saw in Daniel inspired his dislike, and Daniel understood this. "There's some rock-bound intolerance in that lad," he had told Patrick. "He'll never compromise for the sake of his own advantage. Funny thing, though, he's at war with something or someone, in his mind, or his soul, if you will."

Daniel dutifully attended Mass with his uncle. He did not see Jason there very often, and when he did, Jason would sit with his eyes unswervingly regarding the great crucifix above the high altar. When he prayed, it was with a strange intensity. It was as if a devoted son contended with a capricious or incomprehensible father and demanded answers to unanswerable questions.

In his spirit he is a priest, Daniel would think with a curious mixture of compassion and mirth.

That such a young man should be in love with Patricia Mulligan was inexplicable to Daniel. Patricia was both stupid and shrewd, sly and meanly obdurate. That a whole world existed beyond her and was unconcerned with her did not enter her mind. She was pretentious, haughty with those she considered her inferiors, and devoted a great deal of time to her appearance. Daniel had never seen her reading even a newspaper, except for the local society column. She was pettish too often, would sulk if crossed, and had a hysterical temper if anything displeased her, which it did often. But if she wanted something, she could be sugary sweet to her father, for whom she had much contempt as well as fear.

Daniel admitted that she had style and a certain cultivated flair, and that she could quote what she had been taught in school with a superficial facility, though he doubted she fully understood what she was quoting. Daniel found her boring, and he disliked her. He knew the dislike was strongly returned. Patricia had a quickness about her; her intuition had warned her that Daniel would never find her admirable.

When Jason, on his Sundays on duty, would stop at Patrick's table and politely inquire if anything else was desired, Patricia would give a small flounce on her chair and avert her eyes as if from an offending spectacle or intrusion. But Jason would helplessly linger, looking at her, and Daniel felt annoyance at this. Jason was intelligent; how did it happen that he did not really see this girl? But then, Daniel would conclude, does any of us ever really see the obvious, or care to see it?

Daniel was an astute observer and was deeply interested in his fellowman, partly because it was necessary in his profession and partly because he had the Irish tendency to look for meanings beyond the merely patent. In the short time he had been in Belleville, he had completely absorbed his uncle's affairs and knew more about people than the genial Patrick would ever know.

A little over a week ago Molly had come into Daniel's office with a downcast face and an unusual timidity. He was very pleased; she had never entered before unless called. He stood up and smiled, his polished-marble eyes alight. He offered Molly a chair, but she preferred to stand before his desk, her hands nervously clasped before her. He waited. She did not speak, but he saw the anxiety and trouble on her freckled face, that face which he was coming to find endearing.

"Is there something I can do for you, Molly?" he asked.

Now she looked at him. Her firm mouth actually quivered. She swallowed. "I don't know how to begin," she said, her voice shaking and subdued. "I suppose I should talk to Mr. Mulligan...and then I somehow feel I shouldn't."

Daniel was delighted. She had come to him instead of to Uncle Patrick. That implied trust of a kind. "Well," he said, "do you want to tell me?"

She glanced over her shoulder. She had closed the door. She wet lips he saw were dry. "This is confidential, Mr. Dugan," she said. "Please."

"Of course, Molly. You can trust me."

Now she lifted her head and regarded him sharply. "Can I, Mr. Dugan?"

"You can, indeed. I give you my word."

The clean white and starched shirtwaist was trembling over her breast. Everything was so crisp about Molly except for that riot of red curls, which even the ribbon tying them back in a huge blue bow could not completely control. The curls seemed to twinkle and laugh, shimmering with copper highlights. The piquant features were very sober now. She studied him as if begging mercy, but there was pride on her face also. "It would be terrible if you said anything, Mr. Dugan. But...I think I need help."

"Go on, Molly, speak up." All his interest was engaged now.

Again she wet her lips. "It's about Miss Mulligan. Patricia. You're her cousin. I thought you might help..."

Daniel sat down and took up a pencil in his fingers and twiddled it. "Patty? Something wrong with Patty?"

Molly almost whispered, "I don't know. But I'm afraid it will be."

Daniel waited, and then he said with gentle impatience, "For God's sake, Molly, speak up."

Molly drew a deep breath, and her eyes never left him. "It was two weeks ago. I had rented a buggy for a ride, on a Sunday. I'd saved the money. It was a beautiful day, and my mother told me to go out for a while. She's an invalid. So I rented the buggy and took it out on Cleveland road."

Daniel smiled. "That's where I wanted you to ride with me, Molly."

She was silent a moment. "I drove, all by myself. And then Patricia passed me fast on her bicycle."

Daniel's alertness increased. "Yes? She often rides on it."

Molly apparently did not hear him. "I called to her, but I think she didn't hear, or if she did, she ignored me. Patricia and I aren't really friends. Anyway, she...came to a break in the trees. She was quite a distance beyond me now. She got off her bicycle...went through the break. The trees and the shrubbery are very thick, you know. She disappeared. And then...And then..."

"Yes, Molly?"

"I...A minute later my brother, Lionel, passed me. I was very surprised. I called to him, but there was a lot of traffic and he didn't hear." She paused again, and now her eyes were somber with trouble. "He...went through the same break in the trees. Both of them—they acted as if they knew the place. I think they did."

So, thought Daniel with cold alarm. That explains many things.

"I...I'm not a spy, Mr. Dugan. I think that's...despicable. But I was frightened. You see, I know my brother, Mr. Dugan. He isn't...well, the kindest person. Please understand. And I know that Patricia is..."

"Very stupid," said Daniel.

"I'd say she doesn't know, perhaps, how to take care of herself. Mr. Mulligan has always sheltered her. She's never had to take care of anyone but herself; she's never worked

183

out in the world. She's like a child, in spite of all her ... airs. Forgive me. I hate to criticize people. It's not my business. But I thought of Mr. Mulligan; he's such a good man, such a good father. And so I drove on a little, and then I hitched the horse to a tree and went back to the break. I was really frightened about Patricia. She ... she never seemed to notice Lionel at the Inn-Tavern or in church. She ... doesn't pay attention to any of the people who work here." Molly gave him a tentative smile. "She thinks we're beneath her, I suppose. And yet, there she was meeting my brother. I wanted to make sure."

"And so you followed them," said Daniel when she became silent. Her fingers were twisting together in agitation.

"Yes. I did. I went through the break, very quietly. I just had to see. I just had to!"

"I understand," said Daniel.

She sighed in despair. "There's a kind of open space, quite a way from the road. Patricia ... Lionel—they were standing there, hugging each other, and Patricia ... well, she was sort of crying and laughing and saying, 'My darling, my darling!'"

Molly looked at Daniel as if waiting for an explosion. But he was only nodding, and his square face was thoughtful. "That was all?" he said.

"No." Now there was a rush of violent color into Molly's distressed face. "I don't know how to say this. But Lionel took her hand, and they went to the other edge of the space, under a willow tree. The branches and leaves covered them. They just disappeared in there. I didn't hear anything. I went away."

There was silence in the neat office.

Daniel twiddled the pencil faster in his fingers. He wondered about Molly. How much did she know about these things? "What do you think I should do, Molly?"

She threw out her hands. Her honey-colored eyes were filled with tears. "I thought ... I thought you might tell Patricia about my brother. Mr. Dugan, he isn't a good man, my brother! I couldn't talk to him. He'd only laugh at me or call me names. Lionel ... he doesn't care about anything but himself. I know it's terrible for a sister to talk this way about her brother, but it's true. He ... he'll hurt Patricia terribly. I ... I like Mr. Mulligan. He'll be hurt, too, if he knows. I'd do anything for Mr. Mulligan, anything! He's such a good kind man, like a father to me. It's Mr. Mulligan I'm afraid for, but I just can't tell him."

"You don't want me to tell him?"

Molly was aghast. She leaned on the desk and gazed at Daniel imploringly. "No! That would be dreadful! I know he wants Patricia to marry Jason Garrity, but she doesn't...Patricia wouldn't even look at Jason." Molly was almost sobbing. "I just don't understand why she should meet my brother like that! She doesn't know the slightest thing about him. When I saw them together, I couldn't believe it." Molly, who was never distraught, was incoherent now. "I thought...perhaps you could say something to Patricia, but not telling her about this. In a conversation, perhaps about the Inn-Tavern, and tell her about Lionel. In an offhand way. Never letting her know you know. Mr. Mulligan...he relies on my brother, and Lionel is very smart and ambitious. I...I don't want to hurt my brother, either, Mr. Dugan."

"Um," said Daniel, looking at the pencil. He leaned back in his chair. "You've tied my hands pretty well, Molly."

"I suppose," she said miserably. "I just don't want anyone to be hurt. But Patricia should be warned."

Now Daniel was curious. "What do you think could happen to her, Molly?"

Molly swallowed very hard and averted her face. "Well, if she...if she fell in love with my brother...if she loves him...it would be terrible for her. He...he's in love with Joan Garrity. He's planning on marrying her when he has more money. I know that. And she's in love with him, too. They're the same kind of people. It's hard to explain, Mr. Dugan, but they are. Patricia isn't Lionel's kind. I don't know why he is meeting Patricia. I still can't believe it, really. Why is he?"

Daniel smiled grimly. "I'm sure I don't know either, Molly."

Molly looked exhausted. "Well, I know that Mr. Mulligan is raising Lionel's salary next week."

"He's raising Jase Garrity's, too."

Molly nodded. "And times are so bad. Even at dinner now, the dining room is not over half-filled during the week. It's just Saturdays now. And people aren't buying much whiskey or wine, either. I don't understand why Mr. Mulligan's raising their salaries, except that he's such a good man." She hesitated, then forced herself to speak. "I think Lionel's using Patricia!"

Daniel could not help himself. "In what way, Molly?"

"To...to advance himself. And I think he got Patricia to

ask her father, and so she had to ask for Jason, too. And I think Lionel put her up to all that! I really do."

"And, to do that, he's making love to her?"

Scarlet washed over Molly's face. Then she cried, "I wouldn't put it past him! I know my brother. I think he's telling Patricia he cares about her, and so he's using her."

Daniel was still curious. He said again, "Um. Well, Molly, girls will be girls and boys will be boys. As for Patricia—what's a silly flirtation, anyway? She flirted with a lot of young men in Philadelphia. There's no harm in that. Is there?" He leaned toward Molly, somewhat amused at her confusion.

"But what if Patricia fell in love with him and he married someone else, Mr. Dugan?"

Daniel sighed. For God's sake, didn't the girl know anything? Now he was no longer amused. He said, "Do you think Lionel might really want to marry Patricia for her money, for a big position with her father?"

Molly shook her head wretchedly. "Under other circumstances, I'd suspect that. But Lionel wants Joan; he's always wanted her. If he could marry Patricia for her money, and have Joan too, he'd do that. I know he would. But, there's Jason, her brother, among other things. No. Lionel wants only Joan. I've watched them for years. They are...one person, really."

Daniel tapped his very white teeth with the pencil. "If Lionel is truly ambitious, and all for himself, he'd marry Patricia and forget Joan. Other men have done that."

"But...Mr. Mulligan. He'd never consent. I know that. Lionel...he's very strange. He'd never give Joan up, never. You'd think he would, but he wouldn't. It would be like cutting half of him off." She added, "And there's the new hotel. When that is built, Lionel will have money too. He's...I don't know the word for what he feels for Joan..."

"Obsessed, perhaps?"

Molly considered. Then she nodded. "Obsessed. It was always that way. Lionel can be reckless, too. It doesn't show often, but it's there."

Daniel sighed. "I see I have to be tactful. I'll do all I can, Molly, I promise you. And thank you for telling me.... Molly, you can't control other people's lives, you know."

"But he's my brother!"

Daniel was touched. "Yes, Molly, I know. I'll do my best. And then I'll report to you."

He stood up and took her hand and looked down at her, and she was comforted and reassured. She wiped her eyes and blew her nose, then tried to smile. "Thank you, Mr. Dugan."

She pulled her hand away and left the room lightly and swiftly. Daniel stared at the closed door. What a hell of a situation. Stupid Patty.

Then all at once he knew that he was in love with Molly Nolan, and he was amazed at himself.

14

The next Sunday threatened rain, and Patricia, Daniel saw, kept glancing anxiously through the window of the dining room as she, her father, and Daniel were eating breakfast. They had just returned from Mass. The day had darkened; the mountains looked rough and brown and there were wisps of fog drifting through the lower reaches of the great hills. The air had become chill, and a new wind was battering the walls of the big, ugly house; wood had been lighted in the fireplace. As yet, there was no rain. The gaslight in the overhead chandelier glimmered on the silver dishes on the table.

"I hope it doesn't rain," said Patricia. "I promised the Comstock girls to drop in on their mother's at-home today."

"You can take the buggy, love," said Patrick, eyeing more sausages on the silver platter. "You don't have to use the 'cycle. And Ben can drive you."

"Oh, it's Sunday, and I don't want to bother him. I'll just wear my mackintosh if it rains." There was a slash of autumn lightning and Patricia became more anxious. "Elsie, the housemaid, says, 'If it rains before seven, it will clear by eleven.' And it rained before seven this morning. It's"—she looked at the watch pinned to her blouse—"it's nearly eleven now. I do enjoy the exercise on my bicycle, Dada. It makes me feel so fresh, after this stuffy house and the Inn-Tavern."

"Glad you visit the Comstock girls now," said the doting Patrick. "You used to look down on them, love."

Patricia glanced at him covertly. She said, "Well, I'm more tolerant of silly people now." Thunder followed the lightning, and Patricia stared through the windows, almost visibly praying.

Daniel watched her closely. "You aren't friends with Molly Nolan, Patty?"

"Oh, dear, no," said Patricia. "And please don't call me Patty, Daniel. After all, she just works for Dada. You don't cultivate employees. Very injudicious. They do take advantage."

"Oh, I don't know about that," said Daniel. "Now, there's her brother. What's his name? Yes, Lionel. Your father treats him like a son, and he never takes advantage, as you call it."

Patricia's face changed subtly. She sipped at her coffee.

Patrick said, "Oh, and it's a grand rascal that Lionel is!" He smiled widely. "A real card, he is. But bright as new steel. The ladies all love him at the Inn-Tavern."

"So they do," said Daniel, glad of this opportunity. "An Irish Don Juan. Love 'em all, leave 'em all. That's his style. He's the kind of dancing scoundrel who will use women for his own purposes, with no more regard for them and their delicate feelings than a young fox. I've met many a man like him. Schemers. Opportunists. Adventurers. They love no one but themselves; they don't really have any honest human sensitivities. The world, they think, is their oyster, and they try to eat it up. Yes, I've known many, here and abroad. Women are to be cultivated for their usefulness only. If women don't have any position or money these men can exploit, then they aren't worth a second look."

Patricia's face closed, as if guarding a secret. But her eyes were stealthy and knowing.

"Jase told me that Lionel is in love with Joan Garrity," said Patrick, succumbing to a seventh sausage.

Patricia suddenly exclaimed, "That's a lie—it's not true!" Her voice was high and emphatic, and she put her coffeecup down on its saucer with a clatter. Her father regarded her with innocent astonishment. "Lionel wouldn't even look at that...thing!" Patricia added with more emphasis.

"Now, then, how would you know that, love? I've never seen you talking to Lionel, and you know very little about that beautiful cripple. Face like an angel. Pity. Burden on poor Jase and his grandfather."

Daniel shrugged. "I still don't know much about all these younger people. But I, too, have heard that Lionel is infatuated with Joan Garrity."

"Never!" cried Patricia, outraged.

"How do you know?" asked Daniel with an air of indifference. He chose another muffin and regarded it critically and so did not see the glance of hatred his cousin gave him.

"It's just common sense!" she said. "Lionel's going to be quite well off when the new hotel is built. Why should he want a beggarly cripple? It's an insult to him."

"Hah," said Patrick, hovering over the basket of muffins. "Jase is going to be rich, too, and so is his sister, through him. They'll all have money. And that lovely colleen Joan could melt any man's wits, with that face of hers. Like an angel's. I hear she's very smart, too. She looks like a grand

189

princess in church. People look at her. No holy statue is as perfect. If she hadn't been crippled, she'd have turned the heads of crown princes." He tapped his flushed forehead. "One thing I know, love, is people. That girl has a mind. I shouldn't wonder the gossip about her and Lionel is true."

Oh, what stupid, absurd lies! thought Patricia with profound scorn. She was about to say something with furious anger when she felt an enormous wave of nausea, something she had been suffering lately. Indigestion, of course. It had been that immense dish of spareribs and sauerkraut she had eaten last night. She could never resist it. And the morning eggs and ham and bacon were frequently stale, she was sure. She had such a sensitive digestion. Anything not quite fresh always did upset her. She must speak to Dada about the kitchen, not only here but also at the Inn-Tavern. He was so careless and too amiable with the help. She would have to speak to the family doctor about her morning nausea and her frequent vomiting.

The nausea mounted. She clapped her hand over her mouth and ran from the dining room. Patrick's round pink face wrinkled with concern. "I don't think my Patricia is well," he said. "She's run a few times after breakfast. Must call Dr. Hanrahan tomorrow."

Oh, my God, thought Daniel with genuine alarm. Didn't that bastard protect her? Or is that one of his schemes? I should break his neck, thought Daniel, and maybe I will. What if he's forced to marry that idiotic wench? That would break Uncle Pat's heart. I know him; he's set on Jason Garrity as a son-in-law. Good God, what a mess. What could he himself do? Nothing.

Elsie, the crafty and inquisitive housemaid—a little sinewy girl with a vicious face—found Patricia vomiting helplessly in her bathroom, kneeling on the tile floor and clutching the seat of the commode, heaving, as Elsie thought, all her guts up. Elsie had seen this before, and had wondered. Miss Patricia was very healthy for all her skinniness, and a big eater. She said with false solicitude, "Miss Patricia? Something wrong?"

Patricia gulped. She was very white and trembling. She wiped her mouth and looked up at the servant. "Elsie, there's something wrong with the food! I think I have ptomaine or something." She shivered. "I'm going to the doctor tomorrow to find out. I have a very delicate stomach." She glared with accusation at Elsie.

"Nobody else's sick, Miss Patricia. Nobody's been complaining."

"Nobody has a stomach like mine," said Patricia with a touch of pride.

"And that's bad, isn't it? Let me help you to bed so you can lie down."

Patricia's sweat had left her face slimy and cold. She stood up, weaving. Elsie put her hand on Patricia's shoulder with pretended concern and guided her to the bedroom. Patricia collapsed on the edge of her silk-covered bed, wiped her face with a damp handkerchief, and panted. "Maybe typhoid," she said with terror. "There have been cases lately, in Belleville."

"Oh, dear," murmured Elsie. "Here, let me take your shoes off, dearie. You do need the doctor. I've seen you like this other mornings."

"It's Mass," said Patricia, hitting the bed with her clenched fist. "I get so hungry. Nothing to eat from midnight Saturday until after Mass on Sunday. I get so faint. No wonder I throw up after I've finally eaten."

"Shame," said Elsie, kneeling and taking off Patricia's fine kid slippers with their black ribbon bows. "Thank God I'm Protestant."

Patricia leaned back carefully on the lace pillow shams, still gulping. She stared at the ceiling. "I must really be ill," she said. She paused, and her pale face colored slightly. "Elsie, I...I haven't come 'sick' for two months. Do you think that's part of it?"

Elsie's face became alert. She sat back on her heels and looked closely at Patricia, trying not to smile. But...when? The wretched thing was always guarded by her father. But she was a sly one, she was. There were the Sundays on the bicycle. Like all servants with empty lives, Elsie was inordinately curious about her "betters," and with vindictiveness. She pretended growing concern.

Patricia sat up. "Do you think it's typhoid, Elsie?" Her terror grew.

"Could be." At eighteen Elsie was an expert dissembler. She lowered her eyes with assumed modesty. "But I did hear...only ladies, married ladies, get this sometimes when they are going to have a...baby."

Patricia became rigid. Her slender throat tightened with a new convulsion. A baby! But that was impossible. A woman had to do certain things—but what were they? Surely not just...that! It had to be arranged and decided upon. But she

191

and Lionel had neither arranged nor decided on anything much, and certainly not *that*. She had mentioned marriage often, and Lionel had sighed and said, "Not just yet, darling, not until I am worthy of you."

Patricia thought about the breakfast conversation, and her whole spirit writhed in violent denial. Lionel loved her, but she felt despair and a gigantic fright through all her body. She whispered, "What if you don't want the...baby, Elsie?"

Elsie grinned. "Oh, Miss Patricia! I shouldn't be talking to you about such horrible things! But Mrs. Lindon knows; she's got all those girls there."

"What does she know, Elsie?"

"Well, there are doctors with knives...They take the baby away."

Patricia shuddered and was freshly nauseated. Her head whirled; she had to clutch the side of the bed to keep from falling off. Everything rocked and swayed. She felt she was in a nightmare, grotesque, ominous. But it couldn't be! She and Lionel had done nothing to make a baby!

"But how do you get a baby in the first place, Elsie?"

Elsie stood up, trying not to burst into laughter. She lifted her skirts and pointed lasciviously and with certain gestures up between her legs. Patricia watched her, turning as white as snow.

"No more than that?" she whispered.

Elsie giggled. "It's enough!" she said. "But what am I doing talking to a lady like you about such nasty things, Miss Patricia? Shame on me." She bit her lip with assumed contrition. "You didn't know about it?"

"No. I didn't." Patricia's whole body was running with sweat. "Are you sure...that's all, Elsie?"

"Yes, indeedy. A girl's got to be very careful, Miss Patricia. Men ain't no good, ever. Get a girl into trouble all the time. Sometimes they marry the girl, but not often. Just run off and let the whole town make fun of her, pointing. And sometimes she goes away and has the kid...or gets rid of it."

"But that's murder," said Patricia.

Elsie shrugged. "Better than having the kid, anyways. But you got to be careful. You can die under the knives. Blood poisoning. That is, if you can get a doctor to do it. He charges a lot of money and could go to prison if he's found out. So can the poor girl, too. It's a shame. Men!"

But not Lionel, not her beloved Lionel. All at once Patricia experienced a spasm of overwhelming joy. She would tell

Lionel today. And they would be married. Her eyes began to sparkle with brown lights. She smiled feebly. She looked through the window. There was pale yellow sunlight peeping through the eddying clouds. Lionel. But how should she tell him? She turned crimson with shame. She and Lionel had never discussed what had happened during their rendezvous in the glade. It was too precious, too exciting, too ecstatic. It was...sacred.

Lionel would marry her. She almost laughed in a sudden huge delight. She would whisper to him...Her color deepened. He would be so happy. They would tell no one, no one, until they were married. Of course Dada would go out of his mind. But he loved his daughter, and he would be reconciled. But he mustn't know what had brought about the marriage. He wouldn't believe it, anyway.

"Are you sure, Elsie?" she asked, with a great hope that it was true.

"Sure." She watched Patricia sit up and run the bag of rice powder over her flushed face. She watched as Patricia smoothed down her navy-blue skirt with the rows of black silk braid just over the instep. What was the crazy thing thinking now? The rich ought to be shot. They had everything. The poor had nothing. It wasn't fair. Elsie wished she could tell the other servants. But she would lose her job, and jobs were hard to find.

Patricia went downstairs and found her father dozing over his newspaper in the library, which was filled with books no one ever read. "Dada," she said, and he started awake and beamed at her fondly.

"Dada, I don't think I should go to the Inn-Tavern with you today." The very thought of food made her retch again. "I think I should just rest. And then, when I feel better, I'll go to see Amy Comstock and her sisters."

"Good," said Patrick. "Rest. Ladies are very weak, need all the rest they can get. But take the buggy today. There's a cold wind up."

"Yes, Dada," said Patricia.

Later, she wheeled out her bicycle. The day was too threatening for many people to be on the road. The dun-colored sky was darkened rather than lightened by the intermittent thin yellow sun. It was also sharply windy, and the trees moved restlessly from side to side. Patricia's felt hat veiled her face; the mackintosh was none too warm even over her dark blue wool suit with the white silk shirtwaist; the thin black kid gloves could not seem to keep out the chill. She pedaled fast against the wind. She began to plot what she would say to Lionel. It was only when she thought of him that her body warmed.

She glanced anxiously at the sky. "Oh, please don't let it rain!" she said aloud. She was glad that when she was married they would no longer have to be out in the open for love, but safe in the rich house her father would build for her. In the meantime she and Lionel would live with her father. She gave little or no thought to the child slumbering in her womb; she felt no maternal thrill or anticipation. There was only Lionel. Like a colossus he stood astride her soul; she was possessed by him. As she pedaled eagerly to the rendezvous, he filled her entire universe. "Please don't let it rain!" she prayed to some amorphous deity. If it rained, Lionel would not come. The very thought was devastating. She hungered and ached for him with the most powerful desire she had ever known and would ever know. Not for an instant did she believe he would abandon her. He had assured her too often of his deep love. No. Rain or not, he would come, for he would know she was waiting for him. He would be as desirous of meeting as she was.

She came to the break in the blowing trees and pushed her bicycle through the brush. Nettles caught at her silken ankles; she hardly felt them. When she saw Lionel's bicycle against a tree, she laughed aloud in joy. She stood her own beside his, then ran into the glade. He was there, standing and smoking and looking up at the sky, his hands in his pockets, his hair a ruddy glow in the increasing gloom. To Patricia he seemed like a god, tall, restless, beautiful beyond describing. Her heart clenched with rapture and adoration and she sang, "Lionel! Lionel!"

He turned. He was frowning. He was thinking: So, the little idiot came on a day like this. I should have known. She hasn't any sense at all. He smiled and opened his arms, and she ran into them and nestled her face against his shoulder and clutched her hands behind his neck, murmuring incoherently.

He was wary at once. Never before had she greeted him with such a fierce display of emotion. He pushed her face from his shoulder and looked down at her. Her cheeks were flushed under the dark blue veil, her eyes glittering as if with a fever. His alertness increased, and his self-protectiveness closed about him. He said, "What's the matter, dear? Didn't you think I'd come on this kind of day?"

She gulped with sudden jubilation. "Oh, I knew you'd come. You knew I would be coming!"

She was still clutching him, still breathing as if she had run all the way. He had decided this would be the last time he would meet her. It was too damned dangerous. He had been rehearsing, just before she came, what to say to leave her with her dignity—so that she would not be vengeful and ruin him—to give her the impression that she had relinquished him, not he her. He had abandoned his plan to use her, though she had caused his wages to be substantially increased. For only yesterday Patrick Mulligan, in a fit of expansiveness, had mentioned positively that he would marry his daughter off to Jason Garrity very soon.

It was odd that Lionel, the exigent, had wanted to say, "No, not Jase for your daughter! Jase is my friend. He deserves better." He had been both aghast and amused at his impulse; he had not thought he loved Jason that much. Human entanglements. They could raise hell with a man.

He gently removed Patricia's arms from his neck and looked critically about him. "Do you think we ought to stay?" he asked, pretending concern for her. "It looks like rain, and you wouldn't want to get lung fever. I should have got word to you not to come—"

"Oh, I don't care about the rain!" cried Patricia, her eyes glowing with passionate love. "Storm, wind, snow, rain—it doesn't matter so long as I'm with you, Lionel! Nothing matters!"

His uneasiness heightened to alarm. He saw she was trembling. His lips felt cold and stiff, and he looked at her with something like ferocity, trying to discover the reason for her sudden wildness, the shaking of her mouth, the fast rise and fall of her breast. That she was exultant and elated frightened him even more.

He said with caution, "You act as if you've got a wonderful secret. What is it, darling?" He forced himself to smile.

She clapped her gloved hands together in joy, and her smile was wide. "I have, I have!"

"Tell me," he said, and wanted to slap the silly fool. An awful premonition came to him. There had been that one time, just that one accident. Though one time was enough to knock a woman up.

"We're going to be married!" she exclaimed, and now tears rushed into her eyes, tears of happiness. "Right away!"

He said, and even his knees felt cold with fear, "Right away?"

She wanted to say, "We're going to have a baby."

But she could not. Her throat worked, but a hot shame came to her, an enormous embarrassment, a trepidation. He would want to know how she knew, and she simply could not explain her new knowledge. It would be shameful, unlady-like, obscene. Good girls never talked of things like that to a man, even a man one was going to marry. She had heard some whispers in her aunt's house to the fact that young Mrs. So-and-So was "enceinte," but even women alone together did not speak openly of such things. She was appalled at the thought of telling Lionel, like a disgusting shopgirl. Her face turned red, and seeing that, Lionel was aghast. He thought of Patrick Mulligan. He was ruined, ruined, because of this idiot, this...creature. He wanted to kill her! He lusted to take her by the throat and strangle her, and leave her here alone in the glade for animals to find. But he would not give up his last hope. He said, and his voice was hoarse, "You haven't told anyone of this...have you?"

"No, no. Not yet. Not until after we are married."

He breathed a little easier and studied her with an intensity filled with hatred and disgust. But he forced himself to take her face in his hands. She turned her head suddenly and kissed one of his palms. He shuddered. He wanted only to leave her, to forget that she ever lived and that he had been fool enough to get embroiled with her.

He forced himself to speak tenderly. "Your father would never permit it, Patsy. You know that. He wants you to marry Jason Garrity."

"Oh, I know, I know!" she cried. "But I'd never do that. I love only you, Lionel, and he is only a clodhopper. He's got Dada mesmerized, the crafty thing! Lionel, we'll go away somewhere, tomorrow perhaps, to a little town—how about Spring Valley?—and we'll find a minister to marry us at once, and then when it's done we'll come back and tell Dada, and he'll forget all about Jason and be so pleased for us. After all, he's so fond of you already; you know that's true."

"A minister?" said Lionel incredulously. "Why, we're Catholic, Patsy. We can't do that. And you know how priests are. They want to know everything, and ask lots of questions, and they'd want to talk to your father first."

"Oh, I . . . I've thought about that, too. We could say I'm an orphan. But what's wrong with a minister? If Dada objected to that, after we were married we could always be remarried before a priest." She was jumping with excitement. "Lionel, don't you see? It's so easy. And then, when all the hubbub is over Dada will build us a beautiful house and we'll be so happy together!" She was again seized with ecstasy and took his arm and shook him almost fiercely. "Don't you see?"

Yes, I sure as hell see it, thought Lionel with fresh hatred. He said, "I can't do that to your father, Patsy."

Again the extreme impatience took her. "Why not? He'll be happy for me, knowing how much I love you."

"You haven't told him that, for God's sake?"

"Of course not!"

The tight muscles of his chest relaxed and he could breathe without that iron band across it. He said, "Let's be reasonable, Patsy. Let's . . . wait. A year or two. By then the hotel will be built, and I'll have enough money, and a strong position, and in the meantime I'll get around your father and make him understand—"

"We can't wait!" Patricia almost sobbed in her agitation and fear.

"Why not?" Once more he was terrified.

The red swept over her face again. She almost told him. But she controlled herself. "I . . . don't want to wait, Lionel. I love you too much. I'm twenty years old. I want to have our life begin now! Now! In a beautiful new house of our own, the one Dada will build for us."

"Patsy," he pleaded. "Let's be sensible. When I'm soundly established, your father won't be so against it. It won't be more than a year, I hope."

Patricia paused. Oh, if it weren't for that . . . condition, it would be so wonderful! It would be only a matter of a little waiting, and in the meantime they would meet like this, every other Sunday, in a sheltered spot somewhere. But that baby, that horrible baby! It threatened to come between her and Lionel, and she tensed with her hate of it, her tremendous repudiation of it, her denial of its existence, and she felt a longing for it to die. A tempest of thought roared into her mind. Elsie had mentioned Mrs. Lindon and had hinted that Mrs. Lindon would probably know a doctor. Patricia no longer thought of "murder." She wanted only to rid her body of this vile intrusion into her happiness, and again she knew hatred for the thing in her womb. A memory like lightning slashed

197

into her tumbling mind, a remembrance of words she had repeated hundreds of times without any consideration of their meaning: "...and blessed is the fruit of thy womb..." It had never occurred to her what a womb was in all reality, though she had had a vague idea that it was something in her body which would later contain an infant, still later to be born. But the process had been lost on her. Besides, she had believed that Plans were made for such an occurrence, special measures, until Elsie had enlightened her that morning.

Knives. Blood. Blood poisoning. Death. And for what? She was struck by a maddened frenzy of despair. She was beginning to remember whispers of "bad girls," of "girls sent away." Servants. She had been curious, but no one had explained, and the subject had been changed abruptly. She herself was not a "bad girl." Her thoughts became incoherent, jumbling around in her mind like leaping, insane balls. She twisted her gloved hands together, staring up at Lionel with a face stark and white.

He took a step back from her. Yes, it was possible. She looked mad. But why didn't she *say* something, if it were true? When confronted by such things, girls were never reticent about voicing their fears.

Mrs. Lindon, thought Patricia in her frantic groping for a solution. But Mrs. Lindon was Dada's friend, an investor in the new hotel. Mrs. Lindon wouldn't help her. At the thought of Clementine, Patricia cringed. Mrs. Lindon would tell Dada. Dada would then know... Patricia almost screamed in her terror. Dada would kill Lionel. Or he would throw poor Lionel out, to walk the streets. It would be all her fault, not his. No, it was the baby's fault, for daring to be conceived, for entering into her bright magic world of love and hope.

Lionel was watching her with a fiery acuteness. "You see how it is, Patsy," he said, and his voice was actually trembling.

She whimpered, "Let's get married, Lionel. Dada will come around. I know he will. We'll—"

"Patsy. I'm a poor man just now, a very poor man. My mother, who's never got over my father's death, is an invalid in her bed. It takes nearly all the money I earn, and nearly all Molly earns, to have someone take care of Mum so we can work. We live in a three-room cottage, Patsy. You've never seen poverty. A shack. Ice-cold in winter, a furnace in the summer. I haven't any money, Patsy. Where would we live if we were married now? In that shack that leaks when it

198

rains? You'd have to sleep with me on a cot in the kitchen. You'd have to help the woman who takes care of my mother, washing her clothes, feeding her ... You'd be a drudge, Patsy, as poor as death. You don't know what poverty is!" His hatred grew as he contemplated the past years of his lean and deprived life.

That stark, still face stared up at him, slowly comprehending.

"I know your father better than you do, Patsy, much better. He'd never forgive us. He wouldn't give you a cent. Within a few months you'd be ragged, your hands sore, your shoes broken. He wouldn't let you take a coat from his house. And, Patsy, he'd throw me out. Where would I go? Who would give me a job? We're in the midst of a Panic. There's no work to be had. We'd be in the breadlines, at the door of the soup kitchen. Think! Think just for a minute, for God's sake!"

His own terror was mounting, and he was sweating with his urgency. He took Patricia by her stiff shoulders and shook her. "You must understand!"

That ... thing would destroy my Lionel, thought Patricia. Dada would ruin Lionel's life. It was a measure of her love for Lionel that she did not think of herself just then. But she felt a consuming flame of savage hatred in her for her baby—and for her father, who would see Lionel and herself homeless, starving. She believed Lionel implicitly. Men knew more about men than women did. There had been times when she herself had had to confront her father on some trivial thing he opposed, and he had been like a stone wall, inexorable in his refusal. How could she have forgotten?

In a last pathetic convulsion of despair, as she saw her whole life going down into a black chasm, she whispered, "I wouldn't care where I lived if I was with you, Lionel...."

He stood straight and stiff and assumed a noble expression. "But I would care, Patsy. How could I drag you down to such poverty and degradation? I can't do that to you, dearest, I can't, not even if it kills me to lose you! I'd sacrifice everything, everything I've hoped for, for you. But I haven't anything in that hotel myself except the offer of my services. I haven't even the fourteen acres Jase Garrity is putting into it. I have nothing. What have I to offer you? Nothing but my bare hands. Patsy, I can't do that to you. I would hate myself for all the rest of my life. Don't tempt me any longer, Patsy, my dearest. Don't weaken me. Or I'll be guilty of everything you'll suffer."

There were tears of fear in his eyes, and she believed they were for her.

"Patsy, send me away, now, at once, for your sake. For your dear sake."

No, she thought in her desolate heart. Not for my sake, my darling. For yours.

But the baby remained, and her father would send her away, possibly never to return. The shame. Or...the knives, and possible death. What had Elsie said? There was prison for such girls as herself, if they survived. Prison. There was no escape for her, unless she destroyed Lionel, and she would prefer to die herself rather than to do that.

Suddenly she thought of Jason Garrity. She shivered with horror and revulsion. Dada would be out of his mind with joy if she married him. And Lionel would be safe, safe from hunger and vagabondage. Lionel would be safe.

Patricia closed her eyes, and her face was white and still. There was a menacing rumble of thunder, but she did not hear it. She looked tragic, and for the first time in her life she had assumed a pathetic dignity, the dignity of sacrifice. Lionel was not moved. He felt only the exhilaration of victory. There was a deathly luminousness on the girl's features, and Lionel stepped back from her, dimly intimidated. Then she opened her eyes, and a less implacable man than Lionel would have felt compassion and shame. But he felt nothing but his own triumph, his own release. He was convinced that he had induced her to think of herself, and poverty. So he was safe from retribution.

"For your dear sake, Patsy..."

"No, Lionel. For yours." She held out her hand to him, and he, after a moment's hesitation, took it. Even through the glove her fingers were icy. She said in a voice suddenly mature and strong, "Kiss me just once, Lionel, before we say good-bye."

Again he hesitated. Then he bent his head and kissed her chastely on her cheek. In a moment she sought his mouth, and now tears were gushing down her cheeks. But he was too clever to let her succeed in seducing him. He dropped her hand.

"Good-bye...my darling," he said, and let his voice shake with assumed anguish. "Good-bye."

He turned, and rushed noisily through the shrubbery. He let her hear a terrible moan. Then he got on his bicycle and pedaled away as fast as he could.

Patricia stood alone in the glade. Rain fell heavily, but she felt nothing but her own sorrow, her own grief and despair. Water penetrated even through the mackintosh, drenching her clothes. She began to tremble with cold.

She went home, surrounded by storm and blue lightning and rain, and never remembered it.

She never remembered that while on the way home she kept repeating aloud, as if in prayer, "For you, my darling, only for you. My Lionel. My heart. Lionel, Lionel..."

PART II

And Satan answered the Lord and said:
Doth Job fear God for naught? Hast thou
not made a hedge about him, and about
his house, and about all that he hath on
every side? Thou hast blest the work of
his hands, and his substance is increased
in the land. But put forth thine hand
now...

—Job 1:9–11

15

Bernard Garrity sat with his friend and employer, Saul Weitzman, on a bench in the warm sun of a late-April Sunday, in what was called, by the people of Belleville, "The New Park," but had been named by the town fathers "Mountain View." It was not entirely a grandiloquent label, for the view of the mountains beyond was resplendent in the sunlight, but the park itself was very small and triangular and was surrounded by an iron fence whose gates were severely closed at sundown and never open at all in the winter. It had been a worthy deed to create the park—the only one in Belleville—and an expensive one. Property taxes had had to be raised to level ground in what was once a rocky slum covered with weeds, to demolish the derelict buildings, and to plant trees and flowerbeds and shrubs, and to erect an iron statue of William Penn in the center of it all.

But Belleville, it was argued by the harassed mayor, "deserved a park," like other communities and towns, and besides, what would the grand guests at Ipswich House think of a town that could boast of no such green oasis. Besides, the mayor had added, the hotel would bring prosperity to Belleville. Belleville had only to "clean up, paint up," and shops would open and the value of property would rise, and things would be rich indeed for all and sundry. The mayor did not quite believe this himself, but his prophecy came true in a fine manner that even the carpers could not denigrate.

So Belleville had its park, and more than half the houses now used electric power. Many new houses were built, and new people moved into them to enjoy the prosperity also, and some elegant little shops appeared—elegant to the inhabitants of the town at least—and there was even a medium-sized new factory producing "crafts of the region" and other mendacities, and it did an excellent business among the "summer people," who declared the products "quaint." There was also a very popular restaurant called the Amish House, where one could dine on shoofly pie, "country" ham, scrapple, and "distinct delicacies" invented by "our Amish neighbors." The fact that the nearest Amish settlement was some forty miles away was not known by the summer people, who relished "the lavish food of the region." They also loved Patrick Mulligan's "old-country" Inn-Tavern, and the gentlemen loved the young relatives of Mrs. Lindon, and Mrs. Lindon loved the generous patrons of her establishment. The inspired mayor did not agree to having all the main streets covered with macadam. He insisted that some should be kept bricked and cobblestoned, so the lady summer visitors could gush over the "unspoiled" charm.

Almost no houses now had backyard privies, except a few on the outskirts, and these, at the mayor's urging, were wreathed in vines during the summer, and kept whitewashed and comparatively odor-free. Belleville began to respect itself. Bernard once said, "They should have put up an iron statue to old Johnny Myers instead of Bill Penn." He was referring to the mayor, of course, who would have agreed with him, though the mayor had just been elected a state senator by a grateful people, whom he promptly forgot.

Guests came to Ipswich House as early as mid-April from as far away as Philadelphia, Scranton, Wilkes-Barre, and, to the awe of the inhabitants of the town, even from New York and New Jersey. On a clear day, it was boasted, one could stand in the gardens of the hotel and see three states, or a reasonable suggestion thereof. The railroad had put in a spur that reached almost to the foot of the mountain, to provide easy access to the hotel for the summer people, and the hotel met the guests at the pretty little depot with a string of glittering carriages and two large automobiles. A bicycle trail had been added to the road, meandering down through an avenue of tidy trees and pruned flowering bushes. A brook had been discovered, smothered in earth and wild growth, and it had been enlarged and cleared and now tumbled down in a very pleasing fashion to the river, over artful little dams. "Weirs," Bernard called them.

In short, in just slightly over five years, Belleville had been quite "transformed," to quote the more ecstatic inhabitants. It was all due, of course, to Patrick Mulligan, on whom affection was bestowed on all occasions. There was talk about electing him mayor, but the more restrained inhabitants of Belleville objected. "An Irish mayor? Heaven forbid!" That silenced the enthusiastic.

Bernard, with his friend and employer, was enjoying this unusually mild April sunlight, "warming our old bones," as Saul said. "Who's old?" grunted Bernard. "Speak for yourself, Saul, and you six years younger."

"You'll never grow old," said Saul with admiration, his voice carrying the thick accents of his native Germany.

"Quite right," said Bernard. "The Irish don't believe in it."

Saul chuckled, shifting his fat buttocks on the slats of the bench. The blue smoke from his treasured meerschaum pipe rose contentedly in the shining air. Bernard smoked a cigar, a very large one. It had cost ten cents, which he considered outrageous. "The Jews don't believe in it, either," said Saul. "Too busy running all the time from pogroms. Got to have young legs." New, tentative leaves, a soft yellow-green, threw dancing shadows on the two old men below. The winding paths through the park were of zealously raked gravel, which people said was picturesque; flowerbeds, showing rows of buoyant tulips, mostly red, bordered the walks. Later there would be other flowers in season, lovingly cared for and very neat. No child dared to stamp on those beds or pick any blossoms. Activity among children was severely kept in check by parents proud of the park if not of their offspring. No picnics were allowed, and a shower of chewing-gum wrappers brought swift punishment to the offender. "Keep Off the Grass" signs were meticulously obeyed. Dogs were outlawed in the park. Even the birds looked disciplined as they flashed through the sun and to the refuge of their new nests.

Bernard was eighty-four now, a vigorous and lively eighty-four. Always spare, his body was still hard muscle, quick and springy when he walked or trotted, a quick marching step he had learned in the British army. It was nearly as fast as it had been in his youth. But his flesh now resembled the driftwood washed up on the stony shores of the sea, dark and with a dim silvery shine. His gray eyes were still vital, even if nested in deep wrinkles, and his large nose was as arrogant and defiant as ever. The plow of years might have cleft his sunken cheeks, but the mouth between them was stern and forbidding and the teeth within were strong and clean as always. His totally white hair had diminished, but the crest-like way it rose over his forehead was still like the crest on a Roman helmet. His chin had retained its pugnacity. He had not lost his formidable look. The years had not gentled him. Rather, they had increased his native ferocity. He was one who would never mellow into tolerance for sloth, lies, cruelty, weakness, or general ineptitude. The world was "a bastard of a place," he would say, "and I don't know why the good Lord hasn't smashed it by now." His mind was like a knife, sharp and brilliantly honed. He did not need glasses to read.

His hand, now roped with veins, lifted to his cigar. He raised his eyes to the distant view. "Age," he remarked, "is a matter of opinion. I've seen buckos in their fifties and sixties whining about the long years they have lived. They are 'tired,' they say. Tired of what? Living, perhaps. But then, I'm thinking, they never really lived."

"Work," said Saul, "keeps a man young."

"Depends," said Bernard, who hated platitudes. "I've seen work kill, that I have. It's how a man looks at things. Does he want to endure, or does he not? Simple as that, then."

He studied the far scene with little visible pleasure. But few things had ever pleased Bernard, and Saul suspected that this was the source of Bernard's vitality. He would never be complacent or sentimental. Saul considered him fondly, as one would a brother. In contrast with the tall gaunt Bernard, Saul was like a plump small cushion, extremely trim and turned and comfortable, rosy as a peony in full bloom. His three round chins were excellently barbered, as was his thick white hair, and he had a rigorously trimmed white mustache which did not hide his kind smiling mouth. He might be poor, but his blue serge suit was pressed—by himself—at least twice a week, and his striped shirt daily knew an iron, and his stiff white collar and cuffs—celluloid—never had a stain upon them. Though it was only April, he wore a shining white straw hat with a gay red band around the crown, and it looked jaunty and pleasingly defiant. He had sweet round brown eyes that seemed to be perpetually smiling. He was a childless widower of many years and hardly remembered his Anna, who had had a stringent tongue and had stood at least a foot taller than himself. She had also kept kosher. Saul had long forgiven her that, but he had never forgotten. He would sometimes remember with a shudder, especially around the time of Passover. However, in her memory, he ate matzohs and prepared gefilte fish for himself, both of which he deplored but which Bernard found tasty and enjoyable.

"When in Rome," he would say to Bernard, "do as the Romans do; that's what I read. I'm American now."

"And Americans cook as bad as the English, I'm thinking," said Bernard as he would spear another piece of fish. He shook his fork admonishingly at Saul. "Niver forget the ould ways. D'you want the world all one color, one culture? The good Lord never intended that, then. He wanted variety, and that he did. Think of flowers of only one color, say, purple, which I hate. Who would want a garden, if so?"

Saul's cheery face would grow momentarily sad. "It would be safer," he said.

Bernard had snorted. "And what's a world without danger? Tell me that, bucko. Damned dull place. That's why I niver could stomach the talk of heaven and pearly gates and streets of gold. Who would want it? Give me battle, every time." And he thought of his youth and his fists and his sturdy kicking boot, and he smiled nostalgically. He would then talk of Ireland and the "cursed Sassenagh" and would embellish his bloody stories, relishing the many confrontations, which he usually had won. His slate-gray eyes would become like glittering stones on which lightning had suddenly struck.

The two old gentlemen, on this warm April day, sat in peaceful silence together, Saul listening to the birds, Bernard looking up at the mountain, where, on its plateau, stood the completed hotel, Ipswich House.

It was a sight, Bernard admitted to himself dourly, to please the most contentious eye, though he would never confess that to anyone. The architect had agreed to pale yellow brick and stucco and a red-tiled roof and bronze doors, and there the great hotel stood like an enormous U, on its noble acres, half-hidden by clusters of timber oaks and firs and maples and linden trees, with here and there a royal elm. The immense lawns were greening, as they sloped and stretched with the curve of the mountain meadow. Flowerbeds, even this early, gleamed with the satiny heads of narcissus and tulips of many colors. The hotel was open all winter, too, for the new fad of skiing, and sledding and skating, and was particularly gay at the Christmas holidays, "with guests from a dozen states," the brochure stated proudly, exaggerating only slightly. With fires blazing in almost every room—though there were adequate coal furnaces—and holiday greens at every window and enormous Christmas trees in the public rooms dancing with tinsel and glass balls and toy reindeer and Santa Clauses, and ballroom music every night and liquors and wines donated by the management, it was a joyous and resplendent time at the resort. Only during the holidays were children permitted in any number, on the wise advice of Mrs. Lindon, who firmly believed children sabotaged any attempts at adult enjoyment. In short, Ipswich House was a haven for those males who were in flight from exigent wives and untidy offspring, and who were usually accompanied by lovely young ladies who answered to the name of "Mrs.," though everyone knew they were not married to their escorts. Younger males, however, still filled with illusions, arrived with their legal spouses, to return every year for several years, until they, too, discreetly brought with them more amiable ladies with dash and spirit and much happy laughter.

There had not been an empty room in summer after the first year, and guests made reservations long in advance, and returned season after season. Though it was only five years old, guests referred to it as "an institution." The rooms were furnished as shown in the English model, all very expensive and all over the objections of the prudent Patrick Mulligan. But Jason had stubbornly insisted, and when Patrick was congratulated on the splendor and beauty of the hotel, he would say with a grand wave of his hand, "No money spared. Elegance for elegant people." He finally included that phrase in the brochure Lionel had prepared, which was illustrated by photographs. The rates were staggering, but few complained.

Sometimes, though not very often, Patrick forgot that this was all the doing of Jason Garrity, whom he loved more than he did his daughter and grandchildren. When his nephew Daniel reminded him of this fact, Patrick would say with irritation, "Don't I know it, then? Am I a fool? Ah, that's a grand bucko, my Jason." He would pat his growing belly, now of a formidable size, and look loving and thoughtful.

They had come a long way, all of them, he would think when alone in his enormous black-walnut bedroom in his own house, which was also occupied by his daughter and Jason and their three children, Sebastian, the eldest, and the twins, Nicholas and Nicole. Patricia, who endlessly read romantic novels, had picked those names for her children, much against Jason's will. But Jason invariably pampered and indulged her, much to Bernard's disgust and disbelief.

They were all in debt, of course, to the two local banks and a large one in Philadelphia, but Patrick had been able to pay off the mortgage he had taken on the Inn-Tavern during the early days of financing. Mrs. Lindon had been of tremendous advantage here, and was, in her way, a partner in the profits. She had persuaded the two bankers in Belleville, her devoted friends, to sell her the extra acres needed—for cash—and had almost completely managed the financing of Ipswich House with the assistance of Daniel Dugan, who was now business administrator of the "corporation." Bernard was not certain of all the "finagling," as he mistrustfully called it, for he hated debt of all kinds, and "obligations," especially to bankers, and lawyers, whom he loathed above all other men. Hadn't they been influential in the passing of the new amendment, the Federal Reserve System, which would become active in 1913? Hadn't they stolen the right of Congress to coin money, as asserted in the Constitution? Bernard never failed, at any opportunity, to denounce "those international robbers." He was also aware that the "damned stupid people" had voted for the Sixteenth Amendment, a federal income tax, many times declared unconstitutional by the United States Supreme Court. They had voted for this because of the lying promises of politicians. "They'll know, every man jack of them," Bernard would say, "when they, as Thomas Jefferson predicted, would eventually be taxed in their comings and their goings, with their food and their drink, their property and their shelters, and the fruits of their labor taken from them."

Mr. Elmer Schultz, of Pittsburgh and Philadelphia, had been induced by the knowledgeable Mrs. Lindon and her banker friends to become part of the corporation and invest money, and had brought in his best architects to design Ipswich House in exact accordance with Jason's wishes and his grandfather's picture book detailing the English establishment. They had deplored the expense, but Jason, quoting Bernard, said, "In for a penny, in for a pound," which Mr. Schultz had considered, and then had reluctantly agreed to.

Jason was now manager of Ipswich House at a large salary, and in view of the fact that he had contributed his vital fourteen acres, was given fifteen percent of the net proceeds, which were growing year after year. Lionel, in charge of the dining rooms and the purchasing of foods and wine and liquors, and the supervision of the kitchens, and all those employed in the work of purveyance, also received a large salary—not as large as Jason's, for Jason was the final authority in all things at Ipswich House, except for Patrick Mulligan, who rarely interfered. He had his own hands full with the management of the Inn-Tavern, which also was flourishing. Lionel was given, in addition to salary, one percent of the net profits and an annual bonus because of his priceless genius in stimulating business. He wrote the flamboyant brochures. He also kept the workers under his rule honest, to a great extent, and that was no light struggle.

All concerned were ebullient and optimistic, sometimes

even Jason, who had become unnaturally cautious and morose.

Bernard knew nothing of the intricacies of mortgages and financing and bonuses and profits and expansion, and so was less than enthusiastic when Jason would attempt to enlighten him. He would wave his hand dismissingly and say, "When a man's in partnership with bankers, he's mortgaged himself to the Devil, and that he has. Niver was a banker a friend of man, except if that man had a lot of money and didn't need a bank." His mistrust had become greater the last year or so, when Jason had announced that the corporation had bought one thousand acres of land forty miles away, also in the Poconos, for "a family hotel, for all seasons," a hotel at least twice as large as Ipswich House. The foundation had already been dug and contractors engaged.

"Mark my words," Bernard had said with gloomy alarm, "you'll all end up in debtors' prison. And don't tell me there are no debtors' prisons in America! You'll have them soon, with this new federal-income-tax business."

"Oh, Da," Jason would reply. "You're too pessimistic. Weren't we all promised that the new federal-income-tax amendment would apply only to the very rich, and then only two or three percent? The government doesn't want to kill the goose that lays the golden egg."

"They always do!" shouted Bernard. "And why, tell me that, boyo! Because to tax is to ruin. Lord Acton said that himself, and even if he is a Sassenagh, he spoke truly. 'The power to tax is the power to destroy.' Read your history, damn you. What are you doing with all those books I gave you? No man should vote unless he knows what he's voting for and knows what is good for his country."

"A new Jeremiah is heard in the land," Jason said, but not without some uneasiness.

"About time," grunted Bernard. "But too late, I'm thinking."

"The Irish never trusted governments," said Jason.

"With damned good reason!"

Beside Bernard, Saul was half-dozing in the unseasonably warm April sun. Saul had comforting silences, and Bernard reflected that he himself needed comforting. Once, a man of his years had peace. Now there was no peace anywhere. Like an Irish farmer who could smell snow long before it arrived, Bernard smelled trouble in the world, putrid trouble. Weren't the newspapers now denouncing the German kaiser because he was building up his armed forces? "That German feller," Bernard would confide to Saul, "knows something we don't. But you can wager he probably has reason for his suspicions. Perhaps because Germany is so prosperous, with no slums, and the rest of us are always in and out of Panics."

Bernard had taken to reading *Das Kapital*, by Karl Marx, but no one would listen to his views on Communism but Saul Weitzman, who would nod soberly. "It's an old tyranny," Bernard would say. "It crops up, eventually, in every country, and that's the end of the poor sods. Goes back to Egypt and Babylonia. I'll give you another book. Eugene Debs, American socialist. In prison for conspiracy to kill. They do love their killings, these humanitarians. Killing's their ultimate way of proving they love mankind." And Bernard would laugh bitterly. "I'm glad I'm not a day younger. It's Jason and his children I think about, and what they're going to face. I'll be thankfully dead."

Three youths wandered by, giggling among themselves as they told each other salacious stories. They kicked up the gravel and guffawed. Bernard studied them grimly. The Farrell lads—Joe and Mike and Matthew—the oldest sixteen and a worker in one of the mills, Mike, fifteen, on his first job in a new small factory, and Matt, the youngest, a hellion of about twelve. Their dada, thought Bernard, was a good and prosperous man, with a hardware store and a blacksmith shop which also catered to those who owned automobiles, and a sound little body of a wife who beamed happily at everyone. How did two such get sons like these, always in mischief. Dennis, their father, had wanted the two oldest to finish high school, but they were too dull of wit to continue, and the youngest, who was the most intelligent, was always playing truant. They had all been firmly disciplined by their father, who had been born in Ireland, and though they feared and obeyed him most of the time, they also hated him for his sternness. They despised their mother, who adored them, and exploited her generous and tender heart. Kathleen Farrell reminded Bernard of his dead daughter-in-law, Katie.

Bad blood somewheres, Bernard would think, when he encountered them. They were afraid of Bernard, to some extent, and the cane he carried with him. They wandered off, but a moment or two later young Matt crept up behind Saul and smashed down his gay straw hat over his ears. "Kosher kike!" the boy yelled, and at a distance, his brothers laughed like jackasses. Bernard sprang to his feet, clutching his cane, but the boys ran off like hares.

"Never mind," said Saul, ruefully examining his ruined hat. "Only boys. They mean no harm."

Bernard shouted, "They don't, eh? And it's wrong you are. They mean only harm. They're always in trouble, in spite of their dada's leather belt, and it's sorry I am for Dennis and his lady." He sat down, breathing heavily, his grayish face mottled with dangerous color. "I'd like to beat the shit out of them, myself. Could do a better job than their dada, whose arm is always being held back by Kathleen. Wimin! They should niver have the rearing of men-children, niver. My mum niver dared raise her voice to my faether, or interfere. And many's the time he laid us boys out, though he left the colleens to Mum."

He took Saul's hat from him, and cursed. Saul was a poor man; he paid Bernard eight dollars a week for six days in his shop, and could not understand why Bernard remained in the old shanty when his son, Jason, was only too anxious—as was Patrick Mulligan—to have the old man live in the ugly luxurious house where Patrick still lived with his daughter and Jason and their children—despite Patricia's endless tears and nagging for a new home.

"In the old country, the generations live together, and everybody is happy," Saul would urge.

"I doubt it," Bernard would answer. "I'm independent, I am, and I like living alone. Niver was one for stumbling over a family."

He said, now, "It's your birthday coming, Saul. I'll buy you another hat. With a green ribbon," and he chuckled sourly, and weighed his heavy cane in his hand with some wistfulness.

There was a coolness these years between him and Jason. Bernard never explained why. But he would think: And it's a grandson of mine who got his wife in the family way for two months before he married her! I thought better of Jason. Not a sneaking rascal—I thought. Not one to take advantage of a poor trusting girl—I thought. Then suddenly running off with her to a justice of the peace in Riverton one fine day, unbeknownst to poor Pat, and not a priest until two weeks later to sanctify the marriage, and not the lovely wedding for his girl that Pat had dreamed of since she was born. Thought better of Jason. And everyone saying, and the doctors, that Sebastian was a seven-month baby, and everyone believing

213

it but me. You don't have a fine boy like Sebastian being born weighing over seven pounds, if he's a seventh-month baby. But fools believe what they want to believe, and Pat's a power in Belleville and brought prosperity here. Wonder if he's fooled himself. Probably. But only too glad to have Jason as his son-in-law, no matter how it came about.

Father Sweeney had remarried the two renegades—as Bernard called them—and Father Sweeney had baptized the children, and never said a word. Discreet, thought Bernard, and did not know whether to be grateful or not. But the priest had been vehement enough when he had persuaded his lordship the bishop not to inflict John Garrity on him as an assistant, after John had been ordained. There was a meek little German lad now as Father Sweeney's assistant. The parish had grown over these years. John was assistant pastor to an old arthritic priest in Scranton, in a depressed parish, and as the old priest "had taken to the bottle, poor soul, for his pains," and John was very vigilant and active and seemed everywhere at once, no one complained.

Jason could not understand the coolness between him and his grandfather. As he was reticent by nature, he had not asked. Jason believed his older son to be his own, and that Sebastian was indeed a seventh-month child. He had been told so by two physicians, very prudent men who knew the truth but who were afraid of Patrick Mulligan. They too surmised that Jason had got Patricia into "a delicate condition" at least two months prior to the marriage. Patrick, the innocent, also believed in the fable of the premature baby. He would never have believed that his sheltered darling had been immoral and had bared herself, before marriage, to any man.

Only three knew the truth: Daniel Dugan, now married to Molly Nolan, and Lionel and Joan Garrity. Lionel had married Joan four months after he had abandoned Patricia. He adored her almost abjectly; he trusted her absolutely, and she trusted him. A cynic by nature, Joan had accepted with celestial equanimity Lionel's confession that he most probably was Sebastian's father. "Well, it's over and done with," she had said, "and the girl is a fool and always was, and because Sebastian is your own, my darling, I love him also." This was no lie. Unable to bear children herself, she did indeed love the child, as his mother did not. He was Lionel's. Joan did not pity her deceived brother. She had never considered him of much consequence, anyway, and had even despised him. She was totally convinced that without Lionel he would be nothing, and she resented her brother as a result, and her hatred grew with the years.

Daniel had not told Molly of his knowledge. Molly had a sharp tongue, and under all that adorable independence and intrepid demeanor was a soul easily outraged at injustice and betrayal. Some might have blurted out the truth, and would never have understood that some things are better hidden.

Once Molly had said, innocently, "He's very big, the baby, for being premature, isn't he, Dan?" And Daniel, looking gravely thoughtful, had replied, "But Jason is a big man, my love, and Patty is no midget. And Jason's grandfather is a giant, too."

Molly was glad that her brother, Lionel, and his wife, Joan, had no children. "There's enough wickedness in this world, Dan, and those two are genuinely wicked, without adding to their number." Daniel agreed. Molly was still childless after three years, and this saddened them both.

Bernard, sitting with Saul on the sun-warmed bench in the park, was thinking of his great-grandchildren, Sebastian, four, whom he loved devotedly, and the twins, Nicholas and Nicole. Idiotic names! Bernard knew that Patricia did not even try to hide the fact that she disliked Sebastian, ignored and slighted him, and complained of him always. There were times when one saw real hate in her eyes as she looked at the little boy. Yet, he was gravely handsome, tall for his age, and always courteous and obedient and unfailingly kind. To Bernard he had "a lovely face," for it was square and serious, with good bones, large agate-colored eyes like his mother's, a short sharply defined nose, a faintly smiling mouth which did not detract from his usual gravity, and thick curling brown hair with a hint of deep red in the clustering waves. A true Garrity, Bernard would think. The boy was already being tutored at home, and he had intellect as well as intelligence. He kept his childish thoughts to himself, but Bernard suspected that they were not childish at all, and in this he was right.

The three-year-old twins were another matter.

Nicholas was, as Bernard described it, "disjointed." He was small even for three, and incessantly in motion, giving the appearance of a crudely carved marionette held by uncertain but vibrating strings. He ran and moved very fast and was always falling, for despite his smallness and his compact frame, he was clumsy. He also wailed, even though not hurt by these mishaps, and then would spring feverishly to his feet and scamper off, his arms and legs not quite coordinated, and thrown out as if he was in flight. He had a rectangular face, sallow and bony, with the large Garrity nose, a tremulous excited mouth, and dark slate-colored eyes protruding as if he were out of breath, which he usually was. He had Patricia's thin fine hair, perpetually in disarray and always drooping over his forehead and into his eyes. He had large ears which were strangely a bright pink. He gave the impression of incurable dishevelment.

He was "harmless, I'm thinking," to quote Bernard, "but no brains at all." When Patricia mentioned that he had a delicate nature and was exquisitely sensitive, Bernard would snort to himself. "An artist," Patricia would declare with passionate love, "and always trying to draw pictures."

It was his twin sister, Nicole, who had "the brains." But to many people she was a most ugly little girl, for she was even shorter than her brother, and at three a veritable fat dumpling of a child, shapeless and all belly, with thick arms and legs and a round fat face. Her skin was coarse, though she was hardly more than an infant, with no rosiness of cheek or mouth. But her face was perpetually resolute, her lips extremely firm and controlled, her chin heavy and dimpled. She had the look of a matron, which amused Bernard, for she resembled his grandmother amazingly. Her brown hair was harsh if abundant, and without light. No nonsense about the little colleen, Bernard would say fondly. She had one excellent feature—truly beautiful and radiant gray eyes with long dark lashes like stars.

Despite her fatness, which was mostly muscle, she moved with surety, like Sebastian, and always with purpose. No pretty frocks could conceal that stalwart little body with its square shoulders and large belly and broad chest. Frills and bows, on which Patricia insisted, mocked the strength that was so evident, and made her look like a parody of a frivolously bedecked doll. When she walked, one could hear her steady footsteps even on the heaviest carpets. Bernard watched Nicole with affectionate amusement. "A tartar," he said once, without disapproval. "She'll make her way, but God help the man she'll marry. He'll know who's in charge, from the start."

Patricia thought her daughter "adorable" and a beauty, and never noticed the ridiculous disparity between the dainty name and Nicole herself.

From babyhood Nicole had understood her twin brother. Even at three, she was sorry for him, and protected him and brushed him off when he fell and wiped away his endless tears. All her actions, with him, were maternal. In spite of Patricia's rebukes, Nicole called her brother Nick and he called her Nickie.

It infuriated Patricia that between Sebastian and Nicole there was a profound sympathy, and that both children had made themselves the guardians of the disorganized Nicholas. When Jason, exhausted from long hours of dealing with mutinous workers, from maids to gardeners and cleaners, to window washers and laundresses, arrived home, he would inevitably be greeted by Patricia's tinny but emphatic complaints about Sebastian, and how he was inciting the twins to many numerous crimes, especially against her.

Jason loved his children, but between him and Sebastian there was an unspoken compatibility, a mature tenderness. He would take Sebastian with him to the library and shut the door, not to administer punishment, as Patricia hoped and believed, but to sit in gentle silence with the child on his knee, their hands clasped together warmly, their eyes communicating in wordless comprehension and consolation. Then they would emerge, Sebastian too often to a lonely dinner in the kitchen with an indignant cook, and the other children to the firelit nursery with their special nursemaid, or even with their parents occasionally.

Jason could not understand—nor did Bernard—the hatred Patricia had for her older son. But always, to Bernard's exasperation, Jason endured her whims, complaints, and evident dislike of him and was infinitely tender and patient with her. Jason firmly believed that Patricia was of ineffable substance, above other women as a flowering tree is above ordinary grass. Can't he see how stupid she is? Bernard would ask himself. How vulgar, how cunning, how selfish and self-centered, how incapable of tolerance and consideration of others? But Jason did not see all this, just as he could not know the source of Patricia's aversion to Sebastian. He had persuaded himself that it was all due to "birth difficulties" and incompatible differences of temperament. He was certain time would solve these things nicely, an attitude astonishingly different from his usual realistic outlook.

Besides, he was always so tired now. He would fall into bed overcome with weariness, only to find his mind spinning with problems, with doubts, with conflicts and worries. He and Patricia had separate bedrooms, at her insistence—she needed her rest since she was very high-strung. They had not slept together since the birth of the twins. Jason understood that she feared more pregnancies. She was too fragile for this world, he would think.

It was odd that he had not as yet recognized how similar he and Sebastian were in nature, just as he was never doubtful of the child's paternity. Patricia's pettiness toward Jason, her not hidden resentment, her frequent ridicule of his person, her implied contempt for his intelligence, her cruel accusations that he had no social graces, never truly entered his consciousness. He was always trying to win her admiration. This, too, enraged Bernard, who thought of her as a silly and pretentious fool and a woman of no delicacy.

Always thin, she was now emaciated, though she had retained her style and taste. She loathed her father's house just as she increasingly scorned Patrick himself and deprecated him frequently to Jason. That she was desperately unhappy was not apparent to Jason, nor did he ever know of her tears and yearnings when alone in her bed. Bernard, in moments of rare empathy, suspected that something "ailed" her, but he could not guess what. It was unnatural for a woman who had so much to be so miserable.

Bernard was thinking of all this now, and he sighed. Saul said, "We go back to the shop and have a little lunch, eh? Made some gefilte fish, for Passover, next week. You like it, eh? And some matzohs, and chicken soup. Not kosher." He chuckled.

"Good," said Bernard.

It was then that the Farrell youths returned, crunching on the gravel as they ran toward the two old men. They stopped at a distance, nudged each other, grinned, then began to chant: "Ido sheeney, Ido sheeney!" One picked up a stone and hurled it at Saul. He dodged, pale and trembling.

"Off with you, damn you!" Bernard shouted, and half-rose, seizing his cane. "And you at Mass this morning, with your dada and mum!"

"Aw shut up, you old man!" the elder boy shouted with an obscene curse. "Want a stone down your gullet?"

Bernard stood up. His cheeks turned crimson and the veins in his temples swelled. Saul caught his arm. "They are only children," he pleaded.

Bernard shook off his hand and glared down at him. "They're devils," he said. "The kind who murdered old Joe Maggiotti. God damn their souls."

"Bernie..." said Saul.

The eldest boy turned a face of gleeful malice on him. "Wait till you see what we did to your kosher shop!" he shouted in delight. "Peed on all your groceries and sausages!"

Saul became white. He said in a choked voice, *"Oi gevalt!"*

Bernard rushed at the two older youths, grasped them by the necks, and pounded their heads together. They howled and struggled. He held them with hands like iron. He looked at the youngest, Matt, who was suddenly alarmed. "Matt," said Bernard, "I want to see your dada now, in the shop. With these spalpeens I'm taking with me. You go for your dada or I'll... I'll kill your brothers." He longed for the sight of blood. Saul got heavily to his feet, his kind face twisted. Matt ran off, whimpering.

Bernard banged the youths' heads together again, over and over, until they cried like infants. "Curse you," he muttered. "Damn the law. I'd like to kill you, but you're not worth hanging for." His lips were engorged with purpling blood. He could hardly breathe; there was a terrible pain in his head. He wanted to press his hand against it, but he could not set loose the youths he now had again by their throats. "March," he gasped in a hoarse voice. "Down the street. To the shop. Saul, come." Saul picked up the discarded cane, and weeping, followed the old man and his captives back to the shop.

The door was open. A barrel of pickles had been overturned on the immaculate floor. Many eggs had been tossed at walls, and their contents were oozing over Bernard's bright green paint. Loaves of bread had been stamped and crushed. Cans had been thrown about in fierce abandon. Milk had been poured out on every surface. Small blocks of ice had been taken from the icebox and sent skidding over the floor and under counters. Dress goods had been unfolded, befouled, and thrown about recklessly. Many were torn.

Saul openly wept now, covering his face with his hands. He was poor and lived frugally by necessity. He saw months of profits hopelessly destroyed. But worst of all was the evidence of foulness in the human soul, of monstrous cruelty and hate. He felt that his heart was crushing between stones. Bernard stood with the youths in the midst of all this, and resumed banging their heads. "Damn your souls to hell!" he said, and he poured out his own hate on them with a string of imprecations.

"Bernie," Saul stammered. "You're killing them. Their noses bleed. Bernie—"

"Shut up," said Bernard, but he halted the banging. A numbness ran down his right side, and his legs buckled. However, he did not release the youths, whose faces were streaming with blood and tears. It was then that Dennis Farrell, their father, rushed in. He saw everything immediately.

"Oh, God damn," he said. He was a tall, very lean man, muscular from hard labor. He had a dark narrow face and belligerent black eyes. "God damn," he repeated.

"Yes," said Bernard. The two youths looked imploringly at their father. "We didn't do nothing," the older sobbed. "Nothing at all. This crazy old man—"

Dennis walked calmly over to his son and struck him, backhand, on the face. He did the same to the younger one. They fell to the filthy floor and curled up like fetuses. Dennis said, "Bernie, do you want to thrash them, or shall I?" He removed his belt slowly, deliberately.

"It's your place," said Bernard. He was leaning heavily against a counter, struggling for breath. The pain in his head increased unbearably. For a moment he shut his eyes. His breathing was like a groan. "But who's to pay for all this destruction, Dennie?"

"I will," said the younger Irishman. "Saul, you make out a bill. Get you the money from the bank tomorrow." He added, "Never raised them this way. Don't know...More and more, it's like this with the kids. Who's doing it, teachin' them these things? Where's the Church, the priests? It's not the parents, though they say it is. It's Original Sin."

"Always was," said Bernard. "Always will be. You can't cure humanity." He could speak no more.

Dennis Farrell walked to the youths on the floor, who looked up at him with affrighted eyes. Without rage, without words, he began to beat them, methodically, unsparingly. They were too afraid to scream, though they cried feebly and tried to writhe away. At last his arm tired. He put his belt back on. He said, "Now, you bastards, on your feet, and clean up here, every inch, or you'll get more."

"Mr. Farrell..." said Saul, who had watched, horrified. It was not the beating so much that had overcome him. It was the dispassionate calmness of the stern father. He glanced down at the youths with pity. So young, so bad.

"Go on upstairs, Mr. Weitzman," Dennis said. "Saul. You and Bernie, you go up. When it's clean down here, I'll call you."

It was then, with a dreadful cry, that Bernard Garrity

collapsed on the floor, cans rolling about him, his face turned into the pickle brine.

Jason had asked his friends and relatives to leave him alone with the dying man for a few minutes.

The April afternoon had a sky of deep gray marbled with black streaks, like the lid of an ancient tomb. Lightning writhed through it, but there was no thunder. A long and angry wind hammered at the windows of the large hospital room, and steely rain tried to pierce the glass like arrows. Jason had donated this room to the Sisters' Hospital, and other Catholics had "been squeezed" by Jason, to quote Patrick, to enlarge the building and improve it. "Do you want the proprietary hospital to be better and cleaner than ours?" Jason had demanded, and Patrick and Daniel had paid up, grumbling that they would be bankrupted. Now they were proud of the hospital, with its excellent nursing staff, an operating room, and two physicians on call, a fine big kitchen, and a small chapel which could hold twenty people.

The room was warm, for new furnaces had been installed and the radiator hissed comfortably. The wooden floor had been scrubbed white, and there were gay curtains at the windows and a thick rug at the side of the high narrow bed. Everything smelled of beeswax and soap. A lamp stood on a table nearby, and its gentle light streamed on Bernard Garrity's face. The paralyzed man could move only his head, but his eyes were as alive and aware as always. He was awake, but he did not look at Jason.

"Da," said Jason, leaning forward in his chair, "I want to know something. Blink once for no, and twice for yes. Do you hear me, Da?"

The fallen head on its snowy pillows turned to Jason, and the vital eyes were full of accusation. Jason's stricken face quickened with pain and grief. "All right, Da. I don't know why there's been a...division between us. I never asked. I should have. You'd have told me the truth. Was it something I did?"

Bernard blinked twice.

"My God," said Jason, almost groaning. "I don't know. It can't be the new hotel. We talked that over many times, a long time ago. Da," and Jason leaned closer, "I never deliberately hurt anyone in my life. I never committed the sins of false witness, theft, blasphemy, or envy. I never blackened a man's name. I've tried all my life to be just and decent and

221

patient, even at the worst of times." He smiled weakly to keep from crying. "And . . . I never wronged a woman, either."

He never knew why Bernard's face changed so strangely or why his eyes, though still piercing, became brighter. "Do you understand, Da?" A long moment or two passed; it was as if Bernard were thinking.

The dying eyes blinked twice, for yes, and softened. The dying man struggled to speak. The dry white lips moved, but there was no sound. And then, to Jason's astonishment, Bernard, fighting with his last dying efforts, raised one wavering hand. It seemed to beckon. Jason, trembling, fell on his knees beside the bed, and the hand descended and gently lay on his thick black curls as if begging for forgiveness.

"Oh, Da," Jason moaned, and turned his head to kiss the cold dry palm of his grandfather. Now he was crying, gulping to keep back sobs. He took that feeble hand, raised with a last mortal effort, and held it tightly in his own. Oh, God, if Da could only speak, only one word! But Jason knew that the rift between them had gone, and all was forgiven. Then the hand fell. Jason looked up, eyes filled with tears. Incredibly, Bernard, for the first time since his stroke, was smiling, a smile of infinite love and remarkable tenderness. Jason had seen this expression only a few times before, and it was always for Katie.

Bernard had been given the last rites, for his death could occur at any moment. That great face might be sunken, but it remained indomitable. For Bernard in his dying did not forgive humanity for its crimes against the innocent and the helpless. To the last he questioned him whom he considered the adversary of man. God might forgive—but not Bernard Garrity!

Jason's friends and relatives came in now, moving silently, with only a faint rustling. Jason rose to give Father Sweeney the one chair. The priest now looked prosperous and well-fed. His clothing was the best silken broadcloth, and his cheeks, for the first time in his life, were pink and full. The auburn hair had faded until streaks of white appeared in it, but he had two modest chins and a considerable potbelly. He was eating well and regularly, thanks to Jason and the bounty of Patrick Mulligan. He looked almost benign. Standing at his shoulder was the young priest John Garrity, with his triangular face shining like bone in the lamplight and his pale eyes as censorious as ever, austerity like a grim shadow over his features. He stood, rigid and rigorous, as if at attention, and he gazed at his grandfather, who would not return his look, and his mouth was a white slash and his Garrity nose, attenuated, reminded one of the edge of an ax blade.

Behind him was Lionel Nolan, standing beside his wife's wheelchair, the antic face sober, the yellow eyes secretive and telling nothing. Joan looked as always, like some celestial apparition, pure, immaculate, blue eyes filled with heavenly luster, black waving hair dressed beautifully under a wide brown felt hat. She was wrapped in expensive furs. A single great jewel twinkled on her perfect hand. She looked, indeed, like some angelic visitor clothed in modern style, and an aura of light seemed to surround her. She gazed at her grandfather, and the gaze was the gaze of a compassionate saint, though in fact she felt nothing at all but impatience.

But she held the hand of the little boy she so dearly loved, Sebastian Garrity. The child's face had a maturity far beyond his age, and was full of his usual gravity. He had been crying, for he loved Bernard and knew that he was Bernard's favorite great-grandchild. The lamplight brought out red lights in his brown hair, and the tendrils that crept about his ears and forehead were the color of fire. Occasionally Lionel could not help but glance at his secret son. However, discretion had long been one of his well-practiced traits. He was kind and affectionate to the son he loved more than even Joan could know, but though he often wished to, he did not embrace him, not even when the two were alone. Sebastian leaned against Joan's arm, and she gazed at him with a passion of love only Lionel had ever seen before.

Patricia was not there, nor were her other two children. "I just can't go, Jason," she had told her husband. "Your grandfather never did like me and I never liked him, either. Death and illness depress me; you know how sensitive I am, and Nicholas, too. I'm sorry this has happened, but your grandfather is a very old man, and it really was stupid of him to do what he did at his age. No, really. Don't press me. I wouldn't even go to my own father's funeral."

Jason, as usual, forgave her and watched as Patrick came in with Saul Weitzman, Patrick grim and vengeful, remembering how his friend had come to this state.

Bernard looked long at his grandson Jason. With the acute perception of the dying, he saw Jason's broad dark face, so impassive, so contained, the eyes so like his own, slate-gray and brave, the quiet mouth, the strong nose. His integrity, his sureness, even his somewhat unbending nature, were quite apparent even to the most stupid observer.

A tear slowly gathered at the corner of Bernard's left eye; his mouth quivered. Love for Jason filled him like a wave. He detested himself for his earlier coldness and withdrawal; he said to a God in whom he hardly believed, "Well, then, forgive me, dammit." He turned his silent eyes slowly on those about him. He tried to smile at Saul, his eyes flickered with fond amusement when he saw Father Sweeney, but they became chill when they touched Joan, and turned away. He saw Sebastian, and the last smile, full of tenderness, rested on the child.

Then those searching eyes saw Lionel, and saw instantly what he had not known before—that here was Sebastian's father. Only Joan had seen this resemblance, the hair, the touch of yellow in the agate eyes, the quickness of expression. But only Bernard knew, now, that Sebastian's nature was neither his father's nor his mother's. He was complete in himself. Another tear formed at the corner of Bernard's eye. He felt, with the acuteness of those who are dying, that the child was more of himself, and Jason, than of Patricia and Lionel. There was the "blood" of a spiritual kinship, the kinship of the soul.

"Pray, God, and O Christ, and Blessed Mother," was Bernard's dying thought, "that my grandson never knows, never knows."

He looked at Saul then, and again tried to smile encouragingly, but his mouth sagged and could only grimace. A sudden anvil fell on his chest; he could not breathe. His big body heaved, shuddered. His last glance was on Jason, and Jason never forgot that look, which seemed to pierce his very heart, to stay there forever.

Father Sweeney fell to his knees, and so did everyone else, even Saul, and the priest began the litany for the dying. "Go forth, Christian soul..."

Bernard's soul flew to the God with whom he had always argued, and Father Sweeney was certain—as he thought later with a sad smile—that the Almighty was probably receiving another rebuke from an innocent. And the priest was sure that God listened attentively and with divine understanding. Whether Bernard returned the courtesy was a moot point.

After all, hadn't our Lord himself asked his Father why he had forsaken his Son?

Saul whispered to himself, "Eli...Eli...Adonai. The Lord gives. The Lord takes away. Blessed be his name."

That night, as he lay alone, Jason thought: The cornerstone has gone from my life.

And he was filled not only with sorrow but also with rage. He hated the thought that his brother would co-celebrate the requiem Mass with Father Sweeney, John Garrity, who, to the last, had stared, even on his knees, with cold reproach at his grandfather.

16

Today was the first day of May, a day which Bernard would have welcomed as a "grand morning, and that it is." Overnight the mountains had become almost summerlike, with a sky like a glowing aquamarine against which every tree was distinct. The distant Ipswich House was so vivid that one could almost count every pale brick and every chimney. It was half-past seven, and Jason had slept late; he was usually up at six and would leave the house no later than half-past. He looked through his bedroom window at the narrow garden; roses of every color were already in thick bud, and all the trees sparkled with life as green leaves danced in a soft breeze. A dogwood tree offered her bouquets of white flowers like a bride, and three redbud trees glowed bright pink with masses of blossom. Peonies, like small cabbages, bobbed heavy pink and white heads as in greeting.

Jason, somber though he was, felt a reluctant lift of heart, in spite of his sorrow for his grandfather and his growing hatred and desire for vengeance. He went into Patricia's room; she always ate breakfast alone, and in bed, and considered herself a partial invalid who needed quiet and long hours of sleep. But the truth was that she wished to avoid Jason as much as possible and did not want him to see the enormous amount of food she ate. As he usually came into her room much earlier, she always pretended to be asleep, even if she had been awake for some time. She was not expecting him this late and had just finished devouring a honeyed grapefruit, a large dish of bacon, two eggs, a mound of hot toast and butter, a glass of milk, and several cups of tea thick with yellow cream and several spoonfuls of sugar, and half a pot of strawberry jam and half a pastry. She still felt hungry. At ten o'clock she would eat again, and at half-past one would have a huge lunch; then would come afternoon tea and a gargantuan dinner. Before she would go to bed she would have one or two thick sandwiches, cake, and at least two glasses of milk. She thought no one noticed her prodigious consumption of food, but all the servants did, though Jason did not know. She was always complaining of having no appetite.

Despite all this, she was so thin that her collarbones were conspicuous, her arms and legs scrawny to emaciation, her body like a preadolescent girl's. Her long face was very pale, and the attenuated bones were sharply prominent, especially her nose. She lay peacefully back on her big white pillows lavishly edged with lace, and contemplated the last half of the pastry with contentment. But her eyes were not surfeited; they were avid. Her scanty fine brown hair was braided in two meager plaits; she wore a white nightgown of satin and cascades of fine lace and pink ribbons, and her slight breast hardly raised the shining fabric.

She could not get her way with the rest of the ponderous heavy furniture in the house, which she considered abominable and tasteless, but she had prevailed in her bedroom and dressing room, which were exquisitely furnished in the Louis XV style, all pale rose and blue and yellow, with an Aubusson rug in the same colors on the polished floor. The soft wind blew white lace curtains back into the bedroom, and the blue draperies gleamed against the wall where they had been drawn. The wallpaper was a pale yellow, the color of daffodils, with a ceiling border of blue-green ivy. The expensive lamps were genuine cut crystal with white silk shades bordered in gold.

Even in bed she was trim; there were no wrinkles in her nightgown or pale rose quilted bed jacket. Nor was her braided hair untidy. The tiny pink ribbon bows at the ends of her braids looked freshly tied and neat.

Her eyes widened with displeasure when she saw Jason. A slight flush appeared on her cheeks, and she hastily threw her napkin over the ravished breakfast tray. "I thought you'd left by now," she said. "It's late."

Like a lover fearful of a rebuke, he came to her canopied bed, with its blue silk curtains edged with gold braid, and bent and kissed her cheek. She shut her eyes with distaste for a moment and then said petulantly, "I was awake half the night." She averted her face from him and sighed. "I really must see Dr. Conners. *Crises des nerves.*" One of her novels of True Love and virginal heroines and fascinating but ruthless men was open on her bedside table.

Jason looked at her with the devotion Bernard had thought grotesque and degrading to Jason. But it was not the real Patricia whom Jason saw; it was his mind's image. He quite believed his wife had to "force" herself to "eat anything," as she said, and he was always in terror that her "delicacy"

227

would cause her imminent death. Had she been an early Victorian she would have had "the vapors." Jason was certain that if she fell she would break like fine glass. Bernard was not the only one who thought Jason's delusion incredible, though he shared his delusion with Patrick Mulligan himself. All others knew exactly what Patricia was, especially Nicole. The servants jeered at her in the kitchen, and guffawed among themselves, but they feared her tongue, which could be endlessly shrill with recriminations. Jason and Patrick could not understand why the servants were always leaving, sullenly or in tears, in spite of high wages.

"Yes, lovey," said the infatuated young husband, "go to Dr. Conners. Are you taking your iron pills regularly?" He stood near her, humbly adoring and anxious. He saw fragile beauty where none existed; he saw refinement which was not there, and a superb intelligence Patricia had never possessed. He had trembled to approach her on their wedding night; he felt he was befouling a pure young nun whose thoughts were always ethereal. Patricia, with her shrewdness, had guessed this at once and so later had used this fantasy to escape her conjugal duty. When Jason touched her, she endured only because it was desperately necessary to deceive him. Her marriage to him had been a cruel charade.

She had gone alone after her anguished last meeting with Lionel, to the Inn-Tavern one afternoon, where she had found Jason supervising some servants in a corridor upstairs. She had urgently whispered to him that she must see him alone, and at once. Literally trembling, he had taken her to the end of the corridor and had waited for her to speak.

He saw that she was very white, and that her eyelids were red and her manner distraught. He did not know that this was but two days since her "renunciation" of Lionel, and he was never to know. He only saw that she was in unusual disarray of both body and emotions. He wanted, in dismay, to take her in his arms and comfort her. He wanted to cry out to reassure her. But he could only stand in silence, ready to die for her if it could diminish her air of fright and distraction.

Her shrewdness prevented her from sobbing out at once some wretched tale of fabrication. She was afraid of scaring him, and she needed him. So she tried to control herself, forced herself to smile, though the smile was ghastly. She took his arm and drew him nearer to her, and now his trembling was visible, for he both worshiped and desired her.

"You know Dada wants me to marry you, Jason," she said, fighting for a beguiling tone of voice.

His gray eyes were startled and imploring. "Yes, Miss Patricia, I know. He's mentioned this a few times." He could barely speak. "I...I couldn't dare to hope, though. I don't even dare now." If Patricia had not been in such a terrified state, even she might have had compassion on him.

She clutched his arm tighter. "I...I'm awfully shy, Jason. I...I told Dada...you know, the calling of the banns for several weeks in church, and everybody listening and staring...I just couldn't bear it. I'm...awfully shy. I shrink from people. I...yes, I've always wanted to marry you—I knew what you felt for me. But I'm so afraid of people. Even you..."

He could not believe it. His dark handsome face turned very white. "Miss Patricia!" he said.

"Weeks of banns," she repeated, hardly hearing him. "Weeks. And before that, an engagement period of not less than three months. Dada would say it was improper for fewer. Perhaps he would insist on six months. And then, the wedding. He wouldn't have it private...you know. It would be a spectacle." She thought of Lionel, whom she had dreamed would be her groom, she in a Paris bridal gown with a cathedral train and a misty veil and orange blossoms, and he adoringly beside her, kneeling before the high altar, and the bishop celebrating the nuptial Mass himself, and the choir solemnly rejoicing, and the cathedral—it would be in Philadelphia, of course—full of sunshine and flowers. The radiant vision shattered and tears filled her eyes, her color faded. She wanted to die for an instant, in her grief and despair. She shut her eyes and gulped.

"Miss Patricia," said the incredulous Jason, who could not credit this miracle. He put his hand over the hand on his sleeve; it convulsed under his fingers, but she held on.

"So," she whispered, like one renouncing life and welcoming death, "let's run away...to another town...and be married by a justice of the peace. Tomorrow. Jason, please. Please?"

"But your father. It would be wrong to deceive him, with all his plans. He would be very angry, you know, at both of us, running off like that, as if...as if..." He could not say the insulting words. "I wouldn't blame him if he were angry at us. It isn't fair to him. All his plans, his only daughter. Like a laborer and a shopgirl who had to..." He swallowed again. What did such a lovely innocent young girl know of hasty, forced weddings?

Jason's eyes were pleading. He still could not believe this was happening.

She clutched him tighter. "For my sake, Jason. Please. You don't know how I feel about such vulgar displays. I love Dada, but he hasn't any taste, or sensibilities. I...I would just die, Jason. A justice of the peace. And then we can be remarried before a priest—Father Sweeney—quietly, privately. It can be arranged. If Dada gets angry, it won't last. He'll be so delighted. Believe me, he'll be so delighted! He'll scold at first, and then be reconciled. We'll explain it to him. Oh, Jason, for God's sake, please!"

Even Jason, in his befuddled state, saw her terror. He did not understand it. But he believed in her shyness, her aversion to crowds. What a delicate girl she was, and how poignant.

Overcome, wanting to protect and hold her and comfort her, he whispered, "How can we arrange it?"

"We can go on the train in the morning, tomorrow morning, and then back on the afternoon train—five o'clock. Jason? Oh, God, Jason, say you will!"

The white tendons in her throat stood out under her skin. She thought of knives and blood and doctors and death, and of pain and shame and degradation. She became frantic. Now she clutched both of Jason's arms, and he saw her wide eyes, the distended irises, the gasping mouth, the desperate and frantic fear. Had he been less infatuated, he would have drawn back and wondered at such frenzied vehemence.

"Yes," he said finally.

She uttered a deep sigh of relief and leaned against him. Oh, Lionel, she whispered to herself. Oh, my Lionel, my darling. Jason's strong arms were about her. He hesitated, then bent his head and timidly kissed her ice-cold cheek. He tasted her tears. "Thank you, Lord!" he murmured. He was like a grateful child whose father had given him a gift after long suffering.

He had no doubts, no hesitations. He was blessed.

And so it happened. Even when the hastily bought wedding ring was on Patricia's finger, in the dark study of an indifferent justice of the peace, Jason could not believe that Patricia was his bride. He was in a daze all the way back to Belleville on the gritty train. He tried to hold Patricia's hand, but she pulled it away. Shy little girl, thought Jason with compassion.

Patrick, after his first rantings, was elated. He kissed Jason on both cheeks, and tears brightened his bright blue eyes. "What a hasty rascal you are, Jase! Stealing my little colleen right from under my nose! What a scandal!" He shook his big head. "And what'll people say about all this? Running off. Well, now, what's to do? We'll see Father Sweeney. In the meantime, it's no valid marriage, I'm thinking, justice of the peace! Off with you, Jason, back to your grandfather. Until you're properly married to my child, in a month or two. Only right."

But Patricia, counting the weeks of her pregnancy, wildly refused to let her bridegroom leave her. Again she was frantic. Patrick, who could deny her nothing, finally consented. Patricia and Jason spent the night in the best guest room of Patrick's house. Bernard, at home and unaware of the marriage, said to himself. "Good. The boy's out for once. Let him enjoy himself."

Patricia thought she had suffered before, but this night was terrible to her. Jason had had little experience with women; when the need had previously arisen, he had sheepishly gone to Mrs. Lindon's house and had been ably serviced by one of her young "nieces." He had no way of knowing that Patricia was no virgin on her wedding night. He only knew that she cried in his arms, shaking sobs of despair and sorrow. He thought it quite natural, even when, at last, she repulsed him. But his love and desire and tenderness were finally too much for her, and she knew this had to be, for her own sake, and Lionel's. But as she submitted, she thought death might have been preferable to this, after all.

When Jason had done and the ecstatic passion and joy and wonder had left him for a while, he felt that he had committed an unpardonable crime in taking this holy girl. He wanted to cry, to beg her forgiveness. She only lay rigid, sobbing quietly, and then turned from him. He thought that natural, too. Brides were always shocked on their bridal night.

He told Bernard the next day. He was bewildered at Bernard's horror, outraged by his oaths and condemnations. Didn't Jason know that marriage was not entered into lightly, but was a sacrament? And, that girl . . . She wasn't a one he would choose for Jason—had he been daft, then? There was that lovely girl Molly, always in the house, visiting Joan, though it was plain to see it was Jason she wanted. Jason swore. Molly!

The estrangement began then, only to harden at the birth of the "seventh-month" baby.

But Jason, standing diffidently by his wife's bedside this May morning, could only think how unusually fortunate he was to have such an extraordinary wife and delightful children and a father-in-law who doted on him. He said to Patricia, "If you're unwell today, Patricia, stay in bed and rest. Your health is not too good, you know."

"I think I'll take your advice," said Patricia, looking languid. But she had no intention of canceling her luncheon engagement with some young ladies of "the best families." They had Bristol cream sherry, and Patricia, who would never indulge in "strong spirits," drank vast quantities of that sherry, which lifted her pain for a few hours and made her laugh senselessly. That she was becoming the object of talk among her friends, who listened eagerly to the alcohol-released confidences, and that they gossiped among themselves when she was gone, she did not know. But never did she speak of Lionel except in passing and in cautious indifference. Of Joan, his wife, she said much, and all in malicious ridicule. "That cripple." She was certain that Lionel had married Joan on "the rebound" after her own "renunciation" of him, and out of gentle pity or probably Jason's pressure. So she consoled herself, but was not reconciled.

After leaving his wife, Jason went to the nursery, where his children were finishing their breakfast. Nicole was rigidly supervising Nicholas' manners, sitting upright like an infant Queen Victoria in her small chair at the table. Sebastian, who had a precocious mind, was reading a book. When Jason entered the room, Nicole was saying to her elder brother, "It's not polite to read at the table, Bastie." (It was a nickname to which Patricia objected, it having vague invidious suggestions.) "And, Nick, you use a fork with your omelet, not a spoon. You're not a baby now."

Jason was amused. The children ran to him, Nicholas breathlessly babbling and flailing his arms, Nicole sedate as always, and Sebastian with a shining expression of love. Jason kissed them all. He lifted the heavy Nicole in his arms, where she immediately said, "Tsk," and brushed off a minute thread of lint from his broad shoulder. She then devoted herself to correcting the placement of the tight black tie under his high, stiff white collar. This occupied her completely, it would seem, but she listened to every intonation of his voice and her stern little heart was sentimentally awash. She felt that her father and her brothers were children who would disintegrate except for her attentions.

The nursery was filled with warm sunlight and pleasant cretonne furniture and blackboards and toys and braided rugs—all Patricia's doing. The scent of new-cut grass floated in on the light breeze. Miss Flowers, their nursemaid and governess, looked severe. She was always disputing with Nicole, who had very definite opinions about the correctness of all things. "A damned little old woman," Miss Flowers would confide to the other servants. "Obstinate. Always interfering."

Nicole gave Jason a very damp kiss just before he put her down and lifted Nicholas, who was clamoring for attention. Then, gravely, he shook hands with Sebastian in a manly fashion. "Be good, children," he said as he prepared to leave.

"They will," said Nicole with strong emphasis and a quelling look at Nicholas, who was still clamoring. "Quiet, please, Nick." The little boy immediately subsided. He obeyed his sister as he obeyed no other. She had a hard hand which was always in readiness, even for Sebastian, whom she dearly loved. All her feelings were adult and measured and astute. "The little colleen has a lot of common sense," Bernard had said of her. "She'll niver make a mistake, if she can help it. All rules and regulations. A proper tartar." He would laugh and think again of his grandmother who had survived the Famine by sheer willpower, even though very old at the time. "Nickie's a sergeant," he would add. "Worse than my own," and laughed when she had corrected him, respectfully but firmly. He once said to Jason, "It's not reincarnation I believe in, though the Jesuits do, but if I did, I would say the little one is the reincarnation of my grandmother."

I'm really blessed, thought Jason as he got in his car in the converted stable and drove up the winding road to Ipswich House. A wife like no other, remarkable children, and money. If only Da had lived... He drove a very large Packard of a brilliant red, which Patricia thought vulgar. She preferred her dainty electric automobile, which did not smell or snort or backfire, and which had a polished black elegance like an expensive buggy.

The morning was beautiful, but Jason's spirits became darker as his car climbed the road. He had an unpleasant task to do this morning, and nothing would ease him unless he accomplished it. Like many of the Irish, he did not forgive, but bore great grudges when his sense of justice was outraged.

He paused for a moment to contemplate Ipswich House and to remind himself that but for him it would not exist and he would still be impoverished. For only an instant he was gratified. The door was opened for him and he entered the great flagged hall, then proceeded to the offices at the rear of the left wing. Lionel, he had observed, was already present, for his Oldsmobile was outside, and so was Daniel Dugan's Cadillac. It was to Daniel's office that he went, and his face became more set as he proceeded.

Daniel's office was discreetly lavish, and expensive, with black lacquered furniture, cool white draperies, and a white rug. His secretary, a young man, was taking dictation. On seeing Jason, Daniel said good morning and dismissed his secretary. Jason sat down, looking formidable. "Well," he said, "I got your message, and here I am. What do you want to say?"

Daniel calmly lit a cigar and leaned back in his chair, studying Jason. "Let's be reasonable," he said. "Dennie Farrell has more than repaid Saul Weitzman. He thrashed his sons. Let's look at the law—"

"Damned to the law," said Jason. "I want those bastards sent to prison." His voice was rough, edged with emotion. "They've got to learn a lesson"—he thought of old Joe Maggiotti, who had been murdered—"or they'll soon be trying to kill other people."

"They didn't kill anybody; they didn't even try," said Daniel. He frowned at his cigar. "I know how you feel, Jason, and I don't blame you. But let's not get feelings mixed up with facts. They are young, still—"

"They committed an adult crime," said Jason, his face growing darker by the moment. "So they should be punished as adults. They killed my grandfather. Are you forgetting that?"

"They didn't set out to do that. It isn't even manslaughter, according to the law. He was an old man and had high blood pressure. I talked to Dr. Conners, and he said he had told your grandfather a year ago not to get excited."

"Those bastards excited him. They caused his death."

Daniel said, "Mr. Garrity had a bad temper. His neighbors will testify to that if you go ahead with your plans. I've heard the boys are sick over what happened to him."

"I will make them sicker," said Jason.

"You'll make yourself resented, or ridiculed. And it will be remembered that your grandda brutalized them before their father even arrived." Daniel added, "People are becoming soft over children these days."

"Yes," said Jason. "I know. They are going to be an example."

Daniel shrugged. "I can only give you my advice. Let it drop, Jason." He spread out his hands. "It'll come to nothing."

Jason stood up. "Yes, it will. I'll use everything I can. And Mr. Mulligan is with me. There are ways..."

Daniel said, "With the law, or without it?"

"What the hell does it matter!" Jason shouted. "One way or the other."

Daniel looked at him. He saw Jason's flushed face, his enraged gray eyes, his clenched fists. He said, "Just be careful, Jason, be careful."

"Careful, shit," said Jason, and stamped out of the office.

We Irish never give up, thought Daniel. And perhaps that's good, too.

Jason went to his own office near Daniel's. Though equally lavish, it was more somber than the other's, all heavy polished furniture and dark rug and deep maroon draperies. He found Father Sweeney and Dennis Farrell and the latter's wife, Kathleen, and Patrick awaiting him. Jason wasted no time. He looked at Dennis and said, "I am going ahead today and have your sons arrested."

Mrs. Farrell, a little plump woman with fair hair and sober clothing, began to cry. Her face was blotched with earlier tears and her eyes swollen. Her husband stood beside her, his hand on her shoulder.

"Yes!" shouted Patrick, his small eyes dancing with blue fire. "I'm with you, my boy!"

Father Sweeney said, "Jason, please listen to Dennis a moment."

Jason swung on the parents. Dennis' narrow dark face was twisted in an expression of pain. He patted his weeping wife's shoulder.

"I'm not listening to anybody," said Jason. "Justice is justice. My grandfather is dead, Farrell, because of your sons. They're going to prison, no matter what I have to do."

"Yes!" said Patrick. "It's about time, with the spalpeens the way they are these days."

235

"You're going to have them arrested, Mr. Garrity?" said Dennis. He sighed. "You've got to catch them first."

"What the hell do you mean by that?"

Dennis said, "I'd give everything I have to know where they are, my sons. They didn't come home Monday night. The next day I went to where they work." He paused. "They hadn't reported for work for a whole month. A whole month. Not one day. But they brought home their usual...wages."

Jason frowned and was silent for a few moments. Then he said in a changed voice, "Where did they get their money?"

Dennis turned aside. "They stole it. There's been robberies in the neighborhood. I think that's where they got it, but the police don't know yet." He drew a deep breath, almost a moan. "I don't want to get the police yet. I want them found. I'm their dada." He took his hand from his wife's shoulder.

"Mr. Garrity. I wanted my lads to go to the nuns' school. But Kathleen here said they were too strict—corporal punishment. So, off they were sent to the public schools, where the teachers can't whip the kids anymore. Can't force them to behave. No discipline. When Mike was in school, he complained to the school nurse—yes, they've got them now—that I beat him when he was bad. Only, he told the stupid bitch that I beat him when I was drunk, and I took the pledge twenty years ago! She came to the house flourishing papers in her fist, threatened me with the Society for the Prevention of Cruelty to Children. God damn. Never whipped my lads unless they needed it, and Kathleen pleading for them even then. 'Only children,' she said. A man isn't a child after he's twelve. The Jews say that—only, it's thirteen with them. So do we, when a kid's confirmed. But tell the mothers that, these days!"

He turned on the priest. "Father Sweeney! What are you telling the kids? Why aren't you giving them hell?"

The priest said, "Dennis, we do our best. But the secular school boards are interfering, and we're afraid. They're trying to put parochial schools out of business, destroy our authority. A godless society. That's what they want. If I were more emotional, I'd say it is a plot."

"It is," said Patrick. "Old Bernard told me. He gave me books to read." He snorted. "Separation of church and state. That's what they're muttering. And where in the blessed Constitution is it said that God should be outlawed from education? Doesn't Congress open with prayer to Almighty God? Wasn't all our colleges, and all public schools, opened under religious auspices." He turned to Dennis. "You should have sent them to the sisters' school."

"Yes," said Dennis. "Kathleen, stop crying. It's too late now."

"The nuns are so strict!" Kathleen sobbed. "Whipping the children. I remember, meself."

"It did them no harm," said her husband, and now his voice was harsh.

"Where are my lads?" Kathleen cried suddenly, her swollen face dripping with tears. But her husband turned to Jason, who had been listening with a strange expression, and not with belligerence.

Dennis said, "Don't think it was you who made them run away, Mr. Garrity. They just knew I'd find out about them." Again his face twisted and his hard realistic black eyes filled with sudden tears. "My lads. I tried to teach them. Wan't any use. What's got into the children these days?"

Jason said, and it was involuntarily, "What ever gets into men? It's always there. Da told me. It just needs to be set loose, and it's being set loose now."

"Deliberately," said the priest. "I hear reports from the sisters."

Jason went to his large window and looked out at the glowing early-summer gardens, filled with a tumult of flowers and swaying trees and green grass spreading everywhere. How long has it been since I noticed it? thought Jason, shaken by what he had just heard. It came to him that he really had no peace in himself, and he did not know why. I have everything—and perhaps I have nothing, he thought.

Then something mysteriously changed before his eyes. The gardens became more intense in color, and seemed to possess a meaning, something he had once known but could not remember. He only knew that the scene before him moved closer, surrounded him, and it was filled with love and passion and grandeur and the authority of a Law beyond the law of man. A tremendous light appeared to have fallen on the gardens, dazzling, overpowering, trembling with portent. Then he, too, felt small and affrighted, but exultant.

But the adversary remained. However, Jason was stirred with compassion. God had no pity on men. It was man's duty, then, to have pity on his fellows. He turned back to those in his office. He said to Dennis, "And you don't know where your sons are?"

"No, Mr. Garrity."

237

"My lads!" wept Kathleen, and now her husband turned to her. "Don't worry, Kathleen. They'll come back when they're hungry."

"They'll go to jail for stealing!" she wailed.

"And they'll be punished. It may save them."

Jason doubted it. He said to Dennis, "Let's hope so. I...won't do anything against them. Perhaps I'm wrong. The thing is to get them back. I'll offer a reward..."

Would old Bernard have done that? Jason asked himself. Then he remembered what Bernard had once said: "We've got to stop men from corrupting men. Break the bloody chain." With surly reluctance he had added, "And return them to God—if he'll have them. Better still, to the Blessed Mother. She understands. Her Son, I'm thinking, has too much on his mind."

17

Patricia dressed with her usual fastidious care to go to her luncheon engagement. She put on a brown silk dress with a hobble skirt bordered with a wide band of brown satin at the hem and at the waist. The neck was bordered in the same fabric. Her slippers were of the finest French kid, also brown, with simulated spats of light tan with brown buttons. She looked at herself closely in her long pier mirror, and was satisfied. She had been told often by her father that she was a beauty, called enchanting by fortune hunters, and was adored by Jason. Aided by her own self-love and the flattery of the local tradespeople, she could find few flaws in her appearance. She saw, not a very ordinary young woman in her mirror, but an apparition of taste and seductiveness. If she had one regret it was that she was still too slender, for while Lillian Russell's vast breast and large hips were not so stylish now, plumpness was still fashionable in women.

Patricia opened a locked drawer, to which only she possessed the key, and contemplated her trays of jewels. On her last birthday Jason had given her a long string of gold beads which reached to her knees, and to match, her father had given her a bracelet of the same beads, three rows of them, and a pair of yellow-gold earrings set with big topazes. She put them all on. She then finished her costume by setting her wide brown hat, with the yellow silk roses, down over her brow and putting on brown silk gloves and a brown silk cape.

After a final satisfied glance in the mirror, she went dutifully to the nursery, which was on the third floor, where she found her children in the brightness of their playroom with the scent of new grass blowing through the windows. Miss Flowers sat at a table with Sebastian and Nicole; she was teaching the boy in an irritable voice as shrill as Patricia's own. Nicole sat quietly, listening, sometimes turning the pages of her picture book. She already knew many words in it. Miss Flowers disliked both children for different reasons—Sebastian had a way of looking at her with an enigmatic directness which disconcerted her, and Nicole, never a hypocrite, was frank in her critical stare. If Miss Flowers had a favorite, it was Nicholas, who was restlessly pushing a red toy train over the polished floor, making puffing noises like a small engine. Disheveled as usual, he darted his restless eyes everywhere, but without interest. Seeing his mother, he jumped up, shouting, throwing his arms wide, his Buster Brown rompers slipping down to his hips under the long belted tunic with the sailor collar.

"Careful, dear," said Patricia as the child embraced her thighs. But she was pleased by his noisy greeting, and she preferred him over his twin, whom she lovingly called "my old lady." Nicole stood politely, tidy as always, in a tight maroon frock with a starched pinafore. Her brown hair was curled by a hot iron every day—duty of Miss Flowers—but the curls did not shine. They were topped by a flaring butterfly bow of white silk ribbon. Patricia thought the child looked beautiful, but it was strange that she never saw the real beauty of the magnificent gray eyes, clear and shining as pond water, depthless in their expression, lucent and thoughtful and perceptive.

Sebastian also stood at the table, his face impervious. He knew he would not receive a kiss from his mother, and probably not even a smile. He had trained himself not to feel too much pain. A sunbeam struck his brown hair and made a reddish halo over its curls and brought out yellow sparkles in his eyes. He was aware that his mother had a profound aversion to him. He had persuaded himself that it was because of some defect in his character, and he was always trying to discover what it was. Sometimes he was quite overwhelmed by guilt. If his mother did not love him as she loved his brother and sister, then it was his fault.

As Patricia affectionately adjusted the bow on Nicole's head, the child studied the mother's attire; she thought the long string of beads was ridiculous, clinking at the knees like that, and rattling as it swung. But as Papa had given it to Mama, it did not receive a word of criticism. She looked at the simulated spats, and her small thick nose wrinkled disapprovingly. Patricia's heavy scent discomfited her. But she smiled amiably at her mother, for she was a courteous child by nature. Nicholas, in the meantime, was excitedly jabbering about the new train, and tugging at his mother's arm for her complete attention.

"You'll wrinkle my cape, sweetheart," she said, patting him on his hot twitching cheek. But he clung to her as a squirrel clings to a branch swinging. "Mama! Mama!" he shrieked. "It's got a bell—ting-ting! Ting-ting! Look, look!" His agate eyes, so like Patricia's, bulged.

"Wonderful, dear," said Patricia with genuine fondness. Such a delightful little fellow, so lively, so endearing! So unlike...Her glance fell on the silent Sebastian and her expression changed to one of cold malevolence. Here was the cause of her never-ending sorrow, her unassuaged grief, her thwarted hunger, her renunciation of the only creature she had ever passionately loved. His insistence on being born would never be forgiven by her, for he had destroyed her happiness and left her wedded to a man she often detested or, at best, contemptuously endured. Her love for Lionel was as tumultuously alive in her as ever, and this intruder had parted her from all she had ever wanted.

Sebastian saw that malign glance and looked aside, his young heart trembling with pain. Patricia said nothing to him this morning. She kissed the twins gently, told them to be "good," and smiled at Miss Flowers, a small wiry little woman who Patricia sometimes thought resembled a starved bird. The governess smiled in an attempt at friendliness, though she had nothing but envious scorn for the other woman. Such an idle, useless, silly thing, with her airs and graces, and so unworthily rich, too! It just was not fair.

Nicole, young as she was, was sorry for her mother even though she did not know why. Acute of eye and mind, she only knew that Patricia was always tense and nervous and without ease, especially when her husband was present.

After Patricia had left, Nicole sat at the table again, and quickly leaned across it and patted Sebastian's hand in a motherly gesture of comfort. "Stop that, Nicole!" cried Miss Flowers. "Your brother is difficult enough without your pampering! Sebastian, are you being deliberately stupid, or is it natural?"

Nicole said with staid calm, "It's you who's stupid, not Bastie."

"Don't you call him 'Bastie'!" shouted Miss Flowers with fury. "Your mama doesn't like it! What a disobedient, obstinate child you are, to be sure! Perhaps that's because you are so plain!"

Nicole smiled; her little face suddenly bloomed with dimples, and the gray eyes were brilliant. "Mama thinks I am beautiful," she said. Miss Flowers seethed. "Never mind," said Nicole. "I know I look like a liver dumpling." There were times when she could be quite tolerant.

"You're lovely," said Sebastian with a look of devotion. "Your eyes, Nickie—they look like one of Mama's crystals. All shiny."

Nicholas rushed to the table, banging against it and causing the books and papers to leap. "Nickie! Play with my train." He jumped up and down, and tugged at his sister's arm. She looked down at him like an indulgent mother. "Run away, Nick, dear. I'm busy with my book."

Nicholas promptly thrust out his arm and swept books to the floor and shrieked. "Nickie, come!"

Nicole sighed. She climbed down from her chair, picked up the train, and followed by her leaping brother, went into his bedroom, carefully closing the door after her. She ruffled her twin's disordered hair. "What a trial you are," she said, and began to play with the toy. Nicholas flung himself on his knees, screaming with excitement, and pushed the train up and down on the polished floor while Nicole watched with bored affection. But Sebastian needed quiet for his lessons. She thought about her mother and frowned. She hoped Mama wouldn't be too "tired" after the luncheon with the ladies. Nicole knew all about Patricia and had developed her own euphemisms.

Patricia went slowly down the long and narrow staircases. The house was not totally quiet. Even the May sunlight was bleak and flat here, as it was stringently admitted through the little windows. Though the day was warm, the air in the huge house was chilly, and Patricia shivered. Black depression crept over her like a fog. She was not yet twenty-seven, but she felt that her life was over. Her eyes filled with tears. On the last step of the stairs she hesitated, shivering. Then she tiptoed into the dining room, hesitated again, and finally opened a cabinet and helped herself to a large glass of Patrick's potent burgundy. She swallowed slowly, her eyes closed, waiting for the warmth to gather in her vitals. When it did, at last, she went to the garage for her electric automobile and drove away.

The Schofield house, where her new "best friend" lived, was not far away, and Patricia trundled there in a warming haze. Elizabeth Schofield was a small blond girl, five years Patricia's junior. Elizabeth's parents lived in a very modern house, "Greek restoration," all white brick with white pillars and tastefully furnished, which inspired both Patricia's envy and admiration. What Elizabeth's father did was a subject for speculation in Belleville. He had "offices," but what his occupation was, no one seemed to know exactly. It was enough for Belleville, however, that he was apparently rich and had a number of servants and a fine new Cadillac, and his wife, a fashionable woman, was a socialite. Elizabeth herself had the face of a wicked child, at once innocent and evil, and her gossip was charmingly malicious. Winking at the other young ladies after Patricia had had two small glasses of sherry, she would add a large measure of strong bourbon to the succeeding ones. Patricia's subsequent indiscretions at the luncheon table proved unfailingly amusing.

She would always refer to Jason as "that oaf I'm married to," and tell of his more private ineptitudes. A luncheon with Patricia served for giggling discussion for at least a week. Oddly enough, Elizabeth's father would listen attentively, and often question his daughter with shrewdness. Patrick Mulligan and Clementine Lindon were the only ones who had some idea of Mr. Schofield's activities. Clementine would refer to him as "that confidence man" to her dear trusted friend. But Mr. Schofield was a regular visitor to her establishment and so she would say nothing more even to Patrick, who was under the impression that Mr. Schofield was a legal thief. Daniel Dugan, his nephew, was less amiable on the subject, but said nothing much to his uncle. He merely watched alertly. He had heard of Mr. Schofield in Philadelphia and New York. Mr. Schofield had offices there, too, equally as ambiguous. What he was doing in this backwater was a matter on which Daniel speculated to himself.

Patricia rarely remembered her return home; she only knew that she was sleepy and relieved of her chronic suffering. She would leave her automobile in front of the house, stagger inside, sway up the stairs to her room, and there throw herself on her bed to fall into a heavy slumber. A few hours later she would awaken in a state of fierce hysteria with recriminations of all and sundry, particularly her father and her husband. There would be an odor of Sen-Sen about her. Strangely enough, neither Patrick nor Jason was suspicious. Patricia was careful. Her clothes were always neat, even if her face was drawn and haggard and her eyes red and sore from tears unconsciously shed during her drunken sleep. She never recalled what she had said at the luncheon, except that the occasion had been pleasant. As for Patrick and Jason, they would murmur together solicitously about Patricia's tenuous health and her too-acute sensitivity, and treat her with tenderness.

Each morning, on his rounds at the resort, Jason went into Lionel's office, where he was always greeted with the old smiling affection. Only lately had a peculiar flicker briefly appeared in Lionel's lupine yellow eyes. It was not there all the time, and Jason never noticed.

Jason dutifully inquired about his sister, Joan. As always, Lionel's face lighted at the mention of his wife's name. Joan was splendid, even after five years of marriage. Joan was faultless in every way. Jason listened with a smile. He liked Lionel's offices, even if unlike his own. They were spare but attractive, all gleaming wood floor and light airy draperies and brass electric lamps. The room held an astringent if agreeable odor that seemed to emanate from Lionel himself.

Jason sat down, a massive figure in his mourning black, and he and Lionel discussed business matters. Lionel had taken to smoking a pipe, and he leaned back in his swivel chair and contemplated the smoke. Because of the warmth of the day, he had removed his coat and sat in his fine percale white shirtsleeves, though he had not loosened his narrow red tie, only a few shades darker than his fiery hair. His black silk vest, patterned and rich, was neatly buttoned, and a gold watch chain twinkled over his stomach. Despite his snub nose and freckles, his native appearance of compact elegance had increased greatly. His hands were quick and restless and stroked a folded newspaper on his desk as he talked with Jason.

"We're having a little trouble again, I hear, with Mr. and Mrs. Adrian Schlecter, Jason, in Suite 5-G."

"Yes. I found a sheaf of their complaints on my desk this morning. I'm getting exasperated with them. We've told them over and over that they can't bring their little grandsons here except at Christmas. I'm about ready to tell them to get out—now—and not come back. I showed them what the oldest grandson did to the cabinets in the living room of the suite, and what another one did to the expensive French wallpaper in his bedroom. 'Only dear little children,' Mrs. Schlecter said, with that foolish grin of hers. She didn't offer to pay for the damage, though. I reminded her that we had made a concession in letting those damned kids here for Easter, and that she could not entertain them again. She then accused me of 'not loving the little ones.'"

"They're our most generous guests," said Lionel thoughtfully. "And they have the most expensive suite and stay here most of the year. They give good tips, too."

"We're running a hotel for adults," said Jason. "Except at Christmas, we don't want our guests annoyed by kids. The Ipswich House is regarded as a retreat."

Lionel laughed. "Especially for gentlemen who've had enough of their wives for a while."

Jason frowned. He was never at ease even with these discreet arrangements. "What the hell," Patrick had said. "Jase, it's not our business, provided they behave themselves and act...decorously. Is that the word? Yes. A gentleman has a right to bring a female guest, if the gentlemen and the ladies always occupy separate rooms and are sufficiently discreet. If they...ah...visit their friends in their rooms, whose affair is that?" Patrick had chuckled. "Human nature. You'll never be able to outlaw that, Jase, not even with the blue laws here. Anyway, they always leave the bedroom or sitting-room doors open."

"Until midnight," Jason had said.

Patrick had coughed. "Well, they don't want their neighbors to be disturbed by...conversation. Besides, over half our guests are legally married."

"Even if they seem to have a new wife every year, some of them."

"Well..." Patrick had spread his hands and had smiled.

"People talk, Mr. Mulligan." Jason still called him that.

"It doesn't keep the guests away. I haven't heard our shopkeepers complain, either." He had patted Jason's shoulder. "Never mind. The new hotel we're building will be a family one—rugged and simple. Come on, Jase. This hotel here is a happy place."

"I feel like a whoremaster," Jason had grumbled, and Patrick had laughed. "Irish priggishness," he had commented. "We may all be devout Catholics, but there's a lot of Calvinism in us, too. That makes sin even more interesting."

Today Jason said to Lionel, "Mrs. Schlecter has another complaint. She said their neighbors were roistering all night and kept her and her husband awake to all hours. When I checked, I found there were two married couples quietly enjoying an after-dinner drink together in their sitting room. At eight o'clock. But Mrs. Schlecter likes to go to bed at eight to be 'up with the dear caroling birdies,' as she says. I told her that other neighbors object to her singing at four or five

A.M. Before God gets up. She then said something about sinful people wasting God's blessed time."

"I know," said Lionel. "She has tried to wheedle the room-service waiters to bring breakfast for her and her husband at five, an hour before the kitchen is even open. I suggested she have sandwiches wrapped to take upstairs after dinner, and she agreed, then wanted a hot plate to make coffee in her room. That, I said, was forbidden. I'm more tactful than you, Jason. I said the fire department has rules and we can't violate them."

"I'm ready to throw them out."

Lionel examined his pipe. "They bring at least six other couples here, friends, who come here every year with them. That would be a loss of several thousand a month, if they all marched out and never came back again." He looked at Jason. "My business is feeding the guests. Just don't be too rigid."

While Jason fumed, Lionel opened his newspaper. "Look at this," he said. "Just when we wanted to install oil heat instead of coal, Washington warns—they're always warning—that our oil resources will be exhausted by 1930. And coal soon after."

"We should heat with wood?"

Lionel chuckled. "And here's another thing. Natural gas, according to them, is already running short. I've noticed the heat did go down several times in the gas stoves this winter. Another funny thing. When my men went down to the markets this morning for supplies, they were told the last delivery of sugar, meat, and butter was a third less than two weeks ago. And they were offered graham flour instead of the white. They couldn't get a full supply of ham and bacon, either."

Something stirred darkly in Jason's mind, something old Bernard had said once. Jason could not remember. "The railroads aren't on strike again."

"No. But it's funny. Well, probably nothing to worry about. Time we got back to work."

Jason encountered Daniel Dugan in the lower hall. Daniel smiled at him and said, "Carrying the world on your shoulders again, Jason?"

Jason shrugged. He still did not trust or like Daniel. They exchanged a few casual remarks. Daniel said, "We're doing better business this year than last, for this time of the year. But prices of everything are going up, I see."

"They usually do," said Jason, and went to his own offices. The glory of the May day was no longer glorious to him. He

246

at thinking at his desk for a long time and came to himself with a heavy feeling of depression. What was it that Bernard had said long ago? "Taxes are garnered for wars, and that's really the thought behind that new Sixteenth Amendment, the federal income tax. Mark my words. Taxes mean wars and tyranny. Four Horsemen of the Apocalypse. That's the way the big boys get power—through wars and taxes. Power bought with blood and confiscation. I know my history."

Well, thought Jason, taxes won't bother me. I'm not a rich man. And war with whom? America won't ever engage in foreign wars. We've got too much sense. And Washington's too small and feeble to push us into one.

Jason settled down to the papers on his desk. More and more guests were arriving every day. Even in his distant offices Jason could hear the hubbub of new arrivals and the sound of automobiles on the drive. He worked steadily until six, when he was interrupted by the assistant manager, who did all the hiring and, when necessary, the discharging. Edward Griswold was an earnest young man, dedicated to his employers. There was something celibate about him. He talked only business, and conducted his work in privacy, usually without consulting anyone. Therefore, Jason was surprised when Edward knocked apologetically at his door and then entered. "Mr. Garrity. We have a problem."

"When didn't we have?" asked Jason wearily. He wanted to go home for dinner. The day had been arduous. It was his duty to greet the more important guests on arrival, and there had been a number of them today and there had been some dissatisfaction about assigned rooms and suites. Jason, never at ease, as was Lionel, had had to keep his temper, and that had been hard. "What do you want, Eddie?"

"We advertised for a first-class cook," said Mr. Griswold. "Old Emil, our best, has given us notice for the first of June. We put advertisements in all the newspapers, in Philadelphia and New York." He paused. "Only the best, we stated. Experienced in French cooking. We have an applicant, only one qualified. The others were ... well, not up to it." Mr. Griswold had borrowed some English phrases from his reading of Victorian novels.

"You have a qualified applicant? Well, why don't you hire him? What has it to do with me? That's your job, Eddie."

"That's the problem." He fell into gloom. "The only one qualified, and he has references from Delmonico's and the Waldorf in New York, excellent references. The only thing...I'm afraid everyone in the kitchen will quit if I hire him."

"What's he got? Leprosy?" Jason was impatient. He looked at his watch.

Mr. Griswold did not smile. "No. He...he's a Negro, Mr. Garrity. I felt I couldn't hire him without your approval."

Jason vividly remembered some of the old signs in Belleville, and there were still some: "No Irish. No Catholics. No Foreign-Born." His gorge rose. "Send the man in."

Mr. Griswold, after an astonished stare, scuttled out. A moment later a tall young Negro, slender and stiff of demeanor, entered. He was very black, very distinguished-looking, with fine features and a haughty glance. He was dressed like a rich gentleman in black silky broadcloth, and with a diamond pin in his tie. His hair was thick and smooth. There was a diamond ring on his finger. He stood in silence before Jason's desk, and the two young men studied each other for a few moments. Then Jason said, "Don't you have an ass, and knees? Sit down!"

The young Negro hesitated, then sat down, crossing long legs. His feet wore polished boots. "Your name?" asked Jason. The other ceremoniously reached into his pocket and brought out a card case. He slowly removed a thick cream-colored card and presented it to Jason. It read: "Edmund Patterson. Chef Suprême. Cordon Bleu." His eyes challenged Jason, large lustrous black eyes with lashes as long as a woman's. The engraving on the card was in Old English script.

"I understand you've worked in New York and Philadelphia, Mr. Patterson."

"Yes. For a number of years." His voice was mellifluous and tinged with an English accent. "Before that, in Johannesburg, South Africa, where I was registered in a gourmet cooking school."

"I see," said Jason, who did not. He was becoming irritated at the other's manner. "You were born in South Africa?"

"Yes." The man's hauteur increased. "I belong to the Bantu tribe. But...I am a Zulu."

Jason was more at sea than ever. "Zulu?"

"We Zulu men are the best chefs in the world. We are not like the Bantus."

Jason leaned back in his chair and found himself broadly smiling. But the other man simply stared at him with a slight affront.

"You were a chef in Johannesburg. What, may I ask, did they pay you there?"

"Four thousand gold rand a year. Equal to dollars."

Jason whistled. "That's a lot of money. And . . . in New York and Philadelphia?"

"About the same . . . sir."

"We pay our head chef—I mean, cook—two thousand a year, Mr. Patterson."

The young Negro's face held instant disdain. "Possibly not a good chef. Or a chef at all."

"We're not a stylish town in Belleville, Mr. Patterson. How did you get here?"

"I saw your advertisement in the New York *Times*. I like New York, sir, but my wife, Sue Ann, doesn't. I met her four years ago, when I was attending a convention in New York. She's a fine dressmaker, and employed four women. She was born in New York. We have two children. Sue Ann wants to live in a small town. For the sake of our children. She visited once, here, and likes it. What am I to do?" he asked with sudden desperation and in masculine confidence. "Sue Ann has a very strong will, and she is afraid to bring up children in New York. A bad influence, she says. Sue Ann—she can be very assertive at times, like all Zulu women. Yes, she is Zulu too. I wanted to return to Johannesburg, where men like myself are respected for their accomplishments. But Sue Ann is an American, and refused to leave." He sighed. "I was much appreciated at Delmonico's. I was offered much more money if I would remain there."

"Women can be difficult," said Jason, trying not to smile again.

Mr. Patterson sighed. "Yes. Can't they? I should have put my foot down. I did try. But Sue Ann put two feet down."

Jason looked through his window reflectively. "America is a very prejudiced country, Mr. Patterson."

"No more than elsewhere, I assume, sir. I worked one year in London. I don't understand prejudice."

Jason looked at him with concealed amusement. "You've said you aren't like the . . . the Bantus."

"Indeed not! Very ignorant people. We Zulus have a proscription against intermarriage with them. We have our own apartheid."

Jason struggled with his amusement. "I'm afraid you are a very prejudiced man, Mr. Patterson."

"There is such a thing as not intermingling with your inferiors, sir."

Mankind, thought Jason, is congenitally stupid. He said, "And what makes a man inferior to other men?"

"It's a matter of intelligence, sir."

"Well, on that I agree. You speak like an educated man."

"I'm a graduate of a university for the Zulus in Pretoria." The musical voice was rich with pride. "I speak English, French, and Afrikaans."

Negroes, reflected Jason, did not attend universities in America, at least not good ones. "You won't find life easy in Belleville, Mr. Patterson. We have only about half a dozen Negro families here."

"I am a Zulu!"

Jason waved his hand. "That is a distinction white Americans won't understand."

"I'm willing to try. If I may ask the salary?"

"Two thousand a year."

"Impossible. I am willing to start for three thousand, for one year, and then an increase."

He brought forth references from the Savoy Hotel in London, from Delmonico's in New York, and another from Philadelphia, one of the best restaurants. Each was laudatory and expressed regrets that Mr. Patterson was leaving. Jason studied them. He said, "You won't find good accommodations here."

"I will build my own house. I have catered, too, in the best establishments in Johannesburg and New York. My own house, in South Africa, was a very nice one."

"It won't be easy."

"Nothing is easy, sir." He added, "But you, perhaps, sir, would not understand that."

Jason suddenly lost his temper. He leaned forward in his chair, and his eyes were bright with anger. "And how would you know that, then? I am Irish. My people suffered through a famine. We are under English rule, and the English treated us like dogs with fleas because of our race and religion. When we rebelled, our women and children were beaten on the streets by English soldiers! And raped. My grandfather's little sister was hanged because she tried to defend her faith—a little girl, Mr. Patterson! My people died of hunger in the cities and on the roads and in the country. No one helped us. We suffered for centuries..." Jason's breath came heavy and fast and his face was engorged with rage. Mr. Patterson listened with astonishment.

"It's a long and terrible story," said Jason. "Too long to tell you now. Those of us who could get on ships came to America. Most of us weren't admitted, for we were suffering from consumption and famine fever. We were left to die— men, women, and children—on the docks of New York. We who survived lived in caves, in the winters, in Central Park. No one would employ us, or if we were employed, we were paid very little—so little that we starved again. We thought we had come to a free country! Free, hell! Can't you read? Almost all factories in America—still—have signs on them: 'No Irish. No Catholics. No Foreign-Born.' We're pariahs, outcasts, and we are still despised. For many years no one would rent to us. We lived in hovels. What do you know about this, you with your fine university, your education, your large salary, your grand clothes. I tell you, the slaves in the South were better treated than we Irish. And better than the Jews and the Hungarians and the Poles—all white men. And the hate still exists. What do you know?"

He threw himself back into his chair, and his face was swollen with anger. "Not too many years ago a fine old man, an Italian, was murdered in this town, a poor old man who had a shop near where I lived. Only a few weeks ago a poor Jewish shopkeeper was attacked—right here. My grandfather died protecting him. Only a few weeks ago. And you say I wouldn't understand! Let me tell you this: I am a man. You are a man. We have to deal with human evil all our lives, without whimpering. Or, we aren't men at all."

The young Zulu's face had changed, become shocked, moved. He said in a low voice, "Forgive me. I didn't know."

"It's time you did," said Jason, and coughed. "Here in America, in Belleville, we lived in a hovel, my grandfather, my father, my mother, my brother and sister, and I. My old grandfather worked until the day he died. My mother died of consumption. There was no money to cure her, to feed her. We had to fight...Well, never mind. But unless we are born fortunate, all of us, we are going to suffer from our dear fellowman. Learn that once and for all, Mr. Patterson."

After a moment he said in a drained voice, "You've got to get over your own prejudices, Mr. Patterson, as do we all." Then he said, "Unlike you, I never attended a university. I've worked hard since I was a young child. Do you know that until a very few years ago children in America were forced to work in factories and mills, even mines, when they were as young as five and six? Tens of thousands died of injuries, of starvation or disease. No one cared! Oh, my God. What do you know?"

The young Zulu swallowed convulsively. In a humble voice he said, "I didn't know anything. I'm sorry, sir. Would you like a glass of water?"

Suddenly Jason wanted to laugh, but without mirth and only with bitterness. "No. But I should like some whiskey. Have a glass with me." He got up, and discovered he was trembling. He went to a cabinet and brought out two glasses and a bottle of bourbon. He filled the glasses and lifted his. "To humanity, and may God's wrath visit it!"

"Amen," said Mr. Patterson, and drank. Jason said, "Wait here," and left the room. He went to the kitchen. The evening meal was in preparation and the huge kitchen was full of steam, delicious odors, and hurrying men. Jason lifted his voice and shouted, "Everybody stop! I have something to say!"

It was rare for the manager of the hotel to enter the kitchen, and all the men stared. Jason said, "I'll make this short. I have just hired a chef, a real chef, to take charge of all the meals here. He is a Zulu, a black man, an African, and he has worked in the best restaurants in the world, in South Africa, London, New York, and Philadelphia. He has class, as you'd say, and education. You'd call him a nigger. I call him a superior man.

"Now, if any of you'd like to quit, say so now. You won't get work at the salaries you get here. In fact, you won't find jobs at all if I can help it, and I can. Understand that right now. If you make Mr. Patterson's life miserable, you'll answer to me. You will be working under Mr. Patterson.

"Well? Are you going to quit?"

There was a deep sweltering silence in the room, and all the men stared at each other, dumbfounded.

Then one man stepped forward, a Hungarian. "Mr. Garrity," he said, "you don't need shout at us. We got good jobs here, yes? We like this place. I do pastry. We treated right here, by everybody. We work with this...this black man. Yes." He turned to the others.

There was another silence. Then some said sullenly, and some with smiles, "Yes. Yes."

Then all were laughing and shaking their heads as they went back to work. Their attitude now was that Mr. Garrity had been absurd.

Jason returned to his office. He said to the Zulu chef, "It's all right. You can start tomorrow, if you want to. But there's one thing you have to know, Mr. Patterson. Every man in that kitchen thinks he is better than any other man there, and far superior in every way. That's human nature. If you look for slights, you'll get them. But for God's sake, don't insult them, either!"

18

Jason went to the little Holy Cross cemetery on his way home, in the last brightness of the May day. He stood at Bernard's grave, which was still raw, though little tufts of wild grass were already sprouting on it. The mound had not settled yet. When it did, there would be a large marble cross on it. The cemetery had that strange eerie silence only graveyards have, as if filled with watching eyes and sentient presences. Where was Bernard now, if anywhere? It was as if he had never lived, that ferocious and gallant old man. Jason said aloud, "Da?" Was this all that was left of a heroic life, of any human life—a mound of brown wet earth? For what was a man born? For what did he endure living? For what did he die? The earth was one vast tomb, and there were no answers from it. Let priests expound, explain. They were shouting in a universal darkness, deluded, perhaps even afraid.

Jason got into his automobile and went home. He had but one life to live and he would live it as best he could. Still, he thought, I am blessed in many ways, with my dear wife and my children and my fortune. I could have nothing. He tried to lighten his mood, and forced himself to think of his new Zulu chef and finally could smile. No matter a man's race or color or religion, he was one with the rest of his wretched fellows, and they all had one terrible adversary—God. And each other, of course, sad to say.

The house was very quiet except for the sounds in the kitchen and the voices of servants. Jason went upstairs to his wife's room. He found her, as he did so often, fast asleep on her bed. She had removed only her slippers. Her fine hair had fallen over her face. Her arms were flung out as if pleading. How thin the poor girl was! She ate almost nothing. She looked lost, sprawled on her bed in her brown dress. One topaz earring lay beside her, and Jason picked it up and put it on her dresser. He then stood and gazed at her tenderly, his darling, his fragile wife. She was so ineffable, so easily hurt. He still could not believe that this delicate creature had married him, with all her daintiness and feminine emotions. His smile was almost humble.

She had no strength, he reflected, no endurance, or she

would not be so tired this often, so enervated after a mere lunch with friends. Everything, it seemed, exhausted her. The fine hair puffed up and down with her irregular breathing. She would have her regular migraine tonight. Patricia moaned; then, as if feeling Jason's eyes on her, she started awake. She sat up, swaying, looked at her husband, and pushed back her hair. "Oh, good heavens," she murmured. "I've missed tea, and I haven't eaten all day." She clutched her temples. "Oh, what a headache I have! And I'm sick to my stomach."

Jason went into her bathroom, and, as usual, mixed her a dose of Bromo-Seltzer. She drank it greedily, licking the last drops from her dry lips. She averted her eyes from him, and her mouth became sullen. "Shall I ring for tea for you, dearest?" asked Jason.

Patricia shuddered. "No." She smoothed her wrinkled dress and yawned abruptly.

"You should have stayed in bed, as you promised," he said.

"I didn't promise. How tiresome you are, Jason. You expect me to spend my whole life in this awful house and go nowhere. Not that there is anywhere interesting to go in this town." She found one of the rats which bolstered up her hair in the latest Irene Castle fashion; it was under her elbow. She pushed it under a slight buttock, and her sallow cheek flushed with vexation.

"Why don't you stay in bed tonight?" asked Jason. "You can have a tray up here. I'll call Joan and say we won't be there for dinner."

Patricia gave him a glance that was purely vicious. "Oh, you would like to imprison me here all the time, wouldn't you! Never seeing anyone but you and my father and my children. What fun! What time is it? Seven! Oh, do go away and let me get ready. Joan is expecting us in half an hour."

She and Jason had dinner with Lionel and Joan once a week, and that occasion, combined with Joan's and Lionel's weekly visit, was almost all Patricia lived for with real happiness. All the days between meant nothing to her. To sit in the presence of Lionel—and to watch him "suffer" too—was to know hours of meaning and painful joy.

"Are you sure you are well enough to go?" asked Jason with anxiety, noting the drawn pallor of her face. "We were out late last night with Daniel and Molly."

"Oh, how I *did* enjoy that!" Patricia cried, and slapped the pillow near her vindictively. "Daniel and Molly! I can't stand either of them! Daniel's sly and Molly is stupid. They have no conversation. And Molly watches me all the time. Like a thief. And then she looks at you like a cow, all big eyes. Everyone knows she was in love with you. It makes me laugh."

"Molly? In love with me? Patricia, that's ridiculous. We've never even liked each other." Jason laughed. He was amazed at the very thought.

"Well, she was, and probably still is. In a way, I'm sorry for my cousin, marrying such a vulgar unattractive thing as Molly. He could have had the best in Philadelphia. I could never understand it. Oh, do go away, Jason! I've got to change and freshen up." Her voice was shrill, and she shrank when Jason lovingly touched her brow.

Jason went away, to see his children. He found Patrick romping with them. Nicholas was swinging from one of his arms in a monkeylike fashion, and shrieking, Sebastian was standing nearby, smiling, and Nicole was holding his free hand, smiling at him like a fatuous mother. Patrick was fatter and pinker and balder than ever. He resembled a giant Kewpie doll, paunchy and joyously smiling. His little bright blue eyes shone happily as he played with the children. They sparkled even more on seeing Jason, whom he loved dearly as a son, for all Jason's "John Knox" convictions. To a jovial Irishman like Patrick, the "black Irish" were formidable, and could be daunting, especially to those of a more flexible bent.

Nicole ran to Jason, and before she held up her short arms to him, she scrutinized him in her usual fashion, seeking his mood. She felt that something had disturbed him today, had aroused his anger, which could be awesome at times. He picked her up and she gave him a kiss, murmuring into his neck. The murmur was as consoling as the hand-pat she had given Sebastian this morning. Nicholas, yelping as customary, rushed to his father, bouncing up and down, demanding to be picked up too. Jason set Nicole down and took his wriggling son up; Nicholas squirmed in his arms. Though it was cool now in the nursery, the child was sweating vigorously, his hair damp, his mouth uttering panting incoherencies. Sebastian approached but stood at least two feet away, and the man and the child smiled at each other in silence, the warm understanding flowing between them without words. Jason had the sudden thought that if he told Sebastian of his encounter with the new Zulu chef, Sebastian, even at his age, would comprehend entirely, and with sympathy.

"Expected you earlier, Jason," said Patrick. He thought it was a grand sight, the big dark man and his children together.

"I visited Da's grave," said Jason.

"Oh," said Patrick, and gave his son-in-law a sharp and searching look. So, the bucko had been annoyed or upset about something today and had gone to the grave for some comfort, then. Patrick waited for some hint of this, but Jason was disentangling himself from Nicholas' fervid grip and it appeared to take all his attention. Patrick said, "And where's Patricia?"

"She had a migraine," said Jason.

Nicholas clung to his knees, still jabbering. Then Nicole firmly pulled him off. "Enough," she said. "Be quiet, Nick." Instantly the little boy sucked in his breath and was still, though he gave the impression of vibrating like a struck violin string.

"She gets them too often," said the concerned Patrick.

"Yes. I tried to persuade her that we shouldn't go to Lionel and Joan's tonight, but she insisted."

"Always mannerly," said Patrick. "And considerate." But he frowned a little. He was fond of Lionel, trusted him and appreciated his acumen and many talents, but he did not like the beautiful Joan, with her misleading composure and apparent serenity. He did not find them soothing; he had come to the conclusion that "that angelic lady has more to her than seems, and it's not good, I'm thinking." He had guessed long ago that Joan had nothing but remote derision for Patricia, and this offended him. When Patricia was particularly inane, Joan's heavenly blue eyes would seek out Lionel's, and for an instant or two the expression in them was not so celestial. Patrick did not think his daughter inane; he thought her childlike and trusting. Joan, he was now convinced, was neither; once Mrs. Lindon had expressed her opinion to him that Joan was spiritually corrupt, and though he had been horrified at this remark, he had lately almost come to believe it. Always moved by feminine beauty, he had told himself that Lionel had corrupted her, if corrupted she was. As for Lionel, Patrick genially accepted his corruption; most men were so, except Jason, of course.

The two men then remarked on the increase of early arrivals this year at Ipswich House. Jason mentioned Lionel's information that food supplies had been short lately. Patrick frowned. "I wonder what's up," he said. "Heard the farmers were doing well, and there's lots of beef and pork and butter. Maybe our suppliers haven't been ordering enough."

"Maybe," said Jason. Miss Flowers then appeared to summon the children for their supper in the little dining room connected with the nursery, and so Jason had no time to express his amorphous uneasiness.

"Tired, Jase?" asked Patrick as they went downstairs together.

"A little. The new arrivals were pettish, more so than usual."

Patrick chortled. "They always are. You've got to have patience."

"I'm not as tolerant as you, Mr. Mulligan."

"And that I know, lad. You never were." On the bottom step he put his hand affectionately on Jason's arm. "When you're my age, nothing much will rile you. I promise. How was my darling Molly last night?"

"Astringent—as usual."

Patrick nodded. "Irish tongues, like knives. All Irish women have them. I love that colleen. Danny's very lucky, for all her sharpness. But a great heart it is she has, a great heart. Lovely."

Patrick went into the dining room and Jason went to the library to wait for Patricia and to read his newspaper. He saw an inconspicuous item: The French government had ordered early military maneuvers and were increasing the draft of young men. Britain had ordered ten new warships. The Balkans were again in an uproar, but then, when were they not? Czar Nicholas had addressed the Duma yesterday in "a closed session." But when were the Russians, always ambiguous and full of mystery, ever candid with anyone? Winston Churchill, the item added, was inspecting the Dardanelles at the government's request. Well, the mighty British Empire was always vigilant. Nothing sinister there. The exiled Communist, Lenin, was in Germany at the present time, and so was his friend Trotsky. The German kaiser was not noted for his intelligence; none of the Hanovers were, which included the present King of England, George V, another grandson of the late Queen Victoria who had not been particularly bright.

To cover his uneasiness, Jason turned to more conspicuous items in the newspaper. The rift between President Taft and Theodore Roosevelt was becoming wider. Teddy was roaring about the country giving flaming speeches concerning his

"New Nationalism." "I stand for the Square Deal!" In Cleveland he had announced that he was a candidate for the presidency. He had scornful words for Elihu Root, who had "given" the nomination to President Taft at the Republican convention. The Progressive party, Teddy's own, had nominated Mr. Roosevelt. Taft was incensed. "I have been a man of straw long enough!" he declared with unusual fervor. Politics, thought Jason. Roosevelt had divided the Republican party; if he was not its candidate, then, by God, he would stop Taft.

Wilson, thought Jason. He did not know why he felt a thrill of something like fear. Patricia then entered, pulling on her gloves, and he stood up. She looked fresh and glowing, he was happy to see. He did not know that the slight rosiness of her cheeks and lips was not her own, but had been applied with a careful piece of cotton. Only her eyes remained slightly reddened and swollen. The veil on her pink velvet hat mostly concealed this, however. She wore a very Parisian dress, which Jason had not seen before, of gray silk, tight of skirt, and draped with silver bugle beads over the bodice. She had put on her aquamarines, and a full capelet of white fox was flung over her shoulders. If her figure was too meager, she did have style and her waist was flexible and slender. Jason regarded her with loving admiration. "How pretty you look, Patricia," he said. "Is the headache gone?"

But she cried in anger, "Oh, Jason, how could you! You didn't change; still in that old black serge, and you haven't even shaved tonight!"

"What of it? It's only Lionel and Joan. No other guests tonight."

"But how insulting to your ... host!"

"For God's sake, Patricia! I see Lionel every day, and he's only family, as is Joan."

"You can be sure Lionel's changed!"

Jason smiled indulgently. "Well, he's always 'the glass of fashion,' always was even when he had only two dollars to rub together."

"He's elegant!"

"Always was." Jason held out his arm to his wife, but she brushed by him in a pet. She refused his help in getting into the automobile, pushing aside his hand. The exceedingly tight skirt pulled up on her leg and showed the thin and nearly shapeless calf. Jason thought it indecent. Women's fashions! It wouldn't be long before they displayed their knees, and knees were unsightly objects.

The long mauve twilight had settled over the little city, and the mountains had turned a dull plum. Patricia held her hat in the nimble breeze. "I do wish you'd put up the top, Jason. That wind is blowing my hair about, and if my hat wasn't pinned on, it would blow away." She smelled of lilacs and face powder. Jason was silent; he was listening. In the distance an organ-grinder was grating out an unfamiliar air. It had a sorrowful and poignant sound. "You know music so well, Patricia. What is that tune?"

"Oh, Jason, you are so ignorant! If only you would go more often to concerts with me in Philadelphia, and the opera. But no. Always business, always some excuse. Lionel takes even Joan, and she a cripple." Patricia paused, seething again. "That's the Miserere."

"Miserable?" said Jason, controlling his temper.

"Not quite, for heaven's sake. It's a mourning song, in a way. The Catholic Church uses it sometimes, at a different tempo. A sort of tolling."

A mourning song. Jason listened, and it seemed to echo the pain in his chest. The city darkened; a lamplighter was running about like a cricket, attending to the streetlamps. The houses Jason drove by looked shut and ominous. What nonsense. He was seeing omens everywhere. There was no sound just now but of that majestic, slow, and lost music echoing through the quiet streets. Jason felt cold. He was in no mood for Lionel and Joan tonight. He thought of his grandfather and the old shack on the derelict street where he had spent his wretched childhood. All at once that little house seemed, to Jason . . . What? Safe. Now, what the hell do I mean by that? he thought. He had never remembered it before without gloom, but suddenly it possessed peace, in spite of the hunger and dire poverty.

"I suppose you didn't even notice you got a letter today from your brother, the priest," said Patricia. "It was on the hall table in the tray, where all mail is put."

"Jack?" Jason considered. "No. I just passed the table. I didn't look."

"You are the most unobservant person I ever knew! Really, Jason. Do slow down. We are approaching their house."

They were now in the newer part of the city, quite close to the mountains, which had become black shadows against a darkly starred sky. Patricia looked about her with her usual umbrage and envy. Every house was new, modern, attractive, set on wide lawns with old trees which had been carefully

260

preserved. The houses were not mansions; they were solid-middle-class. "New money," Mrs. Lindon had called it. But they had no wooden fretwork, no tall narrow windows, and, in most cases, no verandas. That was the latest style—no verandas, no porches. They had a light look, which Jason thought seemed impermanent, even frivolous. Well, it was a new age; things did change.

The Nolan house was set back from the street, which was wider than the older streets in Belleville. Mr. Schultz' architect had been consulted by Lionel and Joan, and the building was handsome, of pale rose brick with white doors and shutters. The front door was embellished by shallow wide steps and pale polished stone. On each side was a slender wooden column, painted white, which gave the house a slight Regency air. The windows were quite large and glimmered with the light of two or three electric chandeliers. Patricia thought of her father's house and almost cried. What a struggle she had had to make Patrick install electricity! "Harsh? What do you mean, Dada? You want that horrible old gaslight still, so smelly, so dangerous?"

A neat little maid of some fourteen years opened the door. She wore a black dress and a frilled white apron and cap and had the innocent face of a young colt. Jason smiled at her, but Patricia rustled past with a haughty uplifted face as if the girl was not human. Lionel came into the hall, smiling, in a dark gray suit excellently cut, his lean figure like that of a ballet dancer, his red hair smoothly combed into glistening waves, his gray tie pierced by a modest diamond pin, his linen immaculate. At the sight of him Patricia's heart lurched, as always, with deep pain mingled with aching joy, and her lips trembled, remembering. The little maid took her hat and her cape and Jason's deplorably battered fedora.

"Lionel!" said Patricia, as if it had been years since she had seen him. She gave him her hand. He held it for a long moment, and her flesh had a powerful desire to become one with his. He pressed her fingers, then turned to Jason and struck him affectionately on the shoulder. "Nice night, isn't it?" he said in the most beloved voice in the world to Patricia. Her face was transformed; it had become so radiant that she was almost pretty. While Jason and Lionel exchanged some casual remarks, she stared at Lionel fixedly, until Lionel became aware of her gaze and, taking her elbow, led her into the parlor, where Joan was waiting.

Here was no heavy mahogany or walnut furniture. It was

261

all delicate French reproductions, upholstered in pastel colors, the lamps of crystal or subdued gilt, the rugs good if imitation Aubussons, the draperies airy and fresh, and spring flowers everywhere in crystal vases. There was a faint flowery scent in the warm air, and apple wood burned in the marble fireplace. An exceptionally fine print of a Madonna and Child hung above the mantel, on which stood an ormolu clock.

In a lady chair near the fire sat Joan, beautiful in a blue velvet robe embroidered in gold. She looked like a child perched there; her masses of gleaming black hair were knotted in a classical fashion, but tendrils had escaped to frame her perfect face, giving her an aspect of innocence and defenselessness. But there was nothing defenseless in the large dark blue eyes. They were keenly aware and observant. Her little white hands were folded in her lap.

Lionel, on his wedding night, had been delighted to discover that Joan's legs were not twisted or shriveled, but due to Kate's assiduous massaging were perfectly formed and round and white, even if small and without strength. They could have belonged to a child, the knees dimpled and smooth, the toes rosy. Patricia, even as she kissed Joan's cheek, was filled with resentment of her sister-in-law's dazzling appearance, and seething with envy of the house and its furnishings.

"What an exquisite dress," said Joan in her soft and fluting voice. "Paris, no doubt."

"Yes. Dada bought it for me in New York." At least, thought Patricia, it was more expensive than that robe she's wearing. Belleville!

Joan smiled. She never talked very much; her features were expressive enough, but she never revealed her emotions or thoughts except to Lionel. She said, "And how are the dear children?"

"Splendid," said Patricia. "The twins are adorable. Nicole said to me, yesterday, 'Mama, you're more stylish than the ladies in *Harpers Bazaar!*' She sees so much, the dear little thing. At her age, too. And Nicholas! He is so artistic. He draws all the time and colors with crayons. Miss Flowers says he's very gifted. An artist in the family! I always wanted to paint, to do something creative."

Joan's mouth lifted in a gentle smile. "And Sebastian?" The smile was somewhat malicious.

Patricia's face changed, became almost ugly. "Sebastian? Oh. He does well enough, though Miss Flowers thinks he is very slow. I do hope he has all his wits. So unlike the twins.

He never chatters like Nicholas, who just bubbles with ideas and observations. Did I tell you what Nicholas said to me a week ago?"

"I believe you did," said Joan. "He is always talking, isn't he?" Her tone was neutral, but Patricia flushed. How she hated this miserable cripple who had stolen Lionel on the "rebound"! It was just like her to favor Sebastian over the twins, Sebastian, who rarely remarked on anything and who was so very sly. One never knew what was in his mind, if anything. Come to think of it, thought Patricia, annoyed, he resembles his dear auntie, Joan. How I should like to tell this cripple that she isn't his aunt at all, but his stepmother! The thought made Patricia smile, and the smile was not attractive. Joan saw it and perceptively had an idea what had inspired it. She was amused, though her face remained bland. But her heart, never attuned to anyone but Lionel, and now Sebastian, was not calm at all. What could this fool know about the dear child, that most loved child? Joan felt that Sebastian was her own, for he was Lionel's, and the thought of him under Patricia's influence angered and outraged Joan, though her face remained inscrutable in its smoothness.

"Sherry, Patricia?" Lionel was saying.

Patricia seated herself on the other side of the fire and looked up at Lionel, and he was embarrassed at the slavish adoration of him in her eyes, her attempt to communicate that adoration. "Always sherry," she said. "I take nothing stronger, you know. I don't approve of it."

Lionel nodded. "Joan?"

"Whiskey, love, as usual, with a very little water." Patricia wrinkled her nose in a condescending fashion. Lionel, who knew all about Patricia, added whiskey to the sherry. Then Lionel poured whiskey for himself and Jason, who had seated himself at a little distance. He had kissed his sister mechanically. He was no longer enchanted by her. He thought his friend Lionel could have done much better than Joan, who could not be a real wife to him. He would have been amazed, and aghast, to know of Lionel's and Joan's passionate and intoxicated coupling, the ecstasy, the joy, the becoming of one flesh, body, and spirit, the profound rapture and sweetness, the unshakable faithfulness. He had never known this with Patricia, and suspected there was something missing in his life, but he did not know what it was. He was convinced that true ladies possessed no passion. That was reserved for immoral women, of whom he knew almost nothing.

Lionel sat near Jason. "I heard, before I left the office, that you had hired a nigger as chef," he said. "I thought that was Griswold's job, and that he would report such an applicant to me. I do have charge of the kitchens, you know, friend."

Jason's mouth tightened. "True. You do have. But Eddie had looked for you. You weren't around just then, and this needed immediate attention." He paused. Jason hated to confront anyone with unpleasant facts, especially not Lionel, who was like a brother. "And I am manager, you know ... friend." He regretted the mimicry immediately, but he was disturbed tonight and did not quite know why.

Lionel made an eloquent gesture of submission. Joan had heard this, and while she smiled at Patricia, she began to listen.

"Patterson has credentials of the very best," Jason continued. "We're lucky to get him."

"I read them, after you'd left."

"Then you know." Jason's deep voice became hard. "And I object to Patterson being called a 'nigger.' He is an educated gentleman."

"But a Negro, just the same."

"What the hell has that to do with it?" asked Jason. "I remember something Saul Weitzman told Da, that the Jews were admonished to treat the stranger in their midst with kindness, 'for you were strangers in Egypt, also.'" He paused. "Coming down to it, we're all strangers to each other. Da used to say that no man had a friend, and I'm beginning to believe it."

Patricia had heard. She exclaimed, "Oh, that awful old Jew! He caused your grandfather's death, Jason! Have you forgotten that?"

Jason said, "We all cause each other's death one way or another," and was astonished at himself. He was beginning to sound like Da, and then he smiled. I hope so, he thought. He said, "Da left all the money he had in the world to Saul—eight hundred dollars he'd stashed away in his famous tin box under his bed. Da knew what he was doing."

"Senile old man," said Patricia.

"No one here has his acuteness, his intelligence," said Jason. He was rarely annoyed at Patricia, but tonight he was. "And it wasn't Saul who caused Da's death. It was two young criminals."

"Just children," said Patricia in a sentimental tone. She

assumed a maternal gentleness, all soft smirks and tilted head.

"No one is a child," said Jason. "Da used to quote the Holy Bible. 'A child is evil from his birth and wicked from his youth. The heart of a child is deceitful.' Or something like that. I'm beginning to believe that, too."

Lionel laughed. "I've known that since I was a kid. I remember my thoughts even when I was five years old. Nasty. Purely evil. Well, coming back to our new chef. I heard you bullied the kitchen cooks into compliance."

"I didn't threaten them. I told them they had to act like men, or quit. I also warned Patterson that he mustn't be prejudiced, either. He has a very high opinion of himself, probably deserved." Jason paused. "But that doesn't give him license to patronize the other help, either, and I made that plain."

There was a subtle charge in the air. Jason rarely exerted his authority and had never done so before to Lionel. Now he had a cold, threatening appearance, and even Joan was impressed. A peculiar flicker appeared in Lionel's yellow eyes as he looked at Jason, and for the first time Jason became aware of it and was confused. He knew Lionel was secretive, but this was different. It was affectionate, that flicker, but it was also enigmatic. Jason could usually read Lionel, but now he could not. Lionel was looking into his glass with a disturbing thoughtfulness.

What a dolt my brother is, thought Joan with contempt. And to think he is over Lionel! It's outrageous.

Lionel replenished the contents of the glasses, moving with his usual foxlike grace. He said, "I forgot to tell you. We have two other guests tonight."

"Oh, no!" cried Patricia, giving her husband an accusing look. "And Jason didn't change!"

"Who?" asked Joan.

"Mr. and Mrs. Chauncey Schofield."

Jason frowned. "I've heard of him. How did you meet him?"

"At the house of friends."

"Wonderful people!" exclaimed Patricia, giving her dress a quick look. "Rich. Sophisticated. Cultured. From Philadelphia. I met them when I visited their daughter, Elizabeth."

"If they're like that, what are they doing in this backwater?" Jason asked. "I had the impression—I don't know where I got it—that there's something fishy about Schofield Enterprises. What does 'Enterprises' mean?"

Lionel grinned. "Only he knows, exactly, but they seem to have a lot of money and they bought a very fine house. We've been there. He 'dabbles,' he says, in real estate, politics, finance, enterprises of all sorts which will make him money. He invests in them."

Jason repeated, "What is he doing in Belleville, then? Nothing here to interest him."

Lionel shrugged. "He thinks Belleville has a future."

"Very interesting people," said Joan. "Perhaps Belleville has possibilities after all. Mr. Schofield has offices in New York and Philadelphia." She smiled. "Perhaps he likes this backwater."

"Patricia's friend Elizabeth isn't really his daughter," said Lionel. "He's only about thirty-two, not much older than we are. His wife is at least fifty. Old enough to be his mother. I think she is the one who had all the money to begin with. A rich widow. He used it, I suppose, to make money for himself."

"I've heard about men like that," said Jason, and was surprised to discover he was being disagreeable. "Opportunists. Adventurers. Not nice characters at all. They marry susceptible women for their money. Mrs. Schofield is fortunate that he hasn't run off with all of it."

Lionel laughed, his very endearing laugh. "She has good lawyers in New York, who administer her late husband's estate. And she's not as foolish as she seems. She burbles on like an idiot and is infatuated with Chauncey, but I think there's some cunning in her, too. He's a very attentive husband, and a charmer. And a good father to Anita's daughter by her first husband. She takes Chauncey's name. Elizabeth is a beauty and she's only ten or so years younger than Chauncey. He has a great influence over her."

"Lawyers or no lawyers, Mrs. Chauncey and her daughter had better watch out."

"You're being uncharitable," said Lionel, grinning. "Ah, I hear the bell. They've arrived." He rose and went to greet his guests. Patricia looked at Jason inimically. "I don't think you should judge Mr. Schofield that way. I'm beginning to think you married me for my money, yourself."

Jason colored, but he had no words to reply to her. He could only say, "Now, Patricia." But he was wounded. He could never make Patricia understand that he had loved her from boyhood. She would only shrug. What did she really want? He was always trying to please her, always giving her gifts. She was never satisfied. She accepted everything as if she were doing him a favor.

"Besides," said Patricia with loftiness, "why shouldn't a man marry money? Why should he marry a pauper?" And she looked at Joan, who was highly amused. Patricia fingered her jewels. Her gown no longer pleased her. She remembered that Mrs. Schofield was always magnificently dressed, and with better jewelry. Patricia was feeling her liquor.

Jason waited, fuming. He was prepared to dislike the Schofields even before meeting them, and he did not know why. It was not like him to judge people before knowing them. But there had been something tonight...For some unrelated reason he was remembering that odd flicker in Lionel's eyes.

Jason could hear a man's rich, mannered voice in the hall, accompanied by a woman's high-pitched rush of greeting. She was expressing, Jason supposed sourly, her joy on encountering Lionel. The man with her laughed; it had an unctuous sound, and then Lionel spoke and it was his "public" voice, as Jason had once called it with mingled amusement and impatience. I'm certainly in a fine mood, he thought, and I think it is all the fault of that damned conceited stuck-up Zulu. He glanced at Patricia; he was always glancing at her. She was listening avidly, already adjusting her society expression of pleasant politeness. Poor girl, so shy, so diffident—it was difficult for her to be with strangers for long. Jason suddenly glanced at his sister. She was watching him with a faint smile of derision, as if she knew a disreputable secret about him, and he thought, as he had thought years ago with humiliation, that Joan regarded him with disdain.

The new guests, led by Lionel, were entering the room, and Jason got to his feet. Joan thought how ponderously he moved now, and how rumpled he was, and how unkempt he looked with that faint blue-black shadow of a beard. How different he was from Lionel, who was all grace and lightness, and who appeared years younger.

Jason looked intently at Mr. Schofield, and he knew what Lionel had meant when he had called the other man "a charmer." He was very tall, almost as tall as Jason himself, and as lean as Lionel in his black broadcloth suit, impeccably tailored and obviously not from Belleville. He had broad fine shoulders, and his linen was beyond any criticism. But Jason noticed, with distaste, that his jewelry was a little flamboyant, including a little-finger ring with a diamond just a carat too large. He also wore a Harvard class ring and a diamond stickpin, also too conspicuous. Yes, a confidence man.

Jason studied his face. It was large and smooth and tanned and of an extraordinary handsomeness. The nose was strong, the mouth was full, humorous and expressive, with a somewhat heavy underlip. But it was his forehead that fascinated Jason, for it sloped down like a shelf over dark brown heavy eyebrows, so that those brows seemed pressed too closely to the eyes. Under that ledge, his green eyes, unusually large, were active and compelling. His brown hair was full and had been cleverly trimmed.

He wore an air of extreme assurance and strength. Jason could understand why women would adore him, and even men would be attracted to all that healthy charm. He had a way of looking frankly and openly at others, as if he had never had anything to hide in his life, and it was a warm look intimating that he found nothing but friends in the world and was himself a sincere friend to all mankind. He was smiling widely now, and his teeth were big and white.

Yes, thought Jason, a mountebank if I ever saw one, and the hairs on the back of his neck bristled.

His wife, Anita, was obviously his senior by some twenty years. As if she knew this was evident, she assumed a girlish vivacity and manner, all animation and flutterings, much smiling and laughter, and much fast chatter and breathlessness. She was of medium height and very tightly corseted so that her plumpness was well-restrained, giving her a rather nice figure in its elaborate evening dress of silver satin and lace. Her bosom was full, as were her hips, but the waist was not bulky, again due to the corsets. She had a round babyish face, with cheeks like ripe peaches under a skin only slightly webbed with little wrinkles, round blue eyes like a staring child's that mirrored a child's candid greed, and a mass of golden hair whose color was suspect. She glittered with a diamond necklace, diamond earrings, a diamond bracelet, and two large diamond rings.

Compared with her, Joan was a demure Mona Lisa in her blue velvet gown and patrician aura, and Patricia was quite extinguished, like a brown hen.

"Oh, my darling angel!" cried Mrs. Schofield, running to Joan as fast as her hobble skirt would permit. She gave Joan's cheek an audible kiss, and Joan endured it with one of her sweetest and most affectionate smiles. "You look too heavenly for this bad, bad world! As usual!" Patricia had risen and was waiting. She had lost her style and appeared awkward, like a schoolgirl caught among adults, improperly dressed, and embarrassed.

Mrs. Schofield became aware of Patricia. She flung out her hands to the younger woman, and Patricia timidly took them.

"Dearest Patricia!" proclaimed Mrs. Schofield. "Elizabeth told me how sweet, positively ravishing, you looked at luncheon. You've been so kind to my poor lonely little girl for the three years we've been here. So kind! And introduced her to so many of your dear little friends! We're so grateful."

Joan watched this with her faint smile. Patricia was overwhelmed. Mrs. Schofield was always cordial, but she was exceeding herself now.

"It was nothing," said Patricia, flushing with gratification. Her voice was barely audible. "Everyone loves Elizabeth."

"Yes, don't they! She's so ingenuous, so artless, so confiding. No guile at all! Like a baby." Mrs. Schofield patted Patricia's thin shoulder, and looked about her, gasping with all her efforts. Lionel had already introduced Jason to Chauncey Schofield and was busy preparing a glass of whiskey for the latter and refilling Jason's own glass.

What a foolish woman, Jason was thinking. Or is she? Jason remembered the lawyers in New York who guarded her inheritances. Then he caught the expression in those round blue eyes, and he changed his opinion about the intelligence of the lady. Here was no fool; there was a cunning awareness behind the apparently gullible face, a cynical shrewdness. He hated emphatic and noisy women. She and her husband were well-matched, and she was at least as crafty as he. Whatever business they are up to, thought Jason, she's an able partner. He approached the lady. "I must be invisible," he said. "Nobody's introduced us. I'm Patricia's husband, Mrs. Schofield."

She broke into a blazing smile. "Anita!" she cried. "I'm Anita to my friends!"

"And I bet you don't have an enemy in the world," said Jason with an honest look. Joan turned and studied him sharply, and then bit her lip to keep from smiling in appreciation.

"Oh, you are so kind!" burbled Mrs. Schofield. "The whole world is so kind, really, this great, wide, beautiful, wonderful world, as the song goes."

"Give love and you'll get love," said Jason, and again Joan

bit her lip. Patricia regarded her husband with astonishment; he was actually being civilized for a change.

"True, only too true!" cried Anita. She clapped the palms of her hands together in rapture. "You are a dear man, Mr. Garrity. I've heard so much of you from Lionel and Joan, so much."

"And all of it flattering, no doubt," said Jason.

"Indeed!" Now she was regarding him closely. Taking my measure, thought Jason.

She said, "What a handsome man you are, sir! I do like big manly men. And you have a look of power, so attractive to poor women like me. We can't resist you."

"Do try," said Jason, and Joan suddenly put her fingers over her mouth. Patricia was even more astonished. How could Mrs. Schofield really be interested in Jason, who had no polish, no culture or formal education? But Mrs. Schofield was probably just being gracious and amiable, as always.

Lionel had been listening intently, and his red brows had risen and his foxlike grin had widened. Mr. Schofield was also studying Jason with enormous concentration, and kept a smile on his face, even though suddenly convinced that Jason was not quite so stupid as Joan had intimated. Chauncey, whose business was the manipulation of others, became cautious the more he scrutinized Jason. Lionel was right. There was more to this bumbling Irishman than appeared to the casual eye. The Irish might be violent and sentimental and quick to take offense, but there was something disconcertingly deep about them. Lionel was Irish, too, but he was quite open in his villainy when it came to business. He had said of Jason, "Don't underestimate my brother-in-law when you meet him. He could disagreeably surprise you." Anita's right, thought Chauncey. There *is* a look of power about him. Bitter power. And he looks older than he is.

"He's a man of principle, God help him," Lionel had said. "But far from a lump. He was a trusting kid when we were at school together, but something happened to him later. I don't know what it was. He's hard to know now; even I can't always figure him out. I've even suspected a latent ruthlessness. But he'd never do anything he'd consider dishonorable."

"Ah," Chauncey had replied. "Men like that can be easily fooled."

"Well, good luck, Chauncey, but don't be too confident."

Chauncey had given Lionel his wide-eyed sincere look, and then they had laughed together.

The little maid appeared and in a frightened voice announced dinner. Joan said, "Corned beef and cabbage. And boiled potatoes. Jason loves it." Jason looked at her incredulously. He had not eaten this since his mother had died, remembering, with pain, his birthday party and Kate's fever-flushed and loving face. Mrs. Schofield clapped her hands in delight. "I love it, too!" Patricia, who loathed it, said eagerly to her friend's mother, "So do I." She was almost fawning, and this discomfited Jason and made him feel vaguely ashamed for her.

The large dining room was brightly lit by a very expensive crystal chandelier with electric candles. The furniture was an expert reproduction of Sheraton, and there was a genuine lace tablecloth and much silver, crystal, and fine china. Jason was bemused. He had watched Lionel pick up Joan in his arms as if she were a child. He had seen Joan put her little arms softly about her husband's neck; he had seen them look deeply at each other, forgetting everyone else. Joan's eyes, so transparently blue, had gazed into Lionel's for a long moment and her face was suffused with an unearthly light, and Lionel had looked back and there was a tremulousness on his face. Jason had always believed that only the good could love profoundly, but now he saw love in all its tremendous passion. Patricia, he thought, never gazed at him like that, and coming down to it, he had never responded the way Lionel had responded to Joan. For a little it was as if the two knew there was no one else in the world but each other. God might be love, he commented to himself, but it seems Satan can love, too, and perhaps more abundantly, and with selflessness.

Lionel tenderly deposited Joan at the foot of the table. They touched each other's hands before Lionel went to the head of the table and waited until the ladies had been seated before seating himself. Mrs. Schofield was on his right; Patricia, his left. Then the men sat down and Jason felt as if his weight would crush the delicate chair under him. Suddenly he hated this house and did not know why. He wanted another drink, and not wine, and a slight film of sweat dampened his forehead.

The dinner might have been plebeian, but it was served superbly, and everyone talked pleasantly and laughed. But Jason felt danger in the atmosphere, as if inimical eyes were watching, and waiting, and all directed at him. He tried to divert his thoughts. Lionel's income was far less than his, and Lionel had house expenses, which Jason did not. Patricia had her own large income, left to her by her mother, but Joan had married with very little, and that given to her by Jason, who had had not much himself then. For the first time Jason wondered how Lionel could handle the big house and the maid and cook and the new automobile. Debt, probably, he thought with gloom, for he himself had the austere Irishman's detestation of debt. He became more and more uneasy. He kept glancing at Chauncey, and said little himself. The food reminded him of his grandfather, and his pain increased. Da, he thought, I wish to God you were here, and perhaps you could tell me why I feel so wary. Why was I invited tonight with these strangers? He did not yet suspect Lionel of ulterior motives; he did not doubt Lionel's affection for him. Lionel was exigent, and had always admitted it, but his dealings with Jason had been open and untarnished. Never once had he taken advantage of his friend. He might be devious with others, but never with Jason. Until now? Jason became deeply depressed. He found a fresh glass of whiskey at his elbow. He drank it gratefully. Patricia gave him an admonishing glance, but he noticed that she was drinking the wine, and that her voice had risen to a higher and more insistent pitch, and that she was laughing too much and looking only at Lionel.

Jason turned his head and saw that his sister, who was next to him, was amusedly watching Patricia, and the amusement was not kind. Jason became angry. He glared at Joan, and feeling his look, she turned to him with a smooth inquiring face. He looked away. His glass was miraculously filled again, and he lifted it. Then he felt a cold warning in himself, and he put the glass down. He turned his eyes to Chauncey and Anita. They were too urbane, too easy, too casual—weren't they? Jason pushed his glass of whiskey farther away. What had Chauncey Schofield to do with Lionel? He was not a man to waste time, Jason had judged. "Enterprises!"

Jason caught Chauncey's attention. "Just what are 'enterprises'?" he asked. Chauncey looked politely surprised. He said, smiling his charming and seductive smile, "Everything. Finance. Managing the investments of others. Investing in property for myself and others. Politics. Development of land." He waved an elegant hand. "Everything."

"In Belleville?" Jason's smile was dour.

"Not quite, though there are possibilities here. I was a guest a short time ago at Ipswich House. I was much impressed. Wonderful. An innovation. I hear you arranged it all...Jason."

Jason said nothing to that, and his stare became more piercing. "What possibilities?" he asked.

Chauncey looked down the table. "Well, I must confess something. I stopped at Ipswich House three years ago on the way South. Very much impressed. So I brought Anita here for another few days. We didn't see you then...Jason. She was so delighted, she fell in love with Belleville. Rural, in a way, and she was brought up on a large farm near Boston. Quaint, she said, and wanted to live here, away from the noise and bustle of the city. A sort of refuge for her and Elizabeth. Once we moved, I began to think Belleville did have possibilities."

"Such as what?"

Chauncey involuntarily glanced again at Lionel, who kept his face without expression. Then he shrugged. "I get 'feelings.' Sometimes they're right, sometimes they are wrong. We'll see. In the meantime, we are enjoying living here. At least Anita and Elizabeth enjoy it; I do, too, on visits. I have my main offices in New York and Philadelphia and just...dabble here, for my own amusement."

Jason took up his glass of whiskey and drank it swiftly. He became aware that everyone was watching him now and not speaking.

"Dabble...in what?" said Jason.

"Nature." Chauncey laughed. "I like to hunt and fish and boat on the river and watch the people. So simple, so without complications. So...sincere."

"What makes you think they are?"

"Jason," said Patricia in a quelling tone; her eyes were glazed the way they often were, lately, especially after her luncheons.

"I'm a city boy," said Chauncey. "Perhaps I'm imagining simplicity and honesty here."

"You are," said Jason. His tone was heavy. "Small towns are quite as vicious as the cities."

"How do you know that?" cried Patricia, and her intoxication made her voice too loud, almost fierce. "You almost never go to Philadelphia or New York! You imprison me here in this awful town, with nothing worthwhile to do!"

"Patricia," said Jason.

She glowered at him. "No opera here, no concerts, no symphonies! Nothing. Only dull, stupid people. No class, no style, no fashion. Dull, dull, dull!" She hit the table with a clenched fist. "I hate it."

"Patricia," he said again, and this time—and for the first time ever with Patricia—his tone was formidable. She looked at him in half-drunken stupefaction, then turned to Lionel as if for protection. But he kept his face averted, thoughtful. Joan was watching; a Mona Lisa smile curled her mouth, and it was cruel.

Lionel thought it time to direct the conversation. "Among other things, Jase, Chauncey is becoming interested in the hotel business. After seeing Ipswich House."

Chauncey looked eager and boyish. "Yes! Since seeing your hotel, Jason, I've bought over one thousand acres in the Poconos, nearer to New York by eighteen miles or so."

"To build your own hotel?" One thousand acres!

"I've thought of it. A different kind of hotel. I can get the financing from New York. A grand hotel, such as they have in Europe. If it works out, I am going to call it Honeymoon Haven."

"Marvelous!" exclaimed Mrs. Schofield, and clapped her hands. "Chauncey, dearest, you never told me about that!"

"Honeymoon Haven?" said Jason, making a mouth. "What does that mean?"

"Well, sir, something different. There are family hotels in Pennsylvania. And Ipswich House, which is unique." Chauncey looked very disarming and earnest. "A refuge for tired businessmen. And their . . . wives. To renew their first . . . love."

"Ipswich House isn't a family hotel, Mr. Schofield."

"I know that! That's what interests me, that's what inspired my idea! A grand hotel, very large, very luxurious, very sophisticated, and easy for New York men to reach. Ipswich House inspired me. But I thought on a far bigger scale. The railroad is already near my land. I intend a real palace!" He looked down for a moment. "I hope it doesn't seriously interfere with Ipswich House, which, of course, is considerably farther from New York and more inconvenient to reach."

Ah, thought Jason. He said, "Do you know how much your hotel will cost?"

Chauncey looked rueful. "I know, I know. It'll be millions, at least twenty. I've raised eight."

"You don't use your own money?"

Chauncey laughed. "There are three classes of entrepre-

274

neurs who never use their own money—thieves, bankers, and private investors!"

Jason wanted to ask him in which category he placed himself, but decided that was too rude. He returned to the subject of the new hotel. "Honeymoon Haven. Sounds like a cathouse to me." He smiled. "A great big luxurious, stylish cathouse."

"Jase," said Lionel. "Ladies present."

"Never mind, Lionel," Chauncey said with humor. "We know what we are talking about, even if the ladies don't. Jason, I hear Ipswich House isn't entirely pure. I have friends who come here—with ladies of the moment. Very discreet."

"But you don't intend to be discreet."

"Jason, this is a new era. We'll advertise carefully. Come on. Men are men. You should know that. But there'll be nothing vulgar about my hotel. Everything very elegant and very costly. Tired businessmen deserve that. It'll be very expensive, very, to keep the lugs out."

"Men like Diamond Jim Brady, of course."

Chauncey showed all his white teeth. "If they can pay, who cares?"

"Do you intend to recruit...the ladies too?"

There was a silence. Lionel and Chauncey looked quickly at each other. Then Chauncey said, "Hardly. I don't know what you're thinking, Jason."

"Yes, you do. I think it's disgusting." He added, "You'll never be able to do that in Pennsylvania. We're very moral here."

Chauncey gave his charming smile and rubbed his fingers together. "I have friends among the state senators who are all for progress."

"Progress to what?"

"To admitting human nature."

"And confessing we are not above the beasts of the field?"

"Well, are we?" Chauncey winked, and Jason wanted to hit him.

He said, "I've heard about some of the big cities. The gentlemen see their wives safely to bed, and then they go out. To places where they have young girls, eight and ten years old, who are chloroformed so their screams of agony can't be heard outside the bedrooms. Sold, like cattle, for money, by their parents. Ruined, even crippled, for life. Often they die of their injuries...."

"Do you really have to talk like that?" shouted Patricia, shuddering. "I don't believe a word of it!"

"Life is hard, Patricia," said Jason. "My grandfather, may he rest in peace, told me much of this world, and the men in it. I thought, sometimes, that he was exaggerating. I don't now. Not since tonight."

"So unchristian!" wailed Patricia.

"It always was, Patricia. Someone once said, 'There was only one Christian, and he was crucified.' Patricia, you don't look well. Shall we excuse ourselves and go?"

"I meant you were unchristian, Jason! So uncharitable. Misinterpreting what was said here."

"Shall we go?"

"No," she whimpered. "Let's talk of something pleasant."

Joan exchanged a look with Lionel. Chauncey sighed. He said to Lionel, "Tell Jason, please."

Lionel said, his yellow eyes intent, "Jason, I've invested twenty thousand dollars in Chauncey's new venture. He's talked to the bankers here. They are willing to lend him two million. And the banks in Philadelphia and New York are negotiating. They think it is a very profitable idea."

"They would," said Jason, and pushed back his chair.

"Bankers are in business to make money. They're not here to watch public morality."

"I know. Patricia?"

But Lionel said, "We thought you might like to invest too, Jason."

Jason was incredulous. He stared at his brother-in-law. "I? Are you insane?"

Chauncey lifted his hand placatingly. "All right. Jason doesn't want to invest. He doesn't want to be rich. He's a simple man; no greed for money. Let it go at that."

There's something else, thought Jason, and pulled up his chair again.

"Well," said Chauncey, "perhaps you don't need to worry, Jason, and have your morality offended. But there is that one thousand acres we own. Next to it is another thousand, even more desirable. We need them."

Ah, thought Jason.

"But we don't know who owns them. We've tried to find out. They're registered under the name of the Brothers Company. We can't find out who the Brothers are. We thought perhaps that you might know."

Jason kept his face expressionless. He thought of what Patrick had bought. No one was to know. Of course, there was a large mortgage on it, but the lenders agreed to secrecy.

Why Patrick had insisted on this, Jason had never learned. Had he known about Chauncey Schofield? Patrick had said, "You've a fine mind, Jason. I've left it all to you. Yes, it's a risk, with all we own in Belleville. Kept it from the banks here. Don't talk. But it'll be yours, Jason, all of it, when I'm dead."

Jason said, "I don't know who owns that property and I don't care. And I couldn't invest in your hotel, Mr. Schofield. I doubt I could raise a hundred thousand dollars. We owe everything and everybody."

"But you're building a new hotel forty miles from here."

"Already heavily mortgaged."

"You've a reputation for hotel business, Jason. I've heard that all over."

So, they want me, too, for their rich whorehouse. Jason smiled, and it was a forbidding smile. "I'm glad to hear I have a good reputation. It is worth something in the banks—who own us at present. But not for long. Patricia?"

"But there is dessert," said Joan, speaking for the first time. "A special dessert. Patricia's favorite."

"What is it, Joan?" Patricia was immediately absorbed.

"English trifle."

Patricia threw up her hands. "Oh, good, good!"

"Patricia?" said Jason, and his face was set.

Mrs. Schofield leaned toward him. "Jason, dear, don't deprive the dear girl of a treat. You businessmen are always in such a hurry. And I love trifle too."

Jason looked at the two men present. "I don't," he said, and stood up. "Patricia. We are leaving now."

He was dismayed. Did they suspect who owned those other thousand acres? If so, how had the information leaked? He must talk to Patrick immediately.

277

19

"I told you he was a man of principle and narrow prejudices," said Lionel when he and Chauncey sat alone in the library.

"I also told you he is exactly what we need. A man of principle. Who'd suspect anything then?"

"Well, you aren't going to get him, Chauncey."

Chauncey laughed. "There are...pressures. No one can resist the pressures. It'll take some time. Perhaps years. But we're young." He lit a cigar. "And we'll get that acreage, too."

"Are you sure about that land?"

Chauncey reflected. "Pretty sure. My information was guaranteed authentic."

"He usually tells me everything," said Lionel, hurt.

Chauncey roared in laughter. "This time he didn't!" He added, "Of course, I could be mistaken. It'll take some time to investigate more thoroughly."

Later that night, in bed, after a rapturous half-hour, Joan said to Lionel, "We all know my brother. He should have been the priest, not Jack. What a fool Jason is! He sounded like a Christian Brother, and he doesn't go to Mass."

"Well, Joan my love, an Irishman can take himself out of the Church, but you can't take the Church out of an Irishman."

"You succeeded, my darling."

"But I'm different." He ran his hands passionately over her small body, and she clung to him.

"Thank something-or-other for that," she said, and began to gasp.

She had a breast like a white dove. Lionel nestled against it, moaning. Joan, Joan, he thought. For a while he forgot everything but his wife.

"I have never seen or heard anything so rude in all my life," Patricia sobbed on the way home.

"You're still young, old girl," said Jason. "You'll learn someday."

"There's nothing I want to learn from you! Such a display of ill-breeding and crudeness, to say the least! And to important, superior people like the Schofields, who know everyone!" Her sobs grew louder and tears poured down her cheeks.

Usually her reproaches would make Jason immediately contrite and he would exhaust himself begging her pardon over and over and calling himself a brute. But tonight he did not feel one twinge of regret or concern over offending her. He was startled at this, and hardly heard her continuing diatribes of shame, anger, and contempt. Something had caught his ear in her voice, and he wondered about it. He had heard this slurring before when they had gone out or after she had visited her friends for lunch, and he had thought it "mere nerves." But—and it came to him like a cold shock—he had heard that blurring of words in taverns and in Mrs. Lindon's house.

It was the voice of drunkenness, stumbling over multi-syllabic words. He also recalled, again with shock, that Patricia's face, after going out, would look quite bloated, her eyes glazed, her lips wet, and that her irritability, always so close to the surface at the best of times, would become more shrill, more emphatic. She would scream like a Fury then, insulting beyond reason, and her laughter, not merry, would be as ear-shattering as the ripping of metal.

Patricia, drunk? What had she had? Only two little glasses of sherry and two glasses of wine at dinner. Not enough to make even a teetotaler tipsy. How often, he thought with a new coldness, had she been... like that? Too many times, and it had been getting worse lately. Surely not. Wasn't she always making disdainful remarks about her father's drinking? Didn't she call "strong spirits" the drink of the unlettered and generally worthless? As for a woman who drank, such a person was not to be mentioned by ladies, since drink was probably the least of her sins. No lady "drank," except for a small glass of sherry before dinner or a little wine with the dinner itself. Though gentlemen drank strong spirits... well, gentlemen were gentlemen—if they kept it all within bounds and did not become coarse in the presence of ladies. Even then, it was hardly admirable.

Jason had never been particularly tactful; he was too honest for that. He said in an incredulous voice, "Patricia, have you... have you... been drinking whiskey?"

"What?" she said, wiping her dripping eyes. "What did you say, interrupting me?"

"Whiskey, Patricia. Did you have any whiskey tonight?" He was horrified at his very words.

There was a sharp silence. Patricia's wet eyes blinked. Of course she had not had any whiskey, for God's sake! Two little sherries, one or two glasses of wine. Her affront made her speechless. Then, in more of a rage than she had ever felt, she clenched her thin hand into a fist and struck Jason on the arm, crying out in horror and insult, "How dare you, how dare you, you beast! Wait until I tell Dada!" She had turned to him on the seat of the car, and a wind whipped her breath to him. The unmistakable sour odor of whiskey.

"Patricia," he said, "you are lying."

She raised her hand to strike him again, and her white face was fiendish in the passing lamplight. "Oh, you monster!" she cried. He caught the hand flailing at his face and almost crushed it in his grip, for he was both enraged and terribly afraid. A drunken man was to be held in contempt. A drunken woman was to be both pitied and despised.

Patricia's screaming voice flew along the street in rattling echoes. "I never even tasted whiskey in all my life, except once when I was eight years old and had a toothache and Dada poured a spoonful of it on the tooth! Never before, never since! You...you..."

Her breath struck him again, the sour effluvia assailed him, stronger than ever. Yet, there was verity in her voice. Patricia was a very poor liar; she lacked the imagination. Again Jason was jolted. But he could not understand. There was only one solution; someone had been giving it to her without her knowledge. Lionel. Why?

This time the shock was physically as well as mentally painful. He was hurt enough at Lionel's implied interest in the "rich whorehouse." He had not once come to Jason's aid, nor had he agreed with him tonight. He had only watched and listened, his yellow eyes jumping with secret hilarity. Jason had thought the hilarity was directed at Chauncey. No, he told himself now with increasing pain and a sense of awful bereavement. It was at me. My friend. He was making fun of me, in his mind. Jason's grief was nearly as overwhelming as at Bernard's death.

He almost collided with a tree, and Patricia screamed, "It's you who's drunk, or mad! You just about killed us then! You're insane."

Where else, going back now years, had she had whiskey? Who had slyly given it to her? What had anyone to gain by this? Patricia had no secrets; she knew nothing much of her father's or husband's affairs so that she could be induced to babble them. She was a gossip, but all women were gossips, and she was too ignorant of the world to absorb the low degradations to which so many could descend. But some people had been cruel enough to do this to her. Evil was not always directed at importance. It was banal, small, too. She had been given whiskey frequently, at least twice a week lately. But why, in the name of Christ, why?

"I hate you, I hate you!" she was sobbing. "I'll never forgive you!"

Poor girl, he thought with pity, but without his usual urge to appease her. I'll get to the bottom of this!

She fought him as he carried her upstairs to her bedroom. She tried to get off the bed on which he had gently laid her, then suddenly collapsed, bubbles gathering at the corners of her mouth. But a moment later she was heaving and he ran to the bathroom for a basin. He was just in time; she was leaning over the edge of the bed and retching. Chewed food and wine poured out of her, and now the stink of whiskey was stronger. There had been more than sherry in those glasses. Two? Perhaps she had had more. When he was talking to Chauncey, Lionel had been busy refilling glasses, and Jason had not even noticed when his own was refilled. Lionel was deft.

Lionel. Jason held his wife's struggling head; her hair was damp, and so was her forehead. Her slight body was convulsed. Jason wanted to kill whomever was responsible. "There, there, dear," he said. "I'll get a wet cloth." She had fallen back on her pillows, panting, her eyes bloodshot and suffused.

He wiped her mouth. "Oh, God," she groaned. "It was that...awful corned beef; it always makes me sick. Joan knows I hate it. She should have had something else for me."

"Yes," said Jason, watching her. His grief and fear sickened him. Somebody would pay for all this. He recalled being awakened at night in his own room next door, hearing something like moans from Patricia's, and then the running of water. This was not new.

Patricia abruptly fell asleep, her mouth sagging open. Jason removed her dress and her slippers. How thin her body was, even more so than after the twins had been born.

Jason felt rage and terror, but no longer tenderness. He was never to feel tender toward Patricia again, only pity and the solicitude of a friend who no longer loves but because of past affection offers compassion in sorrow and loss.

As Chauncey and his wife, Anita, drove home from Lionel's house, Anita said, "Well, dearie, your charm didn't accomplish anything tonight, did it?"

"Not directly, pet, not directly. But I learned something. I learned that Garrity can't be made to do anything just for money. He's like a rock. So...I will have to use other means, more strenuous ones, ones he'll never know about until it's too late." Chauncey laughed. "And then he'll wonder what has hit him."

"You really are a very naughty boy, sweetheart," said Anita, and laughed fondly. He patted her hand, and she moved against him and put her head on his shoulder.

"And you're a naughty girl, and a very lovely one, and I love you, love you," he murmured, and made his voice low and husky, and Anita shivered and snuggled closer to him. How she loved him, the dear pet, so handsome, so engaging, so full of charm. She held his hand tightly before releasing it and after kissing him strongly on the mouth.

He smiled to himself. He had outmaneuvered men like Garrity before, and had reduced them to bewildered bankruptcy. It had been all their fault, not his, the idiots. He only wanted to make his fortune—and theirs, if they were willing. Their rejection was their own doing. Life had no place in it for men of principle and conscience.

He had no resentment toward Jason, no animosity. Jason had had his chance and had refused it, unlike Chauncey's friends in New York and Boston who were as wily and conscienceless as he, Chauncey, and knew good chances when they saw them and expressed their gratitude by putting more opportunities in his hands.

"You never did tell me how you found out about who owned that property you want," Anita said.

"Well, I'm not sure, myself. But I'll find out pretty soon. It's probably Garrity and Mulligan. In fact, it's almost certain. I watched Garrity when I mentioned the land. He's easy to read; his face changed in a way I'm familiar with. Don't worry, sweetheart."

"The only thing I worry about, dearest, is that perhaps you might stop loving me."

He made an incredulous sound, and laughed. "Stop loving you, Anita? Why, dammit, you're my whole life! If there was a God, I'd thank him for letting me find you, you silly little girl. You've made my whole existence," and his voice broke most sincerely.

They reached their house, which was partway up one of the mountains, a new house and a splendid one, that Anita had furnished with the help of an interior decorator from Philadelphia. People now called it "a showcase." Chauncey looked up at Ipswich House. It was late, but almost all the windows shone with light. A splendid place. A model for other hotels. Chauncey's handsome mouth literally watered for it, and he nodded and smiled to himself.

When he and Anita were up in their lavish gold-colored bedroom, he said, "I'll give you your nightcap, sweetheart. You look a little tired."

She was disappointed, but she knew that disappointment made her look older and gave her lines. Chauncey yawned. "And I'm tired myself."

He went into the bathroom, opened the cabinet, and took out a packet of sleeping powders. Anita often had headaches, but she would not wear her glasses when with other people, nor would she wear them regularly in front of him. He poured one of the powders carefully into a glass, opened another powder and put it into the glass, too. He watched it fizz, then carried it into the bedroom. Anita was already in her most seductive nightgown, and he said admiringly, "That's lovely, beautiful! Is it new?" Her flesh bulged against the silk and lace and ribbons.

"Yes. I'm glad you like it, dearest."

He bent and kissed her fully on the mouth, and she put up her arms and clung to him. Her perfume was stale. She had removed her cosmetics, and the web of little lines on her babyish face was very visible.

Chauncey kissed her again, even more soundly. "Well, drink this up, sweetheart, and sweet dreams!"

Her infatuated and enchanted eyes stared at him, and her heart filled with love and gratitude that he was hers and that he loved her. Still looking at him, she obediently drank the draft to its dregs. She made a coy face and said, "What a terrible taste. But it does help me sleep."

Chauncey stood near her, smiling. He had removed his clothes and had put on a silk nightshirt and a crimson satin robe. He glanced at himself in the mirror, winked at his image, and ran his hand over his abundant crisp brown hair. His heart began to beat with a familiar excitement.

He lay down beside his wife. He put his arm under her

and drew her head to his shoulder. He yawned very widely and rubbed his eyes. Then he turned his head and kissed Anita deeply. She was already half-asleep. He stroked her hair and cheek, and she sighed happily and held his hand.

He waited half an hour, impatiently. Finally Anita, drugged heavily, fell asleep. Her mouth opened; she began a soft snoring. Carefully, inch by inch, he withdrew his arm, lifted her head from his shoulder, and slowly laid it on her pillow. He turned off the bedside lamp. He slipped even more carefully from the bed. He stood up. At the door he paused to listen. The snoring was louder. He opened the door and crept out, closing it after him. Again he waited for a murmur or movement. It did not come.

He walked lightly down the long hall, and his excitement grew, but he did not hurry. He tapped on a closed door. It opened.

Elizabeth, with her pretty face and long fair hair, stood before him, clad in a nightgown the color of diaphanous moonlight and a robe of light silk embroidered in silver. She smiled radiantly at him, and without a word he entered her room. She closed the door.

She put her arms about his neck and clung to him, and he held her almost savagely and rubbed his body against hers. Her flesh was warm and sweet. She held up her face to him, and they kissed long and with rising passion. "Oh, my God," Elizabeth whispered against his mouth, and kissed him again. She smelled of violets.

He carried her to her bed and lay down with her. He turned off the lamp and took her in his arms.

Jason could not sleep. He finally got up and moved silently into Patricia's room. She was as he had left her, in a drunken stupor, snoring, and motionless. She had a night light on, for since childhood she had been afraid of the dark; it was a feeble yellowish light, but adequate for what he felt he must do.

Hardly making the whisper of a sound, and always listening for a break in the heavy snoring, he opened drawer after drawer in her dresser and dressing table. The old furniture did not creak; the drawers moved as if on water. There were her lacy drawers, her petticoats of satin or light creamy wool, her nightgowns in silken envelopes, her corsets stiff with bone and dripping with cords, her camisoles with all their ribbons. To Jason, they had a sort of innocence, a naiveté, and for a few minutes he felt he was violating something childlike and undefended. But he went on, grimly searching. He opened closet doors to peignoirs, to flannel gowns, to rows of slippers and hats. The dressing table was full of her scents and powders, and, hidden in one drawer, some tiny pots of paste rouge. For some reason this seemed to him the saddest of all.

He did not find what he was looking for, though he searched under the cushions of chairs, on the backs of shelves, under the bed. He opened empty traveling cases, found a huge unlocked wardrobe trunk and looked in every crevice and in all the drawers. Nothing. He felt behind draperies and over valences. Nothing but dust. He saw his ghostly face in a long mirror, its haggard lines, its anxious eyes, and the hard set of his mouth. He went back to the bed and stood looking down at Patricia. "What is it, dear?" he asked her in his mind. "Who's done this to you, and why?" Her eyelashes flickered as if she had heard him. Then she moaned and said faintly, "My darling, my darling." There was agony in her muttered voice. She moved restlessly, and moaned again.

Jason frowned. Not for an instant did he think she was addressing a man. Nor, he thought, was she speaking to him. One of the children? Yes, little Nick, her favorite. Jason wanted to kiss her cheek, touch her hand. His deep and incredible love for her had gone forever, and he knew it. It was replaced now with a protective affection, the love of a brother involved with her well-being but not with her emotions. There was an emptiness, yes, but not a desolate one. Jason felt stronger for the release, yet very alone.

He went downstairs into the dining room and to the liquor cabinet. There were wines there, Patrick's, but the compartment that held whiskey was surely locked, padlocked, in fact, for, as Patrick had often said, "Servants go for the hard stuff, not the tasty ones." Jason knew that only he and Patrick had the keys to the musty cellar, where extra supplies of liquors were kept. Patricia had never gone down there in her life, for she was terrified of spiders and mice and webs and dead flies.

Jason, dusty and exhausted, went back upstairs. So Patricia was not getting any whiskey in this house. Where was she getting it, then? At the homes of friends. Jason cursed under his breath. Why? But he knew why—the pointless but boundless malevolence of humanity, the mindless malice which sought only to hurt, to mock, to ridicule. Da had been quite right: man was not worthy to live. Someone had secretly put whiskey into Patricia's sherry, first as a joke, perhaps, to have revenge on her prissiness or to punish her for her arrogance, or perhaps even in envy. Her susceptibility had then been discovered, and her trustingness, and so the giggling and delighted whisper had spread. Patricia, under the influence, would reveal titillating tidbits of her personal life and the life of her family. Jason felt his face burn with wrath, and he clenched his hands and his breath came fast.

Lionel had heard of Patricia's misfortune. He would not think it a misfortune—he would think it amusing. He had never liked Patricia, and had always, until Jason had married her, ridiculed her lightly even to him. He had actually turned white when Jason told him of the marriage. He had stared at Jason strangely. Then he had said, "No, no," in an odd voice. But he had made himself smile, and shaken hands with Jason, and had congratulated him. However, for some weeks thereafter his manner had been guarded, and Jason often found Lionel looking at him with an expression of mingled affection and dismay. Lionel had attended the reception after the church wedding, and Jason had caught him staring at him from a distance, as at a beloved brother who has been betrayed or injured.

As Jason finally undressed, very slowly and wearily, he remembered these things. Lionel knew of Jason's love for Patricia; he would not willingly hurt Patricia, for that would hurt his friend. Lionel was naturally malicious, but it was a light and jesting malice. He was not one to play practical jokes just for his own amusement. That he was capable of malignancy, Jason had long suspected, but he had not as yet shown it. Lionel certainly had no reason to hate Patricia; even if he had, he would not attack his best friend through her. Besides his friendship for Jason, Lionel would also remember that Patricia was his employer's daughter. Yet, he had given her whiskey tonight. And he had brought the Schofields to meet them. Were the two connected? He, Jason, would find out, and his thoughts about Lionel were for the first time both anguished and vengeful. He lay awake until it was time to get up. He listened at Patricia's door. There was no sound but that of snoring.

Patrick had left for his office at the Inn-Tavern. Jason went into the hall telephone closet, carefully shut the door, and called his father-in-law. He said, "Mr. Mulligan. I've got to see you and Daniel in your office the very first thing this morning. In an hour. Would you call him for me, please? It's a matter of extreme importance."

20

"It's a grand girl, our Molly," said Patrick Mulligan to his nephew Daniel. His voice was fond. "Severe, and sharp-tongued, and no-nonsense. It's happy I am that she comes here every week to look over the work and see the girls are not lying down on the job and that every file is in place."

"Something of a slave driver, Molly," said her husband, also fondly. "And a big conscience. She feels that if she isn't supervising your office, and you, too, Uncle Pat, everything will collapse and you'll be robbed of your last dollar. She hasn't much faith in men's intelligence, thinks we're lack-adaisical."

Patrick sighed. "Ah, if you had a son! A fine broth of a boy he'd be with Molly as his mum and you as his dada. Well, then. With all the debt we're in, Molly has the right to be worried about us."

Daniel laughed. "Molly would rather starve than go into debt. I constantly tell her money doesn't grow by hiding it in a mattress—or in a bank, for that matter. I wanted her to go to New York last week for some new clothes; she hasn't bought even a pair of shoes since we 'ran into debt and into the hands of the money lenders,' as she calls it. I keep re-assuring her that we are doing splendidly, paying off the mortgages, and that, in fact, the Inn-Tavern is mortgage-free. That doesn't satisfy her enough. There's Ipswich House, still, and the new hotel we have under way. Anyway, she refused to buy clothes she badly needs. She mends her stockings, too, and her drawers, and I found her patching the elbows of an old coat. Don't laugh, Uncle Pat. I'm serious, even if I'm laughing myself. Dear Molly."

"Dear Molly," echoed Patrick. "But she is right. We're still heavily in debt, even if struggling well with it."

"Well, Molly's no advertisement of our solvency and success," said Daniel. "I tell her to keep out of sight of our bankers, or they might call in their notes. When she went to Sunderland's first grandchild's baptism party last week, she wore a dress five years old, and far out of style. It was clean and pressed, but that is all you could say about it. I was embarrassed."

"Still," said Patrick cheerily, "that will show the bankers that we're not profligate with their damned money."

"Then," said Daniel, laughing again, "I undermined their confidence. I myself was dressed even more splendidly than Lionel Nolan, that rascal. And Joan looked impossibly exquisite, as usual, and as transcendent as a saint in stained glass. And Patty, as usual, was...stylish. Why weren't you and Jason there, too?"

"We had work to do. An emergency," said Patrick with virtue.

"What emergency?"

Patrick scratched a pink ear. "I don't remember me, just now. But, sure and it was an emergency. What else?"

Daniel leaned back in his chair and carefully lit one of his expensive cigars after giving one to his uncle. His eyes, looking even more like bright brown marbles than they had six years ago, musingly fixed themselves on Patrick. He was still solidly handsome, if losing some of his hair, and he gave the impression of alert strength and agility. He said, "I wonder why Jason is in such a sweat, wanting to see us this morning."

"Now, then, I don't know. It isn't like Jason to get his bowels all stirred up like a silly woman. I've tried to think what it is." Patrick spread out his hands. "If it was something about Patricia, he wouldn't ask that you be here too, Danny. So it's nothing personal."

Daniel thoughtfully watched a coil of blue smoke rise toward the ceiling; it coiled sluggishly, for the day was quite hot and the little office was steamy with heat and smelled even more strongly of dust than usual, and was far more untidy than when Molly was the "typewriter." Only one change had been made: the files, growing all the time, had been removed to another room, as well as the two stenographers of whom Molly did not entirely approve. "I did all the work myself," she often told them, her honey-colored eyes cold and rebuking, "and now there are two of you, and you are always complaining there is too much work. The trouble is that you work only nine hours a day and a half a day Saturday, while I worked ten hours and all day Saturday for half of what you each get now."

"Times have changed," one girl remarked pertly.

"So they have, Miss Gradz, and for the worse. No one wants to work anymore, or earn an honest dollar." Her stare at the younger girls was daunting. They hated and resented her, but they gave her grudging respect.

Daniel said, "You've never told Jason that you put him on the deed to that thousand acres, have you, Uncle Pat?"

"No. That was the agreement between you and me, Danny. I did tell him I'd left it to him in my will."

"And I told you that was redundant. He's on the deed, and that's more than enough. Right of survivor, of course. Well, that's a safeguard for you, I must admit, if the unforseen should happen and he predeceases you, which isn't likely. I explained to you at the time you put him on the deed that you couldn't sell, later, without his signature and agreement. It does put you in an awkward position, though, if you wanted to sell and he balked."

"Why should he, in the name of saints? He's married to my daughter; he's like a son to me. Jase would never oppose me in a simple sale, if we decided not to build on it ourselves. I did buy it for speculation, though."

"I heard a rumor that Schofield bought the adjoining thousand acres."

"No! Did he, then?" Patrick sat up in his chair. "I wonder why. There's a scoundrel if there ever was one!"

"It's just a rumor. Schultz told me last week. And Schultz also told me that Schofield's sniffing around to find out who owns the other thousand acres—which we own, or rather, you and Jason own."

Patrick smiled widely and rubbed his thumb against his index finger. "But we made sure the owner's name wouldn't get out, didn't we? No use letting the banks in this town get a whiff of that news; they'd be crying over our notes they hold. Calling me reckless, and such, taking on another big mortgage. Well, my da always said land is the only security."

"Even with mortgages up to your...crotch, Uncle Pat."

"Ha," said Patrick, "higher than that, bucko, higher than that. And once I was so damned careful and never owed a penny. Land fever." He considered. "Wonder what Schofield is doing away out there. He speculates, they tell me. I've tried to get some idea about him from Sunderland and the other banks, but they said they didn't know what he does, and it was none of their business."

"Which means it is," said Daniel, and frowned at his cigar. "When a banker pretends indifference, you can be sure he's got his finger in the pie, too. But what pie? Nothing in Belleville, I've heard, or not as yet. An interesting situation.... Where's Jason, by the way? He's fifteen minutes late." Daniel paused. "We don't even know if Schofield really owns those other acres."

Jason was entering the outer office, where Molly was still sternly examining what had been done the past week in the files. He burst into the room, and Molly looked up, startled at the crash, and then her fine skin flushed. Her eyes opened wide, her hands trembled slightly, and all at once her sensible clear-featured face was tremulous. "Hello, Jason," she said.

"Hello," he said shortly. He often encountered Molly here, and considered her a "busybody." "Daniel and Mr. Mulligan here?"

Molly nodded. Jason was about to pass her abruptly, and then, for some mysterious reason, he halted and turned to her again. They looked at each other in a sharp silence broken only by the fast rattle of the two typewriters.

Molly certainly wasn't stylish. Her shapeless brown suit was obviously out-of-date; the skirt was wide and unfashionably low, and her blouse with its plain white jabot looked wilted and tired. Her hair was not arranged in the present Irene Castle fashion, which simulated, without cutting, the dancer's "bob." Patricia wore it that way. Molly's brilliantly red hair, shining and fiery in the sunlight, was severely braided, then wound on top of her small head like a coronet. But her eyes, Jason noted, seemed filled with a radiant light.

Patricia's contemptuous words of last night returned to Jason. "She's in love with you and always was!" It was as if the words were freshly spoken, and Jason's first reaction was amusement. Molly Nolan, now Mrs. Dugan. Molly. And then: Molly!—incredulously. He could only stare, as if seeing her for the first time. She did not move, yet her eyes appeared to come closer, flashing like sunlit gold.

It's ridiculous, thought Jason, feeling suddenly confused. Molly Nolan, pigtailed Molly Nolan with the sharp tongue— the same little girl I knew and disliked all my life. Never a sweet word or a sweet smile. Just...Molly, who disliked me as much as I disliked her and was always underfoot, visiting Joan, helping Joan with her lessons. Why?

Jason saw something now that he had never seen before— that Molly was beautiful, that she had a "good" face without guile or trivial meanness, that her figure, even under those deplorable old clothes, had curved and lissome lines, and that her hands, wearing only a plain wedding ring, were soft and white, yet eminently capable. They were useful hands, deft and quick.

The clattering typewriters invaded Jason's ears almost painfully. He came to himself and felt a line of dampness over his long Irish lip. He said, "They're here?" Molly nodded again. Now she was smiling, and her steady lips were shaking a little. It was a smile Jason had never seen before, full of womanly emotion and sweetness. He turned quickly and went to the other office's door, opened it, then shut it behind him.

Molly leaned weakly against the files, and her heart was jumping. Something like ecstasy flowed over her. She felt drunk and did not know why. She only knew that something had passed between her and Jason, with soaring sparks.

Patrick and Daniel looked up when Jason exploded into the office, a most unusual entrance for the customarily quiet and deliberate young man. Even on this hot day he wore his mourning uniform of thick black wool, and he looked rumpled and ominous. Patrick was in shirtsleeves, Daniel cool and well-tailored in a light tan Palm Beach suit with a brown-and-white-striped shirt fresh from the iron. Every brown hair was in place, and his florid face was calm. Both men smiled at Jason, though somewhat warily. Jason, Daniel now often said, "could be difficult at times," and unbending when a matter of principle was involved.

"Well," said Patrick, "and a good morning to you, bucko, and here we are, as you asked, and waiting." Daniel nodded pleasantly, and relit his cigar and leaned back in his chair. Jason flung himself down in another chair, glaring. "It's a long story," he said with abruptness, and plunged into it. The two other men listened in attentive silence. He was not one to gesture, but now he gestured vehemently, and his fists were clenched. Then he was finished, and he coughed stridently, catching his breath.

Patrick and Daniel regarded each other significantly. Patrick's full cheeks had turned crimson; Daniel's eyes were full of meaning. "Well, well," said Patrick in a genial tone, "so now we have a little idea of what Schofield does, then. A gambler. A chance-taker. Something like you, Jase."

Jason was aghast and freshly enraged. "Me?" he shouted. "Me?"

Patrick nodded happily. "Yes, like you, bucko. Look what you did with Ipswich House and the other hotel we are building. Chances, and me crying in my breakfast porridge over it all. But you were right, even if we are up to...well, our necks in debt."

"You're putting me in the same class with that thief?"

"Now," said Daniel, "who says he is a thief? Where's your proof, Jason?"

Jason turned to him suddenly, his chronic dislike plain in his face. "There's something about him, dammit! I have an instinct about such men. But that's not the only thing. It's the sort of hotel he wants to build, with investors' money. A big, luxurious whorehouse."

Daniel said softly, "Oh, my God."

Patrick was undisturbed, but now his bright blue eyes sharpened. He said, "Jason, my boyo, when did God set you up as a censor on the morals of other people? Wait a minute, please. What has it to do with you? Sure and it has, you've as much as said. Because of the land I've left you in my will, next to his land?"

Jason turned red with frustration. "You don't understand, Mr. Mulligan. I—we—intend, I hope, to build still another hotel on that land. Think what having such an unsavory place next door will do to the value of our land."

Patrick's usually good-tempered face became hard and cynical. He lifted a plump pink hand. "Listen to me, Jase. Sin doesn't only pay, but it pays handsomely. Never let the priests tell you different. Crime flourishes because it pays high interest and is solvent. I could tell you many tales of the rascals in New York, in politics and such, who have fine mansions on Fifth Avenue with fleets of servants and yachts and gold and jewelry and wives above reproach. They are respected by senators and presidents and honored everywhere, with eulogies in their churches when they die. How did they make their money? By honest dealing, then? By going to Mass on Sunday and supporting orphans and widows and feeding the poor, and such? Is that why they are honored? No, boyo, no. And many they are who own expensive brothels into the bargain, and they are the protectors of chorus girls and beautiful whores. Many of those fine gentlemen, Jase, made their money by cheating the people out of public funds, selling rotten stone for buildings, and financing dangerous trains. Does anyone despise them, then? Look at Tammany Hall, for instance..." He paused, shook his head admonishingly. "Jason, how old are you? A grown man, and you know no more of the world than a baby in his nappies."

Jason's rage only increased. He tried to keep from shouting

as he said, "Your property, Mr. Mulligan! It won't be worth a damn with Schofield's hotel next to it."

"I disagree," said Daniel. "As Uncle Pat has tried to tell you, it will increase the value. But land value isn't exactly what you have in mind, is it?"

Jason knew he was being made to look like a fool, and this infuriated him even more. "No," he said. "But Schofield—he makes me sick, sick to death. He...he tried to buy me; his offer of an investment was just an excuse."

"Well," said Patrick, "he appreciates a good man when he sees him, and you ought to be flattered, Jase. Now, now. Calm down a minute."

Jason almost yelled, "He wants me as a front for his disgusting proposition! That's all! I didn't think that before, but now I see it. The hell with him. I can't understand your position, Mr. Mulligan, I can't."

Patrick leaned toward him, and his face was one Jason had never seen before; it was tight and knowing and not too kind. "Laddie, you know that not all of our guests are nice virtuous married folk. You've known that for years."

"But we don't blatantly advertise that illicit couples are particularly invited! We don't imply we're running a brothel! If we have to shut our eyes to some...things, well, as you once said, Mr. Mulligan, 'that's business.'" Jason's voice had become bitter. "I don't like it, I never did. I'm not a seminarian, Mr. Mulligan. I do know something of the world. I know we can't demand that every couple who comes to Ipswich House show us a marriage certificate, dammit! But we do try to run a decent place, and that's why we have a good guest list of respectable people, mainly. But literally to advertise—"

"You mean 'implying,' not 'advertising,' Jason," said Daniel. "Not even Schofield would be so blatant."

Jason gave him a scathing glance. "He isn't actually going to advertise what the place will be in the newspapers! He'll just spread the word! I accused him, and he never denied it. Word of mouth is almost as good as advertising outright."

"Who knows?" said Daniel, and shrugged and looked at his uncle.

Patrick said, "You're not as white as snow yourself, Jase. You visited Mrs. Lindon's establishment before you married my daughter. And you've visited there since, I hear. Now, now. Let me finish. I know that Patricia's delicate, always was. I know it would kill her to have more children. I don't condemn you, laddie, not at all. Men are men, and women are women. But you're not one to sit in judgment, either."

Jason had become very pale.

"I'd rather see you in some nice clean place like Mrs. Lindon's than killing my daughter, making her have more children. I know you love my colleen, and you're sparing her. It's glad I am you are, Jason. You're a considerate husband, not a bad one. And how many men do you think are like you? If you blame anyone, I'm thinking you should blame nature, who did it all. It's not of our choosing."

Jason said, "And it's nature that makes us shit, too, but we do it privately, not publicly with music and fanfare, and special decorations and sports and banquets."

Patrick smiled. "It's not the same kind of pleasure, Jase."

Jason's fists clenched again; he was still pale. "Have you given a thought, Mr. Mulligan, to the young girls who will be involved in all this?"

"Jase," said Patrick, "no one forces any girl into what is called a 'life of sin.' Never mind the tales of white slavers. That's very rare. A girl chooses her life. I doubt that Schofield's hotel will be filled with streetwalkers and sluts and cheap whores. Men who go there will be rich enough to afford the best. Naughty ladies, no doubt, but beautiful and stylish ones. Like many who come to the Inn-Tavern and Ipswich House." His eyes narrowed on Jason, and they were not too friendly, and Jason felt something close to despair.

"Ladies such as Uncle Pat mentions usually retire on rich estates," said Daniel, smiling. "They're not innocent country girls. They're seasoned courtesans. Don't break your heart over them, Jason. Many are well-paid actresses and chorus girls. The Florodora sextet did very richly for themselves. I've seen many of them in splendid Cadillacs on Fifth Avenue. They also live in little mansions, with servants, and travel abroad, after their 'retirement.' Some have famous shops, exclusive restaurants, or own jewelry stores. Some even married wealthy men."

"I see I'm getting nowhere," said Jason.

"What I am interested in," said Patrick, "is, has he any idea who owns my thousand acres?"

Jason felt very tired. After all, he had not slept all night. "I don't think so," he said in a dull voice. "But he'll find out. And that's why I want to see you, sir, to ask you not to sell to him if he offers."

295

"He won't find out," said Patrick. He paused. "Did he hint how much he would pay?"

"No." Jason saw a deep look being exchanged between uncle and nephew and felt sicker than ever. "Think," Patrick mused to Daniel. "A thousand dollars an acre." He pulled a paper toward him, and a pencil. He figured. Then he whistled. "Damn," he said.

"We could ask more. He probably wants it badly enough," said Daniel.

"We could pay off the mortgage on Ipswich House and finish the new hotel! And more!"

Jason said, "Have you thought what will happen if he won't buy, at your price, Mr. Mulligan? We couldn't build a respectable hotel next to his."

"He'll buy," said Daniel. "I say at least fifteen hundred dollars an acre. It's choice property. I'll look into it at once."

Jason stood up. His eyes were sore with sleeplessness. He turned slowly, defeated. He saw Molly near the door, and started. How long had she been there, unnoticed? Her eyes encountered his, and her face was both compassionate and understanding. He wanted to go to her and hold her. The longing was like a terrible hunger in him; it was a desire for a refuge in a strange and alien land, a desire for love and companionship and surcease.

But as he went toward the door, she moved aside, though she did not look away from him. He left the office. The two men and Molly watched him go. Then Daniel said coldly, "I knew it was wrong of you, Uncle Pat, to put him on the deed. He'll never agree."

"There are ways," said Patrick, and thought of his daughter, who loved money even more than she did her children. Patricia was a sensible girl. For a considerable time now, Patrick had been aware of Patricia's shrewdness, a trait he had not known earlier in her life. He was quite pleased.

Lionel whistled through his teeth when Jason's secretary handed him a peremptory note from Jason. "Come to my office immediately." Well, well, thought Lionel. He never wrote to me like that before. Lionel's keen mind became sharpened. So, old Jason was going to "take him down" because of Schofield last night. Lionel did not smile. Jason was not only manager of Ipswich House but also son-in-law of the owner. For the first time Lionel lost his confidence in the profound friendship between himself and Jason. Still, he was married to Jason's sister. Jason would not hurt his brother-in-law for fear of hurting Joan, so Lionel was a trifle more encouraged as he stood up and put on his jacket. He remembered everything that had been said in his house last night and prepared rebuttals. However, a strong uneasiness remained with him as he adjusted his tie and smoothed his cuffs. He recalled what Joan always told him: "It is shameful that you are subordinate to my brother, who is such a grim fool and hasn't half your brains, my darling. In fact, he plucks your brains. I know. What would he do without you? He's used you all your lives. You have the intelligence, not he. It's shameful. Sometimes I can't bear it."

Lionel had at first laughed, knowing the truth. But lately he had started to listen to Joan. He had initially believed she spoke only out of her love for him. But insidiously his dissatisfaction had started to grow. He was no longer willing to "just plug along." Besides, he had gone into debt to please and pamper Joan, to give her what she deserved. He had not done it lightly, but he had done it, even though it had assaulted his Celtic nature. The Irish avoided debt like the plague, for they had long memories, he would think to himself. He had put all his money into Schofield's scheme. Though he was optimistic by nature, he was also prudent. He had many wakeful hours worrying about that twenty thousand dollars saved so painfully.

Well, there was nothing for it but to face Jason—Jason, whom he had never feared before; Jason, who had suddenly become formidable. Lionel remembered the long-ago episode of the gold piece Jason had rejected on his fourteenth birthday, money desperately needed by himself and his family. Principle! There were more men of principle in the county poor farm than there were villains or fools.

Lionel tried to stroll easily on the way to Jason's office, and he forced himself to smile when he knocked on the door and then entered. He had expected an angry greeting, but he felt a sharp consternation when he saw Jason in the flesh. There was something like hatred in his flashing eyes. Jason saw that Lionel, as usual, was beautifully and stylishly dressed in a light blue Palm Beach suit, bought in New York. His white shirt and cuffs glistened. His red hair was perfectly groomed, his manner insouciant and casual. "Hello," he said.

"Sit down," said Jason, and Lionel sat, and now his fear increased. He saw the clenched fists on the big desk, and the white clenched lips, the distended nostrils, the fierceness in the eyes that looked at him as at a hated stranger.

"If it's about last night..." Lionel began.

Jason struck his desk with his fist. "It is." He hardly parted his lips. "Why did you give Patricia whiskey last night, and make her drunk?"

Lionel was astounded, and Jason saw it. He did not know that Lionel had expected an attack because of Chauncey Schofield.

"But that's what she always drinks, mixed with sherry!" Lionel blurted.

"What?"

"She drinks that everywhere, for God's sake, Jason! Didn't you know? I thought you gave it to her yourself, for Christ's sake!"

Jason stared at him in a silence that seemed to charge the air. All at once Jason knew that Lionel was speaking the truth. Lionel never lied to him; he never had. Lionel might be devious and avoid answering directly, or evade any question he did not want to answer. But he never lied to Jason. To others, yes. But not to his friend.

Jason slowly swiveled in his chair, and his profile was set. "What do you mean, 'everywhere'?"

"It's common talk, Jason, I swear to you. I heard it from Joan first, of course, and then from others. Patricia's been drinking that mixture for years. I swear to God she has. And everyone thought you knew."

Jason was silent. He did not turn back to Lionel. He stared at the wall. Then he said slowly, "I didn't know. And neither does her father."

Lionel was so relieved that he felt faint. "Think for a minute, Jason. What would I have to gain doing something like that?"

"You never liked Patricia." Jason's voice was abstracted, for he was thinking.

"No, I never did. I never pretended to, friend. I was shocked when you married her. You want the truth, don't you? I knew you... liked her and wanted to marry her, but I had the idea... the idea that she was against it, and I was glad. I'm sorry, Jason. I really am. But, good God, I wouldn't do anything to Patricia so as to hurt you. And I don't believe you think I would, either. And if you did, did you ask yourself why?"

"I've thought a million things," said Jason, and put his

298

head in his hands. "I believe you, Lionel. But you should have told me."

"I thought you knew, and so did Joan! Why should I have embarrassed you?"

Jason did not speak.

Lionel went on, "Again, it's common knowledge. I don't know when it started, except it was long ago. She goes to lunches with her friends...and she always drinks whiskey with sherry. I don't know how it began. Do you mean Patricia doesn't know, either?"

"She doesn't. I accused her last night, and she almost went out of her mind. She hit me, and screamed. I believe her. She doesn't know. But why...What does she...do when she... drinks with others?"

Lionel examined a cuff. "She prattles, I heard. About her family. Other people find it amusing."

Jason's averted cheek twitched. "Do you know what she prattles about?"

Lionel hesitated. Jason turned suddenly to him, and his voice was frightening. "Tell me, if you know."

"I don't know, personally. Only what I've heard. Jason, do you want the truth or some nice lies?"

"The truth."

"Well." Lionel sincerely hesitated. "You know she dislikes Sebastian, don't you?"

"No. I...did...not." The words came painfully, slowly. "I knew their natures weren't...compatible. Patricia thinks he's too...quiet, and she distrusts quiet people. It's only her way. She thinks Sebastian is mischievous, too. I think she...misunderstands him. The kid loves his mother. But Patricia can be...impatient with people she doesn't understand. Dislike her own child? No. I can't believe that."

Lionel said nothing. He thought of his little son being abused and mistreated by "that damned fool of a woman." The thought had always angered him. Now he felt a surge of hatred for Patricia, a longing to take his son from her and her ugly house. But he swallowed quickly and controlled himself. "Well, Jason, that is the impression she gives other people—that she can't stand the poor kid. Perhaps she doesn't really mean it—I don't know. But she talks always of the twins. She really loves them, especially Nick. I prefer Nicole, myself," and he smiled honestly.

But Jason hardly heard. He said, "Does she...prattle about me?" When Lionel did not answer, Jason again fixed him with those unrecognizable eyes, which demanded an answer, and a truthful one.

"Yes. To tell the truth." Lionel was actually coloring. "Not as much as she does Sebastian. She feels that you don't... well, understand her. She is always complaining of not having a house of her own, and she thinks you are partly to blame. She thinks you don't appreciate what she calls 'the finer things of life.' She says she is... stifling. Her own words. But, you know how women babble—"

"No, I don't." Jason wondered why he did not feel much pain at this news of his wife's betrayal. "Does she talk about her father, too?"

"Yes. Quite often. She links you with him, as frustrating her, or some damn thing. But mostly she babbles gossip she has heard, or imagined. And talks of clothes and jewelry and fashion and actresses and actors she has seen or read about. Just chatter."

"And people find it amusing, I suppose."

"Well, you know how people are. And a lot are envious, too."

Jason nodded as if his head had become too heavy to be held upright. "Anything else?" When Lionel did not answer, the hard fierce stare returned again. "Tell me."

"Oh, goddammit, Jason! She tells everyone that she doesn't... that she sleeps alone. That you are... gross or something." Lionel's color deepened. "I wish to God you hadn't forced me to tell you!"

Jason's chin fell on his chest.

Lionel's voice had become accusing. "You made me tell you. I didn't want to. It's a hell of a thing for a husband to hear, especially one who loves his wife."

Jason's gaze did not waver as it rose again to Lionel's face. "But I don't love Patricia," Jason said. "I'm only sorry for her now. She's the mother of my three children. There's that. I suppose I still feel some affection for her, but that's about all. I found that out last night." He added, "And I found out that she never cared about me, either."

Lionel felt another jolt of fear. "Did she... want... someone else?"

"I don't know. If she did, I never knew. And now I don't care. In a way, it's a relief to me."

He suddenly realized that he was confiding in Lionel as he always had, and was ashamed of himself. He turned back

300

to his desk and gazed down on it. "I wonder who started it, and why. The whiskey with sherry."

"God only knows. Maybe it started out as a joke. But she seemed to like it."

"I detest women who drink whiskey. I think they're contemptible."

"Do you, now," said Lionel, and felt some anger. "Joan drinks whiskey, openly, and you know it. Your sister, my wife. Do you think women different from men? I don't like your insinuation that there's something wrong with a woman who prefers whiskey to wine." He went on, "There's something straitlaced about you, Jason. These are new days."

"I've been reminded of that, several times." His thoughts were so confused, he found himself saying, "I never asked, never knew. Why did Molly marry Dugan?"

"There's no secret about it! A woman knows she needs a home and a husband. Molly knew that there was nothing else for her here but marriage. She may look and act like an old maid—we never did get along—but she's a woman, after all. And Dugan, she reasoned, would be able to do things for our mother which we couldn't do, at that time. And she liked him, I suppose. He's a good catch for Molly, though what he saw in her, I don't know." Lionel smiled. "He could have married anybody. Perhaps she has hidden charms no one else ever saw. She's a homely girl."

"No," said Jason. "Molly's beautiful."

Lionel thought nothing would astonish him after what he had already heard, but he was astonished again. "Molly? Beautiful? When did you find that out? It isn't visible to anyone else." Lionel laughed a little. Then, all at once, his foxlike eyes became yellow slits, watching.

"Well," said Jason, "I think I always thought she was very goodlooking. I don't know. It doesn't matter. Well. Thanks for telling me about Patricia, Lionel."

Lionel stood up. Then Jason said, "You'll regret lending Schofield that money, friend. I'm sorry to have to say it."

Lionel gave him a whimsical salute. "Thanks for your concern. But I have a feeling it will return to me a dozen times over."

And that was all that was said of Chauncy Schofield. After Lionel left, Jason sat all alone in a turmoil of thought.

He felt unbearably and incurably betrayed, rejected, and lonely beyond words. His pain increased. He had no one he could truly confide in, who would console him or cheer him, or who gave a damn about him.

Molly.

21

It was, to Jason, astonishingly curious that that evening he went into Patricia's quarters without his usual trepidation and hope for a smile or a word of conjugal kindness. The hope, he realized now, was never fulfilled and never would be. He could not understand his feeling of relief on this realization, his feeling of sudden freedom. He was like a man who had never known liberty and was all at once precipitated into it. It was confusing, but exhilarating too.

It was also curious to him that Patricia had not only consented to marry him but had urged him into that marriage. Why? Had it been because of the genial pressure of her father, and his own urgency? He no longer believed that Patricia's nature was vulnerable and delicate, so she had not succumbed out of exhaustion or persuasion. There was a wiry strength, he had discovered, in his wife, an obstinacy which would not yield, or, if yielding, remained obdurate and sullen. There had to be some hidden reason why she had consented to marry him, and Jason began to wonder what it was. Had her father bribed her? She had a large inheritance of her own, but Patricia was always susceptible to money.

He was no longer deceived that she had a fragile appetite, for now he remembered the ruins of the huge breakfasts he had overlooked until now. He had loved her for what he had believed to be her daintiness, refinement, and fragility, all the feminine virtues he found enchanting. In the last twenty-four hours he had had a revelation: Patricia possessed none of these characteristics, and this astounded him. But it had set him free of an almost lifelong slavery.

So he went with resolution and calm into her quarters. She was sitting at her dressing-table mirror, staring thoughtfully at her image and rearranging her hair with a concentration he found faintly ludicrous. Her reflection was no longer exquisite to him. It was plain, and touched with a certain selfish grossness. What did she see there? What I once saw, he thought, with mingled pity and bitter amusement.

She turned to him abruptly, and frowned. But he was no longer disturbed at this expression. He said quietly, "I want to talk to you, Patricia, and please don't interrupt until I am finished." He sat down, but not too near her. He had not given her his usual pleading kiss. Patricia began to speak in her customary irritable fashion, and then she paused, staring. Jason had changed. He was looking at her with only remote interest, and she was startled. Patricia might not be too intelligent, but she was acute. She liked power. All at once she realized that Jason had escaped her.

He said, as she half-faced him on her stool, "I believe you, that you did not think that you were drinking whiskey last night."

"You ought to be ashamed," she said. "You know how I hate spirits, and only drink wine. Yet you accused me—"

Jason lifted his hand with authority, and startled again, she subsided, but with umbrage.

"For a long time, Patricia, you have been given whiskey mixed with sherry, everywhere you go."

She gasped, affronted and incredulous. "How preposterous! Don't you think I'd have known?"

"Of course you couldn't have known. Sherry can hide any adulteration. You had only two or three small glasses of sherry before dinner last night, and one or two glasses of wine during dinner. Not enough to put you in that...condition. You were drunk. Do you hear me? You were drunk!"

"A lie, a lie, a filthy lie!" she cried, and her long face turned a furious red. "You think anyone who laughs or jokes is drunk! If someone smiles, you think he is drunk! You and your grim face, like a stone!"

"Quiet, Patricia. Hear me out."

She struck her dressing table with a clenched hand. "It's your ugly, crippled sister who told you that lie, that disgusting cripple! She's always hated me, because I'm sound! How Lionel could have married her..."

Jason said, as if she had not spoken, "It was Lionel who told me about the whiskey in the sherry this morning. He said it was common knowledge. He thought I knew. But I didn't. He thought that was what you wanted, and so he gave it to you."

A strange look came over her face. "Lionel?" she said, and the name was a caress, something Jason missed, though he was aware of the sudden quiet which had come to Patricia. She was almost smiling.

"Yes, Lionel. We had a talk this morning. I accused him of tricking you last night. You know how mischievous he is. But he's never lied to me on important things. He's my friend.

He said *everyone* knew about your sherry and whiskey. Some enemy, years ago, began it, to hurt you."

"Lionel said that?" Her voice was soft and trembling.

"Yes."

"He thought it was done to hurt me? And that he gave it to me because he thought I wanted it?"

"Yes."

Patricia's eyes filled with tears. The softness of her expression, her faint smile, made her almost pretty. Jason was puzzled. He had expected any reaction but this. His wife seemed to be not only touched but also happy. "How kind of him," she murmured, "to want to help me."

"I suppose so," said Jason, still puzzled.

Patricia's head had dropped. She was deep in reflection. Her love had tried to protect her; her love had given her only what he thought she desired. So he had not forgotten those Sundays in the glade. He would never forget, as she would never forget. But why hadn't he behaved like the romantic heroes she had read about in the novels—remaining celibate out of grief? Patricia's lips trembled with emotion. Her small breast rose and fell rapidly. She was both sorrowful and unbearably happy.

Jason waited. He had never seen such an expression on Patricia's face before, gently tender, exalted. Then she changed again and faced him with hard coldness. "Your sister drinks whiskey, and no one accuses her of being drunk!"

"Joan is used to whiskey, ever since she was a child. Da would give it to her when she had a toothache or stomachache, in hot water with lemon juice and sugar. You aren't used to it, Patricia. And whiskey can be lethal for the Irish, more so than for any other race. Your father drinks it, because he is used to it, and so am I. But we're careful. We know just how far to go, though we're tempted, often, to exceed that. We know how vulnerable we are. You are especially vulnerable. You'll never get used to it, Patricia. Well. You must now be on your guard with your 'friends.' You have enemies, as everyone else has, and they look for soft spots where they can hurt you. People aren't good, no matter what the priests say. No, they are not good. They'd prefer to hurt than to help."

"I have no enemies!" she shouted. "I have only friends! You are the one who has enemies! No one likes you or loves you, as they do me!"

Jason sighed. How silly she was. He said, "There is such

a thing as envy, Patricia, and it's cruel. You are probably envied."

This pleased her. Her fast breath slowed. Jason saw his advantage. "Yes, you are envied, dear, for your position and...style. So, be careful after this, won't you?"

Her pleasure increased. She actually gave him a friendly smile. In a meek voice he had never heard before, she said, "Well, thank you, Jason. I will be careful. But why anyone should envy me..."

He stood up. "They do, dear. Envy is a common human sin. And so, be careful."

He touched her shoulder but did not kiss her. He went out, somewhat reassured. Patricia did not even see him go. Lionel. He had wanted to protect her. He never forgot. Lionel, Lionel. She thought of writing him a loving note in gratitude. But her native caution advised against this. She would remember, however, to whisper her thanks to him the next time they met, and to press his dear hand tightly.

She felt an urgent thirst for sherry. She looked forward to it. It did not occur to her that it was not sherry she now so ardently desired; she only knew she must have a glass almost immediately. Humming, smiling at her image in the mirror, she continued her toilet. Natural color touched her cheeks and lips. Her chronic depression lifted. She was a girl again, waiting for the meetings in the glade, in enchanted sunlight and summer warmth.

She often ate dinner alone, for her father and husband frequently dined at the Inn-Tavern or Ipswich House, with guests. She drank her two glasses of sherry alone in the library, musing happily, and thinking. Then she looked at her glass. What insipid cheap sherry her father served! It was bland and tasteless. She wondered. She looked at the bottle. Her favorite Bristol cream. She suspected Patrick of filling the original bottle with thrifty substitutes. Scowling, she went to the wine cabinet in the dining room and looked for a sealed bottle. She furtively opened one and drank from it without a glass. Bland. Strange she hadn't noticed it before. She drank some wine, a large glass of it. It warmed her. But still she was unsatisfied, and it came to her that when she had dinner at home she had experienced this dissatisfaction before, this mysterious craving.

Then she shrugged. When did whiskey ever hurt anyone? Especially small amounts she had been drinking in sherry? Hesitating, afraid, she thought of the dank dark cellar, with spiders, where Patrick kept his hard liquor. She looked at the locked part of the dining-room wine cabinet, then furtively knelt and examined the lock. It could be opened by unscrewing the hinge. She went upstairs for a steel nail file. Then, kneeling again in the dim silence, she hurriedly, almost frantically turned the screws. The door opened; the screws dropped on the carpet. She filled her wineglass with a large portion of whiskey, then cleverly replaced the screws and locked the door.

She sat in the library, and the familiar euphoria soon embraced her. She thought only of Lionel, and she was filled with joy and desire and passion. She sipped. Then she dozed, still smiling, until the dinner bell rang more and more peremptorily. Sluggishly she obeyed its call, and ate alone, staring with shining eyes into the distance. She ate very little tonight. After dinner she climbed upstairs to her room and fell onto her bed, dreaming happily of the glade and Lionel's embraces.

When she awoke at midnight, and the house slept, she went downstairs and again opened the whiskey cabinet. This time she shrewdly replaced the loss with water so her father would not suspect. If he did, he would blame the servants. That would never do. He would only buy a lock that could not be picked. Then she thought of Tim, the handyman. He was a sly, exigent man. He could be bought—and he could buy her the whiskey she now knew she could not resist. But whiskey never hurt anyone. Did it? One just had to be careful. It was not that she drank. She just needed the surcease from pain—and the visions of Lionel. Everyone needed something, didn't they? Life was very dull at its best, especially in Belleville.

Jason forgot to go into his wife's bedroom the next morning for the first time since they were married. He ate breakfast alone with Patrick. On the hall table he found another letter from his brother, John. He made a mouth. Letters from the priest exasperated him, always, and he usually delayed reading them. He put it in his pocket and went upstairs again to see his children.

It was Decoration Day. Jason had taken the day as his holiday, and Lionel would take Independence Day. Nicole and Nicholas and Sebastian were already waiting for him, corpulent little Nicole sedate in spite of her absurd dress of fluffy Swiss eyelet voile with its rows of stiff French lace on almost every inch, and her slippers with immense black silk bows, and her curled hair topped by another huge bow of white silk. She wore a sash of bright pink silk about her thick waist, and the great bow perched on her substantial rear like a rudder. She was quite aware of the grotesquerie of her mother's choice, but bore it with her customary resignation and dignity. Her gray eyes this morning were the color of a sunlit sea at dawn, and Jason, looking fondly down at her, felt a warm glow of love for his small daughter. "Hello, Grandma," he said, gently pinching her cheek.

She smiled at him, and her face flashed with dimples. "Hello, Sonny-boy," she said, and held her face for his kiss. Nicholas bounced up on the balls of his feet, fervid and flushed as always and shouting incoherently. Nicole put a firm hand on his shoulder, and he subsided a little. He pushed a new toy, a jack-in-the-box, at his father, making the lid slap up and down. "Look, look!" he shrieked. "It jumps, bang, bang, bang! Look, look!"

"I see," said Jason, and smoothed the damp lank hair back from his son's forehead. The child bounced like the toy itself, and he gasped and his eyes gleamed senselessly. Nicole took his arm, murmured something, and the boy looked at her as at a strong-minded mother and fell silent. Sebastian, as usual, waited quietly. Jason felt quite foolish at the surge of love he felt for his older son and the recognition of fellowship and, indeed, friendship. He held out his hand to the young boy, and Sebastian gravely took it. They shook hands like men who understand each other.

The nursery was full of blazing light and a hot wind heavy with the scent of roses. A few days ago Patricia had said with vexation, "Are you going to take the children to the cemetery this year, Jason?" "Yes," he had replied.

The gardener had prepared two large bunches of flowers, wrapped in wet paper. Jason took his children downstairs, not pausing at Patricia's door as he would have done only last week. It was not deliberate; he simply did not think of her. The man and his children got into the waiting red Cadillac, with its fawn canvas top folded down. He guided the automobile through the silent sunlit streets, under the dancing shade trees, over rough cobbles and then smooth macadam. It was very early. A few men were out hosing down the hot grass; a very few children sat on porches under awnings. It was a pleasant day. Jason thought that, after all, it was good to be alive, it was good to know and feel this splendid day, it was good to have such children, it was good to be prosperous, even if in debt. He sweltered in his somber black mourning suit, but even that was not unbearable.

It was exactly the sort of day, he thought, to visit a cemetery. Even sorrow was almost sweet on a day like this, and if the dead knew of it, they would rejoice, too. He smiled at the idea. The dead knew nothing; they were beyond joy and pain, sadness and celebration, and perhaps that was good, too. He had not gone to Mass this morning. There was nothing to pray for in church, where the adversary lived with an unchanging face and a changeless heart—if he indeed had one.

Only Sebastian remembered last Decoration Day, for the twins had been too young to go to visit Kate's grave. "This time," said Sebastian, "we see Grandpa's grave, don't we?"

"Grandpa, Grandpa!" screamed Nicholas, and bounced on the hot leather seat of the automobile. "I didn't bring my jack-in-the-box to show Grandpa!"

"Grandpa's in heaven," said Nicole severely. "Do be quiet, Nick."

Nicholas bounced even more fervently. "In heaven, in heaven, we all go to heaven!"

"Perhaps," said Nicole, and again, and more firmly, quieted him. Sebastian sat beside Jason, leaning against his shoulder. "Do you think Grandpa will know we are visiting his grave, Papa?"

Jason knew he should say, "Of course he will know." But one did not lie to Sebastian or croon reassurance that a child like Sebastian did not need anyway. So Jason said, "I don't know, dear. No one knows."

Nicole said in her steadfast voice, "Everybody knows, Papa."

Jason thought of what Lionel had said lately about the little girl: "What a reverend mother she will make, if she decides she has a vocation. God help the poor young nuns under her rod, and the innocent little novices. She reminds me of old Sister Agatha." With which, after a moment's reflection, Jason had to agree, laughing. "If there is such a thing as reincarnation, then Nicole is either my great-great-grandmother or Sister Agatha." Sister Agatha had died six years ago, indomitable and irascible to the very last, even when she had listened with daunting attention to Father Sweeney's litany for the dying. "It was an intimidating experience," he confessed later to Jason. "I felt as if I were still stumbling over my catechism." He had paused. "I expected her to reach for her switch, paralyzed though she was."

They reached the cemetery, Holy Cross. It was very small and filled with cheap little headstones and small crosses and crumbling urns. But it was crowded with people, old and young, bearing flowers and pots of geraniums. The silence was broken by voices praying aloud, chatting to friends, and even scolding children. It made for a festive atmosphere. A conscientious soul was running a clattering lawnmower over some graves, and it was a comforting sound in this little garden for the dead. Jason led the way first to his parents' grave. Kate lay beside her husband, Peter, and Bernard lay next to her. There was a very small headstone on the first two graves—"Katherine Garrity, Peter Garrity. RIP." Jason had put a temporary wooden cross on Bernard's grave, until the marble one would arrive.

He let the solemn Nicole lay the flowers on her grandparents' graves. Her dignity was never more manifest, her movements slow and careful. She then watched her father place flowers on Bernard's grave. Jason looked down at the still-raw earth, and his face darkened and tightened. Sebastian took his hand in wordless sympathy. No one noticed, at first, that Nicholas had run away among the gravestones. It was Nicole who first was aware of his absence.

"Oh, that awful boy!" she exclaimed. "I hear him screaming. I'll get him, Papa." She moved away with amazing speed on her short fat legs, and soon reached Nicholas, who had paused beside an elderly weeping couple, man and wife, who were kneeling by a new grave and sobbing. He was demanding to know why they were crying, and his shrill voice vexed the mourners, who stared at him. Nicole reached him, took his arm in a hard grip, apologized to the annoyed couple, and led her brother away, scolding him quietly. "You mustn't disturb people," she said. "They come to be with their dead."

"I'm not dead, dead, dead!" he shrieked excitedly, and tried to tear himself loose. But Nicole's grip was too strong, and she almost dragged him back to her father and brother. He began to cry loudly, and tears ran down his twitching face. Released, he ran to Jason and clutched his thighs and jabbered fresh incoherencies, pointing to Nicole accusingly. Jason patted his head. Then he saw Saul Weitzman approaching with a pot of small pink flowers and a trowel.

"I bring flowers for Bernie, Jason," he said. He smiled

under his trim white mustache and looked shyly at the younger man. "And say a prayer for the repose of his soul."

"If he has one, he isn't reposing," said Jason. "He's probably somewhere else, raising hell," and he smiled his gratitude at Saul. "Or having a drop of the creature while arguing with the Devil."

Saul smiled in silence and shook his head. The children watched him as he stiffly knelt and dug a small hole for the flowerpot. When it was planted, Saul replaced his hat, stood up, bent his head and clasped his hands, and quietly prayed in Hebrew. Then, to Jason's curiosity, he looked about him, found a smooth white stone, and laid it on an arm of the wooden cross.

"What does that mean?" asked Jason.

Saul hesitated. "Well, we believe that if you put a stone on a grave the sleeper knows you have been there. You haven't forgotten him."

"Oh," said Jason. He did not know why tears flooded his eyes. He blinked hard and turned to his children. "Saul, you know my older boy, Sebastian, and the twins, Nick and Nickie. Nickie's the girl, an old lady."

Gravely Saul and Sebastian shook hands. Nicole made an awkward curtsy. Nicholas stared and hummed. It came to Jason that the child was never quiet. If not screaming demandingly, he hummed like a telephone wire in a wind, and as meaninglessly. His eyes never ceased their jumping. For the first time Jason felt a twinge of uneasiness. The child was never really still, not even when he slept. He churned up his bed and tangled his sheets with his small thin arms and legs. He often dangerously choked when eating, for he could not stop chattering.

"You have dear children, Jason," said Saul.

"I know." But he continued to watch Nicholas.

"You are blessed," said Saul.

"I hope so," said Jason. Nicole had taken her brother's hot little hand and was holding it still, like a controlling mother. Sebastian was looking at the stone on the cross. His tall young body, clad in a white suit with brass buttons, was motionless, and all at once Jason thought that the child was not really a child. He was a man in a child's body. Tears gathered again in Jason's eyes.

Nicholas screamed, "I want to go pee-pee! Now!"

"All right," said Nicole, and looked toward the distant fence, where a few bushes bristled, and led her twin away.

Saul and Jason and Sebastian laughed. They watched the little ones hurrying away. "Nickie's really his mother," said Jason. "She's the only one who can subdue him."

Sebastian watched his brother and sister until they disappeared behind the bushes. The sun was getting hotter; the headstones shimmered with light.

"I must get back to the shop," said Saul. "Even on a holiday, the people, they come. For milk and bread they've forgotten, though it's illegal to sell." He spread out his hands. "But one must live."

He shook hands with Jason and Sebastian and trotted off, natty as always in his old pressed suit, carrying his trowel. "He's a good man," said Sebastian.

"And that makes him rare," said Jason. Sebastian glanced up at him quickly, his agate eyes understanding, and again Jason had the thought that his son was a man, not a child. Jason said, "Two weeks ago, Sebastian, some bad people came here and overturned the urns and the headstones and scrawled obscenities on them. They don't like Catholics."

Sebastian nodded, as if accepting the wickedness of humanity. "People don't like each other, Papa."

"I wonder why." But Sebastian did not answer.

The two other children were returning. Jason felt a hard jolt in his chest. They were accompanied by Molly Dugan, whose arms were filled with flowers. Molly had bent her head and was listening intently to Nicole, and smiling. Nicholas had begun to run in tight circles down the path and over the grass. He was like a wound-up top which never stopped whirling.

Molly looked at Jason and smiled. "Hello," she said in her quiet voice, as firm as Nicole's. Jason could not answer. He could only look into Molly's golden eyes and admire her tall pretty figure clad in a pale green linen dress, simple and unadorned. Suddenly he was aware of no one else, not even his children. His heart had set up an intense throbbing. He felt a mixture of immeasurable joy and pain and longing and harsh desire. His mouth had become dry, with a metallic taste.

Molly's eyes widened on him. She was flushing like a startled young girl. Then she half-turned aside. "I brought flowers for my parents," she said. Her voice was unsteady, her wide mouth uncertain. She plucked a rosebud from her bunch of blossoms and bent and laid it gently on Bernard's grave. "I loved him, too," she said. She looked up at Jason, and her eyes were wet. "I loved him..."

"Everybody loved Da," said Nicole, who was looking from her father to Molly, and seeing everything. "He said he knew you when you were little, like us, Aunt Molly."

"Yes, dear," said Molly. She looked only at the grave. "I used to visit your Auntie Joan."

("Why do you think she was always in your house?" Patricia had cried.)

Jason's voice was hoarse. "Where's Daniel?" he asked.

"He's in Boston. Some hysterical client asked him to come." Molly's tone was neutral.

"There's a bench over there," said Jason, "in the shade. Nickie, watch Nick, and Sebastian, you watch them both." He was trembling.

Molly seemed startled again. She glanced up and saw Sebastian clearly, as she had never seen him before. There had been times when she had sensed a vague resemblance to someone in the child, but the recognition invariably fleeted away, leaving her uneasy and unsettled and puzzled. Sebastian was looking at her seriously, and the sun lit up his curls, and they were on fire in the sun, as fiery as her own hair. And she saw, in that light, the yellow flashes in his large eyes, the band of ginger freckles across his nose and over his pale fine cheeks, and the graceful posture of his child's body.

Forgetting even Jason and her joy in the sight of him, she said to herself, in real anguish, "Oh, no, no, no!" She was remembering her alarm over Patricia's meetings with Lionel; she was remembering the plea she had made to Daniel to "do something." She was remembering her denunciations of her brother, her fear for Patricia. Now she could not take her terrified gaze from Sebastian; she was remembering, too, that he was a "seventh-month child."

A full-term child—Lionel's son. Her own flesh and blood. And that surprising and precipitate marriage of Patricia and Jason. She had been numbed by it, had been unable to feel much after she had heard of it. For a long time, reality had become blurred, for her grief had been overwhelming. She had never fully remembered the next few months. They had been like a long and deadly nightmare, with shadows voiceless and inchoate. She had moved among them.

As she stood near Jason now, she felt cold and insubstantial. Jason was watching her. He saw her pallor. Only her

313

dress and her hair and eyes had color. She looked desperately sick. He moved closer to her and put his hand on her partly bare arm. It was as chill as ice in spite of the heat. There were icy drops on her forehead, too. "Molly," he said. "Is there something wrong?" He was frightened.

She tried to speak, but it was some moments before she could. Then she almost whispered, "No. Not really. No. I think it's the sun." She could look at him now; her eyes were great with suffering, and he did not know it was for him. Then her eyes filled with tears. She felt his warm hand on her flesh. She wanted to put her hand over his, to press it closer to her. Then she turned away. "I must go," she said. She had dropped her flowers on the grave. Then, before Jason could speak again, she stumbled blindly away.

Jason watched her go. An enormous emptiness surrounded him, an enormous loneliness. He watched until she disappeared through the gate. "Molly," he said aloud, and the sun seemed to have lost its brightness.

He was stunned into immobility by the power of his own emotions. He had known Molly since early childhood; he had disliked her, avoided her, condemned her in his boy's irrational judgment. He had thought her ugly and uncouth. When had he stopped believing all this? He could not remember. All these years he had reiterated his old aversion for Molly. When had he stopped? It must have been a long time ago, though he had been unaware of it himself. Had he been trying to avoid the truth? Surely his "new" indifference to Patricia had not been sudden, but had been growing over the past few years, while he consciously tried to deny it.

Jason, standing alone and almost unbearably desolate in the little cemetery, recalled his grandfather's real horror and grief at his marriage to Patricia. He had mentioned Molly; Jason had been repelled. Was it then that he had begun to think of Molly, and had obliterated the thought because of his old illusions concerning Patricia? God help me, he thought, I don't know. But he felt these emotions had existed for a long time, working like diligent moles in the very center of his ordered essence, his tidy lawn that he had cultivated. Had that cultivation contained a little frantic desperation?

It seemed to him, as his desolation increased, that he had always loved Molly, even while fighting against that love. The recognition had not been an abrupt holocaust. The meeting in Patrick's office had been a volcanic explosion of truth that could no longer be denied.

But at least, he thought, I am now free of the fantasy of what I thought a woman should be. There was some sadness in this thought; one does not relinquish dreams that easily, but he knew now that Molly loved him, too, and probably always had.

He felt no betrayal of his marriage. In reality, he had never really been wedded to Patricia. He had married a lie, but the deception was his, not Patricia's. She was only herself, which, he thought grimly, is not true of me. Molly was also married. Why? Why had Molly married Daniel, if she had loved him, Jason? Stop it, he thought. Am I trying to condemn her again? What right have I to criticize? What right have I to feel doubly betrayed? I betrayed Molly from the very beginning. I betrayed both myself and Patricia.

All at once the sun became brilliant as it had never been brilliant before. He was suddenly filled with an ecstatic trembling. What did it matter if conditions were impossible? He was in love for the first time in his life. Everything took on meaning, excitement and promise.

He did not ask himself, as yet, what the promise was which so illuminated everything around him. He only knew that life had become infinitely richer, more significant. The world had become a joyous place, a gorgeously painful place, where pain was only part of rapture and enhanced it. He felt reborn.

He called his children to him. Sebastian and Nicole, side by side, walked sedately, a middle-aged couple. Nicholas came running and jumping. Again, in the very midst of his happiness, Jason felt uneasy and watched the little boy racing toward him. "Lively, alive," Patricia had said of him.

But Nicholas did not fit these easy phrases. There was something wrong.

When the family returned home, Jason was informed that his wife wished to see him in her bedroom. Jason frowned. He had no desire to see Patricia now. But he had no right to destroy her. He went upstairs to her rooms, and she was lying on her chaise longue in a mannered posture of melancholy abandonment which Jason now recognized as one of her many affectations. But he was patient. After all, what had happened was not her fault; the fault lay with him.

"Yes, Patricia?" he said. He felt nothing at all for her

except a faint compassion and a faint guilt. He stood near the door. He did not rush to her as he always had in the past, full of anxious concern and solicitude.

Patricia half sat up, peering at him, startled, as at an intruding stranger. "It's late," she said, and he noticed the shrill whining note in her voice. "Have you forgotten we go to the Clarks' for dinner tonight?"

He looked at his watch. "Not for three hours."

She stared at him, frowning. He was different. He was not the abject slave she had known from childhood, always wanting to appease her.

"Why take children to a cemetery, Jason? They should be spared the knowledge of death."

"Why?"

She was taken aback. "Why? It isn't healthy."

"Death is as natural as life. It's part of living, Patricia. Kids can't be taught that early enough. Why fill their lives with bogeymen?"

"My father never used to take me to my mother's grave."

"He was wrong."

She became angrily animated. "I don't think so! How can a child live with the thought of death?"

"Oh, for God's sake! They see it every day in the world around them. Do you think they are stupid? To deny death is to make a liar of a parent, Patricia. And kids always see through lies, and then they begin to despise their parents for telling them."

"You've changed," she said.

"Have I?" He did not know that his usually impassive face was glowing like a youth's.

"Yes. And I don't like it."

He turned away. He said involuntarily, "You'll have to get used to it." He left the room.

Patricia fell back on her cushions. He was not the man she had known only yesterday. He had escaped her. She felt powerless. This enraged her. She got to her feet, went to her locked dressing table, and took out a bottle of whiskey. She did not wait to get a glass. She lifted the bottle to her lips and drank avidly.

"I'll show him!" she said aloud, and drank again. "He'll find out!"

She thought of her father, and smiled vindictively. Her father always listened to her, even if sometimes he frustrated and denied her. It was time he got over his infatuation for Jason.

"I'll see to it!" she said, and triumphantly raised the bottle like an avenging sword. Then all at once it became a toast to Lionel, and her face was alive and happy.

22

It was Jason's habit, and duty, to make a tour of Ipswich House every morning. He consulted the housekeeper, a very diligent and intelligent widow, who ruled the maids with a stern hand. She never smiled, except at Jason. He called her "Sergeant," to which she didn't object. Her name was Mrs. Gruber, and she was spare and gray and convinced of the evil of humanity, and was never tolerant of foibles. She knew what often happened in the hotel, and while she disapproved, much of the time she accepted it as part of the "sinfulness" of mankind. God would judge—one of these days! She lived for that.

In the meantime, she had a shrewd eye for trickery and lies. Especially if they involved money and the cost of insurance to the hotel. In many ways she regarded the hotel not only as her responsibility and domain, but as her very own. She deeply respected Jason, even if she did believe he was a little careless at times about the "goings-on." Men!

She met him this morning when he was on his rounds, her arms folded over her flat breast, her face forbidding. Seeing this, he said, "Now what, Sergeant?"

"It's Mrs. Bristol—again, sir." Mrs. Gruber's face, the texture and color of wood, became darker than ever. Her hair was gray and thin, though, incongruously, the tiny knot on the back of her head was set off by an elaborate Spanish comb crowded with glass jewels of various colors. It had a jauntiness at odds with her character, which was uncompromising and humorless. She wore a gray calico dress over her slatlike body, and a stiff white apron with another incongruity—an embroidered frill of pink.

"What's her complaint this time?"

Mrs. Gruber looked justified. "I'm sure it's not my business, sir, but I always had my doubts about Mrs. Bristol."

Mr. and Mrs. Bristol were from New York, and the most elaborate suite in Ipswich House was usually occupied by them from June first until long after Labor Day, and they often returned then for the Christmas holidays. Mr. Bristol was a financier, treated by several New York banks with awe. He was a handsome and impressive man, about sixty years old, with white hair and what people called a "fine figure." He was a considerable athlete, and had a courtly manner and rich voice. "Fruity," Jason described it. He also had a way of touching one when he was speaking, which was somewhat patronizing.

Mrs. Bristol was almost young enough to be his grand-daughter, and indeed he had a granddaughter her age, about twenty-one. She was his third wife, and had been a chorus girl with Ziegfeld's *Follies*. She was very beautiful and svelte, with pale gilt hair that shone even in faint light, a square exquisitely tinted complexion, widely spaced large blue eyes, a tiny nose, and a voluptuous pink mouth. She possessed a quantity of jewelry which an empress would not have despised, and a wardrobe that screamed of Worth and was very daring. In short, she was distracting, the envy of all the ladies and the dazzlement of every gentleman. She was almost illiterate, and her grammar and syntax made the less enchanted wince, including Jason. Her voice was almost a screech, and her laughter raucous.

In ten years, Lionel once said, she would look like a haggard whore, for even now her manners were coarse and cheap for all her finery and furs and gems. She was flirtatious and had a habit of tapping gentlemen archly on the cheek with a distressingly big-knuckled hand. She had originated in Hoboken and it was whispered that her father was a "gandy dancer," one who worked on the beds of railroads. However, Mrs. Bristol boasted that her paternal parent had been a "fame-us" physician, and her mother a familiar of Lillian Russell.

She was often alone, for Mr. James Bristol was absent a great deal on business in New York, leaving his young wife for considerable periods. She was never seen during the day, during which she slept luxuriously in her silken bed, and appeared only at night in one of her magnificent gowns that revealed half her full breasts. The gentlemen did not mind; the ladies said uncharitable things. Mrs. Bristol was accompanied by her maid, a shrewd-faced little woman with a French accent that occasionally slipped into the cadence of pure Brooklynese. Her name was Elise. Mrs. Bristol's name was Flora, and she was always asking bewitched gentlemen to call her that, though she never requested it of ladies. With the latter she was very haughty and supercilious.

Lionel was amused by her airs and said she hardly added "tone" to Ipswich House. But the suite cost a fortune by the week, and so no one, except Mrs. Gruber, objected. Flora Bristol, however, was a trial to the hotel help, for she alleged to have a very sensitive stomach—like Patricia, Jason often reflected. She was never served a dish which did not have to go back to the kitchen in exchange for another, and she was critical of the wines. Her husband adored her, it was most obvious, and never returned from New York without a costly gift. When she wished, she was most ingratiating and made what the waiters called "eyes." She also danced like a sylph and was much in demand in the ballroom.

"What seems to be the trouble, Mrs. Gruber?" Jason asked this morning.

"She's howling. She says someone stole her diamond lavaliere and earrings and her diamond bracelet. Worth, she says, one hundred thousand dollars."

"Good God!" said Jason, aghast. It was the first theft ever reported at Ipswich House. "When did she miss them?"

"Just an hour ago. She suspects Hattie, the chambermaid, and the waiter who brought her her breakfast two hours ago—in bed." Mrs. Gruber emphasized the last two words as if they were more reprehensible than the claimed theft. She drew a heavy breath. "I don't believe a word of it."

Jason, still shaken, scrutinized the little woman, whose intelligence he never underrated. "Why not?"

"I think it was her...brother, Mr. Carstairs, if that's his name."

"Her brother?"

"Yes, sir. He came four days ago. Mr. Bristol's away, as usual. Mr. Carstairs checked in after Mr. Bristol left. He's a businessman, she says. He left early this morning. He occupied Mr. Bristol's bedroom." Mrs. Gruber sniffed roughly. "She says."

"I never saw him," said Jason. "He checked in? That can be verified, of course."

"I checked. He did, sir."

"Good. What sort of a man is he?"

"Very elegant. Very handsome. Looks like Francis X. Bushman. Of the moving pictures, sir. Him who plays with Beverly Baine in all those love stories. Scandalous. People ain't got any shame these days, sir, and the moving pictures are all to blame. People kissing in them and huggin' and whatnot. Police should stop 'em. Bad for children to see."

But Jason was perturbed. While he was considering, Mrs.

Gruber added, "Don't look the least like Mrs. Bristol. Her brother. Got black hair and brown eyes and dark skin."

"You don't think he is really her brother?"

Mrs. Gruber hesitated. "Well. No. I got two daughters; one's fair, like...her, and the other's darker, but there's a family resemblance. Nothing like that with Mrs. Bristol and her...brother."

"He's never been here before?"

"No, sir. And he don't talk like Mrs. Bristol, who's got that funny New York accent. He talks almost like a gentleman."

"Like Mr. Bristol? Mr. Bristol is also from New York." Jason could not help smiling.

Mrs. Gruber tossed her head. "Mr. Bristol is a cultured gentleman, and this man sounds a little like that, only like a stage actor. Like he's pretending, or imitating. Like Mrs. Bristol's maid, who pretends she's French, when half the time she forgets and sounds like Mrs. Bristol."

The suite consisted of two large bedrooms, finely and distinctively furnished, an even more royal sitting room, and a huge marble bathroom with gilt fittings. The maid, Elise, occupied a small bedroom on the fourth floor, where other live-in servants slept, those from other towns.

"I think I'd better talk to Mrs. Bristol at once," said Jason.

"Knock hard on the door, sir. She don't often wear clothes when she's in there. Chambermaid told me."

Jason had a fleeting vision of the delectable Flora Bristol in the nude, and for an instant had the hope he could surprise her. He went up the marble stairs to the second floor 'and knocked on the carved and ornate door of the suite. He heard a loud sob, a woman's consoling voice; then the door opened, to show the wizened face of Elise and her scowling little black eyes. She dropped a curtsy and said, *"Entrez, s'il vous plaît, m'sieu."*

Flora was in bed, in a froth of silk and lace and, alas a satin bed jacket. Her pale gilt hair was loose down her back and over the pillows, though her lovely breast was far from being entirely concealed. She looked delicious, for all her tears. The great bedroom was filled with wafts of perfume; very expensive. Though there was moisture on her roselike cheeks, her blue eyes were oddly without redness. She smiled wanly at Jason, whom she considered to be very attractive, though obdurate to her charms. She held out a languid hand to him. He noticed, as he had before, that her hands were very large for all they were smooth, and that the nails were flat and broad.

"I'm sorry to hear about your jewelry, Mrs. Bristol," said Jason, sitting down near the bed while Elise kept an alert distance. "Tell me about it. I understand your brother was here for a few days. Did you notice the loss before or after he left?"

"Theo. It was before. Wasn't it, Elise?"

"Oui, madame."

"And he didn't report it to the desk?"

"I . . . I don't know. I don't think so. He was in a hurry for his train. He has big business in New York. He's a broker. I just told him I'd report it myself." Her voice was husky, in considerable contrast with her dainty appearance. "So I told Mrs. Gruber, the housekeeper. I just know who took it! Hattie, the chambermaid! She's always staring around, looking for something. Or it could be the breakfast waiter, that Herman. Has a sneaky look on him; and he can't talk English, either. Just German, I think."

Hattie Eisen was a middle-aged farmwoman of great integrity, and had worked for years in the Inn-Tavern. Her husband's farm was poor, and she "helped out," as she called it. Patrick also "helped out," by buying almost all the hotel's fresh fruit from the little farm, and sweet butter for the guests who preferred it. Herman Heinz, the waiter, was quite old, a silent and earnest bachelor, also a longtime employee of Patrick's, and of honorable Mennonite stock.

"That Hattie was fiddling around my dressing table this morning with her duster," said Flora Bristol, raising her voice indignantly. "She took a long time, longer than usual. And Herman loitered around there, too. That was just a minute after Elise came in. Wasn't it, Elise?"

Elise moistened thin purplish lips and said, *"Oui, madame."* She looked at Jason with cunning cruel eyes. Then she said, without an accent, "I wondered what they both were doing there, right at that dressing table, together. Now we know. They were in it together."

Jason said sternly, "That's a dangerous accusation, Elise. You didn't really see anything, did you?"

"I saw them moving their hands, side by side. The jewelry was laid out, where Madame left it last night before she went to bed."

"You saw her lay it there?"

The eyes shifted. Then the woman said, "Well, m'sieu, she

always lays it there, for me or Mr. Bristol to put it in their little safe. Sometimes at night, sometimes in the morning."

Jason pounced. "Isn't it your duty to help Mrs. Bristol get to bed?"

Again the eyes shifted, and this time nervously. The woman darted a look at her mistress. "Well, not last night, sir. It was late, and Mrs. Bristol said I needn't stay up after eleven, waiting for her, and I could go to bed, as she'd be dancing most of the night."

"So you don't know if the jewelry was there last night, as usual?"

Jason's voice had become hard.

"What're you trying to insinuate, Mr. Garrity?" cried Flora, sitting straight up in bed.

"I'm not insinuating anything, Mrs. Bristol. I'm just trying to get a clear picture of when the jewelry was last seen. You saw it last?"

"Yes, I did! What do you mean?"

Jason shrugged. "Elise, you don't know if the jewelry was there last night?"

Flora screeched.

Elise said, "If it hadn't been, Mrs. Bristol'd have noticed it. She had to take it off herself, didn't she?" Her tone was challenging and impudent. "If it had been gone before she went to bed, she'd have noticed, wouldn't she?"

"I don't know. I'm the one asking questions, if you please." Jason turned to Flora, whose great blue eyes reflected anger and ... Was it fear, too? He wondered. "Have you notified your husband, Mrs. Bristol?"

"Elise is going to send him a telegram and ask him to come back right away." Flora fell against her pillows and wiped her eyes. "He'll be so mad. It cost a fortune. My wedding gift three years ago. Made by Cartier's."

"I'll send the telegram myself," said Jason, standing up. "In the meantime, you should look for it. You might have placed it somewhere else."

"We looked everywhere! Under the bed, in the bathroom, under the rugs, and on the windowsills. Everywhere! It's gone!"

"I think we should call the police," said the maid.

Flora sobbed. "We'll wait till Mr. Bristol gets here and takes charge of things. He wouldn't want trouble. The police are so nasty, so nosy."

"Yes, they do ask embarrassing questions, don't they? Mrs. Bristol, what is your brother's address?"

She dropped her lace handkerchief, and now he definitely saw fear in her eyes. "My brother? His address? He...he's just moved. I guess he put his new address on the book downstairs. When he checked in."

She moistened lips which had gone quite dry. "Mr. Garrity..." Her voice was pleading. "My husband doesn't like Theo. You see...well, Daddy left a lot of money, and Theo doesn't have to work, but he went on the stage. It's in our blood, the stage. Ma worked with Lillian Russell, though she didn't need to. Mr. Bristol don't like stage people."

Jason smiled without humor. "He liked you, didn't he, Flora?"

"Well, yes." The frightened eyes dropped demurely. "He insisted on taking me away from it, though. I was only seventeen. He...he met me at a party. Oh, Mr. Garrity, please don't tell Mr. Bristol Theo was here! It would make him so mad!"

"I thought you said your brother was a broker."

"I...well, he was. Then he went on the stage. Just for fun."

"But your brother is really a stockbroker?"

"Yes, yes! He's just on the stage, for fun, for a little while."

"What's the name of the play in New York?"

"It's...well, it's not in New York yet. Just trying out in Pittsburgh."

"What's the theater?"

"Oh, Jesus! What has *that* to do with it?"

"Nothing, perhaps. And the jewelry was gone before he left?"

"Yes! No. Oh, Jesus, you've got me all mixed up! Maybe it was before or afterward."

Jason fixed his sharp gray eyes on her. "Mrs. Bristol. The name of the theater, please, and the play. In Pittsburgh."

"I don't know! Oh, God, get out of here! I thought you'd help, and have that Hattie and Herman arrested, with no fuss! But all you want to do is make trouble for me and Mr. Bristol and my brother! Get out! You just wait until my husband gets here, that's all!"

"What are you going to tell your husband?" Jason's voice was inexorable.

"Tell him? That one of your help took my jewelry, that's what! Practically saw them do it myself!"

The stupid thing isn't the best of liars, thought Jason. He looked at Elise. She was enjoying herself. There's no love lost there, thought Jason, again grimly amused. I wonder how much she bribed the woman to lie? The fool doesn't know she's laid herself open to blackmail for life.

He said, "Mrs. Bristol, I'd like to talk to you alone, if you please. Alone." He felt a little pity for the girl, married to a man old enough to be her grandfather. She had married him for money and position, of course, and it had been a bad bargain, perhaps. James Bristol was entirely too "fruity," and there was sometimes a brutal glint in his eyes. At one time, it had been reported to Jason, he had literally dragged his young wife from the dance floor when she had been somewhat too provocative with her partner. But a hotel manager doesn't interfere between husband and wife, unless matters became very suspicious and sinister.

The girl was almost beside herself. "I don't want to talk to you alone, for Christ's sake! You don't want to help, you bastard! All you want to do is save your damned hotel from trouble. Frig you, mister! Get the hell out of here! My husband will deal with you, and it'll cost you a fortune!"

Jason studied her. Now all the sweetness and daintiness were gone, and a tough young harridan was there, full of obscenities as well as fear. He said, "Do you want me to talk to you in front of Elise, Mrs. Bristol, or would you prefer private interrogation? From me, or the police? If you won't talk to me, then I'm calling the police immediately. Make up your mind. I want to help you, if you'll let me. I want to save you from embarrassing questions by the police and stories in the newspapers. Your husband is a very prominent man, and I don't think he'd like the publicity...and all the scandal."

"Scandal!" she yelled. She pushed her perfect legs from under the silken sheets, and Jason had a good look at them. The full white breast was almost bare now, and heaving. Her lovely face had lost all its color. "What do you mean, scandal?"

"I'd like to discuss that alone with you."

She looked at Elise. "All right!" she screamed. "Get out! Don't come back until I ring for you, dammit!"

There was a charged silence while Elise, with visible regret, left the room and closed the door. Flora regarded Jason with fear and hatred. Then she said, "Well, go ahead. Ask me. Ask me anything, you...you..." And she called him an epithet Jason had heard only twice before, from rough and crude railroad men. He felt a little less sympathy for young

Mrs. Bristol. He wondered where Mr. Ziegfeld had recruited her, or perhaps it had been one of his agents.

"Has your husband ever met your...brother?" The pause was deliberate.

"Yes! We went to a play a year ago in Boston. Why?"

"And Mr. Bristol knew he was your...brother?"

"I...I...Of course he did."

"And met him?"

"Goddammit, yes! How many times—?"

"Did he know him by the name of Carstairs?"

Flora rolled up her eyes, beseeching the ceiling. "Hell, yes."

"Is that his real or stage name?"

A long hesitation. "Well, if you want to know, it's his stage name. Everybody knows him by that name."

Jason let a moment or two elapse. Flora looked at him imploringly, and genuine tears began to roll down her cheeks. She clasped her hands together, as if praying. "Mr. Garrity, please don't tell my husband Theo was here! For God's sake! Please, please."

"But he'll have to know, won't he, when he finds out about the jewelry? He'll have to report it to the police first of all, then to the insurance company. Quite a mess. Your husband doesn't look like a meek man. He might look for your...brother."

She licked her lips. Jason was disbelieving. Hadn't she given the slightest thought to this at all? The girl was an idiot. Little Nicole was a genius in comparison. Nicole would have thought of all the consequences and made clever plans.

"And the police will question your...brother too. Probably with your husband present."

Her whole face had shrunk as she began to realize all the ramifications.

Jason let her think—if it was possible for her to think. Then he said almost gently, "I do want to help you. And I want to save the reputation of the hotel, too. And save your husband embarrassment. He isn't the sort of man who'd stand for stories in the newspapers, is he? I need your help, Flora. And you need mine. So let's help each other, and no more lies. What do you say?"

She nodded, and gulped. He said, "Carstairs isn't your brother, is he?"

She started to nod again, then stopped. Then she whispered, "No. He's a...chorus boy. I've known him four years. We...we were always good friends, the best. We wanted to get married, but there wasn't no money, and Jimmy, he wants money, and so do I. His name ain't really Theo..."

"I didn't think it was. Do you want to tell me his real name?"

She moaned. She put her hands over her face. "No, I don't. What good would it do? I...I love him, Mr. Garrity. We've always loved each other."

Jason reflected. Then he leaned to the bed and took one of her hands, and she clung to his fingers helplessly, like a child.

"Is Theo in trouble, Flora?"

She dropped her head, and her hair hid her face. She was crying silently. Then in a broken voice she whimpered, "He's in trouble, yes. Gambling. When his play closed—two months ago, it wasn't any good, and he only got twenty-five dollars a week in the chorus, anyway—he didn't have a cent. I sent him some money. Mr. Bristol, he's kind of cheap, Mr. Garrity. Doesn't give me much to spend. All charge accounts. I...I bought some things and charged them, and then I sold them. I told Mr. Bristol maybe someone took the clothes, and he was so mad! He fired our housekeeper, but he couldn't prove she'd taken them, so he couldn't have her arrested, though he wanted to. And Theo—he gambled away what I gave him, hoping he could have some luck and pay it all off. He lost. And now they're after him."

"Who?"

She shrank. "Gamblers. He owes them."

"The Black Hand?"

She nodded. Then she tossed back her damp hair and looked at Jason with anguish. "They'll kill him, Mr. Garrity! You know what they are! He owes a lot of money..."

"And he came to you and asked you to help him."

"Yes! And I only had two hundred dollars, and he owes thousands! He's scared to death."

Jason thought. "How do you know he's told you the truth?"

"I know he did. This isn't the first time. He's always gambled. This time he promised to stop. To sell the jewelry and keep the rest of the money and get into some little business."

I wonder, thought Jason. Well, it was none of his affair. He had the hotel to protect. Still, his compassion for this beautiful imbecile was strong. "Don't you think it's time to stop helping Theo? For your own sake? Don't you think you shouldn't see him anymore?"

"I suppose so," she murmured. "I sure got a scare this time. But I love him, Mr. Garrity! What shall I do?"

"You can do only one of two things. Never see Theo again. Perhaps when he knows he can't come to you again, he will reform. That's the best you can do for him. Or you can leave your husband right now, today, and join Theo. What good would that do either of you? You have only two hundred dollars..."

She was shaking her head over and over, despairingly. "No. I gave that to Elise—to tell all those lies."

"I thought it was something like that." Jason's voice shook with rage. "Where did you find that woman?"

"She answered an ad my husband put in the papers."

"References?"

"Well, in a way. That is, I liked her, and the others were awful. I gave her the reference, a false name. That is, I had a friend of mine give it. She'd married a man like Mr. Bristol, too. She never saw Elise. I just asked her."

Jason marveled at this naiveté. "Do you know if she was ever in trouble?"

"No." The blue eyes looked at him with fresh fear. "I didn't ask. I just liked her. You should have seen the others!"

"Did she ever steal anything from you?"

"No. Never. I'm real good to her, Mr. Garrity. Even if she didn't have any references. Said she'd just come over from France."

Jason shook his head slowly from side to side, again marveling. The girl was incredibly stupid. When she lost her stupendous beauty, Bristol would surely divorce her. Jason hoped she would be shrewd enough to find a good lawyer and get a sound settlement, unless she again embroiled herself with one such as "Theo" and was discovered. Then it would be the streets. She would be too old for the Mrs. Lindons.

Women, he thought suddenly, aren't the most fortunate creatures in the world, and we men have pretty much exploited them. And without pity. We want either our illusion of them, or their money. I wonder how often we really want the woman herself. Sometimes, perhaps, but not very often, dammit. It's the rare man who'll get himself in a mess like this one for a woman, but it's quite common for a woman to do it for the man she loves.

He said, almost gently, "Mrs. Bristol, I am going to give

you some good advice. But first I want to ask you a question. Who was Mr. Bristol's second wife? And his first one?"

She stared at him openmouthed, wondering. "Well, his first wife—she had a lot of money, and he didn't. He didn't tell me. I just heard. She had two children, girls, and then she died, and she left him all her money. Then he married somebody like me—I heard. A chorus girl. I don't know her name. She had a friend..." The blue eyes opened enormously, with shock and realization. "And...and...Mr. Bristol found out. He threw her out. Not a cent, either. Just the clothes on her back, and then he divorced her. And then...and then...three years ago he married me. Oh, my God." Her voice fell to a whisper.

"Yes," said Jason.

"And anyway, she wasn't pretty anymore. And kind of old. Thirty."

"Yes," said Jason.

She was silent. He let his comments sink in. Then he said, "If Mr. Bristol...if you and he should part, it would be a good idea to have a smart lawyer, Flora. And keep your skirts clean in the meantime."

"Yes, yes!" she said passionately.

"Well, now, what are you going to tell your husband about the jewelry?"

She came back to the present with a start. "I'll...I'll tell him I put it down...somewhere and couldn't find it again. In New York. We go to a lot of places. He'll be mad, but it'll be better than what I thought up, won't it?"

Jason smiled. "And you're still very pretty, Flora. And young."

"I know what you mean." She actually smiled, and it was a wiser smile.

"What are we going to do about Elise, Flora?"

"What? I gave her two hundred dollars—she knew about Theo."

"That wasn't very bright of you to let her know."

"She didn't know—all the other times. Theo and I meet in New York, in his rooms. This is the very first time I let him come to my place—he just had to have money! He couldn't wait."

"Did you ever hear of blackmail?"

She turned a ghastly white, and her eyes seemed to fill her face.

"You mean...?"

329

"Yes. Elise could strip you, threaten to tell your husband about Theo being here, and the jewelry, and the bribe you gave her."

"Oh, Jesus, Jesus! What am I going to do?" She wrung her hands.

"Will you let me take care of her, and not say one single word?"

She was shivering. "Oh, yes, yes!"

"Then ring the bell for her."

Elise came in, moving as silently as a shadow, and closed the door. She looked quickly from her mistress to Jason, then back to Flora. Jason said, "I have only a few words for you, Elise."

"What?" Her tone was impertinent.

"When you came to work for Mrs. Bristol, you had no references. She falsified one for you, because she liked you. You must have worked somewhere before. How old are you? About thirty-five, forty? Where did you work before?"

"None of your business."

He leaned toward her, implacable. "A crime has been committed here, and not the crime about the jewelry. I am going to have your background investigated, Elise. I am going to find out all about you—whether or not you have ever been in trouble, for instance."

She turned an ugly scarlet. "I never was in trouble! I kept house for my father until he died!"

Jason nodded, as if he approved. "Good. But we'll find out, anyway. We'll find out where you and your father lived; all about you. Your old friends. Your reputation. Everything. Then, when it is all...clear, you and Mrs. Bristol will get along together very well."

The woman leaned toward him like a vicious cat, snarling. "Is that so, sir? Well, no, thank you. I'm quitting, and right now!"

She turned to Flora. "And it's all your doing, you little bitch! I'll fix you!"

Jason stood up and seized the woman's black-clad arm and swung her around to face him. "No, you won't. You've already blackmailed Mrs. Bristol. That's a very serious crime. Have you blackmailed others, too? We'll find out. You see, Mrs. Bristol has told me everything. She is going to tell her husband everything, too. Aren't you, Mrs. Bristol?"

Flora looked at him with horror. Then she saw him wink. "Yes," she muttered. "Right away."

"And he'll throw you out on the street!"

"For what, Elise?" Jason asked. "Because Mrs. Bristol had a friend visit her? You saw nothing; you heard nothing. You weren't here."

"I know she gave him her jewelry!"

Oh, hell, thought Jason, did the little fool actually tell her? But Flora said, "How do you know? I never told you; you only know the jewelry is gone. I...I just gave you that money so you wouldn't make a fuss about it and get Mr. Bristol madder than he's going to be. I don't know why I gave you that money in the first place! Maybe just to keep you from going to the police, as Mr. Garrity wanted me to. You never saw a thing!"

So the little imbecile does have a few brains tucked away, thought Jason with relief. He said, "If you ever bother Mrs. Bristol, or try to cause her trouble, she will have you arrested. That money you received from Mrs. Bristol was in lieu of notice. Now, leave this hotel at once, or you'll find yourself in prison. Judges don't like blackmailers, and if you try anything anonymously, we'll still find you. I promise we will."

The woman screamed, "Is that so! If everything was just dandy, why'd she give me that money?"

Jason pretended impatience. "Because, somehow, the jewelry has disappeared. Carelessness, perhaps. And Mrs. Bristol didn't want the police called."

"I saw that man in these rooms!"

"What if you did?"

"And he slept here!"

"In Mr. Bristol's room. He's an old friend." Then Jason added, "In the meantime, your background is going to be investigated. I have an idea you won't like that. So get out, *now*."

The woman spat at Flora and at Jason. Then she ran from the room, muttering threats under her breath.

Flora flung herself on her pillows, crying with exhaustion and release from terror. Jason watched her cry for a few minutes. When she sat up, he said, "There may be some mention—you can't tell—of Theo being here, anyway. You took him to the dining room, didn't you? Of course. You'd better make up a good story to tell your husband."

She rubbed her eyes with her knuckles and frowned in concentration.Then she brightened. "I know! I'll tell him the actor husband of a friend stopped in to give me some messages from...let me see...Clara! He was on his way to join her in... where? Pittsburgh. Rehearsing, both of them, for a play. James doesn't like stage people. That's the truth, Mr. Garrity. I've talked about Clara to him; he never met her, though. I'll write to Clara—"

"Oh, no you won't! You'll just be getting yourself into more complications and lies. Don't write. Just tell him that simple story, then change the subject. As fast as you can, as if it isn't important. And pray hard."

She nodded solemnly. "I can't tell you how grateful I am for what you've done, Mr. Garrity."

His voice became cold. "I did it for the reputation of the hotel, and to save two innocent people from your accusations. Two innocent people, Mrs. Bristol. I bet you never gave a thought to the possibility that they might have gone to prison."

She stared at him, blank-faced. Then she bowed her head. "No. I didn't think."

"You'd better start to think. I know it'll be hard for you, Flora, but it'll help you in the future."

He left the room. He found Mrs. Gruber on the next floor and tried to smile at her cheerily. "It's all settled, Annie."

"Oh? She found her jewelry, then?"

"Not exactly. But she thinks she knows where she left it. In New York."

The housekeeper regarded him shrewdly. "She does, eh? And her brother?"

Jason kept his face very straight. "He really is her brother, dear."

"Hah!" Mrs. Gruber looked at him with a very slight smile. "Well, I guess you can call anyone your brother, can't you? Says so in the Bible."

Jason grinned. He patted her shoulder. "And I can call you sister, can't I?" He held out his hand, and she shook it with a warmth that would have astonished her underlings. Then she sobered. "What about poor Hattie and Herman? They've already heard about the fuss."

"They'll get something extra in their pay envelopes on Friday."

Mrs. Gruber inclined her head, satisfied. "Well, they do say that money heals all things. Better'n love anytime." She paused. "You're a good man, Mr. Garrity." She left him abruptly.

Jason went to his office. He found Lionel waiting for him with a gleeful smile. "Jase, you've got trouble again."

"Again? I've just gotten rid of one trouble. What's it this time?"

Lionel spread eloquent hands. "Ordinarily, this would be my business. But you hired the man, he's all yours."

"Patterson? I thought everything was just peachy. We're getting compliments from people who know good food. Our menu has even been noted in New York. What is the damned trouble anyway?"

"It's a matter of béarnaise sause."

Jason looked stupefied. "Béarnaise sauce? Are you serious?"

"Yes indeed. Very serious." Lionel chuckled. "You see, it got spilled all over Horace, Patterson's assistant. A whole big kettleful."

"Is he hurt?"

"Medium, I'd say. His feelings are hurt worse, and the men are with him, to a man. Two of them took him to a doctor."

"I don't understand. How is it Patterson's fault?"

"Well, it seems that Patterson thought the sauce was an insult to him, seeing it's his recipe. He dumped the whole kettleful over Horace. Churlish, I think." Lionel stood up, laughing. "I'll send him in to you. The kitchen's in an uproar. I'll have to calm the men down. There are hints of lynching our Edmund. Worse still, of drawing and quartering him. Messy."

Edmund Patterson entered the office like a stately African king, all black burnished skin and noble expression. Jason surveyed him in silence for a moment or two, then said, "All right. Sit down."

Edmund obeyed, sitting stiffly in the chair, his lustrous eyes revealing cold affront.

"Why did you pour a boiling kettle of sauce over Horace, your assistant?"

"He committed a sacrilege, sir. Besides, it wasn't hot; it was just warm in a large double boiler."

"Sacrilege?"

"Yes. The béarnaise sauce, for which I am famous. I have a variation on it, my own. It was greatly admired and acclaimed in London, Paris, and New York. I taught it carefully to Horace. Then today he omitted the vital ingredient—white Graves. He now claims that 'alcoholic beverages' are against his religion and that his vicar exhorted him not to touch them even for cooking purposes. So he omitted the wine." Edmund's eyes dropped as at a blasphemy, and he shuddered visibly.

"We have several orders for lobster dinners tonight, and for filet of sole, and more for steak. Yes, it is quite amusing for steak, though pale and made with a white wine. Many gentlemen relish it. Think if those dishes were served without my famous béarnaise! There would be a small riot."

Jason bit his lips to keep from laughing.

"The orders, sir, for fish, have increased tremendously lately. The most expensive dishes, too. All because of my sauce, which is incomparable."

He speaks, thought Jason, as if mentioning the Host. "Yes. I've tasted it myself."

Edmund regarded him with suspicion. "And you found it good, sir?" The tone was condescending.

"Yes indeed." Jason's eyes were watering, and he wiped them. "Makes even filet of sole edible. In fact, I'd prefer the sauce without the fish."

The stern black face relaxed. "Thank you, sir. It is a sauce for connoisseurs only."

"And thank *you*, Edmund." Jason appreciated the fact that chefs considered their art somewhat holy. He said, "I hope you have time to make more sauce."

"Indeed, sir. If I am permitted back into that kitchen of... of barbarians, who seem somewhat annoyed at present."

Jason recalled some phrases from an English guest. He said, "Edmund, it was hardly cricket to pour sauce over Horace. Not done, you know."

"It is done regularly, sir, in England and France! No one dares to tamper with a head chef's recipes! It is outrageous, unconscionable! Not to be countenanced for a moment!"

"I understand that. But, there are Horace's feelings to consider."

"Really, sir. Such a hullaballoo. A bit of butter and tarragon essence on his face and neck, and only what he deserved for his sacrilege. I talked with a policeman who was summoned by the ignorant wretches in the kitchen. Assault, they said. I explained to the policeman, who was quite understanding, though he did seem to have difficulty with his voice."

"I can imagine," said Jason.

"I will also pay for the physician who is seeing to Horace's complaints, Mr. Garrity. Horace should be grateful."

"I'm sure he will be—eventually," said Jason.

"You seem to comprehend, yourself, sir."

"Oh, I do, I do. Quite."

"And I will recompense Horace for his inconvenience. I think twenty dollars should do it."

"You'll make him happy."

Edmund was now prepared to be charitable. "It really is not his fault, Mr. Garrity. Where, in this town, could he have learned to cook? Such dishes as the others prepare! It is—pardon me—vomitous."

Jason knew that since Edmund had arrived, diners came in droves, even on the railroad, and that Patrick had asked for the services of Edmund occasionally in the Inn-Tavern on special occasions, and that Mrs. Lindon had indeed called Edmund "incomparable." It was rumored that she had tried to lure him away for her own table. He said, "Is there anyone in the kitchen you'd prefer to have instead of Horace, who may still feel indignant?"

Edmund hesitated, like a king considering the merits of a new courtier. Then he shook his head. "But I have a friend, a former assistant, in Delmonico's, quite a talented white man, who yearns for the rural life, which is natural, I suppose, for a New Yorker born and bred. If you would care—"

"Another perfectionist like you, Edmund?"

"No, sir. But amenable and appreciative and eager to learn."

"Well, write to him, and perhaps we'll have peace in this establishment." He added, "Better get back to the kitchen and that sacred sauce."

Edmund rose. "Thank you, sir."

"Wait a minute, Edmund. What are you doing about accommodations for your family when they arrive?"

Edmund looked down his nose in contempt. "I have studied the Negro families here, sir. Pure Ivory Coast. Not Bantus, and certainly not Zulus. One would not associate with them, except to employ them as servants."

"I'm afraid you're still very intolerant, Edmund."

"One has to draw lines, sir, or life becomes intolerable." He sighed. "If only my wife...But she has a very strong mind and is insistent on coming here, and when a woman is insistent, it is time to capitulate."

"Women can be difficult, Edmund."

Edmund sighed again.

"And you found no decent house for your family?"

"None to which I would bring them."

Jason considered. "Well, Edmund, you are living in the hotel. There is a suite which doesn't have a view of the mountains and the valley, but does look out on the gardens. Four somewhat modest rooms, but very comfortable. The only problem is your children. We don't encourage children here, as you know."

The stern thin face suddenly split in a wide smile. "Sir, *my* children are not *American* children. They are disciplined, respectful, do not speak unless spoken to, and never romp in the house. Very studious, even at their small ages. Are you offering me that suite, sir?"

"Yes."

Edmund considered. "But only if you permit me to pay the regular rental."

"Done."

Jason stood up and offered his hand, which Edmund took with gratitude. "I suggest," said Jason, "that if another...sacrilege happens in the kitchen, you consult me or Mr. Nolan, and not take action yourself."

Edmund frowned. "But one needs discipline in the kitchens, sir."

"One doesn't need mayhem. We don't do those things in America. The police frown on it."

"Sad," said Edmund. "A most unruly country, I am afraid."

"Let us hope it will improve." Jason thought of Holy Cross cemetery, and his face became harsh. He told Edmund of the vandalism, and Edmund listened in horror. "But you are a white man, sir!"

"Just try to persuade most people here of that, Edmund. Well, good luck." He walked to the door with Edmund. Then he smiled. "I enjoy having you here. The only comic relief I have in my life is you and my little daughter, Nicole. Thank you."

Edmund was not certain this was a compliment, but he bowed with ceremony and departed as if accompanied by a train of attendants.

Still smiling, Jason sat down at his desk and saw a pile of paper heaped with troubles on his desk. The life of a hotel manager was no paradise. He summoned his secretary.

Three days later he was forced to intervene between Mr. Bristol and Flora. Mr. Bristol was administering a beating to his wife, and her screams had aroused the whole hotel at midnight. Jason had been called, and found Mr. Bristol purple-faced with rage and full of blasphemies. He shouted at Jason, who had forced himself between the bruised and bleeding girl and her husband, "What would you do with a stupid

336

careless cunt who lost her jewelry 'somewhere' in New York? Give her a medal, Garrity?"

"I'd remember she was young and careless. I'd behave as a gentleman, and get in touch with my insurance company. Look at the poor girl! On the floor, bleeding like a stuck pig. You ought to be ashamed. I must ask you to leave at once. We don't stand for things like that here, Bristol. We detest wife-beaters. In fact," said Jason, raising his fists, "I think I'll give you a taste of your own medicine."

Mr. Bristol stepped back. "You wouldn't dare." But he looked with apprehension at the big young Irishman.

"I would. I'm just aching to give you a beating. And the police, who've been called, would agree with me. Now, pack and get out. Both of you, if your wife can walk." He looked at the sobbing girl. "Mrs. Bristol, I advise you to talk to a lawyer in New York. Immediately."

The girl wept, "Yes, Mr. Garrity, I will! Right away! And I'll get a divorce, too!"

Mr. Bristol had suddenly became a middle-aged man, rumpled and subdued. He bent over his wife. "Now, Flora, I'm sorry I lost my temper, even if you deserved it. Let me help you up, darling. And you can't get a divorce in New York State, except for adultery, so be a good sensible girl."

She flung off his hands. Her blackened eyes sparkled furiously. "What about Linnie Merrill? I know all about her!"

"Flora, dear."

"Aw, shut up. You ain't even good in bed, you dirty old man!"

Jason decided it was time to leave. The Bristols left within two hours, but to where, he did not know or care. The first train was at six in the morning.

At least, he said to himself, Bristol had not uncovered anything about "Theo." Jason hoped that Flora would be prudent and get that threatened divorce quickly, before her husband discovered the naughty fact and denied her a settlement. She was really very beautiful. And she did have a gutter wisdom, under all that delicious flesh.

23

Old Bernard had once said, "When a politician, anxious for office, talks of 'reforms,' it's time for citizens to inspect their guns. Something dirty is afoot, and dangerous."

"Well," young Jason had asked, "what politician would you trust, Da?"

"None, and that's the truth. But I would be less suspicious of a man who talked of the 'ancient verities,' such as patriotism, honor, sobriety, hard work, respect for authority, constituted law, decency, manhood—if there's any of that left in this country. But I would be afraid if a man were too pious; I'd investigate him, and that I would." He had added, "And beware of the rich man who cries for the poor! He is a cannibal. Like the tearful walrus who ate all the trusting oysters in that book *Alice in Wonderland*."

Bernard had puffed at his cheap cigar for a moment, then had said, "But the worst of all is the rich politician who 'suffers' for the common man. No, you can't trust a politician. You can't trust a government."

"You don't trust anyone, Da."

"Sure, and that's true. Humanity can't be trusted, boyo."

Jason was remembering that conversation of long ago. He was also reading the newspapers with some alarm. One prophesied, with enthusiasm, that Teddy Roosevelt would be elected president this autumn. Another acclaimed Woodrow Wilson. And a third declared that Mr. Taft was sure that he would be elected.

Jason felt impatience for all three candidates, but he feared Wilson, the professor with the grim pale face of fanaticism. Why the Democratic party, which had a reputation for common sense, had nominated such a man was bewildering. Unless...And Jason remembered Bernard's belief that evil and invisible forces often were in command of governments, and politicians. Da certainly was convinced that the "powers of darkness" existed, but not the powers of light. And he, Jason, was becoming convinced of that also.

Jason had bought a few shares in the past year. He turned to the stockmarket report from Wall Street. The Dow Jones average was mysteriously "down," except for the manufacturers of steel—and munitions. Jason focused sharply on the rise of Barbour-Bouchard, the great American munitions industrialist, who had interlocking European cartels and subsidiaries. They showed a heavy rise. Why? There was another small item that caught Jason's eye. The munitions factories in Europe were extremely active just now. "Chimneys are smoking in every country," said the report. Why?

Jason restlessly turned the pages of the newspapers. Hell! thought Jason. What can I, as a single individual, do to prevent calamity? Nothing. Taft is the safest man. He is not an imperialist, like Roosevelt. Nor a social fanatic like Wilson. I'll vote for Taft. At least he has some reason in his rhetoric, some steadfastness.

But Jason had more immediate troubles, all baffling. Coal for the hotel furnaces was unaccountably delayed. It was August, and the furnaces would need fuel by the end of September, when the cool mountain days would arrive, and the cooler nights. Usually supplies were delivered no later than the early part of July; now there were only vague promises that "deliveries will be made in the near future." Edmund Patterson was complaining that lately the gas stoves seemed unable to produce steady flame and often failed in the late afternoon. This complaint was not simply at Ipswich House. As Jason had noted earlier in the summer, it was reported from many of the larger Northern cities. State governments "explained" that "there seem to be some shortages." The cause of this was unknown, and the shortages seemed confined to the large oil-, coal-, and gas-producing states. To add to the puzzle, the steel mills had suddenly become active again, but what they were producing was not explained. It was all very vague, but Jason's uneasiness was growing.

There was nothing vague about the reports concerning the new hotel. Delays in the deliveries of bricks, mortar, wood, stone, marble, and equipment had been lengthening over the past months. Angry calls to contractors either brought no replies or weak apologies that they had been too optimistic concerning dates of delivery, but "hoped" to have the situation resolved very shortly. "What the hell?" Patrick had asked. "This never happened before. Is everybody becoming too lazy to work?"

That spring there had been the mysterious "shortage" of sugar and wheat, "due to unseasonable frosts," said the newspapers. Dark sugar appeared in the markets, full of impurities, and dark flour, which customers did not like. The newspapers appeared equally baffled and annoyed. Odd to say, Mr. Roosevelt, usually the first to explode during national events which did not please him, was silent. The cost of living began to rise, and, as was customary, the poor and the low-paid working class suffered.

Jason tried to improve his mood by turning to the lighter sections of the paper, the articles Patricia always read. These ranged from Mary Pickford, "America's Sweetheart," the songs of Irving Berlin, and the new dances, claimed to be immoral by the "guardians of American virtue," to the antics of suffragettes and stories of the "injuries to the nation's morals and health" by the local saloons, and the other "purveyors of the Demon Rum." There were editorial diatribes against the "laxness of modern parents" and the "growing indifference of youth to decorum, sobriety, religion, and authority." There were also editorials concerning the "Yellow Peril." One got the impression that the Oriental people were about to inundate the white population of America, and there were sinister queries as to the reason.

Jason also noted that more and more girls and women, even married women with children, were entering the factories and were wretchedly paid. "A new freedom for women!" some newspapers exulted. It was progress. The same story also made light of the increase in racial tension. It seemed to Jason that the Negro was either affectionately derided in popular songs or genially lynched in the South. He remembered hearing a song recently that went:

> When you ain't got no money,
> well you needn't come round,
> Ef you is broke, Mister Nigger,
> I'll throw you down.

The tune had originated in 1898, and was revived with enthusiasm.

Disgusted, Jason was about to throw down the paper when his eye fell on an excerpt from a speech by Roosevelt. "We stand at Armageddon, and we battle for the Lord!"

That sentence seemed even more portentous than anything else in the news, and the glowing August sunset suddenly seemed bleak and cold. Did Mr. Roosevelt anticipate something the rest of the country did not? What Armageddon, what battle?

Jason stood up, filled with unease.

At least one evening a week now he came home to have dinner with Patricia. His conscience induced him to do this. Had he not done his wife a terrible wrong in marrying her? He had thought he loved her. He forgot that she had implored him to marry her, and so he was full of pity for her now. Still, the marriage had given him Sebastian, and the twins, so something good had come of it. He would try even harder to mitigate his guilt for making her his wife. In the meantime, he was resolutely trying now to avoid thinking of Molly, for when he did so he would feel a profound wave of despair, and despair was not a familiar emotion. "We Irish may weep, but we never despair," Bernard had often said.

Jason went into the dining room, where the servants were laying the dinner dishes and silver. He poured a large measure of whiskey for himself and drank it, standing up near the cabinet. It seared his throat and stomach, but it comforted him. He thought of Patricia. At least, he reflected, the episodes of her drunkenness were over. As he had rarely encountered drunken women before—and they all, when he had seen them at Mrs. Lindon's, had appeared jolly, noisy, and profane—he did not recognize Patricia's chronic torpidity and long sullen silences as drunkenness. Moreover, she did not go out regularly anymore for endless lunches, and when she and Jason visited friends, she drank only one glass of sherry and one glass of wine at dinner. He did not understand that her chronic exhaustion was a sign of both intoxication and suicidal depression. If she was surly and silent in his presence and had a new habit of fixing her eyes unblinkingly on some spot in the distance, he felt that she was rightfully reproaching him for his lack of devotion. So he tried to be kinder than ever. She did not seem to notice. Or she would make an impatient gesture of repudiation, as if engrossed with her own thoughts.

Dinner would not be ready for at least half an hour, and Jason went up to the nursery, where his children were having their supper. Nicholas was the first to see him; the child overturned his glass of milk, pushed his plate onto the floor with a crash, and jumped at his father, his small face contorting in the evening light. "Papa, Papa, Papa!" he screamed. "What...what...Peaches, ice cream! Come, come!" He threw himself into Jason's arms and kissed him, but his hot and protuberant eyes were unseeing. He writhed in Jason's grasp, and renewed his shouting. When Jason tried to put him down, he clung to his father's neck and slobbered against it. A low animal-like burbling came from his pulsing throat, a new manifestation. Jason held him tighter and said, "Now, now, Nick." He did not know why he added, "It's all right, son, it's all right." Though it was not too warm in the nursery, the child was sweating. He clutched Jason and seemed to struggle, but any movement to set him down made him frenzied, and excited that strange cry. Then Jason felt a liquid warmth through the Buster Brown bloomers, and the stench of urine rose in the pleasant air.

Concerned, Jason looked down to find Nicole standing before him. The little girl's round face was unusually grave. She said very quietly, "Nick, get down and come with me. Nick!" She put her small hand on his leg and tugged at him, and instantly he was quiet. He slid down from Jason's arms and went away with his sister.

"Dear me," said Miss Flowers, embarrassed. "The child does get so excited, Mr. Garrity." She added, "Excuse me, please sir," and followed the two children, saying, "Tsk, tsk."

"Well," said Jason, to Sebastian, who had gotten down from his chair politely and was waiting in his usual grave silence. Jason wiped his hands on his handkerchief, looked at it helplessly. Sebastian came and took it away from him. He said in his gentle manly voice, "I think Nick is sick, Papa."

"Has he a cold...or something?"

"I don't think so, Papa. I think something's wrong with Nick."

Jason was instantly alarmed. He said, trying for lightness, "Now, what could be wrong? He's very excitable, but he's only a little boy, after all. And little boys do have accidents, you know, Sober Face."

Sebastian disposed of the wet handkerchief. He went to the table and poured a glass of lemonade for Jason, and drew out a chair for him. Then he looked at Jason and said, "Nick is out of control. I think he should see a doctor."

"Do you, then," said Jason, almost like his grandfather, and with an effort at indulgence. "If he were sick, Miss Flowers would have told me. He looks very healthy; he's just too active for a sultry day."

Jason tousled Sebastian's hair. The boy absently smoothed it back. He was thinking. Then he said, "Papa, I don't care what anyone says. Nick needs a doctor. He doesn't say one word, anymore, that's sensible. And he wets the bed every night, and cries in his sleep. I hear him, right across the

342

room. And I dry him off and change him, and he jumps and jumps. Papa. Please."

"You're an old man, Bastie," said Jason, but he was more alarmed. "What does Mama say? Have you told her?"

Sebastian looked him straight in the face, and once again Jason thought he was confronted by a man and not a child. His agate eyes, so like Patricia's, were all at once suffused by an intense yellow light. "I've told Mama," he said in a low voice, and looked quickly away. "So has Nickie. So has Miss Flowers."

"And?"

The boy was visibly hesitating. "I don't think Mama is well, either, Papa. She...she didn't listen...much. She..." Sebastian did not add that Patricia had shouted at him and had slapped his face and had called him a fool, and that she had upbraided Miss Flowers for being too strict with "little Nicholas," and had scolded Nicole for not "caring" for her brother and taking him to the toilet in time.

"A mother always knows if there is something wrong with her child, Sebastian."

Sebastian looked away for a moment, and said nothing. Jason drank some lemonade and watched the boy. Patrick had said only recently, "The little spalpeen, God bless him, is too quiet. Too many wimin about him. Needs his da more. Take him hunting in the autumn, with us."

The huge red August sun, setting to the west, glowed outside the nursery windows. The scent of newly mown grass entered the room. As if to reassure himself, Jason said again, "Your mother would know if something ailed Nick, dear. That she would. She is a very good mother and loves you all."

Sebastian did not speak. He merely watched Jason with a mature pity.

"I'll talk to her about a doctor," said Jason. "Hope that will make you feel better, Bastie."

"Thank you," said Sebastian. He went to the table again, fetched the pitcher, and refilled Jason's glass. Jason regarded him with love. The boy was entirely too old for his years. Something must be done. Patrick was right. Miss Flowers and Nicole came back into the room, Miss Flowers annoyed, Nicole thoughtful.

"Where is Nick?" asked Jason.

"I put him to bed, the naughty boy," said Miss Flowers crossly. "Dear me, at his age! He is almost four."

"He can't help it," said Nicole. "He didn't eat half his dinner, either. Sometimes he throws up."

"A delicate digestion," said Miss Flowers, glowering at the girl. "Like his dear mama. I've heard her complain of it."

Nicole stared at her with scorn. "He gets upset at nothing. And he runs and runs all the time, and cries too much."

"Dear me," said Miss Flowers, "he's only a baby."

"I'm almost four, too, and I'm not a baby," said Nicole. She turned to Jason, innocently absurd in her flounced dress and ruffled pinafore. "Papa, take Nick to a doctor."

"You and Sebastian," said Jason. "Is Nick asleep?"

"He screams one minute," said Sebastian, "and the next minute he is asleep and you can't wake him."

"So energetic," said Miss Flowers, fuming at them. "So unlike..." She glanced at Sebastian with no liking at all.

Nicole slipped her hand into Sebastian's and held it tightly. The light in the room reddened, and Jason all at once felt afraid. He said to Miss Flowers, "Take Nick to Dr. Conners tomorrow."

"Dr. Conners wouldn't know," said Nicole. "He only knows colds and bellyaches."

Jason smiled. "Dr. Garrity, what do you think is wrong with Nick?"

Nicole did not respond to this attempt at lightness or to Jason's smile. "I don't know, Papa. But it's something. Not a bellyache, not a cold. It's something."

"Just a surplus of energy," said Miss Flowers with a spot of crimson on her cheeks. "Dear me, Nicole, you talk like an old lady."

"I *am* an old lady," said Nicole with emphasis.

"You do seem so, dear," said the governess. She almost winked at Jason. Nicole ignored her and waited for Jason to speak. Miss Flowers simpered at Jason this time. "So precocious, this dear child, Mr. Garrity."

Jason's alarm was growing. "Miss Flowers or your mother will take him tomorrow to Dr. Conners. Let him examine Nick first of all."

"A healthy, normal little boy!" cried Miss Flowers, giving Sebastian a look of affront. "Sebastian, you do try to cause trouble all the time, don't you? It is very bad of you, indeed, and no wonder your poor mother suffers! You are always agitating poor little Nicole, too, over nothing."

"He does not!" said Nicole in an unusually loud voice. "We

both love Nick, and we know there's something wrong with him."

Both Nicole and Sebastian were silent then, studying Jason with ponderous attention. He stood up, touching one child and then the other on the cheek. "Tomorrow. I promise," he said. Then he bent and kissed them. They smiled at him gravely, and Jason got the impression that he was the most naive person in the room, and it amused him for a moment. Then he went downstairs to dine with Patricia.

When Jason entered the room, Patricia was already at the table, one hand aimlessly toying with a fork. The air in the large gloomy room was stuffy, pervaded by the odors of yesterday's roast pork and fried potatoes.

"Good evening, Patricia," he said as he sat down. Her unseeing eyes touched him a moment, then resumed their staring; she did not answer him. She was no more aware of him than if he had been a fly on the ceiling. He looked at his wife more closely than usual. When had she become so thin, so emaciated? Her customary appetite had failed of late; she would merely push her food absently about the plate, drink a glass of wine, break a piece of bread she would not eat, and nibble at dessert. Her lassitude in these last weeks had become extremely noticeable, and when questioned, she would reply that it was only the heat. Her long and usually colorless face had taken on a constant flush; in the mornings her face was puffy and her eyes ringed with deep circles. But in some way she contrived to keep her meticulous grooming, though in the past weeks her clothing had seemed to hang on her.

Then there were times when she appeared very vivacious, laughing, talking loudly and with a feverish rapidity, and even singing abruptly on the most untimely occasions, especially when visiting Joan and Lionel.

Jason was often perplexed and disturbed by these unaccountable and sudden changes of mood, but he did not know the reason. Patrick, anxiously fond, would wonder, but if he questioned his daughter, she would laugh and throw her arms about his neck, then dance away. This reassured Patrick; it did not reassure Jason. About Patricia now lingered a sweet scent that neither man suspected was a new disguise for a breath saturated with alcohol. It was not Sen-Sen, nor cloves, and so they had no suspicion. Once Patrick said, "Nick resembles his mother more every day, the boyo! Lively as crickets, both of them." Jason was no longer reassured by such a remark. A week ago he had asked Patrick to force Patricia to see Dr. Conners, for he knew his own suggestion would be ignored or treated with contempt. The old physician had his own shrewd conjectures, but no absolute evidence. As he was old-fashioned, he could not bring himself to believe that a lady like Patricia Mulligan would "indulge" to the point of blind intoxication, and Patricia was careful. Besides, she preferred to drink alone now, especially before she went to bed, when she was safe from detection.

But alcohol was not the only cause of her lassitude. The reason for her chronic intoxication was fixed in her despair, which grew steadily and was alleviated only in the presence of Lionel. Then she became unnaturally animated, her hands plucking at her handkerchief, her eyes too bright and ardent, her gestures too lavish. Her flush would become brighter, her lips feverish. Only Joan knew and smiled to herself and was amused. Lionel had a growing suspicion and was careful to seat himself at a distance from Patricia; she would then direct all her conversation, sometimes stammering and disordered, at him, and she would gaze at him knowingly and with a terrible hunger.

"The fresh raspberries with cream are very good," Jason said now after a long oppressive silence at the table. He noticed that Patricia had scarcely touched her food, and his anxiety grew.

She started, looked at him as if jolted. "Are they?" she said listlessly, and then surveyed the berries with a faint frown. She picked up her spoon, took two berries on it, and put them into her mouth. Then she stared dumbly at her plate. Her eyes were dry and dull.

"You should eat more," said Jason.

Patricia shrugged, without lifting her eyes. "The heat," she said. She drank a fourth glass of water, then seemed to study the cut design on the glass.

Jason said, "I have to go to New York next week. Would you like to come along?"

Only two months ago she had aroused herself to assent with eagerness when Jason had suggested this. Now she said in an indistinct voice, "No."

"Why not?" Jason leaned toward her over the cluttered table. "You always liked New York."

"No," she said again. With an obvious effort she focused her gaze on Jason. "Too hot."

346

"The fall styles will be in, Patricia. You were always interested in them."

She shrugged and did not answer. Now his alarm quickened. "Are you taking the tonic the doctor gave you?"

"Yes."

"Lively as a cricket," Patrick had said with paternal love. But it was a sporadic liveliness, and even this had diminished lately. Jason saw that Patricia now had practically no breast at all, that the slender waist had become a mere stem, that her flushed skin was dry and faintly tremulous.

"I think you should see a better doctor, such as young Tim Hedges," said Jason.

Alarm flickered in her eyes. She said in a raised voice, "No! There's nothing wrong with Dr. Conners! He's taken care of me all my life!" There was a hint of fear in her vehemence.

"But Dr. Hedges has had a more modern education in medicine."

"No!" She began to get to her feet.

Then Jason remembered Nicholas. "Just a minute, dear. I must talk to you. It's about Nick."

Patricia slowly subsided into her chair. "What about Nick, for heaven's sake?"

"Well, dear, he does seem too strenuous, let us say, for his age. Too... active, and he's too thin, too. It's hard to get his attention—"

"He's not a secret sneak like your dear Sebastian! He's a real little boy! He doesn't creep around listening. He's not crafty, sneaky, like—"

"Patricia. You know that isn't true about Sebastian."

She threw up her hands, and Jason caught a whiff of that sweetish odor as she uttered a short laugh. "Oh, everyone knows he is your pet, and the twins might not exist, for all you care!"

"That's not true. How can you say that?"

Her eyes were wide and glittering, and all at once Jason thought: She hates the child! My God, she hates the child! Why?

Now Patricia was dangerously excited. Her hands became tight fists on the table, and she leaned toward Jason, her teeth bared in anger. "The way he's always looking at you. Looking at me. Trying to catch us in something! And stupid! I've never known a child to be that stupid. Even Miss Flowers says he is, to me, his mother! I wish...I wish...I wish he'd never been born!"

"Patricia!" Jason was horrified.

"I wish you'd send him away, out of my sight! I can't bear him!"

Jason leaned back in his chair, his horror growing.

"I never wanted him to be born!" Patricia's voice was loud and shrill, and the servants in the kitchen halted their work and listened.

"Why?"

"He...he..." Then the years of careful discretion came to her aid. She fell back in her chair, swallowed convulsively, and momentarily shut her eyes. She whispered, "He came too soon." She swallowed again. "There wasn't any time just for us—to be alone."

Jason frowned. Then he was touched. So that was the trouble. "But the twins came very quickly, too, only a year after Sebastian. You didn't resent them, Patricia."

She was desperately trying to control herself. "I was used to being a mother by then. That's all. But I...I don't think I ever wanted children anyway."

"That's because you were always Dada's little girl." Jason's compassion grew. "You didn't want to grow up that fast."

She looked at him for several seconds, then said, "I suppose."

"Well, dear. I'd really like for Nick to see Dr. Conners tomorrow. Please, Patricia. It may be as you say, that he's just an overactive little boy, but I'd like to make sure. I'm worried."

She smiled at him scornfully. "A perfectly healthy, cheerful little boy, who's interested in everything! Unlike your pet, who has as much perception as a turnip. He hardly talks, he hardly runs, he hardly smiles or laughs. I think he's feeble-minded. He's the one who needs to see the doctor, not Nicholas. I think he should be put away, in an institution. What do they call people like him now? Idiots or morons. Which do you think your pet is, Jason?"

"Patricia, you never talked about Sebastian that way before." He was profoundly shocked. "I know you've often been impatient with him, and called him 'slow.' You've often ignored him, because you don't understand him. He's a very quiet child, and thoughtful and studious. He doesn't make a noise. That's his nature. And he and Nicole adore each other."

Patricia became excited again. "Nicole's just sorry for him!

She as much as told me so! She knows what he is, even if you don't."

"We're getting nowhere, Patricia. If you or Miss Flowers won't take Nick to the doctor, I will. In fact, I think I will."

"No!"

"Yes." Jason stood up. "It might interest you to know that Nickie—Nicole—asked me to take Nick to the doctor. Little Nicole."

"I don't believe it! But she's just a baby, and she's devoted to Nicholas."

"I know. And the kid is worried about him."

"Don't be ridiculous. She isn't even four years old yet. How can such a baby think of anything?"

"She's a very intelligent young lady. Well? Will you take Nick, or will I?"

Patricia was quickly frightened. "You're serious, aren't you?"

"Yes, I am."

Patricia had always evaded responsibility, thought Jason, or perhaps she had never been forced to take it. Now she was looking at him with growing terror. She put her hands over her eyes. "I...I'm afraid. There's nothing wrong, but I'm afraid. You'd better take him yourself. I...I don't feel well, and I can't seem to get up easily in the morning anymore. Take him. You'll find out there's nothing wrong."

"I hope so. I believe so. Patricia..."

But she had literally flung herself from her chair and was running out of the room, to the closed silence of her bedroom and the hidden bottle. As she drank from it, she began to cry, sobbing deep in her chest. Then she whispered, "Oh, Lionel, Lionel!"

She drank deeper, and as the night came on swiftly, she fell on her bed and wept into her pillow until she sank into a stupor.

Dr. Conners was an old man with shaking hands and pale blue eyes and a small white Vandyke beard. But he was no fool. What he lacked in more modern learning he had made up for in that invaluable wisdom—experience. He motioned Jason into his examining room and looked at him with a troubled expression.

"I'm just a family doctor, Jason," he said as they both sat down. They could hear Nicholas burbling in the other room

349

as Miss Flowers dressed him. It was an aimless chittering, like a squirrel's, and very loud.

"Well?"

"In every way, Nicholas seems a healthy little boy, if a little thin. Perhaps too active. He could grow out of that. His heart beats a little too fast, but then, he's excitable. A lot of children are that way. You've told me he often wets his bed. That's not unusual for children like him. Boys need more training than girls. I'll bet Nicole never does," and the old doctor smiled.

Jason did not smile. "Is there anything abnormal about Nick, Ben?"

Dr. Conners hesitated. "Well, there's the way he talks. Of course, girls talk much more coherently at that age than boys do. He seems unable to get out the words fast enough. In too big a hurry to express himself clearly. I've seen that before in children his age, especially if they have a very active mind, too."

Jason waited, and his eyes did not leave the doctor's face. Dr. Conners carefully lit his old pipe and puffed at it reflectively. He did not appear to want to look at Jason. When the silence became too heavy, the doctor said, "I've not had much experience..."

"In what?" Jason's own heart began to thump too hard.

"Let me say this: the human mind, or personality, is very mysterious, very...delicately adjusted. I've seen dull little boys, unable to learn in school, suddenly become scholars and make their mark in the world. I've seen little girls who did not talk, even at four, open their pretty little mouths one day and speak like ten-year-olds. No one knows why. There are some men in Austria—alienists, they are called. They are probing these cases; they have theories. Some of them seem absurd to me, some of them not."

Jason felt sick. "You mean they treat insane people?"

"No, no! Please don't misunderstand me! What is sanity, what is insanity? I've heard it said that an intelligent mind can reject an irrational world, make up one of its own in self-defense. The alienists call that schizophrenia, a complicated term. I don't understand it, myself. It needs toughness to stand this world, Jason. Or it needs absolute stupidity. In fact, the 'sanest' people I know are the most stupid."

"Ben, what are you trying to tell me, for God's sake?"

The doctor hesitated again. Then he sighed and rubbed

his chin. "If Nick were m⟩
to a neurologist, first of all.

Jason's body felt numb. "Yo⟨
me! I'm the child's father!"

The old doctor sighed again. "The⟨
I couldn't put my finger on it. It was ⟨
I'm probably wrong. We doctors frequen⟨
It's a kind of look in the child's eyes, a l⟨
slightest concentration. He...jabbers, Nick—a⟨

"As if there's nothing there." Jason's voice was ⟨   ⟩d
flat.

"Now, now, don't put words in my mouth, Jason. I'd say
that Nick has no...control—not even a very young child's
control of himself. He stares at things, but I don't think,
forgive me, that he's really interested in them. If he touches,
it isn't to get the feel; it is just an aimless touching, another
physical activity."

"He's got schizophrenia, then?"

"No, no. He hasn't that kind of a mind. I shouldn't have
mentioned the term; it has no relevance for Nick. I was just
trying to explain the mysteries of the human mind. Nick
hasn't rejected the world; it just doesn't seem to reach him."

"Like an infant."

"Infants are curious almost from the day they are born,
Jason. Nick...isn't." He puffed at his pipe. "Let me call the
neurologist now. It may be a very simple thing. In the meantime, I'll give you an elixir for Nick which will help to calm
him. That may be all he needs."

"What in God's name shall I tell his mother, Ben?"

"The truth. That I'm only a general practitioner and that
the little boy needs a more advanced examination. Don't let
Patricia get frantic. Be as detached as possible. Tell her Nick
is wearing himself out with too much activity, and you need
advice. That he needs building up. Remember, I may be
wrong, and Nick may be perfectly normal. Besides, who
knows what is normal or abnormal? Sometimes I, too, think
the world was created by a divine madman."

"You're not alone, Ben." Jason tried to smile. "I think that,
too."

24

Saul Weitzman had rented the rooms over his shop to a young widow with three small children; she was a seamstress and a general dressmaker of no great talent but with much diligence. He had let the premises for almost nothing, out of pity, and had then rented the Garritys' old rear cottage for himself. He had retained the old furniture, including a buffet on which he displayed his few treasures, such as an ancient silver menorah, a red Venetian glass decanter and three matching goblets, and a beautiful plate or two, and some English bone-china teacups. Somehow he had infused the rooms of the cottage with a bright warmth, and he kept everything polished and excessively neat.

To Jason, it was a refuge. He did not ask himself why, and he no longer confided very much in Lionel; in fact, he rarely saw Lionel alone. When he did, Lionel would look at him with the old affection and humor, but that flicker in his eyes was still there, accompanied recently by a sort of furtive wariness. In Saul, Jason found the perfect confidant, paternal, patient, and kind. Saul was very old, but his eyes were bright and understanding, his words always sensible and to the point. He was hardly more prosperous, but his boots shone with polish and his linen was always trim and snowy and his ancient suit pressed. He would say, "I have all I need. What more does a man want?" He would rock in his chair and listen to Jason like a father, nodding his head judiciously at times, comprehending even when Jason spoke with difficulty. Saul would speak of Bernard, not implying the past tense but the present, and when he did so, Jason felt the presence of his grandfather in the little room.

Saul had not known Kate Garrity, but he spoke of her as of an old friend, valued and admired and loved. He rarely mentioned Joan or John, and when Jason did he would just listen and smoke his pipe.

Jason had come to see Saul late this hot September night, and it was evident to Saul that Jason was not only upset but also sick with some almost unendurable pain. It was a while before he could speak other than in a desultory fashion, sipping a glass of port. The windows were open; there were stiffly starched white muslin curtains over them, which blew out into the room with a soft rustle. Thunder complained in the passes of the mountains and lightning flickered in the distance. There was no rain as yet. The air was heavy, hard to breathe, and the gaslight burned languidly. Saul rocked in his chair with the linen cover and waited. He had rarely seen Jason so distressed, so burdened with words he could not yet say. He had aged in one week, his gray eyes weary with sleeplessness and suffering. At one moment he appeared to be about to speak, and then he would sink back into silence, as if he had no power to reveal what he wanted to say.

Saul poured him another glass of port. Jason's torment was almost palpable, a presence that touched both of them. For some time there had been total silence between the two men, and Saul wondered if at last Jason would decide to say nothing at all. There were times when speech could not encompass a man's agony.

The thunder came nearer and the lightning grew more frequent.

Then Jason said in a voice filled with sorrow, "It's my little boy, Nick."

Saul regarded him solemnly through his polished glasses.

"You know Nick," said Jason. He tried to light a cigarette, and it slipped from his hand. "He was very active, always running—as if he wasn't going anywhere. Jabbering. You've seen and heard him." Jason looked at his friend now, and the stark grief in his eyes was appalling.

"Yes," said Saul.

"I just brought him back from Philadelphia yesterday. Nick...His mind will never be more than four years old."

Saul's face became very old, almost stern, in the shared pain.

"I took him to the best neurologist, and he sent me with Nick to a team of alienists. They all examined him. He'll always have the mind of a four-year-old. Always."

Saul murmured something like a prayer in Yiddish.

"They don't know..." said Jason, his voice lower and hoarser than before. "They don't know what causes it. Nick isn't exactly an idiot. He's what they call a...a low-grade moron. Moron. Some people have a euphemism for it now. They are calling it 'slow.' But it's feebleminded! He can learn a little more—a very little more. Take care of himself, perhaps better. But hardly more than an idiot. Never be able to read, to think as a human being. He...his body is healthy. He will

353

grow to manhood, but he'll still be a little child. Nothing can be done."

Jason put his hands over his eyes and rubbed them. Then he looked at Saul, and his pain was like a wound.

"They've given me some medicine. It will keep him...better, under control. One of them suggested an institution, where he'll be trained. But the alienists said he would do better for a time in his home with his family—more secure, protected. They said he may never be—oh, God—dangerous to himself or others. They can't tell. We...I...just have to watch. If the time comes. Oh, God, he's my child, my little boy. What in the name of Christ can I do?"

Very slowly Saul relit his pipe, contemplated it, bent his head. He said, "They call them God's fools. He'll never know all the misery we know, Jason. He'll always be happy, a child, like a child, Jason."

"In other words, he'll never be alive! Is that what you're saying?"

Saul sighed. "He's alive in his own way, happy, too, Jason. This world isn't the best place, is it? Don't they all say that the life of a child is the sweetest and happiest? You and me, Jason, we can't look back and say it was, for us. But for Nick, it can be, and it's so, isn't it? He seems like a happy little boy. There's worse things than not growing up, Jason. Didn't King Solomon say, 'Better the day of your death than the day of your birth'? That's for men, old in the world. Little Nick, he won't have that suffering. For him life will always be sunshine and love and no worries."

But Jason said in a groan, "God damn God!"

Saul winced. "Let me tell you something. I had a brother like that, in the old country. Happy as a lark, all his life; we all loved him. He lived until he was forty, gentle and sweet. What does a happy child see? Love and care, that's it. Jason, there's worse lives than that."

But Jason shook his head over and over in increasing torment. "But not for his parents; there's no joy or peace, watching somebody like that. A waste of life..."

"Is it a waste to those children? Is a bird a waste, or a butterfly, or a flower? Who can say it is?"

"He won't be a man."

"'The days of a man's life are full of trouble. Like the grass he is cut down.' Job cursed the day of his birth. Nick will never do that."

"It's better to suffer," said Jason. "Then you know you are

354

a man. It's better to have pain than endless childhood. At least you know you are alive."

Saul shook his head wearily. "I'm an old man. I wish I'd never been born. It was God's will—blessed be his name—and here I am in my old age, with none of my own. I'll go to my grave and thank the Lord."

Jason turned to him sharply and really saw his friend for the first time, and they gazed at each other mutely in the awful light of revelation. Then Saul reached out his hand and took Jason's, and together they listened to the thunder that rattled the sky like an enemy threatening the frail house of their lives. "It's no bargain," said Saul at last. "No, it's no bargain."

He looked at Jason, and the saddest smile touched his face. "From this, then, Jason, your son was spared. This knowing."

The rain poured down as if in uncontrollable surrender to despair.

"I know women, I know Patricia," said Dr. Conners in the library of Patrick's house. "Many women, on being forced to confront a disastrous or even a trivial problem, run screaming from the room in denial, hoping to be pursued and placated, persuaded it is 'nothing' or just a nasty joke. They want to be treated as children, sheltered from all unpleasantness; they want their world to be sweet. If this is denied them, and they must face reality, more often than not they will soon behave sensibly. They will grow up." He paused. "Let's hope Patricia does, though she has been protected by you both all her life." The old physician looked with cold accusation at Patrick and Jason.

"We want her to be responsible for Nicholas and help us," he continued. "So, under no circumstances must you console Patricia; sympathize, yes, but not console. She must accept what Nicholas, her favorite, is, and help the child, too."

He lifted his hand warningly to the stricken father and the devastated husband. "Under no circumstances," he repeated, "treat her like a hysterical child. It's time she was a woman."

"God help us," said Patrick. "Help us all. And you don't know what causes this?"

"No, no. And while Nicholas can be trained to do simple things for himself, like a well-disciplined child of four or five, he'll never be a man. We can give him medicines to keep him quiet most of the time, but we'll never know when he will become uncontrollable, as his body grows to maturity. He will have the strength of a man, with a man's physical demands, yet his mind...You may have to consider an institution later, a fine private institution."

"No," said Jason.

"No," said Patrick in a husky voice. "This is his home, with people who love him."

The doctor sighed. "We'll see. If he becomes a danger to himself or others, the law might intervene. Or you could get a 'keeper,' a strong man, to watch him all the time, one who has experience with these unfortunates."

"A jailer," said Patrick. "Do they...always need to be 'watched'?"

"Usually, when the imperative needs of a man are under a child's lack of control. Well, then. Call Patricia."

Patrick rang for a maid, and she was told to send down Mrs. Garrity at once. Then the three men waited in a desperate silence. Patrick puffed at a cigar he had not lit; Jason turned a cigarette in his trembling fingers. The doctor looked at each man with compassion. Long minutes passed. Patricia did not appear. Patrick rang impatiently again. The maid came down and said, her eyes downcast, that Mrs. Garrity "did seem to sleep very sound" but that she had been aroused at last and was dashing cold water on her face and combing her hair.

"She's not well," said Patrick. "Always so frail, yes. All her life. Too delicate for this world."

The doctor glanced aside; his white hair glistened like snow in the bleak light of the early-September sun that came through the windows. The trees were fading; only the late annual flowers, in brilliant profusion, kept the garden as colorful as summer. The mountains beyond had paled to a dim lavender. A new family, with four girls and one boy, had recently bought the house next door and their laughing voices drifted into the room like a mockery. Sebastian and Nicole had had their first encounters with their neighbors two or three weeks ago and had not recovered from this unusual experience. Patricia had never wanted her children to "associate" with inferior people, but on investigation she had discovered the newcomers "acceptable if a little rowdy and heedless." She had been introduced to the mother, Mrs. Crimshaw, at a "welcoming tea," and on finding out that she was from New York and of a "good, well-to-do family," had graciously condescended to be friends. Mr. Percy Crimshaw was "retired." That is, he was on the boards of two banks in Philadelphia, but had been forced to move to the country after a heart attack. He was a semi-invalid, though of a very robust appearance and given to long hunting and fishing trips. His health also did not prevent him from discreet visits to Mrs. Lindon's establishment or business trips to Philadelphia. His wife was a fat pink-cheeked woman, good-tempered and devoted to her family, although not very perceptive. She was what Bernard would have called "simple." She had already begun to adopt the Garrity children without question or criticism, and believing Sebastian to be timid, she had become his second mother. She did not know that Sebastian, who was only very fond of her, treated her as if she were younger than Nicole, and that Nicole affectionately tolerated her for her very goodness.

To Jason, this early evening, the children next door seemed too loud, too exuberant, too painful a reminder of his own flawed son. He suddenly exploded, "Why the hell can't they keep those brats quiet for once!" Dr. Conners said nothing, but Patrick said, "Now, then, Jase, they're only playing. D'you want them to be grieving, too?"

Patricia came down, walking slowly and carefully, with the new sweet scent floating about her. All her motions were lethargic and sluggish; her face was pale and without expression; she concentrated all her efforts on walking straight. The hair about her face was damp but combed. She had put on a fresh frock, a dark blue linen with a sailor collar and a black silk tie. She stood in the doorway; the men rose. She blinked, then said feebly, "What's the matter? I was resting. Is it important?"

"Yes," said Dr. Conners. "Sit down, Patricia. I want to talk to you." She did not look at her father and husband, but fumbled for a chair and sat down. "I hope it's important," she said with resentment. "I'm tired. Such a hard day at the Altar Society bazaar." Her voice was uncertain.

"You do too much, my darlin'," said Patrick, kissing her cheek. But Jason could not look at her. He sat down again. It was ridiculous, but he felt guilty, as if her coming anguish were his own fault.

"You know that Jason took Nicholas to Philadelphia for examination," said Dr. Conners, "and that they returned this morning."

Patricia gave Jason a glance of pure venom. "Yes! How

ridiculous! Jason, you knew it was absurd! And it was humiliating for me."

Dr. Conners lifted his hand. "My dear, it wasn't ridiculous at all. It should have been sooner."

Patricia turned on the doctor. "You're all wrong! He's just too active a child! He's alive, not like some children." She gave Jason another venomous look.

"Patricia," said Dr. Conners. "Listen to me. There's something wrong with Nicholas. He...he'll always have the mentality of a four- or five-year-old. Always."

Patricia shrieked. She clutched the arms of her chair, the cords straining in her neck. Her face was wild and frantic, turning from one to the other. "A lie, a lie, a lie! I don't believe it! It can't be! You are trying to make me sick, suffer! Dada...!"

Her father came to her again and tried to take her hand, but she pushed him away and glared up at him with frenzy. "Dada! Why do you let them lie to you about Nicholas! They must hate us, Dada. Jason's just trying to hurt me. Even his sister says he's sly and stupid! People like that want to hurt, because they know they're cheap and inferior—they try to take revenge on us!"

Her head swung round to Jason. "I hate you, hate you, hate you! I always did! Now you're trying your tricks on my father, who loves you like a son! How can you be so vicious, so cruel, you and your pet, Sebastian! He's another trickster, like you, always wanting to make people feel miserable! He's made my life a curse—he's the one who should be sent away! Even Miss Flowers..."

Patrick and the doctor were appalled; Patrick stood immobile near his daughter, looking down at her. Patricia's eyes were still on her husband, gleaming with hatred. "Yes, yes, I know all about you! That's why I hate you."

She seized her father's hand, and her face grimaced convulsively. "Dada, Dada, save me! Don't listen to these lies about a perfectly normal, happy little boy, full of life! And so bright, too! Never making trouble, always loving, always laughing. Dada, help me. Send Jason and Sebastian away, out of this house. Then we'll have some peace. Just you and me and the twins, Dada. Oh, God, just us four! Peace!"

"Patricia," said Patrick in a faint voice, "don't talk like that. You don't mean it, darlin'. You're just upset. You—"

She flung his hand from her with savagery. "Oh, they've got you believing those wicked lies about my child! You're in it with them, Dada, or you're fooled. Why do you want to do this to me?"

So, thought the physician, she's known instinctively something was wrong with the child, and that's what she's denying.

Patricia literally leaped from her chair, screaming, and ran from the room. No one tried to stop her. She pounded into the hall, then halfway up the stairs. In her distraught state she expected at least one of the men to come running into the hall, calling to her. But there was silence. She stopped, gasping, leaning over the balustrade, sucking in her breath in order to hear. There was no sound. She pushed back her damp hair and listened more intently. She tried another scream, beat her feet on the stairs. She might have been alone in the house. She groaned and looked about hopelessly. No one was coming to embrace and pet her and say it was "nothing," as had been done during her childhood when she was asked to face a crisis.

She clutched the railing, and not since that day of her "renunciation" of Lionel had she felt such despair. Her eyes filled with tears. She searched the hall for one loving face. She was helpless, no one was coming. She had the sensation of walls crashing about her, leaving her open to catastrophe. She could not by cajoling, weeping, or protesting make the terrible fact disappear. But she continued to whisper to herself, "No, no. Of course not. It's all wrong. They'll see!" She glanced up the stairway and thought: I'll take Nicholas away with me, somewhere lovely and quiet, and he'll be all right, and we'll laugh together. We'll be...safe.

She sank down on the stairs and dropped her head on her knees. Then a new thought struck her. She sprang up and raced down the stairs and into the library.

"Patricia, darlin'," said Patrick, rising. His eyes were streaming, and all at once he looked old and broken. But she did not look at him. She looked at Jason, and her eyes burned with hatred.

"You!" she exclaimed. "You did this to my child! There's bad blood in you. Your hateful crippled sister! Your crazy grandfather! Your consumptive mother! Bad blood, diseased blood! You gave it to my baby, my poor little Nicholas!"

"No," said Dr. Conners, standing up. "No, Patricia. No one knows why this happens to a child. You must simply accept it. Nicholas will always be a happy little boy in his mind. He needs all the love he can get. And such children are often very lovable. They can bring much happiness to a family."

Patricia flung her hands over her face and wept loudly. Jason came to her but did not touch her. He wanted to share her suffering. He wanted her to know she was not alone and that they needed mutual help.

"I'll take my child away, and some decent doctor will tell me you all lied," Patricia moaned. "There are good doctors, better doctors—if anything's wrong, and there isn't."

It's natural that she should frantically look for a way out, thought Dr. Conners. But to turn on her husband and father with such hatred, such accusations—that's also a sickness. He said, "I'm sure your father and your husband will help you, Patricia. They'll find someone else—I can give you other names." He did not like to give her false hope.

"Operation?" Patricia sobbed, without removing her hands from her face.

"No. No. I don't think so. But we'll find out."

Dr. Conners pitied her, but he felt a greater compassion for her father and her husband. The doctor led Patricia to a chair, where she crouched and moaned like a wounded animal. After a few minutes he deftly gave her an injection, a sedative. The very thin arm lay limply in his hand, and she did not start at the prick. Her pale face took on a tragic shine in the gloom. Her sobs abated, while the men watched her in silence. Then her head fell back against the chair.

Dr. Conners sighed. "Well, someone put her to bed. She'll sleep for a long time. When she wakes up, she'll be more...composed. Able to face this and make plans."

It was Jason who carried his wife to bed and undressed her, suffering at the sight of her thin body and shriveled flesh. He put on her nightgown, covered her with the sheet and the soft blanket. She was beginning to snore. He looked down upon her and thought of what she had said in the library, and forgave her. In some obscure fashion, he believed he was guilty, guilty of not loving her, of loving another woman, and perhaps she had known this for some time and was heartbroken. Perhaps she had known it before he had done so himself.

The three men went up to the nursery, where the children were having their early supper. Nicholas came running, shouting. "Choo, choo, choo! We go on choo-choo, Papa. Now! Nickie and me and Bastie!" He danced with frenetic excitement, eyes bulging. "Papa, come!"

"In a little while, Nick," said Jason.

Nicole, approaching, looked at her father with deep concern. It was not possible for the little girl to know, but she sensed some terrible disaster. Sebastian came over also, and took Jason's hand without speaking. Jason looked down at him, and his eyes filled with tears. He had no doubt now that Patricia hated her eldest son, as she hated him. But it was Sebastian for whom he felt sorrow. Nicholas was still shouting and jumping and clutching Jason's thighs. Dr. Conners studied the little boy. There was no question about it, none at all. The physician sighed.

It was Patrick who took Nicholas from Jason and hugged him with desperation and despair. The boy bobbed in his arms, screeching, "Choo-choo-choo! Ding-a-ling, ding, ding! We go on choo-choo. Now, now, now! Mama, Papa, Nickie, Bastie, Grandpa! Now!" and his voice rose to a yell and his mouth frothed and his eyes darted here and there without ever focusing.

Miss Flowers, who had been out of the room, now returned. The servants had heard everything; she had come from the kitchen and had just been informed. Her gray face was tight, vindictive, and she tossed her head. "May I have a moment alone with you, Mr. Garrity?" She stared at him like a triumphant enemy.

"Certainly," Jason mumbled. He withdrew from the other two men. Nicole was again calming Nicholas, but not so successfully this time. He had become impatient with her efforts and had tried to kick her in the face.

"See that, Mr. Garrity," said Miss Flowers. "I always suspected he was a loony. Dangerous. He'll get worse."

"What?" said Jason. He had not at first understood her. Then he did, and his haggard face flushed with anger.

"He's a loony, sir, and you know it. Everybody else did, long ago. Now I'm frightened. Please accept my notice at once, Mr. Garrity."

"Get out," said Jason in a low, passionate voice. "Now."

She tossed her head. "Gladly. I wouldn't spend another night in this house. And don't think the other servants won't leave. The laundress is getting tired of all those dirty sheets and dirty filthy clothes. No one wants to work around crazy people."

She gave little Nicholas an ugly glance. "Look at him, wiggling like a snake in Mr. Mulligan's arms. He's strong as a lion; they usually are. Look at him trying to kick his sister in the face! And I shouldn't wonder Sebastian is a loony, too. The quiet ones are the worst."

Within two days all the servants had left. Jason, in spite of the lull in the economy, had difficulty in getting replacements, though he offered far more than the current rate. Patricia lay sodden in her bed for several days, not speaking, turning her face away when anyone entered the room. When alone, she moved feebly out of bed and resorted to whiskey, which, with the sedatives, effectively made her unconscious for hours. Nicole brought her trays, and Patricia seemed more responsive to the child, who sat with her and tried to give her comfort. Nicole knew there was "something wrong" with Nicholas. She and Sebastian shared the same secret, though they did not speak of it. They only consoled each other and gave Nicholas a larger share of love.

The little boy was calmer when he took his syrup from Nicole. He would take it only from his sister. He now clung to her and in a lesser degree to his brother. Jason excited him with dim memories of a train. Patrick was too emotional, and the child sensed this and responded with screeching laughter. When comparatively calm, he gave evidence of his innate sweet temper.

Jason hired a young teacher who not only was a competent instructor but had had experience with children such as Nicholas. His name was Francis Doherty and he had the composure of a young Dominican priest, was kind but rigorous. The children liked him at once. Nicholas would perch on his knee and hum to himself while Sebastian and Nicole had their lessons. Often he fell asleep in the teacher's arms, and Mr. Doherty did not remove him. He acted as if this was all very ordinary. He especially liked Sebastian and knew instinctively that the child was sorrowful. He called Nicole "Reverend Mother." He was a short, slender man with a monk's face, pale blue eyes, a Roman nose, a severe mouth, and much formality.

Patricia, on the rare occasions when she saw Nicholas now, would involuntarily shiver. It was not that she had an aversion to the child, but he had become vaguely threatening to her, and she tried to avoid him even though she loved him more than ever. To her, it was looking on the dying. She mourned as if for the dead and did not leave the house for over a month, and then only for a drive with her father.

She would not come down for her meals for another month, and then only if Jason were not there. She did not honestly believe his "blood" was the cause of her son's condition, but as her hatred for her husband was now so intense, she could not bear to see him.

In some twisted way she thought that he was responsible for all her suffering, that in some fashion he had deprived her of Lionel, that if "things had been different," Nicholas would not have been born this way.

She once went alone to see Joan. By this time the whole town knew of the Garrity "affliction," and many there were who felt pleased. Not that they actively detested Jason; they simply did not like him and therefore condemned him. As this was a weekday, Lionel was not with his wife. Joan received Patricia tranquilly, ordered tea for them both. She looks as old as death, Joan thought without compassion.

She had never been moved by anyone but her brother John and her husband, and was not stirred now. But her face expressed sympathy as she listened to Patricia's sobs. It was not until Patricia began to speak with alarming viciousness of Sebastian that Joan quickened from her supernal calm.

She interrupted the stream of vituperation, saying sharply, "How is Sebastian to blame for any of this, Patricia?"

Patricia beat her bony knees with her fist. "He's just... just... an evil influence, Joan! I honestly think if he were sent away, Nicholas would get better. I've heard of people like Sebastian. Dada told me stories when I was a child. They can cause... cause such things, with their wicked souls."

Joan's heart literally trembled for the boy she loved so dearly. "What nonsense," she said in a hard voice. "You talk like a fool, Patricia. I sympathize with you, but such nonsense! Sebastian is a wonderful, intelligent, really noble child, and he will be a fine man. I know you hate him; I've always known that. But I must protest. He's given you no reason to detest him, but you've hurt him terribly all his life."

"Oh, you don't know, the wickedness, the way he creeps about the house!"

"He's only looking for affection," said Joan, and her cheeks flushed. "You've always tried to turn Jason against him; I've seen that, and even his grandfather. I don't know your reason." Joan paused. "And I don't want to know. But it's not natural. People speak of it; you've been quite open about what you feel concerning Sebastian. They don't admire you for it."

When Lionel came home to dine with her, she said to him,

363

as she nestled in his arms, "That horrible, contemptible woman! I wish to God, Lionel, there was some way we could take Sebastian away. I'm afraid for him there."

"So am I," said Lionel with a rare sincerity. "So am I."

25

In November Woodrow Wilson was elected president of the United States. Mr. Roosevelt had effectively divided the Republican party and showed no regret. Some of his friends muttered that "Teddy seems to be interested in Greater Things." He had a look of avid anticipation.

In 1913 Mr. Wilson signed into law the Federal Reserve System and the Internal Revenue Act.

Lenin, in Russia, wrote to friends: "We have the world! Taxes and wars and the power to control the currency of the American nation will result in universal Communism. America will fall into our hands like a ripe plum. We will smash her face with an armored fist!"

Dr. David Starr Johnson, director of the World Peace Foundation, said, "What shall we say of the impending war in Europe? We believe that it will never come. Humanly speaking, it is impossible." A newspaper in the state of Maine published an editorial to the effect that "the outlook for universal brotherhood of man was never brighter than today, not since Christ was born in the manger!"

Only in Washington did some quiet men know the prospect for peace was dim. While the rest of the country was lulled into false security, many American bankers and financiers made many discreet journeys to consult the great munitions makers in several countries, including Germany.

Occasionally there were small ominous items in the newspapers, but the vast majority of the American people did not read them. They were more fascinated by the articles about one Sigmund Freud, and read those with libidinous eagerness, for he "proved" that there was no genuine human love anywhere. A boy, even in infancy, "lusted for his mother." A girl hated her mother and longed to have intercourse with her father. An adult, embracing a child, even his or her own, was "an unspeakable scandal." A worshiper of Christ was accused of adoring a phallic symbol and was prompted only by "a lust of the flesh."

The spiritual corruption of America and in most of the European world had begun. Only in Russia were Freud's teachings not permitted. The czar found them "disgusting."

Lenin agreed. It was not his plan to permit this perversion to enter his country. But it would be used sedulously to destroy the soul of other peoples.

At the same time, the German kaiser was warned by his generals not to act hastily in any crisis. He was incredulous. Who would attack Germany? And why? He loved military displays and invited his cousin, King George of England, to be his guest for the "presentation." He invited Mr. Roosevelt for the same purpose. There was something dangerously innocent about his pride. But when whispers reached him of "The War," he thought it absurd.

In the meantime, the German people were as industrious as ever. The English raced to build their navy, and the French, cynical and sophisticated, detected something sinister in the world.

Only two nations suspected nothing at all: Russia and America. This was no accident.

Jason Garrity detested receiving letters from his brother, victorious letters now. The old pastor in John's parish had died, and he had been elevated to monsignor. He never forgave Jason for not attending the ceremony. But Jason was obsessed by his growing troubles. He was not in any mood to be "proud" of his brother. He had written John of Nicholas' affliction, and John had mentioned it, almost impatiently, as "God's will." He was far less interested in his brother's children than in the sin in his own community. It sounded, Jason thought morosely, like Sodom and Gomorrah. John monitored his communicants like a top sergeant, and Jason sourly remarked to Lionel that he was certain that John never slept but patrolled the streets and searched for heresy.

Jason had sent a handsome check to his brother on the occasion of his sacred honor, and John wrote with his usual tone of admonishment: "I thank you most sincerely for your check and trust it has caused you no financial embarrassment." A sneer? thought Jason. "The ladies of the parish have formed a society, with my approval, for the Protection of the Souls of Our Children. They intend to hold discussions on the Lack of Morality in Modern Life, and the perils of moving pictures and other secular entertainment. I have warned them not to be too intrusively zealous." You *did?* thought Jason. "But I praise their dedication to Youth. Accordingly, I have donated a portion of your check to this worthy endeavor." Oh, God, thought Jason. "I am certain you will be pleased at this charity." Guess again, thought Jason. "I will preside." I'm sure, thought Jason. With a pitchfork. "We are particularly incensed by one Mary Pickford, an actress in the moving pictures." What! thought Jason. Did she *kiss* somebody?

"As for the rest of your money, I have given it to the Rosary and Altar Society." Well, it will produce some flowers at any rate, thought Jason. "A contingent of men signed the Pledge this week, and we are hoping for absolute sobriety." What an Irishman! remarked Jason.

John continued: "I trust you and Patricia have resigned yourselves to God's will in the matter of Nicholas' affliction. All things work together for the best. But you were always one to 'kick against fate.' I hope, in this sorrow, that you have attained some small humility as well as resignation. God does not afflict his children without reason." John had scratched out "cause," but scrutiny revealed the original word.

"I am enclosing a Miraculous Medal for Sebastian. Joan seems troubled concerning her nephew, and Joan is usually correct in any situation. She has tremendous Family Feeling, and particularly loves the boy, though I have warned her of the dangers of too much personal involvement in any human affairs. One, only, deserves out love." *You?* thought Jason. "I am glad to hear that Lionel is prospering, and you also. Give thanks where it is due."

Jason could read only portions of his brother's letters at one time. What a comforter! he would think. At least Job wasn't afflicted by one like you. Otherwise he would really have "cursed God and died," and you'd have thought he deserved it.

Frequently, on receiving one of John's letters, Jason would vengefully visit St. John the Baptist Church to grimly stare at the high altar. He no longer conducted a savage confrontation with the Lord. He merely stared like an antagonist. Then, newly embittered, he would go for a long walk, seeking some solace, some peace, which he could not find. He never attended Mass, never went to confession. The adversary loomed larger and larger in his mind, the afflictor of the innocent. What had little Nicholas done to merit this horror? What had his parents done, his brother and his sister? To "submit" with meekness was not worthy of a man. There could be only defiance in manhood if one believed, and indifference if one did not.

Today, a radiant Sunday in May 1914, Jason had returned

from one of many visits with Nicholas' doctors in Philadelphia and New York. Patricia continued to insist on additional opinions. She was "certain" that somewhere there existed "a little doctor that no one knows much about," a physician who has the "right" pill to cure the child. So over and over again, to soothe and calm her, Jason would go on the futile search, encountering many charlatans who talked of electric currents, diets, exercises, and even amulets and esoteric prayers. Even Patrick, her doting father, became impatient, but Jason, heavy with guilt, would do anything to pacify her. If he so much as hinted at protest, she would become hysterical and accuse him "of not wanting our child to get better."

The twins were now five years old, Sebastian six. Nicholas was almost as tall as Sebastian. He was in appearance healthy and vigorous. Only Nicole and Mr. Doherty could control him with any success. The first year Patricia had hardly spoken to the boy out of grief and fear; now she was excessively affectionate, even maudlin. This excited him; he would burst into loud tears, complain like a baby, and for an hour or so after her visits would be completely out of control, running, screaming, and flailing his arms. Patricia intended to take him to Lourdes in late August or September—"just my child and I, alone, and there will be a miracle." She still refused to accept the immutability of nature's failure.

The last medical visit seemed only to confirm her vehement belief that one day Nicholas would be "cured." In some fashion she felt that Nicholas' condition reflected on herself as a mother, and it needed only resolution of will to correct the tragedy. She had almost always gained her own way throughout her life, and she saw no reason why her usual tactics should not succeed again.

"You can't blame her for wanting to try anything," Jason said to Patrick. The older man shook his head. "Lourdes, next," he said, and Jason could not help smiling, though he was not amused. "Well," he said, "there have been some authentic cures, you know." But Patrick, the pragmatic Irishman, did not believe in miracles. In this he was much like Bernard.

"We shouldn't waste money just now," Patrick said. "Curse it. The new hotel is not even half-finished. And the money's going out hand over fist; the prices keep getting higher. Only last week the contractor demanded another increase before he will deliver the new wood. It will be another six months or more before we can begin to send out our brochures. What the hell is the matter with the country?" He cursed again. "And now Patricia wants to go abroad, and I know my girl! It won't just be Lourdes. It will be Paris for a couple of months, then Rome, then England, and maybe Germany 'for the baths.'" He shook his head and turned back to the subject of their hotel. "Schofield seems confident he'll take over that land we own next to his."

"No, he won't," said Jason. "That is, you aren't selling it, are you, Mr. Mulligan?"

Patrick gave him a look which was suddenly dour for so rosy and amiable a man, and Jason, as often before when he mentioned the land, saw that Patrick's glance held some furtive resentment.

"No," he said shortly, and turned away. His manner toward Jason was no longer so paternal and kind. Jason felt heavily depressed. There were so many mysterious things wrong with his life now, and he could not fathom them. Business affairs had a slippery way of evading him; his wife detested him; his child was mentally different, his father-in-law oddly withdrawn, his friend Lionel watchful and curiously wary. Jason had the sensation that he was under a secret surveillance. He no longer even had the pleasure of seeing Molly.

In the past two years he had visited her and Daniel Dugan's house infrequently. He did not know how that came about, but he was at first relieved. Then there had come Nicholas' affliction. Patricia, who had always disliked Molly, had irrationally come to despise and avoid her. Jason had the suspicion that Patricia envied the other young woman for not having any children. Molly had a far more expensive house than even Lionel and Joan. Daniel was also very rich. Molly, in the past two years, had "gone off" several times to Europe, indulged extravagantly by Daniel, and had remained abroad for months at a time. This added to Patricia's vindictiveness. Even when Molly was in Belleville, Patricia tried to avoid her, and visits between the two couples had dwindled to no more than once a month. Even then there was a puzzling uneasiness in the atmosphere. Daniel made some efforts to ease the strain, but by himself could not do much. Jason had little light talk. The two women were silent antagonists, and when Molly tried to be agreeable to Patricia, the latter would become snappish and contemptuous.

It appeared to Jason that Daniel did not particularly enjoy his company, though he was urbane as always. Molly avoided

Jason's eyes, though he noticed that when she thought she was undetected, she would gaze at him intently. But if he faced her quickly, she turned her regard away and resumed talking to Patricia.

Molly no longer seemed as fond of Jason's children. Until two years ago she had been exceptionally interested in Sebastian, then had incomprehensibly changed. She was kind to Nicholas; if she had a favorite, it was Nicole. But she never asked about Sebastian.

Jason had decided, especially since Nicholas' infirmity had been discovered, that it would be too selfish to indulge his love and longing for Molly. He had felt more and more guilt because of Patricia. She was his wife; she was the mother of his afflicted son; he owed her first duty, as he termed it. To desert her now, even if only in his thoughts, was a kind of abandonment, a cruelty she did not deserve. He had been guilty enough of loving Molly.

This morning he decided to take a walk to be alone with his thoughts. Often these days he would take his elder son. Sebastian was still a comfort. He was generally silent but gave Jason the sensation that he was "there," an understanding, stalwart companion. Two years ago Patrick and Jason had taken him hunting, which he did not like, though he became expert with the rifle. "We'll only hunt what we can eat," Jason told him. "Mama likes partridge and rabbit." Patrick had been much pleased with him until he had gotten sick when Patrick shot a deer. "Dammit!" Patrick said, "you've got to keep the numbers down or they'll starve during the winter! D'you think, Bastie, it's kinder to let them die of hunger than to kill them?" "No," said Sebastian. Then he had added, "Why's there so much pain?" Patrick did not understand, but Jason did.

Jason reflected on the boy's words when he took his walk. Yes, why? Was it a childish question? It presupposed that there was a sentient force which delighted in pain, both of man and beast. As God was the creator of all things, was he not the creator of torment? Jason did not want Sebastian to revolt against God, for he wished that his children would be happy. If only I were an atheist, Jason would think, I would explain that death and suffering were accidents of nature, and there would be no question of "why." There would be only acceptance of the natural condition.

Jason knew the religious answer: that man had brought sorrow and pain and death into the world, and it was none of God's doing. It was the sin of disobedience. He could not reconcile this with the premise of God's omniscience. Jason had once read a Jesuitical explanation: that it was what transpired in the soul of a man—free will—over which God had no control, and not his mere actions.

Jason had struggled most of his life to not believe in God. He knew it would make his existence less burdensome.

Still—and he considered it a perversity—he wanted his children to believe in God. He could not understand why. At least, he would think, it can make life endurable and give some easy answers to the human condition. And what would I be if I couldn't blame God for everything? he would say with bitter humor. Still, he would be more content, less anguished, if he did not believe.

He thought: I would be free. No regrets, no matter what I did. I would be the hunter—and not the hunted, the way most men are. No consciousness of "sin," no prohibitions. I would be happy, knowing there was no responsibility, no command to be more than a man. Or would I?

He would consider, almost with hatred, his brother, John, the priest, who believed he knew all the answers, and never doubted, as Father Sweeney did. In a way, he is the perfect atheist, Jason would say to himself. Even Christ, in his agony on the cross, questioned. To question is to be a man. Unthinking faith is not faith at all. Job, he recalled, had been full of questions and lamentations. He was a man, which was more than you could say for the "faithful." They preferred not to meditate, not to exercise their divine gift of thought. If there is sin, Jason would reflect, that is the sin. I'll bet Satan gets his best harvest from the pious.

Saul Weitzman had told him of the *yetzer hara,* the spirit of evil. "God," said Saul, "doesn't want weak slaves. He wants us to fight against wickedness. That's why he created Satan."

Jason was thinking of all these things when Dennis Farrell interrupted him at breakfast. One glance, and Jason knew that here entered the spirit of tragedy, and sorrow.

"What is it, Dennie?" asked Jason. He took his visitor's arm and led him to a chair. "Coffee? No?" Jason sat down and braced himself, as he had done all his life, in anticipation of bad news.

"It's me lads," said Dennie. His sturdy workingman's shoulders dropped. He averted his face. "The police in Indianapolis wrote me. They saw your ad in the papers asking

371

for information. The lads were killed two years ago—railroad accident." Dennis huddled in his chair. "They...they were robbing a freight car—fell under the wheels when it moved. They were buried in paupers' graves. Then some policeman remembered your ad, and sent me photographs of my lads— dead. And some trinkets they had with them. For identification. They were my lads; there was a jackknife I had given Mike, with his initials. No doubt."

He looked at Jason, heartbroken. "The worst—the very worst—that my lads were thieves, and they old and strong enough to work honestly. My dada used to say a man who'll steal is a man who will kill."

"My God," said Jason. "Dennie, you shouldn't have come here. You should have called; I'd have come to your house. Your wife—"

Dennis lifted a quick hand. "No. You see, she blames you for what happened to the lads. She said they was scared of you, and so ran away, and they became thieves because they couldn't find work. Work! Any man who wants to work can find it, even in bad times! And you didn't have anything to do with them running away. They went off a couple of times before, when I thrashed them for doing wrong. So, my woman's hysterical. She has to blame somebody."

He drew a deep breath. "She doesn't want to blame herself for coddling and pampering them and defending them, as she says, from the nuns. And me. And all we wanted them to do was grow up to be good and sober and hardworking Christians! That's our crime. I don't want to say anything to her; she's suffering enough. I don't want to tell her she's responsible..." He wrung his hands, and his haggard face turned from side to side. "She knows she's guilty."

"There's a new attitude in the country," said Jason, hoping to relieve his pain. "Your wife's probably been reading about it in the newspapers. Children mustn't be 'hurt' or disciplined. They must just be 'loved.' That's why we have so many young criminals now. I read a little poem once; don't know who wrote it:

> Let love come last, after the lesson's learned.
> Love, like all things else, must be earned.

"And that goes for children, too. Saul Weitzman. He told me that it is Jewish teaching, from the Holy Bible, that a man owes his children an education, but above all he must teach them righteousness. Parents are not commanded to 'love' their children. Children have to earn their parents' love. But kids are commanded to honor their parents." He waited a moment and said, "And the Church teaches that also. If your boys had loved their mother, they'd not have run away, or they'd have let her know where they were. But they didn't love her because she loved them too much."

He put his hand heavily on the stricken father's shoulder. "Your sons are victims of the new child philosophy. But your wife's the real victim. When she can listen to you, tell her."

Dennis said simply, clenching his fists, "I hate her for what she did to my lads. Mr. Garrity," he said, standing up, "you are a good man. The best I ever knew. If it wasn't for you, I'd never have known where my lads were."

He stumbled wearily from the room, and Jason watched him go. He thought, involuntarily, of what Christ had said to a young man who had called him "good": "No one save God is good." Then he thought of his brother, John, who considered himself perfect in all his judgments. Jason felt that he need not go to the church to accuse God of "victimizing" Dennis' two sons. Their mother had been expert in doing that. But... An uneasy thought came to him, and he shouldered it aside with gloom. That way led to intricate theological philosophy, and he was in no mood for that or for counting how many angels could dance on the head of a pin. He was too realistic a man.

Instead he wrote an offering for Masses for the souls of the Farrell boys. Then he went to the church and deposited it in the poor box.

He stood on the hot sidewalk in front of the church. He felt overpoweringly restless. The bells in the church began to ring for the raising of the Host. Jason walked away quickly. The town was quiet, for most of the people were in church this Sunday morning. The shadows of new leaves danced over the sidewalks. A warm breeze ruffled the grass and whipped the curtains at open windows.

Jason walked through the glittering streets, which were almost deserted. His thoughts became more somber, crushing. Suddenly, without warning, he was invaded by the litany.

Christ have mercy,
Lord have mercy,
Christ have mercy...

He felt the winds of evil blowing over the world, and he ran from them. He ran to the narrow shining stream in the midst of the city. He was breathless when he arrived.

It was peaceful here. Then why did he not feel peace? He looked over the narrow water, sparkling blue and white in the sunlight. The grass along the banks was high, filled with buttercups and dandelions like small yellow suns. The air was pungent. Birds conversed among themselves. Why was everything so innocent except man? He was the destroyer. And yet he was given "dominion" over the earth, to filthy its streams and its oceans with his children's poisonous offal, to murder everything in it that was blameless and lovely, to drown the music with his raucous voice, to build his cities on its noble meadows, to imprison its rivers and invade the sanctities of its forests, to bare its mountains for his ugly houses, to erect walls where no walls had existed. *That* was "dominion"?

Then a terrible thought came to him: Man is the Evil. And Satan is his god. Man was at war with all that was pure and beautiful, and he would never cease his destruction. Unless... Unless what?

"I have repented that I made man." So said God.

Jason stood very still as he remembered that. What did that do to God's omniscience? We have no answers, Jason said to himself. He gazed at the beauty about him, the unprofaned beauty, and felt sick at heart. A flicker of red down the bank suddenly caught his eye. For a moment he thought it was a fire, it shone so brightly against the green. He went slowly toward it and saw that it was a woman's head resting in the grass, and that the head belonged to Molly Dugan.

Jason halted. Molly alone. As the wind moved the tall grass, he could see her profile, strong and clear and pensive. Then all at once an ineluctable light fell on every blade of grass, on every buttercup, on every tree. It dazzled him. He felt like crying out; he could hear his heart beating in his chest, feel its throbbing in his temples. Molly. Her name was a sound of ecstasy to him, of longing he had never known before, of hunger mingled with despair and delight. It seemed to him that the rapturous and unearthly light had penetrated all things and that Molly was illuminated in it.

He would have gone away in silence had she not sensed a presence. She sat up in the grass and brushed her hair from her eyes. She said, as if she had expected him, "Jason."

He said her name as he slowly went toward her. She looked up at him gravely. He wore a madras jacket of blue and white over dark trousers, and his white shirt was collarless, like a workman's, and he was hatless, his crisp black curls bare to the sun. His dark Irish face was eloquent, though he did not know it, his gray eyes shining like sunstruck granite, his large mouth trembling at the corners.

"Jason," Molly said again, and her voice was a husky whisper.

He sat down beside her in the aromatic grass near the stream, and they looked long at each other, as they had never done before. It was a naked gaze full of wordless speech. Molly's eyes were pure brilliant gold, and Jason could see himself reflected in the black pupils. He could see every freckle across the bridge of her pugnacious little nose. He could see how tender her smiling mouth was. She wore a green linen dress with white braid about the throat and on the short sleeves, and it emphasized the startling color of her hair, which had escaped the neat crown of braids.

She had clasped her hands about her knees, and those hands seemed the loveliest Jason had ever seen. Then she slowly put one into his, and they looked at the little river, which suddenly seemed to Jason to roar triumphantly. Their fingers clung together as if they were sealed.

A rabbit ran near their feet and scampered away on seeing them. A robin sang to the sky. The warm breeze rustled reeds near the water. A vast contentment came to Jason, a feeling of fulfillment. I'm not alone, he thought, and did not know exactly what he meant. He only knew that he was experiencing the one real joy of his life, untarnished by any sadness or doubt or uneasiness. He looked at Molly, who was smiling faintly as she gazed at the water, as if she, too was feeling the rightness of his presence here.

She said, "I was thinking of you."

"Were you? I'm glad, Molly. When did you get back from Europe?"

"Two days ago. Daniel is still there. He's clearing up things, he says. He thinks something is about to . . . well, a crisis. I even felt it, and I don't know why. England and France were never more peaceful, more beautiful. Yet, there was something . . . as if everything was just stage scenery, and the real movements hidden behind. Isn't that silly?"

"No," said Jason, and did not know he held her hand tighter. "I've felt it myself, right here."

He told her of the "scarcities" plaguing Ipswich House and of the mysterious delays in the delivery of materials for the new hotel. "I don't know if they are connected, or if they are two different things, one impersonal, one personal." He looked at her, smiling. "But somehow, today, it doesn't matter."

"No. Not today," said Molly, and her voice was soft and comforting.

Again they were silent, and Jason had never known such peace, such completion. He had never felt so understood—no, not even by Bernard—yet he and Molly had not exchanged a significant word. He realized that sympathy needed no words. It simply was.

"I don't see you very often, Molly," he said at last.

She was silent. Her hand moved in his as if she would take it away. Then it clung tighter. A shadow ran over her profile, and he was reminded of Sebastian. He thought she would offer a polite excuse, but she said directly, "You seemed to be avoiding me—us."

He bent his head. "Yes."

She did not ask why. She said nothing.

Jason said, "I love you, Molly."

She smiled, her face still in profile. "And I've loved you all my life."

Jason pondered on that for a moment. "So Da said."

Molly nodded. "Yes, he knew. Everybody did but you."

"Why did you marry Daniel, then?"

Molly took her hand from his. She was pale under her sunburn. Her face was stern. "Why did you marry Patricia?"

He felt a sad pain in his chest. "I thought I loved her."

Molly sighed. "I don't even have that excuse for marrying Dan. But...I had no one. No one at all. I only had a dying mother. Dan was kind. He, at least, loved me, and still does in his way. He helped me; no one else ever did. My mother—he made her last months comfortable, and that was before we were married. You don't know what it means for a woman to be alone. I didn't think of Dan's money; I still don't. But he was there when I needed someone. We have a good marriage. A tranquil marriage. We're friends."

She took her hand from his firmly, and now her voice was almost passionately bitter. "What do you have, Jason Garrity?"

He hesitated, feeling her withdrawal in more ways than one. "I have my children," he said.

Her face immediately became sorrowful. She turned to him, and her golden eyes were bright with tears.

"Especially Sebastian," he said.

He was bewildered when Molly suddenly put her hands over her face. "What's the matter? You always seemed to love Bastie."

She dropped her hands, and her face was very white. "I do," she said, "believe me, I do." Her eyes were full of torment. He was more bewildered than ever.

"Then why don't you come around to see him... and the twins?"

He had never known Molly to be evasive, but he believed she was evasive now. "Patricia—she's never liked me, Jason. And lately she's given me the impression that she'd appreciate my absence. I don't like to go where I'm not wanted."

"I want you." He smiled, trying to make her smile also.

But she did not. The shadow on her face deepened. "You mustn't say that." She made a motion to rise.

Jason felt despair and a frantic need to keep her. He caught her arm. "Don't leave me, Molly, for God's sake, don't leave me!"

She was struck by his anguished expression, by the dread in his voice. Without willing it, she put her arms about his neck, murmuring her love over and over, her cheek pressed to his. "Oh, Jason, Jason, Jason."

He could feel her heart pounding against his chest. He felt the warmth of her breast, the fullness of it. His pain was still there, but joy returned greater than ever, and with it came so intense a passion that everything about him became indistinct except for Molly's face and hair. There was now only one imperative in him, a shouting urge that could not be resisted. This was the culmination of his life.

He wondered, later, if Molly had also felt that the melding of their bodies in the sweet grass, with the sound of the stream a counterpoint to the surging of their flesh, was the supreme and inevitable fulfillment.

Certainly when he looked down at her smiling face, he thought he saw the whole world in her eyes. Her arms nested lightly on his shoulders. She held him and kissed his mouth and eyes with intense tenderness. Jason could only say, "Molly, Molly, Molly..."

They lay side by side, hands clasped, and looked up at the pattern of light through the leaves, and to Jason it was as if he had reached the summit of his existence. He was at peace for the first time in years. He did not want time to move from this spot. He knew himself to be loved as he had

377

never been loved; he had realized an ecstasy which was more than carnal, which had made him whole.

"Molly..." he said.

"Yes, love," she answered.

Everything had been said. But he added, "Now I can stand anything. I have you."

Molly's shining face dimmed. She released his hand and sat up. She rebuttoned her dress, shook her hair free of grass blades and crushed buttercups, and gazed at the stream.

At last Jason, disturbed by her look, said, "Molly?"

She smiled somewhat mournfully but did not look at him. "Jason, I don't regret it. I'm glad. But...there are...others to consider."

She half-expected him to say, "That doesn't matter." However, he sat up too and said, "I know. I know only too well."

Then he suddenly smiled, and she was surprised. He said, "I'm thinking of what Da said to Father Sweeney, that the real adultery was living with someone you didn't love. It was, he said, the adultery of the soul."

"Did Father Sweeney agree?" Molly could not help smiling.

"He could never win an argument with Da."

Molly sighed. "This hasn't been fair to Dan."

Jason felt so buoyant that he said, "We'll get divorces."

Molly glanced at him quickly. "We are both Catholic. And you have children."

"I wonder if the Church really issues a life sentence of unhappiness to anyone," said Jason. "Unhappiness can eventually destroy a man, and even make him a vicious person. How many men and women are actually 'joined by God'? Only love can make a marriage, not just a young infatuation. The Church should put more obstacles in the way of marriage, say, a year between calling of the banns and the ceremony."

Molly did not look at him when she said, "Would that have prevented you from marrying Patricia?"

Jason frowned, considering. "I thought I loved her, ever since I was a kid. I just remembered something. I was dazed when she came to me and begged me to marry her quickly; she said her father would want a big wedding, and she wanted a quiet, modest one. She wanted to be wed at once, by a justice of the peace...What's the matter, Molly?"

Molly said simply, "Oh, God." She clenched her lips together to keep from blurting out the truth. But—there was Sebastian, who was innocent. To mortally injure a child was unpardonable. Jason was all he had, except for Joan, who

378

probably knew, or she would not be so tender toward the child. God damn Lionel, Molly thought. And Patricia, too. She turned quickly to Jason and said, "Oh, my dear..." Her voice was full of angry compassion. She took his face in her hands and kissed him hard on the mouth.

He said, "We'll work it out. Molly, will you marry me?"

"I can't do that to Dan. He's not at fault."

"Neither was Patricia." He stared at her in surprise, for her expression was strange.

"I'm not so sure!" she cried.

"What do you mean?"

She put her hand on her mouth. She said, "Tell me, honestly, Jason, did you...did you...had you...did you sleep with Patricia before you were married?"

"Christ, no! She isn't that kind of a girl. What makes you ask that?"

Then, her last hope gone, Molly said, "I just wondered. The hurried marriage," she said, and stopped. Jason became alarmed at her expression. But he tried to make a joke of it. "Did you sleep with Dan before you were married?"

"No. Of course not. And Dan—he's been very good to me. As I said before, we are friends. And I can't hurt a friend."

She stood up. Jason got up also and brushed off her dress. She put her head on his shoulder and could not help the silent tears, for all her efforts.

Jason said, "Will you tell Dan?"

"No," Her voice was unexpectedly firm and resolute. "Will you tell Patricia?"

"I'd like to. She blames me for Nicholas' condition. I think she'd like to be free of me. She even said so, in front of her father and Dr. Conners."

Molly said, "But Dan deserves better of me, Jason. I don't think there is any solution. You have your children, in spite of Patricia."

"And my children will be happier living with parents who despise each other? That'll make for a joyous home?"

"Don't talk like that, please. You...you have to be there, to protect Sebastian...the twins."

Jason half-turned away. "She wants to send Sebastian away. Ever since she learned of Nicholas' illness. She'd like me to go with him."

"I think that would be best, for you and the boy."

"Then I wouldn't see my other children, and there is Mr. Mulligan, who would be hurt. He loves Sebastian too, and

379

me, though he's been acting a little peculiar in the last two years. But so is everybody else!" He laughed ruefully and shook his head. "So there's no solution."

She took his hand, and they walked slowly away together.

"Where shall we meet again, alone?" asked Jason.

"We won't," said Molly. "We can't."

Jason looked down at her. Her face was pale but resolved.

"We can't. There are too many involved with...us. Let's cherish what we had. Who knows? There may be a merciful God."

She took her hand from his and sprang off as swiftly as a butterfly in a dazzle of green and gold, and Jason watched her go and felt as if half his soul had gone with her. Yet, he was not too unhappy. He would see Molly, at the very least. She would not be gone from his life. He felt no guilt. It was as if he had been married for the first time.

26

One morning in early June, Lionel came into Jason's office. It was a slumberous day of warm green grass and tranquil sun. It was reported that almost all of Europe knew this beatitude, and later it was remarked that this June was a time to remember, to cherish, for there would never be another so bright with promise.

There was a rumor of trouble in Bosnia, but the Archduke Francis Ferdinand of Austria would soon smooth things over. He was planning to visit the area later in the month with his morganatic wife, the Duchess of Hohenberg. In short, though Slavic Bosnia had been newly acquired, or seized, by Austria-Hungary, it was said that the people in general were quite complacent and reconciled. At least "spokesmen" said they were. The international financiers agreed—though they smiled, and shuffled their papers, and looked long and significantly at each other. The plotted conspiracy was in motion. Lenin, in Russia, received the first bulletin of the visit and was jubilant.

In America President Wilson naively drafted a new set of proposals for his "New Freedoms." The American people had never felt such ebullience. The latest depression seemed to have ended. Even the farmers were almost contented. The summer portended unusually rich crops. There was some concern about two Mexican generals, Carranza and Villa, who were threatening war on each other. But there was much more excitement at "the hot debate" over women's corsets. Americans were also involved in a discussion as to whether or not to permit Sunday baseball. The Reverend Billy Sunday opened a campaign in Scranton, Pennsylvania, on this sinful subject.

These were the subjects of interest to Americans in June 1914, along with immense excitement over a series of moving pictures called *The Perils of Pauline*.

Everything seemed peaceful. Millions of happy young men considered their future, made love, and attended sports events.

Lionel visited Jason in his office this lovely June day and said, "I'm going home. It's four o'clock. Joan will pick up

Sebastian for his usual Sunday visit. Too bad you have to work." He sat on the edge of Jason's desk and nonchalantly lit a cigarette. He did not quite meet Jason's eye, a habit he had acquired some time ago.

"I forgot," said Jason. "I thought he was going to the new park with Mr. Mulligan."

"He has more fun at my house, Jase."

"And he hasn't any 'fun' at his own?" Jason leaned back in his chair.

"I didn't say that. You're becoming snappish lately, Jase."

"And why not? We're a year behind on the new hotel, and we're having new difficulties getting supplies for Ipswich House and the Inn-Tavern. People are asking why."

Lionel shrugged. "It's worse in other cities. It's not just here."

"I know." Jason frowned. He was not yet twenty-eight, but there were patches of gray at his temples and he appeared much older. He glanced at Lionel and noted Lionel's resemblance to Molly. What had happened between Lionel and himself? The affection was there, but not the confiding friendship. Well, he thought, we are both growing older, and things change. But he had not changed toward Lionel. Or had he? He said, "Dan Dugan's come back. He came in this morning."

"I know." There was that new evasiveness in Lionel's voice. He stood up. "Well. I'm going. Have a happy Sunday, working." He waved his hand amiably.

Why do I feel so uneasy? thought Jason, then applied himself to his work. But an image of Molly lingered in the back of his mind, and he felt both exhilaration and sadness.

Instead of going home as he had told Jason, Lionel went to visit Chauncey Schofield in his elegant house that was the envy of half the town. They sat in the June-scented garden, which was very private and shrouded with trees. Anita Schofield sat with them working on needlepoint. In the sunlight of the garden her dyed hair took on an astonishing orange tinge. She had taken off her glasses when Lionel had arrived, and greeted him with her usual enthusiasm. "How very nice, dear Lionel!" she exclaimed, giving him both her hands. It was as if he had paid an unexpected and welcome call. "How wonderful to see you again!" She swung their hands together, and beamed. It seemed she produced affection at will, and Lionel often wondered how she contrived it. He could simulate warmth, but not as convincingly as Anita Schofield.

He also knew that she was far shrewder than her husband,

and he often marveled how he could deceive her. Then Lionel deduced that she was infatuated with him, and even the cleverest of women could be blinded by love.

Anita was always present at business conferences, and she listened to every word, though coquettishly denying any real interest in "gentlemen's affairs."

"Well," said Chauncey after giving Lionel a large whiskey, "I've seen Senator Georger again. He confirmed that Jason Garrity is on Mulligan's deed, though Jason doesn't know it. Mulligan doesn't want him to know it, either."

"So? Then what do we do?"

"Wait."

"We've been waiting more than two years, and we're not getting any younger."

Chauncey knew Lionel's debts to the dollar. He was trying to discover some way to use that knowledge to his advantage, but so far had not succeeded. He had delicately approached Mrs. Lindon with the suggestion that she buy up Jason's paper, but Mrs. Lindon had cryptically said, "Let's wait and see." Chauncey was certain that she was not moved by any consideration for Jason but by some motive of her own, and he was uneasy. But it was part of his successful facade that he never allowed his feelings to be perceptible. His air of assurance never faltered.

He said, "Mulligan and Jason know very well by now that it wouldn't be profitable to build another hotel right next to ours—that's why we built so close to the line. That's why Mulligan is so mad at Jason. By the way, I have the plans now for our hotel 'cottages, luxurious homes away from home.' For guests wanting a great deal of privacy—where they can hold consultations in peace. Businessmen do like retreats, you know."

"Away from their wives." Anita smiled.

"Can't we get through to Dan Dugan?" asked Lionel.

Chauncey sighed. "We already have, don't you remember? At least we tried. He's all for selling us those acres—but there is the deed. I thought it wasn't wise to tell Dan that my good friends are behind the delays in delivering the supplies for Mulligan's new hotel. After all, he is involved in it."

"So am I," said Lionel.

"So are the local banks, and Mrs. Lindon."

Lionel's eyes were narrow slits as he studied his friend. "I need money," he said.

"Don't we all!" Chauncey laughed. Then he said, "My

friend in Washington hinted there'll be some 'disturbance' in Europe that will affect all of us."

Lionel snorted. "Doomsday Downers! You all sound like Jason."

Chauncey was alerted. "What does he say?"

"That there'll be a war!" Lionel laughed.

But Chauncey leaned forward, and there was no smile on his face now. "What makes him think so?"

"He gets all the newspapers and business magazines. He says he 'reads between the lines.' He keeps clippings, and almost has me convinced."

"There's been a rumor of a big European war for a long time. France wants Alsace back."

"Well," said Lionel, "I can't imagine why France's affairs would push the whole continent into war."

But Chauncey only smiled. "Buy munitions stocks."

"What with?" Lionel had just bought Joan a necklace of opals in New York.

"Borrow, if you have to. I'm giving you inside advice."

Lionel was gloomy. There was no question of his borrowing.

Chauncey asked, "Is Jason buying munitions stocks?"

"No. He says wars are immoral and aren't fought for what politicians say they are. He thinks there's a conspiracy behind modern wars, that they are organized by bankers rather than governments." Lionel stood up. "Oh, hell. I always thought Jase had his head on right. Now I'm not so sure."

He paused. "Do you think there is going to be a war?"

Chauncey made a disarming gesture. "I'm just guessing. I read the newspapers too.... It's just a hunch. Probably just another Balkan tempest in a teapot, as the saying goes." Chauncey stood up also and put his hand on Lionel's shoulder. "Let things work themselves out. I'm optimistic about the hotel and the land. We'll get the acreage one way or another. Just takes a little time." He assumed an expression of concern. "Does Jason know a lot of people who think as he does?"

"Some. Of course, most are like old Saul, and he hardly counts." Lionel laughed and said good-bye.

As soon as he left, Anita turned to her husband and said seriously, "Can't they be stopped?"

" 'Freedom of speech,' " said Chauncey. "But no one listens to them. Nobody in their right mind." He walked into the house and went to his library. He called a private number in Washington. "We might run into trouble here, right in

Belleville," he said. "A man named Garrity....Yes, you helped delay supplies for the hotel he's building."

Joan sent the automobile for Sebastian. She no longer called for him and accompanied him to her house, for she wished no encounter with Patricia or with her brother. But she sat at her window waiting impatiently. When the automobile drove up, she struggled with her canes and crept into the hall, her face shining with anticipation and love. She embraced the boy, and he clung to her as she murmured, "My little darling." There was a fragrance of lilies about her, and her smile lit up her face.

Sebastian thought his aunt the most beautiful woman in the world, and the most kind and loving. Once Nicole had been included in the invitations, for she amused Joan, but recently she had declined. Sebastian got no satisfactory reply from his sister except that she was "needed to take care of Nick." That had to content Sebastian, for Sundays were Mr. Doherty's days off and Sebastian finally conceded that in the absence of his father, Nicole was indeed needed. There were times when the little boy ran screaming through the house like a young colt. He sometimes knocked ornaments from tables and cabinets in a wild frenzy of destruction, and even Nicole was unable to stop him. He never appeared to understand that this was "wrong." When a servant reprimanded him, he would only stare in confusion. Later, if Nicole corrected him, he would burst into tears and hide.

Patrick had finally come to the conclusion that the boy needed institutional care, but there was Patricia who must be considered. When he mentioned the matter to Jason, his son-in-law had said, "What about Patricia? Let her try Lourdes. Then perhaps..."

Sebastian was pleased to be away from the tension.

When he visited his aunt, Joan would always search him for resemblances to Lionel. She often wondered why Jason did not see them and she was gratified when strangers remarked on the resemblance and were surprised when Joan informed them that Lionel was "not a blood relative," and that the boy was her nephew. She held the secret carefully, in protection of the only two people she had ever loved. But she rejoiced when she found some new attribute which linked Sebastian to Lionel, either in character or appearance.

She held his hand in the sitting room, now, and listened to his every word. She thought that Sebastian's voice had taken on Lionel's intonations. My child, my child, she said to herself, and held the boy's hand more tightly. Her emotion conveyed itself to Sebastian, who looked at her wonderingly. She was smiling like an angel. Then she felt the old despair that Sebastian was not her son. Had she not already hated Patricia, she would have hated her now.

A bright red fire burned in the crest of the trees. The Sunday quiet came clamorously alive with bells for early service, each competing with each other. Joan said, "My dearest, do you go to Mass regularly?"

"Yes, Aunt Joan. And so does Nickie. Sometimes Grandpa takes us, sometimes Mr. Doherty when he stays home."

Joan, who had a great sense of humor, laughed at herself. She was pleased, and relieved, that Sebastian attended Mass, though she and Lionel considered themselves atheists, except in the presence of Father John Garrity. She squeezed the boy's hand and said sincerely, "That's good."

She did not see the quizzical and loving glance Sebastian gave her; she was everything that was beautiful, wise and desirable in a woman, as Lionel was everything that was strong and interesting in a man. But he detected subtle ironies. He said, "Aunt Joan, when Father Sweeney came to see you and Uncle Lionel a month ago, he asked you why you don't attend Mass or at least make your Easter duty."

Joan was an expert in dissimulation, but she never lied to Lionel or Sebastian. She uncomfortably deliberated on her reply. She considered Sebastian as an adult who deserved respect. Finally she decided to answer with humor. "I think your Uncle Lionel and I are perfect!" Then, seeing the boy remained serious, she said, "We aren't good Catholics, I'm afraid."

"Why?" The boy was interested.

"Why? I don't really know. You remember your great-grandfather? He wasn't either. It must run in the family. Skeptics."

"And Papa doesn't go."

"You see? It runs in the family. The Irish are either very, very religious, or they are complete skeptics. No halfway with us. We go to Mass with absolute faith or we don't go at all." She looked at him fondly.

"Mama doesn't attend Mass either anymore, not even if Grandpa scolds," said Sebastian. "But then, she's so sick."

"More than usual?"

Sebastian hesitated. He was always reticent when it came

to his mother. "Sometimes," he said. He was sharply intuitive. He had learned much earlier that Joan detested Patricia and that his mother disliked his aunt with an almost insane hatred. She never referred to Joan except as that "repulsive cripple." He had also learned that no love existed between Jason and Joan. The families visited each other, but there was an antipathy between aunt and mother that was almost visible. Patricia, as an antagonist, was no rival of Joan's. Joan could reduce Patricia's arguments to incoherence in minutes, even if the disagreement were only over a popular song. And Joan was quietly mirthful at her success in goading Patricia, and would glance at Lionel in a droll fashion which did not escape Sebastian and made him miserable. Why did not Mama and Aunt Joan like each other? Papa also looked wretched and often motioned with his head for Uncle Lionel to retreat to another room with him. This then left the child in limbo until Joan would call him to her, take his hand, or give him a kiss.

Then Mama would look very strange, smiling a vicious smile as if she possessed a dreadful secret. She appeared to be "making fun" of Aunt Joan in an ugly way, and Aunt Joan was seemingly ignorant of it. After kissing Sebastian, she would turn to Mama in the most tranquil way and say in her lovely voice, "Let's not quarrel, Patricia, over such a silly thing."

The boy received undercurrents, but what they were, he did not know. Once Patricia was particularly excited and when Joan mentioned "a silly thing," Patricia had said loudly, "Yes, a silly thing, a silly thing!" and she had cried, "A stupid thing!" and had glanced maliciously at Sebastian. This had puzzled the child, for he had not been the object of conversation, and Lionel had thought: The goddamn bitch! She'll blurt out everything one of these days and the fat'll be in the fire. He and Joan talked of it later, and Joan had said, "Oh, she's insane and drunk, but she's very self-protective. She might, at times, want to destroy Jason and Sebastian and me, especially me, but she knows it'll be the end of her if she does." She had added, as she always did, with sincere passion, "How I wish Sebastian was my child!" Her eyes would fill with tears.

Now Sebastian said in a low voice, "I want to tell you something, Aunt Joan. I...I want to be a priest. I think I have a vocation."

Joan had marvelous self-control. She only said, "Why? You

haven't even made your First Communion. So how could you know?" But beneath the blue silk of her dress, she clenched her hands together.

"I just know, Aunt Joan. I haven't told anyone yet but you."

"Do you want to be like your Uncle John?"

Sebastian gave her a somber glance. Then he said, "No."

Joan was not deluded by her brother; she knew all his faults, though she loved him deeply. She said, "Then who?"

"I just want to be a priest."

"What gave you that idea?"

"I just have it. Ever since... I don't know just when, but it was a long time ago."

She looked at his young profile, the beautiful lips set firmly, the grave expression, the long lashes shading the agate eyes, the soft hair turning redder through the years to red, the set of his shoulders so like Lionel's, and the hands, above all, like Lionel's, eloquent, yet restrained, as Lionel's were not. Impulsively she held his hand to her cheek, too moved to answer immediately. She was not touched, but alarmed, at the idea of the child becoming a priest.

"You must give it a lot of thought," she said, telling herself that all Irish lads wanted to be priests at some time in their lives. It was the national affliction. Only Lionel had not claimed it. "Every Irish boy wants to be a priest. We're a priestly people." She smiled, but Sebastian did not smile.

The charming house always affected Sebastian deeply; he often felt he had come home, and was immediately guilty that he had felt so. He sat at the dining-room table, though at home he did not, except on holidays, with the other children. Lionel would glance at him with genial affection and would sometimes touch the boy's cheek. Then the atmosphere would become charged with a feeling of love and security that Sebastian never knew in his own house, not even with Jason, for whom he felt such devotion. It was not that Sebastian was deceived by Lionel; he sensed what he was, though he had not yet put it into words. But he encountered acceptance in this house, total acceptance, from everybody. His mother tainted the other atmosphere for him. Even Patrick would give him a dubious glance from time to time when Patricia had been more than usually accusatory. According to Patrick, it was not "natural" for a mother to hate her child without some definite reason, and so he wondered about Sebastian.

Patricia often said, with anger at her father's defense of the child, "Oh, he's deep! Sly, like Jason!"

Patrick also wondered if Jason had discovered that he was on his father-in-law's deed, and the conviction had inserted itself into his affection, like a thin, poisonous blade.

But in Lionel's house tonight there was no question that Sebastian was sincerely loved. When it was time for Lionel to drive him home, Joan was reluctant to part with him. Lionel did not speak much on the journey, but Sebastian basked in what he knew as his uncle's great affection and understanding. Sometimes Lionel teased the boy for being an "old man," but Sebastian never doubted that Lionel loved him.

"So you want to be a priest!" said Lionel on this occasion, for Joan had persuaded the boy to "tell Uncle Lionel." "What the hell for, kid?"

"I told you, Uncle Lionel. I think I have a vocation."

"Piffle," said Lionel, who wanted to use a stronger word. He paused, then said, "Shit."

He was immediately concerned, but Sebastian smiled and said nothing. "Look here," said Lionel, "it's just a whim. You need some fun in your life. Your sister is a hundred years old; your mother is taken up with your brother. Your grandfather is old and now has heart trouble. And your father has all the burden of his family on him, and his work besides. He has to work much harder than I do. And there's Nicholas again, a worry, to say the least. Not too much good for fun, all that. How would you like to go on a vacation with your aunt and me this summer?"

Joy shone on the boy's face. "I'd love it!" Then he sobered. "I can't leave Nickie all alone with Nick."

"She's not alone. She has her mother to help, and Mr. Doherty, and sometimes her...your father and Mr. Mulligan."

"Nick doesn't always pay attention to them. He does to me and Nickie. Then there's Mama. She's sick so much."

The drunken, foolish bitch! thought Lionel vindictively. He had never even liked Patricia at the best of times. Now he saw her as the enemy of his son, probably the worst enemy he would ever have.

"You've got to live for yourself sometime," Lionel said.

But Sebastian said nothing, and Lionel knew that he had made an adult decision. "Now, look," said Lionel, "do you want to be like your Uncle John?"

"No."

"That's good, anyway." Lionel laughed. "I'd hate to think he was your model! Well, it'll be a long time. A long time." He was not given to a display of any emotion in public, but he leaned sideways and kissed his son's cheek. Sebastian put his head on his father's shoulder, with a great content. The sparkling stars sailed through the treetops, and from a nearby house there came the faint poignancy of a Chopin nocturne.

Sebastian felt peace as he had never known it in his own home. He did not know the word, but it was an ineffable peace, held in his father's arm as he was, and they did not speak again.

When Lionel came home, he said to his wife, "Do you think your brother Jack has something to do with perverting Sebastian's mind?"

"No. Jack doesn't like children. He doesn't like anyone but me." A peculiar expression passed over her face. "He never notices Sebastian when he's here visiting, except to tell the child that all children are 'evil from their birth and wicked from their youth,' or something like that. As though he were the entire vessel of Original Sin."

"Who, then, dammit?"

"You know that when we were children ourselves"—and Joan smiled—"Father Sweeney said God chooses his priests when they're born."

Lionel was angered, a rare thing for him. "If he's been talking to Sebastian, he'll hear from me!"

Joan glanced at him with surprise. His face was intensely serious. He said, as he had said so many times before, "There's nothing I wouldn't do for my son. *My* son."

Joan felt no jealousy, no resentment. She took her husband's hand and kissed it and held it against her cheek. She said, "And I, too."

For she believed that she was more the mother of Sebastian than Patricia, who hated him. She, Joan, would give her life for him. For he was Lionel's son.

"We are his parents," she said. "Oh, yes, we are his mother and his father. He has no one else."

Patricia blew into Patrick's bedroom on a gust of hot windy air. She was screeching at the top of her lungs.

Patrick had been forced to return to his house, during the past six months, to rest for an hour or two during the afternoon because of his heart ailment. He fumed over it but conceded it was necessary. He would not limit the amount of food he absorbed at the table nor his lavish drinking of wine and whiskey, nor his vigorous visits to his amiable mistress. "Hell," he would say, "if a man cannot live the life he loves, then he'd better not live at all. Life bought at the price of pleasure isn't worth it." But he did rest because of his growing exhaustion.

He was napping when Patricia banged open the door, screeching imprecations, and she did not notice that her father was lying naked on his bed. He half sat up, blinking, and pulled the sheet over him hastily. He thought suddenly that she seemed shockingly like her son, Nicholas, and that she sounded much like him in her violent and explosive words.

"It's the very worst, the very worst! Irreplaceable! The only decent artistic thing in this whole damned hideous house! And what was he doing in Mama's bedroom anyway! Snooping! He hates anything beautiful because he's so ugly himself! He's got to be sent away, right away!" She was gasping, her face dangerously red, her usually sleek fine hair tousled, her brown linen dress only partly buttoned, her eyes insane with hatred and wrath.

"What is it?" asked Patrick, putting his hand against the ominous pain in his chest.

Through her hail of words her father gathered that Sebastian, on a curious visit to Patricia's mother's room, had "deliberately" destroyed a very large and valuable piece of Meissen china set in the middle of a black walnut table. It had been delicately painted with dolphins, exquisitely wrought cupids twined with gilt and pink ribbons in strategic spots, bouquets of incredibly tiny flowers, small woods animals and birds by the flock, miniature trees, and baskets with infinitesimal fruits in them. It was a veritable museum piece and was at least two hundred years old.

No servant was permitted to dust the object, only Patricia herself, ever since she was a child, and it was a task she enjoyed. What little imagination she had, had been inspired by that object. She had been a lonely child, for no contemporary had been able to endure her arrogance, and the china ornament had been her companion. She had given names to the cupids, the dolphins, and the animals.

Patrick sat up straighter, for he well knew what the ornament had meant to his daughter, and he was extremely angry and compassionate. Patricia, weeping convulsively, sank on her knees and cried over and over that "he must go, go, go, and at once, before he does worse mischief!" It seemed that Sebastian, who was found alone in the room—servants, hearing the crash of the heavy ornament, had come running—explained that he was looking for Nicholas and had accidentally bumped into the table.

"That big piece!" exclaimed Patrick. "I can hardly lift it meself! And the table is heavy; needs a man to move it!" His face became crimson and swollen.

"He confessed! He could do nothing else, being caught there, Dada!"

Patrick thought of the slender boy. The enormous ornament was not only very heavy; it was almost as large as the boy himself. He shook his head and then smoothed his daughter's hair and said, "There, there, mavourneen. 'Twas your puir mither's pride and joy, and that it was." When deeply disturbed, he lapsed into his childhood's brogue. "Send the lad to me, I'll get to the bottom of this, then." He kissed his daughter and wiped her tears with the edge of the sheet.

Patricia threw her arms about his neck and screamed, "Send him away, Dada, send him away, even if he is Jason's pet. Jason doesn't even try to help poor Nicholas! Tries to stop us from going to Lourdes so Nicholas can be cured!"

"Send the lad to me," said Patrick, and Patricia flew out of the room like a Fury. Patrick, groaning, pulled on his trousers, but it was much too hot to put on a shirt, and so he sat again on the bed, his pink and hairy chest heaving with his rapid heartbeat, his head hammering. The room was suffused with Patricia's perfume, which nauseated him. He retched once or twice and rubbed his fat sweating face and groaned again. He reflected miserably that everything had gone wrong lately, and he thought of his debts and his heart and Patricia's ill health and how hard it was to grow old when one felt young. He closed his eyes for a minute or two. Bright sparks ran about the inner lids and frightened him.

Patricia ran shouting into the nursery, where a subdued duo awaited her, Nicole and Sebastian. Nicholas was suddenly asleep in his room. He did this often after a period of sustained violent activity, and it was almost impossible to wake him later.

The two children looked in silence at Patricia as she stormed into the pleasant schoolroom. Patricia flung out her arm and pointed toward the door. "Get to your grandfather's bedroom, you sneak," she shouted at Sebastian. "He wants to talk to you, and I hope he beats you almost to death!"

"Mama," said Nicole. But Sebastian caught her arm and squeezed it, so she was silent. Patricia began to scream again. "He'll send you away, as I always wanted, and then we'll have peace in this house! You cause nothing but trouble here, and always did! Mischief-maker, liar, sneak. No wonder poor Nicholas is sick! *You* make him sick! I swear you do! He'll be all right after you're gone! You're possessed of the Devil!"

Unfortunately, Mr. Doherty, who was permitted a walk after lunch, was not present at the time of the breakage or for this hysterical scene.

Nicole turned silently and imploringly to Sebastian, but he shook his head and gave her a warning look. Her beautiful gray eyes flooded in tears. He walked to the doorway near where Patricia stood trembling with rage. When he passed near her, she swung out her arm and struck him fiercely on the face, so that he staggered and almost fell.

"Mama!" cried Nicole.

"Nickie," said her brother, holding his bruised face and turning toward her. "Nickie!" His young voice was loud and commanding. The child burst into tears and went into her bedroom. Sebastian watched her go, then left the room. When he had gone, Patricia followed her daughter. She found Nicole sobbing on her white-dotted-swiss bed, and Patricia sat beside her, still panting. But Nicole moved away from her in silence.

"Darling," said Patricia. But Nicole shut her wet eyes and did not speak. She had never done this before, and Patricia felt abandoned.

"He's made you treat your mother like this, the wicked boy."

But Nicole opened her eyes and stared somberly at the wall. She let Patricia stroke her hair, but it was as if her mother were not present and she was caught up in a sorrow more than she could bear.

Patrick, in his bedroom with Sebastian, rubbed his smarting eyes. He felt unutterably weary and sick. He had always loved Sebastian, his first grandchild, but for a considerable time, due to Patricia's tales, he had come to be suspicious of the boy and extremely troubled and doubtful, for the first time, of his own judgments. No mother could so loathe her own child and accuse him so monstrously without cause, not even Patricia, who was sometimes guilty of hysterical ex-aggerations. There was also the matter of the destroyed ornament. No one, Patrick reflected, could get around that. He looked sharply at the boy and said, "What've you got to say for yourself, then, Bastie? That lovely work of art, your Mum's treasure."

The boy looked at Patrick seriously. "It was an accident," he said. He had never told a lie in all his life before. But he and Nicole had hastily invented a story, and he hoped it would be believed.

"Come, now," said Patrick, and was deeply vexed. "A heavy object like that! Sure, I could hardly lift it meself."

The boy shut his eyes for an instant, then looked directly at his grandfather. He was very pale and very resolute. "Nickie and I—we missed Nick for a minute. We didn't hear him. Then we went looking for him. Everywhere. And he"— the young voice weakened—"he was in Grandma's room, looking at the ornament. He thought it was pretty. Nickie and I took his hand to take him back to the nursery, and I...I slipped and fell against the table. Hard. And it rocked...it rocked, and the ornament fell off and broke. That's all. I'm sorry. Mama liked it so much. And Nick cried. He honestly did. He was sick over it. And we took him back and put him to bed."

Patrick listened to this in absolute silence, and his little bright blue eyes were keen. He had heard thousands of prevarications before, and something sounded flase in the account of the child. He said, "Sure, and you wouldn't be diddling me would you, Bastie?"

He was not prepared for the stark terror that suffused Sebastian's face. He sat up in alarm, all his instincts alert. "Are you lying to me, child?"

"Why should I lie?" cried Sebastian. "You can ask Nickie, Grandpa! Why should I lie? It was my fault, all my fault."

"Maybe Nickie will tell the same story you've told her to tell."

The blue eyes became piercing and formidable. Sebastian began to tremble violently. Patrick said, "Only a maniac with the strength given him by the Divil himself, or a very strong man, could tip that table over, then. Were you spalpeens, the three of you, racing around the table and knocking it, in your divilment?"

Wildly Sebastian thought that this would have been a better story. He gasped audibly, and shook his head. "Only me! Only me!" His voice was desperate. "You can ask Nickie. Mama, she said you would punish me, Grandpa. I wish you would and then let me go!" He clenched his small hands together. "Let me go!" he cried beseechingly.

"Let me go!" a little boy had cried in Patrick's hearing when he was a child himself. But the boy had been savagely beaten by an English soldier and eventually died. He had stolen a loaf of bread from a shopkeeper in the soldier's presence, for he had been starving. The echo rang dolorously down the decades, and Patrick felt sick, seeing the bright red blood of his playmate as vividly as if it had just been shed.

He held out his hand to Sebastian, and the boy took it and cried helplessly. "I'm sorry, I'm sorry," he mumbled between his sobs. Patrick wanted to weep himself, over the long-dead child and over Sebastian.

"Don't cry, then," he said. "It's all right, lad." He wiped the child's eyes with a corner of the sheet. Then he took Sebastian in his arms and held him tightly. "It's a man you are, Bastie, not a little colleen, and there'll be time enough for sorrow. There, there, now." He rocked the boy in his arms, crooning. Sebastian was now on Patrick's knees, and his tears wet Patrick's chest. Patrick felt an enormous grief, the grief that all fathers feel for their children, a grief darkened with guilt that they had brought their sons into the world at all. "Weep not for myself," the good Lord had said on his way to Calvary, "but for your children." Patrick had not understood that before, but now he did in all its poignancy.

With intense clarity he thought of Patricia. He knew now that all her tales of the child had been lies, but why she lied was a profound mystery. A terrible thought came to him: had Nicholas inherited some dementia from her? Was she mad herself? There was a certain extreme excitability common to both mother and child. But Patricia's was for effect. A different and agonizing pang assailed Patrick's head, and the room swayed about him and he felt frightened as it became unreal to him. He shut his eyes.

When he opened them, Sebastian was no longer crying but was sitting up on Patrick's knee, his young face concerned. "What is it, Grandpa? What is it?"

"Nothing, then. A headache." Patrick tried to smile. He was still dizzy. He pushed Sebastian off his knee, then smacked him affectionately several times on his buttocks. "Tell Mama I thrashed you. It's no lie."

When Sebastian was gone, Patrick lay back on his hot pillows. He did not think of his oldest grandchild. He thought of Nicholas, and he knew the truth. God help us, he thought. He cried again, an old man's tears.

Sebastian found his mother with the still-silent Nicole. The little girl sat up abruptly in her bed, and when she saw the traces of tears on her brother's face, she burst forlornly into tears herself. She ran to him and embraced him, clutching him convulsively. Patricia laughed, an ugly laugh. Sebastian looked over his sister's shoulder at her.

"Did he thrash you, as you deserved?"

"Yes, Mama."

She stood up, satisfied, and gave him an evil glance of triumph. Suddenly she felt an uncontrollable desire for whiskey, and almost ran out of the room, shouting, "And that's just the beginning! You're going to be sent away, where you'll be thrashed all the time!"

Nicole had quieted into silent sobbing. Sebastian whispered, "Grandpa didn't hurt. Nickie, he took me on his knee."

She looked up into his face. "Then he won't send Nick to some hospital? He doesn't know? You didn't tell him?"

"No. Of course not, Nickie. I thought of Mama all the time. What she'd do if Nick was sent to a hospital. Poor Nick."

Nicole thought of the scene in her grandmother's room and shuddered at the memory. She and Sebastian had found Nicholas there jumping maniacally up and down on the heavy table and slobbering with glee. When the other two children had gasped with dismay, seeing the huge ornament rocking beside the child's leaping feet, Nicholas had glanced at it with mad eyes, and then, with incredible strength, had pushed it off. It fell with a splintering crash, and Nicholas howled again as he jumped to the floor, overbalancing the table, which rolled on its rim.

The two other children trembled and clung to each other as Nicholas danced about them, shouting, "No more pretty! Boom, boom! Boom, boom!" And he howled once more.

Sebastian said with horror, "Quick! Take him back to the nursery! Put him to bed!" He heard the servants pounding up the back stairs, and he pushed Nicole fiercely. "Hurry! I'll say it was an accident—I was looking for Nick, I'll think of something—get out of here!"

"No! You're not going to take the blame this time!"

"Mama. She'll die if Nick's sent away! And so will Nick, alone with strangers. Please, Nickie, please!"

Nicole had obeyed, dragging the dancing, giggling Nicholas with her, just as the servants burst into the upper hall.

Once in the nursery, the girl had put her brother to bed, and he had fallen into one of his abysmal sleeps.

Then Nicole, shivering, had sat down and awaited calamity.

27

Jason thought that he could deal well enough with great problems, but trivial ones exhausted him. It was their very pettiness that was exasperating, devouring time and seeping away a man's energy. This day had been full of such trivia. He was thankful to close his desk and stretch and prepare to leave at six. He was almost out the door when Edmund Patterson entered, as regal and stately as always. Jason put out his hand defensively. "Not now! Besides, you should consult Mr. Nolan."

"Sir," Edmund said, "it is a matter of hotel management."

Jason sighed. "Get us a drink from that cabinet. I'm too tired to do it." Edmund prepared the glasses and the whiskey with immense ceremony. Then he sat down; his chef's uniform after a full day's work was as crisp, Jason resentfully thought, as if cut out of fresh white paper. They drank in silence, and Jason decided that the chef was one of the handsomest men he had ever known; Edmund made him feel sweaty and rumpled.

"What area are you proposing now for improvement?" Jason finally asked sarcastically.

"I thought of picnics."

"We have picnics for those who like them."

"Informal, primitive ones, sir."

"That's the great American picnic, with bugs and wet grass and sprained ankles on the mountain trails and paper plates and warm beer."

"I am proposing, Mr. Garrity, an elegant picnic—for two. Only two. A lady and a gentleman, with cushions on the grass, white linen, the best silver, the thin-stemmed glasses, cold champagne, gourmet viands, formal china. Instead of walking, the couple would be driven by one of the hotel grooms."

"That's a *picnic!*" exclaimed Jason, laughing. "Ridiculous. No inconveniences, no mud, no bees and hornets and wasps, no poison ivy—why, Americans would be insulted by being deprived of these pleasures. Go on, Edmund!"

Imperturbable, Edmund said, "We could charge a lot for them, as a luxury. They would be unique, grand, lavish."

Edmund coughed. "Quiet. Poetic. You've not thought of romance, sir."

"We get enough of it in some of the rooms."

Edmund smiled. "Americans are naive. They believe romance is only conducted at night. A lady and a gentleman leaving at midday, decorously, in a carriage—it is only for the view."

"Edmund, are you conniving at vice?" Jason laughed, but he was interested.

"In romance."

Feeling less tired and much entertained, Jason reflected. Edmund said, "Not all our guests come from Philadelphia and Pittsburgh."

It was a novel idea, and the more Jason thought about it, the more intrigued he was. Edmund said, "Ladies in their prettiest dresses and hats and slippers. No walking shoes, no walking skirts. No sunburn. They would love that. If ladies pretend to like ruggedness and informality, it is only to please gentlemen. But a browned skin—vulgar—and a burned nose doesn't please the gentlemen at all. They prefer their ladies to be delicate, not milkmaids."

"Women are getting more manly by the day, Edmund."

"Alas," Edmund said. "And the gentlemen don't like it. A true lady is still the masculine ideal, and nothing will ever alter that."

"You've had experience, then?"

Edmund lowered his eyes. "Daisies won't tell, to use the vernacular, sir. And no gentleman will."

Jason refilled the glasses. He thought again. "It might be an experiment, Edmund."

Later, it turned out to be a great success, and Jason raised Edmund's salary.

Now Jason said, rising, "I expect you to take charge of the kitchens in the new hotel, Edmund, if it is ever built."

Edmund's face broke into a charming smile. "With cooks I will recruit in New York, sir."

On the way out, Jason stepped into Daniel's office. Daniel was talking genially to his secretary, but when he saw Jason, his expression became cold. Jason was certain that Molly had not "confessed," but his face became warm. Even before that episode, Daniel was less friendly, and the coolness had increased over the past few months, to Jason's bafflement.

"Good afternoon," Jason said. "I am going home. Dinner with you and Molly?"

"Yes." Daniel leaned back in his chair. His brown eyes became enigmatic. "By the way, Uncle Pat did not come to the Inn-Tavern this afternoon. He called to say he wasn't feeling well. His heart, you know."

"He hasn't missed a day for years! He was feeling all right this morning." Jason was troubled.

Daniel shrugged. "Well, his age, you know. A man gets tired. I think he needs a holiday."

Daniel paused. He appeared to scrutinize Jason, and Jason had the impulse to say, "What's the matter between us, Dan?" But guilt kept him silent. He half-saluted and went out. Well, he thought, Dan and I were never buddies, in the best of times. But he used to like me. Now he doesn't at all. Hostility is there like unexploded dynamite. I can feel it.

A little depressed, Jason walked out into the late sunshine. He got into his automobile. The mountains were the color of jasper against a pale blue sky, and basked in serenity. The trees rushed up the hills in a green tide, ranging in shades from emerald and aquamarine to a lively olive, like a sweetly turbulent ocean. The black mood quickened in Jason. He stopped the automobile and glanced up at the hotel. The late sun ignited blond walls. It was a proud sight, but for the first time, Jason was not proud. Dejection overcame him, and he started the automobile again. He could not give a name to his dejection. He shook his head as if to get rid of a swarm of flies. God, what is the matter with me? he asked himself with exasperation. I will be invoking druids, as my ancestors did, next! To ward off evil spirits!

Suddenly a radiance fell over mountain, river, sky, trees, blinding Jason with its effulgence. A sea of light engulfed him, bearing his soul upward to ecstasy, becoming one with the brilliance he thought he saw with his eyes. The light became rapture, the rapture light. They flowed into one another, pulsing, blissful, without boundaries, without end. Above all, they brought joy. All was transformed, charged with grandeur. A thought came to Jason unbidden: "Be still. And know that I am God."

The glory ebbed. The familiar scene became small, ordinary, merely pretty. The majestic revelation faded. Jason felt as if he had been wakened in some fetid valley after falling asleep in Olympia.

He did not know when he came to the main road; a honk of a startled car came to him like the squawk of a gigantic and indignant goose. A Model-T Ford abruptly came to a stop, and Jason vigorously applied his brakes. Dazed, he saw the opposing motorist rapidly approaching him, frightened and angry. He smiled; it was Father Sweeney, nearly as fat as Patrick Mulligan himself, and nearly as bald now. "Dreaming, Jason?" he actually bellowed, red of face. "Sending me to meet with my ancestors in a hurry, without a shriving?"

"Sorry, Father," said Jason. "I was thinking."

"You nearly wrecked the car you gave me!"

"And it cost all of eight hundred and fifty dollars. I couldn't afford it." Jason smiled somewhat ruefully. The priest did not smile. His eyes, not so ingenuous lately, fixed themselves seriously on Jason. He had heard rumors.

"Worried, lad?"

Jason studied him. He was still somewhat dazed. Then his big face smiled with mischief, though his eyes seemed far away. "No. Not more than ordinarily. Coming down the mountain road, I thought I had a . . . vision."

"Vision of what?" Father Sweeney's eyes now became sharp.

"I don't know. I wish I did."

Father Sweeney paused. If someone like John Garrity had come to him and talked of "visions," Father Sweeney would have been highly suspicious and skeptical. Jason was a different matter. He was not a dreamer or a fanatic. He was pragmatic and sensible. Father Sweeney had come to appreciate Jason during the past years, and to have a deep affection for him. He knew all about Patricia, and about the tragedy of Nicholas. He knew Jason's secret charities; he knew Jason's agnosticism. Nevertheless, he knew Jason was "God-haunted," like Bernard. Unknown to Jason, the priest often had observed him in the empty church sitting and grimly contemplating the crucifix over the high altar, which he had given to Father Sweeney. The priest had not approached him. He had respected his thoughts, though he suspected they were not pious. It was as if Jason had confronted a formidable antagonist, and challenged him.

So the priest was thinking that if Jason had a "vision," it would have been an interesting one at least.

Jason laughed now. "Daydreaming, Father," he said. "Just daydreaming. Better get the car going, or someone will smash it up."

"How's Nick, Jason?"

Jason turned his head away. "As usual. He seems . . . healthy, thank God."

"And how's Reverend Mother Nickie?"

Jason turned back to him. "Manages." He chuckled.

"And Sebastian?"

Jason's face softened and his gray eyes actually glowed. But he only said, "Well enough. For a kid." He paused. "Crank up your car for you, Father?" He left his own automobile and started the priest's. Father Sweeney watched him, sighing. A massive young man, never complaining, proud and private, as were all the Irish, yet he could be dangerous if aroused. Father Sweeney had rarely seen Jason gentle, except with his mother and his children. But as the priest knew, he could be merciful.

Father Sweeney did not know why he silently prayed. "Guard him, Lord." On the way home, he wondered what Jason's vision had been. He doubted that John Garrity ever had a vision in his life, priest though he was.

Jason went at once to the library when informed that Patrick was resting there. Patrick was dozing in a red leather chair; Jason paused to study him. The older man looked pale and exhausted, even in his sleep, jowls drooping, mouth open, hands clasped over his huge belly. Drops of sweat dripped from his forehead. The air was close; the red sun glared sullenly in a window before falling to the rim of the mountains and setting them afire. Jason became alarmed at Patrick's appearance. There was no sound in the house, not even a servant's voice. Then Jason became aware of the ticking of the grandfather clock. It seemed to be counting, measured stroke after measured stroke, and in ominous cadence. The mountains were now crowned with a dull flame, like the dying embers of a burning city noiselessly collapsing into ruins. Jason shivered as if the room were cold.

Dusk swiftly invaded the library.

I love him as a father, Jason thought. I love him almost as if he were Da. What has come between us? The troubles? Patricia? I share them with him. It must be something else. He is sick. I didn't realize it before; I thought it was just his age. When Da was his age, he was still a young man.

Patrick stirred and groaned dimly. He opened his eyes with an enormous effort, as if against his will. He saw Jason standing before him and motioned sluggishly. Jason sat down. Patrick briefly closed his eyes again. "We have trouble." Jason remained silent. When did we not have? he thought. Patrick was utterly exhausted again, and braced himself with the arms of his chair. He regarded Jason with a new intensity.

Then the older man told him about the accident. The words pained him, and he began to sweat. Jason listened with horror, not speaking, until Patrick had finished. Then he said, "I don't believe Bastie and Nicole."

Patrick sighed and said, "I don't believe them either."

"Then it was...?"

Patrick nodded.

A heavy silence fell. The two men could hardly see each other in the dusk, and they communicated without speech for some time. A maid noiselessly entered and lit a lamp. They did not notice her. Patrick's eyes filled with tears, and Jason, moved, averted his gaze. He felt that Patrick had drawn closer to him, with something of the old trust and affection.

Then Patrick said, "I didn't tell you before, Jase. But I am thinking it over. Nick...should be sent to a...school that deals with his illness." He paused. "I've spoken to the teacher."

Jason said loudly, "No!" He rose suddenly, in protest. "Think of Patricia. Separated from the boy. She'll grow worse."

Patrick sat up straighter. "Then you know something I do not. Tell me." He added, "I'm her father."

Jason was silent.

"Tell me, damn you! I'm not some old lady that needs to be soothed and coddled and protected. Sure, and the instincts bothered me..." The little bright blue eyes flashed, and wrath blotched his fat face with patches of scarlet. Jason felt despair. Patrick thumped the table nearest him and shouted, "Tell me!"

"I thought to spare you—"

Patrick screamed an obscene and blasphemous oath. "Tell me, curse you!"

Jason half turned away and told him. Patrick listened, at first denying, incredulous, then throwing himself back in his chair, weeping the hard dry sobs of grief, covering his face with his hands. Jason told him all. "I don't know where she gets it. Alcoholics are clever. You can't keep it from them."

"Christ! 'Alcoholics'! My daughter is a drunk!"

"Mr. Mulligan. They're sick people."

An obscenity came from Patrick. "What's she sick of? Before she even knew of Nick, this was going on, you tell me.

403

Nothing was denied my colleen. Nothing. You tell of 'despair.' Why is she desperate?"

"I don't know. But she is. For a long time."

"Get to the bottom of this, then."

"I've tried. Dr. Conners has tried. Ask him."

"Send her down to me!" Patrick gasped. "I'll cure her if it takes a whipping!" He gagged, as if about to vomit.

Jason listened in consternation. "She isn't a child, Mr. Mulligan. To be whipped when she's naughty. Father Sweeney approached her with tact. She denies everything. Whatever it is, she won't confess it. She's sick. Have mercy."

Patrick glared with something like hate at Jason. "You're her damned husband! Hasn't she confided in you?"

Jason did not speak for a moment. Then he said, "I don't know why she married me. She didn't love me; I've found that out. She never confided in me. For a long time—it comes to me—she hated me. From the beginning."

"Why, then, did she marry you?"

Jason shook his head. Patrick literally leaped from his chair and confronted his son-in-law with clenched fists. "Did you fuck her before, and then had to get married? I'll kill—"

"Mr. Mulligan." Jason spoke quietly.

Eventually Patrick dropped his hands and found his chair and closed his eyes. "I'm sorry," he whispered. "Oh, Christ." He pondered, then suddenly sat upright. "A seven-month child! It minds me..." He choked.

"Mr. Mulligan! She had no opportunity—guarded as she was. You insult my wife. She was a virgin when I married her."

Patrick contemplated him with compassion. "How do you know?"

Angered, Jason said, "A man knows. I never will forgive you. An insult, an unpardonable insult, to my wife."

Patrick reached out and took his hand. "Jase. Forgive me. I'm a distracted father, that I am. My daughter...an alcoholic. My grandson a...a...I'm an old man. Jase, send Nick to a school..."

"No," said Jason, and left him with a face like iron.

Patrick collasped in his chair when he was alone. His thoughts tormented him. Who? I'll kill...He reached for a glass of whiskey. God help us all. Troubles never ended for the Irish.

As Jason started up the stairs, he said to himself: How long have I known about Patricia and covered it up—her

404

drinking? And whatever ails her? In despair he asked himself: What ails her? Before Nick was taken sick she hated me. Was afraid to face something?

He turned on the chandelier at the top of the stairs and hesitated, looking around him, feeling a weight on his shoulders as if he were an old man. Then he went on slowly to the children's quarters. He found Sebastian and Nicole being read to by Francis Doherty, the children unusually grave and tense in the lamplight. They got up out of their chairs and stared at him with apprehension. He smiled and patted Nicole on the head and squeezed Sebastian's shoulder reassuringly. He said to Francis, "Leave us alone, please. I want to talk to my children privately."

He seated himself and motioned the children to approach him. He took their hands. He said, "You've both been taught not to be liars, that lying is cowardly and sinful. Good. I approve. But when a lie is spoken to protect someone helpless, or to spare pain of grief, it is merciful and good. Truth, under these circumstances, would be cruel and unpardonable. Do you understand me?"

They nodded cautiously. They don't trust me, Jason thought with sadness. It's because of their mother; I've always taken her part even if wrong. He said, "I've talked to your grandfather. He's told me all about it. Nick will not be sent away."

Nicole's sturdy face showed joy, her dimples flashing and her beautiful gray eyes growing bright with tears, and Sebastian smiled and blinked. Both children leaned against Jason's knees, and he hugged them. They hid their faces in his shoulders. Never had Jason loved his children so much and with such profound tenderness.

Suddenly an animal roar sounded from the boys' bedroom. A chair was knocked over, feet scrambled rapidly, and gasping, Nicholas, in his nightshirt, leaped explosively into the room. He was a whirlwind; he twirled frantically, shouted, bounded, arms like windmills, eyes unseeing, with a maniacal glittering, mouth open and drooling. Nicole ran to him and grasped his arm, but he thrust her off and kicked her savagely with his bare feet, then resumed his yelling and convulsive twirling about the room. Jason, horrified at this violence, stood up and said, "Nick!" The boy lowered his head like a beast, and with a mad and an inhuman screech he charged his father.

Jason caught him. He was appalled at the child's demented strength. He had to struggle to hold Nicholas in his arms. The boy bit him in the neck. Jason had difficulty retaining his grip on the boy and avoided the gnashing teeth. He had one thought: Possessed! Nicholas was no longer Nicholas, Jason thought despairingly! What was he? He heard Nicole cry out, a forlorn cry, and Sebastian's distressed exclamation. For the first time Jason decided Patrick was right.

Mr. Doherty appeared at the doorway, staring, aghast. Then he ran into the boys' bedroom and emerged holding a bottle and a spoon. His face was white and strained. As Jason held Nicholas, Francis pinched the child's nose, and forgetting the spoon, poured a measure of the red liquid down the boy's resistant throat.

"He'll be all right in a minute," Francis said. "Whew!" He wiped his brow with the back of his hand and shook his head. "It grows worse."

Nicholas spat, beat his fists against Jason's chest. Then all at once he subsided, smiled a beatific smile, and said, "Pretty, pretty. Boom boom!" He kissed Jason with enthusiasm, over and over, hugged him around the neck. "Papa, Papa!" he shouted. "Nick loves Papa! Nick loves Nickie! Nick loves Bastie! Nick loves Mama!"

God help my son, thought Jason, and put the child gently down. Nicholas embraced his knees. He ran off and kissed his sister, then his brother, then Francis Doherty. His little face glowed with affection. He was oblivious of the rivulets of urine that accompanied him.

Jason asked, "How long has this been going on?" He was weak and sick and had to sit down abruptly.

Mr. Doherty said, "Why, sir, over a month!" He added, "I thought you knew, Mr. Garrity."

Jason was silent.

Mr. Doherty said, "Your neck is bleeding, sir! I'll get some iodine."

"His medicine, what is it?"

"Tincture of morphine. It quiets his...excitement."

"Morphine! Has it come to that?"

Francis did not reply. He went to the children's bathroom for a washcloth and a bottle of iodine. Jason was barely conscious of the ministrations. He said absently, "Thank you."

Nicole had taken Nicholas into his bedroom, to change him, and Sebastian went with her. Jason looked at the pool of urine on the rug. Then he went to his wife.

Patricia's bedroom was completely dark. She had drawn shades to keep out any light; it was as if she desired to burrow in a cave, to hide, like an animal that had bitten itself in unbearable distress. A dim reflection came from the hall lamp. Jason stood by her bed in silence. She was huddled up in a blanket despite the heat, which was smothering. The sweet and overpowering effluvium was sickening. Jason finally admitted to himself what it was.

He felt a huge repugnance and disgust. Then suddenly he thought of Bernard's remark: "The good Lord says, Who knows the travail of the heart which is being condemned? We're all strangers to one another." Jason considered it. Then he made a gesture of denial. A sufferer should not inflict his suffering on the innocent. After all, who does not suffer in one way or another? He thought of Molly, and a spasm of acute desolation struck his chest.

There was a virtue in suffering in silence. But Patricia screeched aloud in her sorrow over Nicholas. She shared it with the other children and her husband and father. However, prior to Nicholas' affliction, his mother had been drinking, at first unknowingly and then deliberately. Alcoholism. Jason felt renewed repugnance in spite of what he had told Patrick, that alcoholics were sick people. Jason thought of Bernard again. "There comes a time when men have to choose self-control or pain," the old man had said. "If the pain gets bad, then the hell with the self-control! It's no righteousness to bear unbearable pain, though some think it is. It can lead to murder or suicide. The bottle seems safest."

Jason had come to the conclusion that his wife was stupid, selfish, shallow, and pretentious, in short, a trivial woman. A man's capacity for pain varies in the individual. Patricia's pain, mysterious as it was to father and husband, might be the result of mere egotism or a more serious malady. Whatever it was, she was either incapable of expressing it, due to her lack of intellect, or she dared not.

Patricia groaned in her drunken sleep, and the groan seemed to come from unendurable torment. Jason was confused, and he said aloud, "What is it, Patricia? Tell me!" He turned on the bedside light, fumbling in his agitation. It started to fall, and he barely caught it.

Patricia sat up, disheveled and stupefied. Her face was haggard and old; she drooled, like Nicholas, and she wiped away the saliva. Her cheek was crumpled, her hands tremulous. Her frock was twisted and creased, her fine hair unpinned. She had a dazed look, and while she struggled to orient herself, she gulped dryly. Suddenly she shivered violently. An aura of sour alcohol surrounded her and Jason recoiled. Her eyes were dull and lifeless and far away.

Then she came fiercely alive and glared at Jason with such malignance that he was afraid. Her hair actually rose on her head, and she bounded to her feet and confronted him wildly, her teeth glittering in the lamplight. Jason stepped back.

"You!" she screamed. "You and your pet! You'll both go! Dada agrees with me. Out, out, out, both of you! Bag and baggage!" She smiled now with mad glee and pointed her finger at Jason. "Out!"

"Wait," said Jason. "I know all about it. Your father has just told me." He wanted to grasp Patricia by her arm, but she danced away from him like an insane dervish. He began to shout, attempting to control her. "Sebastian didn't destroy your ornament! It was an...accident."

Patricia abruptly stopped her whirling dance. She threw back her head and screamed again, one tearing shriek after another. Then she picked up a crystal bottle from her dressing table and hurled it at Jason. He dodged. He could not control his rage. He strode to Patricia and grasped her by her shoulders and shook her over and over. "Listen to me, you fool! Nick did it, only Nick, and you know as well as I do! Nick, Nick. Sebastian only took the blame—"

"He confessed! The sneak. He was forced to confess he did it! He tried to lie his way out of it! He knew how I loved Mama's ornament and wickedly smashed it. He took revenge!" Patricia's hair, a tangled mass, fell around her face. "Why would he take the blame?" She moaned, "You broke my neck; wait till I tell Dada! He'll kick you out!"

"Sebastian took the blame to spare you, and to keep Nick from being sent away—as your father advised me dozens of times. I'm half-convinced of that, in the last few minutes. Yes, I am. A drunken mother is bad for him."

Immediately Jason was sorry he had spoken so, and broken his word to Patrick and to himself. But the disastrous words could not be recalled.

Patricia was absolutely still. She put both hands to her cheeks and stared at Jason. She muttered, "A drunken...Nick, Nick, my baby. He'll be sent away—all the fault of your pet, Sebastian. He's always lying about Nick, blames him for everything he does himself—trying to send Nick away, my

408

poor baby! Next he'll try to send Nicole away, me away! So he can have it all to himself, Dada's money..." Her voice became hysterically shrill. "A drunken mother! Me, a drunken mother! You—"

"Yes. A drunken mother," and now Jason was contrite. "I knew it for a long time. Your father didn't; I hid it from him, for both your sakes. Now it's out. Why do you do it, Patricia?"

She shrieked, and tears flew from her eyes. "Because I can't stand being married to you! I hate you!" She clutched her head in her hands and groaned over and over, "I can't stand being married to you. I never could."

Jason knew he was hearing the truth from Patricia for the first time. I always knew it, he thought with extreme pain. I lied to myself. No excuse. Then he became conscious of Patricia, who had clapped both her hands over her mouth and was staring over them at him. Her eyes glistened in terror—there was no mistaking it for anything else.

"Why, then, did you marry me? You proposed to me, not I to you. You said you wanted to marry me right away. Why?"

"Because of Dada," she mumbled. The terror grew brighter in her eyes, and Jason knew she again spoke the truth, but it was curiously ambiguous. "He wanted me to marry you."

"You said you loved me, Patricia." Jason's voice broke with pity for himself and his wife, and a deep grief.

"I...thought I might love you in time—it was all for Dada. To please him. That's all."

"And to please your father you sacrificed yourself, me, our children and ultimately your father himself. What devotion. I thought you weren't capable of it." He spoke with immense bitterness.

"Now you know, Jason. Why don't you leave—with Sebastian?" She actually put her hands out pleadingly to him, like a beggar.

He was amazed. "Divorce?" Something like elation stirred in him.

"No!" Horror sounded in Patricia's voice. "Dada wouldn't stand for it! We're Catholic. A divorced woman—his daughter. I couldn't bear the disgrace. I'd say...I'd say...you left me at my request. Yes! a legal separation."

Jason watched her narrowly. "I'll leave. But all three of the children leave with me."

"No! Nicole and Nicholas remain with me!"

409

"No." In his pain he taunted her. "With a drunken mother?"

"I'll take the pledge!"

"What will that be worth, in your state?"

"If you leave, I swear I shall not take a drink again, not even wine."

Jason pondered. His acute Irish perceptions were aroused. "It's not only being married to me, the cause of your ... drinking. There's something else, too. Why don't you tell me? Patricia, once I loved you. I'm still your friend, your husband. Tell me."

She clasped her hands tightly together. "There's nothing else."

"And I know you're lying."

Renewed terror jumped brilliantly to her eyes. "No! No!"

Jason turned from her. "Bastie stays. I stay. The other children stay. I can't hope that you'll stop your drinking, but I'd advise you to not make it as obvious. For all our sakes. I suspect all the children know it, God help them. And I insist you treat Bastie with more justice. Or"—he turned to her— "I'll take the children and leave."

She studied his face, grim and hard and resolute, and she caught her breath audibly. She knew he meant it. "I'm warning you, Patricia."

Now she turned away. "I'll take Nicholas to Lourdes in August. Then ... he'll be cured. Things'll be better then. Jason ... ?"

He struggled against his pity and tried to feel contempt. "Yes. August. The twenty-eighth. I've already bought your tickets." Patricia mutely mouthed something, but he made a gesture and left.

The house was silent. A maid informed him that Mr. Mulligan had had a dinner tray in his room, and Mrs. Garrity had ordered one. The children were in bed. Jason dined alone.

All at once he was filled with foreboding. The June night was tranquil. The scent of roses came through the windows on the warm breeze. Jason forgot that he and Patricia were to have dined with Daniel and Molly.

The Archduke of Austria and his wife prepared for their journey from which they would not return.

28

Mrs. Lindon, more bosomy and imperious than ever, smiled with amusement at Chauncey Schofield. "Rome wasn't built in a day," she said as if she had invented the cliché. "We'll get what we want. It's worth waiting for. Old Patrick can't live much longer."

"Then the thousand acres will belong to Garrity, and good-bye to our scheme," Chauncey said.

"Not so fast, dear. We have other resources of which I told you. Jason was always simple-minded; he believes in honor, even among bankers. Behind his cynical Irish facade he believes in the loyalty of friends. He can't learn that a man has no friends, especially when it comes to money. That is why I take care to remain solvent! You extend yourself too much, a masculine fault."

Chauncey's too-handsome face was smooth as glass, charming and conciliatory. He put on an expression of admiration. "Guilty, as charged, Clementine. Did you take my advice six months ago and invest in munitions stocks?"

"I did, and thank you, Chauncey. Doubled in value. You have knowing friends in Washington. Did you take your own advice?"

"Anita did. I wish I had. My money is all tied up in previous commitments."

They were in Clementine's private parlor, richly furnished but too crowded with knickknacks and furniture. She fanned herself and was slightly "rosy" and too fat, but her figure had remained impressive. She reminded her admirers of a ship in full sail, grand and imposing. She wore her new Sunday dress of gold-threaded red silk, by Worth, an original, and there were egret plumes in her dyed hair attached to a circlet of genuine diamonds; this and a splendid diamond bracelet and diamond earrings created a blaze in the late sunlight. Clementine could not be accused of restraint, for she was a lusty woman who believed in display. "Restraint is for the shabby," she would remark. "And decorum for women who have not been tempted. Necessity is the virtue of those who can't afford luxury. And righteousness is for people who have nothing else for which to pride themselves. But knowledge of human nature has made me tolerant; I know what motivates it. And it amuses me. But I'm not Irish, as is our friend Jason Garrity. He'll become bitter."

"He is already displaying signs of it." Chauncey laughed. "It is the fault of his wife. Thank God Anita has more sense."

Clementine became thoughtful, and she studied Chauncey in his light blue Palm Beach suit and gaudy tie, which was the latest fashion in New York, though not approved in more conservative circles. Aware of the scrutiny of his hostess, Chauncey became innocent and attentive.

She tapped his hand lightly with her fan. "I advise you to be a little more discreet," she said. "You were seen by my youngest 'cousin,' Arabelle, down near the river; she was taking a constitutional with a friend. Last Sunday, in the late afternoon. You were with Elizabeth, Anita's daughter, in a compromising position, let us say." Clementine delicately cleared her throat and reached for her whiskey glass. Her corrupt eyes were cool and intent. "If Anita gets wind of it, you'll be ruined, and disagreeable things could happen to your associates also. Including me."

Chauncey became pale. Clementine nodded. "You can rely on Arabelle to keep her mouth shut; she likes you and knows I am your friend. She confided only in me, I assure you. But if you're seen by some of the other townsfolk... What on earth possessed you? In the daylight, in the bushes? An uncomfortable place and time."

Chauncey smiled weakly. "We were carried away. It won't happen again."

"Be carried away in a more secret place than down by the river." Clementine smiled, but her eyes remained hard. "Men are so reckless. But I gave Elizabeth more credit for discretion."

"We are in love," said Chauncey.

"Hah. I don't believe in love. I have had too much experience with men. A haughty sex, and fickle. Don't try to diddle me with talk of love." She shrugged. "I read your mind. I'm no blackmailer, though I was once, a long time ago. But I warn you: I'll not be jeopardized by anyone injudicious enough to create a scandal."

"I promise to be more careful." Chauncey felt panic. The old bitch! he thought. She'll use it, when it serves her purpose.

Clementine said, "You visit my girls from time to time. Why aren't you satisfied? They're safe. Closemouthed." When

Chauncey did not reply, she said, "Is it that Elizabeth inherits her father's fortune if her mother dies?"

"You do me an injustice, Clem."

"Hah. When a man puts on a virtuous expression with regard to money, women should be wary. Money comes first with men, and I don't blame them. I can't stand hypocrisy. Anita is healthy. Do you plan to murder her?" Clementine laughed. "Her lawyers are too suspicious of you."

Chauncey stood up, much agitated. Clementine again laughed. "Sit down. Have another drink." She said, "We are all murderers, one way or another. Oscar Wilde said, if I remember, each man kills the thing he loves—the coward does it with a kiss, the brave man with a sword. Not only should Anita beware. But Elizabeth, too, if you love her. She is in the greatest danger."

The June day was hot, as hot as midsummer. The earth seemed in a state of jubilation. It was ironic, Lionel repeated with amusement in the following months, that Jason, long known to him as "Doomsday Jase," felt more cheerful than he had in years. Lionel said, "Jase was forever speaking of a 'Grand Conspiracy' which would lead to war, but when it happened, Jason was humming Irish ballads in his office. He even smiled as I happened to pass by the door. I said, 'Well!' and he said, 'Pippa Passes,' though God knows what he meant."

Jason could have told him. That morning Molly Dugan came to visit her husband, Daniel, in his office, and encountered Jason in the hall at Ipswich House. They exchanged a few words, and these only casual, but all at once Jason felt elated. He stared down in Molly's eyes and they both smiled. Moments passed in silence, and then they began to speak, and neither one remembered what they said, but neither one forgot the encounter. Molly continued on her way, but she had pressed Jason's hand in parting, a gesture full of consolation and sympathy and love. He watched her go; she turned a corner and he was still bemused and joyful; he was not alone any longer. He had a companion and friend, and Molly had not forgotten him after all. He was convinced that she knew all his recent travail and had tried to convey comfort and hope to him, and her steadfastness. He began to hum. The mood lasted well into the day, in slowly diminishing effect, but it left him with a sense of tranquillity.

At the end of the day, just when he was leaving, Edmund

Patterson knocked and entered. Jason did not protest and say, "Speak to Mr. Nolan." Instead he asked, "Now what is it?" in a tone of great good humor. "Have a drink." Edmund proceeded to the cabinet and filled two glasses with whiskey. He dropped a newspaper beside his chair, gravely saluted Jason with his glass, and drank in silence, as though he had forgotten where he was. His handsome black face was preoccupied.

Jason watched with fond amusement and drank also. Edmund said, "Mr. Garrity. You remind me more and more of a Roman centurion."

"Formidable?"

"Yes. But at this moment"—Edmund smiled—"not as formidable."

"Well, it's a beautiful day."

Instantly Edmund's face changed and became grave. He glanced at the evening's newspaper beside his chair. He said, "I'm in trouble."

Jason smiled and sighed. "Now what?"

Edmund did not smile. "It's my children. Gilbert is eight years old and Jennifer six. My wife teaches them; she is well-educated and disciplines them well. A man, a truant officer, visited her yesterday and insisted that my children be enrolled in the public-school system. Now, my wife visited the public schools several months ago." Edmund raised his hands and closed his eyes as if confronted with a scene of horror. "Suffice it to say the students are years behind in their learning compared with my children. Gilbert reads the books by Charles Dickens and I teach him French at night. And Jennifer is not far behind."

"But the truant officer demanded that you send your intellectuals to the public school?"

"Yes. I am resisting. After all, my children deserve a good education, as all children do—provided they have minds. I do not believe in compulsory education. Those who do not wish to learn or who cannot learn should not be subjected to an education they can not absorb."

"I agree with you, Edmund."

Edmund sighed. "The truant officer, whom I visited today, does not agree. I give him credit when he said, 'If all the congenital ignoramuses were eliminated from the classroom, three-quarters of the schools would be compelled to close and the poor teachers would lose their jobs.' He was quite the cynic. Nevertheless, he insisted upon my children entering public school the next term." He hesitated. "I brought out the fact, when protesting, that you yourself, Mr. Garrity, did not send your children to any school, but have a tutor, Mr. Doherty, for them. The officer commented, 'That's different.' How is it different, Mr. Garrity?"

"Mr. Doherty is an accredited teacher, Edmund."

"My wife, unfortunately, is not."

"That's it."

"I was under the impression that it was because my wife is a Negro."

"The trouble with you, Edmund, is that you are prejudiced."

The chef raised his head proudly. "I admit it. I am prejudiced against fools and injustices. The world is full of them, sad to say."

"I agree. How do you propose to combat them?"

"I will not send my children to the public school."

"You will be arrested, and if you resist, the children will be taken away from you." Jason was alarmed. He considered. "What about sending your children to my house, to be taught by Mr. Doherty?" Jason frowned. He was already anticipating Patricia's screeching objections.

Edmund's austere face broke into a smile. "I thought of that, Mr. Garrity." He cleared his throat. "Pardon me, but I've already been in communication, by telephone this morning, with Mr. Doherty."

"You have? What did he say?"

"He is willing, if you are. For the same stipend you pay him for teaching your own children. I consented, eagerly."

Jason was amused. "Well, then, there is no trouble."

Solemnly Edmund rose and extended his hand to Jason. Jason said, with hesitation, "There's my son Nicholas. He's...not well. Your children could be disturbed by him."

"I've heard of his affliction, Mr. Garrity. My children are mature in their outlook."

"Not prejudiced like you, Edmund?"

"I try to be tolerant, even of fools, sir."

Jason said, smiling, "Alas, you're not succeeding, Edmund. By the way, my little daughter, Nicole, is quite a martinet. She's as prejudiced as you are, Edmund, in her way. Your children will come under her rule."

"I know of your children, Mr. Garrity."

Jason's face became somber. He seemed about to speak, then was silent. Edmund said with compassion, "People will

415

talk, sir. Primates chatter all the time, humans as well as monkeys." He shook his head, deploring. "Little to choose between the species."

Jason nodded. "The only difference is that humans have no tails."

"Yes, they do, Mr. Garrity. On their souls."

He reached down and retrieved his newspaper. He held it in his hands and became heavy with import. "My father," he said, "fought in the Boer War. On the side of the Boers, not the side of the English. After all, he belonged to the Dutch Reformed Church. He said it was really a war fought for gold and diamonds. He said there was a conspiracy among evil men dating back to the French Commune."

Jason was stunned. Edmund misinterpreted his expression and said defensively, "My father was a very intelligent man. He always quoted Matthew, chapter twenty-four, about the end of the world. And the first two chapters of the prophet Joel."

"I've read them, Edmund." Jason paused. "It's becoming clearer. The financiers, the elite, as they call themselves, want to rule the entire human race."

Edmund opened his newspaper and handed it to Jason. "It begins," he said.

Jason read the big black headlines dated yesterday: "ARCH-DUKE OF AUSTRIA AND WIFE SLAIN IN BOSNIA!"

Jason closed his eyes. "God help us. God help us all."

"Amen," said Edmund.

A sense of calamity pursued Jason as he drove home, unaware of the bright June evening. He paused a few blocks from his house. An organ-grinder with his monkey stood there, an old man. The music was loud and dolorous, the man fiercely mustached. Jason was caught by the tune, poignant and sorrowful. He leaned from the window of his automobile and called to the man. "What is that you're playing?"

The old man smiled broadly; he removed his dusty fedora. "Si, signor! Pretty tune, eh? Called 'The Children's Prayer.' Big War! Napoleon's War. Eighteen-twelve? My wife always cries when she hears it."

Jason found a silver dollar and gave it to the delighted man. "Play it again, please."

The old Italian complied, and the silent street echoed the music. Jason drove on. The serene large houses seemed unreal to him, like facades hiding untold soundless violence.

The falling sun, to Jason, was falling on his world, all mankind.

The little monkey let out a wild and piercing scream. Jason heard it and shivered. "The Children's Prayer." Much good it would do them!

29

On July 28, 1914, Austria-Hungary declared war on Serbia. On August 1 Germany declared war on Russia; on August 3, France declared war on Germany; and the next day Great Britain joined her allies.

In America newspapers announced the news with big black headlines, but few Americans felt concerned. It was "exciting." War had nothing to do with the average American. It merely served to enliven conversation over teacups and pastries. A patriotic madness, however, filled the capitals of Europe, with parades, martial music, and student demonstrations.

The people were delivered from the boredom of daily work and the petty frustrations of their private lives, and for that they were fervently grateful. Men exploded from their prosaic cocoons thirsting for adventure. The romance of war colored millions of drab existences. At first the people did not know who the "enemy" was. It was sufficient to be gloriously threatened. Danger was unreal to the mobs. Confusion added to the exhilaration. Those who dared to express trepidation were howled down or accused of lack of patriotism, or worse, of treason.

The conspirators smiled. They were very intelligent and knew the psychology of the masses. Robbed of adventure by the industrial revolution, they understood that men found the sword preferable to monotony. Later mankind would weep and claim to be victims, but by then it would be too late.

The German kaiser and the Russian czar invoked God as their ally. They, too, were innocent. Max Wolfe, in *Der Berliner,* protested desperately. He was jailed as a subversive. The German ambassador to the United States wrote many letters to the kaiser. They were ignored. The ambassador wrote to the newspapers, warning Americans not to visit Europe, but Americans ignored them, smilingly, and continued to sail, looking for excitement. They did not care that the ships were loaded with contraband for England.

On August 12, Daniel Dugan paid a surprise visit to Jason's office. Daniel was not a frequent visitor, and because of Molly, Jason felt embarrassment and guilt whenever he saw the man.

Daniel seated himself and stared at Jason for long moments without speaking. "You have trouble," he said finally.

"When have I not?" Jason braced himself.

Daniel waved his hand. "The shortages for our kitchens and furnaces are over—temporarily. This has nothing to do with you personally. The government has been declaring 'shortages' for some years—coal, oil, grains, gas, and other essentials."

"Preparing for war?" Jason said with grimness.

Daniel nodded. "Preparing for war. You were right. It began in 1908 or earlier. Teddy Roosevelt knew of it and planned for it, gloriously. He implied it was time for America to move 'imperially.' You knew that; I've listened to you talk. But I have the facts; I know politicians and bankers throughout the world; I've spent half my life traveling, and have access to them all, because of my international investments."

Jason interrupted. "Da knew all this, too; he used to talk to me when I was in knickers! He not only had the 'intuition of the Irish,' to quote you, but he read books and newspapers and periodicals and listened to the mouthings of politicians. He didn't have the 'friends' you had and have. But he was wise, and distrusted all governments, with good reason."

Daniel smiled a small smile. "I can quote your own quotation from George Washington: 'Governments are not reason; they are not eloquence. Like fire, they are a dangerous servant and a fearful master.' True. And politicians are ambitious; Julius Caesar knew that; he was the consummate politician. You were right when you said it all goes back to the French Revolution—the enslavement of nations under the self-called elite." He yawned. "I am well prepared. You're not, Jason."

"I know. All these debts, and the new hotel is not even built yet."

"The delays have been deliberate."

Jason sat up. "I suspected that! But who?"

Daniel shrugged. "You have made enemies. I have too, but I invested in power for myself and am reasonably invulnerable. And I know when to keep my mouth shut. You don't. You also don't know how to adjust to the inevitable. I keep my warnings to myself; I know when I'm powerless. You don't."

"Stop this mumbo jumbo, Dan! Who?"

419

Daniel deliberately lit a cigarette and stared at the wall beyond Jason. The steamy August day caused Jason to sweat, but Daniel remained cool and calm. He said, "You are too damned emotional for your own good. You give the impression of being impassive and objective, but you boil inside. You have to guard against your own impulsiveness. You are all for honesty and honor, but they don't exist except in the feverish minds of romantics."

Jason raised his voice. "I don't need you to analyze me!" His face was red with mortification. "Make your point!"

"I will. You've come to the attention of Washington. The Greeks had an old saying: 'The wise man does not evoke the notice of gods, or governments.' "

Jason was incredulous. "An obscure man in an obscure little city! Go on, Dan!"

"You underestimate yourself, Jason. An honest man provides a great danger to governments, no matter how 'obscure' he is. And you are not *that* unknown. Six weeks ago, you spoke before an audience of German-Americans urging American neutrality. The papers quoted you in full. 'Prominent businessman and hotelier warns against involvement in the war! He asserts there is an international financial conspiracy promoting this conflict.' "

"Well?" challenged Jason. "It's true."

Daniel sighed. "Pontius Pilate said, 'What is truth?' That is the question. Imitating Pontius, I wash my hands. I can't do anything. Nor can you. Well, your speech appeared in the Washington newspapers. I've brought clippings. 'HOTELIER AGREES WITH PRESIDENT WILSON!' My dear young friend, you don't agree with Colonel House and Company, though they assert their complete agreement with the president. And they're watching you closely."

"Ridiculous. The American people are vehement against being involved in Europe's war."

Daniel raised his brows; he looked amused. Then he was sober. "I will advise you; no more public lectures. It's dangerous—for you. Keep your mouth shut." When Jason was speechless with temper, Daniel said, "Despite your cynicism, you believe in Judeo-Christian goodwill. It's a delusion. The world's not made that way, and never was and never will be. You're a good man. Therefore you will be always confused and outraged, and a victim. Get along with your government; that way is survival."

Jason said, "The price is too high for a man with honor.

420

Survival is not the point. I believe the Bible says 'Resistance to tyrants is obedience to God.'"

"In whom you do not believe!" Daniel gave an abrupt laugh, and Jason reluctantly laughed with him. Daniel said, "Well, anyway, compromise, for your own safety. Compromise is the mark of a civilized man."

"Then I'm not civilized. I don't compromise with evil."

Daniel made a restrained if eloquent gesture and regarded Jason with a little compassion. "By the way, Molly met Patty downtown. Patty says she is going to Lourdes, with Nicholas, the twenty-eighth."

Jason gaped, amazed and with disbelief. "I thought she had a little intelligence! She knows there is a war... she reads the newspapers..."

"Does she?" Daniel spoke with a quiet brutality. "I've known my cousin all her life. She reads only letters to the lovelorn, the fashion news, and gossip. Forgive me. If the war penetrated her consciousness, she has lightly brushed it off. As she brushes off anything which inconveniences her or threatens to inconvenience her. Didn't you and Uncle Pat ever discuss the news in front of her?"

"I don't remember. She... avoids me." Jason spoke with difficulty. "But she must know her trip must be canceled."

"I doubt it. She spoke to Molly about attending the Paris 'showings.' 'Then off to London,' she said gaily, 'after Nicholas is cured at Lourdes.' The world revolves about Patty and her concerns. Didn't you know that?"

"I thought that she realized the situation," muttered Jason.

"Not with Patty. I don't want to offend you..."

"No offense taken." Jason was alarmed and freshly incredulous about his wife. I knew she was a fool, but I never thought she was an idiot! I overestimated her.

On reaching home, Jason heard Patricia's voice in the library, screaming hysterically, and Patrick's weak protests. Patrick apparently was trying to soothe her and not succeeding. Now what? Jason thought resignedly. He entered the library, and Patricia pounced upon him.

"You! Agreeing to have little niggers in my house, attending school with my children! My children! Mr. Doherty told me. You must be mad! It's all right for your pet, but not for Nicholas and Nicole! Niggers! I wouldn't have them in my house even as servants!"

Jason was seized with a powerful urge to choke the life

out of her. Hatred swept over him like a scarlet tide. Her sweet effluvium suffocated him.

Patrick got up, holding on to his chair. "Now, mavourneen. Now, be calm." He swayed. "Now, Jason. Don't—"

Patricia turned on him. "You! Consent to this! Have you no pride? Niggers! Sitting down with your grandchildren! The whole town will laugh! 'Good enough for the Irish!' they'll say." She screamed again. "Children of hired help, kitchen scum!"

"The Irish," said Patrick, "were treated like scum in their own sacred country, and starved to death in their own fields, their women and children raped in the streets, their sons and daughters hanged in public...Mavourneen, all people are God's children—"

"The Irish are not apes!"

Jason seized her by the arms and shook her savagely. "Listen to me, you drunken slut! Edmund Patterson is an educated man. He's a renowned chef, in demand in London and New York. I'm lucky to have him. He's a gentleman, and his wife is a lady. His children are superior. If anything, I'm afraid for Edmund's children. Afraid of them associating with Nick, who is...dangerous. You know it, damn you, except you want to hide, as you have always hidden from the truth!"

"Dada, help me!" Patricia shrieked. "He's going to kill me!"

"Jase..." Patrick tried to loosen Jason's arms. "Oh, God..."

Jason hurled his wife from him, and she tottered backward and fell with a thump in a chair. She screamed over and over, and the servants listened avidly in the kitchen, and giggled. Jason put his shaking hands over his face and groaned.

"The drunken...I wish to God I'd died before I married her!"

Patrick said, "There, now, you don't mean it, I'm thinking. Stop, my darling"—this to Patricia. He staggered, and Jason gripped his arm. Patricia, diverted, stopped her screaming and looked at her father. Patrick leaned on Jason's shoulder, and gasped. "Marriage...is...a...sacrament. Quarrels—that's nothing. Man and wife often disagree. That's normal. Jase..."

Jason was alarmed by Patrick's appearance. "All right, Dad," he said. He never had used the word to Patrick before, and the older man's eyes shone with pleasure. "I'm sorry. I've had a bad day. But Patricia must learn—Edmund's children are going to study in this house. He has taken an objection to the public schools, and I don't blame him!" He turned to Patricia and said, with a terrible face, "And I warn you, don't insult his children. Or I'll remove my own kids from this house, and you won't ever see them again. I mean it."

"You wouldn't dare!" cried Patricia. "Dada?"

Patrick recovered himself. "Children belong to a father, mavourneen—when their mother is...unfit."

Patricia sat up. "Unfit?" she cried. "Dada."

Patrick walked slowly and painfully to his daughter and laid his hand on her head. She saw his tears, and gaped with shock and disbelief. He nodded sluggishly, as though his strength was exhausted. "Jase and I know all about the...drinking. Known it a long time. Pity you. I wanted...Jase said you are a sick girl; it's a sickness. That's what he said. Pleading for you. I wanted to...punish you."

Patricia shrank in her chair. She whispered, "A little drink now and then, and you treat me as a criminal."

Patrick said, "No. It's a secret sorrow, I'm thinking, but I won't pry. You'd best keep it to yourself." Patrick's voice expressed profound pity. Patricia stared, and then suddenly burst into tears, lowering her head almost to her knees. Patrick sighed. Her sobs filled the otherwise silent room.

When she grew quieter, Jason said, "There's another thing. There's a war in Europe. I've heard that you still plan to sail on the twenty-eighth, as originally intended. You can't be such a fool!"

Patrick turned around quickly. "No! Patricia knows...she reads. That's a lie you heard, Jase. Malicious. Gossip."

But Patricia sprang up and confronted Jason with renewed energy. "You hate Nicholas! You don't want him to be cured at Lourdes!" She whirled on her father. "I'm going. Try to stop me!"

Jason made a gesture of futility. He said, "Dad, I'll leave your daughter to you. I've resigned."

He left the room, followed by Patricia's frantic screams and Patrick's beseeching protests.

30

"It's painful for me," said Dr. Conners, "to have to admit that a lady—a lady—can indulge. Working-class women and...women who have loose morals, but not a lady like Patricia."

Patrick, who was becoming more feeble day by day, and Jason sat silently in Patrick's library this hot August of 1915.

"Perhaps it would have been better to let her go to Europe last year, with Nicholas," resumed the doctor, "and satisfied herself that nothing could be done for the boy. Despite the war, despite the sinking of the *Lusitania,* Americans persist in visiting Europe. If Patricia had gone..."

Jason said to himself: I almost wish she had gone on the *Lusitania!* Solved all our problems, and poor little Nick's, too.

"I don't need to tell you," said Dr. Conners, "that Patricia's 'problem' has gotten worse. I recommend a hospital, a private sanatorium. They call her condition a nervous breakdown, avoiding scandal."

"The scandal's all over town!" groaned Patrick. "She never goes out except to visit Lionel and Joan. Deserted her friends, takes no interest in clothes—why, she used to live for clothes. Doesn't even...wash. The chambermaid told me. Her bedroom is dirty, disordered. Her hair—rat tails. My beautiful colleen! I had such hopes for her."

Dr. Conners sighed. "Typical of her condition."

"Tell me! Truly and honestly, Ben. Is she...insane? Like Nick?" Patrick's words were a desperate cry.

"No. Patricia isn't insane. She has normal intelligence. Years ago, she was healthy in her mind and body—it is the drink that has destroyed her. Something must have driven her to it."

The doctor's tired eyes moved swiftly to Jason, who said dully, "Not guilty. I loved her when I married her. I loved her when I was a child. I tried to make her happy. You heard her: she hated me all that time. Lately I've had the feeling that she was in love with someone else. Probably nothing to it. Perhaps some man in Philadelphia who was unavailable."

"No," said Patrick, who shook his head over and over. "She'd have told me. She loved Jason, she said. She couldn't wait until they were married. Something happened. What was it, Jase?"

Jason said with deliberate hardness, "You've asked me that a hundred times, and I said I didn't know, and I still don't know. She asked me to marry her, in a hurry. But we've been over all that in the past year or two! I'm sick of repeating the same words!" Losing control, he said in a louder voice, "And I'm sick, myself, over the life your daughter's led me ever since we were married. I . . . I . . . loved her, until I realized it was no use—no use at all. My marriage has been a hell. I only stand it for my children. And I am pretty near the edge now." His anger increased. "Let me alone, or I'll take my children and get out and leave you alone with your daughter. I never had a life and it's time I did. I've never had any joy— except once." His voice became husky. "Just one day. In a lifetime—just one day. And I only realized it recently! I don't blame anybody. I was a fool to put up with your daughter all these years."

"Now, Jason," said the doctor. "Pat's sick—"

"*I'm* sick! Do you think I'm made of stone, and have no emotions, no feelings? That I live only to serve a woman who hated me from childhood? Mr. Mulligan, let's understand this once and for all. I loved your daughter, but I thought it was hopeless. Then came a day she insisted on marrying me without your knowledge."

The doctor got up. "I think I must go," he said.

Jason turned furiously to him. "Hear me out! It's time I took my own part. I've even accused myself, trying to discover what I did wrong. When I realized, after years of abuse, contempt, and ridicule, that I no longer loved her, I tried desperately to blame myself. But now it's time to save my own life." He almost choked with rage. "I refuse to participate in these discussions any longer. It's up to you what you do with your daughter. I don't care. Do you hear me! I don't care!"

"Jase . . ." Patrick seemed to lose substance. "The marriage sacrament—"

"Sacrament! Our marriage was not a 'sacrament.' At least, so far as your daughter was concerned."

He struggled for breath. "I not only have my debts to worry about, but the ruin of my marriage. I'm incapable of carrying the load anymore. Send her to a sanatorium; send her anywhere! I'm not interested any longer."

"Jase . . ." Patrick was weeping, the tears of an old stricken man. "I'm sorry. I'm beside myself. Forgive . . ."

Jason felt a twinge of compassion, but he suppressed it. Too often had he been betrayed by pity. "I'm beside myself, too, Mr. Mulligan. Did you ever think of that?"

"You're strong, Jase..."

"I've been strong long enough. I'll do a little whining from now on. Perhaps it'll make people realize that I'm a human being, too."

"Jase, will you help persuade Patricia that she should go to a private hospital?" Patrick held out his hands pleadingly.

"No! She's not my wife anymore!" He turned to the doctor. "Don't bother me with your consultations in the future. I must save my own life."

He almost ran from the house. He came to the little park, which was deserted, and threw himself on the grass and sobbed. "Molly. Molly. Molly." He hid his face in his arms. The grass felt as parched as his life.

"A secret sorrow she has," pleaded Patrick to Dr. Conners. "My little colleen."

"Sorrow is the natural condition of man," said the doctor, with some severity. "People with character conceal it from each other." But out of compassion for Patrick, he talked to Patricia sternly and without compromise.

She went to a private sanatorium a week later, near Wilkes-Barre. She left her father's house in stunned silence. She did not even speak to her children. Her father and her doctor accompanied her. Jason was not there.

On the journey, Dr. Conners thought about Jason: "Beware of a patient man when he comes to the end of patience."

Jason visited Saul Weitzman at least once a week, for he felt Saul and Edmund Patterson were his only friends, since he rarely saw Molly these days. One cool evening in September he stopped by Saul's little house. Jason settled himself in the old rocking chair which had belonged to Bernard. Saul regarded him with concern, for he had aged. His gray eyes were sunken and exhausted, and he was too quiet.

"How is Mrs. Garrity?" Saul asked.

"Gaining," said Jason, and the muscles of his face became hard.

"And the children?"

Now Jason actually smiled. "Reverend Mother has taken over the household, including the servants. They obey her! She strikes terror in them. And Mr. Doherty—he consults her with the lessons and problems with the other children, Nick, Sebastian, and Edmund's children, Jennifer and Gilbert. She lays down the law. Even Nick...even Nick has some control over himself. Reverend Mother has a hard hand."

"A tartar," said Saul, with love. Then he said, "I need some advice; I can't afford a lawyer, and you have troubles enough of your own."

"Nonsense," said Jason. "I brood too much on my own. Tell me."

Saul hesitated. "I'm not an American citizen."

"I thought you were." Jason was surprised.

"I *feel* as if I were American-born, Jason. A feeling for a country makes her your motherland, *nein?*"

Jason nodded. "I suppose so. Why didn't you become a citizen, then?"

Saul shifted uncomfortably and played with a tiny crumb on his immaculate tablecloth. "There is a difficulty. I first came to Canada. A work permit in the harvest. It ran out. Canada is very...very stern with aliens." He paused. "I slipped across the border to America. From Alberta. Illegal." His chest expanded, and he gave a beautiful smile. "I came home!"

"In spite of the prejudices you met?"

Saul gestured eloquently. "In spite of. Men are always prejudiced." He hesitated. "The world is at war. I'd like to vote. I went to an office—the U.S. Immigration Bureau in Scranton. 'I want to become an American citizen! I been here twenty-nine years! From Germany.' I was honest. No records of my arrival? they asked me. No, I said. I didn't leave the country after I came, not a single day. A man came from an inner office. He was sharp, no smiles. 'From Germany, eh?' he says. 'We'll investigate.' What is this 'From Germany,eh?' 'We are not at war with Germany,' I said. He waved me out." Saul looked dejected. "I came home afraid."

Jason reflected with anxiety. "I have a friend, a lawyer. I'll speak to him. It won't cost you anything, Saul."

"I pay," said Saul.

"He is my friend. At the most, ten dollars."

"This I can afford." Saul smiled in relief. "Lawyers—they cost so much. But, a friend. I come also."

"I'd rather you didn't," said Jason. "For many reasons."

Saul was puzzled, but Jason did not explain.

The next morning he had his secretary call the office in

Wilkes-Barre, not Scranton, to tell the inspector in charge that Mr. Jason Garrity, the hotelier, wished to talk to him at once. The inspector, he knew, was an Irishman himself; Jason had had occasion to talk to him before, in regard to a Pole he employed as one of the gardeners. A severe man, James Fogarty, and aware of the majesty of government, but "human," as Bernard used to put it. Inspector Fogarty, who remembered Jason, was cordial over the telephone. Jason armed himself with a bottle of the finest Irish whiskey and drove to Wilkes-Barre.

"Top of the morning, Jimmy," said Jason, discreetly handing over the bottle. Mr. Fogarty deftly disposed of it in his desk.

"When you speak Irish," said Mr. Fogarty, who was Irishborn, "it means trouble for me. What is it, then?" He leaned back in his chair. The office was shabby and water-stained from the ancient radiator. Mr. Fogarty's uniform was not fitted; he was a spare man with a grim disillusioned face and red hair like Lionel's. He was fifty years old; his brown eyes were sharp and he had a Spanish cast to his features.

Jason cleverly opened the conversation by referring to the inspector in charge of the Scranton office, whom Mr. Fogarty bitterly hated. It seems that Mr. Fogarty's hometown was Scranton, and he had anticipated becoming inspector in charge there. Mr. Fogarty had been assistant inspector and well-liked by his men. "Then, out of nowhere, this Sassenagh appears," Mr. Fogarty never tired of complaining with anger, "from a shitty little burg no one has ever heard of, near International Falls, Minnesota! And he's elected! Over me. Politics! I stood him for a year, then applied for a transfer, and here I am."

After patiently waiting for the story to be retold and making sympathetic sounds, Jason explained Saul Weitzman's plight. Mr. Fogarty listened intently, a light of combat in his eyes. He leaned back in his chair, assumed a judicial expression, and tapped his desk with a pencil.

At last he said, "Well, now it seems this bastard exceeded his authority and doesn't know the latest rulings. Twenty-nine years, you say, your friend lived in this country? He arrived in the days of contract labor, no records were kept then; millions came in. The country was glad of cheap labor. Your friend is being persecuted by that... that son of a bitch just because he's German!"

"I suspected that, Jim."

"Hates Germans as much as he hates the Irish, if possible. His father came from England; stands to reason. Well, then, send your friend in, and I'll process his papers and send them to Philly, and his troubles are over." He reflected. "Any danger of us getting into this war?"

"Yes."

"No doubt?"

"No."

Mr. Fogarty raised an eyebrow. "Love to see old England get a beating, that I would."

Jason carried the good news to Saul, who embraced Jason lavishly. "How much it cost?" When Jason told him "nothing," he was incredulous and eyed Jason suspiciously. "Nothing? A government official—no money?"

"And don't you offer him anything, either. You'll land in jail or be kicked out of the office and denied your papers."

"You're a good boy, Jase, the best. I wish I could be of use to you. Maybe the time will come."

Jason smiled. "Do you have five hundred thousand dollars lying around, Saul?"

"Bad as that, Jase?" Saul was grave.

"Nearly. Never mind. I worry enough."

It was two hours after his return to Belleville that Jason was startled to remember that he had been near Patricia's sanatorium and had never once thought of her.

Americans of German descent watched with consternation, and in extreme cases, terror, as the propaganda generated by many prominent newspapers continued to build. When independent newspapers related alleged atrocities by the French and British also, they were attacked viciously by their more powerful competition.

Despite pleas from the German embassy that Americans refrain from traveling to the war theaters, pointing out that American ships carried contraband for the "Allies" as well as excited American passengers, travel persisted. If any papers carried an item to this effect, the others shouted "FREEDOM OF THE SEAS THREATENED BY GERMANY!" Or they denied that American ships carried contraband.

British war songs became extremely popular, particularly in the Eastern cities, and were sung everywhere to applause and emotional tears. Moving-picture studios and theaters competed with each other to rush out horrendous productions showing a German conquest of America. The films depicted the raping of little girls, the bombing of American churches, massacres in the streets, and the destruction of cities.

But despite the propaganda, millions of American mothers of sons sang, "I didn't raise my boy to be a soldier!" Millions of sober Americans, informed and intelligent men, protested against American violations of neutrality, and formed peace societies. Rural America, led by Midwestern newspapers, declared that the sinking of the *Lusitania* was not a cause for military action. It was the Northeastern portion of the country that clamored for war as the conspiracy against humanity gained momentum.

Jason joined Bulwark America in 1916, one of the myriad peace societies springing up about the country. Events in Europe were no longer a matter of smiling excitement but of terrified speculation and suspicion that America was being manipulated into joining a conflict it did not want. Many Americans felt themselves victims of forces which were inimical to their freedom, and were frightened despite governmental protests that America would remain neutral. But the more Washington became vehement, the more people became alarmed.

Jason not only joined Bulwark America but also became its chief officer in the part of Pennsylvania in which he lived. Daniel Dugan said, "You are a fool. Do you think a peace society can have any influence at all? Didn't you believe your own words and the words of your grandfather?"

"It's a matter of principle," Jason said.

Daniel laughed. "More people have died for a 'principle' than in the wars. Don't be an idiot. Protect yourself." He added, "I've booked passage on a ship to England to rescue my investments in London." When Jason mentioned the possible danger, Daniel just smiled cynically. "When did an Irishman consider danger?"

"You've just advised me to 'survive' and be safe. A contradiction of your own advice. What does Molly say?"

Daniel did not reply for several moments, and Jason was made uncomfortable by the long enigmatic stare with which Daniel regarded him. "Molly says it is foolish. Molly is not given to hyperbole. We respect each other's opinions and...lives. We don't interfere with one another." For some inexplicable reason, he looked sad. "Think you can manage in my absence, Jason?"

"You have a good manager. I expect no crises." He was relieved at Daniel's changing the subject.

"Patricia any better?"

"We expect her home for Christmas."

"And Nick?"

"No change, except for the worse. Doherty and Nickie appear to be in control the majority of the time."

Daniel said, "I am worried about Uncle Pat. He's failing rapidly. It's a sorrowful thing, a strong man falling into ruin. He acts so vague at times."

"He's worried about his daughter, though I think she is...cured." Jason did not add that he himself had visited Patricia only twice in a year. She had raved at him, and the hospital doctor had delicately advised Jason that his visits "had better be infrequent" in order to avoid "upsets."

"And Sebastian?"

"He grows more like a priest every year. God forbid!"

"Your brother doesn't visit very often?"

"He sees Joan and Lionel." Jason's voice was reserved. "I avoid him as much as possible. We weren't very friendly as children, and we always fought as adults." He added, "Dan, when do you leave on your damn-fool ship?"

"Next week. England will never be the same after this war. Lloyd George and the other socialists will take care of that. This is their opportunity. And America will not be the same either. I predict she'll enter the war sometime in 1917." He paused, then said, "The investment I have in England is important. I shouldn't have left it as long as I did."

The skeptical Irishman went to confession the day before he left for New York—the first time Father Sweeney had ever seen Daniel take Communion. The priest was moved. He had long suspected that Daniel was unhappy, though he did not know the cause, for Daniel was invariably cheerful and confident.

The priest said, "Take care of yourself, Dan."

"I will." He seemed about to add to this, but then remained silent.

Daniel never returned. His ship was torpedoed near the coast of Ireland, by a U-boat. Its hold was full of explosives. The fire flared like a sun above the black waters before it sank into the December sea.

On a snowy January day a memorial Mass was celebrated for Daniel Dugan by Father Sweeney in St. John the Baptist

Church. Numerous relatives and friends came from Boston and New York. Most of the mourners from Belleville were business acquaintances. Molly was not popular, despite her husband's wealth and her impressive house. The women claimed she was not "friendly or warm"; she belonged to no women's organizations, no clubs. She did not even belong to the Rosary and Altar Society, and she was seldom seen at Mass. The rare times she "socialized," she had "nothing to say of interest." In short, she did not gossip.

"She puts on airs. She thinks she is better than we are, because she married a rich man from Boston. But she is only shanty Irish!" But Molly even as a child was discriminating; fools bored her; she could not bring herself to be falsely cordial to people or pretend interest in them, as could her genial brother. She was not hypocritical, and as a consequence, people did not like her. She talked forthrightly; if she did not favor something, she said so.

But Lionel's and Joan's friends crowded the pews. Joan was considered an "angel and a saint for bearing her painful cross with dignity and pious resignation." Joan was always tactful, and her secret scorn and disdain were hidden beneath her celestial smile. Her physical beauty was taken for beauty of soul. She was patient with Molly, and people approved. She rarely expressed a strong opinion. While Molly had a well-hidden compassion, Joan was cruel and loved no one except her husband and Sebastian. Joan had a reputation for concern and affection. Molly gave great sums to the hospital and the parochial school, and gifts to the priests and numerous other charities, but people did not admire her for this. "She can well afford it." Joan gave meagerly, and was celebrated.

At the memorial Mass, Molly was surrounded by people, yet she gave the impression of being alone. Jason sat beside her, and their clasped hands were hidden by their coats. Only Jason knew that her hand trembled and was very cold. She was not tearful as she seemingly concentrated on the ceremony. "No feeling" was the general consensus. Patrick Mulligan sat on her other side, as if in a stupor. Monsignor Garrity, in his distant parish, sent prayers and assurances that he would include Daniel in special Masses. Jason had requested it, and sent a donation, out of respect. And guilt.

Mrs. Lindon was there, with a contingent of beautiful new nieces, and their decorum was exemplary, as was their rich and subdued clothing. Some knelt, with rosaries in their exquisitely gloved hands. The little church was filled with a profusion of flowers—a gift of Mrs. Lindon. Father Sweeney had accepted them with grace. He was very tolerant these days, and charitable. After all, Mary Magdalen's gift was accepted by our Lord. Father Sweeney could do nothing less.

Chauncey Schofield and his wife and his wife's daughter, Elizabeth, were there. Elizabeth, with her wicked child's beautiful face, had not married, though she had suitors from as far away as New York and Philadelphia. She was an "old maid," and her friends wondered. She was "devoted to her mother," so the story was told. Joan and Elizabeth were great friends.

In spite of the Irish tradition, Molly gave no dinner, as was customary. She returned alone to her silent house and refused visitors. Only there did she give herself up to tearless sorrow. She knew Daniel had loved her deeply; she knew that he had known she had only regard and affection for him. She had not deceived him as to that. Dan, Dan, she thought in her quiet bedroom. If only I had loved you as you loved me!

Condolence cards received no acknowledgment from Molly.

Daniel had left his whole fortune of five million dollars to "my beloved wife," save for some charities in Boston and the purchase of Masses for the repose of his soul.

Molly put her house up for sale, with no explanations to anyone, and when it was sold she moved to New York to a small and luxurious town house on Fifth Avenue. She wrote infrequently to her brother and a few acquaintances. She never wrote to Jason. In time she was forgotten, but never by Jason; she continued to haunt his life with increasing desire and despair. He did not know where she lived; he never inquired.

Patricia had returned home for Christmas with a nurse. She had sunk into a silent immobility that nothing could disturb. She did not come down to meals. She sat in her room, and when her father and children would visit her, she only stared at them dumbly and seemed unaware of their presence. But she had gained weight and was neat, and Patrick was heartened. "My colleen is home, and there she will stay! She's herself again!"

But she returned to her sanatorium near Wilkes-Barre in January 1917, after Daniel's funeral, which she did not attend. Dr. Conners advised her return, and Patrick was devastated and bewildered.

Dr. Conners had said to Jason, "She is far from cured. They keep alcohol from her, and she's physically improved. They tell me she employs her time writing letters, but to whom, they do not know. And sleeping. She cries a lot, but she won't confide in the doctors and nurses or the new psychiatrist. No, she isn't cured. The last days she was home, she was extremely agitated, in spite of being guarded from visitors. Best she return."

"Will she ever be cured?" asked Jason, but with no real interest.

Dr. Conners hesitated. "Not until she gets rid of what bothers her and has bothered her for years. A secret sorrow, as Pat says. But she never impressed me as a deep girl. How deceived one can be!"

Mrs. Lindon said to Chauncey Schofield, "Soon we will move. Confidentially, the bankers are almost agreed to my buying up Jason's loans. Ed Schultz has agreed. I won't touch Patrick for now. He may be Jason's father-in-law, but I hear they're open enemies. Patrick blames Jason for his daughter's condition—I hear."

It was late April 1917.

"Jason hasn't done himself much good with his Bulwark America. The people are all for war with Germany. I admire the propagandists. They've done a good job. Besides, it is certain to cure the depression that's dogged us for years. Anyway, Jason's highly unpopular at the moment. He protested the Preparedness Parades here and in Pittsburgh and Philadelphia." She chuckled, shook her head. "Fools never learn that man proposes and governments decree. Jason actually opposed the proposed draft! He advised ignoring it! He financed a mothers' antiwar meeting in Washington, and he's strapped for money. Patricia's costing him a fortune in that sanatorium of hers."

"The new hotel is practically finished, Clem."

"I don't know how he managed it. He's deeply in debt, though we're solvent. It's opening this summer." She added, "It's nothing personal. I'm fond of Jason. After all, he put me in the way of making huge profits. But money is money. Love never should interfere with it. Love is a rose, but money is a fortress."

She studied Chauncey. "I admire your recent discretion with Elizabeth. Hideaways in Philadelphia and New York and country boardinghouses here. I still offer you my house."

434

Chauncey said, "No. It would be too gross."

She laughed richly. "Elizabeth wouldn't think so! Men! You're all puritans at heart. Women are much more pragmatic."

Chauncey smiled, his most charming smile. The old depraved bitch, he thought. "I agree. Men are romanticists." He put on an expert pretense of admiring Mrs. Lindon, but she was not deceived.

She chuckled again. "Dear Chauncey, I don't like your sex. I never did, ever since I was seduced by an uncle when I was twelve years old. And I never extend hospitality to a girl who likes men. I see it as a weakness which will bring only trouble to the girl and my house. You never knew that about me, did you?"

"I suspected that, dear Clem. I never knew a lady in your profession that did like gentlemen."

Mrs. Lindon mused, while turning her wineglass on the table. Chauncey eyed her uneasily. Suddenly she laughed as if at a colossal joke. She refilled Chauncey's glass and laughed again.

After he had left her house, she thought: Dear Chauncey. I don't have anything against you, but the time is coming that you are expendable. Yes, indeed. Sooner than you expect.

That night Chauncey Schofield said to his wife, Anita, "Darling, I've just had a talk with Clem Lindon. The old bitch is up to something, and that's bad news to us. Wish I'd taken your suggestion months ago—asked the trustee of your late husband's estate to talk to Ed Sunderland of the Belleville Savings Association—"

"To buy up Jason Garrity's paper, you mean? Yes. I thought Gary Winslow might be interested. I did talk to him confidentially, without your knowing, love. After all, I am a woman of substance and still officially a resident of New York." She smiled archly, and Chauncey was unpleasantly reminded that in spite of Anita's love for him and in spite of her extravagantly silly affectations, she was a hard, keen woman.

Gary Winslow was her late husband's trustee and the manager of Anita's money. He did not approve of Chauncey, as bankers did not approve of rich widows remarrying, since the new husband might induce his wife to change banks.

"What did the prig say, Anita?"

"Now, now, dear. Gary is a banker. At that time he was

435

dubious, seeing Jason was head and shoulders in debt to the banks. He advised me not to. But suddenly he seems to have changed his mind. He didn't confide in me about it, but advised me to buy up Jason's paper, and he offered to press Mr. Sunderland about it. He suggested a price that exceeds the Philadelphia offer—I don't know that they were interested. Bankers are so devious—like moles, they work in the night."

"Well, well. What else did the mole have to say?" Chauncey was impatient.

"He advised me, as my friend as well as my banker, to buy Jason's paper. If I'm not interested, his own bank will. What a coincidence! He gave me till next week to make up my mind!"

"And you didn't tell me anything about it. I'm hurt, dear."

Anita laughed and fondled his neck. "I intended to tell you when I made up my mind. After all, I managed before I married you, precious, and I've gotten into the habit. And you have, sometimes, a dreary habit of arguing with me—about my own money—and then a tiresome dispute ensues. Finance is a tedious subject, isn't it?"

Seeing Anita's smile, Chauncey was overcome with dislike. He suddenly knew that he had always disliked her. He said meanly to himself: Money bores you? Clem and you are a pair, madams under the skin!

In the past, Anita had financed some of his more clever schemes—and profited by them—for he was a true entrepreneur. He used his own money for riskier investments, and chortled in triumph when they were successful. Anita was generous enough not to remind him that he had money to finance the more precarious due to her financing of the others. But he suspected her of thinking that. When he was disappointed in a venture, her lawyers in New York came to the rescue, and he lost little money or stayed even. Anita paid their bills. She also gave him a decent allowance, "for you do sometimes make me pots, lover, and your allowance is a bonus."

She owned the house they lived in in Belleville, and three other residences, fully staffed, in addition to other property and investments, and the income from her late husband's estate. Elizabeth would inherit the principal from her father's estate, and at least half from her mother's. Anita often talked as if it were settled. It was not. Elizabeth was not aware of this. She thought her own fortune was secure and only Chauncey's might be threatened, and given a choice between Chauncey and her parents' money, Chauncey would be the loser, much as she was infatuated with him, much as he was the first man she had ever faithfully loved.

Consequently Elizabeth protected Chauncey and was much more discreet than he. A divorce would be disastrous to him. Smug at the "security" she fancied to be her own, she worried for him. She had prevailed on him lately to buy a secluded little cottage a mile from Belleville, where they would meet if they considered that Elizabeth's room was too hazardous.

Chauncey and Elizabeth did not dare to use the cottage overnight. That would have led to questions of Elizabeth's whereabouts. Chauncey himself had plenty of excuses for his absence. He was frequently away overnight visiting clients in Philadelphia, Scranton, Pittsburgh, or New York. Anita's anxiety over her daughter's spinsterhood was becoming acute; she believed Elizabeth to be a virgin. She often confided her anxiety to Chauncey, who was indulgent. "Let the girl alone. She's devoted to you. Beautiful women, as well, know their value. She'll make a choice soon, never you fear."

Chauncey was becoming anxious himself. Anita was eminently healthy. He wished he was ruthless enough to . . . The dark shadow remained in his mind, even though it shocked him to realize it was there. If it had not been for Elizabeth, the shadow would not have existed, and he would have settled for temporary liaisons in other cities, or become a more frequent patron of Mrs. Lindon's house. But Elizabeth was too valuable to him. He loved her and believed the rumors that she would inherit a vast estate.

Tonight he had other things to think of.

"At the risk of boring you, Anita, what is your final decision?"

She laughed with surprise. "To buy up Jason's paper, of course!"

"The sooner the better!" Chauncey was exultant. "I suspect Clem of making a move."

"Mr. Sunderland will be informed tomorrow of my bid. Not a moment later. And Gary will call him. I still don't know why Gary changed his mind on this matter. Lawyers and bankers are so mysterious."

It was late, and Anita smiled beguilingly. "You look tired, dearest. Come to bed."

Chauncey sighed. Elizabeth and he had a rendezvous tonight; it would have to be delayed. After all, he was still elated and felt grateful to his wife.

As they prepared for bed, he asked, "Do you think it could be kept a secret from Clem? And from Jason—for a while?"

Anita yawned luxuriously. "When you have money, lawyers and bankers would be drawn and quartered before they'd reveal your secrets. I'll tell Gary."

"I'd like to see their faces when they know—Clem and Jason!" Chauncey's face changed. It had become vicious.

He did not know Mrs. Lindon knew all about the cottage in the woods. She made it her business to know the secrets of her clients. "You may never know when you will need them."

Jason's paper was not the only one the bank held.

31

It was April 1917 and America was at war. President Wilson had been elected in November 1916 on the slogan "He kept us out of war." In March 1917 he had been inaugurated for another term. Some weeks later he solemnly asked congress for a declaration of war against Germany.

The announcement was greeted with great excitement. There was dancing in the streets, parades, and a wild rush to volunteer. The kaiser was burned in effigy, all Germans, even those born in the United States, were regarded with hostility, and the German language was banned in the schools. Famous actors and actresses from Hollywood and New York began appearing in theaters urging the purchase of Liberty Bonds, and "Over There!" was played constantly on the radio.

The nation had gone mad.

Jason Garrity told large numbers of acquaintances, "All Americans who support this war are either total innocents or guilty traitors. The innocent will die on battlefields 'somewhere in France,' and the guilty will come into their own, in power and triumph."

He was reported to the police as a "subversive." The police in Belleville were mainly of Irish and German descent, and their faces, on reading the reports, were enigmatic. Later, Jason's enemies, frustrated at local police inaction, reported him to senators and congressmen in Washington.

Lionel advised him "to keep your mouth shut." To which Jason had said, "A free country?" and laughed bitterly. "It'll never be free again."

Saul Weitzman said, "I am afraid." Father Sweeney said, "I am afraid."

Jason replied, "The whole goddamn world needs to be afraid."

An insignificant corporal in the Austrian army named Adolf Hitler, a man of little stature but with compelling and hypnotic eyes, began watching world events with interest. A youthful Italian named Benito Mussolini regarded the war with Latin humor and dreamed of the ancient grandeur of

Rome. And one Iosif Vissarionovich Dzhugashvili, a Communist, lately released from Siberia, mysteriously disappeared. His comrades called him Stalin, "man of steel."

These men, as early as 1917, had caught the attention of certain individuals. They had "potential."

Patricia was released from her sanatorium the last of April in the custody of a nurse. She was pronounced "cured, though she will need a little care for a while." She still remained in her bedroom and a converted sitting room next to it and did not come down for her meals. But she displayed a renewed interest in the twins, and she insisted on their presence an hour a day, until she tired of Nicholas' "healthy rowdiness." She would take her medicines with smiling obedience from Nicole, but would frequently burst into tears without provocation, or laugh hilariously at nothing.

Physically she had improved, and she had a small appetite. She did not know, Jason suspected, that America was at war. Friends never visited; they were discouraged by the nurse, under doctor's orders.

Lionel Nolan, who intended to take a drive this mellow May Sunday with Joan, was surprised to receive a call from Jason. Jason's voice was hoarse, almost incoherent, and Lionel had difficulty at first understanding him. "I'm at home. I...I was called at my office. I don't know who to call! Goddammit! It's Bastie....No, no, he isn't hurt. God damn, he isn't dead, I tell you! I wish I were. Don't interrupt. It's hard to talk. I know you're fond of him—I don't have anybody else! Mr. Mulligan's in Philadelphia at the heart clinic...I'm all alone. Patricia...Don't interrupt! It seems that Bastie and the twins were playing with the Crimshaw boy next door. Patricia was sleeping, Doherty was taking a walk with his new lady friend; all but one of the servants had the half-day. Bastie...He told me when I arrived home, Patricia was hysterical. Conners gave her a sedative just now, and she is sleeping."

Lionel was surprised at the acceleration of his heart. He raised his voice and said, "You're not making any sense, Jase. Speak louder and take your time."

Jason took a deep breath. "Bastie told me he wanted to show little Herbert Crimshaw the shotgun I bought him. You know he goes hunting with me. He says he broke the lock of the gun cabinet; he didn't have the key. It...doesn't sound

440

like Bastie—he doesn't like guns. He says he didn't know the gun was loaded—I taught him to unload his gun and clean it after every hunt. It's a mystery. Well, little Herbert was killed, two hours ago."

"Christ!" Lionel shouted.

"The servant called me. Crimshaw had a heart attack; he is in the hospital. The police were called, and homicide detective Waters came out. He took a statement, from me, from Bastie. We're now at police headquarters. The chief of police, Leo Schwarz, your cousin, has gone to Crimshaw's house. Lionel, I didn't know who else to call. You're my friend, Joan's my sister. Help... Bastie." Jason added, groaning, "Nickie—she's stricken dumb. Doesn't say a word; dazed. Bastie was the only child who talked. Nickie took Nick home; he's sleeping."

"The hell with Nick and Nickie!" Lionel yelled in his distraction. "I'm interested only in Bastie! I'm coming down to police headquarters, right away. I'll have to call Joan first. It'll be a shock."

"Yes. Well. Thank you, Lionel. I didn't know anyone else to call—" But Lionel had already hung up.

He found Jason and Sebastian in the waiting room at the police station. The sergeant, behind his desk, was glowering at the man and the boy; at intervals he worked busily with reports. He rose when Lionel entered, and gave him a brief smile. "Hell of a thing, Mr. Nolan. The chief's just arrived; he's in his office going over the reports. Hell of a thing."

"Isn't it, sergeant." Lionel turned to Jason and Sebastian and sat down near them. Jason was haggard and white, his big hands trembling on his knees. His gray eyes were turned inward, as if he was remembering the nightmare scene of blood and anguish he had just left. He had difficulty focusing on Lionel; he stared, as if at a stranger he did not recognize immediately. Sebastian was utterly immobile in his blue blazer and matching short trousers. The boy's brown hair with the reddish lights was disordered, his beautiful grave face drawn. He was not crying. But his very immobility expressed a despair beyond his years. He looked as though he feared to move lest he would lose control and start screaming, and all his strength was directed at the effort to keep silent. His small hands were in his pockets. His agate eyes with the yellowish glints were wide, without expression.

Lionel looked at his son with fierce protection, but he spoke to Jason. "I told Joan. Well...?"

Sebastian blinked and sternly swallowed to hold back tears. Lionel put his freckled hand on the boy's arm and pressed it encouragingly. The small room became hotter, the smell of dust more pervasive. The telephone rang, and the desk sergeant answered it.

"Don't be afraid, Bastie," said Lionel. "Tell me about it."

But the boy was mute. His lips moved; no sound came from them.

"He's in shock," said Jason, and his voice was weak. "As we all are."

Lionel kept himself from saying, "The hell with all of you. Bastie is the only one who counts." The Sunday quiet was disturbed only by an occasional policeman and the muttered conversation of the sergeant talking on the telephone.

"I told you before," said Jason. He glanced at Sebastian and appeared about to speak to him; he made an agitated movement with his hands. "Sebastian, you must—"

"Must what?" asked Lionel, alert. But he was taken aback by the look of terror in the child's eyes, and his defiant expression. "What is it, Bastie?"

The boy shook his head over and over. "I told the truth to Papa. I broke into the gun cabinet; it was locked. I got the gun..." He was unable to go on, but his eyes implored Lionel to believe him.

"It was very bad of you," said Lionel tentatively.

The boy nodded. "Very bad." He shuddered. "I...I didn't intend to...shoot Herbert. He didn't know the gun was loaded."

"Herbert?"

Terror leaped into Sebastian's eyes again. Lionel said, "Did Herbert handle the gun?"

"No!" the boy cried, and immediately after, "Yes, yes! He...handed it back to me."

"Did he, Bastie? Did he? Perhaps you boys struggled with the gun and it went off accidentally?"

"Yes. *No!* I mean, *yes!* Nickie saw it, so did Nick!"

Jason gripped Sebastian's arm and shook him. At this point the police sergeant said, "Mr. Garrity, the chief wants your son in his office. Alone."

Jason stood up. "I'll see the chief. Alone." He gave the sergeant a daunting glance. "The child's been through enough today."

Lionel said, "Was Nickie a witness?"

"She told me...it happened that way," said Jason. "Then she refused to say more."

Sebastian sighed and leaned back in his chair and closed his eyes. He appeared to be overcome and Lionel saw this and frowned intently. He said to Jason, "Leo's not so bad. Humor him."

"Hah," said Jason. He hesitated and looked at Sebastian and patted his shoulder without hope. "Stay with Uncle Lionel. I'll soon be back."

"I'll speak to Leo after you do," said Lionel.

Jason left the room, and the sergeant watched him inimically. He said to Lionel, "Kids. They make all the trouble in the world. I wish I didn't have any." He spoke emphatically.

Lionel smiled. "Tom, you were a kid yourself."

"And I was a little bastard. Wonder the old man didn't beat me to death. I deserved it."

The chief of police, Leo Schwarz, was waiting. Mr. Crimshaw was one of his favorite people, which Jason was definitely not. A short and burly man, he had a sullen and belligerent expression which no doubt came from his necessary dealings with the public. It was also a Sunday, and he had promised his wife to take his five children "off her hands" and to the park. Partly relieved at being denied his paternal duty, he was vexed at being called to his office, which was stuffy and airless and extremely unattractive. Jason had voted to give the chief of the fire department not only a new building but a fine airy office with electric fans and two telephones, and had agreed to outfit his men with tailored uniforms. But he joined those who had voted down doing the same thing for the police department. "Not enough money in the city treasury." Mr. Crimshaw disagreed with the majority opinion and had given the Police Relief Association a handsome sum.

The chief was properly and genuinely horrified at the "murder" of little Herbert Crimshaw. He regarded all killings, no matter how accidental, as "murders," and was justified at least half of the time. He had joined the police force twenty-eight years ago and quickly decided that the public were murderers at heart, "every man jack of them." The years had not proven him wrong.

He entered his office like an avenging executioner, seated himself in his ancient chair, which he managed to make creak exceptionally loudly and caused Jason, in the midst of his distress and horror, to have regrets for being so benign to the fire department at the expense of the police. After all, what was a burning house compared with the death of a little boy?

The chief had not greeted him, and this was ominous. After all, Jason was the son-in-law of Patrick Mulligan, who was a pet of the police department, and Sebastian was Patrick's grandson. The chief bent over his desk and his sparse red hair—he was a first cousin to Lionel Nolan—was matted with sweat and seemed to accuse Jason.

The chief had small, pudgy features that had been cherubic in his youth but were now brutal. He had put on his spectacles and was studying the papers his men had prepared for him. "Goddamn! Christ Almighty! Unbelievable! God Almighty!" he muttered, shaking his head. Occasionally he looked at Jason with furious incredulity. Jason felt despair. The chief was a formidable man even when he attempted to appear genial, but when outraged, was truly implacable. His ice-blue eyes never smiled even at his wife, and his men said they were "snake eyes." He had an abhorrence of lawbreakers, however mild the offense. Confronted with violence, he could be truly forbidding, like a primitive force, merciless and fearful. Judges cowered before him, and even hardened criminals soon became terrified in his presence. Appearing occasionally in the courtroom, he frequently reduced lawyers for the defense to tears. He was not eloquent, but his mere presence inspired dread.

Patrick heartily admired him, and so had Jason—until now.

The chief had finished the reports, and he threw himself back in his chair and surveyed Jason with loathing. "Where's the little bastard?" he growled.

"Outside. I left him with his uncle, Lionel Nolan." Jason said huskily, "Leo—"

The chief stopped him by lifting a meaty and inexorable hand. "Chief Schwarz, if you please." He paused. "Do you realize the horror of this tragedy, Mr. Garrity?"

"More than you do, chief." Jason's Irish temper was rising. "And I'll thank you not to call him a 'bastard.' He's my legitimate son."

The chief ignored that. "Where's your lawyer?"

"In New York, at the moment."

"Bring the little . . . your son in here."

"He's only nine years old."

"Old enough to commit murder."

"It's not murder."

"What do you call it?"

"It was an accident."

The chief eyed Jason with renewed hatred. "He confessed, didn't he? He was acquainted with firearms, wasn't he? He didn't think the gun was a toy, or a peashooter? He's gone hunting with you for years, hasn't he?" The chief banged his fist on the reports and leaned toward Jason over the desk. "You're pleading this was just a boyish prank?" The chief breathed strenuously. "The fact remains that a little boy was killed!"

"Yes." The nightmare was vivid before Jason. "I saw him."

"So did I. And his parents." The chief shook his head. "The mother collapsed."

"Yes. I wish to God that I had died. Instead."

The chief suddenly grinned with malevolence. "Before this over, you'll be wishing it regularly. Well, bring your son in."

"He's answered all the questions before."

"Send him in, I tell you!"

Jason stood up. All at once the cruelty of fate seemed to culminate in the events of this tragic day. His very helplessness increased his rage. His face swelled, and the veins in his temples beat visibly. He clenched his raised fists. Looking at him, the chief was alarmed, and he fumbled at his revolver in its holster. "Eh!" he said.

But Jason no longer saw or heard him. He turned and left the office. Outside the door, he leaned against the wall, breathing with difficulty. He closed his eyes. There was a huge pain in his chest. "God, God, God," he repeated. Several policemen eyed him curiously and exchanged glances. It was several minutes before Jason could trust his legs to carry him to the waiting room.

At the sight of his face, Lionel involuntarily jumped up, releasing Sebastian's hand. "Jase!"

Sebastian was mutely white. Only his hair and eyes held color; he stared at Jason, and his mouth trembled. Jason made a disordered gesture, tried to speak, and failed. Lionel came to him, frightened.

Jason said in a hoarse whisper, "The son of a bitch...the son of a bitch...I've known him all my life, the bastard, the..." He became aware of Sebastian and broke off. "He...wants Bastie, alone."

Lionel said, "I'll go with him." He put his hand on Jason's shoulder. "After all, Leo's my cousin."

445

"The swine," said Jason. "The goddamn swine. I...I'd like to kill him, sure and I would." Jason was gasping. With an anguished cry Sebastian seized Jason's hand and looked up at him with the first tears of this terrible day. "Papa, Papa! Don't look so...Papa!"

Jason clutched the child's arm. "Bastie, listen. You'll have to tell the truth, the truth."

Lionel became rigid. "What truth? Bastie told it, didn't he?"

Jason clutched the boy harder. "The truth. No matter who's hurt. Goddammit! The truth!"

Lionel whistled softly, and his fox's face became shrewd. "The truth. What's the truth, Jason?" His light voice was insidious and sly.

Sebastian was frantic. "I told the truth, Papa!"

"You lie, Bastie. As you've lied before. This time..."

Lionel turned to the child and forcibly removed him from Jason's grasp. He squatted before Sebastian in one flexible movement.

The boy stared into the dilated eyes of his real father. But he spoke to Jason. "I told the truth, Papa! It...it was an accident! I got the gun to show Herbert—I didn't know it was loaded..." Sebastian shook uncontrollably, but he could not evade Lionel's glare.

Jason reached out and slapped the child heavily across the cheek. Sebastian reeled and would have fallen if not for Lionel's grip on his arm.

Lionel sprang up, and his freckles jumped out on his suddenly pallid face. "Hit my...my nephew again and you'll answer to me!"

"He's got to tell the truth! That pig in there is out to send him to jail." Jason turned to the boy. "I'm sorry, Bastie. But you've got to tell the truth. It was Nick, wasn't it?" He was full of shock and sorrow.

"Mama! Nick!" Sebastian was nearly out of his mind with fear. "They'll die!"

So, thought Lionel. He actually smiled. Sebastian threw his arms around Jason's waist. He lifted a frenzied face, and his eyes were filled with despair. The vehement suffering in his face caused Lionel to glance aside, moved almost intolerably. Lionel thought: My son is protecting that drunken bitch and her idiot son. He said, "Jase. I'll go with Bastie to Leo. Jase? It'll be all right. Jase?"

But Jason, with tears in his eyes, stooped to give Sebastian a kiss. He had never struck the child before. "I'm sorry, Bastie," he said in a broken voice. "Go with Uncle Lionel."

He watched the child walking to the door. Sebastian was gulping sobs and Jason closed his eyes and collapsed into a chair. Lionel, graceful and confident as always, uttered soothing words to the boy, and Jason heard them with gratitude and also a feeling of loss. After a while numbness spread over his exhausted emotions.

Lionel entered the chief's office wearing an easy smile. "Hello, Noddie," he said affectionately, using the nickname of his youth, for all the years the chief was senior to him.

"Don't call me 'Noddie' around here," the chief grunted. "I have trouble enough keeping my men in line. Why did you come in, anyway? I want to see the little bastard alone. Well. Have a seat, Lionel. And don't you interfere, hear me?"

"Have a cigar. Mulligan's best. You can't afford them with five kids, on your salary." Lionel struck a match on the sole of his shoe and lighted the cigar the chief had ungraciously accepted.

"No call for you to be here, Lionel. You're only uncle by marriage to the little murderer. How's Joan, by the way?"

"Beautiful as ever."

"My wife, Dolores, will be sorry to hear that," and the chief smiled sourly. "She thinks beauty is sinful, and prides herself on not being so 'cursed.' " He chuckled. Then he glanced at Sebastian, who was standing by Lionel's side. "Proud of yourself, using your father's shotgun?"

"Now, now, Leo," said Lionel. "That's in all the reports you have on your desk." He turned to Sebastian, who was now leaning against him, and he squeezed the boy's hand reassuringly. Sebastian hid his face on Lionel's shoulder and heaved with silent sobs. Lionel put his arm about him. The chief arched his brows. "Didn't know you had it in you, Lionel! For a brat that isn't blood relation! Oh, I know Joan's dippy over him, though I never understood why. She's not crazy about his father, and she hates his mother. People talk. His father! He's not got a friend in this town, except you and old Mulligan, and I heard Mulligan's not so friendly anymore." He puffed on the cigar. "And to hear the gossip, you're not, either."

"Talk," said Lionel. "You're an old gossip, Leo. Jase and I have been friends since we were kids. And speaking of friends, I've heard priests say that two thousand years ago

Christ had no friends, except his blessed Mother. The penalty for being good."

"No call for being blasphemous, Lionel."

"But Jase is good." Lionel made a wry mouth, as if he had tasted something nasty. "And a good man deserves kicking for his asininity, which is what he usually gets. I'm not 'good,' and that's why I have tons of friends, eager to do me favors. There's nothing offends sensible men like a righteous man. Offends their sense of proportion. It's irrational, that's what it is."

"Sure and Garrity's irrational! Look what he did to me!"

Lionel smiled. "Think of what I did for you, Noddie. Helped you get where you wanted."

The chief shifted his bulk in the chair. He growled, "Not that I'm ungrateful, Lionel. But a little kid lies murdered. It's at least manslaughter in the first degree. The district attorney is on his way home. It's out of my hands."

"No, it isn't." Lionel's arm tightened about Sebastian. "It's all in your presentation. You know that."

The chief banged his fist on the desk. He shouted, "And I say the little bastard should be sent to the juvenile reformatory in Philly! And I aim to send him there, after his trial!"

The two men gazed at each other in silence, the chief's face scarlet with rage, and Lionel's grim. Lionel was first to speak. "Mulligan's grandson."

"The hell with Mulligan! He don't even belong to the right party!"

"He's got lots of influential friends."

The chief sneered. "Past tense. I hear talk. On the verge of bankruptcy. Nothing like bankruptcy to set your friends a-running. The hell with Mulligan." He pointed his finger to Lionel. "Take my advice. Have nothing to do with that family."

Lionel got up, and he seated Sebastian in his chair. Then he turned to the chief with a narrow smile. "Take me to the washroom, Leo. I've got something to say to you, privately." He turned to Sebastian, who was freshly terrified, and said gently, "Don't worry, Bastie. Nothing's going to hurt you."

"Don't leave me, Uncle Lionel!" The boy cried.

"Just for a minute. To wash my hands."

Sebastian cowered in his chair. "Uncle Lionel..." He clutched Lionel's hand. "Nick...Mama..." His tearstained face held stark terror, and Lionel winced.

"Don't worry," Lionel repeated. He patted the boy's shoulder. "Be a man. And wait for me."

The chief grumbled, "Nothing's going to change my mind. You're my cousin, Lionel, and I feel real kindly toward you, and what you've done for me, but what's this brat to you?"

The men went to the washroom, the chief expostulating all the way. He repeated, "Nothing'll change my mind." The washroom was fortunately empty, and the chief closed the door. "Now, then," he said truculently.

Lionel dipped his index finger in water and rubbed it on the soap bar. The chief watched with curiosity. Lionel wrote on the mirror, "He's my son." And washed it off immediately.

The chief gaped. Stunned, he turned to Lionel. "Jesus!"

"True." Lionel wiped his hands on the soiled roller towel. "Your own second cousin, Noddie. Your own flesh and blood."

"Jesus," whispered the chief, again. After a pause he grinned. "You and that drunken Mulligan bitch! Thought you had better taste. She snubbed my wife." Leo shook his head. "Does Garrity know?"

"No."

The chief howled with laughter and slapped his knees. "The eyes and hair the brat has! Suddenly minds me of Molly! Lovely colleen, nice to my own children, Dolores too. They're great friends. Well, well."

"And Molly's late husband, Dan Dugan. You owed a lot to him, Noddie."

The chief sobered. Then he held out his hand to Lionel. "Done," he said. "Get the...my cousin out of here."

"And not a word?"

"What! Against my own kin?" He shook his head. "What a joke on Garrity!"

Lionel and Sebastian returned to Jason, and the boy ran to Jason and hugged him. "He let me go, Papa!" Jason lifted him in his arms, but he looked at Lionel with disbelief.

Lionel nodded, "I talked sense to Leo. He's not all bad."

"Bastie told him the truth?"

"He didn't even question him."

Jason looked steadfastly at Lionel and was silent. Then he said, "There's something here that I don't understand."

Lionel spread out his hands. "Leo and I are cousins. It's as simple as that."

"Nothing's 'simple' where you are concerned," said Jason. Then he smiled in passionate relief. He held out his hand. "Thank you, Lionel, thank you. That's all I can say."

449

Lionel found Joan at home in a state of agitation unusual for a young woman famous for her aplomb and self-control. Lionel had rarely seen her upset. She despised hysterics in other women, particularly if they were indulged in before men, and she controlled herself now enough to say, "Tell me all about it." If her voice trembled, it was only slightly. Her hands, though, were clasped tensely together on her blue velvet lap.

Lionel told his wife in detail, his hand on her knee. She asked him no questions, did not interrupt. Her eyes never left his face; they were enormous, filled with a shining blue light. At last, when he was finished, she closed those eyes briefly as though their concentration had exhausted her.

Lionel made one of his eloquent gestures. "So," he said, "Bastie was nearly sent away in place of the loony. To spare Patricia and Nick! We can't let Bastie live there any longer. The tutor threatens to leave, and Bastie hasn't been sleeping lately as it is; he's always on the alert because of his brother. His health is suffering."

"And our son exists under the stigma of having killed a little boy. A lifelong stigma!"

"I offered to take Bastie in our own house, but Jase was adamant. People would talk. So I suggested St. Mary Amelia's School; it's just five miles away, and he can come here weekends and holidays and we can drive out to see him. Better than that house! I persuaded Jase, and he sounded relieved. Bastie is his favorite child."

"Our child."

Lionel bent forward and kissed her. "Our child. Frankly, I'm relieved, too. We'll see Bastie more often than we do now. As for the stigma—people forget. It will be listed as an accident."

"And this is not the first time he's taken the blame for one of these accidents. I wish Patricia was dead. Dead!" Joan's quiet voice rose in passion.

"I do, too. She's a disaster. To her father, husband, children, to herself. And she contrives to get everything she wants."

In her distress Joan cried, "Including you!"

Lionel's face became ugly. "She never had me. I used her." He stood up and paced the room, and Joan watched him, contrite. "I'm sorry," she said. "Sometimes I can't stand thinking of it. I never told you. But Bastie is the result; and that comforts me."

Although Lionel had rarely experienced compassion, the emotion suddenly washed over him. He knelt down beside his wife's chair. Usually fluent with words, he was speechless. After a moment she embraced him tearfully. "Things will work out for the best," he said. "Hush, darling. We'll have a drink to Bastie's liberation, and it really is liberation."

"He's devoted to Nicole."

"And she'll see him often, I promise you. She's a sensible child."

"And I pity her, in that house with that mother! No wonder she acts like an old woman, poor thing." Joan was sincere. "Things don't 'work out for the best.' I'm surprised at you, darling! Mr. Pollyanna."

They laughed for the first time.

When he recovered, Mr. Percy Crimshaw sued Jason for half a million dollars for the death of his little son, Herbert.

32

Jason's lawyer was a young breezy man named Henry
McWilliams, exigent, expensive, cynical, who made light of
problems, including even murder. He was practical and ruthless, and dismissed emotions as irrelevant and muddying. He
believed in facts, law, more or less, and loathed hysterics and
personalities and "extenuating circumstances," except where
they concerned a client. He was a consummate actor, which
no one suspected, for his demeanor was open and frank; he
was polite even if he faced hostility and derision. His appearance was fresh, boyish, and ingenuous; he deceived even
old experienced judges and opponents. He was hurt when a
client's or witness's testimony was received with skepticism;
he would imply by his aspect and lowered head that he was
deeply wounded. "What?" he appeared to be saying. "Can you
possibly infer that I would take any case that is not bona fide
and above reproach? I am distressed beyond words." He had
a triangular smile, with excellent teeth.

In consultation with a client, however, he used no pretense
of sympathy or belief. "Clarity, clarity, and in as few words
as possible. I have no time to waste, and I presume you have
no time, either." The smile was not in evidence as he briskly
named a costly retainer. He was a rogue, as were all lawyers,
disillusioned, merciless, and very successful. He rarely lost
a case. Daniel Dugan had recommended him. He had an office
in Belleville, but his main office was in Philadelphia, where
he had four partners, older than he. He was only forty.

He appreciated Jason at once as a client, for Jason related
all facts without discursive interpolations of emotion, without
incoherences, without visible agitation, and with control.
Henry took notes and approved of Jason. When Jason had
finished, Henry leaned back in his office chair and gave rapid
and intent thought to Jason's story.

"First of all, no interruptions, please. I agree that Sebastian's story should at once be refuted. I agree he should not
appear as a witness. If we had women as jurors, which we do
not, my advice would be different. Women are sentimental
rather than just, and a kid melts their hearts. Your daughter
should not appear as a witness, either. We will stick to the

bare facts. You will relate Nicholas' condition. I want the neurologists and the psychiatrist who examined him to testify to your younger son's affliction. But above all, they should admit—and I'll see that they do—that they advised keeping the boy at home. Which you did, following their informed advice.

"You will testify that you followed their opinions and advice, and in addition, you employed a male tutor who has dealt with other such children. You have also employed, recently, a male nurse. I hope the prosecutor will not insist on the time element; I'll do what I can to head him off. You will testify that Nicholas is now entered into a private institution in Philadelphia, which treats those of his affliction—"

Jason interrupted. "What private institution? I never thought—"

"You will. I'll name you one, and no time should be lost before he enters it. Immediately." The cold hazel eyes were not smiling. "You will testify as to Sebastian's innocence, and relate incidents when he took the blame for your younger son's violence, to spare his mother and brother. His mother in particular, she being a very sensitive and fragile personality. I will try to get jurors that have mothers or wives or daughters like her. You will display grief as to her suffering. She is, at present, confined in a private hospital where she was sent, overwhelmed by nervous prostration due to the recent tragedy and shock."

"She was confined before that, Hank."

Mr. McWilliams dismissed this with a wave of his hand. "No need to mention that. As we have changed venue to Philadelphia because of extreme local bias, no one will know Mrs. Garrity was previously confined, unless you blurt out the information. If it comes out, however, you will say—and it appears to be the truth—that her son's condition preyed on her mind for years. If it comes out that alcoholism is her problem, and the institution staff is questioned, which is unlikely, we will press them to testify that Mrs. Garrity's...disease was brought on by Nicholas' condition. 'In their informed opinion.' After all, they wouldn't try to antagonize a patient whose husband lavishly pays the fees.

"We will get your father-in-law to testify as to Nicholas' actions in the past, and his advice to you that your son be institutionalized, adding that you preferred to follow expert opinion. Mr. Mulligan will testify that Sebastian took the blame of his brother's violent behavior on numerous occasions

453

to spare his mother. Mr. Doherty will be a witness to Nicholas' violent behavior, too, and the housekeeper, and the male nurse."

"But we have no actual witnesses to the tragedy except Nickie and Bastie—"

"True. But there are witnesses to Sebastian's intelligent and exemplary conduct, plus Mr. Doherty's testimony, the servants' testimony, and that of his new teachers in St. Amelia's School. His uncle—Lionel Nolan—who's well-thought-of in Belleville and Philadelphia, is eager to testify in Sebastian's behalf. Lionel can imply...er, that Sebastian... hinted to him that Nicholas fired the gun, and was responsible for previous destructions—"

"It's a lie. Sebastian would not hint even to me, his father. And Lionel would not lie under oath."

The lawyer smiled. "You'd be surprised at the information witnesses can recall when under oath. Perfectly amazing. And I know Mrs. Nolan will testify also. She is a great beauty; I hear she is very saintly, too. The jurors will be extremely moved, especially if she cries."

"I never saw Joan cry, not even when we were children," said Jason bitterly.

"She'll cry. I guarantee that."

Jason sighed wearily. "I haven't a half-million dollars! I haven't even a million cents! Mortgages, debts, taxes, Patricia's expenses, Nicholas' expenses...And Mr. Mulligan is plagued the same. We're overextended. And now the war, with increased taxes. And interest! I'm broke."

Mr. McWilliams was not one to waste sympathy on clients' financial troubles. He knew his worth; he fingered the check Jason had given him as a retainer. "It'll cost you money, Jason, even when you win the case. After all, the plaintiff's son was killed—by your own son, even if he is not legally culpable. I hope to get away with fifty thousand dollars, to the plaintiff, in the verdict. Plus my fee, of course."

Jason smiled ruefully and thought about taking out another loan. "Even when you win, you are a loser," he said.

Mr. McWilliams shrugged lightly and said, "That's life, Jason. You can't win."

"Only lawyers and bankers can."

Mr. McWilliams laughed in appreciation. "One last bit of advice to you, Jason. Don't give any more speeches against the war before the trial. You are notorious even in Philadelphia and I suspect even in Washington."

"What can a man of principle do?"

Mr. McWilliams laughed again and rose. "Cut his throat."

Molly Dugan had no interest in the war, which disgusted her. Daniel had told her too much. She avoided newspapers, speeches, parades, and the public excitement which had made New York delirious. She traveled to quiet places and read books and took walks in the country, to escape. She spent prolonged periods in the Amish country; she heard no talk of war there. The Amish people lived in peace, with no newspapers or magazines and no marches. It was a world apart, tranquil, engaged in the earth, and God, the eternal verities.

She was not happy, and did not forget. When thoughts of Jason became too unbearable, she moved, always in flight. She was too sensible to feel guilt over Jason. After all, she had been honest before she married Daniel; she said she did not love him but had loved Jason all her life. She was fond of Daniel, and grateful to him, she said. But that was all. He loved her, so he married her. It was not her fault that she found it impossible to forget Jason; she had made Daniel an excellent wife, solicitous and affectionate and considerate. It was not her fault that after a while he found this not enough, and she grieved. She wished that she had been able to love him, but she did not feel guilty. That was for sentimental people who enjoyed being punished for what they could not help. Wallowing in self-pity, Molly thought of them, with scorn. Feeling virtuous for their masochism! Molly thought of Spinoza's axiom, that to feel guilty for one's acts is to be twice guilty. The subtlety did not escape her.

But she had not confessed to that joyous day by the river. It would have hurt Daniel unforgivably, and he did not deserve that for loving her.

She came back to New York after Labor Day. The tumultuous city wearied her, and she found refuge in long walks in Central Park, alone. She had few friends; in fact, only acquaintances. The dislocations of public entertainment disconcerted and annoyed her. She had been looking forward to the Ring Cycle, only to learn the tenor—a German—was no longer employed, his contract canceled. What had Richard Wagner to do with this present war?

A particular New York newspaper, fervid and passionate, called for the internment of all Germans, whether American- or foreign-born, as "potential traitors." But there was this impediment: millions of Americans were of German extraction; hundreds of thousands had lived here before the War Between the States. Thousands belonged to the Sons of the American Revolution! And hundreds of thousands had fled Bismarck and his socialism. It was hard to hate them—but the government in Washington tried, particularly Colonel House, who was also covertly interested in Russia and the secret information about Communist unrest, which never was printed in American newspapers. They were not informed.

President Wilson was not informed, either. The idealist could only think of a "league of nations" which should abolish war forever and bring the world to a millennium of peace and brotherhood and universal love—after this "holy conflict," of course. He dreamed of a world government, too, ignoring the fact of proud human diversity and resplendent different cultures. He was not aware of Moses' warning, that nations should not intrude on other nations, races, religions, or customs. Uniformity, he believed, led to love. "Difference" led to war. His slogan, "Self-determination of small nations," would come later, when he was close to death.

It was shortly after July 4 that Molly received one of Lionel's infrequent letters. It was unusually thick, and when Molly opened it, a mass of newspaper clippings fell out. She read the letter and the clippings with extreme consternation.

"Hotelier's insane son absolved in accidental shooting of neighbor's child in Belleville! Crimshaw consented to jurors' verdict of fifty thousand dollars as recompense for death of little boy! Defendant, Mr. Jason A. Garrity, who pleaded insolvency, expressed profound sympathy for the bereaved family but was spurned by the dead child's father.... It is rumored that Mr. Garrity is in extreme financial trouble. He has been sued by the defendant's lawyer, Mr. McWilliams, who refused to accept his $50,000 fee in time payments."

A period of intense thought ensued for Molly. Then she telephoned her banks in Belleville, Philadelphia, and New York. She did not telephone her brother. She set her beautiful lips resolutely, and her eyes were filled with golden fire.

A few days later a New York banker appeared in the office of Henry McWilliams and offered him a certified bank check for sixty thousand dollars, provided he would send a letter to Jason Garrity stating "On reconsidering your fee owed to me, I am presenting a bill for two hundred dollars. The publicity was invaluable to me. Thanks for your patronage. Call upon me if you have any other problems. I will be glad to serve you. Cordially yours..."

"Who?" asked Henry curiously.

"You'll never know," said the banker. "Accept or not."

Henry accepted with avidity. He made out the bill for two hundred dollars to Jason, signed it, sealed and stamped it, and gave it to the banker, who mailed it. Henry thought: Bankers are more clever than lawyers. They're much more closemouthed.

He acquired much respect for Jason, and more respect for his benefactor. He wondered who he was.

Jason telephoned his lawyer in enormous relief. "Thank you, Hank, thank you! You've saved my life! Two hundred dollars, your bill! I'll pay the rest, that I will, in time."

Mr. McWilliams was tempted. But that friend of Jason's— maybe he would be valuable in the future. "No, Jason," said Henry. "Paid in full. God bless you."

He felt very magnanimous.

Belleville, which did not like Jason, had meanly rejoiced over his troubles with his family, and his rumored financial predicament, and above all, over the tragedy of little Herbert Crimshaw, while pretending to stunned horror. Patricia, formerly ridiculed, was the object of hypocritical sympathy.

The city was disappointed at the verdict in Philadelphia. ("All politics," it was said.) Nor was it much appeased when "the loony" was sent away "to a prison school," which was false, of course, and Sebastian was enrolled in a school "far away." It was said that St. Amelia's was a "correctional institution."

33

Anita Schofield was in hysteria when her husband returned from Philadelphia, and he was aghast at the unusual sight.

Elizabeth was there, helplessly pleading with her mother, and the first thing that Chauncey thought, with a terrified heart, was that Anita "knew." Elizabeth, comprehending his terror, silently shook her head and winked. But her large blue eyes were concerned, her smooth face worried, for all her deliberate composure. She wore a white linen dress that managed to remain unwrinkled in spite of the humid day and the clutching of her mother's frantic hands. The pretty drawing room was airless, and too bright with sun; Elizabeth's pale hair shone in it like silver gilt, polished and glossy in its coils.

Elizabeth said in her charming voice, when her mother had subsided in her chair, "Chauncey, it seems that when Mother went to the bank to buy up Mr. Garrity's paper, Mr. Sunderland informed her 'someone' had already done it. Yesterday. Gary Winslow confirmed it. He and Mr. Sunderland protest they don't know who, but we think they are lying."

"God," said Chauncey. He was sick. "Clem!"

"No," said Elizabeth. "She accused Mother; such language. I hope Central was not listening in. Then she came over personally. Vulgar thing. I thought she was refined—at least she pretends she is." Elizabeth put her hand to her mouth to suppress an involuntary laugh. The young woman had a sense of humor. "Such a scene. I thought they would come to blows; the servants were crowding to the door as if they were attending a prizefight."

"I think that the bankers are lying. An anonymous party, eh? I don't believe it."

"Mr. Sunderland also visited Mother, just an hour ago. His agitation seemed genuine. Mr. Winslow called Mother back; he was also agitated. Seemed genuine, too. The sale was made through the New York City Bank, and they refused to name their client. They say it was no one in Pennsylvania; I forced them to give me that much information. Mr. Sunderland was heartbroken, really. He anticipated such a profit. And Mr.

Winslow's chagrin was honest, I think. Banks are not averse to profits."

"That 'someone' gave someone a huge profit! Bankers can't resist. Funny business."

"Clem Lindon doesn't love you anymore, Chauncey. She accused Mother of lending you money to buy up the paper, after she had told you, specifically, that she was interested in it and she was going to buy it herself, and you had seemed pleased. She departed breathing flames and vowing vengeance. Mr. Sunderland swore to her you were not 'guilty' and calmed her down after an hour's visit to her—in tears, he said. But Mrs. Lindon says she isn't convinced. She talked to Gary Winslow too, by telephone, here in this house." Elizabeth cleared her throat delicately. Her blue eyes lifted. "What drama. Too bad you missed it, Chauncey. Worthy of Sarah Bernhardt. Mother and Mrs. Lindon. The windows rattled." Elizabeth implied her entertainment, in spite of her concern for Anita.

"Then all our plans are smashed," said Chauncey miserably. "The Inn-Tavern, Ipswich House, the new hotel, and the thousand acres of land—all gone up in smoke. Ruined." He sat down near his wife, and his green eyes flared inimically, as if she were to blame. "Stop that noise, Anita! Did you talk to anyone in New York, or here, about buying Garrity's paper? Someone who has two million to spare?"

"Good God, no!" Anita shouted. "No one but you and the bankers! I'm not a fool! Elizabeth didn't even know. Only you! If anyone did any talking, it was *you!*"

"You know me better than that. I'll go and see Clem."

"She says," said Elizabeth, her eyes sparkling with amusement, "that if you ever darken her door again, she'll set her dogs on you. Doberman pinschers. She means it, too. She's looking for a scapegoat in spite of the bankers' denials. You're it, Chauncey."

"The woman is mad, the whore is mad!" wailed Anita, seeking her husband's clammy hand contritely.

"I wonder if Garrity knows," said Chauncey.

"He hasn't a friend in the world who possesses two million dollars—or even an enemy, except Mother and this horrible Clem. Mr. Mulligan is in no position to buy out Mr. Garrity," said Elizabeth. "I wonder who that 'someone' is. At any rate, Mr. Garrity is ruined."

"So are we," said Chauncey.

"You weren't invested."

"No. Only anticipating. And that's worse."

Mr. Edward Sunderland was in a dilemma. He knew Gary Winslow personally and he was Anita Schofield's esteemed trustee and banker. He had believed Gary was acting on behalf of Anita when he bought—at a huge profit—Jason's paper. When Gary told him, yesterday, that Jason's paper had been sold to an anonymous buyer through the New York City Bank, he had been shocked. Mr. Sunderland was well aware that that bank could put pressure on Gary's bank; three of its directors were on the board. (Mr. Sunderland kept the secret; after all, bankers do not tell their clients everything.)

Jason now had to be told the situation, for Mr. Sunderland's bank had held considerable of Jason's paper, and the Philadelphia banks also. Mr. Sunderland's duty and responsibility was to inform Jason. He did so, by discreet letter, and immediately afterward found he had to depart on urgent business in Pittsburgh.

"We found it necessary, Jason," he wrote, "to sell your paper to the New York City Bank. You already owed one hundred thousand dollars in interest and were twelve months in arrears. We carried you as a friend, hoping and believing in your ultimate solvency. In the last month, however, we were pressed to show a better cash balance, and we reluctantly sold your paper. Time was of the essence. Only an extreme emergency forced us to do as we did, believe me. I had warned you you were overextended."

Jason, on receiving this letter addressed to his office, found himself unable to move due to shock and stunned disbelief. He felt himself ruined, a beggar. His whole world crashed about him, leaving him on the verge of an abyss with an unseen enemy who was trying to make him fall to his death. He was prostrated, incredulous. Things didn't happen that way! He literally could not move. A whole life's work come to nothing! He was reduced to his boyhood poverty. His shares in Ipswich House and what investments he had owned he had put up as collateral. The unseen enemy could sell him out at a moment's notice, call in his paper, and he was not in a position to redeem it! And he owed interest. Despite the unseasonably hot September day, he was dripping with cold sweat. He saw the house of his childhood and youth vividly, smelled the stenches of the street. It was always winter there, and he felt the cold blasts and saw the black icy nights. He was running, again, to deliver newspapers, and his mother's laundry; his nostrils were filled with the harsh odor of soapsuds. He heard the dolorous dripping of faulty eaves; he was shoveling snow and shivering. His hands were frozen in his thin mittens, his feet numb, his nose wet, his ears aching, his muscles twinging, his chilblains itching and smarting. The bell of the church tolled.

"Oh, God," he said aloud. And then a strange deep voice seemed to echo in his ears, a harsh derisive voice: "There is no God." There was a sound of inhuman laughter.

Jason put his hands over his face and wept.

Worse than anything he had experienced was a sense of stupendous loss. He felt absolutely alone, desolate, abandoned. He was a child, and his father had deserted him, never to return. He was driven to a wilderness, silent and utterly arctic, where no life existed and his was the only beating heart, and no sun arose over windy spaces on the edge of black soundless seas. He thought vaguely: I am in hell, isolated from God.

It seemed to him that the same inhuman laughter assailed him again, coming from enormous distances, from the end of the world. And the emptiness alone had meaning, and the rest was delusion.

"Curse God and die!" the voice said in a wind like a hurricane.

Jason felt that he was literally dying; his eyes held no vision and his body was powerless. He felt that he had left his flesh and was floating in a sightless void, and the void was in him as well as without. There were drums beating somewhere, a roar that curiously contained a dread presence, a presence frightful beyond imagining, tremendous and puissant, beyond human minds to comprehend, merciless, grandly intelligent and all-knowing, immortal, and riding storms and holocausts.

Jason experienced a terror he had never known before, a terror of ultimate oblivion, a terror not born of flesh but of the soul. For he found himself succumbing to evil.

It was fear that saved him—a fear of what, he did not know. He came to himself, dazed, paralyzed, but in touch with reality in some measure. The old familiar walls were around him, the pictures, the rug, the chairs, the files, and the windows which opened upon a placid sun. There was a ringing of a telephone somewhere, the sound of footsteps, a laugh, a voice, the smell of grass and trees, a warmth, a breeze, the hum of an elevator. Dear and normal sounds! Jason was rescued—he sensed that; but from what he was rescued was hidden from him. I had a nightmare, he thought.

His telephone rang, and he reached out to it, dimly amazed that he had recovered the dominance of his hand.

A cultured masculine voice said, "Mr. Jason Garrity? Good afternoon, sir. My name is Manley Morrison, president of the New York City Bank.... Are you there, sir?... Good, I thought we were disconnected by Central.

"Mr. Garrity, I know you heard the news, that my bank had bought your paper, for a sum in the neighborhood of two million dollars. Hello? Yes. We have a bad connection, I am afraid. My bank sold your paper to a client, an anonymous client whose name I fear we cannot divulge. You'll know the person in time.

"I will write you a letter today, giving all details. You will pay the interest on the paper—no increase in interest, hah—in care of this bank. I will convey the money to the proper person—What?... Does the person intend to call in the paper immediately? I regret I do not know. It is out of our hands, sorry.... Why did we sell your paper? Why, sir, the person wanted it specifically, and I do not know why."

The enemy, the enemy, thought Jason. Who? Chauncey Schofield with his wife's money? Probably. Curse him. He's won at last.

His hand shook as he called Lionel to summon him to his office. He closed his eyes in exhaustion. He did not, in his extremity, notice that Lionel's face was grim and drawn and that his freckles were like a ginger snow over his face. "Sit down, Lionel. I have something to tell you. Bad news."

"I know it all," said Lionel. "Well, talk away. I'm ruined, too."

He listened to what Jason told him. Jason's voice was weak but steadfast, and his gray eyes never left Lionel's face, condemning. He talked for a long time, and Lionel stared fixedly at him, not moving, expressionless.

"So, it is probably your friend Schofield who did this to me, with his wife's money. You are involved with him. You are in the plot."

"No," said Lionel. He lit a cigarette and screwed his face up, and Jason noticed for the first time his appearance of shock. Lionel's fingers trembled.

"Don't ask where I heard—I won't tell you, Jase. I heard—

that's all. Clem Lindon and Chauncey—damn their souls—tried to buy up your paper, each of them separately. It was already sold." Lionel permitted himself a fiendish smile. "They're at each other's throats." Lionel paused. "Chauncey's satisfied with my own paper, for what it's worth, and it isn't worth much. At least he says he is. We're both in the same boat, Jase."

Jason sat up. "I don't believe it!"

Lionel shrugged. "Believe it. I'm going to sell Joan's jewels to save my paper. They won't cover it, and Sunderland said he 'can't' renew my loan."

Jason's eyes bulged. Suddenly he burst out into wild laughter, and tears ran down his face and he rocked himself in his chair, slapping his arms.

"I'm glad you think it's funny," said Lionel. "Chauncey's out for revenge, and I'm handy. I did nothing to him—"

"You were his friend!" Jason's voice was hoarse with his Hogarthian mirth. "Hoist with your own petard!"

Lionel was still. "What do you mean by that?"

"My instinct tells me you were both out to ruin me." Jason's gray eyes glittered. "You, married to my sister!" And now his eyes were deadly and piercing and filled with hate. "You—my friend! I wouldn't save you if I had a million dollars, Lionel. I would see you starve. And I forbid you to see Bastie anymore, and forbid Joan, too, and he's not to visit you. I have means to enforce that."

When he was alone, Jason felt bereft and full of sadness. Lionel was dead to him, irrevocably dead—his oldest friend.

For several minutes he forgot to think of his own plight. Pictures of the young Lionel all about him, whistling, laughing, carefree no matter the circumstance, meeting Jason at the snowy dawn, helping him to deliver papers, sharing his meager lunch, singing.

34

Saul Weitzman's shop was burned down on October 3, 1917; it was arson. "Dirty Kraut!" a placard said. Saul contemplated the black ruins and crimson embers, with Jason, and wept silent tears. His landlord gave him notice to vacate his little cottage immediately. Jason offered him shelter in his own house; Saul had only a black cardboard suitcase. Saul gave his treasured plates and silver and furniture and Venetian glass to the widow who had been dispossessed from the rooms over the shop. He also gave her all he had in the bank.

"You need it and I do not," he said. He had withered and seemed smaller, an ancient man, unusually silent these days. He sat with Patrick, who could get up from his bed only a few hours a day now, and in silence they communicated, men centuries old. Saul gave Patrick his medicine, and they wept together, feeling the weight not only of years but also of affliction.

The house was heavily quiet now. Of the children, only Nicole remained, and she would wander into Patrick's room and sit down near Saul—a childish crone among gnomes. Saul had the whimsical thought that she was older than they, aeons older. She seemed to brood over millennia reflectively and uncomplainingly, and was accepting and of unearthly patience. She dined with her father, and he found the small girl's company infinitely comforting, though she talked little. A maternal presence, he thought, and was moved profoundly.

She talked little of her brothers and less of her mother, and when she did it was as if they were away on a holiday. She talked of Fatima, of the miracle of the sun, as if it were expected. She talked about the Blessed Mother's prophecies, prophecies of doom to the world, and prophecies of Russia— "Russia will spread her errors all over the world with dread results, and upheavals involving all mankind."

Jason listened indulgently. "Superstition. Nickie, Russia is engaged in a desperate struggle in the war, an ally, under the czar. What 'errors' can she spread? Her people are starving and dying on battlefields. Russia is the weakest of our allies."

Nicole replied seriously, "I believe the Blessed Mother."

"Do you believe, Nickie, in the miracle of the sun, dancing?"

"Yes, I do, Papa. Ten thousand people were there."

"Optical illusion. Do you understand what the newspapers say?"

"I am not a child, Papa."

No, you are not, my darling, Jason thought. He said, "Russia! Impotent. We might as well talk about a 'banana republic,' as Teddy Roosevelt calls it, as about Russia. Just about as powerful. And as remote, and as influential. Exiled socialists, and stupefied peasants, poor souls."

"But I believe the Blessed Mother, Papa. Satan uses what comes in hand." Nicole spoke positively. "Satan is the prince of this world."

"He'd have a hard time seducing Russia! Tens of millions of devout peasants!"

Nicole laid down her fork, and her beautiful gray eyes, wide and dominating her plain face, filled with a great light. "The Blessed Mother cannot lie, Papa. And Satan uses the most...most...unlikely people to cause confusion. I read the Holy Bible, also."

"Reverend Mother! God forbid."

Nicole serenely buttered a slice of bread. "I will be Reverend Mother one of these days. I am going to enter the Carmelite order."

Jason laughed, the first time he had laughed in weeks. "I'm going to marry you off to a banker. They're the only powerful men in the world."

He thought about the speech he would give in Pittsburgh three days from now. He thought about the New York City Bank. Amazingly, they had not pressed for the usual interest; they had extended his deadline. Jason suspected a plot by the still-unknown buyer of his paper, and was still numb from his despair. "The earthquake will hit when I least expect it."

The war was driven from his mind. Patricia, Sebastian, Nicholas, Nicole, Patrick, absorbed his attention. A man was fatally distracted from the world when he had a family. "Hostages to fortune." Few family men attained eminence; women could inspire a man, but not children. An intelligent man should acquire mistresses and leave his wife to bear children and attend to domestic concerns. The Muslims were wise: uneducated wives to bear offspring and delightful concubines to entertain with astute conversation.

Jason thought, I'll give the speech in Pittsburgh on schedule, and the hell with what is to come. I'm faced with the necessity of personal survival.

One morning soon after his return from Pittsburgh Jason found Saul to be missing. A note was under his bedroom door. Saul had written, "Almighty God does not pervert justice. Who committed the world to his keeping? Who but he established the whole world? If he were to turn his thoughts inward and recall his life-giving spirit, all that lives would perish on the instant and man return to dust.

"Dear Jason, this is from the book of Job. Remember it. God be with you, dear friend. Do not worry about me. I commit my life to him, blessed be his name."

Jason was devastated. He appealed to the police, and to private agencies, for weeks. He was panic-stricken. He expected a letter from Saul, but it did not come. Saul had vanished from those who had persecuted him and also from those who loved him. It was if he had never been.

Nicole said, "Papa, he had his own life, Mr. Weitzman. But God will be with him and never desert him. He was a good man."

Jason said, forgetting Nicole was a child, "God, if he exists, always deserts the good. St. Teresa of Avila said to him, 'Lord, no wonder you have so few friends. You treat them so badly.' "

Nicole never uttered a platitude. She smiled lovingly. "Papa. You'll find out."

Edmund Patterson requested an interview with Jason. Jason put up his hands and closed his eyes wearily. "What now? The new hotel opens next week. Your wife and children are already in the house near it. Don't tell me you've changed your mind and will go back to New York?"

"No, Mr. Garrity. New York is not attractive to me any longer." Edmund's face shone with determination. He was stately as always, and crisp as always, and resembled a king increasingly, dignified and assured. "I have heard of your ...financial troubles."

"Who has not? It's common gossip. Even the dogs and cats have heard of them." He frowned. "Are you afraid you'll not get your salary?"

"Mr. Garrity. You do me an injustice, besides insulting me. I am your friend, though I am black." Edmund paused.

"Jesus! Will you never forget that?"

"America made me conscious of it, sir. Particularly in the last years."

"Be glad you're not drafted as an army cook! You and your oly sauces! Well, what is it?"

Edmund gazed thoughtfully at Jason's drawn face. "I have wenty thousand Krugerrand on deposit in South Africa, and fteen thousand dollars here. I am thrifty, though Sue Ann, ke all wives, is inclined to be extravagant."

Jason whistled admiringly. "Do you starve Sue Ann and eep her barefoot?"

Edmund did not smile. He rarely smiled. "Mr. Garrity. I ave come to offer you my savings in your troubles."

Jason sat up, astonished. "You what?"

"Without interest. You will repay when you are able."

Jason got up and went to the windows, where he looked ut blindly. His eyes were moist and he was obliged to blink hem. He started to speak, but could only cough. He blew his ose and muttered, "Damn this weather."

"The sun is shining and it is mild," Edmund pointed out.

"I didn't notice," said Jason huskily. He returned to his hair.

He and Edmund gazed at each other, not speaking for some noments. Then Jason said, "Have a drink. I need one, too."

They drank slowly and in silence. Jason fixed his eyes on is glass. He turned in his chair and stared at the wall. Edmund, you're the only friend I have in the whole world."

"'Blessed is the man who has *one* friend.' Old Bantu prov- rb."

"Yes. Come to think of it, it's true. Pour me another drink. ake one yourself."

"There's the matter of dinner, but thank you, sir." Edmund ot up and replenished Jason's glass.

"You smell of soap and eau de cologne, Edmund. A German cent. Careful. You'll offend patriotic Americans."

"Sue Ann buys it for me. Garlic and onions offend her lelicate nose. But what would dishes be if not for garlic, nions, and herbs?"

"What indeed?"

"I buy her attar of roses occasionally, which she favors. Very expensive. Do you know what it costs an ounce, Mr. Garrity?"

"No. I never bought attar of roses for any woman."

"Wise. It is addictive to ladies." He meditated. "If I can

467

put up with the stench of attar of roses, Sue Ann can put up with the fragrance of cooking."

"Did you tell her so?"

"No. I cherish domestic harmony."

"Coward. Like all husbands."

Edmund glanced at his watch. "Mr. Garrity. Will you accept the loan of my money?"

"Edmund, I need nearly two million dollars. I'm in debt. But in December I have to meet my interest payment. I may have to take you up on your offer." He drank. "God knows when you'll get repaid."

Edmund smiled again. "I am not a religious man, sir, but King David did say he never found a just man needing to beg for bread."

They shook hands fervently. Jason had never kissed a man in his life except his grandfather. He kissed Edmund on the cheek. Edmund returned the salute, his hand on Jason's shoulder. He looked grave.

Jason sat motionless for a long time when Edmund had left. Then he called Lionel on the telephone. He said, "You may see Bastie whenever you wish, Lionel."

After a moment Lionel said, "What caused you to change your mind?"

"A friend. But you wouldn't understand."

"A friend?"

"The only one I have."

"Jase, you're lucky."

"That I am. Do you have one?"

"No."

The Bolshevik Revolution exploded in Russia at the predetermined hour, but the rest of the world was aghast. An ally against Germany was lost. The significance escaped the allied nations, which offered the excuse that Russia was weak anyway and that her armies were starving and ill-equipped. The Russian people were confused, terrified, and bewildered. The trained Communist traitors seized power. They were not voted in. The czar was benumbed but after a few days was convinced that his people would turn on the Communists as they had turned on other criminals. War-weary, hungry, desperate though they were, they had a massive common sense and a native cynicism. They would die for Mother Russia gladly, but ideology would not appeal to them. It never had. At once pragmatic and mystical, passionate and stolid, they

468

vere prohibited by fluctuating moods from any permanence of conviction. Only icons held their steadfast devotions; icons lid not interfere with the business of existence. But the czar lid not reckon on those behind the revolution.

Jason, on hearing the news, thought about the conversation he had had with Nicole.

He gave another speech in Pittsburgh to two thousand men and women. He quoted Abraham Lincoln: "The money power preys upon the nation in times of peace, and conspires against it in times of adversity. It is more despotic than monarchy, more insolent than autocracy, more overweening than bureaucracy. It denounces as public enemies all those who question its methods or throw light upon its crimes."

Jason said, "All wars are greed for territory and gold, however 'noble' the perpetrators shout they are, however vehement their slogans. This war is not an exception. As Benjamin Franklin said, 'There is no good war or bad peace.' There are other means for resistance to enemies or invaders. The people should refuse to cooperate. They would suffer fewer casualties than in warfare! And they would win."

He was given great applause, but outside the hall he was picketed by youths who shouted to him, "Traitor! Go back to Kraut Land! Coward! Subversive! You should be hanged!" Jason surveyed them; they were all of draft age, and some were in uniform. Their fresh and earnest and indignant faces aroused his compassion. He called to them, "God help you, boys! You'll need it!"

A few days later he was quietly visited by a federal officer from Washington, who submitted a card and sat down without invitation. He was a young anonymous-appearing man, the typical bureaucrat, and his face was clean and young.

"Well?" said Jason, smiling grimly.

"Your speeches, Mr. Garrity, your letters to the newspapers. We are at war; it may have escaped your attention. He who gives aid and comfort to the enemy is a traitor."

"I don't consider the Germans the enemy of my country. Peoples don't become enemies of other peoples. Governments do; it's only governments that make war against other governments, for gain or for power. The people fight while the men who instigated the war sit safely behind desks and eventually divide up the spoils. As they planned they would.

"George Washington said, 'Eternal vigilance is the price of peace.' Only weak nations invite attack. I don't have any objection to my country being strong and invincible. On the contrary, I advocate this. But aggression—no."

"Not defense, Mr. Garrity?"

"Oh, come on! Germany never attacked us! You will tall about sinking our passenger ships. You know as well as I do that they carried arms to the 'allies,' in violation of the laws of neutrality, in the face of desperate warnings by Germany When you carry contraband, you are aiding one nation against another nation who is not your enemy. You know all that as well as I do. But you don't inform the people. I do."

The agent smiled more broadly. "'My country, may she always be right—but my country right or wrong!'"

Jason said, "My country is made up of individual men. My country is not its government, who usurps power over individuals without consulting them. Government is alleged to be the servant of individuals, *not* their master. The Constitution says so. The American people didn't vote us into this war."

"Congress, their representative, did."

"On such grave matters, the people should vote nationally not Congress. Congress isn't immune to propaganda from the White House."

The agent listened with an inscrutable face. Jason smiled "I will make a rude syllogism: 'All governments are corrupt Washington is our government; therefore Washington is corrupt.' Did you ever hear of Colonel House?"

"I am personally acquainted with him, Mr. Garrity."

"You know, then."

"You are Irish, Mr. Garrity?"

Jason leaned back and contemplated him for a long time. "The government is clamoring that if you call yourself a German-American, an Irish-American, a Polish-American, an Italian- or God-knows-what-American, and if you emphasize your race, you are not an American! I agree. Racial distinctions are a private matter." Jason grinned unpleasantly. "Doesn't that answer your question? I am an American. Nothing else. If some men attempt to divide individuals according to race, I'm their enemy, and all decent people should be their enemy—they're enemies of America. Their aim is to set Americans against Americans—to their own advantage. And to create public disorder. I stand upon my constitutional rights, even in wartime, to dissent. Isn't this a free country?" asked Jason.

The agent got up and retrieved his hat from Jason's desk.

e paused by the door and looked back. "What makes you
ink so, Mr. Garrity?"

The agent did not visit Jason again, nor was Jason har-
ssed. But the newspapers stated that Jason had been in-
estigated "for possible subversion in connection with his
peeches and letters." That did not add to his popularity.
hauncey Schofield and his wife and Elizabeth spread ru-
ors. Ipswich House was half-empty at the Christmas holi-
ays, and the new hotel had its windows broken. Ice and snow
nd wind and rain almost ruined its interior.

"God," exclaimed Patrick feebly, "and sure you got us in
avoc, bucko." He dropped his head.

"What's a man of conscience to do?"

Patrick sighed. "Take out another loan, if the banks will
t you. Conscience is expensive, I am thinking. A man cannot
fford it." He added, and his blue eyes were glaucous, "Any
ews about your paper?"

"No."

"Pray God something else does not happen. I can't stomach
."

Two nights before Christmas, Jason received a telephone
all from Patricia's sanatorium. "This is Dr. Frosby, one of
he attendings. I regret to inform you, Mr. Garrity, that your
vife is very ill with the Spanish influenza and pneumonia.
he is conscious, but that is all. I am afraid she is too ill to
e removed to the hospital. But you and her father should
ome down at once."

Patrick had no words for this fresh calamity, which was
he worst of all. He and Jason took the train together. He had
o strength even to talk. He sat in the train, tears rolling
lown his cheeks unheeded, fingering his rosary, which Jason
ad never seen before. Jason himself was empty of thought
nd emotion, hands slack on his knees, staring out on the
nowy landscape with dead eyes. It seemed distorted to him.
"he mountains had no reality. Time had no reality. He tried
o feel; it was impossible. There was not even a sensation of
ightmare.

They reached Wilkes-Barre, still not speaking, and rode
o the sanatorium in a station hack. It was very cold, and the
streets were slippery with ice. Patrick swayed around in the
ack like a loose-jointed rag doll, his eyes closed, tears still
unning down his cheeks. Jason wished he could comfort him,
ut he had no words.

Jason was informed at the institution that Mrs. Garrit wished only to see her father. Jason made no protest. He sa in the waiting room. The day darkened; snow began to fal There was a Christmas tree in the room, and patients an visitors came in to admire the glittering tinsel and candle and red and green and blue and silver balls. Someone wa singing carols; the wind rattled the windows. Somewhere woman sorrowfully cried. Jason would hear the nurses' sooth ing voices and their quick muffled footsteps. He murmure to himself, "Patricia...my wife." The words had no meanin to him.

Patrick walked like an old man to his daughter's room, hi face masked. He sat down beside Patricia's bed and looke at her. This white-skin-covered skeleton with the closed eye and noisy breathing was not Patricia! God, not his lovel little colleen with her perfumes and grace! He looked at th remote face, dignified by approaching death, withdrawn an aloof, and he tried to find a familiar feature. The braide lifeless hair; this was not his daughter's hair. This sunke mouth and nose—not Patricia! He sought for the hand lyin in the blanket; a fleshless hand. It was cold, ice-cold, an made no response to him.

"Patricia, mavourneen," Patrick whispered. "My darling. She opened her eyes. "Dada," she said almost inaudibly "I am going to die. Glad. Glad." Her eyes were a lifeles brown, red-rimmed. "Dada. Be glad for me."

"My darling..." Patrick sobbed. "Do you want to see Ja son?"

"No. I did him a wrong, and Sebastian a wrong....Dada I've confessed. I'll confess to you. Jason...not Sebastian' father."

Patrick could not speak. But he thought: I knew it, I knev it.

"Lionel is."

Patrick closed his eyes. There was a scarlet whirling befor them.

Now tears floated in the deathly eyes as Patricia foun her last strength. "Dada, I married Jason...Lionel could no marry me. He didn't want to marry me...see that now. Dada I love him, loved him forever. It's not his fault; he al ways wanted...Joan. I...ran after him...ran after him Forgive me. Forgive Lionel...he didn't want me. I drank t forget...I didn't forget. Made you ashamed..."

Patrick groaned. The hand he held came alive, grippe

472

his. Patricia tried to lift her head from the pillow, and gasped. Her eyes seemed to fill her face. Her whispering was hoarse. "Don't tell Jason. Make it up to him. Sebastian, too. I hated him, my child. I tried... to hurt him. He came between me and Lionel, I thought. My beautiful child, my good child. He loved me; I hated him. I sent him away, drove him away. God... forgive... me. The priest... absolution. I... don't forgive myself.... Help me, Dada..."

Patrick gathered her in his arms and crooned an Irish lullaby remembered from his childhood. He sang of the moon and the dark forest and God's love for his children, and safety and the arms of the Mother and peace and rest and green meadows and blue rivers, and joy in the morning.

Patricia listened and smiled and closed her eyes.

After a while Patrick fell on his knees and whispered the litany for the dying. It was the last thing that Patricia heard in this life. Her face assumed the aspect of a child, and her father held her after she was dead. And rocked her in his arms for a long time, until Jason was there, and the priest, and took him away.

John Garrity co-celebrated the requiem Mass with Father Sweeney in Belleville, and Jason sat with Patrick and his children in the little cold church. The children cried silently. But Jason felt nothing at all. He had felt nothing at all since the day Patricia died. He could not make himself feel.

35

Monsignor John Garrity sat with Father Sweeney in the latter's shabby study. John was more rigorous than ever, more ascetic, more righteous.

"Jason brought it on himself, with his godlessness, his selfishness. He thought only of money. Now he is bankrupt, his wife dead, his son in an institution, and his cherished new hotel almost in financial ruins. God will not be mocked. He prepares a snare for the proud and the heedless, the sinful, and the self-absorbed. He lays them low.... He will not be mocked."

Father Sweeney was only a parish priest and John was a monsignor. But Father Sweeney got up on his suddenly trembling legs, and his eyes were fiery. "It's you, Jack Garrity, who are mocking God! You mock him every day of your life, and always did! You mock at his altar! How dare you raise the Host—blasphemy! Anathema! I saw blood on your hands when you distributed the Host at the funeral. Your brother is one of the few good men I have ever known, and you are not worthy to kiss his hand!

"Jason is afflicted, yes. But, when were the good not afflicted? The evil flourish like a green bay tree, and the righteous mourn. But let me tell you this, you false priest: God is with Jason, and always was, and he will not forget his son!"

Father Sweeney left the room, and tears of rage and sorrow filled his eyes. But he did not repent his words. He went to the empty church and prayed, and as he prayed, he felt peace. After a while he chuckled.

He had long wanted to tell Jack Garrity the truth about himself.

Chauncey Schofield left Belleville permanently and closed his office in March 1918. There were whispers. His wife did not go with him. She sold her house in April and went to New York.

Rumor had it that Elizabeth and her mother were "estranged," and the daughter declared her "independence" from Anita. Elizabeth went to Philadelphia, where the "brave girl" was reported to work in an office. Belleville did not see her again, nor did it see Anita and Chauncey.

Mrs. Lindon had had her revenge, but she never confided it to anyone. She alone knew when Anita filed for divorce from her husband and named his adulteries at Mrs. Lindon's house. Mrs. Lindon had supplied the pertinent details to her good wronged friend, as she had supplied the location of Chauncey's little cottage in the woods and other data.

In May 1918 Jason telephoned Molly at her house in New York. She answered somewhat cautiously and with hesitation. "Hello, Jason. I'm glad you called. I'm going to Canada, to Montreal, and then to—"

"Molly?"

"I'm already packed. I'm leaving in an hour...for three months."

"Molly, darling. I've thought and thought about my unknown benefactor for the last months. When I received back my paper, debts paid in full, I got suspicious. I don't know anyone who would do such a thing and has the means to do it. Except you. Molly?"

She began to cry, and Jason heard her sobbing. "I don't know, Jason, and I wonder—"

"Molly, will you marry me?"

He heard her take a deep breath. "I'm sorry about Mr. Mulligan's recent death. Three weeks now, isn't it."

"Yes. Patricia's death was the final blow. He never recovered. Though he was ill and his death was expected at any time, we had hopes. Things were too much for him. Molly, will you marry me?"

"I'll think about it."

"What's there to think about, Molly?"

There was a silence; then Molly sighed. "You haven't told me you love me."

"Oh, God, you are like every other woman! I told you that years ago."

"But not recently. Jason, I don't want a husband who is merely grateful to me."

"If you don't marry me, I will get loans from the bank, no matter if it takes years, and repay you. Incidentally, Mr. Mulligan left his entire estate to me, free and clear, except for a trust fund for Bastie. And the thousand acres, too. I was on the deed, and didn't know it. I want to use that land to build a home and hospital for people like Nick and name it the Patrick Michael Mulligan School."

475

"Good," said Molly with some coldness.

"Molly, I love you and I never loved another woman. Now are you satisfied? I love you, I love you, and always did. And Nickie loves you, and Bastie. They deserve another brother and sister. Will you be so kind—"

Molly said in a bright voice, "I think I'll cancel the trip to Canada. And come home."

Jason went out in the May morning. It seemed to him that the world was new, shining, exultant, though in Europe thousands died on battlefields every day. Come what may, man endures, man survives, and there is joy in the morning.

Jason raised his eyes and smiled. God is good. He moves mysteriously, as the priests say, but he has his ways, he has his ways!

He is not the adversary of man. Man is, Jason thought. God is not to be understood by man. He is just to be trusted.

The bells rang for early Mass, and Jason went into the church, reconciled, and looked at the high altar and genuflected. Sanctus, Sanctus.

ABOUT THE AUTHOR

Janet Miriam Taylor Caldwell, born in Manchester, England, on September 7, 1900, won a gold medal for an essay on Charles Dickens at the age of six before coming to the United States with her parents. She persisted in her writing, against endless difficulties, with *Dynasty of Death,* her first published book, coming out in 1938. Since then she has had 34 bestsellers published along with a number of stories. She lives to write.